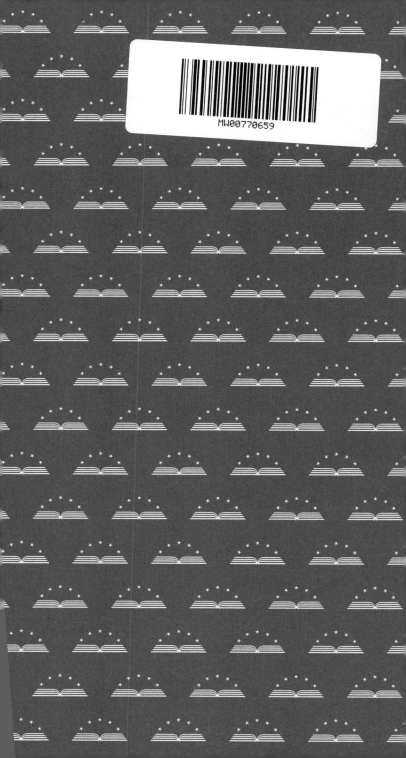

Library of America, a nonprofit organization,
champions our nation's cultural heritage
by publishing America's greatest writing in
authoritative new editions and providing resources
for readers to explore this rich, living legacy.

JOANNA RUSS

Joanna Russ

NOVELS & STORIES

The Female Man
We Who Are About To . . .
On Strike Against God
The Complete Alyx Stories
Other Stories

Nicole Rudick, *editor*

THE LIBRARY OF AMERICA

Contents

THE FEMALE MAN

This book is dedicated to Anne, to Mary and to the other one and three-quarters billions of us.

If Jack succeeds in forgetting something, this is of little use if Jill continues to remind him of it. He must induce her not to do so. The safest way would be not just to make her keep quiet about it, but to induce her to forget it also.

Jack may act upon Jill in many ways. He may make her feel guilty for keeping on "bringing it up." He may *invalidate* her experience. This can be done more or less radically. He can indicate merely that it is unimportant or trivial, whereas it is important and significant to her. Going further, he can shift the *modality* of her experience from memory to imagination: "It's all in your imagination." Further still, he can invalidate the *content*: "It never happened that way." Finally, he can invalidate not only the significance, modality, and content, but her very capacity to remember at all, and make her feel guilty for doing so into the bargain.

This is not unusual. People are doing such things to each other all the time. In order for such transpersonal invalidation to work, however, it is advisable to overlay it with a thick patina of mystification. For instance, by denying that this is what one is doing, and further invalidating any perception that it is being done by ascriptions such as "How can you think such a thing?" "You must be paranoid." And so on.

R. D. Laing, *The Politics of Experience*,
Penguin Books, Ltd., London, 1967, pp. 31–32.

PART ONE

I

I WAS BORN on a farm on Whileaway. When I was five I
was sent to a school on South Continent (like everybody
else) and when I turned twelve I rejoined my family. My
mother's name was Eva, my other mother's name Alicia; I
am Janet Evason. When I was thirteen I stalked and killed
a wolf, alone, on North Continent above the forty-eighth
parallel, using only a rifle. I made a travois for the head and
paws, then abandoned the head, and finally got home with
one paw, proof enough (I thought). I've worked in the
mines, on the radio network, on a milk farm, a vegetable
farm, and for six weeks as a librarian after I broke my leg.
At thirty I bore Yuriko Janetson; when she was taken away
to a school five years later (and I never saw a child protest
so much) I decided to take time off and see if I could find
my family's old home—for they had moved away after I had
married and relocated near Mine City in South Continent.
The place was unrecognizable, however; our rural areas are
always changing. I could find nothing but the tripods of the
computer beacons everywhere, some strange crops in the
fields that I had never seen before, and a band of wandering
children. They were heading North to visit the polar station
and offered to lend me a sleeping bag for the night, but I
declined and stayed with the resident family; in the morning
I started home. Since then I have been Safety Officer for the
county, that is S & P (Safety and Peace), a position I have
held now for six years. My Stanford-Binet corrected score (in
your terms) is 187, my wife's 205 and my daughter's 193. Yuki
goes through the ceiling on the verbal test. I've supervised
the digging of fire trails, delivered babies, fixed machinery,
and milked more moo-cows than I wish I knew existed. But
Yuki is crazy about ice-cream. I love my daughter. I love my
family (there are nineteen of us). I love my wife (Vittoria).
I've fought four duels. I've killed four times.

5

II

Jeannine Dadier (DADE-yer) worked as a librarian in New York City three days a week for the W.P.A. She worked at the Tompkins Square Branch in the Young Adult section. She wondered sometimes if it was so lucky that Herr Shicklgruber had died in 1936 (the library had books about this). On the third Monday in March of 1969 she saw the first headlines about Janet Evason but paid no attention to them; she spent the day stamping Out books for the Young Adults and checking the lines around her eyes in her pocket mirror (*I'm only twenty-nine!*). Twice she had had to tuck her skirt above her knees and climb the ladder to the higher-up books; once she had to move the ladder over Mrs. Allison and the new gentleman assistant, who were standing below soberly discussing the possibility of war with Japan. There was an article in *The Saturday Evening Post.*

"I don't believe it," repeated Jeannine Nancy Dadier softly. Mrs. Allison was a Negro. It was an unusually warm, hazy day with a little green showing in the park: imaginary green, perhaps, as if the world had taken an odd turning and were bowling down Spring in a dim by-street somewhere, clouds of imagination around the trees.

"I don't believe it," repeated Jeannine Dadier, not knowing what they were talking about. "You'd better believe it!" said Mrs. Allison sharply. Jeannine balanced on one foot. (Nice girls don't do that.) She climbed down the ladder with her books and put them on the reserve table. Mrs. Allison didn't like W.P.A. girls. Jeannine saw the headlines again, on Mrs. Allison's newspaper.

WOMAN APPEARS FROM NOWHERE ON
BROADWAY, POLICEMAN VANISHES

"I don't—" (*I have my cat, I have my room, I have my hot plate and my window and the ailanthus tree*).

Out of the corner of her eye she saw Cal outside in the street; he was walking bouncily and his hat was tipped forward; he was going to have some silly thing or other to say about being a reporter, little blond hatchet face and serious blue eyes; "I'll make it some day, baby." Jeannine slipped into the stacks, hiding behind Mrs. Allison's *P.M.-Post*: Woman Appears from Nowhere on Broadway, Policeman Vanishes. She daydreamed about buying fruit at the free market, though her hands always sweat so when she bought things outside the government store and she couldn't bargain. She would get cat food and feed Mr. Frosty the first thing she got to her room; he ate out of an old china saucer. Jeannine imagined Mr. Frosty rubbing against her legs, his tail waving. Mr. Frosty was marked black-and-white all over. With her eyes closed, Jeannine saw him jump up on the mantelpiece and walk among her things: her sea shells and miniatures. "No, no, *no!*" she said. The cat jumped off, knocking over one of her Japanese dolls. After dinner Jeannine took him out; then she washed the dishes and tried to mend some of her old clothing. She'd go over the ration books. When it got dark she'd turn on the radio for the evening program or she'd read, maybe call up from the drugstore and find out about the boarding house in New Jersey. She might call her brother. She would certainly plant the orange seeds and water them. She thought of Mr. Frosty stalking a bath-robe tail among the miniature orange trees; he'd look like a tiger. If she could get empty cans at the government store.

"Hey, baby?" It was a horrid shock. It was Cal.

"No," said Jeannine hastily. "I haven't got time."

"Baby?" He was pulling her arm. Come for a cup of coffee. But she couldn't. She had to learn Greek (the book was in the reserve desk). There was too much to do. He was frowning and pleading. She could feel the pillow under her back already, and Mr. Frosty stalking around them, looking at her with his strange blue eyes, walking widdershins around the lovers. He was part Siamese; Cal called him The Blotchy Skinny Cat. Cal always wanted to do experiments with him, dropping him from the back of a chair, putting things in his way, hiding from him. Mr. Frosty just spat at him now.

"Later," said Jeannine desperately. Cal leaned over her and whispered into her ear; it made her want to cry. He rocked back and forth on his heels. Then he said, "I'll wait." He sat on Jeannine's stack chair, picking up the newspaper, and added:

"The vanishing woman. That's you." She closed her eyes and daydreamed about Mr. Frosty curled up on the mantel, peacefully asleep, all felinity in one circle. Such a spoiled cat.

"Baby?" said Cal.

"Oh, all right," said Jeannine hopelessly, "all right."

I'll watch the ailanthus tree.

III

Janet Evason appeared on Broadway at two o'clock in the afternoon in her underwear. She didn't lose her head. Though the nerves try to keep going in the previous track, she went into evasive position the second after she arrived (good for her) with her fair, dirty hair flying and her khaki shorts and shirt stained with sweat. When a policeman tried to take her arm, she threatened him with la savate, but he vanished. She seemed to regard the crowds around her with a special horror. The policeman reappeared in the same spot an hour later with no memory of the interval, but Janet Evason had returned to her sleeping bag in the New Forest only a few moments after her arrival. A few words of Pan-Russian and she was gone. The last of them waked her bedmate in the New Forest.

"Go to sleep," said the anonymous friend-for-the-night, a nose, a brow, and a coil of dark hair in the dappled moonlight.

"But who has been mucking about with my head!" said Janet Evason.

IV

When Janet Evason returned to the New Forest and the experimenters at the Pole Station were laughing their heads off (for it was not a dream) I sat in a cocktail party in mid-Manhattan. I had just changed into a man, me, Joanna. I mean a female man, of course; my body and soul were exactly the same.

So there's me also.

V

The first man to set foot on Whileaway appeared in a field of turnips on North Continent. He was wearing a blue suit like a hiker's and a blue cap. The farm people had been notified. One, seeing the blip on the tractor's infrared scan, came to get him; the man in blue saw a flying machine with no wings but a skirt of dust and air. The county's repair shed for farm machinery was nearby that week, so the tractor-driver led him there; he was not saying anything intelligible. He saw a translucent dome, the surface undulating slightly. There was an exhaust fan set in one side. Within the dome was a wilderness of machines:

dead, on their sides, some turned inside out, their guts spilling on to the grass. From an extended framework under the roof swung hands as big as three men. One of these picked up a car and dropped it. The sides of the car fell off. Littler hands sprang up from the grass.

"Hey, hey!" said the tractor-driver, knocking on a solid piece set into the wall. "It fell, it passed out!"

"Send it back," said an operator, climbing out from under the induction helmet at the far end of the shed. Four others came and stood around the man in the blue suit.

"Is he of steady mind?" said one.

"We don't know."

"Is he ill?"

"Hypnotize him and send him back."

The man in blue—if he had seen them—would have found them very odd: smooth-faced, smooth-skinned, too small and too plump, their coveralls heavy in the seat. They wore coveralls because you couldn't always fix things with the mechanical hands; sometimes you had to use your own. One was old and had white hair; one was very young; one wore the long hair sometimes affected by the youth of Whileaway, "to while away the time." Six pairs of steady curious eyes studied the man in the blue suit.

"That, *mes enfants*," said the tractor-driver at last, "is a man.

"That is a real Earth man."

VI

Sometimes you bend down to tie your shoe, and then you either tie your shoe or you don't; you either straighten up instantly or maybe you don't. Every choice begets at least two worlds of possibility, that is, one in which you do and one in which you don't; or very likely many more, one in which you do quickly, one in which you do slowly, one in which you don't, but hesitate, one in which you hesitate and frown, one in which you hesitate and sneeze, and so on. To carry this line of argument further, there must be an infinite number of possible universes (such is the fecundity of God) for there is no reason to imagine Nature as prejudiced in favor of human action. Every displacement of every molecule, every change in orbit of every electron, every quantum of light that strikes here and not there—each of these must somewhere have its alternative. It's possible, too, that there is no such thing as one clear line or strand of probability, and that we live on a sort of twisted braid, blurring from one to the other without even knowing it, as long as we keep within the limits of a set of variations that really make no difference to us. Thus the paradox of time travel ceases to exist, for the Past one visits is never one's own Past but always somebody else's; or rather, one's visit to the Past instantly creates another Present (one in which the visit has already happened) and what you visit is the Past belonging to that Present—an entirely different matter from your own Past. And with each decision you make (back there in the Past) that new probable universe itself branches, creating simultaneously a new Past and a new Present, or to put it plainly, a new universe. And when you come back to your own Present, you alone know what the other Past was like and what you did there.

Thus it is probable that Whileaway—a name for the Earth ten centuries from now, but not *our* Earth, if you follow me —will find itself not at all affected by this sortie into somebody else's past. And vice versa, of course. The two might as well be independent worlds.

Whileaway, you may gather, is in the future.

But not *our* future.

VII

I saw Jeannine shortly afterward, in a cocktail lounge where I had gone to watch Janet Evason on television (I don't have a set). Jeannine looked very much out of place; I sat next to her and she confided in me: "I don't belong here." I can't imagine how she got there, except by accident. She looked as if she were dressed up for a costume film, sitting in the shadow with her snood and her wedgies, a long-limbed, coltish girl in clothes a little too small for her. Fashion (it seems) is recovering very leisurely from the Great Depression. Not here and now, of course. "I don't belong here!" whispered Jeannine Dadier again, rather anxiously. She was fidgeting. She said, "I don't *like* places like this." She poked the red, turfed leather on the seat.

"What?" I said.

"I went hiking last vacation," she said big-eyed. "That's what I like. It's healthy."

I know it's supposed to be virtuous to run healthily through fields of flowers, but I like bars, hotels, air-conditioning, good restaurants, and jet transport, and I told her so.

"Jet?" she said.

Janet Evason came on the television. It was only a still picture. Then we had the news from Cambodia, Laos, Michigan State, Lake Canandaigua (pollution), and the spinning globe of the world in full color with its seventeen man-made satellites going around it. The color was awful. I've been inside a television studio before: the gallery running around the sides of the barn, every inch of the roof covered with lights, so that the little woman-child with the wee voice can pout over an oven or a sink. Then Janet Evason came on with that blobby look people have on the tube. She moved carefully and looked at everything with interest. She was well dressed (in a suit). The host or M.C. or whatever-you-call-him shook hands with her and then everybody shook hands with everybody else, like a French wedding or an early silent movie. *He* was dressed in a suit. Someone guided her to a seat and she smiled and nodded in the exaggerated way you do when you're not sure of doing the right thing. She looked around and shaded her eyes against the lights. Then she spoke.

(The first thing said by the second man ever to visit While-away was, "Where are all the men?" Janet Evason, appearing in the Pentagon, hands in her pockets, feet planted far apart, said, "Where the dickens are all the women?")

The sound in the television set conked out for a moment and then Jeannine Dadier was gone; she didn't disappear, she just wasn't there any more. Janet Evason got up, shook hands again, looked around her, questioned with her eyes, panto-mimed comprehension, nodded, and walked out of camera range. They never did show you the government guards.

I heard it another time and this is how it went:

MC: How do you like it here, Miss Evason?
JE (looks around the studio, confused): It's too hot.
MC: I mean how do you like it on—well, on Earth?

JE: But I live on the earth. (Her attention is a little strained here.)

MC: Perhaps you had better explain what you mean by that—I mean the existence of different probabilities and so on—you were talking about that before.

JE: It's in the newspapers.

MC: But Miss Evason, if you could, please explain it for the people who are watching the program.

JE: Let them read. Can't they read?

(There was a moment's silence. Then the M.C. spoke.)

MC: Our social scientists as well as our physicists tell us they've had to revise a great deal of theory in light of the information brought by our fair visitor from another world. There have been no men on Whileaway for at least eight centuries—I don't mean no human beings, of course, but no men—and this society, run entirely by women, has naturally attracted a great deal of attention since the appearance last week of its representative and its first ambassador, the lady on my left here. Janet Evason, can you tell us how you think your society on Whileaway will react to the reappearance of men from Earth—I mean our present-day Earth, of course—after an isolation of eight hundred years?

JE (She jumped at this one; probably because it was the first question she could understand): Nine hundred years. What men?

MC: What men? Surely you expect men from our society to visit Whileaway.

JE: Why?

MC: For information, trade, ah—cultural contact, surely. (laughter) I'm afraid you're making it rather difficult for me, Miss Evason. When the—ah—the plague you spoke of killed the men on Whileaway, weren't they missed? Weren't families broken up? Didn't the whole pattern of life change?

JE (slowly): I suppose people always miss what they are used to. Yes, they were missed. Even a whole set of words, like "he," "man" and so on—these are banned. Then the second generation, they use them to be daring, among themselves, and the third generation doesn't, to be polite, and by the fourth, who cares? Who remembers?

MC: But surely—that is—

JE: Excuse me, perhaps I'm mistaking what you intend to say as this language we're speaking is only a hobby of mine, I am not as fluent as I would wish. What we speak is a pan-Russian even the Russians would not understand; it would be like Middle English to you, only vice-versa.

MC: I see. But to get back to the question—

JE: Yes.

MC (A hard position to be in, between the authorities and this strange personage who is wrapped in ignorance like a savage chief: expressionless, attentive, possibly civilized, completely unknowing. He finally said): Don't you want men to return to Whileaway, Miss Evason?

JE: Why?

MC: One sex is half a species, Miss Evason. I am quoting (and he cited a famous anthropologist). Do you want to banish sex from Whileaway?

JE (with massive dignity and complete naturalness): Huh?

MC: I said: Do you want to banish sex from Whileaway? Sex, family, love, erotic attraction—call it what you like—we all know that your people are competent and intelligent individuals, but do you think that's enough? Surely you have the intellectual knowledge of biology in other species to know what I'm talking about.

JE: I'm married. I have two children. What the devil do you mean?

MC: I—Miss Evason—we—well, we know you form what you call marriages, Miss Evason, that you reckon the descent of your children through both partners and that you even have "tribes"—I'm calling them what Sir ——— calls them; I know the translation isn't perfect—and we know that these marriages or tribes form very good institutions for the economic support of the children and for some sort of genetic mixing, though I confess you're way beyond us in the biological sciences. But, Miss Evason, I am not talking about economic institutions or even affectionate ones. Of course the mothers of Whileaway love their children; nobody doubts that. And of course they have affection for each other; nobody doubts that, either. But there is more, much, much more—I am talking about sexual love.

JE (enlightened): Oh! You mean copulation.

MC: Yes.
JE: And you say we don't have that?
MC: Yes.
JE: How foolish of you. Of course we do.
MC: Ah? (He wants to say, "Don't tell me.")
JE: With each other. Allow me to explain.

She was cut off instantly by a commercial poetically describing the joys of unsliced bread. They shrugged (out of camera range). It wouldn't even have gotten that far if Janet had not insisted on attaching a touch-me-not to the replay system. It was a live broadcast, four seconds' lag. I begin to like her more and more. She said, "If you expect me to observe your taboos, I think you will have to be more precise as to exactly what they are." In Jeannine Dadier's world, she was (would be) asked by a lady commentator:

How do the women of Whileaway do their hair?

JE: They hack it off with clam shells.

VIII

"Humanity is unnatural!" exclaimed the philosopher Dun-yasha Bernadetteson (A.C. 344–426) who suffered all her life from the slip of a genetic surgeon's hand which had given her one mother's jaw and the other mother's teeth—orthodontia is hardly ever necessary on Whileaway. Her daughter's teeth, however, were perfect. Plague came to Whileaway in P.C. 17 (Preceding Catastrophe) and ended in A.C. 03, with half the population dead; it had started so slowly that no one knew about it until it was too late. It attacked males only. Earth had been completely re-formed during the Golden Age (P.C. 300–ca. P.C. 180) and natural conditions presented considerably less difficulty than they might have during a similar catastrophe a millennium or so earlier. At the time of The Despair (as it was popularly called), Whileaway had two continents, called simply North and South Continents, and a great many ideal bays or anchorages in the coastline. Severe climatic conditions did not prevail below 72° S and 68° N latitude. Conventional water traffic, at the time of the Catastrophe, was employed almost exclusively for freight, passenger traffic using the smaller and more flexibly routed hovercraft. Houses were self-contained, with portable power sources, fuel-alcohol motors or solar cells replacing the earlier centralized power. The later invention of practical matter-antimatter reactors (K. Ansky, A.C. 239) produced great optimism for a decade or so, but these devices proved to be too bulky for private use. Katharina Lucyson Ansky (A.C. 201–282) was also responsible for the principles that made genetic surgery possible. (The merging of ova had been practiced for the previous century and a half.) Animal life had become so scarce before the Golden Age that many species were re-invented by enthusiasts of the Ansky Period; in A.C. 280 there was an outbreak of coneys in Newland (an island off the neck of North Continent), a pandemic not without historical precedent. By A.C. 492, through the brilliant agitation of the great Betty Bettinason Murano (A.C. 453–A.C. 502) Terran colonies were re-established on Mars, Ganymede, and in the Asteroids, the Selenic League assisting according to the Treaty of Mare Tenebrum (A.C. 240). Asked what she expected to find in space, Betty Murano made the immortal quip, "Nothing." By the third century A.C. intelligence was a controllable, heritable factor, though aptitudes and interests continued to elude the surgeons and intelligence itself could be raised only grossly. By the fifth century, clan organization had reached its present complex state and the re-cycling of phosphorus was almost completely successful; by the seventh century Jovian mining made it possible to replace a largely glass-and-ceramics technology with some metals (which were also re-cycled) and for the third time in four hundred years (fashions are sometimes cyclic too) duelling became a serious social nuisance. Several local Guilds Councils voted that a successful duellist must undergo the penalty of an accidental murderer and bear a child to replace the life lost, but the solution was too simple-minded to become popular. There was the age of both parties to consider, for example. By the beginning of the ninth century A.C. the induction helmet was a practical possibility, industry was being drastically altered, and the Selenic League had finally outproduced South Continent in kg protein/person/annum. In 913 A.C. an obscure and discontented descendant of Katy Ansky put together various items of mathematical knowledge and thus discovered—or invented—probability mechanics.

In the time of Jesus of Nazareth, dear reader, there were no motor-cars. I still walk, though, sometimes.

That is, a prudent ecologist makes things work as nearly perfectly as they can by themselves, but you also keep the kerosene lantern in the barn just in case, and usually a debate about keeping a horse ends up with the decision that it's too much trouble, so you let the horse go; but the Conservation Point at La Jolla keeps horses. We wouldn't recognize them. The induction helmet makes it possible for one workwoman to have not only the brute force but also the flexibility and control of thousands; it's turning Whileawayan industry upside down. Most people walk on Whileaway (of course, their feet are perfect). They make haste in odd ways sometimes. In the early days it was enough just to keep alive and keep the children coming. Now they say "When the re-industrialization's complete," and they still walk. Maybe they like it. Probability mechanics offers the possibility—by looping into another continuum, exactly chosen—of teleportation. Chilia Ysayeson Belin lives in Italian ruins (I think this is part of the Vittore Emmanuele monument, though I don't know how it got to Newland) and she's sentimental about it; how can one add indoor plumbing discreetly without an unconscionable amount of work? Her mother, Ysaye, lives in a cave (the Ysaye who put together the theory of probability mechanics). Pre-fabs take only two days to get and no time at all to set up. There are eighteen Belins and twenty-three Moujkis (Ysaye's family; I stayed with both). Whileaway doesn't have true cities. And of course, the tail of a culture is several centuries behind the head. Whileaway is so pastoral that at times one wonders whether the ultimate sophistication may not take us all back to a kind of pre-Paleolithic dawn age, a garden without any artifacts except for what we would call miracles. A Moujki invented non-disposable food containers in her spare time in A.C. 904 because the idea fascinated her; people have been killed for less.

Meanwhile, the ecological housekeeping is enormous.

IX

JE: I bore my child at thirty; we all do. It's a vacation. Almost five years. The baby rooms are full of people reading, painting, singing, as much as they can, to the children, with the children, over the children. . . . Like the ancient Chinese custom of the three-years' mourning, an hiatus at just the right time. There has been no leisure at all before and there will be so little after—anything I do, you understand, I mean really do— I must ground thoroughly in those five years. One works with feverish haste. . . . At sixty I will get a sedentary job and have some time for myself again.

COMMENTATOR: And this is considered enough, in Whileaway?

JE: My God, no.

X

Jeannine dawdles. She always hates to get out of bed. She would lie on her side and look at the ailanthus tree until her back began to ache; then she would turn over, hidden in the veils of the leaves, and fall asleep. Tag-ends of dreams till she lay in bed like a puddle and the cat would climb over her. On workdays Jeannine got up early in a kind of waking nightmare: feeling horrid, stumbling to the hall bathroom with sleep all over her. Coffee made her sick. She couldn't sit in the armchair, or drop her slippers, or bend, or lean, or lie down. Mr. Frosty, perambulating on the window sill, walked back and forth in front of the ailanthus tree: Tiger on Frond. The museum. The zoo. The bus to Chinatown. Jeannine sank into the tree gracefully, like a mermaid, bearing with her a tea-cosy to give to the young man who had a huge muffin trembling over his collar where his face ought to have been. Trembling with emotion.

The cat spoke.

She jerked awake. *I'll feed you, Mr. Frosty.*

Mrrrr.

Cal couldn't afford to take her anywhere, really. She had been traveling on the public buses so long that she knew all the routes. Yawning horribly, she ran the water into Mr. Frosty's cat food and put the dish on the floor. He ate in a dignified way; she remembered how when she had taken him to her brother's, they had fed him a real raw fish, just caught in the pond by one of the boys, and how Mr. Frosty had pounced on it, bolting it, he was so eager. They really do like fish. Now he played with the saucer, batting it from side to side, even though he was grown up. Cats were really much happier after you . . . after you . . . (she yawned) Oh, it was Chinese Festival Day.

If I had the money, if I could get my hair done. . . . He comes into the library; he's a college professor; no, he's a playboy. "Who's that girl?" Talks to Mrs. Allison, slyly flattering her. "This is Jeannine." She casts her eyes down, rich in feminine power. Had my nails done today. And these are good clothes, they have taste, my own individuality, my beauty. "There's something about her," he says. "Will you go out with me?" Later on the roof garden, drinking champagne, "Jeannine, will you—"

Mr. Frosty, unsatisfied and jealous, puts his claw into her leg. "All right!" she says, choking on the sound of her own voice. *Get dressed quick.*

I do (thought Jeannine, looking in the precious full-length mirror inexplicably left by the previous tenant on the back of the closet door) *I do look a little bit like . . . if I tilt my face. Oh! Cal will be SO—MAD*—and flying back to the bed, she strips off her pajamas and snatches at the underwear she always leaves out on the bureau the night before. Jeannine the Water Nymph. *I dreamed about a young man somewhere.* She doesn't quite believe in cards or omens, that's totally idiotic, but sometimes she giggles and thinks it would be nice. *I have big eyes. You are going to meet a tall, dark—*

Placing Mr. Frosty firmly on the bed, she pulls on her sweater and skirt, then brushes her hair, counting strokes under her breath. Her coat is so old. Just a little bit of make-up, lip pomade and powder. (She forgot again and got powder on her coat.) If she got out early, she wouldn't have to meet Cal in the room; he would play with the cat (down on his hands and knees) and then want to Make Love; this way's better. The bus to Chinatown. She stumbled down the stairs in her haste, catching at the banister. Little Miss Spry, the old lady on the bottom floor, opened her door just in time to catch Miss Dadier flying through the hall. Jeannine saw a small, wrinkled, worried, old face, wispy white hair, and a body like a flour sack done up in a black shapeless dress. One spotted, veined hand round the edge of the door.

"How do, Jeannine. Going out?"

Doubling up in a fit of hysterics, Miss Dadier escaped. *Ooh! To look like that!*

There was Cal, passing the bus station.

XI

Etsuko Belin, stretched cruciform on a glider, shifted her weight and went into a slow turn, seeing fifteen hundred feet below her the rising sun of Whileaway reflected in the glacial-scaur lakes of Mount Strom. She flipped the glider over, and sailing on her back, passed a hawk.

XII

Six months ago at the Chinese New Year, Jeannine had stood in the cold, holding her mittens over her ears to keep out the awful sound of firecrackers. Cal, next to her, watched the dragon dance around in the street.

XIII

I met Janet Evason on Broadway, standing to the side of the parade given in her honor (I was). She leaned out of the limousine and beckoned me in. Surrounded by Secret Service agents. "That one," she said.

Eventually we will all come together.

XIV

Jeannine, out of place, puts her hands over her ears and shuts her eyes on a farm on Whileaway, sitting at the trestle-table under the trees where everybody is eating. *I'm not here. I'm not here.* Chilia Ysayeson's youngest has taken a fancy to the newcomer; Jeannine sees big eyes, big breasts, big shoulders, thick lips, all that grossness. Mr. Frosty is being spoilt, petted and fed by eighteen Belins. *I'm not here.*

XV

JE: Evason is not "son" but "daughter." This is *your* translation.

XVI

And here we are.

PART TWO

I

*W*ho am I?
    I know who I am, but what's my brand name?
    Me with a new face, a puffy mask. Laid over the old one in strips of plastic, a blond Hallowe'en ghoul on top of the S.S. uniform. I was skinny as a beanpole underneath except for the hands, which were similarly treated, and that very impressive face. I did this once in my line of business, which I'll go into later, and scared the idealistic children who lived downstairs. Their delicate skins red with offended horror. Their clear young voices raised in song (at three in the morning). I'm not Jeannine. I'm not Janet. I'm not Joanna.
    I don't do this often (say I, the ghoul) but it's great elevator technique, holding your forefinger to the back of somebody's neck while passing the fourth floor, knowing he'll never find out that you're not all there.
    (Sorry, but watch out.)
    You'll meet me later.

II

As I have said before, I (not the one above, please) had an experience on the seventh of February last, nineteen-sixty-nine.
    I turned into a man.
    I had been a man before, but only briefly and in a crowd.
    You would not have noticed anything, had you been there.
    Manhood, children, is not reached by courage or short hair or insensibility or by being (as I was) in Chicago's only skyscraper hotel while the snow rages outside. I sat in a Los Angeles cocktail party with the bad baroque furniture all around, having turned into a man. I saw myself between the dirty-white scrolls of the mirror and the results were indubitable: I was a man. But what then is manhood?
    Manhood, children . . . *is Manhood.*

III

Janet beckoned me into the limousine and I got in. The road
was very dark. As she opened the door I saw her famous face
under the dome light over the front seat; trees massed electric-
green beyond the headlights. This is how I really met her.
Jeannine Dadier was an evasive outline in the back seat.

"Greetings," said Janet Evason. "Hello. Bonsoir. That's
Jeannine. And you?"

I told her. Jeannine started talking about all the clever things
her cat had done. Trees swayed and jerked in front of us.

"On moonlit nights," said Janet, "I often drive without
lights," and slowing the car to a crawl, she turned out the headlights; I mean I saw them disappear—the countryside blent
misty and pale to the horizon like a badly exposed Watteau.
I always feel in moonlight as though my eyes have gone bad.
The car—something expensive, though it was too dark to tell
what—sighed soundlessly. Jeannine had all but disappeared.

"I have, as they say," (said Janet in her surprisingly loud, normal voice) "given them the slip," and she turned the headlights
back on. "I daresay that's not proper," she added.

"It is *not*," said Jeannine from the back seat. We passed a
motel sign in a dip of the road, with something flashing lit-up
behind the trees.

"I am very sorry," said Janet. *The car?* "Stolen," she said. She
peered out the side window for a moment, turning her head
and taking her eyes off the road. Jeannine gasped indignantly.
Only the driver can see really accurately in the rear-view mirror; but there was a car behind us. We turned off onto a dirt
road—that is, she turned off—and into the woods with the
headlights dark—and on to another road, after which there
was a private house, all lights out, just as neat as you please.
"Goodbye, excuse me," said Janet affably, slipping out of the
car; "Carry on, please," and she vanished into the house. She
was wearing her television suit. I sat baffled, with Jeannine's
hands gripping the car seat at my back (the way children do).
The second car pulled up behind us. They came out and surrounded me (such a disadvantage to be sitting down and the
lights hurt your eyes). Brutally short haircuts and something

unpleasant about the clothing: straight, square, clean, yet not robust. Can you picture a plainclothesman pulling his hair? Of course not. Jeannine was cowering out of sight or had disappeared somehow. Just before Janet Evason emerged on to the porch of that private house, accompanied by a beaming family: father, mother, teen-age daughter, and family dog (everyone delighted to be famous), I committed myself rather too idiotically by exclaiming with some heat:

"Who are you looking for? There's nobody here. There's only me."

IV

Was she trying to run away? Or only to pick people at random?

V

Why did they send me? Because they can spare me. Etsuko Belin strapped me in. "Ah, Janet!" she said. (Ah, yourself.) In a plain, blank room. The cage in which I lay goes in and out of existence forty-thousand times a second; thus it did not go with me. No last kiss from Vittoria; nobody could get to me. I did not, contrary to your expectation, go nauseated or cold or feel I was dropping through endless whatever. The trouble is your brain continues to work on the old stimuli while the new ones already come in; I tried to *make* the new wall into the old. Where the lattice of the cage had been was a human face.

Späsibo.

Sorry.

Let me explain.

I was so rattled that I did not take in all at once that I was lying across her—desk, I learned later—and worse still. Appeared across it, just like that (in full view of five others). We had experimented with other distances; now they fetched me back, to make sure, and sent me out, and there I was again, on her desk.

What a strange woman; thick and thin, dried up, hefty in the back, with a grandmotherly moustache, a little one. How withered away one can be from a life of unremitting toil.

Aha! A man.

Shall I say my flesh crawled? Bad for vanity, but it did. This must be a man. I got off its desk. Perhaps it was going out to manual work, for we were dressed alike; only it had coded bands of color sewn over its pocket, a sensible device for a machine to read or something. I said in perfect English:

"How do you do? I must explain my sudden appearance. I am from another time." (We had rejected *probability/continuum* as unintelligible.) Nobody moved.

"How do you do? I must explain my sudden appearance. I am from another time."

What do you do, call them names? They didn't move. I sat down on the desk and one of them slammed shut a part of the wall; so they have doors, just as we do. The important thing in a new situation is not to frighten, and in my pockets was just the thing for such an emergency. I took out the piece of string and began playing Cat's Cradle.

"Who are you!" said one of them. They all had these little stripes over their pockets.

"I am from another time, from the future," I said, and held out the cat's cradle. It's not only the universal symbol of peace, but a pretty good game, too. This was the simplest position, though. One of them laughed; another put its hands over its eyes; the one whose desk it was backed off; a fourth said, "Is this a joke?"

"I am from the future." Just sit there long enough and the truth will sink in.

"What?" said Number One.

"How else do you think I appeared out of the air?" I said. "People cannot very well walk through walls, now can they?"

The reply to this was that Three took out a small revolver, and this surprised me; for everyone knows that anger is most intense towards those you know: it is lovers and neighbors who kill each other. There's no sense, after all, in behaving that way towards a perfect stranger; where's the satisfaction? No love, no need; no need, no frustration; no frustration, no hate, right? It must have been fear. The door opened at this point and a young woman walked in, a woman of thirty years or so, elaborately painted and dressed. I know I should not have assumed anything, but one must work with what one has; and

I assumed that her dress indicated a mother. That is, someone on vacation, someone with leisure, someone who's close to the information network and full of intellectual curiosity. If there's a top class (I said to myself), this is it. I didn't want to take anyone away from necessary manual work. And I thought, you know, that I would make a small joke. So I said to her:

"Take me to your leader."

VI

. . . a tall blonde woman in blue pajamas who appeared standing on Colonel Q———'s desk, as if from nowhere. She took out what appeared to be a weapon. . . . No answer to our questions. The Colonel has kept a small revolver in the top drawer of his desk since the summer riots. He produced it. She would not answer our questions. I believe at that point Miss X———, the Colonel's secretary, walked into the room, quite unaware of what was going on. Luckily Y———, Z———, Q———, R———, and myself kept our heads. She then said, "I am from the future."

QUESTIONER: Miss X——— said that?

ANSWER: No, not Miss X———. The—the stranger.

QUESTIONER: Are you sure she appeared *standing* on Colonel Q———'s desk?

ANSWER: No, I'm not sure. Wait. Yes I am. She was sitting on it.

VII

INTERVIEWER: It seems odd to all of us, Miss Evason, that in venturing into such—well, such absolutely unknown territory—that you should have come unarmed with anything except a piece of string. Did you expect us to be peaceful?

JE: No. No one is, completely.

INTERVIEWER: Then you should have armed yourself.

JE: Never.

INTERVIEWER: But an armed person, Miss Evason, is more formidable than one who is helpless. An armed person more readily inspires fear.

JE: Exactly.

VIII

That woman lived with me for a month. I don't mean in my house. Janet Evason on the radio, the talk shows, the newspapers, newsreels, magazines, ads even. With somebody I suspect was Miss Dadier appearing in my bedroom late one night.

"I'm lost." She meant: what world is this?

"F'godsakes, go out in the *hall*, will you?"

But she melted away through the Chinese print on the wall, presumably into the empty, carpeted, three-in-the-morning corridor outside. Some people never stick around. In my dream somebody wanted to know where Miss Dadier was. I woke at about four and went to the bathroom for a glass of water; there she was on the other side of the bathroom mirror, semaphoring frantically. She made her eyes big and peered desperately into the room, both fists pressed against the glass.

"He's not here," I said. "Go away."

She mouthed something unintelligible. The room sang:

> *Thou hast led capti-*
> *i-vi-ty*
> *Ca-ap-tive!*
>
> *Thous hast led capti-*
> *i-vi-ty*
> *Ca-ap-tive!*

I wet a washcloth and swiped at the mirror with it. She winced. Turn out the light, said my finer instincts, and so I turned out the light. She remained lit up. Dismissing the whole thing as the world's aberration and not mine, I went back to bed.

"Janet?" she said.

IX

Janet picked up Jeannine at the Chinese New Festival. Miss Dadier never allowed anyone to pick her up but a woman was different, after all; it wasn't the same thing. Janet was wearing a tan raincoat. Cal had gone round the corner to get steamed buns in a Chinese luncheonette and Miss Evason asked the meaning of a banner that was being carried through the street.

"Happy Perseverance, Madam Chiang," said Jeannine.

Then they chatted about the weather.

"Oh, I couldn't," said Jeannine suddenly. (She put her hands over her ears and made a face.) "But that's different," she said.

Janet Evason made another suggestion. Jeannine looked interested and willing to understand, though a little baffled.

"Cal's in there," said Jeannine loftily. "I couldn't go in *there*." She spread her fingers out in front of her like two fans. She was prettier than Miss Evason and glad of it; Miss Evason resembled a large boy scout with flyaway hair.

"Are you French?"

"Ah!" said Miss Evason, nodding.

"I've never been to France," said Jeannine languidly; "I often thought I'd—well, I just haven't been." *Don't stare at me.* She slouched and narrowed her eyes. She wanted to put one hand up affectedly to shade her forehead; she wanted to cry out, "Look! There's my boyfriend Cal," but there wasn't a sign of him, and if she turned to the grocery-store window it would be full of fish's intestines and slabs of dried fish; she knew that.

It—would—make—her—*sick*! (She stared at a carp with its guts coming out.) *I'm shaking all over.* "Who did your hair?" she asked Miss Evason, and when Miss Evason didn't understand:

"Who streaked your hair so beautifully?"

"Time," and Miss Evason laughed and Miss Dadier laughed. Miss Dadier laughed beautifully, gloriously, throwing her head back; everyone admired the curve of Miss Dadier's throat. Eyes turned. *A beautiful body and personality to burn.* "I can't possibly go with you," said Miss Dadier magnificently, her fur coat swirling; "There's Cal, there's New York, there's my work, New York in springtime, I can't leave, my life is here," and the spring wind played with her hair.

Crazy Jeannine nodded, petrified.

"Good," said Janet Evason. "We'll get you a leave from work." She whistled and around the corner at a dead run came two plainclothes policemen in tan raincoats: enormous, jowly, thick-necked, determined men who will continue running—at a dead heat—through the rest of this tale. But we won't notice them. Jeannine looked in astonishment from their raincoats to Miss Evason's raincoat. She did not approve *at all.*

"So that's why it doesn't fit," she said. Janet pointed to Jeannine for the benefit of the cops.

"Boys, I've got one."

X

The Chinese New Festival was invented to celebrate the recapture of Hong Kong from the Japanese. Chiang Kai-shek died of heart disease in 1951 and Madam Chiang is premieress of the New China. Japan, which controls the mainland, remains fairly quiet since it lacks the backing of—for example—a reawakened Germany, and if any war occurs, it will be between the Divine Japanese Imperiality and the Union of Soviet Socialist Republics (there are twelve). Americans don't worry much. Germany still squabbles occasionally with Italy or England; France (disgraced in the abortive *putsch* of '42) is beginning to have trouble with its colonial possessions. Britain—wiser—gave India provisional self-government in 1966.

The Depression is still world-wide.

(But think—only think!—what might have happened if the world had not so luckily slowed down, if there had been a really big war, for big wars are forcing-houses of science, economics, politics; think what might have happened, what might not have happened. It's a lucky world. Jeannine is lucky to live in it.

She doesn't think so.)

XI

(Cal, who came out of the Chinese luncheonette just in time to see his girl go off with three other people, did not throw the lunch buns to the ground in a fit of exasperated rage and stamp on them. Some haunted Polish ancestor looked out of his eyes. He was so thin and slight that his ambitions shone through him: I'll make it some day, baby. I'll be the greatest. He sat down on a fire plug and began to eat the buns.

She'll have to come back to feed her cat.)

PART THREE

I

THIS IS the lecture. If you don't like it, you can skip to the next chapter. Before Janet
                    arrived on this planet

I was moody, ill-at-ease, unhappy, and hard to be with. I didn't relish my breakfast. I spent my whole day combing my hair and putting on make-up. Other girls practiced with the shot-put and compared archery scores, but I—indifferent to javelin and crossbow, positively repelled by horticulture and ice hockey —all I did was

dress for The Man
smile for The Man
talk wittily to The Man
sympathize with The Man
flatter The Man
understand The Man
defer to The Man
entertain The Man
keep The Man
live for The Man.

Then a new interest entered my life. After I called up Janet, out of nothing, or she called up me (don't read between the lines; there's nothing there) I began to gain weight, my appetite improved, friends commented on my renewed zest for life, and a nagging scoliosis of the ankle that had tortured me for years simply vanished overnight. I don't even remember the last time I had to go to the aquarium and stifle my sobs by watching the sharks. I rode in closed limousines with Janet to television appearances much like the one you already saw in the last chapter; I answered her questions; I bought her a pocket dictionary; I took her to the zoo; I pointed out New York's skyline at night as if I owned it.

Oh, I made that woman up; you can believe it!

Now in the opera scenario that governs our lives, Janet would have gone to a party and at that party she would have met a man and there would have been something about that man; he would not have seemed to her like any other man she had ever met. Later he would have complimented her on her eyes and she would have blushed with pleasure; she would have felt that compliment was somehow unlike any other compliment she had ever received because it had come from that man; she would have wanted to please that man, and at the same time she would have felt the compliment enter the marrow of her bones; she would have gone out and bought mascara for the eyes that had been complimented by that man. And later still they would have gone for walks, and later still for dinners; and little dinners tête-à-tête with that man would have been like no other dinners Janet had ever had; and over the coffee and brandy he would have taken her hand; and later still Janet would have melted back against the black leather couch in his apartment and thrown her arm across the cocktail table (which would have been made of elegant teak-wood) and put down her drink of expensive Scotch and swooned; she would have simply swooned. She would have said: I Am In Love With That Man. That Is The Meaning Of My Life. And then, of course, you know what would have happened.

I made her up. I did everything but find a typical family for her; if you will remember, she found them herself. But I taught her how to use a bath-tub and I corrected her English (calm, slow, a hint of whisper in the "s," guardedly ironic). I took her out of her workingwoman's suit and murmured (as I soaped her hair) fragments of sentences that I could somehow never finish: "Janet you must . . . Janet, we don't . . . but one always . . ."

That's different, I said, *that's different.*

I couldn't, I said, *oh, I couldn't.*

What I want to say is, I tried; I'm a good girl; I'll do it if you'll show me.

But what can you do when this woman puts her hand through the wall? (Actually the plasterboard partition between the kitchenette and the living room.)

Janet, sit down.

Janet, don't do that.

Janet, don't kick Jeannine.

Janet!

Janet, don't!

I imagine her: civil, reserved, impenetrably formulaic. She was on her company manners for months. Then, I think, she decided that she could get away with having no manners; or rather, that we didn't honor the ones she had, so why not? It must have been new to someone from Whileaway, the official tolerance of everything she did or tried to do, the leisure, the attention that was so close to adulation. I have the feeling that any of them can blossom out like that (and lucky they don't, eh?) with the smooth kinship web of home centuries away, surrounded by barbarians, celibate for months, coping with a culture and a language that I think she—in her heart—must have despised.

I was housed with her for six and a half months in a hotel suite ordinarily used to entertain visiting diplomats. *I put shoes on that woman's feet.* I had fulfilled one of my dreams—to show Manhattan to a foreigner—and I waited for Janet to go to a party and meet that man; I waited and waited. She walked around the suite nude. She has an awfully big ass. She used to practice her yoga on the white living room rug, callouses on her feet actually catching in the fuzz, if you can believe it. I would put lipstick on Janet and ten minutes later it would have vanished; I clothed her and she shed like a three-year-old: courteous, kind, irreproachably polite; I shied at her atrocious jokes and she made them worse.

She never communicated with her home, as far as I know.

She wanted to see a man naked (we got pictures).

She wanted to see a baby man naked (we got somebody's nephew).

She wanted newspapers, novels, histories, magazines, people to interview, television programs, statistics on clove production in the East Indies, textbooks on wheat farming, to visit a bridge (we did). She wanted the blueprints (we got them).

She was neat but lazy—I never caught her doing anything.

She held the baby like an expert, cooing and trundling, bouncing him up and down so that he stopped screaming and stared at her chin the way babies do. She uncovered him. "Tsk." "My goodness." She was astonished.

She scrubbed my back and asked me to scrub hers; she took the lipstick I gave her and made pictures on the yellow damask walls. ("You mean it's not *washable*?") I got her girlie magazines and she said she couldn't make head or tail of them; I said, "Janet, stop joking" and she was surprised; she hadn't meant to. She wanted a dictionary of slang. One day I caught her playing games with Room Service; she was calling up the different numbers on the white hotel phone and giving them contradictory instructions. This woman was dialing the numbers with her feet. I slammed the phone across one of the double beds.

"Joanna," she said, "I do not understand you. Why not play? Nobody is going to be hurt and nobody is going to blame you; why not take advantage?"

"You fake!" I said; "You fake, you rotten fake!" Somehow that was all I could think of to say. She tried looking injured and did not succeed—she only looked smug—so she wiped her face clean of all expression and started again.

"If we make perhaps an hypothetical assumption—"

"Go to hell," I said; "Put your clothes on."

"Perhaps about this sex business you can tell me," she said, "why is this hypothetical assumption—"

"Why the devil do you run around in the nude!"

"My child," she said gently, "you must understand. I'm far from home; I want to keep myself cheerful, eh? And about this men thing, you must remember that to me they are a particularly foreign species; one can make love with a dog, yes? But not with something so unfortunately close to oneself. You see how I can feel this way?"

My ruffled dignity. She submitted to the lipstick again. We got her dressed. She looked all right except for that unfortunate habit of whirling around with a grin on her face and her hands out in the judo crouch. Well, well! I got reasonably decent shoes on Janet Evason's feet. She smiled. She put her arm around me.

Oh, I couldn't!

?

That's different.

(You'll hear a lot of those two sentences in life, if you listen for them. I see Janet Evason finally dressing herself, a study in purest awe as she holds up to the light, one after the other, semi-transparent garments of nylon and lace, fairy webs, rose-colored elastic puttees—"Oh, my," "Oh, my goodness," she says—and finally, completely stupefied, wraps one of them around her head.)

She bent down to kiss me, looking kind, looking perplexed, and I kicked her.

That's when she put her fist through the wall.

II

We went to a party on Riverside Drive—incognitae—with Janet a little behind me. At the door, a little behind me. The February snow coming down outside. On the fortieth floor we got out of the elevator and I checked my dress in the hall mirror: my hair feels as if it's falling down, my makeup's too heavy, everything's out of place from the crotch of the panty-hose to the ridden-up bra to the ring whose stone drags it around under my knuckle. And I don't even wear false eyelashes. Janet —beastly fresh—is showing her usual trick of the Disappearing Lipstick. She hums gently. Batty Joanna. There are policemen posted all around the building, policemen in the street, policemen in the elevator. Nobody wants anything to happen to her. She gives a little yelp of excitement and pleasure—the first uncontrolled contact with the beastly savages.

"You'll tell me what to do," she says, "won't you?" Ha ha. He he. Ho ho. What fun. She bounces up and down.

"Why didn't they send someone who knew what he was doing!" I whisper back.

"What *she* was doing," she says unself-consciously, shifting gears in a moment. "You see, under field conditions, nobody can handle all the eventualities. We're not superhuman, any of us, *nicht wahr?* So you take someone you can spare. It's like this—"

I opened the door, Janet a little behind me.

I knew most of the women there: Sposissa, three times divorced; Eglantissa, who thinks only of clothes; Aphrodissa, who cannot keep her eyes open because of her false eyelashes; Clarissa, who will commit suicide; Lucrissa, whose strained forehead shows that she's making more money than her husband;

Wailissa, engaged in a game of ain't-it-awful with Lamentissa;
Travailissa, who usually only works, but who is now sitting very
still on the couch so that her smile will not spoil; and naughty
Saccharissa, who is playing a round of His Little Girl across
the bar with the host. Saccharissa is forty-five. So is Amicissa,
the Good Sport. I looked for Ludicrissa, but she is too plain
to be invited to a party like this, and of course we never invite
Amphibissa, for obvious reasons.

In we walked, Janet and I, the right and left hands of a
bomb. Actually you might have said everyone was enjoying
themselves. I introduced her to everyone. My Swedish cousin.
(Where is Domicissa, who never opens her mouth in public?
And Dulcississa, whose standard line, "Oh, you're so wonderful!" is oddly missing from the air tonight?)

I shadowed Janet.

I played with my ring.

I waited for the remark that begins "Women—" or "Women
can't—" or "Why do women—" and kept up an insubstantial
conversation on my right. On my left hand Janet stood: very
erect, her eyes shining, turning her head swiftly every now and
again to follow the current of events at the party. At times like
this, when I'm low, when I'm anxious, Janet's attention seems
a parody of attention and her energy unbearably high. I was
afraid she'd burst out chuckling. Somebody (male) got me a
drink.

A ROUND OF "HIS LITTLE GIRL"

SACCHARISSA: I'm Your Little Girl.
HOST (wheedling): Are you really?
SACCHARISSA: (complacent): Yes I am.
HOST: Then you have to be stupid, too.

A SIMULTANEOUS ROUND OF "AIN'T IT AWFUL"

LAMENTISSA: When I do the floor, he doesn't come home and
say it's wonderful.
WAILISSA: Well, darling, we can't live without him, can we?
You'll just have to do *better*.

LAMENTISSA (wistfully): I bet *you* do better.
WAILISSA: I do the floor better than anybody I know.
LAMENTISSA (excited): Does he ever say it's wonderful?
WAILISSA (dissolving): He never says *anything*!

(There follows the chorus which gives the game its name. A passing male, hearing this exchange, remarked, "You women are lucky you don't have to go out and go to work.")

Somebody I did not know came up to us: sharp, balding, glasses reflecting two spots of lamplight. A long, lean, academic, more-or-less young man.

"Do you want something to drink?"

Janet said "A-a-a-h" very long, with exaggerated enthusiasm. Dear God, don't let her make a fool of herself. "Drink what?" she said promptly. I introduced my Swedish cousin.

"Scotch, punch, rum-and-coke, rum, ginger-ale?"

"What's that?" I suppose that, critically speaking, she didn't look too bad. "I mean," she said (correcting herself), "that is what kind of drug? Excuse me. My English isn't good." She waits, delighted with everything. He smiles.

"Alcohol," he says.

"*Ethyl* alcohol?" She puts her hand over her heart in unconscious parody. "It is made from grain, yes? Food? Potatoes? My, my! How wasteful!"

"Why do you say that?" says the young man, laughing.

"Because," answers my Janet, "to use food for fermentation is wasteful, yes? I should think so! That's cultivation, fertilizer, sprays, harvesting, et cetera. Then you lose a good deal of the carbohydrates in the actual process. I should think you would grow *cannabis*, which my friend tells me you already have, and give the grains to those starving people."

"You know, you're charming," he says.

"Huh?" (That's Janet.) To prevent disaster, I step in and indicate with my eyes that yes, she's charming and second, we really do want a drink.

"You told me you people had cannabis," Janet says a little irritably.

"It isn't cured properly; it'll make you choke," I say. She nods thoughtfully. I can tell without asking what's going through her mind: the orderly fields of Whileaway, the centuries-old

mutations and hybridizations of cannabis sativa, the little garden plots of marihuana tended (for all I know) by seven-year-
olds. She had in fact tried some several weeks before. It had
made her cough horribly.

The youngish man returned with our drink and while I
signalled him Stay, stay, she's harmless, she's innocent, Janet
screwed up her face and tried to drink the stuff in one swallow.
It was then I knew that her sense of humor was running away
with her. She turned red. She coughed explosively.

"It's horrible!"

"*Sip* it, *sip* it," said he, highly amused.

"I don't want it."

"I tell you what," he proposed amiably, "I'll make you one
you *will* like." (There follows a small interlude of us punching
each other and whispering vehemently: "Janet, if you—")

"But I don't like it," she said simply. You're not supposed to
do that. On Whileaway, perhaps, but not here.

"Try it," he urged.

"I did," she said equably. "Sorry, I will wait for the smokes."

He takes her hand and closes her fingers around the glass,
shaking his forefinger at her playfully: "Come on now, I can't
believe that; you made me get it for you—" and as our methods of courtship seem to make her turn pale, I wink at him and
whisk her away to the corner of the apartment where the C.S.
vapor blooms. She tries it and gets a coughing fit. She goes
sullenly back to the bar.

A MANUFACTURER OF CARS FROM LEEDS (genteelly): I hear so
much about the New Feminism here in America. Surely it's not
necessary, is it? (He beams with the delighted air of someone
who has just given pleasure to a whole roomful of people.)
SPOSISSA, EGLANTISSA, APHRODISSA, CLARISSA, LUCRISSA,
WAILISSA, LAMENTISSA, TRAVAILISSA (dear God, how many
of them are there?), SACCHARISSA, LUDICRISSA (she came in
late): Oh no, no, no! (They all laugh.)

When I got back to the bar, Clarissa was going grimly into
her latest heartbreak. I saw Janet, feet apart—a daughter of
Whileaway never quails!—trying to get down more than three

ounces of straight rum. I suppose one forgets the first taste. She looked flushed and successful.

ME: You're not used to that stuff, Janet.

JANET: O.K., I'll stop.

(Like all foreigners she is fascinated by the word "Okay" and has been using it on every possible occasion for the last four weeks.)

"It's very hard not having anything, though," she says seriously. "I suppose, love, that I'm hardly giving anything away if I say that I don't like your friends."

"They're not my friends, for God's sake. I come here to meet people."

?

"I come here to meet men," I said. "Janet, sit down."

This time it was a ginger moustache. Young. Nice. Flashy. Flowered waistcoat. Hip. (hip?)

Peals of laughter from the corner, where Eglantissa's latest is holding up and wiggling a chain made of paper clips. Wailissa fusses ineffectually around him. Eglantissa—looking more and more like a corpse—sits on an elegant, brocaded armchair, with her drink rigid in her hand. Blue smoke wreathes about her head.

"Hullo," says Ginger Moustache. Sincere. Young.

"Oh. How do you do?" says Janet. She's remembered her manners. Ginger Moustache produces a smile and a cigarette case.

"Marijuana?" says Janet hopefully. He chuckles.

"No. Do you want a drink?"

She looks sulky.

"All right, don't have a drink. And you're—"

I introduce my cousin from Sweden.

"Why do you people catabolize foodstuffs in this way?" she bursts out. Still on her mind, it seems. I explain.

"Sickness," he says. "I'm not an alcohol head; that's not my bag. I agree with you. I'd just as soon see people eating the stuff."

(Amicissa dreams: perhaps he won't have the insatiable vanity, the uneasy aggressiveness, the quickness to resent any slight or fancied neglect. Perhaps he won't want to be top dog all the

time. And he won't have a fiancée. And he won't be married.
And he won't be gay. And he won't have children. And he
won't be sixty.)

"A-a-ah," says Janet, letting out a long breath. "Yes. Aha."

I left them for a while. I was alert to any opportunity. I was
graceful. I smiled.

My brassiere hurts.

When I got back they had reached the stage of Discussing His
Work. He was teaching high school but was going to be fired.
For his ties, I think. Janet was very interested. She mentioned
the—uh—day nurseries in—well, in Sweden—and quoted:

"We have a saying: when the child goes to the school, both
mother and child howl; the child because it is going to be separated from the mother and the mother because she has to go
back to work."

"The tie between mother and child is very important," said
Ginger Moustache reprovingly. ("Excuse me, let me move that
cushion behind your back.")

"I'm sure Swedish mothers really groove on their kids,
though," he added.

"Huh?" said my Janet. (He took it as an ignorance of English and relented.)

"Listen," he said, "some time I want you to meet my wife.
I know this is a bad scene—I mean meeting you here with the
plastic people, y'know?—but *some day* you're going to come
out to Vermont and meet my wife. It's a great, heavy scene.
We've got six kids."

"Six you take care of?" said Janet with considerable respect.

"Sure," he said. "They're in Vermont right now. But after
this work hassle is over I'm going back. You grok?"

He means do you understand, Janet? She thought it simpler
to say yes.

"Hey," said Ginger Moustache, springing to his feet, "it's
been great meeting you. You're a real ballsy chick. I mean
you're a *woman*."

She looked down at herself. "What?"

"Sorry about the slang; I mean you're a fine person. It's a
pleasure—to—know—you."

"You don't know me," she was developing the nasty look.
Not very nasty as yet but frustrated-angry, tapping-the-fingers,

now-look-here-I-want-this-explained. She is quite spoiled, in her own way.

"Yeah, I know," he said. "How can we get to know each other in ten minutes, huh? That's true. It's a formal phrase: pleasuretoknowyou."

Janet giggled.

"Right?" he said. "Tell you what, give me your name and address." (she gave him mine) "I'll drop you a line. Write a letter, that is." (Not a bad fellow this Ginger Moustache.) He got up and she got up; something must interrupt this idyll. Saccharissa, Ludicrissa, Travailissa, Aphrodissa, Clarissa, Sposissa, Domicissa, the whole gang, even Carissa herself, have formed a solid wall around this couple. Breaths are held. Bets get made. Joanissa is praying in a heap in the corner. Ginger Moustache got up and Janet trailed him into the hall, asking questions. She's a good bit taller than he is. She wants to know about everything. Either she does not mind the lack of sexual interest or—as is more likely in a foreigner—prefers it. Though he's got a wife. The harsh light from the kitchenette strikes Janet Evason's face and there on one side, running from eyebrow to chin, is a strange, fine line. Has she been in an accident?

"Oh, *that!*" says Janet Evason, chuckling, bending over (though somewhat hampered by her party dress), laughing, gasping with little feminine squeaks from the top of the compass right down to the bottom, hoarse and musical, "Oh, *that!*" "That's from my third duel," she says, "see?" and guides Moustache's hand (his forefinger, actually) along her face.

"Your what?" says Moustache, momentarily frozen into the attractive statue of a pleasant young man.

"My duel," says Janet, "silly. Well, it's not Sweden, not really. You've heard of me; I was on the television. I'm the emissary from Whileaway."

"My God," he says.

"Ssh, don't tell anyone." (She's very pleased with herself. She chuckles.) "*This* line I got in my third duel; *this* one—it's practically gone—in my second. Not bad, hey?"

"Are you sure you don't mean fencing?" says Ginger Moustache.

"Hell, no," says Janet impatiently; "I told you, duel." And she draws her forefinger across her throat with a melodramatic jerk. This mad chick doesn't seem so nice to Moustache any more. He swallows.

"What do you fight about—girls?"

"You are kidding me," says Janet. "We fight about bad temper—what else? Temperamental incompatibility. Not that it's so common as it used to be but if you can't stand her and she can't stand you, what's to be done?"

"Sure," says Ginger Moustache. "Well, goodbye." Janet became suddenly repentant.

"That—well, I suppose that's rather savage, isn't it?" she says. "I beg pardon. You will think badly of us. Understand, I have put all that behind me now; I am an adult; I have a family. We hope to be friends, yes?" And she looks down at him solemnly, a little timidly, ready to be rebuked. But he hasn't the heart to do it.

"You're a great chick," says he. "Some day we'll get together. Don't duel with *me*, though."

She looks surprised. "Huh?"

"Yeah, you'll tell me all about yourself," Ginger Moustache goes on. He smiles and broods. "You can meet the kids."

"I have a daughter," says Janet. "Baby brat Yuriko." He smiles.

"We got homemade wine. Vegetable garden. Sara puts things up. Great place." (He's into his duffle coat by now after searching in the hall closet.) "Tell me, what do you do? I mean for a living?"

"Whileaway is not here-and-now," Janet begins; "You might not understand. I settle family quarrels; I look after people; it's—"

"Social work?" asks Ginger Moustache, extending to us his fine, shapely, tanned, uncalloused hand, an intellectual's hand, but I have hardened my heart and I peep out from behind Janet Evason with the divine relief of my female irony and my female teeth:

"She's a cop. She puts people in jail."

Ginger Moustache is alarmed, knows he's alarmed, laughs at himself, shakes his head. How wide is the gap between cultures! But we grok. We shake hands. He goes off into the party to fetch Domicissa, whom he pulls by the wrist (she silently protesting) to the hall closet. "Get on your Goddamn coat, will you!" I heard only whispers, vehement and angry, then Domicissa blowing her nose.

"So long, hey! Hey, so long!" cried he.

His wife's in Vermont; Domicissa isn't his wife.

Janet had just asked me to explicate the marriage system of North America.

Saccharissa has just said, pouting, "Po' little me! I sho'ly needs to be liberated!"

Aphrodissa was sitting in someone's lap, her left eyelash half off. Janet was rather at a loss. Mustn't judge. Shut one eye. Peek. Busy, busy couple, kissing and grabbing. Janet backed off slowly to the other side of the room and there we met the lean academic with the glasses; he's all sharp, nervous and sharp. He gave her a drink and she drank it.

"So you *do* like it!" he said provokingly.

"I would suhtinly like," said Saccharissa with great energy, "to see all those women athletes from the Olympics compete with all those men athletes; I don't imagine any of these women athletes could even *come neah* the men."

"But American women are so *unusual*," said the man from Leeds. "Your conquering energy, dear lady, all this world-wide American efficiency! What do you dear ladies use it for?"

"Why, to conquer the men!" cried Saccharissa, braying.

"In mah baby brain," said Janet, imitating quite accurately, "a suhtin conviction is beginnin' to fo'm."

"The conviction that somebody is being insulted?" said Sharp Glasses. He didn't say that, actually.

"Let's go," said Janet. *I know it's the wrong party, but where are you going to find the right party?*

"Oh, you don't want to go!" said Sharp Glasses energetically. Jerky, too, they're always so jerky.

"But I do," said Janet.

"Of course you don't," he said; "You're just beginning to enjoy yourself. The party's warming up. Here," (pushing us down on the couch) "let me get you another."

You're in a strange place, Janet. Be civil.

He came back with another and she drank it. Uh-oh. We made trivial conversation until she recovered. He leaned forward confidentially. "What do *you* think of the new feminism, eh?"

"What is—" (she tried again) "what is—my English is not so good. Could you explain?"

"Well, what do you think of women? Do you think women can compete with men?"

"I don't know any men." She's beginning to get mad.

"Ha ha!" said Sharp Glasses. "Ha ha ha! Ha ha!" (He laughed just like that, in sharp little bursts.) "My name's Ewing. What's yours?"

"Janet."

"Well, Janet, I'll tell you what *I* think of the new feminism. I think it's a mistake. A very bad mistake."

"Oh," said Janet flatly. I kicked her, I kicked her, I kicked her.

"I haven't got anything against women's intelligence," said Ewing. "Some of my colleagues are women. It's not women's intelligence. It's women's psychology. Eh?"

He's being good-humored the only way he knows how. Don't hit him.

"What you've got to remember," said Ewing, energetically shredding a small napkin, "is that most women are liberated right now. They like what they're doing. They do it because they like it."

Don't, Janet.

"Not only that, you gals are going about it the wrong way."

You're in someone else's house. Be polite.

"You can't challenge men in their own fields," he said. "Now nobody can be more in favor of women getting their rights than I am. Do you want to sit down? Let's. As I said, I'm all in favor of it. Adds a decorative touch to the office, eh? Ha ha! Ha ha ha! Unequal pay is a disgrace. But you've got to remember, Janet, that women have certain physical limitations," (here he took off his glasses, wiped them with a little serrated square of blue cotton, and put them back on) "and you have to work within your physical limitations.

"For example," he went on, mistaking her silence for wisdom while Ludicrissa muttered, "How true! How true!" somewhere in the background about something or other, "you have to take into account that there are more than two thousand rapes in New York City alone in every particular year. I'm not saying of course that that's a good thing, but you have to take it into account. Men are physically stronger than women, you know."

(Picture me on the back of the couch, clinging to her hair like a homuncula, battering her on the top of the head until she doesn't dare to open her mouth.)

"Of course, Janet," he went on, "you're not one of those—uh—extremists. Those extremists don't take these things into account, do they? Of course not! Mind you, I'm not defending unequal pay but we have to take these things into account. Don't we? By the way, I make twenty thousand a year. Ha! Ha ha ha!" And off he went into another fit.

She squeaked something—because I was strangling her.

"What?" he said. "What did you say?" He looked at her nearsightedly. Our struggle must have imparted an unusual intensity to her expression because he seemed extraordinarily flattered by what he saw; he turned his head away coyly, sneaked a look out of the corner of his eye, and then whipped his head round into position very fast. As if he had been a bird.

"You're a good conversationalist," he said. He began to perspire gently. He shifted the pieces of his napkin from hand to hand. He dropped them and dusted his hands off. Now he's going to do it.

"Janet—uh—Janet, I wonder if you—" fumbling blindly for his drink—"that is if—uh—you—"

But we are far away, throwing coats out of the coat closet like a geyser.

Is that your method of courtship!

"Not exactly," I said. "You see—"

Baby, baby, baby. It's the host, drunk enough not to care.

Uh-oh. Be ladylike.

She showed him all her teeth. He saw a smile.

"You're beautiful, honey."

"Thank you. I go now." (good for her)

"Nah!" and he took us by the wrist. "Nah, you're not *going*."

"Let me go," said Janet.

Say it loud. Somebody will come to rescue you.

Can't I rescue myself?

No.

Why not?

All this time he was nuzzling her ear and I was showing my distaste by shrinking terrified into a corner, one eye on the party. Everyone seemed amused.

"Give us a good-bye kiss," said the host, who might have been attractive under other circumstances, a giant marine, so to speak. I pushed him away.

"What'sa matter, you some kinda prude?" he said and enfolding us in his powerful arms, et cetera—well, not so very powerful as all that, but I want to give you the feeling of the scene. If you scream, people say you're melodramatic; if you submit, you're masochistic; if you call names, you're a bitch. Hit him and he'll kill you. The best thing is to suffer mutely and yearn for a rescuer, but suppose the rescuer doesn't come?

"Let go, ————," said Janet (some Russian word I didn't catch).

"Ha ha, make me," said the host, squeezing her wrist and puckering up his lips; "Make me, make me," and he swung his hips from side to side suggestively.

No, no, keep on being ladylike!

"Is this human courting?" shouted Janet. "Is this friendship? Is this politeness?" She had an extraordinarily loud voice. He laughed and shook her wrist.

"Savages!" she shouted. A hush had fallen on the party. The host leafed dexterously through his little book of rejoinders but did not come up with anything. Then he looked up "savage" only to find it marked with an affirmative: "Masculine, brute, virile, powerful, good." So he smiled broadly. He put the book away.

"Right on, sister," he said.

So she dumped him. It happened in a blur of speed and there he was on the carpet. He was flipping furiously through the pages of the book; what else is there to do in such circumstances? (It was a little limp-leather—excuse me—volume bound in blue, which I think they give out in high schools. On the cover was written in gold WHAT TO DO IN EVERY SITUATION.)

"Bitch!" (flip flip flip) "Prude!" (flip flip) "Ball-breaker!" (flip flip flip flip) "Goddamn cancerous castrator!" (flip) "Thinks hers is gold!" (flip flip) "*You didn't have to do that!*"

Was ist? said Janet in German.

He gave her to understand that she was going to die of cancer of the womb.

She laughed.

He gave her to understand further that she was taking unfair advantage of his good manners.

She roared.

He pursued the subject and told her that if he were not a gentleman he would ram her stinking, shitty teeth up her stinking shitty ass.

She shrugged.

He told her she was so ball-breaking, shitty, stone, scumbag, mother-fucking, plug-ugly that no normal male could keep up an erection within half a mile of her.

She looked puzzled. ("Joanna, these are insults, yes?")

He got up. I think he was recovering his cool. He did not seem nearly so drunk as he had been. He shrugged his sports jacket back into position and brushed himself off. He said she had acted like a virgin, not knowing what to do when a guy made a pass, just like a Goddamned scared little baby virgin.

Most of us would have been content to leave it at that, eh, ladies?

Janet slapped him.

It was not meant to hurt, I think; it was a great big stinging theatrical performance, a cue for insults and further fighting, a come-on-get-your-guard contemptuous slap meant to enrage, which it jolly well did.

THE MARINE SAID, "YOU STUPID BROAD, I'M GONNA CREAM YOU!"

That poor man.

I didn't see things very well, as first off I got behind the closet door, but I saw him rush her and I saw her flip him; he got up again and again she deflected him, this time into the wall—I think she was worried because she didn't have time to glance behind her and the place was full of people—then he got up again and this time he swung instead and then something very complicated happened—he let out a yell and she was behind him, doing something cool and technical, frowning in concentration.

"Don't pull like that," she said. "You'll break your arm."

So he pulled. The little limp-leather notebook fluttered out on to the floor, from whence I picked it up. Everything was awfully quiet. The pain had stunned him, I guess.

She said in astonished good-humor: "But why do you want to fight when you do not know how?"

I got my coat and I got Janet's coat and I got us out of there and into the elevator. I put my head in my hands.

"Why'd you do it?"

"He called me a baby."

The little blue book was rattling around in my purse. I took it out and turned to the last thing he had said ("You stupid broad" et cetera). Underneath was written *Girl backs down—cries—manhood vindicated.* Under "Real Fight With Girl" was written *Don't hurt (except whores).* I took out my own pink book, for we all carry them, and turning to the instructions under "Brutality" found:

Man's bad temper is the woman's fault. It is also the woman's responsibility to patch things up afterwards.

There were sub-rubrics, one (reinforcing) under "Management" and one (exceptional) under "Martyrdom." Everything in my book begins with an M.

They do fit together so well, you know. I said to Janet:

"I don't think you're going to be happy here."

"Throw them both away, love," she answered.

III

Why make pretensions to fight (she said) when you can't fight? Why make pretensions to anything? I am trained, of course; that's my job, and it makes me the very devil angry when someone calls me names, but why call names? All this uneasy aggression. True, there is a little bit of hair-pulling on Whileaway, yes, and more than that, there is the temperamental thing, sometimes you can't stand another person. But the cure for that is distance. I've been foolish in the past, I admit. In middle-age one begins to settle down; Vittoria says I'm comic with my tohu-bohu when Yuki comes home with a hair out of place. I hope not. There is this thing with the child you've borne yourself, your body-child. There is also the feeling to be extra-proper in front of the children, yet hardly anybody bothers. Who has the time? And since I've become S & P I have a different outlook on all this: a job's a job and has to be done, but I don't like doing it for nothing, to raise the hand to someone. For sport, yes, okay, for hatred no. Separate them.

I ought to add there was a fourth duel in which nobody got killed; my opponent developed a lung infection, then a spinal infection—you understand, we weren't near civilization then—and the convalescence was such a long, nasty business. I took care of her. Nerve tissue's hard to regrow. She was paralyzed for a while, you know. Gave me a very salutary scare. So I don't fight with weapons now, except on my job, of course.

Am I sorry I hurt him?

Not me!

IV

Whileawayans are not nearly as peaceful as they sound.

V

Burned any bras lately har har twinkle twinkle A pretty girl like you doesn't need to be liberated twinkle har Don't listen to those hysterical bitches twinkle twinkle twinkle I never take a woman's advice about two things: love and automobiles twinkle twinkle har May I kiss your little hand twinkle twinkle twinkle. Har. Twinkle.

VI

On Whileaway they have a saying: When the mother and child are separated they both howl, the child because it is separated from the mother, the mother because she has to go back to work. Whileawayans bear their children at about thirty —singletons or twins as the demographic pressures require. These children have as one genotypic parent the biological mother (the "body-mother") while the non-bearing parent contributes the other ovum ("other mother"). Little Whileawayans are to their mothers both sulk and swank, fun and profit, pleasure and contemplation, a show of expensiveness, a slowing-down of life, an opportunity to pursue whatever interests the women have been forced to neglect previously, and the only leisure they have ever had—or will have again until old age. A family of thirty persons may have as many as four mother-and-child pairs in the common nursery at one time. Food, cleanliness, and shelter are not the mother's business; Whileawayans say with a straight face that she must be free to attend to the child's "finer spiritual needs." Then they go off by themselves and roar. The truth is they don't want to give up the leisure. Eventually we come to a painful scene. At the age of four or five these independent, blooming, pampered, extremely intelligent little girls are torn weeping and arguing from their thirty relatives and sent to the regional school, where they scheme and fight for weeks before giving in; some of them have been known to construct deadfalls or small bombs (having picked this knowledge up from their parents) in order to obliterate their instructors. Children are cared for in groups of five and taught in groups of differing sizes according to the subject under discussion. Their education at this point is heavily practical: how to run machines, how to get along without machines, law, transportation, physical theory, and so on. They learn gymnastics and mechanics. They learn practical medicine.

They learn how to swim and shoot. They continue (by themselves) to dance, to sing, to paint, to play, to do everything their Mommies did. At puberty they are invested with Middle-Dignity and turned loose; children have the right of food and lodging wherever they go, up to the power of the community to support them. They do not go back home.

Some do, of course, but then neither Mother may be there; people are busy; people are traveling; there's always work, and the big people who were so kind to a four-year-old have little time for an almost-adult. "And everything's so *small*," said one girl.

Some, wild with the desire for exploration, travel all around the world—usually in the company of other children—bands of children going to visit this or that, or bands of children about to reform the power installations, are a common sight on Whileaway.

The more profound abandon all possessions and live off the land just above or below the forty-eighth parallel; they return with animal heads, scars, visions.

Some make a beeline for their callings and spend most of puberty pestering part-time actors, bothering part-time musicians, cajoling part-time scholars.

Fools! (say the older children, who have been through it all) Don't be in such a hurry. You'll work soon enough.

At seventeen they achieve Three-Quarters Dignity and are assimilated into the labor force. This is probably the worst time in a Whileawayan's life. Groups of friends are kept together if the members request it and if it is possible, but otherwise these adolescents go where they're needed, not where they wish; nor can they join the Geographical Parliament nor the Professional Parliament until they have entered a family and developed that network of informal associations of the like-minded which is Whileaway's substitute for everything else but family.

They provide human companionship to Whileawayan cows, who pine and die unless spoken to affectionately.

They run routine machinery, dig people out of landslides, oversee food factories (with induction helmets on their heads, their toes controlling the green-peas, their fingers the vats and controls, their back muscles the carrots, and their abdomens the water supply).

They lay pipe (again, by induction).

They fix machinery.

They are not allowed to have anything to do with malfunctions or breakdowns "on foot," as the Whileawayans say, meaning in one's own person and with tools in one's own hands, without the induction helmets that make it possible to operate dozens of waldoes at just about any distance you please. That's for veterans.

They do not meddle with computers "on foot" nor join with them via induction. That's for *old* veterans.

They learn to like a place only to be ordered somewhere else the next day, commandeered to excavate coastline or fertilize fields, kindly treated by the locals (if any) and hideously bored.

It gives them something to look forward to.

At twenty-two they achieve Full Dignity and may either begin to learn the heretofore forbidden jobs or have their

learning formally certificated. They are allowed to begin ap-
prenticeships. They may marry into pre-existing families or
form their own. Some braid their hair. By now the typical
Whileawayan girl is able to do any job on the planet, except
for specialties and extremely dangerous work. By twenty-five
she has entered a family, thus choosing her geographical home
base (Whileawayans travel all the time). Her family probably
consists of twenty to thirty other persons, ranging in age from
her own to the early fifties. (Families tend to age the way
people do; thus new groupings are formed again in old age.
Approximately every fourth girl must begin a new or join a
nearly-new family.)

Sexual relations—which have begun at puberty—continue
both inside the family and outside it, but mostly outside it.
Whileawayans have two explanations for this. "Jealousy," they
say for the first explanation, and for the second, "Why not?"

Whileawayan psychology locates the basis of Whileawayan
character in the early indulgence, pleasure, and flowering
which is drastically curtailed by the separation from the mothers. This (it says) gives Whileawayan life its characteristic independence, its dissatisfaction, its suspicion, and its tendency
toward a rather irritable solipsism.

"Without which" (said the same Dunyasha Bernadetteson,
q.v.) "we would all become contented slobs, *nicht wahr?*"

Eternal optimism hides behind this dissatisfaction, however;
Whileawayans cannot forget that early paradise and every new
face, every new day, every smoke, every dance, brings back
life's possibilities. Also sleep and eating, sunrise, weather, the
seasons, machinery, gossip, and the eternal temptations of art.

They work too much. They are incredibly tidy.

Yet on the old stone bridge that links New City, South Continent, with Varya's Little Alley Ho-ho is chiseled:

*You never know what is enough until you know what is more
than enough.*

If one is lucky, one's hair turns white early; if—as in old Chinese poetry—one is indulging oneself, one dreams of old age.
For in old age the Whileawayan woman—no longer as strong
and elastic as the young—has learned to join with calculating
machines in the state they say can't be described but is most

like a sneeze that never comes off. It is the old who are given
the sedentary jobs, the old who can spend their days napping,
drawing, thinking, writing, collating, composing. In the libraries old hands come out from under the induction helmets
and give you the reproductions of the books you want; old
feet twinkle below the computer shelves, hanging down like
Humpty Dumpty's; old ladies chuckle eerily while composing
The Blasphemous Cantata (a great favorite of Ysaye's) or mad-
moon cityscapes which turn out to be do-able after all; old
brains use one part in fifty to run a city (with checkups made
by two sulky youngsters) while the other forty-nine parts riot
in a freedom they haven't had since adolescence.

The young are rather priggish about the old on Whileaway.
They don't really approve of them.

Taboos on Whileaway: sexual relations with anybody considerably older or younger than oneself, waste, ignorance, offend-
ing others without intending to.

And of course the usual legal checks on murder and theft
—both those crimes being actually quite difficult to commit.
("See," says Chilia, "it's murder if it's sneaky or if she doesn't
want to fight. So you yell 'Olaf!' and when she turns around,
then—")

No Whileawayan works more than three hours at a time on
any one job, except in emergencies.

No Whileawayan marries monogamously. (Some restrict
their sexual relations to one other person—at least while that
other person is nearby—but there is no legal arrangement.)
Whileawayan psychology again refers to the distrust of the
mother and the reluctance to form a tie that will engage every
level of emotion, all the person, all the time. And the necessity
for artificial dissatisfactions.

"Without which" (says Dunyasha Bernadetteson, op. cit.)
"we would become so happy we would sit down on our fat,
pretty behinds and soon we would start starving, *nyet?*"

But there is too, under it all, the incredible explosive energy,
the gaiety of high intelligence, the obliquities of wit, the cast
of mind that makes industrial areas into gardens and ha-has,
that supports wells of wilderness where nobody ever lives for
long, that strews across a planet sceneries, mountains, glider

preserves, culs-de-sac, comic nude statuary, artistic lists of tautologies and circular mathematical proofs (over which aficionados are moved to tears), and the best graffiti in this or any other world.

Whileawayans work all the time. They work. And they work. *And they work.*

VII

Two ancients on the direct computer line between city and quarry (private persons have to be content with spark-gap radio), fighting at the top of their lungs while five green girls wait nearby, sulky and bored:

I can't make do with five greenies; I need two on-foot checkers and protective gear for one!

Can't have.

Incomp-

?

You hear.

Is me!

(affected disdain)

If catastroph—

Won't!

And so on.

VIII

A troop of little girls contemplating three silver hoops welded to a silver cube are laughing so hard that some have fallen down into the autumn leaves on the plaza and are holding their stomachs. This is not embarrassment or an ignorant reaction to something new; they are genuine connoisseurs who have hiked for three days to see this. Their hip-packs lie around the edge of the plaza, near the fountains.

One: How lovely!

IX

Between shifts in the quarry in Newland, Henla Anaisson sings, her only audience her one fellow-worker.

X

A Belin, run mad and unable to bear the tediousness of her work, flees above the forty-eighth parallel, intending to remain there permanently. "You" (says an arrogant note she leaves behind) "do not exist" and although agreeing philosophically with this common view, the S & P for the county follows her —not to return her for rehabilitation, imprisonment, or study. What is there to rehabilitate or study? We'd all do it if we could. And imprisonment is simple cruelty.

You guessed it.

XI

"If not me or mine," (wrote Dunyasha Bernadetteson in 368 A.C.) "O.K.

"If me or mine—alas."

"If us and ours—*watch out!*"

XII

Whileaway is engaged in the reorganization of industry consequent to the discovery of the induction principle.

The Whileawayan work-week is sixteen hours.

PART FOUR

I

AFTER SIX months of living with me in the hotel suite, Janet Evason expressed the desire to move in with a typical family. I heard her singing in the bathroom:

> I know
> That my
> Rede-emer
> Liveth
> And She
> Shall stand
> Upon the latter da-ay   (ruffle)
> On Earth.

"Janet?" She sang again (not badly) the second variation on the lines, in which the soprano begins to decorate the tune:

> I know   (up)
> Tha-at my   (ruffle)
> Re-e-edeemer   (fiddle)
> Liveth
> And She
> Shall stand   (convex)
> And She
> Shall stand   (concave)

"Janet, he's a Man!" I yelled. She went into the third variation, where the melody liquefies itself into its own adornments, very nice and quite improper:

> I know   (up)
> That my redee   (a high point, this one)
> mer

Li-i-veth   (up up up)
And She
Shall stand   (hopefully)
And She shall stand   (higher)
Upon the la-a-a-atter da-a-a-y
                                    (ruffle fiddle drip)
O-on Earth   (settling)

"JANET!" But of course she doesn't listen.

II

Whileawayans like big asses, so I am glad to report there was
nothing of that kind in the family she moved in with. Father, mother, teenage daughter, and family dog were all delighted to be famous. Daughter was an honor student in the
local high school. When Janet got settled I drifted into the
attic; my spirit seized possession of the old four-poster bed
stored next to the chimney, near the fur coats and the shopping bag full of dolls; and slowly, slowly, I infected the whole
house.

III

Laura Rose Wilding of Anytown, U.S.A.
    She has a black poodle who whines under the trees in the
back yard and bares his teeth as he rolls over and over in
the dead leaves. She's reading the Christian Existentialists for
a course in school. She crosses the October weather, glowing with health, to shake hands clumsily with Miss Evason.
She's pathologically shy. She puts one hand in the pocket of
her jeans, luminously, the way well-beloved or much-studied
people do, tugging at the zipper of her man's leather jacket
with the other hand. She has short sandy hair and freckles.
Says over and over to herself Non Sum, Non Sum, which
means either *I don't exist* or *I'm not that*, according to how
you feel it; this is what Martin Luther is supposed to have said
during his fit in the monastery choir.
    "Can I go now?"

IV

The black poodle, Samuel, whined and scurried across the porch, then barked hysterically, defending the house against God-knows-what.

"At least she's White," they all said.

V

Janet, in her black-and-white tweeds with the fox collar like a movie star's, gave a speech to the local women's club. She didn't say much. Someone gave her chrysanthemums which she held upside-down like a baseball bat. A professor from the local college spoke of other cultures. A whole room was full of offerings brought by the club—brownies, fudge cake, sour cream cake, honey buns, pumpkin pie—not to be eaten, of course, only looked at, but they did eat it finally because somebody has to or it isn't real. "Hully gee, Mildred, you waxed the floor!" and she faints with happiness. Laur, who is reading psychology for the Existentialists (I said that, didn't I?), serves coffee to the club in the too-big man's shirt they can't ever get her out of, no matter what they do, and her ancient, shapeless jeans. Swaddling graveclothes. She's a bright girl. She learned in her thirteenth year that you can get old films of Mae West or Marlene Dietrich (who is a Vulcan; look at the eyebrows) after midnight on UHF if you know where to look, at fourteen that pot helps, at fifteen that reading's even better. She learned, wearing her rimless glasses, that the world is full of intelligent, attractive, talented women who manage to combine careers with their primary responsibilities as wives and mothers and whose husbands beat them. She's put a gold circle pin on her shirt as a concession to club day. She loves her father and once is enough. *Everyone knows* that much as women want to be scientists and engineers, they want foremost to be womanly companions to men (what?) and caretakers of childhood; *everyone knows* that a large part of a woman's identity inheres in the style of her attractiveness. Laur is daydreaming. She looks straight before her, blushes, smiles, and doesn't see a thing.

After the party she'll march stiff-legged out of the room and up to her bedroom; sitting tailor-fashion on her bed, she'll read Engels on the family and make in the margin her neat, concise, perfectly written notes. She has shelves and shelves of such annotated works. Not for her "How true!!!!" or "oiseaux = birds." She's surrounded by mermaids, fish, sea-plants, wandering fronds. Drifting on the affective currents of the room are those strange social artifacts half dissolved in nature and mystery: *some pretty girls.*

Laur is daydreaming that she's Genghis Khan.

VI

A beautiful chick who swims naked and whose breasts float on the water like flowers, a chick in a rain-tight shirt who says she balls with her friends but doesn't get uptight about it, that's the real thing.

VII

And I like Anytown; I like going out on the porch at night to look at the lights of the town: fireflies in the blue gloaming, across the valley, up the hill, white homes where children played and rested, where wives made potato salad, home from a day in the autumn leaves chasing sticks with the family dog, families in the firelight, thousands upon thousands of identical, cozy days.

"Do you like it here?" asked Janet over dessert, never thinking that she might be lied to.

"Huh?" said Laur.

"Our guest wants to know if you like living here," said Mrs. Wilding.

"Yes," said Laur.

VIII

There are more whooping cranes in the United States of America than there are women in Congress.

IX

This then is Laura's worst mind: perpetually snowed in, a dim upstairs hall wrapped in cotton wool with Self counting rocks and shells in the window-seat. One can see nothing outside the glass but falling white sky—no footprints, no faces—though occasionally Self strays to the window, itself drowned in snow-light, and sees (or thinks she sees) in the petrified whirling waste the buried forms of two dead lovers, innocent and sexless, memorialized in a snowbank.

Turn away, girl; gird up your loins; go on reading.

X

Janet dreamed that she was skating backwards, Laura that a beautiful stranger was teaching her how to shoot. In dreams begin responsibilities. Laura came down to the breakfast table after everybody had gone except Miss Evason. Whileawayans practice secret dream interpretation according to an arbitrary scheme they consider idiotic but very funny; Janet was guiltily seeing how contrary she could make her dream come out and giggling around her buttered toast. She snickered and shed crumbs. When Laura came into the room Janet sat up straight and didn't guffaw. "I," said Laur severely, the victim of ventriloquism, "detest women who don't know how to be women." Janet and I said nothing. We noticed the floss and dew on the back of her neck—Laur is in some ways more like a thirteen-year-old than a seventeen-year-old. She mugs, for instance. At sixty Janet will be white-haired and skinny, with surprised blue eyes—quite a handsome human being. And Janet herself always likes people best as themselves, not dressed up, so Laur's big shirt tickled her, ditto those impossible trousers. She wanted to ask if it was one shirt or many; do you scream when you catch sight of yourself?

She soberly held out a piece of buttered toast and Laur took it with a grimace.

"I don't," said Laur in an entirely different tone, "understand where the devil they all go on Saturday mornings. You'd think they were trying to catch up with the sun." Sharp and adult.

"I dreamed I was learning to use a rifle," she added. We thought of confiding to her the secret dream-system by which Whileawayans transform matter and embrace the galaxies but then we thought better of it. Janet was trying in a baffled way to pick up the crumbs she had dropped; Whileawayans don't eat crunchables. I left her and floated up to the whatnot, on which were perched two biscuit-china birds, beak twined in beak, a cut-glass salt dish, a small, wooden Mexican hat, a miniature silver basket, and a terracotta ashtray shaped realistically like a camel. Laur looked up for a moment, preternaturally hard and composed. I am a spirit, remember. She said: "The hell with it."

"What?" said Janet. This response is considered quite polite on Whileaway. I, the plague system darting in the air between them, pinched Janet's ears, plucked them up like Death in the poem. Nowhere, neither undersea nor on the moon, have I, in my bodiless wanderings, met with a more hard-headed innocence than Miss Evason brings to the handling of her affairs. In the bluntness of her imagination she unbuttoned Laur's shirt and slid her pants down to her knees. The taboos in Whileawayan society are cross-age taboos. Miss Evason no longer smiled.

"I said the hell with it," the little girl repeated aggressively.

"You said—?"

(Imitation Laura was smiling helplessly and freshly over her shoulder, shivering a little as her breasts were touched. What we like is the look of affection.)

She studied her plate. She drew a design on it with her finger. "Nothing," she said. "I want to show you something."

"Show, then," said Janet. I bet your knees turn in. Janet didn't think so. There are these fashion magazines scattered through the house, Mrs. Wilding reads them, pornography for the high-minded. Girls in wet knit bathing suits with their hair dripping, silly girls drowned in sweaters, serious girls in backless jersey evening dresses that barely cover the fine-boned lyres of their small chests. They're all slim and young. Pushing and prodding the little girl as you fit a dress on her. Stand here. Stand there. How, swooning, they fell into each other's arms. Janet, who (unlike me) never imagines what can't be done, wiped her mouth, folded her napkin, pushed back her chair, got up, and followed Laur into the living room. Up the stairs. Laur took a notebook from her desk and handed it to Miss Evason. We stood there uncertainly, ready to laugh or cry; Janet looked down at the manuscript, up over the edge at Laura, down again for a few more lines. Peek.

"I can't read this," I said.

Laura raised her eyebrows severely.

"I know the language but not the context," Janet said. "I can't judge this, child."

Laura frowned. I thought she might wring her hands but no such luck. She went back to the desk and picked up something else, which she handed to Miss Evason. I knew enough to recognize mathematics, that's all. She tried to stare Janet down. Janet followed a few lines, smiled thoughtfully, then came to a hitch. Something wrong. "Your teacher—" began Miss Evason.

"I don't have a teacher," said perspicacious Laur. "I do it myself, out of the book."

"Then the book's wrong," said Janet; "Look," and she proceeded to scribble in the margin. What an extraordinary phenomenon mathematical symbols are! I flew to the curtains, curtains Mrs. Wilding had washed and ironed with her own hands. No, she took them to the cleaner's, popping the clutch of the Wildings' station wagon. She read Freud in the time she would have used to wash and iron the curtains. They weren't Laur's choice. She would have torn them down with her own hands. She wept. She pleaded. She fainted. Et cetera.

They bent over the book together.

"Goddamn," said Janet, in surprised pleasure.

"You know math!" (that was Laur).

"No, no, I'm just an amateur, just an amateur," said Miss Evason, swimming like a seal in the sea of numbers.

"The life so short, the craft so long to learn," quoted Laur and turned scarlet. The rest goes: *I mene love.*

"What?" said Janet, absorbed.

"I'm in love with someone in school," said Laur. "A man."

A really extraordinary expression, what they mean by calling someone's face *a study*—she can't know that I know that she doesn't know that I know!—crossed Janet's face and she said,

"Oh, sure," by which you can tell that she didn't believe a word of it. She didn't say, "You're too young." (Not for him, for her, nitwit.)

"Of course," she added.

XI

I'm a victim of penis envy (said Laura) so I can't ever be happy or lead a normal life. My mother worked as a librarian when I was little and that's not feminine. She thinks it's deformed me. The other day a man came up to me in the bus and called me sweetie and said, "Why don't you smile? God loves you!" I just stared at him. But he wouldn't go away until I smiled, so finally I did. Everyone was laughing. I tried once, you know, went to a dance all dressed up, but I felt like such a fool. Everyone kept making encouraging remarks about my looks as if they were afraid I'd cross back over the line again; I was *trying*, you know, I was proving their way of life was right, and they were terrified I'd stop. When I was five I said, "I'm not a girl, I'm a genius," but that doesn't work, possibly because other people don't honor the resolve. Last year I finally gave up and told my mother I didn't want to be a girl but she said Oh no, being a girl is wonderful. Why? Because you can wear pretty clothes and you don't have to do anything; the men will do it for you. She said that instead of conquering Everest, I could conquer the conqueror of Everest and while he had to go climb the mountain, I could stay home in lazy comfort listening to the radio and eating chocolates. She was upset, I suppose, but you can't imbibe someone's success by fucking them. Then she said that in addition to that (the pretty clothes and so forth) there is a mystical fulfillment in marriage and children that nobody who hasn't done it could ever know. "Sure, washing floors," I said. "I have *you*," she said, looking mysterious. As if my father didn't have me, too. Or my birth was a beautiful experience *et patati et patata*, which doesn't quite jibe with the secular version we always get when she's talking about her ailments with her friends. When I was a little girl I used to think women were always sick. My father said, "What the hell is she fussing about this time?" All those songs, what's-its-name, I enjoy being a girl, I'm so glad I'm female, I'm all dressed up, Love will make up for everything, tra-la-la. Where are the songs about how glad I am I'm a boy? Finding The Man. Keeping The Man. Not scaring The Man, building up The Man, pleasing The Man, interesting The Man, following The Man, soothing The Man, flattering The Man, deferring to The Man, changing your judgment for The Man, changing your decisions for The Man, polishing floors for The Man, being perpetually conscious of your appearance for The Man, being romantic for The Man, hinting to The Man, losing yourself in The Man. "I never had a thought that wasn't yours." Sob, sob. Whenever I act like a human being, they say, "What are you getting upset about?" They say: of course you'll get married. They say: of course you're brilliant. They say: of course you'll get a Ph.D. and then sacrifice it to have babies. They say: if you don't, you're the one who'll have two jobs and you can make a go of it if you're exceptional, which very few women are, *and if you find a very understanding man.* As long as you don't make more money than he does. How do they expect me to live all this junk? I went to a Socialist—not really Socialist, you understand— camp for two summers; my parents say I must have gotten my crazy ideas there. Like hell I did. When I was thirteen my uncle wanted to kiss me and when I tried to run away, everybody laughed. He pinned my arms and kissed me on the cheek; then he said, "Oho, I got my kiss! I got my kiss!" and everybody thought it was too ducky for words. Of course they blamed me—it's harmless, they said, you're only a child, he's paying you attention; you ought to be grateful. Everything's all right as long as he doesn't rape you. Women only have feelings; men have *egos.* The school psychologist told me I might not realize it, but I was living a very dangerous style of life that might in time lead to Lesbianism (ha! ha!) and I should try to look and act more feminine. I laughed until I cried. Then he said I must understand that femininity was a Good Thing, and although men's and women's functions in society were different, they had equal dignity. Separate but equal, right? Men make the decisions and women make the dinners. I expected him to start in about that mystically-wonderful-experience-which-no-man-can-know crap, but he didn't. Instead he took me to the window and showed me the expensive clothing stores across the way. Then he said, "See, it's a woman's world, after all."

The pretty clothes again. I thought some damn horrible thing was going to happen to me right there on his carpet. I couldn't talk. I couldn't move. I felt deathly sick. He really expected me to live like that—he looked at me and that's what he saw, after eleven months. He expected me to start singing "I'm So Glad I'm A Girl" right there in his Goddamned office. And a little buck-and-wing. And a little nigger shuffle.

"Would *you* like to live like that?" I said.

He said, "That's irrelevant, because I'm a man."

I haven't the right hobbies, you see. My hobby is mathematics, not boys. And being young, too, that's a drag. You have to take all kinds of crap.

Boys don't like smart girls. Boys don't like aggressive girls. Unless they want to sit in the girls' laps, that is. I never met a man yet who wanted to make it with a female Genghis Khan. Either they try to dominate you, which is revolting, or they turn into babies. You might as well give up. Then I had a lady shrink who said it was my problem because I was the one who was trying to rock the boat and *you can't expect them to change.* So I suppose I'm the one who must change. Which is what my best friend said. "Compromise," she said, answering her fiftieth phone call of the night. "Think what power it gives you over them."

Them! Always Them, Them, Them. I can't just think of myself. My mother thinks that I *don't like boys,* though I try to tell her: Look at it this way; I'll never lose my virginity. I'm a Man-Hating Woman and people leave the room when I come in it. Do they do the same for a Woman-Hating Man? Don't be silly.

She'll never know—nor would she credit if she knew—that men sometimes look very beautiful to me. From the depths, looking up.

There was a very nice boy once who said, "Don't worry, Laura. I know you're really very sweet and gentle underneath." And another with, "You're strong, like an earth mother." And a third, "You're so beautiful when you're angry." My guts on the floor, you're so beautiful when you're angry. *I want to be recognized.*

I've never slept with a girl. I couldn't. I wouldn't want to. That's abnormal and I'm not, although you can't be normal unless you do what you want and you can't be normal unless

you love men. To do what I wanted would be normal, unless
what I wanted was abnormal, in which case it would be abnormal to please myself and normal to do what I didn't want to
do, which isn't normal.

So you see.

XII

Dunyasha Bernadetteson (the most brilliant mind in the world,
b. A.C. 344, d. A.C. 426) heard of this unfortunate young person and immediately pronounced the following *shchasniy*, or
cryptic one-word saying:

"Power!"

XIII

We persevered, reading magazines and covering the neighbors'
activities in the discreetest way possible, and Janet—who didn't
believe us to be fully human—kept her affections to herself.
She got used to Laur's standing by the door every time we
went out in the evening with a stubborn look on her face as if
she were going to fling herself across the door with her arms
spread out, movie style. But Laur controlled herself. Janet went
out on a few arranged dates with local men but awe silenced
them; she learned nothing of the usual way such things were
done. She went to a high school basketball game (for the boys)
and a Fashion Fair (for the girls). There was a Science Fair,
whose misconceptions she enjoyed mightily. Like oil around
water, the community parted to let us through.

Laura Rose came up to Miss Evason one night as the latter
sat reading alone in the living room; it was February and the
soft snow clung to the outside of the picture window. Picture
windows in Anytown do not evaporate snow in the wintertime
as windows do on Whileaway. Laur watched us standoffishly
for a while, then came into the circle of fantasy and lamplight.
She stood there, twisting her class ring around her finger. Then
she said:

"What have you learned from all that reading?"

"Nothing," said Janet. The soundless blows of the snow-
flakes against the glass. Laur sat down at Janet's feet ("Shall

I tell you something?") and explained an old fantasy of hers, snow and forests and knights and lovelorn maidens. She said that to anyone in love the house would instantly seem submarine, not a house on Earth but a house on Titan under the ammonia snow. "I'm in love," she said, reviving that old story about the mythical man at school.

"Tell me about Whileaway," she added. Janet put down her magazine. Indirection is so new to Miss Evason that for a moment she doesn't understand; what Laur has said is: *Tell me about your wife.* Janet was pleased. She had traced Laur's scheme not as concealment but as a kind of elaborate frivolity; now she fell silent. The little girl sat tailor-fashion on the living room rug, watching us.

"Well, tell me," said Laura Rose.

Her features are delicate, not particularly marked; she has a slightly indecently milky skin and lots of freckles. Knobby knuckles.

"She's called Vittoria," said Janet—how crude, once said!—and there goes something in Laura Rose's heart, like the blows of something light but perpetually shocking: oh! oh! oh! She reddened and said something very faintly, something I lip-read but didn't hear. Then she put her hand on Janet's knee, a hot, moist hand with its square fingers and stubby nails, a hand of tremendous youthful presence, and said something else, still inaudible.

Leave! (I told my compatriot)

First of all, it's wrong.

Second of all, it's wrong.

Third of all, it's wrong.

"Oh my goodness," said Janet slowly, as she does sometimes, this being her favorite saying after, "You are kidding me."

(Performing the difficult mental trick of trying on somebody else's taboos.)

"Now then," she said, "now then, now then." The little girl looked up. She is in the middle of something terribly distressing, something that will make her wring her hands, will make her cry. As a large Irish setter once bounded into my room and spent half the day unconsciously banging a piece of furniture with his tail; so something awful has got into Laura Rose and is giving her electric shocks, terrifying blows, right across the

heart. Janet took her by the shoulders and it got worse. There
is this business of the narcissism of love, the fourth-dimensional
curve that takes you out into the other who is the whole world,
which is really a twist back into yourself, only a different self.
Laur was weeping with despair. Janet pulled her up on to her
lap—Janet's lap—as if she had been a baby; *everyone knows* that
if you start them young they'll be perverted forever and *everyone knows* that nothing in the world is worse than making love
to someone a generation younger than yourself. Poor Laura,
defeated by both of us, her back bent, glazed and stupefied
under the weight of a double taboo.

Don't, Janet.

Don't, Janet.

Don't exploit. That little girl's sinister wisdom.

Snow still blew across the side of the house; the walls shook,
muffled. Something was wrong with the television set, or
with the distance control, or perhaps some defective appliance
somewhere in suburban Anytown sent out uncontrolled signals that no television set could resist; for it turned itself on
and gave us a television salad: Maureen trying unsuccessfully to
slap John Wayne, a pretty girl with a drowned voice holding up
a vaginal deodorant spray can, a house falling off the side of a
mountain. Laur groaned aloud and hid her face against Janet's
shoulder. Janet—I—held her, her odor flooding my skin, cold
woman, grinning at my own desire because we are still trying
to be good. Whileawayans, as has been said, love big asses. "I
love you, I love you," said Laur, and Janet rocked her, and Laur
—not wishing to be taken for a child—bent Miss Evason's head
fiercely back against the chair and kissed her on the mouth. Oh
my goodness.

Janet's rid of me. I sprang away and hung by one claw from
the window curtain. Janet picked Laur up and deposited her
on the floor, holding her tight through all the hysterics; she
nuzzled Laur's ear and slipped off her own shoes. Laur came
up out of it and threw the distance control at the television set,
for the actress had been telling you to disinfect the little-mouse
"most girl part" and the set went dead.

"Never—don't—I can't—leave me!" wailed Laur. Better to
cry. Businesslike Janet unfastened her shirt, her belt, and her
blue jeans and gripped her about the hips, on the theory that
nothing calms hysterics so fast.

"Oh!" said Laura Rose, astounded. This is the perfect time for her to change her mind. Her breathing grew quieter. Soberly she put her arms around Janet and leaned on Janet. She sighed.

"I want to get out of my damned clothes," said Janet, voice unaccountably breaking in the middle.

"Do you love me?"

Dearest, I can't because you are too young; and some day soon you'll look at me and my skin will be dead and dry, and being more romantically inclined than a Whileawayan, you'll find me quite disgusting; but until then I'll do my best to conceal from you how very fond I am of you. There is also lust and I hope you understand me when I say I'm about to die; and I think we should go to a safer place where we can die in comfort, for example my room which has a lock on the door, because I don't want to be panting away on the rug when your parents walk in. On Whileaway it wouldn't matter and you wouldn't have parents at your age, but here—or so I'm told—things are as they are.

"What a strange and lovely way you have of putting it," Laur said. They climbed the stairs, Laur worrying a bit at her trailing pants. She bent down (framed in the doorway) to rub her ankles. She's going to laugh in a minute and look at us from between her legs. She straightened up with a shy smile.

"Tell me something," she said in a hoarse, difficult whisper, averting her gaze.

"Yes, child? Yes, dear?"

"What do we do now?"

XIV

They undressed in Janet's bedroom in the midst of her piles of material: books, magazines, sources of statistics, biographies, newspapers. The ghosts in the windowpanes undressed with them, for nobody could see in at the back of the house. Their dim and pretty selves. Janet pulled down the shades, lingering at each window and peering wistfully out into the dark, a shocking compound of familiar, friendly face and awful nude, while Laur climbed into Janet's bed. The bedspread had holes in it where the pink satin had worn thin. She shut her eyes. "Put out the light."

"Oh no, please," said Janet, making the bed sway by getting

into it. She held out her arms to the little girl; then she kissed
her on the shoulder, the Russian way. (She's the wrong shape.)
"I don't want the light," said Laur and jumped out of bed
to turn it off, but the air catches you on your bare skin before you get there and shocks you out of your senses; so she
stopped, mother-naked, with the currents of air investigating
between her legs. "How lovely!" said Janet. The room is piti-
lessly well lit. Laur got back into bed—"Move over"—and that
awful sensation that you're not going to enjoy it after all. "You
have lovely knees," Janet said mildly, "and such a beautiful
rump," and for a moment the preposterousness of it braced
Laura Rose; there couldn't be any sex in it; so she turned off
the overhead light and got back into bed. Janet had turned on
a rose-shaded night lamp by the bed. Miss Evason grew out
of the satin cover, an antique statue from the waist up with
preternaturally living eyes; she said softly, "Look, we're alike,
aren't we?" indicating her round breasts, idealized by the dimness. "I've had two children," she said wickedly and Laur felt
herself go red all over, so unpleasant was the picture of Yuriko
Janetson being held up to one breast to suck, not, it seemed
to Laur, an uncollected, starry-eyed infant but something like
a miniature adult, on a ladder perhaps. Laur lay stiffly back and
shut her eyes, radiating refusal.

Janet turned out the bedside light.

Miss Evason then pulled the covers up around her shoulders,
sighed in self-control, and ordered Laur to turn over. "You can
at least get a back-rub out of it."

"Ugh!" she said sincerely, when she began on the muscles of
Laura's neck. "What a mess."

Laura tried to giggle. Miss Evason's voice, in the darkness,
went on and on: about the last few weeks, about studying fresh-
water ponds on Whileaway, a hard, lean, sexless greyhound of
a voice (Laur thought) which betrayed Laura in the end, Miss
Evason stating with an odd, unserious chuckle, "Try?"

"I do love you," Laur said, ready to weep. There is propaganda and propaganda and I represented again to Janet that
what she was about to do was a serious crime.

God will punish, I said.

You are supposed to make them giggle, but Janet remembered how she herself had been at twelve, and oh it's so serious.

She kissed Laura Rose lightly on the lips over and over again until Laura caught her head; in the dark it wasn't really so bad and Laura could imagine that she was nobody, or that Miss Evason was nobody, or that she was imagining it all. One nice thing to do is rub from the neck down to the tail, it renders the human body ductile and makes the muscles purr. Without knowing it, Laur was in over her head. She had learned from a boy friend how to kiss on top, but here there was lots of time and lots of other places; "It's *nice*!" said Laura Rose in surprise; "It's so *nice*!" and the sound of her own voice sent her in head over heels. Janet found the little bump Whileawayans call The Key—*Now you must make an effort*, she said—and with the sense of working very hard, Laur finally tumbled off the cliff. It was incompletely and desperately inadequate, but it was the first major sexual pleasure she had ever received from another human being in her entire life.

"Goddammit, I *can't*!" she shouted.

So I fled shrieking. There is no excuse for putting my face between someone else's columnar thighs—picture me as washing my cheeks and temples outside to get rid of that cool smoothness (cool because of the fat, you see, that insulates the limbs; you can almost feel the long bones, the *architectura*, the heavenly technical cunning. They'll be doing it with the dog next). I sat on the hall window frame and screamed.

Janet must be imagined throughout as practicing the extremest self-control.

What else can she do?

"Now do this and this," she whispered hurriedly to Laura Rose, laughing brokenly. "Now do that and that. Ah!" Miss Evason used the girl's ignorant hand, for Laura didn't know how to do it; "Just hold still," she said in that strange parody of an intimate confession. The girl's inexperience didn't make things easy. However, one finds one's own rhythm. In the bottom drawer of the Wildings' guest room bureau was an exotic Whileawayan artifact (with a handle) that Laura Rose is going to be very embarrassed to see the next morning; Janet got it out, wobbling drunkenly.

("Did you fall down?" said Laura anxiously, leaning over the edge of the bed.

"Yes.")

So it was easy. Touched with strange inspiration, Laur held the interloper in her arms, awed, impressed, a little domineering. Months of chastity went up in smoke: an electrical charge, the wriggling of an internal eel, a knifelike pleasure.

"No, no, not yet," said Janet Evason Belin. "Just hold it. Let me rest."

"Now. Again."

XV

A dozen beautiful "girls" each "brushing" and "combing" her long, silky "hair," each "longing" to "catch a man."

XVI

I fell in love at twenty-two.

A dreadful intrusion, a sickness. Vittoria, whom I did not even know. The trees, the bushes, the sky, were all sick with love. The worst thing (said Janet) is the intense familiarity, the sleepwalker's conviction of having blundered into an eruption of one's own inner life, the yellow-pollinating evergreen brushed and sticky with my own good humor, the flakes of myself falling invisibly from the sky to melt on my own face.

In your terms, I was distractedly in love. Whileawayans account for cases of this by referring back to the mother-child relationship: cold potatoes when you feel it. There used to be an explanation by way of our defects, but common human defects can be used to explain anything, so what's the use. And there's a mathematical analogy, a four-dimensional curve that I remember laughing at. Oh, I was bleeding to death.

Love—to work like a slave, to work like a dog. The same exalted, feverish attention fixed on everything. I didn't make a sign to her because she didn't make a sign to me; I only tried to control myself and to keep people away from me. That awful diffidence. I was *at her* too, all the time, in a nervous parody of friendship. Nobody can be expected to like that compulsiveness. In our family hall, like the Viking mead-hall where the bird flies in from darkness and out again into darkness, under the blown-up pressure dome with the fans bringing in the scent of roses, I felt my own soul fly straight up into the roof. We used to sit with the lights off in the long spring twilight; a troop of children had passed by the week before, selling candles, which one or another woman would bring in and light. People drifted in and out, lifting the silk flap to the dome entrance. People ate at different times, you see. When Vitti left for outside, I followed her. We don't have lawns as you do, but around our dwellings we plant a kind of trefoil which keeps the other things off; small children always assume it's there for magical reasons. It's very soft. It was getting dark, too. There's a planting from New Forest near the farmhouse and we wandered toward it, Vitti idle and saying nothing.

"I'll be leaving in six months," I said. "Going to New City to get tied in with the power plants."

Silence. I was miserably conscious that Vittoria was going somewhere and I should know where because someone had told me, but I couldn't remember.

"I thought you might like company," I said.

No answer. She had picked up a stick and was taking the heads off weeds with it. It was one of the props for the computer receiver pole, knocked into the ground at one end and into the pole itself at the other. I had to ignore her being there or I couldn't have continued walking. Ahead were the farm's trees, breaking into the fields on the dim horizon like a headland or a cloud. "The moon's up," I said. See the moon. Poisoned with arrows and roses, radiant Eros coming at you out of the dark. The air so mild you could bathe in it. I'm told my first sentence as a child was See the Moon, by which I think I must have meant: pleasant pain, balmy poison, preserving gall, choking sweet. I imagined Vittoria cutting her way out of the night with that stick, whirling it around her head, leaving bruises in the earth, tearing up weeds, slashing to pieces the roses that climbed around the computer poles. There was no part of my mind exempt from the thought: if she moves in this quicksilver death, it'll kill me.

We reached the trees. (I remember, she's going to Lode-Pigro to put up buildings. Also, it'll be hotter here in July. It'll be intensely hot, probably not bearable.) The ground between them was carpeted in needles, speckled with moonlight. We dissolved fantastically into that extraordinary medium, like mermaids, like living stories; I couldn't see anything. There

was the musky odor of dead needles, although the pollen itself
is scentless. If I had told her, "Vittoria, I'm very fond of you,"
or "Vittoria, I love you," she might answer, "You're O.K. too,
friend," or "Yes, sure, let's make it," which would misrepresent something or other, though I don't know just what, quite
intolerably and I would have to kill myself—I was very odd
about death in those strange days. So I did not speak or make a
sign but only strolled on, deeper and deeper into that fantastic
forest, that enchanted allegory, and finally we came across a
fallen log and sat on it.

"You'll miss—" said Vitti.

I said, "Vitti, I want—"

She stared straight ahead, as if displeased. Sex does not
matter in these things, nor age, nor time, nor sense, we all
know that. In the daytime you can see that the trees have been
planted in straight rows, but the moonlight was confusing all
that.

A long pause here.

"I don't know you," I said at last. The truth was we had
been friends for a long time, good friends. I don't know why
I had forgotten that so completely. Vitti was the anchor in my
life at school, the chum, the pal; we had gossiped together,
eaten together. I knew nothing about her thoughts now and
can't report them, except for my own fatuous remarks. Oh, the
dead silence! I groped for her hand but couldn't find it in the
dark; I cursed myself and tried to stay together in that ghastly
moonlight, shivers of unbeing running through me like a net
and over all the pleasure of pain, the dreadful longing.

"Vitti, I love you."

Go away! Was she wringing her hands?

"Love me!"

No! and she threw one arm up to cover her face. I got
down on my knees but she winced away with a kind of hissing screech, very like the sound an enraged gander makes to
warn you and be fair. We were both shaking from head to
foot. It seemed natural that she should be ready to destroy
me. I've dreamed of looking into a mirror and seeing my alter
ego which, on its own initiative, begins to tell me unbearable
truths and, to prevent such, threw my arms around Vittoria's

knees while she dug her fingers into my hair; thus connected we slid down to the forest floor. I expected her to beat my head against it. We got more equally together and kissed each other, I expecting my soul to flee out of my body, which it did not do. She is untouchable. What can I do with my dearest X, Y, or Z, after all? This is Vitti, whom I know, whom I like; and the warmth of that real affection inspired me with more love, the love with more passion, more despair, enough disappointment for a whole lifetime. I groaned miserably. I might as well have fallen in love with a tree or a rock. No one can make love in such a state. Vitti's fingernails were making little hard crescents of pain on my arms; she had that mulish look I knew so well in her; I knew something was coming off. It seemed to me that we were victims of the same catastrophe and that we ought to get together somewhere, in a hollow tree or under a bush, to talk it over. The old women tell you to wrestle, not fight, or you may end up with a black eye; Vitti, who had my fingers in her hands, pressing them feverishly, bent the smallest one back against the joint. Now that's a good idea. We scuffled like babies, hurting my hand, and she bit me on it; we pushed and pulled at each other, and I shook her until she rolled over on top of me and very earnestly hit me across the face with her fist. The only relief is tears. We lay sobbing together. What we did after that I think you know, and we sniffled and commiserated with each other. It even struck us funny, once. The seat of romantic love is the solar plexus while the seat of love is elsewhere, and that makes it very hard to *make love* when you are on the point of dissolution, your arms and legs penetrated by moonlight, your head cut off and swimming freely on its own like some kind of mutated monster. Love is a radiation disease. Whileawayans do not like the self-consequence that comes with romantic passion and we are very mean and mocking about it; so Vittoria and I walked back separately, each frightened to death of the weeks and weeks yet to go before we'd be over it. We kept it to ourselves. I felt it leave me two and a half months later, at one particular point in time: I was putting a handful of cracked corn to my mouth and licking the sludge off my fingers. I felt the parasite go. I swallowed philosophically and that was that. I didn't even have to tell her.

Vitti and I have stayed together in a more commonplace way ever since. In fact, we got married. It comes and goes, that abyss opening on nothing. I run away, usually.

Vittoria is whoring all over North Continent by now, I should think. We don't mean by that what you do, by the way. I mean: good for her.

Sometimes I try to puzzle out the different kinds of love, the friendly kind and the operatic kind, but what the hell.

Let's go to sleep.

XVII

Under the Mashopi mountain range is a town called Wounded Knee and beyond this the agricultural plain of Green Bay. Janet could not have told you where the equivalents of these landmarks are in the here-and-now of our world and neither can I, the author. In the great terra-reforming convulsion of P.C. 400 the names themselves dissolved into the general mess of re-crystallization so that it would be impossible for any Whileawayan to tell you (if you were to ask) whether Mashopi was ever a city, or Wounded Knee a kind of bush, or whether or not Green Bay was ever a real bay. But if you go South from the Altiplano over the Mashopi Range, and from that land of snow, cold, thin air, risk, and glaciers, to the glider resort at Utica (from whence you may see mountain climbers setting off for Old Dirty-Skirts, who stands twenty-three thousand, nine hundred feet high) and from there to the monorail station at Wounded Knee, and if you take the monorail eight hundred miles into Green Bay and get off at a station I won't name, you'll be where Janet was when she had just turned seventeen. A Whileawayan who had come from the Mars training settlement in the Altiplano would have thought Green Bay was heaven; a hiker out of New Forest would have hated it. Janet had come by herself from an undersea farm on the continental shelf on the other side of the Altiplano where she had spent five wretched weeks setting up machinery in inaccessible crannies and squeaking whenever she talked (because of the helium). She had left her schoolmates there, crazy for space and altitude. It's not usual to be alone at that age. She had stayed at the hostel in Wounded Knee, where they gave her an old, unused cubicle from which she could work by induction in the fuel-alcohol distillery. People were nice, but it was a miserable and boring time. You are never so alone, schoolmates or not. You never feel so all-thumbs (Janet). She made her insistence on change formally, the line of work came through, goodbye everybody. She had left a violin in Wounded Knee with a friend who used to cantilever herself out of the third story of the hostel and eat snacks on the head of a public statue. Janet took the monorail at twenty-two o'clock and sulkily departed for a better personal world. There were four persons of Three-Quarters Dignity in the car, all quiet, all wretched with discontent. She opened her knapsack, wrapped herself in it, and slept. She woke in artificial light to find that the engineer had opened the louvers to let in April: magnolias were blooming in Green Bay. She played linear poker with an old woman from the Altiplano who beat her three times out of three. At dawn everyone was asleep and the lights winked out; she woke and watched the low hills form and re-form outside under an apple-green sky that turned, as she watched it, a slow, sulphurous yellow. It rained but they sped through it. At the station—which was nothing but the middle of a field—she borrowed a bicycle from the bicycle rack and flipped the toggle to indicate the place she wanted to go. It's a stout machine, with broad tires (compared to ours) and a receiver for registering radio beacons. She rode into the remaining night hung between the plantations of evergreens, then out into the sunrise again. There was an almighty cheeping and chirping, the result of one limb of the sun becoming visible over the horizon. She could see the inflated main dome of the house before she reached the second bicycle drop; somebody going West would pick it up in time and drop it near the monorail. She imagined great masses of sulky girls being requisitioned to ride bicycles coast-to-coast from regions that had a bicycle surplus to those crying out for bicycles. I imagined it, too. There was the sound of a machinist's ground-car off to the left—Janet grew up with that noise in her ears. Her bicycle was singing the musical tone that lets you know you're on course, a very lovely sound to hear over the empty fields. "Sh!" she said and put it on the rack, where it obediently became silent. She walked (and so did I) to the main dome of the house and let herself in, not knowing whether everyone was sleeping late or had got up early and already gone out. She didn't care. We found the empty guest room, ate some stirabout—that's not what you think, it's a kind of bread—from her knapsack, lay down on the floor, and fell asleep.

XVIII

There's no being *out too late* in Whileaway, or *up too early*, or *in the wrong part of town*, or *unescorted*. You cannot fall out of the kinship web and become sexual prey for strangers, for there is no prey and there are no strangers—the web is world-wide. In all of Whileaway there is no one who can keep you from going where you please (though you may risk your life, if that sort of thing appeals to you), no one who will follow you and try to embarrass you by whispering obscenities in your ear, no one who will attempt to rape you, no one who will warn you of the dangers of the street, no one who will stand on street corners, hot-eyed and vicious, jingling loose change in his pants pocket, bitterly bitterly sure that you're a cheap floozy, hot and wild, who likes it, who can't say no, who's making a mint off it, who inspires him with nothing but disgust, and who wants to drive him crazy.

On Whileaway eleven-year-old children strip and live naked in the wilderness above the forty-seventh parallel, where they meditate, stark naked or covered with leaves, *sans* pubic hair, subsisting on the roots and berries so kindly planted by their elders. You can walk around the Whileawayan equator twenty times (if the feat takes your fancy and you live that long) with one hand on your sex and in the other an emerald the size of a grapefruit. All you'll get is a tired wrist.

While here, where *we* live—!

PART FIVE

I

I HAD GOT stuck with Jeannine. I don't know how. Also, everybody in the Goddamned subway car was staring at my legs. I think they thought I was a cheerleader. Way up in the Bronx we had waited for the Express, forty-five minutes in the open air with tufts of grass growing between the rails, just as in my childhood, weeds surrounding the vacant subway cars, sunlight and cloud-shadows chasing each other across the elevated wooden platform. I put my raincoat across my knees—skirts are long in nineteen-sixty-nine, Jeannine-time. Jeannine is neat, I suppose, but to me she looks as if she's wandering all over the place: hanging earrings, metal links for a belt, her hair escaping from a net, ruffles on her sleeves; and on that kind of shapeless, raglan-sleeved coat that always looks as if it's dragging itself off the wearer's shoulders, a pin in the shape of a crescent moon with three stars dangling from it on three fine, separate chains. Her coat and shoulder bag are overflowing into her neighbors' laps.

So I remember the horsehair petticoats of my teens, which bounded out of one's hands every time one tried to roll them or fold them up. One per drawer. The train groaned and ground to a stop somewhere between one hundred and eightieth and one hundred and sixty-eighth streets. We can look over the plain of the Bronx, which is covered with houses, to something near the river in the distance—a new stadium, I think.

Petticoats, waist-cinchers, boned strapless brassières with torturous nodes where the bones began or ended, modestly high-heeled shoes, double-circle skirts, felt appliquéd with sequins, bangle bracelets that always fell off, winter coats with no buttons to hold them shut, rhinestone sunburst brooches that caught on everything. Horrible obsessions, The Home, for example. We sat looking over the tenements, the faraway bridge, the ball park. There were public parks on islands in the river where I don't remember there being anything of the kind.

77

Jeannine's giving me gooseflesh, whisper, whisper on the side of the neck (about somebody else's home permanent across the car), never still, always twisting around to look at something, forever fiddling with her clothes, suddenly deciding she just has to see out the window, I'll die if I don't. We changed places so she wouldn't have the bar between the windows cutting off her field of view. The sun shone as if on the Perfect City of my twelve-year-old dreams, the kind of thing you see on a billboard under Pittston, Future Jewel Of The Finger Lakes, the ramps, the graceful walkways, the moving belts between hundred-story buildings, the squares of green that are supposed to be parks, and above it all, in the cloudless modern sky, just one sleek, futuristic Airplane.

II

JEANNINE: Cal is too much. I don't know if I ought to give him up or not. He's awfully sweet but he's such a baby. And the cat doesn't like him, you know. He doesn't take me any place. I know he doesn't make much money, but you would think he would try, wouldn't you? All he wants is to sit around and look at me and then when we get in bed, he doesn't do anything for the longest time; that just can't be right. All he does is pet and he says he likes it like that. He says it's like floating. Then when he does *it*, you know, sometimes he cries. I never heard of a man doing that.

MYSELF: Nothing.

JEANNINE: I think there's something wrong with him. I think he's traumatized by being so short. He wants to get married so we can have children—on his salary! When we pass a baby carriage with a baby, we both run over to look at it. He can't make up his mind, either. I never heard of a man like that. Last fall we were going to go to a Russian restaurant and I wanted to go to this place so he said all right, and then I changed my mind and wanted to go to the other place and he said OK, fine, but it turned out to be shut. So what could we do? *He* didn't know. So I lost my temper.

ME: Nothing, nothing, nothing.

SHE: He's just too much. Do you think I should get rid of him?

ME: (I shook my head)

JEANNINE (Confidingly): Well, he *is* funny sometimes.

(She bent down to pick lint off her blouse, giving herself a momentary double chin. She pursed her lips, pouted, bridled, drooped her eyelids in a knowing look.)

Sometimes—*sometimes*—he likes to get *dressed up*. He gets into the drapes like a sarong and puts on all my necklaces around his neck, and stands there with the curtain rod for a spear. He wants to be an actor, you know. But I think there's something wrong with him. Is it what they call transvestism?

JOANNA: No, Jeannine.

JEANNINE: I think it might be. I think I'll throw him over. I don't like anybody calling my cat, Mr. Frosty, names. Cal calls him The Blotchy Skinny Cat. Which he isn't. Besides, I'm going to call up my brother next week and go stay with him during vacation—I get three weeks. It gets pretty dull by the end of it—my brother stays in a small town in the Poconos, you know—but the last time I was there, there was a block dance and a Grange supper and I met a very, very handsome man. You can tell when somebody likes you, can't you? He liked me. He's an assistant to the butcher and he's going to inherit the business; he's got a real future. I went there quite a lot; I can tell, the way somebody looks at me. Mrs. Robert Poirier. Jeannine Dadier-Poirier. Ha ha! He's good-looking. Cal—*Cal* is—*well*! Still, Cal is sweet. Poor, but sweet. I wouldn't give up Cal for anything. I enjoy being a girl, don't you? I wouldn't be a man for anything; I think they have such a hard time of it. I like being admired. I like being a girl. I wouldn't be a man for anything. Not for *anything*.

ME: Has anyone proposed the choice to you lately?

JEANNINE: I won't be a man.

ME: Nobody axed you to.

III

She was sick in the subway. Not really, but almost. She indicated by signs that she was going to be sick or had just been sick or was afraid she was going to be sick.

She held my hand.

IV

We got out at forty-second street; and this is the way things really happen, in broad daylight, publicly, invisibly; we meandered past the shops. Jeannine saw a pair of stockings that she just had to have. We went in the store and the store owner bullied us. Outside again with her stockings (wrong size) she said, "But I didn't *want* them!" They were red fishnet hose, which she'll never dare wear. In the store window there was a zany-faced mannequin who roused my active hatred: painted long ago, now dusty and full of hair-fine cracks, a small shopkeeper's economy. "Ah!" said Jeannine sorrowfully, looking again at the edge of the fishnet hose in her package. Mannequins are always dancing, this absurd throwing back of the head and bending of the arms and legs. They enjoy being mannequins. (But I won't be mean.) I will not say that the sky ripped open from top to bottom, from side to side, that from the clouds over Fifth Avenue descended seven angels with seven trumpets, that the vials of wrath were loosed over Jeannine-time and the Angel of Pestilence sank Manhattan in the deepest part of the sea. Janet, our only savior, turned the corner in a gray flannel jacket and a gray flannel skirt down to her knees. That's a compromise between two worlds. She seemed to know where she was going. Badly sunburned, with more freckles than usual across her flat nose, Miss Evason stopped in the middle of the street, scratched her head all over, yawned, and entered a drugstore. We followed.

"I'm sorry, but I've never heard of that," said the man behind the counter.

"Oh my goodness, really?" said Miss Evason. She put away a piece of paper, on which she had written whatever-it-was, and went to the other side of the store, where she had a soda.

"You'll need a prescription," said the man behind the counter.

"Oh my goodness," Miss Evason said mildly. It did not help that she was carrying her soda. She put it down on the plastic counter top and joined us at the door, where Miss Dadier was trying—softly but very determinedly—to bolt. She wanted to get back to the freedom of Fifth Avenue, where there were so many gaps—so much For Rent, so much cheaper, so much older, than I remembered.

Miss Dadier looked sulkily up at the sky, calling on the invisible angels and the Wrath of God to witness, and then she said, grudgingly:

"I can't *imagine* what you were trying to buy." She did not want to admit that Janet existed. Janet raised her eyebrows and directed a glance at me, but I don't know. I never know anything.

"I have athlete's foot," said Miss Evason.

Jeannine shuddered. (Catch her taking off her shoes in public!) "I thought I'd lost you."

"You didn't," said Miss Evason tolerantly. "Are you ready?"

"No," said Jeannine. But she did not repeat it. I'm not sure I'm ready. Janet led us out into the street and had us stand close together, all within one square of the sidewalk. She looked at her watch. The Whileawayan antennae come searching through the ages like a cat's whisker. It would have been better to leave from some less public spot, but they don't seem to care what they do; Janet waved engagingly at passersby and I became aware that I had become aware that I remembered becoming aware of the curved wall eighteen inches from my nose. The edge of the sidewalk, where the traffic. Had been.

Now I know how I got to Whileaway, but how did I get stuck with Jeannine? And how did Janet get into that world and not mine? Who did that? When the question is translated into Whileawayan, Dear Reader, you will see the technicians of Whileaway step back involuntarily; you will see Boy Scout Evason blanch; you will see the Chieftainess of the Whileawayan scientific establishment, mistress of ten thousand slaves and wearer of the bronze breastplates, direct stern questions right and left, while frowning. Etcetera.

Oh, oh, oh, oh, oh Jeannine was saying miserably under her breath. *I don't want to be here. They forced me. I want to go home. This is a terrible place.*

"Who did that?" said Miss Evason. "Not me. Not my people."

V

Praise God, Whose image we put in the plaza to make the eleven-year-olds laugh. She has brought me home.

VI

Dig in. Winter's coming. When I—not the "I" above but the "I" down here, naturally; that's Janet up there—

When "I" dream of Whileaway, I dream first of the farms, and although words are inadequate to this great theme, while I live I yet must tell you that the farms are the only family units on Whileaway, not because Whileawayans think farm life is good for children (they don't) but because farm work is harder to schedule and demands more day-to-day continuity than any other kind of job. Farming on Whileaway is mainly caretaking and machine-tending; it is the emotional security of family life that provides the glamor. I do not know this from observation; I know it from knowledge; I have never visited Whileaway in my own person, and when Janet, Jeannine, and Joanna stepped out of the stainless steel sphere into which they had been transported from wherever the dickens it was that they were before (etcetera), they did so alone. I was there only as the spirit or soul of an experience is always there.

Sixty eight-foot-tall Amazons, the Whileawayan Praetorian Guard, threw daggers in all directions (North, South, East, and West).

Janet, Jeannine, and Joanna arrived in the middle of a field at the end of an old-fashioned tarmac that stretched as a feeder to the nearest hovercraft highway. No winter, few roofs. Vittoria and Janet embraced and stood very still, as Aristophanes describes. They didn't yell or pound each other's shoulders, or kiss, or hug, or cry out, or jump up and down, or say "You old son-of-a-gun!" or tell each other all the news, or push each other to arm's length and screech, and then hug each other again. More farsighted than either Jeannine or Janet, I can see beyond the mountain range on the horizon, beyond the Altiplano, to the whale-herders and underground fisheries on the other side of the world; I can see desert gardens and zoological preserves; I can see storms brewing. Jeannine gulped. *Must they do that in public?* There are a few fluffy summer clouds above Green Bay, each balancing on its own tail of hot air; the dust settles on either side of the highway as a hovercar roars and passes. Vittoria's too stocky for Jeannine's taste; she could at least be good-looking. We strolled down the feeder road to the road to the hovercraft-way, observed by nobody, all alone, except that I can see a weather satellite that sees me. Jeannine keeps just behind Vittoria, staring with censorious horror at Vittoria's long, black hair.

"If they know we're here," says Jeannine, the world falling about her ears, "why didn't they send someone to meet us? I mean, other people."

"Why should they?" says Janet.

VII

JEANNINE: But we might lose our way.

JANET: You can't. I'm here and I know the way.

JEANNINE: Suppose you weren't with us. Suppose we'd killed you.

JANET: Then it would certainly be preferable that you lose your way!

JEANNINE: But suppose we held you as a hostage? Suppose you were alive but we *threatened* to kill you?

JANET: The longer it takes to get anywhere, the more time I have to think of what to do. I can probably stand thirst better than you can. And of course, since you have no map, I can mislead you and not tell you the truth about where to go.

JEANNINE: But we'd get there eventually, wouldn't we?

JANET: Yes. So there's no difference, you see.

JEANNINE: But suppose we *killed* you?

JANET: Either you killed me before you got here, in which case I am dead, or you kill me after you get here, in which case I am dead. It makes no difference to me where I die.

JEANNINE: But suppose we brought a—a cannon or a bomb or something—suppose we fooled you and then seized the Government and threatened to blow everything up!

JANET: For the purposes of argument, let us suppose that. First of all, there is no government here in the sense that you mean. Second, there is no one place from which to control the entire activity of Whileaway, that is, the economy. So your one bomb isn't enough, even supposing you could kill off our welcoming committee. Introducing an entire army or an entire arsenal through the one point would take either a very advanced technology—which you have not got—or vast amounts of time. If it took you vast amounts of time, that would be no problem for us; if you came through right away, you must come through either prepared or unprepared. If you came through prepared, waiting would only assure that you spread out, used up your supplies, and acquired a false sense of confidence; if you came through unprepared and had to spend time putting things together, that would be a sign that your technology is not so advanced and you're not that much of a threat one way or the other.

JEANNINE (controlling herself): Hm!

JANET: You see, conflicts between states are not identical with conflicts between persons. You exaggerate this business of surprise. Relying on the advantage of a few hours is not a very stable way of proceeding, is it? A way of life so unprotected would hardly be worth keeping.

JEANNINE: I hope—I don't hope really because it would be awful but just to pay you out I hope!—well, I hope that some enemy with fantastically advanced technology sends experts in through that what-do-you-call-it and I hope they freeze everybody within fifty miles with *green rays*—and then I hope they make that whatever-you-call-it a *permanent* whatever-you-call-it so they can bring through *anything* they want to *whenever* they want to and *kill you all*!

JANET: Now there's an example worth talking about. First, if they had a technology as advanced as that, they could open their own access points, and we certainly can't watch everywhere at all times. It would make life too obsessive. But suppose they must use this single one. No welcoming committee —or defensive army, even—could withstand those fifty-mile green rays, yes? So that's not worth sending an army against, is it? They would just be frozen or killed. However, I suspect that the use of such a fifty-mile green ray would produce all sorts of grossly observable phenomena—that is, it would be instantly obvious that something or somebody was paralyzing everything within a radius of fifty miles—and if these technologically advanced but unamiable persons were so obliging as to announce themselves in that fashion, we'd hardly need to find out about their existence by sending anyone here in the flesh, would we?

(A long silence. Jeannine is trying to think of something desperately crushing. Her platform wedgies aren't made for walking and her feet hurt.)

JANET: Besides, it's never at the first contact that these things happen. I'll show you the theory, some day.

Some day (thinks Jeannine) somebody will get you in spite of all that rationality. All that rationality will go straight up into the air. They don't have to invade; they can just blow you up from outer space; they can just infect you with plague, or infiltrate, or form a fifth column. They can corrupt you. There are all sorts of horrors. You think life is safe but it isn't, it isn't at all. It's just horrors. Horrors!

JANET (reading her face, jerking a thumb upwards from a closed fist in the Whileawayan gesture of religion): God's will be done.

VIII

Stupid and inactive. Pathetic. Cognitive starvation. Jeannine loves to become entangled with the souls of the furniture in my apartment, softly drawing herself in to fit inside them, pulling one long limb after another into the cramped positions of my tables and chairs. The dryad of my living room. I can look anywhere, at the encyclopedia stand, at the cheap lamps, at the homey but comfortable brown couch; it is always Jeannine who looks back. It's uncomfortable for me but such a relief to her. That long, young, pretty body loves to be sat on and I think if Jeannine ever meets a Satanist, she will find herself perfectly at home as his altar at a Black Mass, relieved of personality at last and forever.

IX

Then there is the joviality, the self-consequence, the forced heartiness, the benevolent teasing, the insistent demands for flattery and reassurance. This is what ethologists call dominance behavior.

EIGHTEEN-YEAR-OLD MALE COLLEGE FRESHMAN (laying down the law at a party): If Marlowe had lived, he would have written *very much better plays* than Shakespeare's.

ME, A THIRTY-FIVE-YEAR-OLD PROFESSOR OF ENGLISH
(dazed with boredom): Gee, how clever you are to know about
things that never happened.

THE FRESHMAN (bewildered): Huh?
OR

EIGHTEEN-YEAR-OLD GIRL AT A PARTY: Men don't understand machinery. The gizmo goes on the whatsit and the
rataplan makes contact with the fourchette in at least seventy
percent of all cases.

THIRTY-FIVE-YEAR-OLD MALE PROFESSOR OF ENGINEER-
ING (awed): Gee. (Something wrong here, I think)
OR

"Man" is a rhetorical convenience for "human." "Man" includes "woman." Thus:

1. The Eternal Feminine leads us ever upward and on.
(Guess who "us" is)

2. The last man on earth will spend the last hour before
the holocaust searching for his wife and child. (Review of *The
Second Sex* by the first sex)

3. We all have the impulse, at times, to get rid of our wives.
(Irving Howe, introduction to Hardy, talking about my wife)

4. Great scientists choose their problems as they choose
their wives. (A.H. Maslow, who should know better)

5. Man is a hunter who wishes to compete for the best kill
and the best female. (everybody)
OR

The game is a dominance game called I Must Impress This
Woman. Failure makes the active player play harder. Wear a
hunched back or a withered arm; you will then experience
the invisibility of the passive player. I'm never impressed—no
woman ever is—it's just a cue that you like me and I'm supposed to like that. If you really like me, maybe I can get you to
stop. Stop; I want to talk to you! Stop; I want to see you! Stop;
I'm dying and disappearing!

SHE: Isn't it just a game?

HE: Yes, of course.

SHE: And if you play the game, it means you like me, doesn't
it?

HE: Of course.

SHE: Then if it's just a game and you like me, you can stop playing. Please stop.

HE: No.

SHE: Then *I* won't play.

HE: Bitch! You want to destroy me. I'll show you. (He plays harder)

SHE: All right. I'm impressed.

HE: You really are sweet and responsive after all. You've kept your femininity. You're not one of those hysterical feminist bitches who wants to be a man and have a penis. *You're a woman.*

SHE: Yes. (She kills herself)

X

This book is written in blood.

Is it written entirely in blood?

No, some of it is written in tears.

Are the blood and tears all mine?

Yes, they have been in the past. But the future is a different matter. As the bear swore in *Pogo* after having endured a pot shoved on her head, being turned upside down while still in the pot, a discussion about her edibility, the lawnmowering of her behind, and a fistful of ground pepper in the snoot, she then swore a mighty oath on the ashes of her mothers (*i.e.* her forebears) grimly but quietly while the apples from the shaken apple tree above her dropped bang thud on her head:

OH, SOMEBODY ASIDES ME IS GONNA RUE THIS HERE PARTICULAR DAY.

XI

I study Vittoria's blue-black hair and velvety brown eyes, her heavy, obstinate chin. Her waist is too long (like a flexible mermaid's), her solid thighs and buttocks surprisingly sturdy. Vittoria gets a lot of praise in Whileaway because of her big behind. She is modestly interesting, like everything else in this world formed for the long acquaintance and the close view; they work outdoors in their pink or gray pajamas and indoors in the nude until you know every wrinkle and fold of flesh, until your body's in a common medium with theirs and there are no pictures made out of anybody or anything; everything becomes translated instantly into its own inside. Whileaway is the inside of everything else. I slept in the Belins' common room for three weeks, surrounded in my coming and going by people with names like Nofretari Ylayeson and Nguna Twason. (I translate freely; the names are Chinese, African, Russian, European. Also, Whileawayans love to use old names they find in dictionaries.) One little girl decided I needed a protector and stuck by me, trying to learn English. In the winter there's always heat in the kitchens for those who like the hobby of cooking and induction helmets for the little ones (to keep the heat at a distance). The Belins' kitchen was a story-telling place.

I mean, of course, that she told stories to me.

Vittoria translates, speaking softly and precisely:

"Once upon a time a long time ago there was a child who was raised by bears. Her mother went up into the woods pregnant (for there were more woods than there are today) and gave birth to the child there, for she had made an error in reckoning. Also, she had got lost. Why she was in the woods doesn't matter. It is not germane to this story.

"Well, if you must know, it was because the mother was up there to shoot bears for a zoo. She had captured three bears and shot eighteen but was running out of film; and when she went into labor, she let the three bears go, for she didn't know how long the labor would last, and there was nobody to feed the bears. They conferred with each other and stayed around, though, because they had never seen a human being give birth before and they were interested. Everything went fine until the baby's head came out, and then the Spirit of the Woods, who is very mischievous and clever, decided to have some fun. So right after the baby came out, it sent a rock slide down the mountain and the rock slide cut the umbilical cord and knocked the mother to one side. And then it made an earthquake which separated the mother and the baby by miles and miles, like the Grand Canyon in South Continent."

"Isn't that going to be a lot of trouble?" said I.

"Do you want to hear this story or don't you?" (Vittoria translated) "*I* say they were separated by miles and miles.

When the mother saw this, she said 'Damn!' Then she went back to civilization to get a search party together, but by that time the bears had decided to adopt the baby and all of them were hidden up above the forty-ninth parallel, where it's very rocky and wild. So the little girl grew up with the bears.

"When she was ten, there began to be trouble. She had some bear friends by then, although she didn't like to walk on all-fours as the bears did and the bears didn't like that, because bears are very conservative. She argued that walking on all-fours didn't suit her skeletal development. The bears said, 'Oh, but we have always walked this way.' They were pretty stupid. But nice, I mean. Anyway, she walked upright, the way it felt best, but when it came to copulation, that was another matter. There was nobody to copulate with. The little girl wanted to try it with her male-best-bear-friend (for animals do not live the way people do, you know) but the he-bear would not even try. 'Alas' he said (You can tell by that he was much more elegant than the other bears, ha ha) 'I'm afraid I'd hurt you with my claws because you don't have all the fur that she-bears have. And besides that, you have trouble assuming the proper position because your back legs are too long. And besides *that*, you don't smell like a bear and I'm afraid my Mother would say it was bestiality.' That's a joke. Actually it's race prejudice. The little girl was very lonely and bored. Finally after a long time, she browbeat her bear-mother into telling her about her origins, so she decided to go out looking for some people who were not bears. She thought life might be better with them. She said good-bye to her bear-friends and started South, and they all wept and waved their handkerchiefs. The girl was very hardy and woods-wise, since she had been taught by the bears. She traveled all day and slept all night. Finally she came to a settlement of people, just like this one, and they took her in. Of course she didn't speak people-talk" (with a sly glance at me) "and they didn't speak bearish. This was a big problem. Eventually she learned their language so she could talk to them and when they found out she had been raised by bears, they directed her to the Geddes Regional Park where she spent a great deal of time speaking bearish to the scholars. She made friends and so had plenty of people to copulate with, but on moonlit nights she longed to be back with the bears, for she wanted to do the great bear dances, which bears do under the full moon. So eventually she went back North again. But it turned out that the bears were a bore. So she decided to find her human mother. At the flats to Rabbit Island she found a statue with an inscription that said, 'Go that way,' so she did. At the exit from the bridge to North Continent she found an arrow sign that had been overturned, so she followed in the new direction it was pointing. The Spirit of Chance was tracking her. At the entry into Green Bay she found a huge goldfish bowl barring her way, which turned into the Spirit of Chance, a very very old woman with tiny, dried-up legs, sitting on top of a wall. The wall stretched *all* the way across the forty-eighth parallel.

"'Play cards with me,' said the Spirit of Chance.

"'Not on your life,' said the little girl, who was nobody's fool.

"Then the Spirit of Chance winked and said, 'Aw, come on,' so the girl thought it might be fun. She was just going to pick up her hand when she saw that the Spirit of Chance was wearing an induction helmet with a wire that stretched back way into the distance.

"She was connected with a computer!

"'That's cheating!' cried the little girl. She ran at the wall and they had just an awful fight, but in the end everything melted away, leaving a handful of pebbles and sand, and afterward that melted away, too. The little girl walked by day and slept by night, wondering whether she would like her real mother. She didn't know if she would want to stay with her real mother or not. But when they got to know each other, they decided against it. The mother was a very smart, beautiful lady with fuzzy black hair combed out round, like electricity. But she had to go build a bridge (and fast, too) because the people couldn't get from one place to the other place without the bridge. So the little girl went to school and had lots of lovers and friends, and practiced archery, and got into a family, and had lots of adventures, and saved everybody from a volcano by bombing it from the air in a glider, and achieved Enlightenment.

"Then one morning somebody told her there was a bear looking for her—"

"Wait a minute," said I. "This story doesn't have an end. It just goes on and on. What about the volcano? And the adventures? And the achieving Enlightenment—surely that takes some time, doesn't it?"

"I tell things," said my dignified little friend (through Vittoria) "the way they happen," and slipping her head under the induction helmet without further comment (and her hands into the waldoes) she went back to stirring her blanc-mange with her forefinger. She said something casually over her shoulder to Vittoria, who translated:

"Anyone who lives in two worlds," (said Vittoria) "is bound to have a complicated life."

(I learned later that she had spent three days making up the story. It was, of course, about me.)

XII

Some homes are extruded foam: white caves hung with veils of diamonds, indoor gardens, ceilings that weep. There are places in the Arctic to sit and meditate, invisible walls that shut in the same ice as outside, the same clouds. There is one rain-forest, there is one shallow sea, there is one mountain chain, there is one desert. Human rookeries asleep undersea where Whileawayans create, in their leisurely way, a new economy and a new race. Rafts anchored in the blue eye of a dead volcano. Eyries built for nobody in particular, whose guests arrive by glider. There are many more shelters than homes, many more homes than persons; as the saying goes, My home is in my shoes. Everything (they know) is eternally in transit. Everything is pointed toward death. Radar dish-ears listen for whispers from Outside. There is no pebble, no tile, no excrement, that is not Tao; Whileaway is inhabited by the pervasive spirit of underpopulation, and alone at twilight in the permanently deserted city that is only a jungle of sculptured forms set on the Altiplano, attending to the rush of one's own breath in the respiratory mask, then—

I gambled for chores and breakfast with an old, old woman, in the middle of the night by the light of an alcohol lamp, somewhere on the back roads of the swamp and pine flats of South Continent. Watching the shadows dance on her wrinkled face, I understood why other women speak with awe of seeing the withered legs dangling from the shell of a computer housing: Humpty Dumptess on her way to the ultimate Inside of things.

(I lost. I carried her baggage and did her chores for a day.)

An ancient statue outside the fuel-alcohol distillery at Ciudad Sierra: a man seated on a stone, his knees spread, both hands pressed against the pit of his stomach, a look of blind distress, face blurred by time. Some wag has carved on the base the sideways eight that means infinity and added a straight line down from the middle; this is both the Whileaway schematic of the male genital and the mathematical symbol for self-contradiction.

If you are so foolhardy as to ask a Whileawayan child to "be a good girl" and do something for you:

"What does running other people's errands have to do with being a good girl?

"Why can't you run your own errands?

"Are you crippled?"

(The double pairs of hard, dark children's eyes everywhere, like mating cats'.)

XIII

A quiet country night. The hills East of Green Bay, the wet heat of August during the day. One woman reads; another sews; another smokes. Somebody takes from the wall a kind of whistle and plays on it the four notes of the major chord. This is repeated over and over again. We hold on to these four notes as long as possible; then we transform them by one note; again we repeat these four notes. Slowly something tears itself away from the not-melody. Distances between the harmonics stretch wider and wider. No one is dancing tonight. How the lines open up! Three notes now. The playfulness and terror of the music written right on the air. Although the player is employing nearly the same dynamics throughout, the sounds have become painfully loud; the little instrument's guts are coming out. Too much to listen to, with its lips right against my ear. I believe that by dawn it will stop, by dawn we will have gone through six or seven changes of notes, maybe two in an hour.

By dawn we'll know a little something about the major triad. We'll have celebrated a little something.

XIV
How Whileawayans Celebrate

Dorothy Chiliason in the forest glade, her moon-green pajamas, big eyes, big shoulders, her broad lips and big breasts, each with its protruding thumb, her aureole of fuzzy, ginger-colored hair. She springs to her feet and listens. One hand up in the air, thinking. Then both hands up. She shakes her head. She takes a gliding step, dragging one foot. Then again. Again. She takes on some extra energy and runs a little bit. Then stops. She thinks a little bit. Whileawayan celebratory dancing is not like Eastern dancing with its motions in toward the body, its cushions of warm air exhaled by the dancer, its decorations by contradictory angles (leg up, knee down, foot up; one arm up-bent, the other arm down-bent). Nor is it at all like the yearning-for-flight of Western ballet, limbs shooting out in heaven-aspiring curves, the torso a mathematical point. If Indian dancing says I Am, if ballet says I Wish, what does the dance of Whileaway say?

It says I Guess. (The intellectuality of this impossible business!)

XV
What Whileawayans Celebrate

The full moon

The Winter solstice (You haven't lived if you haven't seen us running around in our skivvies, banging on pots and pans, shouting "Come back, sun! Goddammit, come back! Come back!")

The Summer solstice (rather different)

The autumnal equinox

The vernal equinox

The flowering of trees

The flowering of bushes
The planting of seeds
Happy copulation
Unhappy copulation
Longing
Jokes
Leaves falling off the trees (where deciduous)
Acquiring new shoes
Wearing same
Birth
The contemplation of a work of art
Marriages
Sport
Divorces
Anything at all
Nothing at all
Great ideas
Death

XVI

There is an unpolished, white, marble statue of God on Rabbit Island, all alone in a field of weeds and snow. She is seated, naked to the waist, an outsized female figure as awful as Zeus, her dead eyes staring into nothing. At first She is majestic; then I notice that Her cheekbones are too broad, Her eyes set at different levels, that Her whole figure is a jumble of badly-matching planes, a mass of inhuman contradictions. There is a distinct resemblance to Dunyasha Bernadetteson, known as The Playful Philosopher (A.C. 344–426), though God is older than Bernadetteson and it's possible that Dunyasha's genetic surgeon modelled her after God instead of the other way round. Persons who look at the statue longer than I did have reported that one cannot pin It down at all, that She is a constantly changing contradiction, that She becomes in turn gentle, terrifying, hateful, loving, "stupid" (or "dead") and finally indescribable.

Persons who look at Her longer than that have been known to vanish right off the face of the Earth.

XVII

I have never been to Whileaway.

Whileawayans breed into themselves an immunity to ticks, mosquitoes, and other insect parasites. I have none. And the way into Whileaway is barred neither by time, distance, nor an angel with a flaming sword, but by a cloud or crowd of gnats.

Talking gnats.

PART SIX

I

JEANNINE WAKES from a dream of Whileaway. She has to go to her brother's this week. Everything suggests to Jeannine something she has lost, although she doesn't put it to herself this way; what she understands is that everything in the world wears a faint coating of nostalgia, makes her cry, seems to say to her, "You can't." She's fond of not being able to do things; somehow this gives her a right to something. Her eyes fill with tears. Everything's a cheat. If she gets up right now, she'll be able to make the early bus; she also wants to get away from the dream that still lingers in the folds of her bedclothes, in the summery smell of her soft old sheets, a smell of herself that Jeannine likes but wouldn't admit to anybody. The bed is full of dreamy, suspicious hollows. Jeannine yawns, out of a sense of duty. She gets up and makes the bed, then picks paperback books up off the floor (murder mysteries) and puts them away in her bookcase. There are clothes to wash before she goes, clothes to put away, stockings to pair and put in the drawers. She wraps the garbage in newspaper and carries it down three flights to put it in the garbage can. She routs Cal's socks from behind the bed and shakes them out, leaving them on the kitchen table. There are dishes to wash, soot on the window sills, soaking pots to scour, a dish to put under the radiator in case it goes on during the week (it leaks). Oh. Ugh. Let the windows go, though Cal doesn't like them dirty. That awful job of scrubbing out the toilet, whisk-brooming the furniture. Clothes to iron. Things always fall off when you straighten other things. She bends and bends. Flour and sugar spill on the shelves over the sink and have to be mopped up; there are stains and spills, rotting radish leaves, and encrustations of ice inside the old refrigerator (it has to be propped open with a chair to defrost itself). Odds and ends of paper, candy, cigarettes, cigarette ashes all over the room. Everything has to be dusted. She decides to do the windows anyway, because it's nice. They'll be filthy in a week. Of course nobody else helps. Nothing is the right height. She adds Cal's socks to her clothes and his clothes that she has to take to the self-service laundry, makes a separate pile of his clothes that have to be mended, and sets the table for herself. She scrapes old food from her cat's dish into the garbage, washes the dish, and sets out new water and milk. Mr. Frosty doesn't seem to be around. Under the sink Jeannine finds a dishcloth, hangs it up over the sink, reminds herself to clean out under there later, and pours out cold cereal, tea, toast, orange juice. (The orange juice is a government package of powdered orange-and-grapefruit and tastes awful.) She jumps up to rummage around for the mop head under the sink, and the galvanized pail, also somewhere down in there. Time to mop the bathroom floor and the square of linoleum in front of the sink and stove. First she finishes her tea, leaves half the orange-and-grapefruit juice (making a face) and some of the cereal. Milk goes back in the refrigerator— no, wait a minute, throw it out—she sits down for a moment and writes out a list of groceries to buy on the way back from the bus in a week. Fill the pail, find the soap, give up, mop it anyway with just water. Put everything away. Do the breakfast dishes. She picks up a murder mystery and sits on the couch, riffling through it. Jump up, wash the table, pick up the salt that falls on the rug and brush it up with the whisk-broom. Is that all? No, mend Cal's clothes and her own. Oh, let them be. She has to pack and make her lunch and Cal's (although he's not going with her). That means things coming out of the icebox again and mopping the table again—leaving footprints on the linoleum again. Well, it doesn't matter. Wash the knife and the plate. Done. She decides to go get the sewing box to do his clothes, then changes her mind. Instead she picks up the murder mystery. *Cal will say, "You didn't sew my clothes."* She goes to get the sewing box out of the back of the closet, stepping over her valises, boxes of stuff, the ironing board, her winter coat and winter clothes. Little hands reach out of Jeannine's back and pick up what she drops. She sits on her couch, fixing the rip in his summer suit jacket, biting off the thread with her front teeth. *You'll chip the enamel.* Buttons. Mending three socks. (The others seem all right.) Rubbing the small of her back. Fastening the lining of a skirt where it's torn.

Inspecting her stockings for runs. Polishing shoes. She pauses and looks at nothing. Then she shakes herself and with an air of extraordinary energy gets her middling-sized valise from the closet and starts laying out her clothes for the week. *Cal won't let me smoke. He really cares about me.* With everything cleaned up, she sits and looks at her room. The *Post* says you should get cobwebs off the ceiling with a rag tied to a broom handle. *Well, I can't see them.* Jeannine wishes for the she-doesn't-know-how-many-times time that she had a real apartment with more than one room, though to decorate it properly would be more than she could afford. There's a pile of home-decorating magazines in the back of the closet, although that was only a temporary thing; the thought doesn't really recur to her much. Cal doesn't understand about such things. *Tall, dark, and handsome. . . . She refused her lover. . . . the noble thing to. . . . mimosa and jasmine. . . .* She thinks how it would be to be a mermaid and decorate a merhouse with seaweed and slices of pearl. *The Mermaid's Companion. The Mermaid's Home Journal.* She giggles. She finishes packing her clothes, taking out a pair of shoes to polish them with a bottle of neutral polish, because you have to be careful with the light colors. As soon as they dry, they'll go back in the valise. Trouble is, though, the valise is bloody well falling apart at the seams. Cal, when he comes, will find her reading *Mademoiselle Mermaid* about the new fish-scale look for eyes.

Why does she keep having these dreams about Whileaway?

While-away. While. A. Way. To While away the time. That means it's just a pastime. If she tells Cal about it, he'll say she's nattering again; worse still, it *would* sound pretty silly; you can't expect a man to listen to everything (as everybody's Mother said). Jeannine gets dressed in blouse, sweater, and skirt for her brother's place in the country, while in the valise she puts: a pair of slacks to go berrying in, another blouse, a scarf, underwear, stockings, a jacket (*No, I'll carry it*), her hairbrush, her makeup, face cream, sanitary napkins, a raincoat, jewelry for the good dress, hair clips, hair curlers, bathing suit, and a light every-day dress. Oof, too heavy! She sits down again, discouraged. Little things make Jeannine blue. What's the use of cleaning a place over and over again if you can't make something of it? The ailanthus tree nods to her from outside the window.

(And why won't Cal protect her against anything? She deserves protection.) Maybe she'll meet somebody. Nobody knows— O nobody knows really—what's in Jeannine's heart (she thinks). But somebody will see. Somebody will understand. Remember the hours in California under the fig tree. Jeannine in her crisp plaid dress, the hint of fall in the air, the blue haze over the hills like smoke. She hauls at the valise again, wondering desperately what it is that other women know and can do that she doesn't know or can't do, women in the street, women in the magazines, the ads, married women. Why life doesn't match the stories. *I ought to get married.* (But not to Cal!) She'll meet someone on the bus; she'll sit next to someone. Who knows why things happen? Jeannine, who sometimes believes in astrology, in palmistry, in occult signs, who knows that certain things are fated or not fated, knows that men—in spite of everything—have no contact with or understanding of the insides of things. That's a realm that's denied them. Women's magic, women's intuition rule here, the subtle deftness forbidden to the clumsier sex. Jeannine is on very good terms with her ailanthus tree. Without having to reflect on it, without having to work at it, they both bring into human life the breath of magic and desire. They merely embody. Mr. Frosty, knowing he's going to be left at a neighbor's for the week, has been hiding behind the couch; now he crawls out with a piece of dust stuck on his left eye-tuft, looking very miserable. Jeannine has no idea what drove him out. "Bad cat!" *There was something about her.* She watches the blotchy-skinny-cat (as Cal calls him) sneak to his milk dish and while Mr. Frosty laps it up, Jeannine grabs him. She gets the collar around his neck while Mr. Frosty struggles indignantly, and then she snaps the leash on. In a few minutes he'll forget he's confined. He'll take the collar for granted and start daydreaming about sumptuous mice. *There was something unforgettable about her.* . . . She ties him to a bed post and pauses, catching sight of herself in the wall mirror: flushed, eyes sparkling, her hair swept back as if by some tumultuous storm, her whole face glowing. The lines of her figure are perfect, but who is to use all this loveliness, who is to recognize it, make it public, make it available? Jeannine is not available to Jeannine. She throws her jacket over one arm, more depressed than otherwise. *I wish I had money.* . . .

"Don't worry," she tells the cat. "Somebody's coming for you."
She arranges her jacket, her valise, and her pocketbook, and
turns off the light, shutting the door behind her (it latches
itself). *If only* (she thinks) *he'll come and show me to myself.*

*I've been waiting for you so long. How much longer must I
wait?*

Nights and nights alone. ("You can't," says the stairwell.
"You can't," says the street.) A fragment of old song drifts
through her mind and lingers behind her in the stairwell, her
thoughts lingering there, too, wishing that she could be a mermaid and float instead of walk, that she were someone else and
so could watch herself coming down the stairs, the beautiful
girl who composes everything around her to harmony:

Somebody lovely has just passed by.

II

I live between worlds. Half the time I like doing housework,
I care a lot about how I look, I warm up to men and flirt
beautifully (I mean I really admire them, though I'd die before
I took the initiative; that's men's business), I don't press my
point in conversations, and I enjoy cooking. I like to do things
for other people, especially male people. I sleep well, wake up
on the dot, and don't dream. There's only one thing wrong
with me:

I'm frigid.

In my other incarnation I live out such a plethora of conflict
that you wouldn't think I'd survive, would you, but I do; I
wake up enraged, go to sleep in numbed despair, face what I
know perfectly well is condescension and abstract contempt,
get into quarrels, shout, fret about people I don't even know,
live as if I were the only woman in the world trying to buck
it all, work like a pig, strew my whole apartment with notes,
articles, manuscripts, books, get frowsty, don't care, become
stridently contentious, sometimes laugh and weep within five
minutes together out of pure frustration. It takes me two hours
to get to sleep and an hour to wake up. I dream at my desk. I
dream all over the place. I'm very badly dressed.

But O how I relish my victuals! And O how I fuck!

III

Jeannine has an older brother who's a mathematics teacher in a New York high school. Their mother, who stays with him during vacations, was widowed when Jeannine was four. When she was a little baby Jeannine used to practice talking; she would get into a corner by herself and say words over and over again to get them right. Her first full sentence was, "See the moon." She pressed wildflowers and wrote poems in elementary school. Jeannine's brother, her sister-in-law, their two children, and her mother live for the summer in two cottages near a lake. Jeannine will stay in the smaller one with her mother. She comes downstairs with me behind her to find Mrs. Dadier arranging flowers in a pickle jar on the kitchenette table. I am behind Jeannine, but Jeannine can't see me, of course.

"Everyone's asking about you," says Mrs. Dadier, giving her daughter a peck on the cheek.

"Mm," says Jeannine, still sleepy. I duck behind the bookshelves that separate the living room from the kitchenette.

"We thought you might bring that nice young man with you again," says Mrs. Dadier, setting cereal and milk in front of her daughter. Jeannine retreats into sulky impassivity. I make an awful face, which of course nobody sees.

"We've separated," says Jeannine, untruly.

"Why?" says Mrs. Dadier, her blue eyes opening wide. "What was the matter with him?"

He was impotent, mother. Now how could I say that to such a nice lady? I didn't.

"Nothing," says Jeannine. "Where's Bro?"

"Fishing," says Mrs. Dadier. Brother often goes out in the early morning and meditates over a fishing line. The ladies don't. Mrs. Dadier is afraid of his slipping, falling on a rock, and splitting open his head. Jeannine doesn't like fishing.

"We're going to have a nice day," says Mrs. Dadier. "There's a play tonight and a block dance. There are lots of young people, Jeannine." With her perpetually fresh smile Mrs. Dadier clears off the table where her daughter-in-law and the two children have breakfasted earlier; Eileen has her hands full with the children.

"*Don't*, mother," says Jeannine, looking down.

"I don't mind," says Mrs. Dadier. "Bless you, I've done it often enough." Listless Jeannine pushes her chair back from the table. "You haven't finished," observes Mrs. Dadier, mildly surprised. We have to get out of here. "Well, I don't—I want to find Bro," says Jeannine, edging out, "I'll see you," and she's gone. Mrs. Dadier doesn't smile when there's nobody there. Mother and daughter wear the same face at times like that—calm and deathly tired—Jeannine idly pulling the heads off weeds at the side of the path with an abstract viciousness completely unconnected with anything going on in her head. Mrs. Dadier finishes the dishes and sighs. That's done. Always to do again. Jeannine comes to the path around the lake, the great vacation feature of the community, and starts round it, but there seems to be nobody nearby. She had hoped she would find her brother, who was always her favorite. ("My big brother.") She sits on the rock by the side of the path, Jeannine the baby. Out in the lake there's a single canoe with two people in it; Jeannine's gaze, vaguely resentful, fastens on it for a moment, and then drifts off. Her sister-in-law is worried sick about one of the children; one of those children always has something. Jeannine bangs her knuckles idly on the rock. She's too sour for a romantic reverie and soon she gets up and walks on. Whoever comes to the lake anyway? Maybe Bro is at home. She retraces her steps and takes a fork off the main path, idling along until the lake, with its crowded fringe of trees and brush, disappears behind her. Eileen Dadier's youngest, the little girl, appears at the upstairs window for a moment and then vanishes. Bro is behind the cottage, cleaning fish, protecting his sports clothes with a rubber lab apron.

"Kiss me," says Jeannine. "O.K.?" She leans forward with her arms pulled back to avoid getting fish scales on herself, one cheek offered invitingly. Her brother kisses her. Eileen appears around the corner of the house, leading the boy. "Kiss Auntie," she says. "I'm so *glad* to see you, Jeannie."

"Jeannine," says Jeannine (automatically).

"Just think, Bud," says Eileen. "She must have got in last night. Did you get in last night?" Jeannine nods. Jeannine's nephew, who doesn't like anyone but his father, is pulling furiously at Eileen Dadier's hand, trying seriously to get his fingers

out of hers. Bud finishes cleaning the fish. He wipes his hands
methodically on a dish towel which Eileen will have to wash
by hand to avoid contaminating her laundry, takes off his coat,
and takes his knife and cleaver into the house, from whence
comes the sound of running water. He comes out again, drying his hands on a towel.

"Oh, baby," says Eileen Dadier reproachfully to her son, "be
nice to Auntie." Jeannine's brother takes his son's hand from
his wife. The little boy immediately stops wriggling.

"Jeannie," he says. "It's nice to see you.

"When did you get in?

"When are you going to get married?"

IV

I found Jeannine on the clubhouse porch that evening, looking at the moon. She had run away from her family.

"They only want what's good for you," I said.

She made a face.

"They love you," I said.

A low, strangled sound. She was prodding the porch-rail
with her hand.

"I think you ought to go and rejoin them, Jeannine," I said.
"Your mother's a wonderful woman who has never raised her
voice in anger all the time you've known her. And she brought
all of you up and got you all through high school, even though
she had to work. Your brother's a firm, steady man who makes
a good living for his wife and children, and Eileen wants nothing more in the world than her husband and her little boy and
girl. You ought to appreciate them more, Jeannine."

"I know," said Jeannine softly and precisely. Or perhaps she
said *Oh no.*

"Jeannine, you'll never get a good job," I said. "There
aren't any now. And if there were, they'd never give them to a
woman, let alone a grown-up baby like you. Do you think you
could hold down a really good job, even if you could get one?
They're all boring anyway, hard and boring. You don't want to
be a dried-up old spinster at forty but that's what you will be if
you go on like this. You're twenty-nine. You're getting old. You
ought to marry someone who can take care of you, Jeannine."

"Don't care," said she. Or was it *Not fair?*

"Marry someone who can take care of you," I went on, for her own good. "It's all right to do that; you're a girl. Find somebody like Bud who has a good job, somebody you can respect; marry him. There's no other life for a woman, Jeannine; do you want never to have children? Never to have a husband? Never to have a house of your own?" (Brief flash of waxed floor, wife in organdie apron, smiling possessively, husband with roses. That's hers, not mine.)

"Not Cal." *Ah, hell.*

"Now, really, what are you waiting for?" (I was getting impatient.) "Here's Eileen married, and here's your mother with two children, and all your old school friends, and enough couples here around the lake to fill it up if they all jumped into it at once; do you think you're any different? Fancy Jeannine! Refined Jeannine! What do you think you're waiting for?"

"For a man," said Jeannine. *For a plan.* My impression that somebody else had been echoing her was confirmed by a brief cough behind me after these words. But it turned out to be Mr. Dadier, come out to fetch his sister. He took her by the arm and pulled her toward the door. "Come on, Jeannie. We're going to introduce you to someone."

Only the woman revealed under the light was not Jeannine. A passerby inside saw the substitution through the doorway and gaped. Nobody else seemed to notice. Jeannine is still meditating by the rail: doctor, lawyer, Indian chief, poor man, rich man; maybe he'll be tall; maybe he'll make twenty thou a year; maybe he'll speak three languages and be really sophisticated, maybe. Mister Destiny. Janet, who has none of our notion that a good, dignified, ladylike look will recall the worst of scoundrels to a shrinking consciousness of his having insulted A Lady (that's the general idea, anyway), has gotten out of Bud Dadier's hold by twisting his thumb. She is the victim of a natural, but ignorant and unjustified alarm; she thinks that being grabbed is not just a gesture but is altogether out of line. Janet's prepared for blue murder.

"Huh," says Bro. He's about to expostulate. "What are you doing here? Who are you?"

Touch me again and I'll knock your teeth out!

You can see the blood rush to his face, even in this bad light. That's what comes of being misunderstood. "Keep a civil tongue in your mouth, young lady!"

Janet jeers.

"You just—" Bud Dadier begins, but Janet anticipates him by vanishing like a soap bubble. What do you think Bud stands for—Buddington? Budworthy? Or "Bud" as in "friend"? He passes his hands over his face—the only thing left of Janet is a raucous screech of triumph which nobody else (except the two of us) can hear. The woman in front of the door is Jeannine. Bro, scared out of his wits, as who wouldn't be, grabs her.

"Oh, Bro!" says Jeannine reproachfully, rubbing her arm.

"You oughtn't to be out here alone," says he. "It looks as if you're not enjoying yourself. Mother went to great trouble to get that extra ticket, you know."

"I'm sorry," says Jeannine penitently. "I just wanted to see the moon."

"Well, you've seen it," says her brother. "You've been out here for fifteen minutes. I ought to tell you, Jeannie, Eileen and Mother and I have been talking about you and we all think that you've got to do something with your life. You can't just go on drifting like this. You're not twenty any more, you know."

"Oh, Bro—" says Jeannine unhappily. Why are women so unreasonable? "Of course I want to have a good time," she says.

"Then come inside and have one." (He straightens his shirt collar.) "You might meet someone, if that's what you want to do, and you say that's what you want."

"I do," says Jeannine. *You too?*

"Then act like it, for Heaven's sake. If you don't do it soon, you may not have another chance. Now come on." There are girls with nice brothers and girls with nasty brothers; there was a girl friend of mine who had a strikingly handsome older brother who could lift armchairs by one leg only. I was on a double date once with the two of them and another boy, and my girl friend's brother indicated the camp counselors' cottages. "Do you know what those are?

"Menopause Alley!"

We all laughed. I didn't like it, but not because it was in bad taste. As you have probably concluded by this point (correctly) I don't have any taste; that is, I don't know what bad and good taste are. I laughed because I knew I would have an awful fight on my hands if I didn't. If you don't like things like that, you're a prude. Drooping like a slave-girl, Jeannine followed Bro into the clubhouse. If only older brothers could be regularized somehow, so that one knew what to expect! If only all older brothers were younger brothers. "Well, who shall I marry?" said Jeannine, trying to make it into a joke as they entered the building. He said, with complete seriousness:

"Anybody."

V
The Great Happiness Contest

(this happens a lot)

FIRST WOMAN: I'm perfectly happy. I love my husband and we have two darling children. I certainly don't need any change in *my* lot.

SECOND WOMAN: I'm even happier than you are. My husband does the dishes every Wednesday and we have three darling children, each nicer than the last. I'm tremendously happy.

THIRD WOMAN: Neither of you is as happy as I am. I'm fantastically happy. My husband hasn't looked at another woman in the fifteen years we've been married, he helps around the house whenever I ask it, and he wouldn't mind in the least if I were to go out and get a job. But I'm happiest in fulfilling my responsibilities to him and the children. We have four children.

FOURTH WOMAN: We have *six* children. (This is too many. A long silence.) I have a part-time job as a clerk in Bloomingdale's to pay for the children's skiing lessons, but I really feel I'm expressing myself best when I make a custard or a meringue or decorate the basement.

ME: You miserable nits, I have a Nobel Peace Prize, fourteen published novels, six lovers, a town house, a box at the Metropolitan Opera, I fly a plane, I fix my own car, and I can do eighteen push-ups before breakfast, that is, if you're interested in numbers.

ALL THE WOMEN: Kill, kill, kill, kill, kill, kill.

OR, FOR STARTERS

HE: I can't stand stupid, vulgar women who read Love Comix and have no intellectual interests.

ME: Oh my, neither can I.

HE: I really admire refined, cultivated, charming women who have careers.

ME: Oh my, so do I.

HE: Why do you think those awful, stupid, vulgar, commonplace women get so awful?

ME: Well, probably, not wishing to give any offense and after considered judgment and all that, and *very* tentatively, with the hope that you won't jump on me—I think it's at least partly your fault.

(Long silence)

HE: You know, on second thought, I think bitchy, castrating, unattractive, neurotic women are even worse. Besides, you're showing your age. And your figure's going.

OR

HE: Darling, why must you work part-time as a rug salesman?

SHE: Because I wish to enter the marketplace and prove that in spite of my sex I can take a fruitful part in the life of the community and earn what our culture proposes as the sign and symbol of adult independence—namely money.

HE: But darling, by the time we deduct the cost of a baby-sitter and nursery school, a higher tax bracket, and your box lunches from your pay, it actually costs us money for you to work. So you see, you aren't making money at all. You can't make money. Only I can make money. Stop working.

SHE: I won't. And I hate you.

HE: But darling, why be irrational? It doesn't matter that you can't make money because *I* can make money. And after I've made it, I give it to you, because I love you. So you don't *have* to make money. Aren't you glad?

SHE: No. Why can't you stay home and take care of the baby? Why can't we deduct all those things from your pay? Why should I be glad because I can't earn a living? Why—

HE (with dignity): This argument is becoming degraded and ridiculous. I will leave you alone until loneliness, dependence, and a consciousness that I am very much displeased once again

turn you into the sweet girl I married. There is no use in arguing with a woman.

OR, LAST OF ALL

HE: Is your dog drinking *cold fountain water*?

SHE: I guess so.

HE: If your dog drinks cold water, he'll get colic.

SHE: It's a she. And I don't care about the colic. You know,
what I really worry about is bringing her out in public when
she's in heat like this. I'm not afraid she'll get colic, but that she
might get pregnant.

HE: They're the same thing, aren't they? Har har har.

SHE: Maybe for your mother they were.

(At this point Joanna the Grate swoops down on bat's wings,
lays He low with one mighty swatt, and elevates She and Dog
to the constellation of Victoria Femina, where they sparkle
forever.)

I know that somewhere, just to give me the lie, lives a beautiful (got to be beautiful), intellectual, gracious, cultivated,
charming woman who has eight children, bakes her own bread,
cakes, and pies, takes care of her own house, does her own
cooking, brings up her own children, holds down a demanding nine-to-five job at the top decision-making level in a man's
field, and is adored by her equally successful husband because
although a hard-driving, aggressive business executive with eye
of eagle, heart of lion, tongue of adder, and muscles of gorilla
(she looks just like Kirk Douglas), she comes home at night,
slips into a filmy negligée and a wig, and turns instanter into a
Playboy dimwit, thus laughingly dispelling the canard that you
cannot be eight people simultaneously with two different sets
of values. *She has not lost her femininity.*

And I'm Marie of Rumania.

VI

Jeannine is going to put on her Mommy's shoes. That caretaker
of childhood and feminine companion of men is waiting for her
at the end of the road we all must travel. She swam, went for
walks, went to dances, had a picnic with another girl; she got
books from town; newspapers for her brother, murder mysteries for Mrs. Dadier, and nothing for herself. At twenty-nine

you can't waste your time reading. Either they're too young or they're married or they're bad-looking or there's something awful about them. Rejects. Jeannine went out a couple of times with the son of a friend of her mother's and tried to make conversation with him; she decided that he wasn't really so bad-looking, if only he'd talk more. They went canoeing in the middle of the lake one day and he said:

"I have to tell you something, Jeannine."

She thought: *This is it*, and her stomach knotted up.

"I'm married," he said, taking off his glasses, "but my wife and I are separated. She's living with her mother in California. She's emotionally disturbed."

"Oh," Jeannine said, flustered and not knowing what to say. She hadn't liked him particularly, but the disappointment was very bad. There is some barrier between Jeannine and real life which can be removed only by a man or by marriage; somehow Jeannine is not in touch with what everybody knows to be real life. He blinked at her with his naked eyes and oh lord, he was fat and plain; but Jeannine managed to smile. She didn't want to hurt his feelings.

"I knew you'd understand," he said in a choked voice, nearly crying. He pressed her hand. "I knew you'd understand, Jeannie." She began reckoning him up again, that swift calculation that was quite automatic by now: the looks, the job, whether he was "romantic," did he read poetry? whether he could be made to dress better or diet or put on weight (whichever it was), whether his hair could be cut better. She could make herself feel something about him, yes. She could rely on him. After all, his wife might divorce him. He was intelligent. He was promising. "I understand," she said, against the grain. After all, there wasn't anything wrong with him exactly; from shore it must really look quite good, the canoe, the pretty girl, the puffy summer clouds, Jeannine's sun-shade (borrowed from the girl friend she'd had the picnic with). There couldn't be that much wrong with it. She smiled a little. His contribution is *Make me feel good*; her contribution is *Make me exist*. The sun came out over the water and it really was quite nice. And there was this painful stirring of feeling in her, this terrible tenderness or need, so perhaps she was beginning to love him, in her own way.

"Are you busy tonight?" Poor man. She wet her lips and didn't answer, feeling the sun strike her on all sides, deliciously aware of her bare arms and neck, the picture she made. "Mm?" she said.

"I thought—I thought you might want to go to the play." He took out his handkerchief and wiped his face with it. He put his glasses back on.

"You ought to wear sunglasses," said Jeannine, imagining how he might look that way. "Yes, Bud and Eileen were going. Would you like to join us?" The surprised gratitude of a man reprieved. *I really do like him.* He bent closer—this alarmed her for the canoe, as well as disgusted her (Freud says disgust is a prominent expression of the sexual life in civilized people) and she cried out, "Don't! We'll fall in!" He righted himself. *By degrees. You've got to get to know people.* She was frightened, almost, by the access of being that came to her from him, frightened at the richness of the whole scene, at how much she felt without feeling it for him, terrified lest the sun might go behind a cloud and withdraw everything from her again.

"What time shall I pick you up?" he said.

VII

That night Jeannine fell in love with an actor. The theatre was a squat, low building finished in pink stucco like a summertime movie palace and built in the middle of a grove of pine trees. The audience sat on hard wooden chairs and watched a college group play "Charley's Aunt." Jeannine didn't get up or go out during the intermission but only sat, stupefied, fanning herself with her program and wishing that she had the courage to make some sort of change in her life. She couldn't take her eyes off the stage. The presence of her brother and sister-in-law irked her unbearably and every time she became aware of her date by her elbow, she wanted to turn in on herself and disappear, or run outside, or scream. It didn't matter which actor or which character she fell in love with; even Jeannine knew that; it was the unreality of the scene onstage that made her long to be in it or on it or two-dimensional, anything to quiet her unstable heart; *I'm not fit to live*, she said. There was more pain in it than pleasure; it had been getting worse for some years, until Jeannine now dreaded doing it; *I can't help it*, she said. She added, *I'm not fit to exist.*

I'll feel better tomorrow. She thought of Bud taking his little girl fishing (that had happened that morning, over Eileen's protests) and tears rose in her eyes. The pain of it. The painful pleasure. She saw, through a haze of distress, the one figure on stage who mattered to her. She willed it so. Roses and raptures in the dark. She was terrified of the moment when the curtain would fall—in love as *in* pain, *in* misery, *in* trouble. If only you could stay half-dead. Eventually the curtain (a gray velvet one, much worn) did close, and opened again on the troupe's curtain calls; Jeannine mumbled something about it being too hot and ran outside, shaking with terror; who am I, what am I, what do I want, where do I go, what world is this? One of the neighborhood children was selling lemonade, with a table and chairs pitched on the carpet of dead pine needles under the trees. Jeannine bought some, to color her loneliness; I did, too, and it was awful stuff. (*If anybody finds me, I'll say it was too warm and I wanted a drink.*) She walked blindly into the woods and stood a little way from the theatre, leaning her forehead against a tree-trunk. I said Jeannine, why are you unhappy?

I'm not unhappy.

You have everything (I said). What is there that you want and haven't got?

I want to die.

Do you want to be an airline pilot? Is that it? And they won't let you? Did you have a talent for mathematics, which they squelched? Did they refuse to let you be a truck driver? What is it?

I want to live.

I will leave you and your imaginary distresses (said I) and go converse with somebody who makes more sense; really, one would think you'd been balked of some vital necessity. Money? You've got a job. Love? You've been going out with boys since you were thirteen.

I know.

You can't expect romance to last your life long, Jeannine: candlelight dinners and dances and pretty clothes are nice but they aren't the whole of life. There comes a time when one has to live the ordinary side of life and romance is a very small part of that. No matter how nice it is to be courted and taken out, eventually you say "I do" and that's that. It may be a great adventure, but there are fifty or sixty years to fill up afterwards. You can't do that with romance alone, you know. Think, Jeannine—fifty or sixty years!

I know.

Well?

(Silence)

Well, what do you want?

(She didn't answer)

I'm trying to talk to you sensibly, Jeannine. You say you don't want a profession and you don't want a man—in fact, you just fell in love but you condemn that as silly—so what is it that you want? Well?

Nothing.

That's not true, dear. Tell me what you want. Come on.

I want love. (She dropped her paper cup of lemonade and covered her face with her hands.)

Go ahead. The world's full of people.

I can't.

Can't? Why not? You've got a date here tonight, haven't you? You've never had trouble attracting men's interest before. So go to it.

Not that way.

"What way?" (said I).

Not the real way.

"What!" (said I).

I want something else, she repeated, *something else.*

"Well, Jeannine," said I, "if you don't like reality and human nature, I don't know what else you *can* have," and I quit her and left her standing on the pine needles in the shadow cast by the trees, away from the crowd and the flood-lights fastened to the outside of the theatre building. Jeannine is very romantic. She's building a whole philosophy from the cry of the crickets and her heart's anguish. But that won't last. She will slowly come back to herself. She'll return to Bud and Eileen and her job of fascinating the latest X. Jeannine, back in the theatre building with Bud and Eileen, looked in the mirror set up over the ticket window so lady spectators could put on their lipstick, and jumped—"Who's that!"

"Stop it, Jeannie," said Bud. "What's the matter with you?" We all looked and it was Jeannine herself, sure enough, the same graceful slouch and thin figure, the same nervous, oblique glance.

"Why, it's you, darling," said Eileen, laughing. Jeannine had been shocked right out of her sorrow. She turned to her sister-in-law and said, with unwonted energy, between her teeth: "What do you want out of life, Eileen? Tell me!"

"Oh honey," said Eileen, "what should I want? I want just what I've got." X came out of the men's room. Poor fellow. Poor lay figure.

"Jeannie wants to know what life is all about," said Bud. "What do you think, Frank? Do you have any words of wisdom for us?"

"I think that you are all awful," said Jeannine vehemently. X laughed nervously. "Well now, I don't know," he said.

That's my trouble, too. My knowledge was taken away from me. (She remembered the actor in the play and her throat constricted. It hurt, it hurt. Nobody saw, though.)

"Do you think," she said very low, to X, "that you could know what you wanted, only after a while—I mean, they don't mean to do it, but life—people—people could confuse things?"

"I know what I want," said Eileen brightly. "I want to go home and take the baby from Mama. Okay, honey?"

"I don't mean—" Jeannine began.

"Oh, Jeannie!" said Eileen affectionately, possibly more for X's benefit than her sister-in-law's; "Oh, Jeannie!" and kissed her. Bud gave her a peck on the cheek.

Don't you touch me!

"Want a drink?" said X, when Bud and Eileen had gone.

"I want to know," said Jeannine, almost under her breath, "what you want out of life and I'm not moving until you tell me." He stared.

"Come on," she said. He smiled nervously.

"Well, I'm going to night school. I'm going to finish my B.A. this winter." (He's going to night school. He's going to finish his B.A. Wowie zowie. I'm not impressed.)

"Really?" said Jeannine, in real awe.

"Really," he said. Score one. That radiant look of gratitude. Maybe she'll react the same way when he tells her he can ski. In this loveliest and neatest of social interactions, she admires him, he's pleased with her admiration, this pleasure lends him warmth and style, he relaxes, he genuinely likes Jeannine; Jeannine sees this and something stirs, something hopes afresh. Is he The One? Can he Change Her Life? (Do you know what you want? No. Then don't complain.) Fleeing from the unspeakableness of her own wishes—for what happens when you find out you want something that doesn't exist?—Jeannine lands in the lap of the possible. A drowning woman, she takes X's willing, merman hands; maybe it's wanting to get married, maybe she's just waited too long. *There's* love; *there's* joy—in marriage, and you must take your chances as they come. They say life without love does strange things to you; maybe you begin to doubt love's existence.

I shouted at her and beat her on the back and on the head; oh I was an enraged and evil spirit there in the theatre lobby, but she continued holding poor X by the hands—little did he know what hopes hung on him as she continued (I say) to hold on to his hands and look into his flattered eyes. Little did she know that he was a water-dweller and would drown her. Little did she know that there was, attached to his back, a drowning-machine issued him in his teens along with his pipe and his tweeds and his ambition and his profession and his father's mannerisms. Somewhere is The One. The solution. Fulfillment. Fulfilled women. Filled full. My Prince. Come. Come away, Death. She stumbles into her Mommy's shoes, little girl playing house. I could kick her. And X thinks, poor, deceived bastard, that it's a tribute to him, of all people—as if he had anything to do with it! (I still don't know whom she saw or thought she saw in the mirror. Was it Janet? Me?)

I want to get married.

VIII

Men succeed. Women get married.
Men fail. Women get married.
Men enter monasteries. Women get married.

Men start wars. Women get married.
Men stop them. Women get married.
Dull, dull. (see below)

IX

Jeannine came around to her brother's house the next morning,
just for fun. She had set her hair and was wearing a swanky
scarf over the curlers. Both Mrs. Dadier and Jeannine know
that there's nothing in a breakfast nook to make it intrinsically
interesting for thirty years; nonetheless Jeannine giggles and
twirls the drinking straw in her breakfast cocoa fancifully this
way and that. It's the kind of straw that has a pleated section in
the middle like the bellows of a concertina.

"I always liked these when I was a little girl," Jeannine says.

"Oh my yes, didn't you," says Mrs. Dadier, who is sitting
with her second cup of coffee before attacking the dishes.

Jeannine gives way to a fit of hysterics.

"Do you remember—?" she cries. "And do you remember—!"

"Heavens, yes," says Mrs. Dadier. "Don't I, though."

They sit, saying nothing.

"Did Frank call?" This is Mrs. Dadier, carefully keeping her
voice neutral because she knows how Jeannine hates interference in her own affairs. Jeannine makes a face and then laughs
again. "Oh, give him time, Mother," she says. "It's only ten
o'clock." She seems to see the funny side of it more than Mrs.
Dadier does. "Bro," says the latter, "was up at five and Eileen
and I got up at eight. I know this is your vacation, Jeannine,
but in the country—"

"I *did* get up at eight," says Jeannine, aggrieved. (She's lying.) "I did. I walked around the lake. I don't know why you
keep telling me how late I get up; that may have been true a
long time ago but it's certainly not true now, and I resent your
saying so." The sun has gone in again. When Bud isn't around,
there's Jeannie to watch out for; Mrs. Dadier tries to anticipate
her wishes and not disturb her.

"Well, I keep forgetting," says Mrs. Dadier. "Your silly old
mother! Bud says I wouldn't remember my head if it wasn't
screwed on." It doesn't work. Jeannine, slightly sulky, at-
tacks her toast and jam, cramming a piece into her mouth

cater-cornered. Jam drops on the table. Jeannine, implaca-
bly convicted of getting up late, is taking it out on the tablecloth. Getting up late is wallowing in sin. It's unforgivable.
It's improper. Mrs. Dadier, with the misplaced courage of the
doomed, chooses to ignore the jam stains and get on with
the really important question, *viz.*, is Jeannine going to have
a kitchenette of her own (although it will really belong to
someone else, won't it) and is she going to be made to get
up early, *i.e.*, Get Married. Mrs. Dadier says very carefully and
placatingly:

"Darling, have you ever had any thoughts about—" but this
morning, instead of flinging off in a rage, her daughter kisses
her on the top of the head and announces, "I'm going to do
the dishes."

"Oh, no," says Mrs. Dadier deprecatingly; "My goodness,
don't. I don't mind." Jeannine winks at her. She feels virtuous
(because of the dishes) and daring (because of something else).
"Going to make a phone call," she says, sauntering into the
living room. *Not doing the dishes.* She sits herself down in the
rattan chair and twirls the pencil her mother always keeps by
the telephone pad. She draws flowers on the pad and the pro-
files of girls whose eyes are nonetheless in full-face. Should she
call X? Should she wait for X to call her? When he calls, should
she be effusive or reserved? Comradely or distant? Should she
tell X about Cal? If he asks her out for tonight, should she refuse? Where will she go if she does? She can't possibly call him,
of course. But suppose she rings up Mrs. Dadier's friend with a
message? *My mother asked me to tell you. . . .* Jeannine's hand
is actually on the telephone receiver when she notices that the
hand is shaking: a sportswoman's eagerness for the chase. She
laughs under her breath. She picks up the phone, trembling
with eagerness, and dials X's number; it's happening at last.
Everything is going well. Jeannine has almost in her hand the
brass ring which will entitle her to everything worthwhile in
life. It's only a question of time before X decides; surely she
can keep him at arm's length until then, keep him fascinated;
there's so much time you can take up with will-she-won't-she,
so that hardly anything else has to be settled at all. She feels
something for him, she really does. She wonders when the
reality of it begins to hit you. Off in telephone never-never-
land someone picks up the receiver, interrupting the last ring,

footsteps approach and recede, someone is clearing their throat into the mouthpiece.

"Hello?" (It's his mother.) Jeannine glibly repeats the fake message she has practiced in her head; X's mother says, "Here's Frank. Frank, it's Jeannine Dadier." Horror. More footsteps.

"Hello?" says X.

"Oh my, it's you; I didn't know you were there," says Jeannine.

"Hey!" says X, pleased. This is even more than she has a right to expect, according to the rules.

"Oh, I just called to tell your mother something," says Jeannine, drawing irritable, jagged lines across her doodles on the telephone pad. She keeps trying to think of the night before, but all she can remember is Bud playing with his youngest daughter, the only time she's ever seen her brother get foolish. He bounces her on his knee and gets red in the face, swinging her about his head while she screams with delight. "Silly Sally went to town! Silly Sally flew a-r-o-o-und!" Eileen usually rescues the baby on the grounds that she's getting too excited. For some reason this whole memory causes Jeannine great pain and she can hardly keep her mind on what she's saying.

"I thought you'd already gone," says Jeannine hastily. He's going on and on about something or other, the cost of renting boats on the lake or would she like to play tennis.

"Oh, I love tennis," says Jeannine, who doesn't even own a racket.

Would she like to come over that afternoon?

She leans away from the telephone to consult an imaginary appointment book, imaginary friends; she allows reluctantly that oh yes, she might have some free time. It would really be fun to brush up on her tennis. Not that she's really good, she adds hastily. X chuckles. Well, maybe. There are a few more commonplaces and she hangs up, bathed in perspiration and ready to weep. *What's the matter with me?* She should be happy, or at least smug, and here she is experiencing the keenest sorrow. What on earth for? She digs her pencil vindictively into the telephone pad as if it were somehow responsible. *Damn you.* Perversely, images of silly Cal come back to her, not nice ones, either. She has to pick up the phone again, after verifying an imaginary date with an imaginary acquaintance, and tell X yes or no; so Jeannine rearranges the scarf over her curlers, plays with a button on her blouse, stares miserably at her shoes, runs her hands over her knees, and makes up her mind. She's nervous. Masochistic. It's that old thing come back again about her not being good enough for good luck. That's nonsense and she knows it. She picks up the phone, smiling: tennis, drinks, dinner, back in the city a few more dates where he can tell her about school and then one night (hugging her a little extra hard)—"Jeannie, I'm getting my divorce." *My name is Jeannine.* The shopping will be fun. *I'm twenty-nine, after all.* It is with a sense of intense relief that she dials; the new life is beginning. She can do it, too. She's normal. She's as good as every other girl. She starts to sing under her breath. The phone bell rings in Telephoneland and somebody comes to pick it up; she hears all the curious background noises of the relays, somebody speaking faintly very far away. She speaks quickly and distinctly, without the slightest hesitation now, remembering all those loveless nights with her knees poking up into the air, how she's discommoded and almost suffocated, how her leg muscles ache and she can't get her feet on the surface of the bed. Marriage will cure all that. The scrubbing uncleanably old linoleum and dusting the same awful things, week after week. But he's going places. She says boldly and decisively:

"Cal, come get me."

Shocked at her own treachery, she bursts into tears. She hears Cal say "Okay, baby," and he tells her what bus he'll be on.

"Cal!" she adds breathlessly; "You know that question you keep asking, sweetheart? Well, the answer is Yes." She hangs up, much eased. It'll be so much better once it's done. Foolish Jeannine, to expect anything else. It's an uncharted continent, marriage. She wipes her eyes with the back of her hand; X can go to hell. Making conversation is just work. She strolls into the kitchenette where she finds herself alone; Mrs. Dadier is outside in back, weeding a little patch of a garden all the Dadiers own in common; Jeannine takes the screen out of the kitchen window and leans out.

"Mother!" she says in a sudden flood of happiness and excitement, for the importance of what she has just done has suddenly become clear to her, "Mother!" (waving wildly out the window) "Guess what!" Mrs. Dadier, who is on her knees in the carrot bed, straightens up, shading her face with her one hand. "What is it, darling?"

"Mother, I'm getting married!" What comes after this will be very exciting, a sort of dramatic presentation, for Jeannine will have a big wedding. Mrs. Dadier drops her gardening trowel in sheer astonishment. She'll hurry inside, a tremendous elevation of mood enveloping both women; they will, in fact, embrace and kiss one another, and Jeannine will dance around the kitchen. "Wait 'til Bro hears about *this*!" Jeannine will exclaim. Both will cry. It's the first time in Jeannine's life that she's managed to do something perfectly O.K. And not too late, either. She thinks that perhaps the lateness of her marriage will be compensated for by a special mellowness; there must be, after all, some reason for all that experimenting, all that reluctance. She imagines the day she will be able to announce even better news: "Mother, I'm going to have a baby." Cal himself hardly figures in this at all, for Jeannine has forgotten his laconism, his passivity, his strange mournfulness unconnected to any clear emotion, his abruptness, how hard it is to get him to talk about anything. She hugs herself, breathless with joy, waiting for Mrs. Dadier to hurry inside; "My little baby!" Mrs. Dadier will say emotionally, embracing Jeannine. It seems to Jeannine that she has never known anything so solid and beautiful as the kitchen in the morning sunlight, with the walls glowing and everything so delicately outlined in light, so fresh and real. Jeannine, who has almost been killed by an unremitting and drastic discipline not of her own choosing, who has been maimed almost to death by a vigilant self-suppression quite irrelevant to anything she once wanted or loved, here finds her reward. This proves it is all right. Everything is indubitably good and indubitably real. She loves herself, and if I stand like Atropos in the corner, with my arm around the shadow of her dead self, if the other Jeannine (who is desperately tired and knows there is no freedom for her this side the grave) attempts to touch her as she whirls joyfully past, Jeannine does not see or hear it. At one stroke she has amputated her past. She's going to be fulfilled. She hugs herself and waits. That's all you have to do if you are a real, first-class Sleeping Beauty. She knows.

I'm so happy.

And there, but for the grace of God, go I.

PART SEVEN

I

I'LL TELL you how I turned into a man.
     First I had to turn into a woman.
For a long time I had been neuter, not a woman at all but
One Of The Boys, because if you walk into a gathering of men,
professionally or otherwise, you might as well be wearing a
sandwich board that says: LOOK! I HAVE TITS! there is this
giggling and this chuckling and this reddening and this Uriah
Heep twisting and writhing and this fiddling with ties and fixing of buttons and making of allusions and quoting of cour-
tesies and this self-conscious gallantry plus a smirky insistence
on my physique—all this dreary junk just to please me. If you
get good at being One Of The Boys it goes away. Of course
there's a certain disembodiment involved, but the sandwich
board goes; I back-slapped and laughed at blue jokes, especially
the hostile kind. Underneath you keep saying pleasantly but
firmly No no no no no no. But it's necessary to my job and
I like my job. I suppose they decided that my tits were not of
the best kind, or not real, or that they were someone else's (my
twin sister's), so they split me from the neck up; as I said, it
demands a certain disembodiment. I thought that surely when
I had acquired my Ph.D. and my professorship and my tennis medal and my engineer's contract and my ten thousand a
year and my full-time housekeeper and my reputation and the
respect of my colleagues, when I had grown strong, tall, and
beautiful, when my I.Q. shot past 200, when I had genius, *then*
I could take off my sandwich board. I left my smiles and happy
laughter at home. I'm not a woman; I'm a man. I'm a man
with a woman's face. I'm a woman with a man's mind. Everybody says so. In my pride of intellect I entered a bookstore;
I purchased a book; I no longer had to placate The Man; by
God, I think I'm going to make it. I purchased a copy of John
Stuart Mill's *The Subjection of Women*; now who can object to
John Stuart Mill? He's dead. But the clerk did. With familiar

archness he waggled his finger at me and said "tsk tsk"; all that
writhing and fussing began again, what fun it was for him to
have someone automatically not above reproach, and I knew
beyond the shadow of a hope that to be female is to be mirror
and honeypot, servant and judge, the terrible Rhadamanthus
for whom he must perform but whose judgment is not human
and whose services are at anyone's command, the vagina den-
tata and the stuffed teddy-bear he gets if he passes the test. This
is until you're forty-five, ladies, after which you vanish into thin
air like the smile of the Cheshire cat, leaving behind only a disgusting grossness and a subtle poison that automatically infects
every man under twenty-one. Nothing can put you above this
or below this or beyond it or outside of it, nothing, nothing,
nothing at all, not your muscles or your brains, not being one
of the boys or being one of the girls or writing books or writing
letters or screaming or wringing your hands or cooking lettuce
or being too tall or being too short or traveling or staying at
home or ugliness or acne or diffidence or cowardice or perpetual shrinking and old age. In the latter cases you're only doubly
damned. I went away—"forever feminine," as the man says—
and I cried as I drove my car, and I wept by the side of the road
(because I couldn't see and I might crash into something) and
I howled and wrung my hands as people do only in medieval
romances, for an American woman's closed car is the only place
in which she can be alone (if she's unmarried) and the howl of
a sick she-wolf carries around the world, whereupon the world
thinks it's very comical. Privacy in cars and bathrooms, what
ideas we have! If they tell me about the pretty clothes again,
I'll kill myself.

I had a five-year-old self who said: *Daddy won't love you.*
I had a ten-year-old self who said: *the boys won't play with you.*
I had a fifteen-year-old self who said: *nobody will marry you.*
I had a twenty-year-old self who said: *you can't be fulfilled
without a child.* (A year there where I had recurrent nightmares
about abdominal cancer which nobody would take out.)

I'm a sick woman, a madwoman, a ball-breaker, a man-eater;
I don't consume men gracefully with my fire-like red hair or my
poisoned kiss; I crack their joints with these filthy ghoul's claws
and standing on one foot like a de-clawed cat, rake at your feeble efforts to save yourselves with my taloned hinder feet: my

matted hair, my filthy skin, my big flat plaques of green bloody teeth. I don't think my body would sell anything. I don't think I would be good to look at. O of all diseases self-hate is the worst and I don't mean for the one who suffers it!

Do you know, all this time you preached at me? You told me that even Grendel's mother was actuated by maternal love.

You told me ghouls were male.

Rodan is male—and asinine.

King Kong is male.

I could have been a witch, but the Devil is male.

Faust is male.

The man who dropped the bomb on Hiroshima was male.

I was never on the moon.

Then there are the birds, with (as Shaw so nobly puts it) the touching poetry of their loves and nestings in which the males sing so well and beautifully and the females sit on the nest, and the baboons who get torn in half (female) by the others (male), and the chimpanzees with their hierarchy (male) written about by professors (male) with *their* hierarchy, who accept (male) the (male) view of (female) (male). You can see what's happening. At heart I must be gentle, for I never even thought of the praying mantis or the female wasp; but I guess I am just loyal to my own phylum. One might as well dream of being an oak tree. Chestnut tree, great-rooted hermaphrodite. I won't tell you what poets and prophets my mind is crammed full of (Deborah, who said "Me, too, pretty please?" and got struck with leprosy), or Whom I prayed to (exciting my own violent hilarity) or whom I avoided on the street (male) or whom I watched on television (male) excepting in my hatred only—if I remember—Buster Crabbe, who is the former Flash Gordon and a swimming instructor (I think) in real life, and in whose humanly handsome, gentle, puzzled old face I had the absurd but moving fancy that I saw some reflection of my own bewilderment at our mutual prison. Of course I don't know him and no one is responsible for his shadow on the screen or what madwomen may see there; I lay in my bed (which is not male), made in a factory by a (male) designed by a (male) and sold to me by a (small male) with unusually bad manners. I mean unusually bad manners for anybody.

You see how *very different* this is from the way things used to be in the bad old days, say five years ago. New Yorkers (female) have had the right to abortion for almost a year now, if you can satisfy the hospital boards that you deserve bed-room and don't mind the nurses calling you Baby Killer; citizens of Toronto, Canada, have perfectly free access to contraception if they are willing to travel 100 miles to cross the border, I could smoke my very own cigarette if I smoked (and get my very own lung cancer). Forward, eternally forward! Some of my best friends are—I was about to say that some of my best friends are—my friends—

My friends are dead.

Whoever saw *women* scaring anybody? (This was while I thought it important to be able to scare people.) You cannot say, to paraphrase an old, good friend, that there are the plays of Shakespeare and Shakespeare was a woman, or that Columbus sailed the Atlantic and Columbus was a woman or that Alger Hiss was tried for treason and Alger Hiss was a woman. (Mata Hari was not a spy; she was a fuckeress.) Anyway everyboy (sorry) everybody knows that what women have done that is really important is not to constitute a great, cheap labor force that you can zip in when you're at war and zip out again afterwards but to Be Mothers, to form the coming generation, to give birth to them, to nurse them, to mop floors for them, to love them, cook for them, clean for them, change their diapers, pick up after them, and mainly sacrifice themselves for them. This is the most important job in the world. That's why they don't pay you for it.

I cried, and then stopped crying because otherwise I would never have stopped crying. Things come to an awful dead center that way. You will notice that even my diction is becoming feminine, thus revealing my true nature; I am not saying "Damn" any more, or "Blast"; I am putting in lots of qualifiers like "rather," I am writing in these breathless little feminine tags, she threw herself down on the bed, I have no structure (she thought), my thoughts seep out shapelessly like menstrual fluid, it is all very female and deep and full of essences, it is very primitive and full of "and's," it is called "run-on sentences."

Very swampy in my mind. Very rotten and badly off. I am a woman. I am a woman with a woman's brain. I am a woman with a woman's sickness. I am a woman with the wraps off, bald as an adder, God help me and you.

II

Then I turned into a man.

This was slower and less dramatic.

I think it had something to do with the knowledge you suffer when you're an outsider—I mean *suffer*; I do not mean *undergo* or *employ* or *tolerate* or *use* or *enjoy* or *catalogue* or *file away* or *entertain* or *possess* or *have*.

That knowledge is, of course, the perception of all experience through two sets of eyes, two systems of value, two habits of expectation, almost two minds. This is supposed to be an infallible recipe for driving you gaga. Chasing the hare Reconciliation with the hounds of Persistence—but there, you see? I'm not Sir Thomas Nasshe (or Lady Nasshe, either, tho' she never wrote a line, poor thing). Rightaway you start something, down comes the portcullis. Blap. To return to knowledge, I think it was seeing the lords of the earth at lunch in the company cafeteria that finally did me in; as another friend of mine once said, men's suits are designed to inspire confidence even if the men can't. But their *shoes*—! Dear God. And their *ears*! Jesus. The innocence, the fresh-faced naiveté of power. The childlike simplicity with which they trust their lives to the Black men who cook for them and their self-esteem and their vanity and their little dangles to me, who do everything for them. Their ignorance, their utter, happy ignorance. There was the virgin We sacrificed on the company quad when the moon was full. (You thought a virgin meant a girl, didn't you?) There was Our thinking about housework—dear God, scholarly papers about housework, what could be more absurd! And Our parties where we pinched and chased Each Other. Our comparing the prices of women's dresses and men's suits. Our push-ups. Our crying in Each Other's company. Our gossip. Our trivia. All trivia, not worth an instant's notice by any rational being. If you see Us skulking through the bushes at the rising of the moon, don't look. And don't wait around. Watch the wall, my darling, you'd better. Like all motion, I couldn't feel it while it went on, but this is what you have to do:

To resolve contrarieties, unite them in your own person.

This means: in all hopelessness, in terror of your life, without a future, in the sink of the worst despair that you can endure and will yet leave you the sanity to make a choice—take in your bare right hand one naked, severed end of a high-tension wire. Take the other in your left hand. Stand in a puddle. (Don't worry about letting go; you can't.) Electricity favors the prepared mind, and if you interfere in this avalanche by accident you will be knocked down dead, you will be charred like a cutlet, and your eyes will be turned to burst red jellies, but if those wires are your own wires—hang on. God will keep your eyes in your head and your joints knit one to the other. When She sends the high voltage alone, well, we've all experienced those little shocks—you just shed it over your outside like a duck and it does nothing to you—but when She roars down in high voltage and high amperage both, She is after your marrowbones; you are making yourself a conduit for holy terror and the ecstasy of Hell. But only in that way can the wires heal themselves. Only in that way can they heal you. Women are not used to power; that avalanche of ghastly strain will lock your muscles and your teeth in the attitude of an electrocuted rabbit, but you are a strong woman, you are God's favorite, and you can endure; if you can say "yes, okay, go on"—after all, where else can you go? What else can you do?—if you let yourself through yourself and into yourself and out of yourself, turn yourself inside out, give yourself the kiss of reconciliation, marry yourself, love yourself—

Well, I turned into a man.

We love, says Plato, that in which we are defective; when we see our magical Self in the mirror of another, we pursue it with desperate cries—*Stop! I must possess you!*—but if it obligingly stops and turns, how on earth can one then possess it? Fucking, if you will forgive the pun, is an anti-climax. And you are as poor as before. For years I wandered in the desert, crying: *Why do you torment me so?* and *Why do you hate me so?* and *Why do you put me down so?* and *I will abase myself* and *I will please you* and *Why, oh why have you forsaken me?* This is very feminine. What I learned late in life, under my rain of lava, under my kill-or-cure, unhappily, slowly, stubbornly, barely, and in really dreadful pain, was that there is one and only one way to possess that in which we are defective, therefore that which we need, therefore that which we want.

Become it.

(Man, one assumes, is the proper study of Mankind. Years ago we were all cave Men. Then there is Java Man and the future of Man and the values of Western Man and existential Man and economic Man and Freudian Man and the Man in the moon and modern Man and eighteenth-century Man and too many Mans to count or look at or believe. There is Mankind. An eerie twinge of laughter garlands these paradoxes. For years I have been saying *Let me in, Love me, Approve me, Define me, Regulate me, Validate me, Support me*. Now I say *Move over*. If we are all Mankind, it follows to my interested and righteous and rightnow very bright and beady little eyes, that I too am a Man and not at all a Woman, for honestly now, whoever heard of Java Woman and existential Woman and the values of Western Woman and scientific Woman and alienated nineteenth-century Woman and all the rest of that dingy and antiquated rag-bag? All the rags in it are White, anyway. I think I am a Man; I think you had better call me a Man; I think you will write about me as a Man from now on and speak of me as a Man and employ me as a Man and recognize child-rearing as a Man's business; you will think of me as a Man and treat me as a Man until it enters your muddled, terrified, preposterous, nine-tenths-fake, loveless, papier-mâché-bull-moose head that *I am a man*. (And you are a woman.) That's the whole secret. Stop hugging Moses' tablets to your chest, nitwit; you'll cave in. Give me your Linus blanket, child. Listen to the female man.

If you don't, by God and all the Saints, *I'll break your neck*.)

III

We would gladly have listened to her (they said) *if only she had spoken like a lady*. But they are liars and the truth is not in them.

Shrill . . . vituperative . . . no concern for the future of society . . . maunderings of antiquated feminism . . . selfish femlib . . . needs a good lay . . . this shapeless book . . . of course a calm and objective discussion is beyond . . . twisted, neurotic . . . some truth buried in a largely hysterical . . . of very limited interest, I should . . . another tract for

the trash-can . . . burned her bra and thought that . . . no
characterization, no plot . . . really important issues are neglected while . . . hermetically sealed . . . women's limited
experience . . . another of the screaming sisterhood . . . a
not very appealing aggressiveness . . . could have been done
with wit if the author had . . . deflowering the pretentious
male . . . a man would have given his right arm to . . .
hardly girlish . . . a woman's book . . . another shrill po-
lemic which the . . . a mere male like myself can hardly . . .
a brilliant but basically confused study of feminine hysteria
which . . . feminine lack of objectivity . . . this pretense at
a novel . . . trying to shock . . . the tired tricks of the anti-
novelists . . . how often must a poor critic have to . . . the
usual boring obligatory references to Lesbianism . . . denial
of the profound sexual polarity which . . . an all too womanly
refusal to face facts . . . pseudo-masculine brusqueness . . .
the ladies'-magazine level . . . trivial topics like housework
and the predictable screams of . . . those who cuddled up to
ball-breaker Kate will . . . unfortunately sexless in its outlook
. . . drivel . . . a warped clinical protest against . . . violently waspish attack . . . formidable self-pity which erodes
any chance of . . . formless . . . the inability to accept the
female role which . . . the predictable fury at anatomy dis-
placed to . . . without the grace and compassion which we
have the right to expect . . . anatomy is destiny . . . destiny
is anatomy . . . sharp and funny but without real weight or
anything beyond a topical . . . just plain bad . . . we "dear
ladies," whom Russ would do away with, unfortunately just
don't *feel* . . . ephemeral trash, missiles of the sex war . . . a
female lack of experience which. . . .

Q.E.D. Quod erat demonstrandum. It has been proved.

IV

Janet has begun to follow strange men on the street; whatever
will become of her? She does this either out of curiosity or
just to annoy me; whenever she sees someone who interests
her, woman or man, she swerves automatically (humming a
little tune, da-dum, da-dee) and continues walking but in the
opposite direction. When Whileawayan I meets Whileawayan

2, the first utters a compound Whileawayan word which may be translated as "Hello-yes?" to which the answer may be the same phrase repeated (but without the rising inflection), "Hello-no," "Hello" alone, silence, or "No!" "Hello-yes" means *I wish to strike up a conversation*; "Hello" means *I don't mind your remaining here but I don't wish to talk*; "Hello-no" *Stay here if you like but don't bother me in any way*; silence *I'd be much obliged if you'd get out of here; I'm in a foul temper.* Silence accompanied by a quick shake of the head means *I'm not ill-tempered but I have other reasons for wanting to be alone.* "No!" means *Get away or I'll do that to you which you won't like.* (In contradistinction to our customs, it is the late-comer who has the moral edge, Whileawayan I having already got some relief or enjoyment out of the convenient bench or flowers or spectacular mountain or whatever's at issue.) Each of these responses may be used as salutations, of course.

I asked Janet what happens if both Whileawayans say "No!"

"Oh" she says (bored), "they fight."

"Usually one of us runs away," she added.

Janet is sitting next to Laura Rose on my nubbly-brown couch, half-asleep, half all over her friend in a confiding way, her head resting on Laur's responsible shoulder. A young she-tiger with a large, floppy cub. In her dozing Janet has shed ten years' anxiety and twenty pounds of trying-to-impress-others; she must be so much younger and sillier with her own people; grubbing in the tomato patch or chasing lost cows; what Safety and Peace officers do is beyond me. (A cow found her way into the Mountainpersons' common room and backed a stranger through a foam wall by trying to start a conversation —Whileawayans have a passion for improving the capacities of domestic animals—she kept nudging this visitor and saying "Friend? Friend?" in a great, wistful moo, like the monster in the movie, until a Mountainperson shooed her away: *You don't want to make trouble, do you, child? You want to be milked, don't you? Come on, now.*)

"Tell us about the cow," says Laura Rose. "Tell Jeannine about it," (who's vainly trying to flow into the wall, O agony, those two women are *touching*).

"No," mutters Janet sleepily.

"Then tell us about the Zdubakovs," says Laur.

"You're a vicious little beast!" says Janet and sits bolt upright.

"Oh come on, giraffe," says Laura Rose. "Tell!" She has sewn embroidered bunches of flowers all over her denim jacket and jeans with a red, red rose on the crotch, but she doesn't wear these clothes at home, only when visiting.

"You are a damned vicious cublet," said Janet. "I'll tell you something to sweeten your disposition. Do you want to hear about the three-legged goat who skipped off to the North Pole?"

"No," says Laur. Jeannine flattens like a film of oil; she vanishes dimly into a cupboard, putting her fingers in her ears.

"Tell!" says Laur, twisting my little finger. I bury my face in my hands. Ay, no. Ay, no. Laura must hear. She kissed my neck and then my ear in a passion for all the awful things I do as S & P; I straightened up and rocked back and forth. The trouble with you people is you get no charge from death. Myself, it shakes me all over. Somebody I'd never met had left a note saying the usual thing: *ha ha on you, you do not exist, go away*, for we are so bloody cooperative that we have this solipsistic underside, you see? So I went up-mountain and found her; I turned on my two-way vocal three hundred yards from criminal Elena Twason and said, "Well, well, Elena, you shouldn't take a vacation without notifying your friends."

"Vacation?" she says; "Friends? Don't lie to me, girl. You read my letter," and by this I began to understand that she hadn't had to go mad to do this and that was terrible. I said, "What letter? Nobody found a letter."

"The cow ate it," says Elena Twason. "Shoot me. I don't believe you're there but my body believes; I believe that my tissues believe in the bullet that you do not believe in yourself, and that will kill me."

"Cow?" says I, ignoring the rest, "what cow? You Zdubakovs don't keep cows. You're vegetable-and-goat people, I believe. Quit joking with me, Elena. Come back; you went botanizing and lost your way, that's all."

"Oh *little girl*," she said, so off-hand, so good-humored, "*little child*, don't deform reality. Don't mock us both." In spite of the insults, I tried again.

"What a pity," I said, "that your hearing is going so bad at the age of sixty, Elena Twa. Or perhaps it's my own. I thought

I heard you say something else. But the echoes in this damned valley are enough to make anything unintelligible; I could have sworn that I was offering you an illegal collusion in an untruth and that like a sensible, sane woman, you were accepting." I could see her white hair through the binoculars; she could've been my mother. Sorry for the banality, but it's true. Often they try to kill you so I showed myself as best I could, but she didn't move—exhausted? Sick? Nothing happened.

"Elena!" I shouted. "By the entrails of God, will you please come down!" and I waved my arms like a semaphore. I thought: *I'll wait until morning at least. I can do that much.* In my mind we changed places several times, she and I, both of us acting as illegally in our respective positions as we could, but I might be able to patch up some sort of story. As I watched her, she began to amble down the hillside, that little white patch of hair bobbing through the autumn foliage like a deer's tail. Chuckling to herself, idly swinging a stick she'd picked up: weak little thing, just a twig really, too dry to hit anything without breaking. I ambled ghostly beside her; it's so pretty in the mountains at that time of year, everything burns and burns without heat. I think she was enjoying herself, having finally put herself, as it were, beyond the reach of consequences; she took her little stroll until we were quite close to each other, close enough to converse face to face, perhaps as far as I am from you. She had made herself a crown of scarlet maple leaves and put it on her head, a little askew because it was a little too big to fit. She smiled at me.

"Face facts," she said. Then, drawing down the corners of her mouth with an ineffable air of gaiety and arrogance:

"Kill, killer."

So I shot her.

Laur, who has been listening intently all this time, blood-thirsty little devil, takes Janet's face in her hands. "Oh, come on. You shot her with a narcotic, that's all. You told me so. A narcotic dart."

"No," said Janet. "I'm a liar. I killed her. We use explosive bullets because it's almost always distance work. I have a rifle like the kind you've often seen yourself."

"Aaaah!" is Laura Rose's long, disbelieving, angry comment. She came over to me: "Do *you* believe it?" (I shall have to

drag Jeannine out of the woodwork with both hands.) Still angry, Laur straddles the room with her arms clasped behind her
back. Janet is either asleep or acting. I wonder what Laur and
Janet do in bed; what do women think of women?

"I don't care what either of you thinks of me," says Laur. "I
like it! By God, I like the idea of doing something to somebody for a change instead of having it done to me. Why are you
in Safety and Peace if you don't enjoy it!"

"I told you," says Janet softly.

Laur said, "I know, someone has to do it. Why you?"

"I was assigned."

"Why? Because you're bad! You're tough." (She smiles at her
own extravagance. Janet sat up, wavering a little, and shook
her head.)

"Dearest, I'm not good for much; understand that. Farm
work or forest work, what else? I have some gift to unravel
these human situations, but it's not quite intelligence."

"Which is why you're an emissary?" says Laur. "Don't expect
me to believe that." Janet stares at my rug. She yawns, jaw-
cracking. She clasps her hands loosely in her lap, remembering
perhaps what it had been like to carry the body of a sixty-year-
old woman down a mountainside: at first something you wept
over, then something horrible, then something only distaste-
ful, and finally you just did it.

"I am what you call an emissary," she said slowly, nodding
courteously to Jeannine and me, "for the same reason that I
was in S & P. I'm expendable, my dear. Laura, Whileawayan
intelligence is confined in a narrower range than yours; we are
not only smarter on the average but there is much less spread
on either side of the average. This helps our living together. It
also makes us extremely intolerant of routine work. But still
there is some variation." She lay back on the couch, putting her
arms under her head. Spoke to the ceiling. Dreaming, perhaps.
Of Vittoria?

"Oh, honey," she said, "I'm here because they can do without me. I was S & P because they could do without me. There's
only one reason for that, Laur, and it's very simple.

"I am stupid."

Janet sleeps or pretends to, Joanna knits (that's me), Jeannine is in the kitchen. Laura Rose, still resentfully twitching

with unconquered Genghis Khanism, takes a book from my
bookshelf and lies on her stomach on the rug. I believe she
is reading an art book, something she isn't interested in. The
house seems asleep. In the desert between the three of us the
dead Elena Twason Zdubakov begins to take shape; I give her
Janet's eyes, Janet's frame, but bent with age, some of Laur's
impatient sturdiness but modified with the graceful trembling
of old age: her papery skin, her smile, the ropy muscles on
her wasted arms, her white hair cut in an economical kind of
thatch. Helen's belly is loose with old age, her face wrinkled,
a never-attractive face like that of an extremely friendly and
intelligent horse: long and droll. The lines about her mouth
would be comic lines. She's wearing a silly kind of khaki shorts-
and-shirt outfit which is not really what Whileawayans wear,
but I give it to her anyway. Her ears are pierced. Her mountain
twig has become a carved jade pipe covered with scenes of
vines, scenes of people crossing bridges, people pounding flax,
processions of cooks or grain-bearers. She wears a spray of red
mountain-ash berries behind one ear. Elena is about to speak;
from her comes a shock of personal strength, a wry impressiveness, an intelligence so powerful that in spite of myself I
open my arms to this impossible body, this walking soul, this
somebody's grandma who could say with such immense élan
to her legal assassin, "Face facts, child." No man in our world
would touch Elena. In Whileawayan leaf-red pajamas, in silver
silk overalls, in the lengths of moony brocade in which Whileawayans wrap themselves for pleasure, this would be a beautiful
Helen. Elena Twason swathed in cut-silk brocade, nipping a
corner of it for fun. It would be delightful to have erotic play
with Elena Twason; I feel this on my lips and tongue, in the
palms of my hands, all my inside skin. I feel it down below, in
my sex. What a formidable woman! Shall I laugh or cry? She's
dead, though—killed dead—so never shall Ellie Twa's ancient
legs entwine with mine or twiddle from under the shell of a
computer housing, crossing and uncrossing her toes as she and
the computer tell each other uproarious jokes. Her death was
a bad joke. I would like very much to make love skin-to-skin
with Elena Twason Zdubakov, but she is thank-the-male-God
dead and Jeannine can come shudderingly out of the woodwork. Laur and Janet have gone to sleep together on the couch

as if they were in a Whileawayan common bedroom, which is not for orgies, as you might think, but for people who are lonesome, for children, for people who have nightmares. We miss those innocent hairy sleepies we used to tangle with back in the dawn of time before some progressive nitwit took to deferred gratification and chipping flint.

"What's this?" whispered Jeannine, furtively proffering something for my inspection.

"I don't know, is it a staple gun?" I said. (It had a handle.) "Whose is it?"

"I found it on Janet's bed," said Jeannine, still whispering. "Just lying there. I think she took it out of her suitcase. I can't figure out what it is. You hold it by the handle and if you move this switch it buzzes on one end, though I don't see why, and another switch makes this piece move up and down. But that seems to be an attachment. It doesn't look as if it's been used as much as the rest of it. The handle's really something; it's all carved and decorated."

"Put it back," I said.

"But what *is* it?" said Jeannine.

"A Whileawayan communications device," I said. "Put it back, Jeannie."

"Oh?" she said. Then she looked doubtfully at me and at the sleepers. Janet, Jeannine, Joanna. Something very J-ish is going on here.

"Is it dangerous?" said Jeannine. I nodded—emphatically.

"Infinitely," I said. "It can blow you up."

"All of me?" said Jeannine, holding the thing gingerly at arm's length.

"What it does to your body," said I, choosing my words with extreme care, "is nothing compared to what it does to your mind, Jeannine. It will ruin your mind. It will explode in your brains and drive you crazy. You will never be the same again. You will be lost to respectability and decency and decorum and dependency and all sorts of other nice, normal things beginning with a D. It will kill you, Jeannine. You will be dead, dead, dead.

"Put it back."

(On Whileaway these charming dinguses are heirlooms. They are menarchal gifts, presented after all sorts of glass-blowing, clay-modeling, picture-painting, ring-dancing, and Heaven knows what sort of silliness done by the celebrants to honor the little girl whose celebration it is. There is a tremendous amount of kissing and hand-shaking. This is only the formal presentation, of course; cheap, style-less models that you wouldn't want to give as presents are available to everybody long before this. Whileawayans often become quite fond of them, as you or I would of a hi-fi set or a sports car, but all the same, a machine's only a machine. Janet later offered to lend me hers on the grounds that she and Laur no longer needed it.)

Jeannine stood there with an expression of extraordinary distrust: Eve and the hereditary instinct that tells her to beware of apples. I took her by the shoulders, telling her again that it was a radar set. That it was extremely dangerous. That it would blow up if she wasn't careful. Then I pushed her out of the room.

"Put it back."

V

Jeannine, Janet, Joanna. Something's going to happen. I came downstairs in my bathrobe at three A.M., unable to sleep. This house ought to be ringed with government spies, keeping their eyes on our diplomat from the stars and her infernal, perverted friends, but nobody's about. I met Jeannine in the kitchen in her pajamas, looking for the cocoa. Janet, still in sweater and slacks, was reading at the kitchen table, puffy-eyed from lack of sleep. She was cross-noting Gunnar Myrdal's *An American Dilemma* and *Marital Patterns of Nebraska College Sophomores, 1938–1948*.

Jeannine said:

"I try to make the right decisions, but things don't work out. I don't know why. Other women are so happy. I was a very good student when I was a little girl and I liked school tremendously, but then when I got to be around twelve, everything changed. Other things become important then, you know. It's not that I'm not attractive; I'm pretty enough, I mean in a usual way, goodness knows I'm no beauty. But that's all right. I love books, I love reading and thinking, but Cal says it's only daydreaming; I just don't know. What do you think? There's my cat, Mister Frosty, you've seen him, I'm terribly fond of him, as much as you can be of an animal, I suppose, but can you make a life out of books and a cat? I want to get married. It's there, you know, somewhere just around the corner; sometimes after coming out of the ballet or the theatre, I can almost feel it, I know if only I could turn around in the right direction, I'd be able to reach out my hand and take it. Things will get better. I suppose I'm just late in developing. Do you think if I got married I would like making love better? Do you think there's unconscious guilt—you know, because Cal and I aren't married? I don't feel it that way, but if it was unconscious, you wouldn't feel it, would you? Sometimes I get really blue, really awful, thinking: suppose I get old this way? Suppose I reach fifty or sixty and it's all been the same—that's horrible —but of course it's impossible. It's ridiculous. I ought to get busy at something. Cal says I'm frightfully lazy. We're getting married—marvelous!—and my mother's very pleased because I'm twenty-nine. Under the wire, you know, oops! Sometimes I think I'll get a notebook and write down my dreams because they're very elaborate and interesting, but I haven't yet. Maybe I won't; it's a silly thing to do. Do you think so? My sister-in-law's so happy and Bud's happy and I know my mother is; and Cal has a great future planned out. And if I were a cat I would be my cat, Mister Frosty, and I'd be spoiled rotten (Cal says). I have everything and yet I'm not happy.

"Sometimes I want to die."

Then Joanna said:

"After we had finished making love, he turned to the wall and said, 'Woman, you're lovely. You're sensuous. You should wear long hair and lots of eye make-up and tight clothing.' Now what does this have to do with anything? I remain bewildered. I have a devil of pride and a devil of despair; I used to go out among the hills at seventeen (this is a poetic euphemism for a suburban golf course) and there, on my knees, I swear it, knelen on my kne, I wept aloud, I wrung my hands, crying: I am a poet! I am Shelley! I am a genius! What has any of this to do with me! The utter irrelevancy. The inanity of the whole business. Lady, your slip's showing. God bless. At eleven I passed an eighth-grader, a boy, who muttered between his teeth, 'Shake it but don't break it.' The career of the sexless

sex object had begun. I had, at seventeen, an awful conversation with my mother and father in which they told me how
fine it was to be a girl—the pretty clothes (why are people so
obsessed with this?) and how I did not have to climb Everest,
but could listen to the radio and eat bon-bons while my Prince
was out doing it. When I was five my indulgent Daddy told me
he made the sun come up in the morning and I expressed my
skepticism; 'Well, watch for it tomorrow and you'll see,' he said.
I learned to watch his face for cues as to what I should do or
what I should say, or even what I should see. For fifteen years
I fell in love with a different man every spring like a berserk
cuckoo-clock. I love my body dearly and yet I would copulate
with a rhinoceros if I could become not-a-woman. There is
the vanity training, the obedience training, the self-effacement
training, the deference training, the dependency training, the
passivity training, the rivalry training, the stupidity training,
the placation training. How am I to put this together with my
human life, my intellectual life, my solitude, my transcendence,
my brains, and my fearful, fearful ambition? I failed miserably
and thought it was my own fault. You can't unite woman and
human any more than you can unite matter and anti-matter;
they are designed not to be stable together and they make just
as big an explosion inside the head of the unfortunate girl who
believes in both.

"Do you enjoy playing with other people's children—for ten
minutes? Good! This reveals that you have Maternal Instinct
and you will be forever wretched if you do not instantly have
a baby of your own (or three or four) and take care of that
unfortunate victimized object twenty-four hours a day, seven
days a week, fifty-two weeks a year, for eighteen years, all by
yourself. (Don't expect much help.)

"Are you lonely? Good! This shows that you have Feminine
Incompleteness; get married and do all your husband's personal services, buck him up when he's low, teach him about sex
(if he wants you to), praise his technique (if he doesn't), have a
family if he wants a family, follow him if he changes cities, get a
job if he needs you to get a job, and this too goes on seven days
a week, fifty-two weeks a year forever and ever amen unless
you find yourself a divorcée at thirty with (probably two) small
children. (Be a shrew and ruin yourself, too, how about it?)

"Do you like men's bodies? Good! This is beginning to be almost as good as getting married. This means that you have True Womanliness, which is fine unless you want to do it with him on the bottom and you on the top, or any other way than he wants to do it, or you don't come in two minutes, or you don't want to do it, or you change your mind in mid-course, or get aggressive, or show your brains, or resent never being talked to, or ask him to take you out, or fail to praise him, or worry about whether he Respects You, or hear yourself described as a whore, or develop affectionate feelings for him (see Feminine Incompleteness, above) or resent the predation you have to face and screen out so unremittingly—

"I am a telephone pole, a Martian, a rose-bed, a tree, a floor lamp, a camera, a scarecrow. I'm not a woman.

"Well, it's nobody's fault, I know (this is what I'm supposed to think). I know and totally approve and genuflect to and admire and wholly obey the doctrine of Nobody's Fault, the doctrine of Gradual Change, the doctrine that Women Can Love Better Than Men so we ought to be saints (warrior saints?), the doctrine of It's A Personal Problem.

"(Selah, selah, there is only one True Prophet and it's You, don't kill me, massa, I'se jes' ig'nerant.)

"You see before you a woman in a trap. Those spike-heeled shoes that blow your heels off (so you become round-heeled). The intense need to smile at everybody. The slavish (but respectable) adoration: Love me or I'll die. As the nine-year-old daughter of my friend painstakingly carved on her linoleum block when the third grade was doing creative printing: I am like I am suppose to be Otherwise I'd kill myself Rachel.

"Would you believe—could you hear without laughing— could you credit without positively oofing your sides with hysterical mirth, that for years my secret, teenage ambition—more important than washing my hair even and I wouldn't tell it to *anybody*—was to stand up fearless and honest like Joan of Arc or Galileo—

"And suffer for the truth?"

So Janet said:

"Life has to end. What a pity! Sometimes, when one is alone, the universe presses itself into one's hands: a plethora of joy, an organized plenitude. The iridescent, peacock-green folds of the mountains in South Continent, the cobalt-colored sky, the white sunlight which makes everything too real to be true. The existence of existence always amazes me. You tell me that men are supposed to like challenge, that it is risk that makes them truly men, but if I—a foreigner—may venture an opinion, what we know beyond any doubt is that the world is a bath; we bathe in air, as Saint Teresa said the fish is in the sea and the sea is in the fish. I fancy your old church windows wished to show worshippers' faces stained with that emblematic brightness. Do you really want to take risks? Inoculate yourself with bubonic plague. What foolishness! When that intellectual sun rises, the pure sward lengthens under the crystal mountain; under that pure intellectual light there is neither material pigment nor no true shadow any more, any more. What price ego then?

"Now you tell me that enchanted frogs turn into princes, that frogesses under a spell turn into princesses. What of it? Romance is bad for the mind. I'll tell you a story about the old Whileawayan philosopher—she is a folk character among us, rather funny in an odd way, or as we say, 'ticklish.' The Old Whileawayan Philosopher was sitting cross-legged among her disciples (as usual) when, without the slightest explanation, she put her fingers into her vagina, withdrew them, and asked, 'What have I here?'

"The disciples all thought very deeply.

"'Life,' said one young woman.

"'Power,' said another.

"'Housework,' said a third.

"'The passing of time,' said the fourth, 'and the tragic irreversibility of organic truth.'

"The Old Whileawayan Philosopher hooted. She was immensely entertained by this passion for myth-making. 'Exercise your projective imaginations,' she said, 'on people who can't fight back,' and opening her hand, she showed them that her fingers were perfectly unstained by any blood whatever, partly because she was one hundred and three years old and long past the menopause and partly because she had just died that morning. She then thumped her disciples severely about the head and shoulders with her crutch and vanished. Instantly two of the disciples achieved Enlightenment, the third became violently angry at the imposture and went to live as a hermit in the mountains, while the fourth—entirely disillusioned with philosophy, which she concluded to be a game for crackpots —left philosophizing forever to undertake the dredging out of silted-up harbors. What became of the Old Philosopher's ghost is not known. Now the moral of this story is that all images, ideals, pictures, and fanciful representations tend to vanish sooner or later unless they have the great good luck to be exuded from within, like bodily secretions or the bloom on a grape. And if you think that grape-bloom is romantically pretty, you ought to know that it is in reality a film of yeasty parasites rioting on the fruit and gobbling up grape sugar, just as the human skin (under magnification, I admit) shows itself to be iridescent with hordes of plantlets and swarms of beasties and all the scum left by their dead bodies. And according to our Whileawayan notions of propriety all this is just as it should be and an occasion for infinite rejoicing.

"After all, why slander frogs? Princes and princesses are fools. They do nothing interesting in your stories. They are not even real. According to history books you passed through the stage of feudal social organization in Europe some time ago. Frogs, on the other hand, are covered with mucus, which they find delightful; they suffer agonies of passionate desire in which the males will embrace a stick or your finger if they cannot get anything better, and they experience rapturous, metaphysical joy (of a froggy sort, to be sure) which shows plainly in their beautiful, chrysoberyllian eyes.

"How many princes or princesses can say as much?"

Joanna, Jeannine, and Janet. What a feast of J's. Somebody is collecting J's.

We were somewhere else. I mean we were not in the kitchen any more. Janet was still wearing her slacks and sweater, I my bathrobe, and Jeannine her pajamas. Jeannine was carrying a half-empty cup of cocoa with a spoon stuck in it.

But we were somewhere else.

PART EIGHT

I

W̲ho am I?
     I know who I am, but what's my brand name?
     Me with a new face, a puffy mask. Laid over the old one in strips of plastic that hurt when they come off, a blond Hallowe'en ghoul on top of the S.S. uniform. I was skinny as a beanpole underneath except for the hands, which were similarly treated, and that very impressive face. I did this once in my line of business, which I'll go into a little later, and scared the idealistic children who lived downstairs. Their delicate skins red with offended horror. Their clear young voices raised in song (at three in the morning).
     I don't do this often (say I, the ghoul) but it's great elevator technique, sticking your forefinger to the back of somebody's neck while passing the fourth floor, knowing that he'll never find out that you haven't a gun and that you're not all there.
     (Sorry. But watch out.)

II

Whom did we meet in that matron blackness but The Woman Who Has No Brand Name.

"I suppose you are wondering," she said (and I enjoyed her enjoyment of my enjoyment of her enjoyment of that cliché) "why I have brought you here."

We did.

We wondered why we were in a white-walled penthouse living room overlooking the East River at night with furniture so sharp-edged and ultra-modern that you could cut yourself on it, with a wall-length bar, with a second wall hung entirely in black velvet like a stage, with a third wall all glass, outside which the city did not look quite as I remembered it.

Now J (as I shall call her) is really terrifying, for she's invisible. Against the black curtains her head and hands float in sinister disconnection, like puppets controlled by separate strings. There are baby spotlights in the ceiling, which illuminate in deep chiaroscuro her gray hair, her lined face, her rather macabre grin, for her teeth seem to be one fused ribbon of steel. She stepped out against the white wall, a woman-shaped hole, a black cardboard cut-out; with a crooked, charming smile she clapped her hand to her mouth, either taking something out or putting something in—see? Real teeth. Those disbodied, almost crippled hands clasped themselves. She sat on her black leather couch and vanished again; she smiled and dropped fifteen years; she has silver hair, not gray, and I don't know how old she is. How she loves us! She leans forward and croons at us like Garbo. Jeannine has sunk down into a collection of glass plates that passes for a chair; her cup and spoon make a tiny, spineless chattering. Janet is erect and ready for anything.

"I'm glad, so glad, so very glad," says J softly. She doesn't mind Jeannine's being a coward. She turns the warmth of her smile on Jeannine the way none of us has ever been smiled at before, a dwelling, loving look that would make Jeannine go through fire and water to get it again, the kind of mother-love whose lack gets into your very bones.

"I am called Alice Reasoner," says J, "christened Alice-Jael; I am an employee of the Bureau of Comparative Ethnology. My code name is Sweet Alice; can you believe it?" (with a soft, cultivated laugh) "Look around you and welcome yourselves; look at me and make me welcome; welcome myself, welcome me, welcome I," and leaning forward, a shape stamped by a cookie-cutter on to nothing, with pleasant art and sincere gestures, Alice-Jael Reasoner told us what you have no doubt guessed long, long ago.

III

(Her real laugh is the worst human sound I have ever heard: a hard, screeching yell that ends in gasps and rusty sobbing, as if some mechanical vulture on a gigantic garbage heap on the surface of the moon were giving one forced shriek for the death of all organic life. Yet J likes it. This is her *private* laugh. Alice is crippled, too; the ends of her fingers (she says) were

once caught in a press and are growing cancerous—and to be
sure, if you look at them closely you can see folds of loose, dead
skin over the ends of her fingernails. She has hairpin-shaped
scars under her ears, too.

IV

Her pointed fingernails painted silver to distract the eye, Alice-
Jael plays with the window console: the East River clouds over
to reveal (serially) a desert morning, a black lava beach, and
the surface of the moon. She sat, watching the pictures change,
tapping her silver nails on the couch, herself the very picture
of boredom. Come up close and you'll see that her eyes are silver, most unnatural. It came to me that we had been watching
this woman perform for half an hour and had given not one
thought to what might be happening around us or to us or
behind us. The East River?

("An artist's conception," she says.)

V

"I am," says Jael Reasoner, "an employee of the Bureau of
Comparative Ethnology and a specialist in disguises. It came
to me several months ago that I might find my other selves
out there in the great, gray might-have-been, so I undertook
—for reasons partly personal and partly political, of which
more later—to get hold of the three of you. It was very hard
work. I'm a field worker and not a theoretician, but you must
know that the closer to home you travel, the more power it
takes, both to discriminate between small degrees of difference and to transport objects from one universe of probability
into another.

"If we admit among the universes of probability any in
which the laws of physical reality are different from our own,
we will have an infinite number of universes. If we restrict
ourselves to the laws of physical reality as we know them, we
will have a limited number. Our universe is quantized; therefore the differences between possible universes (although very
small) must be similarly quantized, and the number of such
universes must be finite (although very large). I take it that it

must be possible to distinguish the very smallest differences —say, that of one quantum of light—for otherwise we could not find our way to the same universe time after time, nor could we return to our own. Current theory has it that one cannot return to one's own past, but only to other people's; similarly one cannot travel into one's own future, but only to other people's, and in no way can these motions be forced to result in straightforward travel—*from any baseline whatever.* The only possible motion is diagonal motion. So you see that the classical paradoxes of time-travel simply do not apply—we cannot kill our own grandmothers and thereby cease to exist, nor can we travel into our own future and affect it in advance, so to speak. Nor can I, once I have made contact with your present, travel into your past or your future. The best I can do in finding out my own future is to study one very close to my own, but here the cost of power becomes prohibitive. My Department's researches are therefore conducted in regions rather far from home. Go too far and you find an Earth too close to the sun or too far away or nonexistent or barren of life; come too close and it costs too much. We operate in a pretty small optimal range. And of course I was doing this on my own, which means I must steal the whole damn operation anyway.

"You, Janet, were almost impossible to find. The universe in which your Earth exists does not even register on our instruments; neither do those for quite a probable spread on either side of you; we have been trying for years to find out why. Besides you are too close to us to be economically feasible. I had located Jeannine and not Joanna; you very obligingly stepped out of place and became as visible as a sore thumb; I've had a fix on you ever since. The three of you got together and I pulled you all in. Look at yourselves.

"Genetic patterns sometimes repeat themselves from possible present universe to possible present universe; this is also one of the elements that can vary between universes. There is repetition of genotypes in the far future too, sometimes. Here is Janet from the far future, but not my future or yours; here are the two of you from almost the same moment of time (but not as you see it!), both of those moments only a little behind mine; yet I won't happen in the world of either of you. We are less alike than identical twins, to be sure, but much more alike than strangers have any right to be. Look at yourselves again.

"We're all white-skinned, eh? I bet two of you didn't think of that. We're all women. We are tall, within a few inches of each other. Given a reasonable variation, we are the same racial type, even the same physical type—no redheads or olive skins, hm? Don't go by me; I'm not natural! Look in each other's faces. What you see is essentially the same genotype, modified by age, by circumstances, by education, by diet, by learning, by God knows what. Here is Jeannine, the youngest of us all with her smooth face: tall, thin, sedentary, round-shouldered, a long-limbed body made of clay and putty; she's always tired and probably has trouble waking up in the morning. Hm? And there's Joanna, somewhat older, much more active, with a different gait, different mannerisms, quick and jerky, not depressed, sits with her spine like a ruler. Who'd think it was the same woman? There's Janet, hardier than the two of you put together, with her sun-bleached hair and her muscles; she's spent her life outdoors, a Swedish hiker and a farmhand. You begin to see? She's older and that masks a good deal. And of course she has had all the Whileawayan improvements— no rheumatism, no sinus trouble, no allergies, no appendix, good feet, good teeth, no double joints, and so forth and so forth, all the rest that we three must suffer. And I, who could throw you all across the room, though I don't look it. Yet we started the same. It's possible that in biological terms Jeannine is potentially the most intelligent of us all; try to prove that to a stranger! We ought to be equally long-lived but we won't be. We ought to be equally healthy but we're not. If you discount the wombs that bore us, our pre-natal nourishment, and our deliveries (none of which differ essentially) we ought to have started out with the same autonomic nervous system, the same adrenals, the same hair and teeth and eyes, the same circulatory system, and the same innocence. We ought to think alike and feel alike and act alike, but of course we don't. So plastic is humankind! Do you remember the old story of the Doppelgänger? This is the double you recognize instantly, with whom you feel a mysterious kinship. An instant sympathy, that informs you at once that the other is really your very own self. The truth is that people don't recognize themselves except in mirrors, and sometimes not even then. Between our dress, and our opinions, and our habits, and our beliefs, and our values, and our mannerisms, and our manners, and our expressions, and our ages, and our experience, even I can hardly believe that I am looking at three other myselves. No layman would entertain for a moment the notion that he beheld four versions of the same woman. Did I say a moment? Not for an age of moments, particularly if the layman were indeed *a man*.

"Janet, may I ask you why you and your neighbors do not show up on our instruments? You must have discovered the theory of probability travel some time ago (in your terms), yet you are the first traveler. You wish to visit other universes of probability, yet you make it impossible for anyone to find you, let alone visit you.

"Why is that?"

"Aggressive and bellicose persons," said Janet with care, "always assume that unaggressive and pacific persons cannot protect themselves.

"Why is that?"

VI

Over trays of pre-cooked steak and chicken that would've disgraced an airline (that's where they came from, I found out later) Jael sat next to Jeannine and glued herself to Jeannine's ear, glancing round at the rest of us from time to time to see how we were taking it. Her eyes sparkled with the gaiety of corruption, the Devil in the fable tempting the young girl. Whisper, whisper, whisper. All I could hear were the sibilants, when her tongue came between her teeth. Jeannine stared soberly ahead and didn't eat much, the color leaving her little by little. Jael didn't eat at all. Like a vampire she fed on Jeannine's ear. Later she drank a sort of super-bouillon which nobody else could stand and talked a lot to all of us about the war. Finally, Janet said bluntly:

"What war?"

"Does it matter?" said Miss Reasoner ironically, raising her silver eyebrows. "This war, that war, isn't there always one?"

"No," said Janet.

"Well, hell," said Jael more genuinely, "*the* war. If there isn't
one, there just was one, and if there wasn't one, there soon will
be one. Eh? The war between Us and Them. We're playing it
rather cool just now because it's hard to work up an enthusiasm for something forty years old."

I said, "Us and Them?"

"I'll tell you," said Sweet Alice, making a face. "After the
plague—don't worry; everything you eat is stuffed with anti-
toxins and we'll decontaminate you before you go—besides,
this all ended more than seventy years ago—after the bacteri-
ological weapons were cleaned out of the biosphere (insofar
as that was possible) and half the population buried (the dead
half, I hope) people became rather conservative. They tend
to do that, you know. Then after a while you get the reaction against the conservatism, I mean the radicalism. And
after that the reaction against the radicalism. People had already begun gathering in like-minded communities before
the war: Traditionalists, Neo-Feudalists, Patriarchalists, Ma-
triarchalists, Separatists (all of us now), Fecundists, Sterilists,
and what-have-you. They seemed to be happier that way. The
War Between the Nations had really been a rather nice war, as
wars go; it wiped the have-not nations off the face of the earth
and made their resources available to us without the bother
of their populations; all our machinery was left standing; we
were getting wealthier and wealthier. So if you were not one
of the fifty percent who had died, you were having a pretty
good time of it. There was increasing separatism, increasing
irritability, increasing radicalism; then came the Polarization;
then came the Split. The middle drops out and you're left
with the two ends, hein? So when people began shopping
for a new war, which they also seem to do, don't they, there
was only one war left. The only war that makes any sense if
you except the relations between children and adults, which
you must do because children grow up. But in the other war
the Haves never stop being Haves and the Have-nots never
stop being Have-nots. It's cooled off now, unfortunately, but
no wonder; it's been going on for forty years—a stalemate,
if you'll forgive the pun. But in my opinion, questions that
are based on something real ought to be settled by something real without all this damned lazy miserable drifting. I'm

a fanatic. I want to see this thing settled. I want to see it over and done with. Gone. Dead.

"Oh, don't worry!" she added. "Nothing spectacular is going to happen. All I will do in three days or so is ask you about the tourist trade in your lovely homes. What's wrong with that? Simple, eh?

"But it will get things moving. The long war will start up again. We will be in the middle of it and I—who have always been in the middle of it—will get some decent support from my people at last."

"Who?" said Jeannine crossly. "Who, who, for Heaven's sake! Who's Us, who's Them? Do you expect us to find out by telepathy!"

"I beg your pardon," said Alice Reasoner softly. "I thought you knew. I had no intention of puzzling you. You are my guests. When I say Them and Us I mean of course the Haves and the Have-nots, the two sides, there are always two sides, aren't there?

"I mean the men and the women."

Later I caught Jeannine by the door as we were all leaving; "What did she talk to you about?" I said. Something had gotten into Jeannine's clear, suffering gaze; something had muddied her timidity. What can render Miss Dadier self-possessed? What can make her so quietly stubborn? Jeannine said:

"She asked me if I had ever killed anybody."

VII

She took us topside in the branch elevator: The Young One, The Weak One, The Strong One, as she called us in her own mind. I'm the author and I know. *Miss Sweden* (she also called Janet this) ran her hands over the paneling and studied the controls while the other two gaped. Think of me in my usual portable form. Their underground cities are mazes of corridors like sunken hotels; we passed doors, barricades, store windows, branch corridors leading to arcades. What is this passion for living underground? At one barrier they put us in purdah, that is, some kind of asbestos-like fireman's suit that protects you against other people's germs and them against yours. But this time it was a fake, meant only to hide us. "Can't have them

looking at you," said Jael. She went apart with the border
guard and there was some low-voiced, aggressive byplay, some
snarling and lifting of hackles which a third party resolved by
a kind of rough joking. I didn't hear a word of it. She told us
honestly that we couldn't be expected to believe anything we
hadn't seen with our own eyes. There would be no films, no
demonstrations, no statistics, unless we asked for them. We
trundled out of the elevator into an armored car waiting in a
barn, and across an unpaved, shell-pocked plain, a sort of no-
man's-land, in the middle of the night. *Is the grass growing? Is
that a virus blight? Are the mutated strains taking over?* Nothing but gravel, boulders, space, and stars. Jael flashed her pass
at a second set of guards and told them about us, jerking her
thumb backwards at the three of us: unclean, unclean, unclean.
No barriers, no barbed wire, no searchlights; only the women
have these. Only the men make a sport of people-hunting
across the desert. Bulkier than three pregnancies, we followed
our creatrix into another car, from out that first one, through
the rubble and ruin at the edges of an old city, left standing
just as it had been during the plague. Teachers come out here
on Sundays, with their classes. It looks as if it's been used for
target practice, with holes in everything and new scars, like
mortar scars, on the rubble.

"It has," says Jael Reasoner. Each of us wears a luminous,
shocking-pink cross on chest and back to show how deadly
we are. So the Manlanders (who all carry guns) won't take
pot-shots at us. There are lights in the distance—don't think
I know any of this by hearsay; I'm the spirit of the author and
know all things. I'll know it when we begin to pass the lit-up
barracks at the edge of the city, when we see in the distance the
homes of the very rich shining from the seven hilltops on which
the city is built; I'll know it when we go through a tunnel of
rubble, built fashionably to resemble a World War I trench,
and emerge neither into a public nursery (they're either much
further inside the city proper or out in the country) nor into
a brothel, but into a recreation center called The Trench or
The Prick or The Crotch or The Knife. I haven't decided on a
name yet. The Manlanders keep their children with them only
when they're very rich—but what posit I? Manlanders have
no children. Manlanders buy infants from the Womanlanders

and bring them up in batches, save for the rich few who can order children made from their very own semen: keep them in city nurseries until they're five, then out into the country training ground, with the gasping little misfits buried in baby cemeteries along the way. There, in ascetic and healthful settlements in the country, little boys are made into Men—though some don't quite make it; sex-change surgery begins at sixteen. One out of seven fails early and makes the full change; one out of seven fails later and (refusing surgery) makes only half a change: artists, illusionists, impressionists of femininity who keep their genitalia but who grow slim, grow languid, grow emotional and feminine, all this the effect of spirit only. Five out of seven Manlanders make it; these are "real-men." The others are "the changed" or "the half-changed." All real-men like the changed; some real-men like the half-changed; none of the real-men like real-men, for that would be abnormal. Nobody asks the changed or half-changed what *they* like. Jael flashed her civil pass at the uniformed real-man at the entrance to The Crotch and we trundled after. Our hands and feet look very small to me, our bodies odd and dumpy.

We went inside; "Jael!" I exclaimed, "there are—"

"Look again," she said.

Look at the necks, look at the wrists and ankles, penetrate the veils of false hair and false eyelashes to measure the relative size of eyes and bone structure. The half-changed starve themselves to be slim, but look at their calves and the straightness of their arms and knees. If most of the fully changed live in harims and whore-homes, and if popular slang is beginning to call them "cunts," what does this leave for us? What can we be called?

"*The enemy*," said Jael. "Sit here." We sat around a large table in the corner where the light was dim, snuggling up to the fake oak paneling. One of the guards, who had followed us inside, came up to Jael and put one giant arm round her, one huge paw crushing her bearishly to his side, his crimson epaulets, his gold boots, his shaved head, his sky-blue codpiece, his diamond-chequered-costumed attempt to beat up the whole world, to shove his prick up the world's ass. She looked so plain next to him. She was all swallowed up.

"Hey, hey," he said. "So you're back again!"

"Well, sure, why not?" (she said) "I have to meet someone. I have some business to do."

"Business!" he said fetchingly. "Don't you want some of the real thing? Come on, fuck business!"

She smiled gracefully but remained modestly silent. This seemed to please him. He enveloped her further, to the point of vanishment, and said in a low voice with a sort of chuckle:

"Don't you dream about it? Don't all you girls dream about us?"

"You know that, Lenny," she said.

"Sure I do," he said enthusiastically. "Sure. I can see it in your face whenever you come here. You get excited just looking at it. Like the doctors say, we can do it with each other but you can't because you don't have nothing to do it with, do you? So you don't get any."

"Lenny—" she began (slipping under his arm) "you got us figured out just right. Scout's honor. I've got business to do."

"Come on!" he said (pleading, I think).

"Oh, you're a brick!" cried Jael, moving behind the table, "you surely are. Why, you're so strong, some day you're going to squash us to death." He laughed, basso-profundo. "We're friends," he said, and winked laboriously.

"Sure," said Jael dryly.

"Some day you're gonna walk right in here—" and this tiresome creature began all over again, but whether he noticed the rest of us or saw someone or smelt someone I don't know, for suddenly he lumbered off in a great hurry, rousting his billy-club out of his azure sash, next the gun holster. Bouncers don't use their guns at The Prick; too much chance of hitting the wrong people. Jael was talking to someone else, a shadowy, thin-lipped party in a green, engineer's suit.

"Of course we're friends," said Jael Reasoner patiently. "Of course we are. That's why I don't want to talk to you tonight. Hell, I don't want to get you in trouble. See those crosses? One jab, one little rip or tear, and those girls will start an epidemic you won't be able to stop for a month. Do you want to be mixed up in that? Now you know we women are into plague research; well, these are some of the experiments. I'm taking them across Manland to another part of our own place; it's a short-cut. I wouldn't take them through here except I have some business to do here tonight. We're developing a faster immunization process. I'd tell all your friends to stay away from this table, too, if I were you—not that we can't take care of ourselves and *I* don't worry; I'm immune to this particular strain—but I don't want to see you take the rap for it. You've done a lot for me in the past and I'm grateful. I'm very grateful. You'd get it in the neck, you know. And you might get plague, too, there's always that. Okay?"

Astonishing how each of them has to be reassured of my loyalty! says Jael Reasoner. *Even more astonishing that they believe me. They're not very bright, are they? But these are the little fish. Besides, they've been separated from real women so long that they don't know what to make of us; I doubt if even the sex surgeons know what a real woman looks like. The specifications we send them every year grow wilder and wilder and there isn't a murmur of protest. I think they like it. As moths to the flame, so men to the social patterns of the Army, that womanless world haunted by the ghosts of millions of dead women, that discarnate femininity that hovers over everybody and can turn the toughest real-man into one of Them, that dark force they always feel at the backs of their own minds! Would I, do you think, force slavishness and deformity on two-sevenths of my own kind? Of course not! I think these men are not human. No, no, that's wrong—I decided long ago that they weren't human. Work is power, but they farm out everything to us without the slightest protest—Hell, they get lazier and lazier. They let us do their thinking for them. They even let us do their feeling for them. They are riddled with duality and the fear of duality. And the fear of themselves. I think it's in their blood. What human being would—sweating with fear and rage —mark out two equally revolting paths and insist that her fellow-creatures tread one or the other?*

Ah, the rivalries of cosmic he-men and the worlds they must conquer and the terrors they must face and the rivals they must challenge and overcome!

"You are being a little obvious," says Janet pedantically from inside her suit, "and I doubt that the power of the blood—"

Hsst! Here comes my contact.

Our contact was a half-changed, for Manlanders believe that child care is woman's business; so they delegate to the changed and the half-changed the business of haggling for babies and

taking care of children during those all-important, first five
years—they want to fix their babies' sexual preferences early.
This means, practically speaking, that the children are raised
in brothels. Now some Manlander real-men do not like the
idea of the whole business being in the hands of the feminized
and the effeminate but there's not much they can do about it
(see Proposition One, about child care, above)—although the
more masculine look forward to a time when no Manlander
will fall away from the ranks of the he-men, and with an ob-
stinacy I consider perverse, refuse to decide who will be the
sexual objects when the changed and the half-changed are no
more. Perhaps they think sex beneath them. Or above them?
(Around the shrine of each gowned and sequinned hostess in
The Knife are at least three real-men; how many can a hostess
take on in one night?) I suspect we real women still figure,
however grotesquely, in Manland's deepest dreams; perhaps on
that morning of Total Masculinity they will all invade Womanland, rape everyone in sight (if they still remember how) and
then kill them, and after that commit suicide upon a pyramid of
their victims' panties. The official ideology has it that women
are poor substitutes for the changed. I certainly hope so. (Little girls, crept out of their crèche at last, touching those heroic
dead with curious, wee fingers. Nudging them with their pat-
ent leather Mary Janes. Bringing their baby brothers out to a
party on the green, all flutes and oats and pastoral fun until
the food gives out and the tiny heroines must decide: Whom
shall we eat? The waving limbs of our starfish siblings, our dead
mothers, or those strange, huge, hairy bodies already beginning to swell in the sun?) I flashed that damned pass—again!—
this time at a half-changed in a pink chiffon gown, with gloves
up to his shoulder, a monument of irrelevancy on high heels,
a pretty girl with too much of the right curves and a bobbing,
springing, pink feather boa. Where oh where is the shop that
makes those long rhinestone earrings, objects of fetishism and
nostalgia, worn only by the half-changed (and usually not by
them unless they're rich), hand-made from museum copies, of
no use or interest to fully six-sevenths of the adult human race?
Somewhere stones are put together by antiquarians, somewhere petroleum is transformed into fabric that can't burn
without polluting the air, and won't rot, and won't erode, so

that strands of plastic have turned up in the bodies of diatoms at the bottom of the Pacific Trench—such a vision was he, so much he wore, such folds and frills and ribbons and buttons and feathers, trimmed like a Christmas tree. Like Garbo playing Anna Karenina, decorated all over. His green eyes shrewdly narrowed. This one has intelligence. Or is it only the weight of his false lashes? The burden of having always to be taken, of having to swoon, to fall, to endure, to hope, to suffer, to wait, to only be? There must be a secret feminine underground that teaches them how to behave; in the face of their comrades' derision and savage contempt, in the face of the prospect of gang rape if they're found alone on the streets after curfew, in the face of the legal necessity to belong—every one of them—to a real-man, somehow they still learn the classic shiver, the slow blink, the knuckle-to-lip pathos. These, too, I think, must be in the blood. But whose? My three friends and I pale beside such magnificence! Four lumpy parcels, of no interest to anyone at all, at all.

Anna, with a mechanical shiver of desire, says that we must go with him.

"Her?" says Jeannine, confused.

"Him!" says Anna in a strained contralto. The half-changed are very punctilious—sometimes about the changeds' superiority and sometimes about their own genitals. Either way it works out to *Him*. He's extraordinarily aware, for a man, of Jeannine's shrinking and he resents it—as who would not? I myself am respectful of ruined lives and forced choices. On the street once Anna did not fight hard enough against the fourteen-year-old toughs who wanted his twelve-year-old ass; he didn't go to the extremity of berserk rage, reckoning his life as nothing in defense of his virility; he forestalled—by surrender —the plucking out of an eye, the castration, the throat cut with a broken bottle, the being put out of his twelve-year-old action with a stone or a tire chain. I know a lot about Manlanders' history. Anna made a *modus vivendi*, he decided life was worth it on any terms. Everything follows from that.

"Oh, you're lovely," says Jeannine, heartfelt. Sisters in misfortune. This really pleases Anna. He shows us a letter of safe-conduct he has from his boss—a real-man, of course—and putting it back in his pink-brocaded evening bag, draws around

him that fake-feather Thing which floats and wobbles in the
least current of air. It's a warm evening. To protect his employé,
the big boss (they are Men, even in the child-rearing business)
has had to give Anna K a little two-way TV camera to wear in
his ear; otherwise somebody would break his high heels and
leave him dead or half-dead in an alley. Everybody knows that
the half-changed are weak and can't protect themselves; what
do you think femininity is all about? Even so Anna probably
has a bodyguard waiting at the entrance to The Knife. I'm cynical enough to wonder sometimes if the Manlanders' mystique
isn't just an excuse to feminize anybody with a pretty face—but
look again, they believe it; look under the padding, the paint,
the false hair, the corsetry, the skin rinses and the magnificent
dresses and you'll see nothing exceptional, only faces and bodies like any other man's. Anna bats his eyes at us and wets his
lips, taking the women inside the suits to be real-men, taking
me to be a real-man (what else can I be if I'm not a changed?),
taking the big wide world itself to be—what else?—a Real-Man
intent on worshipping Anna's ass; the world exists to look at
Anna; he—or she—is only a real-man turned inside out.

An eerie sisterliness, a smile at Jeannine. All that narcissism!
Brains underneath, though.

Remember where their loyalties lie.

(Are they jealous of us? I don't think they believe we're
women.)

He wets his lips again, the indescribable silliness of that insane mechanism, practiced anywhere and everywhere, on the
right people, on the wrong people. But what else is there? It
seems that Anna's boss wants to meet me. (I don't like that.)
But we'll go; we maintain our outward obedience until the
very end, until the beautiful, bloody moment that we fire these
stranglers, these murderers, these unnatural and atavistic nature's bastards, off the face of the earth.

"Dearest sister," says Anna softly, sweetly, "come with me."

VIII

I guess Anna's boss just wanted to see the alien poontang.
I don't know yet what he wants, but I will. His wife clicked
in with a tray of drinks—scarlet skintights, no underwear,

transparent high-heeled sandals like Cinderella's—she gave us a homey, cute smile (she wears no make-up and is covered with freckles) and stilted out. Man talk. They seldom earn wives before fifty. Art, they say, has had a Renaissance among the Manlander rich, but this one doesn't look like a patron: jowly, pot-bellied, the fierce redness of an athlete forced into idleness. His heart? High blood pressure? But they all cultivate their muscles and let their health and their minds rot. There is a rather peculiar wholesomeness to the home life of a Manland millionaire; Boss, for example, would not think of letting his wife go anywhere alone—that is, risk the anarchy of the streets —even with a bodyguard. He knows what's due her. Their "women," they say, civilize them. For an emotional relation-ship, turn to a "woman."

What am I?

I know what I am, but what's my brand name?

He stares rudely, unable to conceal it: *What are they? What do they do? Do they screw each other? What does it feel like?* (Try and tell him!) He doesn't waste a second on the pink crosses in purdah; they're only "women" anyhow (he thinks); *I'm* the soldier, *I'm* the enemy, *I'm* the other self, the mirror, the master-slave, the rebel, the heretic, the mystery that must be found out at all costs. (Maybe he thinks the three J's have lep-rosy.) I don't like this at all. J-one (Janet, by her gait) is exam-ining the paintings on the wall; J-two and J-three stand hand in hand, Babes in the Wood. Boss finishes his drink, chewing on something in the bottom of it like a large teddy-bear, with comic deliberation: chomp, chomp. He waves grandly toward the other drinks, his wife having abandoned the tray on top of what looks for all the world like a New Orleans, white-enamelled, bordello piano (Whorehouse Baroque is very big in Manland right now).

I shook my head.

He said, "You have any children?" Pregnancy fascinates them. The rank-and-file have forgotten about menstruation; if they remembered, *that* would fascinate them. I shook my head again.

His face darkened.

"I thought," said I mildly, "that we were going to talk busi-ness. I'd like to do just that. I don't mean—that is, I don't want to be unsociable, but time's passing and I'd rather not discuss my personal life."

He said: "You're on my turf, you'll Goddamn well talk about what I Goddamn well talk about."

Let it pass. Control yourself. Hand them the victory in the Domination Sweepstakes and they usually forget whatever it is they were going to do anyway. He glared and brooded. Munched chips, crackers, saltsticks, what-not. Doesn't really know what he wants. I waited.

"Personal life!" he muttered.

"It's not really very interesting," I volunteered.

"You kids screw each other?"

I said nothing.

He leaned forward. "Don't get me wrong. I think you have a right to do it. I never bought this stuff about women alone having no sex. It's not in human nature. Now, do you?"

"No," I said.

He chuckled. "That's right, cover up. Mind, I'm not condemning you. It's only to be expected. Eh! If we'd kept together, men and women, none of this would have happened. Right?"

I put on my doubtful, slightly shamed, sly, well-you-know, all-purpose look. I have never known what it means, but they seem to. He laughed out loud. Another drink.

"Look here," he said, "I expect you have more intelligence than most of those bitches or you wouldn't be in this job. Right? Now it's obvious to anyone that we need each other. Even in separate camps we still have to trade, you still have to have the babies, things haven't changed that much. Now what I have in mind is an experimental project, a pilot project, you might say, in trying to get the two sides back together. Not all at once—"

"I—" I said. (They don't hear you.)

"Not all at once," (he continued, deaf as a post) "but a little bit at a time. We have to make haste deliberately. Right?"

I was silent. He leaned back. "I knew you'd see it," he said. Then he made a personal remark: "You saw my wife?" I nodded.

"Natalie's grand," he said, taking some more chips. "She's a grand girl. She made these. Deep-fried, I think." (A weak woman handling a pot of boiling oil.) "Have some."

To pacify him I took some and held them in my hand. Greasy stuff.

"Now," he said, "you like the idea, right?"

"What?"

"The aversive therapy, for Chrissakes, the pilot group. Social relations, getting back together. I'm not like some of the mossbacks around here, you know, I don't go for this inferior-superior business; I believe in equality. If we get back together, it has to be on that basis. Equals."

"But—" I said, meaning no offense.

"*It has to be on the basis of equality!* I believe that. And don't think the man in the street can't be sold on it, propaganda to the contrary. We're brought up on this nonsense of woman's place and woman's nature when we don't even have women around to study. What do we know! I'm not any less masculine because I've done woman's work; does it take less intelligence to handle an operation like the nurseries and training camps than it does to figure the logistics of War Games? Hell, no! Not if you do it rationally and efficiently; business is business."

Let it go. Perhaps it'll play itself out; they do sometimes. I sat attentively still while he gave me the most moving plea for my own efficiency, my rationality, my status as a human being. He ended by saying anxiously, "Do you think it'll work?"

"Well—" I began.

"Of course, of course," (interrupted this damned fool once again) "you're not a diplomat, but we have to work through the men we have, don't we? Individual man can accomplish ends where Mass-man fails. Eh?"

I nodded, picturing myself as Individual Man. The "woman's work" explains it, of course; it makes him dangerously irritable. He had gotten now into the poignant part, the mystifying and moving account of our Sufferings. This is where the tears come in. It helps to be able to classify what they're going to do, but Lord! it's depressing, all the same. Always the same. I sit on, perfectly invisible, a chalk sketch of a woman. An idea. A walking ear.

"What we want" (he said, getting into stride) "is a world in which everybody can be *himself.* Him. Self. Not this insane forcing of temperaments. Freedom. Freedom for all. I admire you. Yes, let me say that I do indeed, and most frankly, admire you. You've broken through all that. Of course most women will not be able to do that—in fact, most women—given the choice—will hardly choose to give up domesticity altogether or even" (here he smiled) "even choose to spend much of their lives in the market-place or the factory. Most women will continue to choose the conservative caretaking of child-hood, the formation of beautiful human relationships, and the care and service of others. Servants. Of. The. Race. Why should we sneer at that? And if we find there are certain traits connected with sex, like homemaking, like reasoning power, like certain temperamental factors, well of course there will be, but why derogate one sex or the other on that account? People" (braced for the peroration) "people are as they are. If—"

I rose to my feet. "Excuse me," I said, "but business—"

"Damn your business!" he said in heat, this confused and irritable man. "Your business isn't worth two cents compared with what I'm talking about!"

"Of course not, of course not," I said soothingly.

"I should hope so!"

Numb, numb. With boredom. Invisible. Chained.

"That's the trouble with you women, you can't see anything in the abstract!"

He wants me to cringe. I really think so. Not the content of what I say but the endless, endless feeding of his vanity, the shaky structure of self. Even the intelligent ones.

"Don't you appreciate what I'm trying to do for you?"

Kiss-me-I'm-a-goodguy.

"Don't you have any idea how important this is?"

Sliding down the slippery gulf into invisibility.

"This could make history!"

Even me, with all my training!

"Of course, we have a tradition to uphold."

It'll be slow.

"—we'll have to go slowly. One thing at a time."

If it's practical.

"We'll have to find out what's practicable. This may be—uh—visionary. It may be in advance of its time."

Can't legislate morality.

"We can't force people against their inclinations and we have generations of conditioning to overcome. Perhaps in a decade—"

Perhaps never.

"—perhaps never. But men of good will—"

Did he hear that?

"—and women, too, of course, you understand that the word 'men' includes the word 'women'; it's only usage—"

Everyone must have his own abortion.

"—and not really important. You might even say" (he giggles) "'everyone and his husband' or 'everyone will be entitled to his own abortion'" (he roars) "but I want you to go back to your people and tell them—"

It's unofficial.

"—that we're prepared to negotiate. But it can't be official. You must understand that I face considerable opposition. And most women—not, you, of course; you're different —well, most women aren't used to thinking a thing *through* like this. They can't do it systematically. Say, you don't mind my saying that about 'most women,' do you?"

I smile, drained of personality.

"That's right," (he said) "don't take it personally. Don't get feminine on me," and he winked broadly to show he bore me no ill-will. This is the time for me to steal away, leaving behind half my life's blood and promises, promises, promises; but you know what? I just can't do it. It's happened too often. I have no reserves left. I sat down, smiling brilliantly in sheer anticipation, and the dear man hitched his chair nearer. He looks uneasy and avid. "We're friends?" he says.

"Sure," I say, hardly able to speak.

"Good!" he said. "Tell me, do you like my place?"

"Oh yes," I say.

"Ever see anything like it before?"

"Oh no!" (I live in a chicken-barn and eat shit.)

He laughed delightedly. "The paintings are pretty good. We're having a kind of Renaissance lately. How's art among the ladies, huh?"

"So-so," I said, making a face. The room is beginning to sway with the adrenalin I can pump into my bloodstream when

I choose; this is called voluntary hysterical strength and it is
very, very useful, yes indeed. First the friendly chat, then the
uncontrollably curious grab, and then the hatred comes out.
Be prepared.

"I suppose," he said, "you must've been different from the
start—from a little girl, eh?—doing a job like this. You've got
to admit we have one thing up on you—we don't try to force
everybody into the same role. Oh no. We don't keep a man out
of the kitchen if that's what he really wants."

"Oh sure," I said. (Those chemical-surgical castrati)

"Now you do," he said. "You're more reactionary than we
are. You won't *let* women lead the domestic life. You want to
make everyone alike. That's not what I visualize."

He goes into a long happy rap about motherhood, the
joys of the uterus. The emotional nature of Woman. The
room is beginning to sway. One gets very reckless in hysterical strength; the first few weeks I trained, I broke several of
my own bones but I know how to do it now. I really do. My
muscles are not for harming anyone else; they are to keep
me from harming myself. That terrible concentration. That
feverish brightness. Boss-Idiot has not talked to anyone else
about his grand idea; he's still in First Cliché stage and any
group discussion, however moronic, would have weeded out
the worst of them. His dear Natalie. His gifted wife. Take
me, now; he loves me. Yes he does. Not physically, of course.
Oh no. Life seeks its mate. Its complement. Romantic rubbish. Its other self. Its joy. He won't talk business tonight.
Will he ask me to stay over?

"Oh, I couldn't," says the other Jael. He doesn't hear it;
there's a gadget in Boss's ear that screens out female voices.
He's moved closer, bringing his chair with him—some silly
flub-dub about not being able to talk the length of the room.
Spiritual intimacy. Smiling foolishly he says:

"So you like me a little, huh?"

How terrible, betrayal by lust. No, ignorance. No—pride.

"Hell, go away," I say.

"Sure you do!" He expects me to act like his Natalie, he
bought her, he owns her. What do women do in the daytime?
What do they do when they're alone? Adrenalin is a demanding high; it untunes all your finer controls.

"Get away," I whisper. He doesn't hear it. These men play games, play with vanity, hiss, threaten, erect their neck-spines. It sometimes takes ten minutes to get a fight going. I, who am not a reptile but only an assassin, only a murderess, never give warning. They worry about *playing fair*, about *keeping the rules*, about *giving a good account of themselves*. I don't play. I have no pride. I don't hesitate. At home I am harmless, but not here.

"Kiss me, you dear little bitch," he says in an excited voice, mastery and disgust warring with each other in his eyes. Boss has never seen a real cunt, I mean as nature made them. He'll use words he hasn't dared to use since he was eighteen and took his first half-changed in the street, mastery and disgust mingling. That slavish apprenticeship at the recreation centers. How can you love anyone who is a castrated You? Real homosexuality would blow Manland to pieces.

"Take your filthy hands off me," I say clearly, enjoying his enjoyment of my enjoyment of his enjoyment of that cliché. Has he forgotten the three lepers?

"Send them away," he mutters in agony, "send them away! Natalie can do them," forgetting gender in his haste. Or perhaps he really thinks they are my lovers. Women will do what men find too disgusting, too difficult, too demeaning.

"Look," I say, grinning uncontrollably, "I want to be perfectly clear. I don't want your revolting lovemaking. I'm here to do business and relay any reasonable message to my superiors. I'm not here to play games. *Cut it out.*"

But when do they ever listen!

"You're a woman," he cries, shutting his eyes, "you're a beautiful woman. You've got a hole down there. You're a beautiful woman. You've got real, round tits and you've got a beautiful ass. You want me. It doesn't matter what you say. You're a woman, aren't you? This is the crown of your life. This is what God made you for. I'm going to fuck you. I'm going to screw you until you can't stand up. You want it. You want to be mastered. Natalie wants to be mastered. All you women, you're all women, you're sirens, you're beautiful, you're waiting for me, waiting for a man, waiting for me to stick it in, waiting for me, me, me."

Et patati et patata; the mode is a wee bit over-familiar. I told him to open his eyes, that I didn't want to kill him with his eyes shut, for God's sake.

He didn't hear me.

"OPEN YOUR EYES!" I roared, "BEFORE I KILL YOU!" and Boss-man did.

He said, *You led me on.*

He said, *You are a prude.* (He was shocked.)

He said, *You deceived me.*

He said, *You are a Bad Lady.*

This we can cure!—as they say about pneumonia. I think the J's will have sense enough to stay out of it. Boss was muttering something angry about his erection so, angry enough for two, I produced my own—by this I mean that the grafted muscles on my fingers and hands pulled back the loose skin, with that characteristic, itchy tickling, and of course you are wise; you have guessed that I do not have Cancer on my fingers but Claws, talons like a cat's but bigger, a little more dull than wood brads but good for tearing. And my teeth are a sham over metal. Why are men so afraid of the awful intimacies of hate? Remember, I don't threaten. I don't play. I always carry firearms. The truly violent are never without them. I could have drilled him between the eyes, but if I do that, I all but leave my signature on him; it's freakier and funnier to make it look as if a wolf did it. Better to think his Puli went mad and attacked him. I raked him gaily on the neck and chin and when he embraced me in rage, sank my claws into his back. You have to build up the fingers surgically so they'll take the strain. A certain squeamishness prevents me from using my teeth in front of witnesses—the best way to silence an enemy is to bite out his larynx. Forgive me! I dug the hardened cuticle into his neck but he sprang away; he tried a kick but I wasn't there (I told you they rely too much on their strength); he got hold of my arm but I broke the hold and spun him off, adding with my nifty, weighted shoon another bruise on his limping kidneys. Ha ha! He fell on me (you don't feel injuries, in my state) and I reached around and scored him under the ear, letting him spray urgently into the rug; he will stagger to his feet and fall, he will plunge fountainy to the ground; at her feet he bowed, he fell, he lay down; at her feet he bowed, he fell, he lay down dead.

Jael. Clean and satisfied from head to foot. Boss is pumping his life out into the carpet. All very quiet, oddly enough. Three J's in a terrible state, to judge from their huddling together; I can't read their hidden faces. Will Natalie come in? Will she faint? Will she say, "I'm glad to be rid of him, the old bastard"? Who will own her now? You get monomaniacal on adrenalin. "Come on, come on!" I whispered to the J's, herding them toward the door, buzzing and humming, the stuff still singing in my blood. The stupidity of it. The asininity of it. I love it, I love it. "Come on!" I said. Pushing them out the door, into the corridor, out and into the elevator, past the fish swimming in the aquatic wall, evil, svelte manta-rays and groupers six feet long. Poor fish! No business done today, God damn, but once they get that way there's no doing business with them; you have to kill them anyway, might as well have fun. There's no standing those non-humans at all, at all. Jeannie is calm. Joanna is ashamed of me. Janet is weeping. But how do you expect me to stand for this all month? How do you expect me to stand it all year? Week after week? For twenty years? Little male voice says: It Was Her Menstrual Period. Perfect explanation! Raging hormonal imbalances. His ghostly voice: "You did it because you had your period. Bad girl." Oh beware of unclean vessels who have that dir-ty menstrual period and Who Will Not Play! I shooed the J's into the Boss-man's car—Anna had long ago disappeared—skeleton keys out of my invisible suit with its invisible pocket, opened the lock, fired the car, started up. I'll go on Automatic as soon as we get to the highway; Boss's I.D. will carry us to the border. No trouble from there.

"You all right?" I asked the J's, laughing, laughing, laughing. I'm drunk still. They said Yes in varying musical keys. The Strong One's voice is pitched higher than that of The Weak One (who believes she's an alto), and The Little One is highest of all. Yes, yes, they said, frightened. Yes, yes, yes.

"Now I did not get that contract signed," I said, putting on my sham teeth over my steel ones. "God damn, God damn, God damn!" (Don't drive on adrenalin; you'll probably have an accident.)

"When does it leave you?" That's The Strong One: smart girl. "An hour, half an hour," I said. "When we get home."

"Home?" (from the back)

"Yes. My home." Every time I do this I burn up a little life. I shorten my time. I'm at the effusive stage now, so I bit my lip, to keep quiet.

After a long silence—"Was that necessary?" from The Weak One.

Still hurt, still able to be hurt by them! Amazing. You'd think my skin would get thicker, but it doesn't. We're all of us still flat on our backs. The boot's on our neck while we slowly, ever so slowly, gather the power and the money and the resources into our own hands. While they play war games. I put the car on Autom. and sat back, chilly with the reaction. My heartbeat's quieting. Breath slower.

Was it necessary? (Nobody says this.) You could have turned him off—maybe. You could have sat there all night. You could have nodded and adored him until dawn. You could have let him throw his temper tantrum; you could have lain under him —what difference does it make to you?—you'd have forgotten it by morning.

You might even have made the poor man happy.

There is a pretense on my own side that we are too refined to care, too compassionate for revenge—this is bullshit, I tell the idealists. "Being with Men," they say, "has changed you."

Eating it year in and year out.

"Look, was it necessary?" says one of the J's, addressing to me the serious urgency of womankind's eternal quest for love, the ages-long effort to heal the wounds of the sick soul, the infinite, caring compassion of the female saint.

An over-familiar mode! Dawn comes up over the waste land, bringing into existence the boulders and pebbles battered long ago by bombs, dawn gilding with its pale possibilities even the Crazy Womb, the Ball-breaking Bitch, the Fanged Killer Lady.

"I don't give a damn whether it was necessary or not," I said.

"I liked it."

IX

It takes four hours to cross the Atlantic, three to shuttle to a different latitude. Waking up in a Vermont autumn morning, inside the glass cab, while all around us the maples and sugar maples wheel slowly out of the fog. Only this part of the world can produce such color. We whispered at a walking pace through wet fires. Electric vehicles are quiet, too; we heard the drip of water from the leaves. When the house saw us, my old round lollipop-on-a-stick, it lit up from floor to top, and as we came nearer broadcast the Second Brandenburg through the black, wet tree-trunks and the fiery leaves, a delicate attention I allow myself and my guests from time to time. Shouting brilliantly through the wet woods—I prefer the unearthly purity of the electronic scoring. One approaches the house from the side, where it looks almost flat on its central column—only a little convex, really—it doesn't squat down for you on chicken legs like Baba Yaga's hut, but lets down from above a great, coiling, metal-mesh road like a tongue (or so it seems; in reality it's only a winding staircase). Inside you find yourself a corridor away from the main room; no use wasting heat.

Davy was there. The most beautiful man in the world. Our approach had given him time to make drinks for us—which the J's took from his tray, staring at him but he wasn't embarrassed—curled up most unwaiterlike at my feet with his hands around his knees and proceeded to laugh at the right places in the conversation (he takes his cues from my face).

The main room is panelled in yellow wood with a carpet you can sleep on (brown) and a long, glassed-in porch from which we watch the blizzards sweep by five months out of the year. I like purely visual weather. It's warm enough for Davy to go around naked most of the time, my ice lad in a cloud of gold hair and nudity, never so much a part of my home as when he sits on the rug with his back against a russet or vermilion chair (we mimic autumn here), his drowned blue eyes fixed on the winter sunset outside, his hair turned to ash, the muscles of his back and thighs stirring a little. The house hangs oddments from the ceiling; found objects, mobiles, can openers, red balls, bunches of wild grass, and Davy plays with them.

I showed the J's around: the books, the microfilm viewer in the library in touch with our regional library miles away, the storage spaces in the walls, the various staircases, the bathrooms molded of glass fiber and put together from two pieces, the mattresses stored in the walls of the guest rooms, and the conservatory (near the central core, to make use of the heat) where Davy comes and mimics wonder, watching the lights shine on my orchids, my palmettos, my bougainvillea, my whole little mess of tropical plants. I even have a glassed-in space for cacti. There are outside plantings where in season you can find mountain laurel, a tangled maze of rhododendron, scattered irises that look like an expensive and antique cross between insects and lingerie—but these are under snow now. I even have an electrified fence, inherited from my predecessor, that encloses the whole estate to keep out the deer and occasionally kills trees which take the mild climate around the house a little too much for granted.

I let the J's peep into the kitchen, which is an armchair with controls like a 707's, but not the place where I store my tools and from which I have access to the central core when House has indigestion. That's dirty and you need to know what you're doing. I showed them Screen, which keeps me in touch with my neighbors, the nearest of whom is ten miles away, Telephone, who is my long-distance backup line, and Phonograph, where I store my music.

Jeannine said she didn't like her drink; it wasn't sweet enough. So I had Davy dial her another.

Do you want dinner? (She blushed.)

My palace and gardens (said I) I acquired late in life when I became rich and influential; before that I lived in one of the underground cities among the damnedest passel of neighbors you ever saw, sentimental Arcadian communes—underground, mind you!—whose voices would travel up the sewer pipes at all the wrong times of day and night, shrill sacrifices to love and joy when you want to sleep, ostentatious shuddering whenever I appeared in the corridor, wincing and dashing back inside to huddle together like kittens, conscious of their own innocence, and raise their pure young voices in the blessedness of community song. You know the kind: "But we were having *fun*!" in a soft, wondering, highly reproachful voice while she closes the door gently but firmly on your thumb. They thought I was Ultimate Evil. They let me know it. They are the kind who want to win the men over by Love. There's a game called Pussycat that's great fun for the player; it goes like this: Meeow, I'm dead (lying on your back, all four paws engagingly held in the air, playing helpless); there's another called Saint George and the Dragon with You Know Who playing You Know What;

and when you can no longer tolerate either, you do as I did: come home in a hobgoblin-head of a disguise, howling and chasing your neighbors down the hall while they scream in genuine terror (well, sort of).

Then I moved.

That was my first job, impersonating one of the Manlanders' police (for ten minutes). By "job" I don't mean what I was sent to do last night, that was open and legitimate, but a "job" is a little bit under the table. It took me years to throw off the last of my Pussy-fetters, to stop being (however brutalized) vestigially Pussy-cat-ified, but at last I did and now I am the rosy, wholesome, single-minded assassin you see before you today.

I come and go as I please. I do only what I want. I have wrestled myself through to an independence of mind that has ended by bringing all of you here today. In short, I am a grown woman.

I was an old-fashioned girl, born forty-two years ago in the last years before the war, in one of the few mixed towns still left. It amazes me sometimes to think of what my life would have been like without the war, but I ended up in a refugee camp with my mother. Maddened Lesbians did not put cigarette butts out on her breasts, propaganda to the contrary; in fact she got a lot more self-confident and whacked me when I tore to pieces (out of pure curiosity) a paper doily that decorated the top of the communal radio—this departure from previous practice secretly gratified me and I decided I rather liked the place. We were re-settled and I was sent to school once the war cooled off; by '52 our territories had shrunk to pretty much what they are today, and we've grown too wise since to think we can gain anything by merely annexing land. I was trained for years—we deplore what we must nonetheless use!—and began my slow drift away from the community, that specialization (they say) that brings you closer to the apes, though I don't see how such an exceedingly skilled and artificial practice can be anything but quintessentially human.

At twelve I artlessly told one of my teachers that I was very glad I was being brought up to be a man-woman, and that I looked down on those girls who were only brought up to be woman-women. I'll never forget her face. She did not thrash me but let an older girl-girl do it—I told you I was old-fashioned.

Gradually this sort of thing wears off; not everything with claws and teeth is a Pussycat. On the contrary!

My first job (as I told you) was impersonating one of the Manlander police; my most recent one was taking the place of a Manlander diplomat for eighteen months in a primitive patriarchy on an alternate Earth. Oh yes, the Men also have probability-travel, or rather they have it through us; we run the routine operations for them. So far has corruption progressed! With my silver hair, my silver eyes, and my skin artificially darkened to make me look even stranger to the savages, I was presented as a Prince of Faery, and in that character I lived in a dank stone castle with ghastly sanitary arrangements and worse beds for a year and a half. A place that would make your hair stand on end. Jeannine must stop looking so skeptical—please reflect that some societies stylize their adult roles to such a degree that a giraffe could pass for a man, especially with seventy-seven layers of clothes on, and a barbarian prudery that keeps you from ever taking them off. They were impossible people. I used to make up stories about the Faery women; once I killed a man because he said something obscene about the Faery women. Think of that! You must imagine me as the quiet, serene Christian among the pagans, the courteous magician among the blunt men-o'-war, the overcivilized stranger (possibly a Demon because he was understood to have no beard) who spoke softly and never accepted challenges, but who was not afraid of anything under Heaven and who had a grip of steel. And so on. Oh, those cold baths! And the endless joking about how *they* weren't queer, by God! And the bellicosity, the continual joshing that catches in your skin like thorns and exasperates you almost to murder, and the constant fingering of sex and womankind with its tragic, pitiable bafflement and its even worse bragging; and last of all the perpetual losing battle with fear, the constant unloading of anxious weaknesses on to others (and their consequent enraged fury) as if fear and weakness were not the best guides we human beings ever had! Oh, it was rich! When they found that not a knight in the Men's House could lay a hand on me, they begged for instruction; I had half the warriors of the mead-hall doing elementary ballet under the mistaken impression that they were learning ju-jitsu. They may be doing it still. It made them sweat enough and it's my signature, plain as day, to the whole bloody universe and any Manlander who turns up there again.

A barbarian woman fell in love with me. It's terrible to see that slavishness in someone else's eyes, feel that halo she puts around you, and know from your own person the nature of that eager deference men so often perceive as admiration. *Validate me!* she cried. *Justify me! Raise me up! Save me from the others!* ("I am his wife," she says, turning the mystic ring round and round on her finger, "I am *his* wife.") So somewhere I have a kind of widow. I used to talk to her sensibly, as no man ever had before, I think. I tried to take her back with me, but couldn't get authorization for her. Somewhere out there is a murderess as rosy and single-minded as I, if we could only get to her.

May She save us all!

I saved the King's life once by pinning to the festive Kingly board a pretty little hamadryad somebody had imported from the Southern lands to kill His Majesty. This helped me a good deal. Those primitive warriors are brave men—that is, they are slaves to the fear of fear—but there are some things they believe every man is entitled to run from in abject terror, *viz.* snakes, ghosts, earthquakes, disease, demons, magic, childbirth, menstruation, witches, afreets, incubi, succubi, solar eclipses, reading, writing, good manners, syllogistic reasoning, and what we might generally call the less reliable phenomena of life. The fact that I was not afraid to pin a poisonous snake to a wooden table with a fork (a piece of Faery handicraft I had brought with me to eat meat with) raised my prestige immensely. Oh yes, if it had bitten me, I would have been dead. But they don't move that fast. Think of me in quilting and crinolines—not like a Victorian lady, like a player in Kabuki—holding up that poor little broken-backed dinkus amid general hurrahs. Think of me astride a coal-black charger, my black-and-silver cloak streaming in the wind under a heraldic banner comprising crossed forks on a field of reptile eggs. Think of anything you please. Think, if you will, how hard it is to remain calm under constant insults, and of the genuine charm of playing bullfight with a big, beautiful, nasty blond who goes hartyhar every chance he gets, and whom you can reel in and spin out again as if you knew all his control buttons, as indeed you do. Think of giving the King bad advice week after week: modestly, deliberately, and successfully. Think of placing your ladylike foot on the large, dead neck of a human dinosaur who has bothered you for months and has finally tried to kill you; there he lies, this big, carnal flower gathered at last by Chaos and Old Night, torn and broken in the dust, a big limpid Nada, a nothing, a thing, an animal, a creature brought down at last out of his pride to the truth of his organic being—*and you did it.*

I keep one precious souvenir of that time: the look on the face of my most loyal feudal retainer when I revealed my sex to him. This was a man I had all-but-seduced without his knowing it—little touches on the arm, the shoulder, the knee, a quiet manner, a certain look in the eyes—nothing so gross that he thought it to be in me; he assumed it was all in himself. I loved that part. His first impulse, of course, was to hate me, fight me, drive me off—but I wasn't doing anything, was I? I had made no advances to him, had I? What sort of mind did he have? A pitiable confusion! So I got even nicer. He got madder and guiltier, of course, and loathed the very sight of me because I made him doubt his own reason; finally he challenged me and I turned him into a faithful dog by beating him right into the ground; I kicked that man so bloody hard that I couldn't stand it myself and had to explain to him that what he believed were unnatural lusts were really a species of religious reverence; he just wanted to lie peacefully on the ground and kiss my boot.

The day that I left I went out into the hills with a few friends for the Faery "ceremony" that was to take me away, and when the Bureau people radio'd me they were ready, I sent the others away, and I told him the truth. I divested myself of my knightly attire (no mean trick, considering what those idiots wear) and showed him the marks of Eve; for a moment I could see that stinking bastard's whole world crumble. For a moment he *knew.* Then, by God, his eyes got even more moist and slavish, he sank to his knees and piously elevating his gaze, exclaimed in a rapture of feudal enthusiasm—Humanity mending its fences—

If the women of Faery are like this, just think what the MEN must be!

One of Her little jokes. Oh Lord, one of Her hardest jokes.

If you want to be an assassin, remember that you must decline all challenges. Showing off is not your job.

If you are insulted, smile meekly. Don't break your cover.

Be afraid. This is information about the world.

You are valuable. Push yourself.

Take the easiest way out whenever possible. Resist curiosity, pride, and the temptation to defy limits. You are not your own woman and must be built to last.

Indulge hatred. Action comes from the heart.

Pray often. How else can you quarrel with God?

Does this strike you as painfully austere? If not, you are like me; you can turn yourself inside out, you can live for days upside down, the most biddable, unblushing servant of the Lady since the Huns sacked Rome, just for fun. Anything pursued to its logical end is revelation; as Blake says, The path of Excess leads to the Palace of Wisdom, to that place where all things converge but up high, up unbearably high, that mental success which leads you into yourself, under the aspect of eternity, where you are limber and nice, where you act eternally under the aspect of Everything and where—by doing the One Genuine Thing—you cannot do anything untruly or half-way.

To put it simply: those are the times that I am most myself.

Sometimes I am a little remorseful; I grow sorry that the exercise of my art entails such unpleasant consequences for other people, but really! Hate is a material like any other. If you want me to do something else useful, you had better show me what that something else is. Sometimes I go into one of our cities and have little sprees in the local museums; I look at pictures, I get a hotel room and take long hot baths, I drink lots of lemonade. But the record of my life is the record of work, slow, steady, responsible work. I tied my first sparring partner in enraged knots, as Brynhild tied up her husband in her girdle and hung him on the wall, but aside from that I have never hurt a fellow Womanlander; when I wanted to practice deadly strategies, I did it on the school robot. Nor do I have love-affairs with other women; in some things, as I told you, I am a very old-fashioned girl.

The art, you see, is really in the head, however you train the body.

What does all this mean? That I am your hostess, your friend, your ally. That we are in the same boat. That I am the grand-daughter of Madam Cause; my great-aunts are Mistress Doasyouwouldbedoneby and her slower sister, Mistress Bedonebyasyoudid. As for my mother, she was an ordinary woman—that is to say, very helpless—and as my father was pure appearance (and hence nothing at all), we needn't trouble about him.

Everything I do, I do *by Cause*, that is to say *Because*, that is to say out of necessity, will-I, nill-I, ineluctably, because of the *geas* laid on me by my grandmother Causality.

And now—since hysterical strength affects me the way staying up all night affects you—I'm going to sleep.

X

In my sleep I had a dream and this dream was a dream of guilt. It was not human guilt but the kind of helpless, hopeless despair that would be felt by a small wooden box or geometrical cube if such objects had consciousness; it was the guilt of sheer existence.

It was the secret guilt of disease, of failure, of ugliness (much worse things than murder); it was an attribute of my being like the greenness of the grass. It was *in* me. It was *on* me. If it had been the result of anything I had done, I would have been less guilty.

In my dream I was eleven years old.

Now in my eleven years of conventional life I had learned many things and one of them was what it means to be convicted of rape—I do not mean the man who did it, I mean the woman to whom it was done. Rape is one of the Christian mysteries, it creates a luminous and beautiful tableau in people's minds; and as I listened furtively to what nobody would allow me to hear straight out, I slowly came to understand that I was face to face with one of those shadowy feminine disasters, like pregnancy, like disease, like weakness; she was not only the victim of the act but in some strange way its perpetrator; somehow she had attracted the lightning that struck her out of a clear sky. A diabolical chance—*which was not chance*—had revealed her to all of us as she truly was, in her secret inadequacy, in that wretched guiltiness which she had kept hidden for seventeen years but which now finally manifested itself in front of everybody. Her secret guilt was this:

She was Cunt.

She had "lost" something.

Now the other party to the incident had manifested his essential nature, too; he was Prick—but being Prick is not a bad thing. In fact, he had "gotten away with" something (possibly what she had "lost").

And there I was, listening at eleven years of age:

She was out late at night.

She was in the wrong part of town.

Her skirt was too short and that provoked him.

She liked having her eye blacked and her head banged against the sidewalk.

I understood this perfectly. (I reflected thus in my dream, in my state of being a pair of eyes in a small wooden box stuck forever on a gray, geometric plane—or so I thought.) I too had been guilty of what had been done to me, when I came home from the playground in tears because I had been beaten up by bigger children who were bullies.

I was dirty.

I was crying.

I demanded comfort.

I was being inconvenient.

I did not disappear into thin air.

And if that isn't guilt, what is? I was very lucid in my nightmare. I knew it was not wrong to be a girl because Mommy said so; cunts were all right if they were neutralized, one by one, by being hooked on to a man, but this orthodox arrangement only partly redeems them and every biological possessor of one knows in her bones that radical inferiority which is only another name for Original Sin.

Pregnancy, for example (says the box), take pregnancy now, it's a disaster, but we're too enlightened to blame the woman for her perfectly natural behavior, aren't we? Only keep it secret and keep it going—and I'll give you three guesses as to which partner the pregnancy is in.

When you grow up as an old-fashioned girl, you always remember that cozy comfort: Daddy getting angry a lot but

Mummy just sighs. When Daddy says, "For God's sake, can't you women ever remember anything without being told?" he isn't asking a real question any more than he'd ask a real question of a lamp or a wastebasket. I blinked my silver eyes inside my box. If you stumble over a lamp and you curse that lamp and then you become aware that inside that lamp (or that wooden box or that pretty girl or that piece of bric-a-brac) is a pair of eyes watching you *and that pair of eyes is not amused* —what then?

Mommy never shouted, "I hate your bloody guts!" She controlled herself to avoid a scene. That was her job.

I've been doing it for her ever since.

Now here the idiot reader is likely to hit upon a fascinating speculation (maybe a little late), that my guilt is blood-guilt for having killed so many men. I suppose there is nothing to be done about this. Anybody who believes I feel guilty for the murders I did is a Damned Fool in the full Biblical sense of those two words; you might as well kill yourself right now and save me the trouble, especially if you're male. I am not guilty because I murdered.

I murdered because I was guilty.

Murder is my one way out.

For every drop of blood shed there is restitution made; with every truthful reflection in the eyes of a dying man I get back a little of my soul; with every gasp of horrified comprehension I come a little more into the light. See? It's *me*!

I am the force that is ripping out your guts; I, I, I, the hatred twisting your arm; I, I, I, the fury who has just put a bullet into your side. It is I who cause this pain, not you. It is I who am doing it to you, not you. It is I who will be alive tomorrow, not you. Do you know? Can you guess? Are you catching on? It is I, who you will not admit exists.

Look! Do you *see me*?

I, I, I. Repeat it like magic. That is not me. I am not that. Luther crying out in the choir like one possessed: NON SUM, NON SUM, NON SUM!

This is the underside of my world.

Of course you don't want me to be stupid, bless you! you only want to make sure you're intelligent. You don't want me to commit suicide; you only want me to be gratefully aware of my dependency. You don't want me to despise myself; you only want to ensure the flattering deference to you that you consider a spontaneous tribute to your natural qualities. You don't want me to lose my soul; you only want what everybody wants, things to go your way; you want a devoted helpmeet, a self-sacrificing mother, a hot chick, a darling daughter, women to look at, women to laugh at, women to come to for comfort, women to wash your floors and buy your groceries and cook your food and keep your children out of your hair, to work when you need the money and stay home when you don't, women to be enemies when you want a good fight, women who are sexy when you want a good lay, women who don't complain, women who don't nag or push, women who don't hate you really, women who know their job, and above all—women who lose. On top of it all, you sincerely require me to be happy; you are naively puzzled that I should be so wretched and so full of venom in this best of all possible worlds. Whatever can be the matter with me? But the mode is more than a little outworn.

As my mother once said: The boys throw stones at the frogs in jest.

But the frogs die in earnest.

XI

I don't like didactic nightmares. They make me sweat. It takes me fifteen minutes to stop being a wooden box with a soul and to come back to myself in ordinary human bondage.

Davy sleeps nearby. You've heard about blue-eyed blonds, haven't you? I passed into his room barefoot and watched him curled in sleep, unconscious, the golden veils of his eyelashes shadowing his cheeks, one arm thrown out into the streak of light falling on him from the hall. It takes a lot to wake him (you can almost mount Davy in his sleep) but I was too shaken to start right away and only squatted down by the mattress he sleeps on, tracing with my fingertips the patterns the hair made on his chest: broad high up, over the muscles, then narrowing toward his delicate belly (which rose and fell with his breathing), the line of hair to below the navel, and then that suddenly stiff blossoming of the pubic hair in which his relaxed genitals nestled gently, like a rosebud.

I told you I was an old-fashioned girl.

I caressed his dry, velvety-skinned organ until it stirred in my hand, then ran my fingernails lightly down his sides to wake him up; I did the same—though very lightly—to the insides of his arms.

He opened his eyes and smiled starrily at me.

It's very pleasant to follow Davy's hairline around his neck with your tongue or nuzzle all the hollows of his long-muscled, swimmer's body: inside the elbows, the forearms, the place where the back tapers inward under the ribs, the backs of the knees. A naked man is a cross, the juncture elaborated in vulnerable and delicate flesh like the blossom on a banana tree, that place that's given me so much pleasure.

I nudged him gently and he shivered a little, bringing his legs together and spreading his arms flat; with my forefinger I made a transient white line on his neck. Little Davy was half-filled by now, which is a sign that Davy wants to be knelt over. I obliged, sitting across his thighs, and bending over him without touching his body, kissed him again and again on the mouth, the neck, the face, the shoulders. He is very, very exciting. He's very beautiful, my classic mesomorphic monster-pet. Putting one arm under his shoulders to lift him up, I rubbed my nipples over his mouth, first one and then the other, which is nice for us both, and as he held on to my upper arms and let his head fall back, I pulled him to me, kneading his back muscles, kneading his buttocks, sliding down to the mattress with him. Little Davy is entirely filled out now.

So lovely: Davy with his head thrown to one side, eyes closed, his strong fingers clenching and unclenching. He began to arch his back, as his sleepiness made him a little too quick for me, so I pressed Small Davy between thumb and forefinger just enough to slow him down and then—when I felt like it—playfully started to mount him, rubbing the tip of him, nipping him a little on the neck. His breathing in my ear, fingers convulsively closing on mine.

I played with him a little more, tantalizing him, then swallowed him whole like a watermelon seed—so fine inside! with

Davy moaning, his tongue inside my mouth, his blue gaze shattered, his whole body uncontrollably arched, all his sensation concentrated in the place where I held him.

I don't do this often, but that time I made him come by slipping a finger up his anus: convulsions, fires, crying in no words as the sensation was pulled out of him. If I had let him take more time, I would have climaxed with him, but he's stiff for quite a while after he comes and I prefer that; I like the after-tremors and the after-hardness, slipperier and more pliable than before; Davy has an eerie malleability at those times. I grasped him internally, I pressed down on him, enjoying in the one act his muscular throat, the hair under his arms, his knees, the strength of his back and buttocks, his beautiful face, the fine skin on the inside of his thighs. Kneaded and bruised him, hiccoughing inside with all my architecture: little buried rod, swollen lips and grabby sphincter, the flexing half-moon under the pubic bone. And everything else in the vicinity, no doubt. I'd had him. Davy was mine. Sprawled blissfully over him—I was discharged down to my fingertips but still quietly throbbing—it had really been a good one. His body so warm and wet under me and inside me.

XII

And looked up to see—

XIII

—the three J's—

XIV

"Good Lord! Is *that* all?" said Janet to Joanna.

XV

Something pierces the sweetest solitude.

I got up, tickled him with the edge of my claw, joined them at the door. Closing it. "Stay, Davy." This is one of the key words that the house "understands"; the central computer will transmit a pattern of signals to the implants in his brain and he will stretch out obediently on his mattress; when I say to the main computer "Sleep," Davy will sleep. You have already seen what else happens. He's a lovely limb of the house. The original germ-plasm was chimpanzee, I think, but none of the behavior is organically controlled any more. True, he does have his minimal actions which he pursues without me—he eats, eliminates, sleeps, and climbs in and out of his exercise box —but even these are caused by a standing computer pattern. And I take precedence, of course. It is theoretically possible that Davy has (tucked away in some nook of his cerebrum) consciousness of a kind that may never even touch his active life—is Davy a poet in his own peculiar way?—but I prefer to believe not. His consciousness—such as it is and I am willing to grant it for the sake of argument—is nothing but the permanent possibility of sensation, a mere intellectual abstraction, a nothing, a picturesque collocation of words. It is experientially quite empty, and above all, it is nothing that need concern you and me. Davy's soul lies somewhere else; it's an outside soul. Davy's soul is in Davy's beauty; and Beauty is always empty, always on the outside. Isn't it?

"Leucotomized," I said (to the J's). "Lobotomized. Kidnapped in childhood. Do you believe me?"

They did.

"Don't," I said. Jeannine doesn't understand what we're talking about; Joanna does and is appalled; Janet is thinking. I shooed them into the main room and told them who he was.

Alas! those who were shocked at my making love that way to a man are now shocked at my making love to a machine; you can't win.

"Well?" said the Swedish Miss.

"Well," said I, "this is what we want. We want bases on your worlds; we want raw materials if you've got them. We want places to recuperate and places to hide an army; we want places to store our machines. Above all, we want places to move from—bases that the other side doesn't know about. Janet is obviously acting as an unofficial ambassador, so I can talk to her, that's fine. You two might object that you are persons of no standing, but whom do you expect me to ask, your governments? Also, we need someone who can show us the local ropes. You'll do fine for me. You are the authorities, as far as I'm concerned.

"Well?

"Is it yes or no?

"Do we do business?"

PART NINE

I

THIS IS the Book of Joanna.

II

I was driving on a four-lane highway in North America with an acquaintance and his nine-year-old son.

"Beat 'im! Beat 'im!" cried the little boy excitedly as I passed another car in order to change lanes. I stayed in the right-hand lane for a while, admiring the buttercups by the side of the road, and then, in order to change lanes back, fell behind another car.

"Pass 'im! Pass 'im!" cried the distressed child, and then in anxious tears, "Why didn't you *beat* 'im?"

"There, there, old sport," said his indulgent Daddy, "Joanna drives like a lady. When you're grown up you'll have a car of your own and you can pass everybody on the road." He turned to me and complained:

"Joanna, you just don't drive aggressively enough."

In training.

III

There's the burden of knowledge. There's the burden of compassion. There's seeing all too clearly what's in their eyes as they seize your hands, crying cheerily, "You don't really mind my saying that, do you? I knew you didn't!" Men's shaky egos have a terrible appeal to the mater dolorosa. At times I am seized by a hopeless, helpless longing for love and reconciliation, a dreadful yearning to be understood, a teary passion for exposing our weaknesses to each other. It seems intolerable that I should go through life thus estranged, keeping it all to my guilty self. So I try to explain in the softest, least accusing way I can, but oddly enough men don't behave the way they do on the Late Late Show, I mean those great male stars in their infancy in the Jean Arthur or the Mae West movies: candid, clear-eyed, and fresh, with their unashamed delight in their women's strength and their naive enjoyment of their own, beautiful men with beautiful faces and the joyfulness of innocents, John Smith or John Doe. These are the only men I will let into Whileaway. But we have fallen away from our ancestors' softness and clarity of thought into corrupt and degenerate practices. When I speak now I am told loftily or kindly that I just don't understand, that women are really happy that way, that women can better themselves if they want to but somehow they just don't want to, that I'm joking, that I can't possibly mean what I say, that I'm too intelligent to be put in the same class as "women," that I'm different, that there is a profound spiritual difference between men and women of which I don't appreciate the beauty, that I have a man's brain, that I have a man's mind, that I'm talking to a phonograph record. Women don't take it that way. If you bring up the subject with them, they begin to tremble out of terror, embarrassment, and alarm; they smile a smile of hideous, smug embarrassment, a magical smile meant to wipe them off the face of the earth, to make them abject and invisible—oh no, no, no, no, don't think I believe any of that, don't think I need any of that! Consider:

You *ought to be interested in* politics.

Politics is baseball. Politics is football. Politics is X "winning" and Y "losing." Men wrangle about politics in living rooms the way Opera Fan One shouts at Opera Fan Two about Victoria de los Angeles.

No squabble between the Republican League and the Democrat League will ever change *your* life. Concealing your anxiety over the phone when He calls; that's your politics.

Still, you *ought to be interested in* politics. Why aren't you?

Because of feminine incapacity.

One can go on.

IV

I committed my first revolutionary act yesterday. I shut the door on a man's thumb. I did it for no reason at all and I didn't warn him; I just slammed the door shut in a rapture of hatred and imagined the bone breaking and the edges grinding into his skin. He ran downstairs and the phone rang wildly for an hour after while I sat, listening to it, my heart beating wildly, thinking wild thoughts. Horrible. Horrible and wild. I must find Jael.

Women are so petty (translation: we operate on too small a scale).

Now I'm worse than that—I also do not give a damn about humanity or society. It's very upsetting to think that women make up only one-tenth of society, but it's true. For example:

My doctor is male.

My lawyer is male.

My tax-accountant is male.

The grocery-store-owner (on the corner) is male.

The janitor in my apartment building is male.

The president of my bank is male.

The manager of the neighborhood supermarket is male.

My landlord is male.

Most taxi-drivers are male.

All cops are male.

All firemen are male.

The designers of my car are male.

The factory workers who made the car are male.

The dealer I bought it from is male.

Almost all my colleagues are male.

My employer is male.

The Army is male.

The Navy is male.

The government is (mostly) male.

I think most of the people in the world are male.

Now it's true that waitresses, elementary-school teachers, secretaries, nurses, and nuns are female, but how many nuns do you meet in the course of the usual business day? Right? And secretaries are female only until they get married, at which time, they change or something because you usually don't see them again at all. I think it's a legend that half the population of the world is female; where on earth are they keeping them all? No, if you tot up all those categories of women above, you can see clearly and beyond the shadow of a doubt that there are maybe 1–2 women for every 11 or so men and that hardly justifies making such a big fuss. It's just that I'm selfish. My friend Kate says that most of the women are put into female-banks when they grow up and that's why you don't see them, but I can't believe that.

(Besides, what about the children? Mothers have to sacrifice themselves to their children, both male and female, so that the children will be happy when they grow up; though the mothers themselves were once children and were sacrificed to in order that they might grow up and sacrifice themselves to others; and when the daughters grow up, *they* will be mothers and *they* will have to sacrifice themselves for *their* children, so you begin to wonder whether the whole thing isn't a plot to make the world safe for (male) children. But motherhood is sacred and mustn't be talked about.)

Oh dear, oh dear.

Thus in the bad days, in the dark swampy times.

At thirteen desperately watching TV, curling my long legs under me, desperately reading books, callow adolescent that I was, trying (desperately!) to find someone in books, in movies, in life, in history, to tell me it was O.K. to be ambitious, O.K. to be loud, O.K. to be Humphrey Bogart (smart and rudeness), O.K. to be James Bond (arrogance), O.K. to be Superman (power), O.K. to be Douglas Fairbanks (swash-buckling), to tell me self-love was all right, to tell me I could love God and Art and Myself better than anything on earth and still have orgasms.

Being told it was all right "for you, dear," but not for *women*.

Being told I was a woman.

At sixteen, giving up.

In college, educated women (I found out) were frigid; active women (I knew) were neurotic; women (we all knew) were timid, incapable, dependent, nurturing, passive, intuitive, emotional, unintelligent, obedient, and beautiful. You can always get dressed up and go to a party. Woman is the gateway to another world; Woman is the earth-mother; Woman is the eternal siren; Woman is purity; Woman is carnality; Woman has intuition; Woman is the life-force; Woman is selfless love.

"I am the gateway to another world," (said I, looking in the mirror) "I am the earth-mother; I am the eternal siren; I am purity," (Jeez, new pimples) "I am carnality; I have intuition; I am the life-force; I am selfless love." (Somehow it sounds different in the first person, doesn't it?)

Honey (said the mirror, scandalized) Are you out of your fuckin' *mind*?

I AM HONEY
I AM RASPBERRY JAM
I AM A VERY GOOD LAY
I AM A GOOD DATE
I AM A GOOD WIFE
I AM GOING CRAZY

Everything was preaches and cream.

(When I decided that the key word in all this vomit was *self-less* and that if I was really all the things books, friends, parents, teachers, dates, movies, relatives, doctors, newspapers, and magazines said I was, then if I acted as I pleased without thinking of all these things I would be all these things in spite of my not trying to be all these things. So—

"*Christ, will you quit acting like a man!*")

Alas, it was never meant for us to hear. It was never meant for us to know. We ought never be taught to read. We fight through the constant male refractoriness of our surroundings; our souls are torn out of us with such shock that there isn't even any blood. Remember: I didn't and don't want to be a "feminine" version or a diluted version or a special version or a subsidiary version or an ancillary version, or an adapted version of the heroes I admire. I want to be the heroes themselves.

What future is there for a female child who aspires to being Humphrey Bogart?

Baby Laura Rose, playing with her toes, she's a real pretty little sweetie-girl, isn't she?

> Sugar and spice
> And everything nice—
> *That's* what little girls are made of!

But her brother's a tough little bruiser (two identical damp, warm lumps). At three and a half I mixed sour cream and ice cubes on the window sill to see if they would turn into *ice cream*; I copied the words "hot" and "cold" off the water faucets. At four I sat on a record to see if it would break if pressure were applied evenly to both sides—it did; in kindergarten I taught everybody games and bossed them around; at six I beat up a little boy who took candy from my coat; I thought very well of myself.

V

Learning to
despise
one's
self

VI

Brynhild hung her husband on a nail in the wall, tied up in her girdle as in a shopping bag, but she, too, lost her strength when the magic shlong got inside her. One can't help feeling that the story has been somewhat distorted in the re-telling. When I was five I thought that the world was a matriarchy.

I was a happy little girl.

I couldn't tell the difference between "gold" and "silver" or "night gown" and "evening gown," so I imagined all the ladies of the neighborhood getting together in their beautiful "night gowns"—which were signs of rank—and making all the decisions about our lives. They were the government. My mother was President because she was a school teacher and local people deferred to her. Then the men would come home from "work" (wherever that was; I thought it was like hunting) and lay "the bacon" at the ladies' feet, to do with as they wished. The men were employed by the ladies to do this. Laura Rose, who never swam underwater a whole month in summer camp with goggles on or slept in the top bunk, fancying herself a Queen in lonely splendor or a cabin-boy on a ship, has no such happy memories. She's the girl who wanted to be Genghis Khan. When Laura tried to find out who she was, they told her she was "different" and that's a hell of a description on which to base your life; it comes down to either "Not-me" or "Convenient-for me" and what is one supposed to do with that? What am I to do? (she says) What am I to feel?

Is "supposed" like "spoused"? Is "different" like "deteriorate"? How can I eat or sleep? How can I go to the moon?

I first met Laur a few years ago when I was already grown up. Cinnamon and apples, ginger and vanilla, that's Laur. Now having Brynhildic fantasies about her was nothing—I have all sorts of extraordinary fantasies which I don't take seriously— but bringing my fantasies into the real world frightened me very much. It's not that they were bad in themselves, but they were Unreal and therefore culpable; to try to make Real what was Unreal was to mistake the very nature of things; it was a sin not against conscience (which remained genuinely indifferent during the whole affair) but against Reality, and of the two the latter is far more blasphemous. It's the crime of creating one's own Reality, of "preferring oneself" as a good friend of mine says. I knew it was an impossible project.

She was reading a book, her hair falling over her face. She was radiant with health and life, a study in dirty blue jeans. I knelt down by her chair and kissed her on the back of her smooth, honeyed, hot neck with a despairing feeling that *now I had done it*—but asking isn't getting. Wanting isn't having. She'll refuse and the world will be itself again. I waited confidently for the rebuke, for the eternal order to reassert itself (as it had to, of course)—for it would in fact take a great deal of responsibility off my hands.

But she let me do it. She blushed and pretended not to notice. I can't describe to you how reality itself tore wide open at that moment. She kept on reading and I trod at a snail's pace over her ear and cheek down to the corner of her mouth, Laur getting hotter and redder all the time as if she had steam inside her. It's like falling off a cliff, standing astonished in mid-air as the horizon rushes away from you. If this is possible, anything is possible. Later we got stoned and made awkward, self-conscious love, but nothing that happened afterward was as important to me (in an unhuman way) as that first, awful wrench of the mind.

Once I felt the pressure of her hip-bone along my belly, and being very muddled and high, thought: *She's got an erection.* Dreadful. Dreadful embarrassment. One of us had to be male and it certainly wasn't me. Now they'll tell me it's because I'm a Lesbian, I mean that's why I'm dissatisfied with things. That's not true. It's not because I'm a Lesbian. It's because I'm a *tall, blonde, blue-eyed Lesbian.*

Does it count if it's your best friend? Does it count if it's her mind you love through her body? Does it count if you love men's bodies but hate men's minds? Does it count if you still love yourself?

Later we got better.

VII

Jeannine goes window-shopping. She has my eyes, my hands, my silly stoop; she's wearing my blue plastic raincoat and carrying my umbrella. Jeannine is out on the town on a Saturday afternoon saying goodbye, goodbye, goodbye to all that.

Goodbye to mannequins in store windows who pretend to be sympathetic but who are really nasty conspiracies, goodbye to hating Mother, goodbye to the Divine Psychiatrist, goodbye to The Girls, goodbye to Normality, goodbye to Getting Married, goodbye to The Supernaturally Blessed Event, goodbye to being Some Body, goodbye to waiting for Him (poor fellow!), goodbye to sitting by the telephone, goodbye to feebleness, goodbye to adoration, goodbye Politics, hello politics. She's scared but that's all right. The streets are full of women and this awes her; where have they all come from? Where are they going? (If you don't mind the symbolism.) It's stopped raining but mist coils up from the pavement. She passes a bridal shop where the chief mannequin, a Vision in white lace and tulle, sticks out her tongue at Jeannine. "Didn't do it!" cries the mannequin, resuming her haughty pose and balancing a bridal veil on her head. Jeannine shuts her umbrella, latches it, and swings it energetically round and round.

Goodbye. Goodbye. Goodbye to everything.

We met in Schrafft's and sat, the four of us, at one table, ordering their Thanksgiving dinner, argh, which is so traditional you can't stand it. Gah.

"What's Indian pudding?" says Janet, baffled.

"No, don't, better not," says Joanna.

We munch in silence, slowly, the way Whileawayans eat: munch, munch, gulp. Munch. Gulp, gulp, gulp, Munch. Meditatively. It's pleasant to eat. Janet screws up her eyes, yawns, and stretches athletically, leaning over the back of her chair and working her bent arms first to this side, then to that. She ends up by pounding on the table. "Mm!" she says.

"My goodness, look at that," says Jeannine, very self-possessed and elegant, her fork in mid-air. "I thought you were going to knock someone's hat off."

Schrafft's is full of women. Men don't like places like this where the secret maintenance work of femininity is carried on, just as they turn green and bolt when you tell them medical events are occurring in your genito-urinary system. Jael has got something stuck between her steel teeth and her sham ones, and cocking an eye around Schrafft's, she slips off her tooth cover and roots around for the blackberry seed or whatever, exposing to the world her steely, crocodilian grin. Back they go. In. Done.

"So?" says Jael. "Do we do business?" There is a long, uncomfortable silence. I look around Schrafft's and wonder why women at their most genteel are so miserly; why is there no Four Seasons, no Maxim's, no Chambord, for women? Women are very strange about money, feudal almost: Real Money is what you spend on the house and on yourself (except for your appearance): Magic Money is what you get men to spend on you. It takes a tremendous rearrangement of mental priorities for women to eat well, that is to spend money on their insides instead of their outsides. The Schrafft's hostess stands by the cashier's desk in her good black dress and sensible shoes; women left to themselves are ugly, *i.e.* human, but Gentility has been interfering here.

"This is awful food," says Janet, who is used to Whileaway.

"This is wonderful food," says Jael, who is used to Womanland and Manland.

Both burst out laughing.

"Well?" says Jael again. Another silence. Janet and I are very uncomfortable. Jeannine, one cheek bulging like a squirrel's, looks up as if surprised that we could hesitate to do business with Womanland. She nods briefly and then goes back to building mashed-sweet-potato mountains with her fork. Jeannine now gets up late, neglects the housework until it annoys her, and plays with her food.

"Jeannine?" says Jael.

"Oh, sure," says Jeannine. "*I* don't mind. You can bring in all the soldiers you want. You can take the whole place over; I wish you would." Jael goes admiringly tsk tsk and makes a rueful face that means: my friend, you are really going it. "My whole world calls me Jeannie," says Jeannine in her high, sweet voice. "See?"

(Laur is waiting outside for Janet, probably baring her teeth at passing men.)

To Janet, Jael suddenly says:

"You don't want me?"

"No," says Janet. "No, sorry."

Jael grins. She says:

"Disapprove all you like. Pedant! Let me give you something to carry away with you, friend: that 'plague' you talk of is a lie. *I know.* The world-lines around you are not so different from yours or mine or theirs and there is no plague in any of them, not any of them. Whileaway's plague is a big lie. Your ancestors lied about it. It is I who gave you your 'plague,' my dear, about which you can now pietize and moralize to your heart's content; I, I, I, I am the plague, Janet Evason. I and the war I fought built your world for you, I and those like me, we gave you a thousand years of peace and love and the Whileawayan flowers nourish themselves on the bones of the men we have slain."

"No," said Janet dryly, "I don't believe." Now you must know that Jeannine is Everywoman. I, though I am a bit quirky, I too am Everywoman. Every woman is not Jael, as Uncle George would say—but Jael is Everywoman. We all stared accusingly at Janet but Miss Evason was not moved. Laur came through Schrafft's revolving door and waved wildly; Janet got up to go.

"Think about it," said Alice Reasoner. "Go home and find out about it."

Janet began to weep—those strange, shameless, easy, Whileawayan tears that well out of the eyes without destroying the composed sadness of the face. She is expressing her grief about (for) Alice Reasoner. I think—when I stop to think about it, which is not often—that I like Jael the best of us all, that I would like to be Jael, twisted as she is on the rack of her own hard logic, triumphant in her extremity, the hateful hero with the broken heart, which is like being the clown with the broken

heart. Jael averts her face in a death's-head grimace that is only
a nervous tic of Alice Reasoner's, an expression that began perhaps twenty years ago as a tasting-something-sour look and
has intensified with time into sheer bad-angelry, luminous with
hate. She has cords in her neck. She could put out her captive's
claws and slash Schrafft's tablecloth into ten separate, parallel
ribbons. That's only one one-hundredth of what she can do.
Jeannine is playing an absorbing game with her green peas (she
had no dessert). Jeannine is happy.

   We got up and paid our quintuple bill; then we went out
into the street. I said goodbye and went off with Laur, I, Janet;
I also watched them go, I, Joanna; moreover I went off to
show Jael the city, I Jeannine, I Jael, I myself.

   Goodbye, goodbye, goodbye.

   Goodbye to Alice Reasoner, who says tragedy makes her
sick, who says never give in but always go down fighting, who
says take them with you, who says die if you must but loop
your own intestines around the neck of your strangling enemy.
Goodbye to everything. Goodbye to Janet, whom we don't
believe in and whom we deride but who is in secret our savior
from utter despair, who appears Heaven-high in our dreams
with a mountain under each arm and the ocean in her pocket,
Janet who comes from the place where the labia of sky and
horizon kiss each other so that Whileawayans call it The Door
and know that all legendary things come therefrom. Radiant
as the day, the Might-be of our dreams, living as she does in
a blessedness none of us will ever know, she is nonetheless
Everywoman. Goodbye, Jeannine, goodbye, poor soul, poor
girl, poor as-I-once-was. Goodbye, goodbye. Remember: we
will all be changed. In a moment, in the twinkling of an eye,
we will all be free. I swear it on my own head. I swear it on my
ten fingers. We will be ourselves. Until then I am silent; I can
no more. I am God's typewriter and the ribbon is typed out.

   Go, little book, trot through Texas and Vermont and Alaska
and Maryland and Washington and Florida and Canada and
England and France; bob a curtsey at the shrines of Friedan,
Millett, Greer, Firestone, and all the rest; behave yourself in
people's living rooms, neither looking ostentatious on the coffee table nor failing to persuade due to the dullness of your
style; knock at the Christmas garland on my husband's door

in New York City and tell him that I loved him truly and love him still (despite what anybody may think); and take your place bravely on the book racks of bus terminals and drugstores. Do not scream when you are ignored, for that will alarm people, and do not fume when you are heisted by persons who will not pay, rather rejoice that you have become so popular. Live merrily, little daughter-book, even if I can't and we can't; recite yourself to all who will listen; stay hopeful and wise. Wash your face and take your place without a fuss in the Library of Congress, for all books end up there eventually, both little and big. Do not complain when at last you become quaint and old-fashioned, when you grow as outworn as the crinolines of a generation ago and are classed with *Spicy Western Stories*, *Elsie Dinsmore*, and *The Son of the Sheik*; do not mutter angrily to yourself when young persons read you to hrooch and hrch and guffaw, wondering what the dickens you were all about. Do not get glum when you are no longer understood, little book. Do not curse your fate. Do not reach up from readers' laps and punch the readers' noses.

Rejoice, little book!

For on that day, we will be free.

WE WHO ARE ABOUT TO . . .

Aʙᴏᴜᴛ ᴛᴏ ᴅɪᴇ. And so on.
We're all going to die.

The Sahara is your back yard, so's the Pacific trench; die there and you won't be lonely. On Earth you are never more than 13,000 miles from anywhere, which as the man said is a tough commute, but the rays of light from the scene of your death take little more than a tenth of a second to go . . . anywhere!

We're nowhere.

We'll die alone.

This is space travel. Imagine a flat world, a piece of paper, say, with two spots on it but very far apart. If you were a two-dimensional triangle, how would you get from one spot to the other? Walk? Too far. But fold the paper through the third dimension (ours) so that the spots match exactly—if you were a triangle you couldn't see or feel this, of course—and you *are* at the proper place. We do this in the fourth. Don't ask me how. Only you must be very, very careful, when you fold spacetime, not to sloosh the paper around or let it slide: then you end up not on the spot you wanted but God knows where, maybe entirely out of our galaxy, which is that dust you see in the sky on clear nights when you're away from cities. The glittering breath of angels. Far, far from home. The light of our dying may not reach you for a thousand million years. That ordinary sun up there, a little hazy now at noon, that smeary spot.

We do not know where we are.

At dawn there was an intensely brilliant flash far, far under the horizon, and about an hour later the noise of the thing; I figured the way you do for thunderstorms, the lag between light and sound: one-hippopotamus, two-hippopotamus, three-hippopotamus, four-hippopotamus, five-hippopotamus —there's your mile. Seven hundred miles. That's over a thousand kilometers. In the event of mechanical dysfunction, the ship's computer goes for the nearest "tagged" planet, i.e. where human life is supposed to be possible, then ejects the passenger compartment separately. Lays an egg, you might say. We won't be visited without a distress call, however, now

195

the colonization fever's died down (didn't take long, divide five billion people by twenty and the remainders start getting clubby again).

Goodbye ship, goodbye crew, goodbye medicine, goodbye books, goodbye freight, goodbye baggage, goodbye computer that could have sent back an instantaneous distress call along the coordinates we came through (provided it had them, which I doubt), goodbye plodding laser signal, no faster than other light, that might have reached somewhere, sometime, this time, next time, never. You'll get around to us in a couple of thousand years.

We're a handful of persons in a metal bungalow: five women, three men, bedding, chemical toilet, simple tools, an even simpler pocket laboratory, freeze-dried food for six months, and a water-distiller with its own sealed powerpack, good for six months (and cast as a unit, unusable for anything else).

Goodbye, everybody.

At dawn I held hands with the other passengers, we all huddled together under that brilliant flash, although I hate them.

O God, I miss my music.

• • •

This is being recorded on a pocket vocoder I always carry; the punctuation is a series of sounds not often used for words in any language: triple gutturals, spits, squeaks, pops, that kind of thing. Sounds like an insane chicken. Hence this parenthesis.)

Of the women: myself. A Mrs. Valeria Graham, actually married to Mr. Graham, in the delicate fifties when alimony becomes mandatory upon divorce (who would pay whom is a conjecture here). Valeria Victrix habitually wears the classical Indian sari, usually gold embroidered on royal blue, like a television hostess's; this does not suit a petite chemical blonde. Ditto the many-splendored earrings: bells within cages within hoops.

A dark young woman who does yoga on her head, off to some "unimportant job" somewhere (she said), hates everyone, says she's called Nathalie. Nathalie what? Nathalie nothing. Mind your own business.

Cassie, thirty-ish, beginning to put on weight; you'll find her waiting table in any restaurant or nude bar on any world. She looks like an earlier stage in the life-cycle of Mrs. Graham, but that's an illusion; nothing but a convulsion of nature could let either of these two rise or fall to the other's level. (Hydrogen fusion, which provided unlimited power and should've made us all rich, but of course didn't.)

A Graham child, female, twelve, a beautiful café-au-lait so she is either Mrs. Graham's by a former marriage or Mr. Graham's ditto, or neither. Hors de combat all trip with one of the few bacterial diseases left, or rather the treatment for it, which had made her dreadfully ill. We'd see her only when she'd stagger into the lounge, looking beautiful and hopeless, and then vomit (again). For whoever finds this and has no Greek, an iatrogenic disease is one created by the physician and we have plenty of them. The physicians and the diseases.

This will never be found.

Who am I writing for, then?

The men: Mr. Graham, a big powerful male in his early fifties, hollow and handsome in the same style as his wife: coloring, dress, and person. Three days out (we were on the way to find the first spot we can then fold onto the second spot) Cassie took off the mask, stopped being squeezably-soft, and lost all expression. The Grahams stopped speaking to her. I say "male" because he emphasizes it subtly, so perhaps she's the buyer and he's the bought. Or both: money marries money. Relations with men are still apt to be patterned on a few rather dull models, especially among strangers, so I know less about the men than I do about the women, but in one way I know more: I mean the conception of themselves they find it publicly necessary to live up to.

Alan: a young man with a set of shoulders like unto those of one who plays *le futbol* (says he did). Extremely polite and attentive, with a carefully intent way of listening to everybody and agreeing civilly and much too often ("Oh, I do agree with you, Mr. Graham, I really do"). My theory is that this obviously insincere behavior conceals absolutely nothing; he's rich enough to take the poor man's Grand Tour, poor enough to need a job, decent enough not to hurt anyone unless he's frightened or hurt himself (which could happen pretty easily), and anxious enough to flatter whoever he thinks can help him. The Grahams, you see, are slumming.

An historian of ideas traveling from one University to another and extremely evasive about his work, as they all are, now there's so little of it to go around; he wears Mr. Graham's kind of conservative clothes: shorts and sport-shirts, bright but not daylight-fluorescent (Vic Graham in blue, John Ude in red). The only historical analogy to Alan's costumes is Graustark, all gold braid, epaulettes, and boots (except the shako, which I think he had to leave behind on account of the weight, though he never mentioned it). The professor is John Ude. Thirties. A very minor intellectual. Bland. Often displays The Smile. The first day, in the lounge, when Mrs. Graham actually introduced herself as *Mrs. Graham*—which is rather like presenting yourself as a Dame of the British Empire or a Roman Tribune—Professor Ude displayed (after a blank moment) The Smile. Then he took out from his sporran The Pipe, gesturing at The Pipe with The Smile to show that he was aware of his own self-mockery. He would have received Valeria as Mistress Anne Bradstreet, had she so required, because the Grahams are rich. Black-body-suited, perpetually angry Nathalie said audibly, "*Missiz!* Oh God," and turned away with an unbelieving, outraged, I-knew-it-was-going-to-be-one-of-those-trips look. Alan gaped hysterically, then shut his mouth. I said nothing. Think of it: Valeria and Victor in blue, Ude in red, Alan indescribable, Cassie in two stars and a cache-sexe (both silver), and Lori Graham in body paint, mostly blue (to match her parents' clothes). The arrows of Professor Ude's irony point only down in the social scale, never up; when they occasionally point at himself, he is very careful to blunt them.

Oh, we are a dull bunch! The professor once uncrimped enough to get into a long discussion with Victor Graham about the new lease on life given capitalism by the unlimited power of hydrogen fusion, the poor fool. He believes in free enterprise, competition, achievement-orientation, the meritocracy. He's never been behind the crew panels where the technocrats live. Travel enough and you can make friends with the crew, what's this, what's that, ask questions; they even let you fiddle about in sick bay if you're careful. You see things, then.

Meritocracy? We're being kept off the streets, that's all, rich or poor. (Foundations pay me to lecture on music and play tapes of it; that's why I travel. I'm a scrounge.)

I once said to Ude, "How fast do you think things really change?"

He said, "That's not my field."

Cassie, determined, bitter, exhausted, full-breasted, wanted to know what a musicologist was and what kind of music.

"Very old," I said. "European twelfth century to Baroque. No farther."

"How nice," Mrs. Graham said. "We must tell Lori."

"Who cares," Cassie said.

I wear body-suits and sandals, like Nathalie, and keep a low profile, especially with passengers. This isn't a luxury liner; you don't have to eat with anybody, just dial a meal out of the locker.

And visit the crew. And envy them.

Behold the new irrelevants: parasites, scum, proles, scroungers. People who do nothing real.

No, dinosaurs.

Isn't . . . wasn't, I mean, a luxury liner.

Stranded dinosaurs.

• • •

Day first. I'm sitting in the corner on the empty tool chest after a little nap. Already excited talk of "colonization," whatever that is. Our tiny laboratory tells us the air is safe, although perhaps a little thin; there's nothing directly poisonous outside. Nathalie's unexpected talent for cataloguing and arranging tools (which is why the tool box is empty). The sun up for at least fifteen hours, taking a slow tour of the horizon at what my childhood tells me is 4 P.M. late autumn, so we have either a very great axial tilt or are in very high latitudes. A few weeks' observation and perhaps we can guess if we're approaching the summer solstice or going the other way, which could give us some idea of how long the seasons will be: could be ten years of summer (and it's hot outside now, about 30° C, they tell me). Through the window you can see ordinary green trees, hilly up-and-downish but not much, some little natural clearings. Very much like New Jersey a hundred and thirty-five years ago, when my ancestors came to Ellis Island: about nineteen-aught-five that was. My maternal something-great-grandfather was a plumber, my maternal something-great-grandmother a sheitel-maker. (A sheitel is a wig which Orthodox Jewish women used to wear after marriage, over their shorn hair. But what do you care.) We don't remember the actual genealogy of the other side nearly so far back, but I've inherited their looks; little, dark, Sephardic Jews fleeing the Spanish frontier at night with rubies, emeralds, and uncut diamonds sewn into the hems of their cloaks. At least I like to think of them that way. I carry the modern equivalent, the only currency that passes everywhere, sewn into my jacket, my neckband, my belt, so flat you couldn't detect it. I mean a whole pharmacopoeia. Because you never know what you will need. (I filched a little from the ship, too: nothing important.)

Our equipment isn't good enough to test whether the life here is edible. We're not supposed to do that. Commonly the problem has been people contaminating the planet, but there have been striking instances of vice-versa. We're supposed to stay inside.

Everybody is getting on everybody else's nerves.

Victor, in his hearty, overemphasized, hollow voice: "I believe I should." (Tail end of a conversation about who's to go out first. Not that it matters. We either go out eventually or cut our throats.)

"Why?" says Nathalie instantly.

"Because I'm old. Expendable. Why else?" (Lori Graham is looking adoring and anxious.)

"Very sensible," says Nathalie. "So should Mrs. Graham." (Lori outraged.)

"Well, if there's any harm . . ." This is John Ude.

"The Grahams will go," says Nathalie over her shoulder, and continues putting together our shovels, our hammers, our axes —"half an hour, no less, no more"—and something longer that comes in sections.

The Grahams go out the air-lock, Victor stooping, Alan kindly restraining Lori when she tries to slip out with them. They have an intense, whispered conversation, with Lori close to tears.

"My, you *are* just an ordinary traveler, aren't you!" I say to Nathalie, hoping to get a rise from her, maybe learn something. No answer. She's engaged in jointing together what we both realize at the same instant is a single-passenger hovercraft:

sealed motor, no cab, kicks up so much dust that you have to
wear an air-filter (included in the box; by Saint George, I was
right), flies over any terrain with ease, including water (at under 32 kph, however), and looks like nothing so much as a stick
with a saddle; hence its name.

"A br—" (she catches herself).

"Broomstick," I finish. On her knees, in the midst of spare
parts, in her black skin-tights, Nathalie gives me (for a moment
only) a glance of shock, of wild surmise—*are you one, too?*

"Where were you really going?" I say.

She inspects her fingernails, comes to a quick decision, licks
her lips wolfishly.

"Government trainee," she says in a low voice but so naturally, that is to say pretend-naturally, that Cassie (who is lying
on a bunk, holding to one ear a cheap, battery-powered music
library that will wear out within days, I can tell) can't hear us.

"At what?" say I.

"Doesn't matter," she says sharply. "Not to tell. And I shan't
now, not because it matters but because it doesn't."

For a moment she's a death's-head.

Then "What!" says Lori Graham, a little desperately, with
the natural irritation of someone whose Mummy and Daddy
may, after all, have been eaten by megatheria. "Nothing," answers Nathalie. "Go on screwing with Alan or whatever it is
you were doing." (Lori makes a disgusted face and Alan turns
aside to blush or giggle.) "If he can," she adds. In the low,
trained voice she says to me, "Who are you."

"A musicologist," I say. "Sorry. Nobody like you. I've picked
things up because I've traveled a lot, that's all."

Cassie sits up, shaking her *radio*. She says to Nathalie, "Can
you do something with this thing?"

"The batteries are worn down and they're electric; we can't
recharge them. You've been playing that ever since we started
this trip and you've probably played it before, quite a lot. I
know you've recharged them but the case is worn. So that's
probably two hundred hours and a couple of rechargings; they
do deteriorate each time, you know. And there's nothing we
can do—our gadgets are all sealed and shielded. It's a different
kind of energy; we can't transform the one to the other. Besides if we tried opening any of the powerpacks, we'd probably

go boom, you know, just like the ship." This is me. I add, "I'm awfully sorry, Cassie."

"So if you're a goddamn music student," says Cassie at her most insulting, "where's your goddamn music, huh?"

I'm tempted to answer "in the ionosphere" (reduced to its constituent atoms or even smaller pieces) but I say, "It was in the baggage compartment."

"Oh," says Alan, clearly disappointed. I guess he has been planning on hearing some music. Cassie draws up her knees in the bunk, exasperated, and presses the side of her face against the sealed window.

Alan adds in a friendly way, "Hey, don't you have any of it with you?" Forgetting to be polite, that one.

"Tapes," I say. "Want to use them for ribbons? I have the amplifier and the recorder—see? they fit in my hand—but the speakers are too big. Two meters diameter."

He opens his mouth, probably to inquire why a speaker has to be two meters across, but Lori—who is *very* well educated, as her parents have been telling us for three weeks—breaks in importantly with a disquisition on the physical reproduction of sound, and how the lowest musical note that can be heard by the human ear is fourteen cycles per second and the lowest sounds that can be felt are even lower, and if you want a really good bass, say for Bach's Toccata and Fugue in D Minor for Organ, or Vestal's Electronic Mass, you just have to have these enoormous speakers for your sound environment because otherwise the sounds just won't fit mechanically on the speakers. "Literally," she says.

"O-o-oh," says Alan in mock awe.

Cassie breaks in furiously with, "Your goddamn education—"

(John Ude has been asleep all this time, worn out, poor man; that's why you haven't heard from him.)

Thank God the Grahams come back in. The air-lock jams. We are now testing the atmosphere just as much as they, something Mr. Ude (waked by the noise of Lori's rejoicings and questionings) seems to notice, but nobody's going to call attention to such things in the presence of an hysterical twelve-year-old with the habit of psychosomatic vomiting. (Her Momma says.)

Joy all around.

(I'm not, of course, recording this at the time it happened. I stole half-an-hour from the long, long dawn. Two and a half hours of twilight, then three more of real dark, and again two and a half hours of dusk-turned-backward: slow, creeping, endless, unadvancing grey.)

We're very high on the world's shoulder. Labrador perhaps. Even with the Pole circle. If the sun goes lower, if it sets closer to the place of its rising, if the dark shrinks, if red-sunset evolves without darkness into red-sunrise. Is this spring? Summer? Fall? We might be heading into a ten-month summer, a twenty-year summer. Desert? Everything dead, brown, burned? Think anyway of midwinter with the sun even lower and only three hours of daylight out of twenty-eight. A night twenty-five hours long.

In the brief, black, real dark we all went outside to look at the sky. A shiver of the nerves as the night air struck us, a kind of blind claustrophilia, wishing to get back into our own, closed-in, stale smell, away from the living odors of night coolness. Everyone stayed together. Black velvet, must be overcast; this awful sense of being outside. Vast space.

We looked up.

Nothing.

I mean there was almost nothing in the sky: a few bright stars near the zenith and halfway to the equatorial horizon a far, faint, dim blur. Island universes. From anywhere on Earth (they say) you can see about three thousand stars with the naked eye. You can also see that arch of powder which we call the Milky Way; it's the center of the galaxy. We're located in one of its arms; it's a kind of flattened ellipse. From anywhere near any galaxy, unless one is very far above or below its major plane, and in the wrong hemisphere to boot, you ought to be able to see something. Not that it matters, of course, for space travel. Still. Nothing matched the star maps Nathalie had (she would!) but then on the other side of the Equator, who knows? And none of us is very good at this sort of thing. But six stars and a blur . . . which might be, God knows, the Crab Nebula or our own, or unidentified astronomical object number goodness-knows-what, something so far away that (as I said) the light of our dying will reach you (whoever you are) only after you yourselves are long dead, after your own Sun has engulfed you and then shrunk to a collapsed cinder with no more light in it than what we saw that night.

Whoever, wherever, whenever.

Lori cried in her mother's arms. Mrs. Graham very clumsy at comforting her daughter, perhaps always was. John, the professor of the history of ideas, saying something like "Uh!" low, a sort of groan.

That empty.

Well, we might be visited in a routine check of the tagged worlds in as little as a couple of centuries, a century, eighty years even. Even little Lori will be dead.

John Ude said, "Come on now, come on, dears. It's a tagged planet. It has to be. Too much coincidence otherwise, eh? The air, the gravity. Now if it's tagged, that means it's like Earth. And we know Earth. Most of us were born on it. So what's there to be afraid of, hey? We're just colonizing a little early, that's all. You wouldn't be afraid of Earth, would you?"

Oh, sure. Think of Earth. Kind old home. Think of the Arctic. Of Labrador. Of Southern India in June. Think of smallpox and plague and earthquakes and ringworm and pit vipers. Think of a nice case of poison ivy all over, including your eyes. Status asthmaticus. Amoebic dysentery. The Minnesota pioneers who tied a rope from the house to the barn in winter because you could lose your way in a blizzard and die three feet from the house. Think (while you're at it) of tsunamis, liver fluke, the Asian brown bear. Kind old home. The sweetheart. The darling place.

Think of Death Valley . . . in August.

• • •

Day two. It began. I just couldn't keep my damned mouth shut. Everybody running around cheerily into the Upper Paleolithic. We're going to build huts. We're going to have a Village Fire that Lori Graham will tend because she is the Fire Virgin or something. Mrs. Graham is suddenly person-of-least-value. Victor says, "Excuse me, dear," with immense firmness and then goes about his business. He's going to go somewhere with John Ude to search for water. They won't drink it, of course, but will carry back samples and then we will analyze it, which is impossible because we don't have the equipment.

But it will certainly help the water-distiller; our tanks are almost empty. Mrs. Graham has suddenly become very cuddly
with Lori, who keeps squirming away, saying, "Valeria, *please!*"
With twenty-five hours of daylight there's no rush, and besides
we have to move everything outside (to find out if that will kill
us). Outside it goes, mattresses and bedding (to get rained on
or infested), tools and toolkit, all of this superficially showing
immense order but in fact about as rational as the ooze of algae from a pond. Our nice, destructible laboratory (like litmus
paper, use it once and it's done for) has told us that the sun
will not burn us, although it has a small amount of ultra-violet,
and more than the usual infrared (too low in the sky, anyhow);
that the local vegetation does not contain mineral poisons; that
the (local) air does not, either; and that the gravitation is 0.93,
which is so close to terrestrial as makes no difference.

Nathalie's digging experimental sanitation pits with a collapsible shovel. And every once in a while it does.

I seek out Ude, who's unpacking the first-aid kit, and say,
"Benzedrine and bobby-pins!" but the joke's too old for either
of us to have ever heard it, and too vulgar, base, and popular
for him to have ever read it.

I say, "Look, you've got an anti-pyretic, two wide-spectrum
antibiotics, pain-killers, and a nice little pamphlet about how to
make a splint out of a bunk-rail. *It's not enough.*"

"We'll make do," he said heartily, flashing The Smile.

I said, "My God, man, what will you do when Lori's wisdom
teeth come in?" and the child, who must have clairaudience
(she was a good five meters away) instantly emitted a nervous
"What!" and came over to join us. She had been watching Alan
Bobby Whitehouse ponder about trying to start to learn to just
possibly swing an axe without cutting his own foot.

"Your impacted wisdom teeth," I said. "*Everybody* gets impacted wisdom teeth. I'm the only adult I know whose wisdom
teeth came in straight. Of course I had gingivitis, and dental surgery, and fillings, and your mother has transplants. So
where are we going to get all this?"

"Huh?" said Lori.

"They might just lie there for years," I said. "I know someone who didn't get them until they were thirty. On the other
hand, you might have intense pain for a month before they

die and rot inside your gums and take a couple of molars with
them, which Daddy can knock out with a rock.

"O pioneers," I added rather sourly.

"Now come on," said John Ude.

(Funny. Everyone's around us now. I've attracted a crowd.
The old raise-the-voice bit. And I wasn't even thinking of it.) I
said, "I don't want to make a speech—"

"Then don't," said Cassie, who's been flapping our linens
in the breeze just to make sure we get a nice dose of the local
pollens.

"Well, fuck you then!" I said. "I will."

And I did. I must have talked for five or six minutes. I told
them (and more):

That a tagged planet is not colonizable but means only bear-
able gravity, a decent temperature range, and air that won't kill
you.

That survey teams sample only one square kilometer of a planet,
doubtless not this one.

That there were no mineral poisons, but that we couldn't test
for organics or allergens.

That there could be incompatible proteins, vitamin deficien-
cies, chelating agents, dozens of things that could mess us up bio-
logically in dozens of ways.

That if we could eat the local macro-life, the local micro-life
could eat us.

That we could die of exposure in the winter because we had no
way to make heat after our bungalow wore out and that was in
six months.

That we could die of heat in a summer whose length we didn't
yet know.

That a breech birth could kill. That a three-days' labor and no
dilation could kill. That septicemia could kill.

That heart failure could kill.

That none of us could even recognize flint, let alone know what
to do with it.

That plastic was a lousy building material.

That each of us carried five to eight lethal genes, and that even
without them, humanity had not exactly been breeding for sur-
vival for the past hundred years.

That there weren't enough of us.

And more. So much more.

I stopped. Too much of the old stiff-necked pride coming back. Giant Alan Bobby, with his axe, says, "I think you better go on," and I only hope Nathalie's training has included eye-gouging and larynx-smashing because this boy is beginning to find out—in two days!—that we are far, far from any law. I hope he can be shamed. I said:

"Well, I hope we find volcanic glass, because I could recognize that; I saw it once in a museum."

This falls flat.

"What do you suggest we do?" says the Professor, with The Smile. "You seem to think we have no chance." Humor her.

I nodded.

The professor repeated, "Just what do you suggest we do?"

Silence.

"Well, anything you please," I said. "Only leave me out of it."

"That," says Nathalie, "will make three women and two men, if we exclude Victor, which puts the numbers considerably lower, doesn't it?"

"Jesus," I said; "Oh Jesus Christ, I'm forty-two years old. Do you think I can have my first child now? Besides you don't want me; my father was a bleeder."

"Liar," says Nathalie. "I saw your medical records. You're not the only one who can get past the crew doors."

"All right," I said. (Nathalie the leader. Wait 'til Alan finds out he can beat you up.) "All right, so you think you have the chance of a snowball in hell. Maybe you do. But *I* think that some kinds of survival are damned idiotic. Do you want your children to live in the Old Stone Age? Do you want them to forget how to read? Do you want to lose your teeth? Do you want your great-grandchildren to die at thirty? That's obscene."

Here the ground came up and hit me, as it always does when you get carried away; it was Cassie, standing over me and shouting, "Shut up! Shut up, you!" I don't think she hit me, only pushed. I wasn't ready, that's all. Rabble-rousing that used to work, but that doesn't work now because it's the wrong rabble and the wrong rouse. Well, we all know that.

And in everyone's face the flash of realization: no law.

John Ude said, "Come, come, dears, don't lose your temper. She'll get over it. Nathalie, what do you carry?" And the whole thing was over.

Much later Cassie, her face grey in the grey dusk, woke me accidentally. She's hunting in the first-aid kit, her face drawn.

She says, "Oh, *you*! Go back to sleep."

I said, "What's the matter?"

"Migraine," she said. "I lost my pills. But this stuff is no good." (The last with a little wail; I judged it hadn't come on yet, maybe just the flashes of light or whatever it is she gets first.) I said, "Hold on," and fished something out of my belt. Should help.

"So what's that, cyanide?" she whispered, closing her eyes as if to concentrate. It must be starting.

"No," I said. "It's like your pills. Better than that all-purpose painkiller nonsense, anyway. Go on." I held them out in my palm.

"Bet it's poison," she said, but she took it. I saw her feel her way to the water-dispenser over the uneven ground, cup a little water in her hand, and throw her head back. She came back and lay down on the mattress, out under the nothing sky. Still clear. Still no stars. One keeps getting the oddest feeling that it must be cloudy, though we've only seen morning fog. The temperature doesn't go down much at night. There's too much light, though; it's like living naked. Sometimes this place looks like a stage set or a little alleyway or back yard of somebody's familiar country home; only in the true dark does it become real.

(Like the Australian outback, as I told them in my great lecture, which looks like New Jersey and can kill you in two hours.)

She said, "What happens now, I blow up?" She cocked an eyebrow at me.

"No," I said, smiling (I couldn't help it). "The pain stops, and if it doesn't you won't care; it's got a euphoric in it, too."

"Ooh, I'm gonna get high," she said. "Jollies . . ." (Taking hold already?) "Say, hon, how come you carry all that stuff?"

I explained: it's better than money. And you never know.

"All *you'd* need is a jack-knife," she said, "if you feel like cutting your throat, which is a goddamn cowardly thing to do, if you don't mind my saying so."

"Good night," I said, and turned over. I wasn't facing her anymore.

"Hey!" (comes the voice at my back). "You really want to kill yourself? You like getting hurt?"

"Yes, I want to do it before I get didded," I said. "And no. No follows from yes."

She chuckled sleepily. "Sorry I hit you. Forgive me, huh? What's that you said about the whozis and the old guy?"

(The old guy preached a sermon in his shroud a week before his death. The whozis were the Northmen; they used to say Deliver us from fire, plague, the fury of the Northmen, *and sudden death*. Those crazy people who took months to die. They had things to think about.)

"Go to sleep," I said. "Dream about your migraines."

And all the things. Such a beautiful world, really. But no music, no friends. If Earth had been hit by plague, by fire, by war, by radiation, sterility, a thousand things, you name it, I'd still stand by her; I love her; I would fight every inch of the way there because my whole life is knit to her. And she'd need mourners. To die on a dying Earth—I'd live, if only to weep.

But this stranger has never seen us before. She says: Hey, what are you funny little things? We are (O listeners, note) one quarter the height of the trees, we are hairless, give birth to our young alive, are bipedal with two manipulating limbs, have binocular vision, we regulate our internal temperatures by the slow oxidation of various compounds (food), and we live no more than a century at the very, very most (at least it feels that way, as the joke goes) and we are caught rather nastily, very badly, and sometimes even comically, between different aspirations. That is the fault of the cerebral cortex. (People are turning over, sighing, mumbling in their sleep, as the light slowly grows.)

Note: *ars moriendi* is Latin. It is a lost skill. It is ridiculed and is practiced by few.

It is very, very important.

It is the art of dying.

● ● ●

Day Three. Alan-Bobby found a medallion among my personal effects (he was sorting everyone's; somehow they haven't gone looking for water yet), and being a nice, obedient little boy, took it to Victor Graham, who took it to John Ude.

"What is it?" said they (in chorus, as I imagine).

He told them. He came over to me (I was making a deck of playing cards from Mrs. Graham's collection of antique post cards by first trying to peel the backs off) and swung the medallion at me, just far enough away so I couldn't grab it. Picture one early Christian, sitting cross-legged on the ground with lap covered by bedsheets, in case the cards didn't work out, and one professor—but not John Donne—who has decided to Tease.

"Now we know!" said John Ude, looking much less cosmopolitan than before.

"That? That's not mine," I said. (When in doubt, deny.)

"Come! Who cares?" he said. (Alan and Victor have gone back to whatever they were doing; I'm sure he asked them to leave "so I can get her to talk" or something.) "Be anything you like. Only it explains what happened yesterday, and if *I* explain to everyone else, they might feel a little better about you."

"You mean they'll dismiss me as a nut," I said. "All right, it's mine." He held it out to me, but I really have no particular use for the thing, and the metal chain might be useful to someone else. I said:

"Look, it's only a symbol. You know, the quartered circle, symbol of Earth and all that. Keep it. Use the chain."

"Don't you want it?"

"No. It's only a piece of jewelry."

"Then you're not . . . ?"

"I am. But I don't use the Tarot, believe in the I Ching, tell fortunes, make sacrifices, have rituals, believe in the Bible—not literally, anyway—the Tao Te Ching, or anything else. So keep it."

"An apostate!" he said.

"Oh, don't be silly." And I went on trying my fingernails on the post cards. Don't see why she can't collect holovision cubes like everyone else. Have to use sheets, anyway. I said, "Do you know how to play poker?"

But he had levered himself down on the grass next to me. No poison ivy so far. I said:

"Well, when are you guys going to find water?"

"A Trembler," he said. "My God, a Trembler in our very midst." I shut my eyes.

"The Quakers," I said, "called themselves the Society of Friends. They were called Quakers because some fool heard John Fox say he quaked in the presence of his God. Actually I like to think of myself as a temblor. Never mind."

"But you tremble."

"Oh, all the time."

"Do you believe in God?"

"No."

"But you believe in something?"

"Everywhere. Always. See Lao-tse: Tao is in the excrement, in the broken tile. Cleave the rock and there am I. Now go away."

"But tell me," he said, professional passion rising, "what does your church—"

"No church."

"Well, what do you say about—about, say, sex?"

"Nothing."

Mrs. Graham, within earshot, having found that the tool chest was water-tight by filling it with water and having Lori take a bath in it, along with most of our clothes, caught guess-what-word. She wiped her hands free of suds and strolled over.

"May I join you?"

"I'm asking," said John Donne, "what the Tremblers have to say about sex."

"Oh, that," said Mrs. Graham, looking knowing. It was real knowledge, too; you'd think Cassie, with her silver nipples, was the expert, but I think Cassie's frigid. She only sells it. Mrs. G has been a buyer, and buyers do what buyers want.

"Well, what *do* they say?" says Valeria.

"Nothing," I said. "Look, Mrs. Graham, I think you'd better keep your post cards to entertain your great-grandchildren. My fingers hurt and besides, there's no reason to sacrifice them; they're entertaining. I'll cut up a sheet."

"And about—"

"Look, John," I said, "we are not a church, only an attitude. Our principal subjects are work and mortality, not fucking. On those two I could tell you a lot but you heard it all yesterday and didn't like it. So why don't you get Nathalie to activate the broomstick and let her go look for water on it? It's a hell of a lot faster than walking."

"No, one of us will have to go," said he, "unless Mrs. Graham can drive . . . ?

"You see," he went on, "Nathalie's life and yours and Lori's and Cassie's are too valuable to put in danger. You are child-bearers. What does your religion say about that?"

"Genetic drift—" I said.

"Civilization must be preserved," says he.

"Civilization's doing fine," I said. "We just don't happen to be where it is."

"Your church—"

"My religion," said I, rising from my cross-legged position without uncrossing my legs (which rather surprised him, but it's easy for short people), "says a lot about power. Bad things! It says thou owest God a death. It says that the first thing a sane civilization does with cryogenic corpses is to pull the plug on those damned popsicles, and if you want to live forever you are dreadfully dangerous because you're not living now. It says that you must die, because otherwise how can you be saved? It says that without meaningful work you might as well be dead. It also says death hurts. And it says if you try to be strong and perfect and good and powerful, you're a damned fool and liar and the truth is not in you. So don't try my patience. It also says God is in you and you are in God, as the fish is in the sea and the sea is in the fish. Saint Theresa. It *also* says—"

"You're a remarkably eclectic bunch," said John Ude, laughing. "Do you believe all this stolen theology?"

"Why not?" I said. "I stole it myself."

"Anyway, that's your field," I added. He laughed. Indulgently.

"I'll spread the word," he said. He walked off—even a twenty-five-hour day ends eventually—and happened to pass by Lori in the tool chest, who crossed her arms over herself with great rapidity and looked sheer murder at him. Odd morés: body paint's O.K. but bathing is private. Surrounded by clothes, too, all colors, bobbing about in the water. Barely room enough for the lot of them, her knees under her chin.

Mrs. Graham said, "Do you believe in life after death?"

"No," I said.

"Oh. And when was the last time you slept with anyone?" I stared at her. She did not even look much interested.

I shrugged. "Years ago. Dunno. A long time."

"And *you're* living in the present?" she said, raising her eyebrows. "Well!" Valeria Victrix. My God, yes, she must have been. In her own element.

"There's other things," I said.

"Like—?"

"Oh look, Mrs. G—"

"Don't call me Mrs. Gee," she said. "It's tasteless, don't you think? Call me Valeria. And tell me what all those wonderful other things are, besides sex. And money. Because you can turn money into anything, you know."

Ah. I'm at the bottom of the pecking order now. Well, there are worse places, like the top. Inciting to riot. Destroying government property. (Symbolic?) I got arrested and was in jail overnight but I certainly wasn't at the center of it. No doubt one of those thirty-year cycles of rebellion Our Man John writes about. And as if they had no connection with physical fact. At the bottom you can hide effectively. I said:

"I was a Communist. I was in the 'twenties riots. Not very important, mind you, but it seemed to be going somewhere."

"Just after hydrogen fusion," said she. "Which took the steam out of your sails, didn't it? And made me rich. So you're a Communist. Good Heavens! And a Trembler, too? I thought they didn't go together."

"They do," I said. "Very well. And I'd prefer it if you called me what we call ourselves: Nobodies—I'm Nobody, who are you? Are you Nobody, too? How nice. Which is no bar to being a Communist. Which I was."

"You're not one any longer?" she said.

"Mrs. Gee," I said, "none of us is anything any longer."

"Frigid little woman," she said, stepping back. I said, "Oh, call me a salad, why don't you, that makes as much sense. And think of what I could call you."

"Motherrrr!" (Lori) She's tired of intimacies with everybody's washing.

"Oh, Valeria," I went on, "the heart is deceitful and desperately wicked, who can know it?" (She doesn't recognize, thinks

I'm crazy.) I said, more prosaically, "If you bother me again, I'll poison Lori's mind against you."

She got up slowly, saying, "At least I remember that I had something," and went to pull Lori out of the washtub. A sensible woman, really, but she's going to learn she has no money here. I yelled, "Hey, don't bug Victor, he's bigger'n you!"

"Victor Graham is *my father*," cried Lori, reaching a glass for the cold-water dispenser, to rinse herself. "Agh!" she cried. She shouted at me, "My father would never do anything wrong!"

"Absolutely, love!" I shouted back. That child will grow up in a perfect mess of illusions.

Did grow up.

George Fox went to jail because he could not forbear rushing into Anglican services and denouncing their priesthood as mummery; he said the great bell struck upon his heart. I was not there, of course; read it in a book. The scores of thousands of books and musical compositions that are preserved in nitrogen at the British Museum in London. Prisoners and political exiles write books. Would you write a book if you were alone on a desert island? Would you scratch in the sand?

Note: We communicate by organs that produce vibrations in the air (gaseous medium). We hear, roughly, sounds from 14 to 8,000 cycles per second. "Sound" is a series of concentric rings made of the rarefaction and compression of air, water, or some other medium. We can't exist completely submerged in water (this may come as a shock to you), as the oxygen we use in our metabolisms comes out of the air. We're not equipped the other way. We draw air into ourselves and push it out. We are extremely fragile, propaganda to the contrary. "Speaking" comes from a different place than "breathing." You must understand this. Those marks, "—", indicate speech. Communication. You must listen. You must understand that the patriarchy is coming back, has returned (in fact) in two days. By no design. You must understand that I have no music, no books, no friends, no love. No civilization without industrialization! I'm very much afraid of death. But I must. I must. I must.

Deliver me from the body of this. This body. This damned life.

• • •

Day four. Nathalie finally went off on the broomstick because
nobody knew how to operate it but her and me. I was not
allowed, naturally. I relented and showed Alan-Bobby how
to use the axe without cutting off his feet. He took it away
from me. He was cutting wood and so was Mr. Graham,
with the little hand hatchet; when they managed to collect
some branches, they lit them to see if they could make a fire.
Bravo! It burned. And the smoke gave Lori a violent allergic
reaction; she ran away clawing at her throat, crying, viciously
rotating her fingers in her ears, and making the tongue motions of someone trying (ineffectually) to scratch her soft
palate. Perfect for the long winter evenings. So they put the
fire out.

Mrs. Graham played gin with Mr. Graham, with the cards
I'd made from bed linen; she kept beating him.

Then she played gin with John Ude and kept beating *him*.

He said he wished to walk about, still being gracious; Mrs. G
tried to get Mr. G back into playing. He said, "I don't wish to."

"But I want to, dear," said Valeria quietly. (A simple, domestic request, repeated many times; Valeria in blue and gold, the
nail of her left little finger a gold sheath, inches long, Victor in
blue, the evening game, Mrs. Graham saying, "Get me a drink,
dear," and Victor eager and compliant. Now I know.)

Victor got up and went to talk to Alan-Bobby, who chuckled and nodded; then they got *really serious*, about drainage
ditches or log cabins, or burning other wood, for Victor would
not hurt his daughter, that I do know, not for the world.

Something odd about Valeria's face. See, Victrix?

She said, "Lori, I'm afraid your silly father has given you
hives."

"Daddy isn't silly," (says oblivious young Graham, cleaning
her toenails with a complicated spiral device that was apparently part of her personal baggage) "and I don't think you
should ask him to play cards if he doesn't want to. You can be
awfully mean, Mother."

I walked over to—no, I thought of walking over—

She came over to me. "Do you play gin?" I shook my head.

"You see how they treat me," and she tossed back that old-young face, that surgically lifted neck, with hair that has begun to come in gray at the roots. It's a beautiful gesture and I myself would be quite content simply to admire it no matter the age of the one who makes it, but I don't think the men will feel the same way.

"Oh, they're bored," I said. "It's nothing. Cultural reversion. We're in the late nineteenth century is all. Do you want to bet how far back we'll be next week? Five to ten it'll be the eighth A.D."

"You're crazy," said Mrs. Graham, not without affection, and went into the bungalow to make friends with Cassie.

I hid the crucial parts of my pharmacopoeia under a rock, in the tin box I will use for the vocoder, eventually. I thought of telling them I'm a vegetarian, just to make them discount even more of what I do (and they would!) but I couldn't do it with a straight face.

An endless afternoon.

John Ude: "You play Go? Chess?" I said No, dunno why, never learned.

Lori remarked that she didn't see what was wrong with the Australian outback because she'd been there, in the special hotel, and it was very, very nice.

I donate my mini-sewing-kit to the communal possessions heap.

Finally, after Cassie had walked six ways around a bedsheet, deciding how to cut it up and sew it for herself, after everyone had memorized the kind of tree whose burning had made Lori sick ("This is very important" said her father), after Lori said, "Oh, I am like to die of tedium" only a dozen times, before we all went mad—

Nathalie returned on the broomstick, covered with dust. There's running water not far from here, *that* way (she gestures) which rises (she says) in a spring some two hundred kilometers to the North, in hilly country, and passes us only a couple of km away.

"Did you have to go all that way?" says Alan-Bobby, in grave complaint. "We've been just waiting around."

She throws over her shoulder, "Of course I had to," and sponging off the mask near the water tank, starts drawing on one of my playing cards where the stream is, where we are, and in which direction everything is. "North" is provincial. She means Pole-wards. At this time of year you can't tell East or West from the sun; though perhaps the sunset (a little to the right) and the sunrise (a little to the left) could tell us if we are facing North or South. Arbitrary. I study it very carefully.

"Will you just stop that!" cries Nathalie furiously, for Alan is taking a bath in the tool chest, a real bath (insofar as he can fit in) and singing lustily, though nothing recognizable. He's tune-deaf. Nathalie shouts, "Goddamn it, you're wasting water!"

"But we've got water," says he, bewildered. "You just said so."

"We've got the raw material for the distiller," she said. "That's all. We haven't even measured the flow yet. Now get out of there!"

He does, tipping the soapy water on to the ground, where it might make the grass wither or blow up (but it doesn't) and prepares to fill the tool box again.

"You . . . !" says Nathalie, white. "You imbecile!"

"I don't think," says Alan, slowly, like a man to whom a new idea has just occurred, "that you ought to talk to me like that."

"We could've put that back through the distiller!" (Which is what we've been doing with our chemical toilet.)

"I think you are much too bossy," says Alan, sponging himself off with a few inches of cold water. He's looking at the ground and something's happening in his head. John Ude has backed off, smiling nervously. Victor's frowning.

Nobody likes her, not Cassie, not Mrs. Gee, not her husband, certainly. Lori and I don't count.

Dried off and in his shorts, Alan advances up to dirty, dust-streaked Nathalie, who has always been Top. He looks sly.

"Say, how come you're boss?" he says.

"Brains," she says. "How come you're such a damn fool?"

"I could take you over my knee and spank you," he says.

Nobody is interfering.

"Idiot," says she. Clearly, in government training schools people don't do these things.

She turns her back on him, superbly.

"Look, nobody else can fly that thing," I say, very quickly.

"And since you won't let me because you don't trust me, you'd better—"

"Turn around," he says.

She props the broomstick against a tree, stripping off her shirt and beating the dust out of it.

"Turn around, you bitch!" he says.

Surprised, she does. Not even afraid. Only surprised.

And Alan-Bobby, who could probably uproot a tree, with those shoulders and arms and that neck, and the little face in between looking peculiarly lost—but very angry now—socks her right in the jaw, knocking her down.

He's red. He says, "Maybe now you'll treat other people with respect. Now that you know there's other people in the world."

She whispers, sprawled on the ground, white as one of my playing cards, "You bloody, blazing, impossible ass—"

He hits her powerfully on the side of the face, snapping her head about.

"That's enough," says Victor, he and John Ude, by some mysterious calculus, speaking almost at the same moment, and each coming forward to hold one arm of this baby colossus. Enough for what? Alan looks happy. I mean it: not triumphant, not overbearing, simply happy. He glows. The twenty-first century can't have been kind to this enormous fellow, and now he's discovering other interesting things to do: chopping down trees, lifting rock with his bare hands, fighting, knocking down women. Too bad he's so young; Victor Graham now, there's a hypertensive if I ever saw one; once his medication runs out, we might do a job like the old Jewish story: the Rabbi and the Count both tied to chairs, alone in the Count's cellar for a whole night, and in the morning the rabbi serene and fresh and the Count a dead man. Apoplexy.

But Alan's useful.

Any day now he'll discover Protecting Women. I hope.

Valeria Victrix got the first-aid kit, and she and I anointed and bandaged Nathalie, who was still shaking—more from anger than from shock. Cassie pushed us aside, claiming she could do it better. She was right.

I said, "Nathalie, I thought a government trainee would know—"

"I will, I will," she said.

"My God, why didn't you duck?" I said. "Or just drop under his punch? Or give him a good knee-over when you were on your back? Or stick your fingers in his eyes?"

Well, he had surprised her. Cassie thought any woman who even got into such a position was a fool to begin with. "Just tell him Lori is watching," she said. "And cry a lot. You're both cuckoo."

I said, "Look here, Nathalie, just how much training have you really had?"

Silence.

Of course. She was going *to* it, not coming *from* it.

I said quickly, "Never mind. Don't speak; your mouth is puffing up."

Sitting, holding rags soaked in cold water to her face. Streaked with dirt. John, Victor, and Alan making ecstatic plans how to move everything nearer the stream. We go to bed when the sun reaches a certain clump of trees; there's hours of daylight yet to go and nobody can tell if the day is getting shorter or longer. It remains warm, too light, but better that than that dreadful, empty, black sky.

You see the rewards of being Nobody.

●   ●   ●

The penalty: everybody comes to me for advice. Because my public word would not be trusted, I can be told anything privately. Alan whispers:

"Hey, wake up. Please?"

Dusk all around us. Scarlatti in my head. I said, "What?"

"Are you awake?" he whispered. I mumbled something and opened my eyes. Dusk or dawn, everybody's mattresses scattered all over the ground, farther apart than last night. I've got to get away from these insane people. Alan is lying by my mattress on the damp ground, his woeful face propped in his hands. He says, in a low voice so as not to waken anyone:

"Do you think what I did was really so bad?"

"Yes," I said. "Absolutely."

"Lori chewed me out something awful," he said. "So did Mrs. Graham. And Cassie won't speak to me."

I sat up. I said, "I bet Ude gave you a lecture on civilization and Vic said you'd have him to reckon with if you tried it again."

"How'd you know!"

"Oh, just guessing," I said.

"Well, do you think it was so bad?" Looking anxious.

"Yes. Now let me sleep. Git."

"Hell, you sound just like Nathalie! I'll tell you, maybe it wasn't right, but I bet it taught her something!"

"What did it teach her?" I said. "Never to approach you without a broken bottle in her hand? Now Lori thinks you're real sweet. And Vic Graham knows that some day you're going to pull something like that on him. It taught us all to love and trust you. Right?"

He sat back on his heels. He said sulkily, "I could do it to you, too, you know."

I said, "Really, Victor? Sorry—slip of the tongue," and was on my feet, holding straight out in that treacherous light the screwdriver I had abstracted from the tool chest on day one.

You surely don't think I'm fool enough to walk about without a weapon, do you?

He reached for it, and I gave his hand a good slash. He withdrew it, extremely astonished.

"Oh, go away," I said. "I haven't the slightest intention of hurting you and you don't have the slightest intention of really hurting me. You're just showing off. You're a good, big, strong, decent, beautiful man, and you can pride yourself on that all you like. But don't forget; even though she's exasperating, *Nathalie is smart* and if you start throwing your weight around nobody else will like you and she'll take advantage of that. Remember: you're not stronger than all of us put together. Besides, Lori's stuck on you."

He lit up. "Yeah!"

"So go to sleep now, huh?"

He said, "How old do you think Lori would have to be before she can have babies?"

"Sixteen," I said (guessing). "Now go to sleep."

Day five: we'll move everything nearer the river, like lemmings. Nathalie will start turning bruise-blue in the face. Alan will creep about like a wounded pup, ostracized by all, scorned by Lori Graham, the worst burdens loaden on his back, meke as the knyght that suffereth for his ladye's sake.

Which won't last.

• • •

Day five: we worked eighteen hours, slept, worked again. Alan
has reverted to the intensely polite, self-suppressing youth everybody knew and loathed. My feet hurt. I tried to explain
about orthopedic malfunctions and was told I was malingering.
Then my ankles swelled out most satisfactorily in the evening,
looking distressingly like small cantaloupes, and everyone was
most apologetic. I said No, no, I had to carry my share. Then
my ankles got even more so. Cassie washed them, the great
nurse, sexpot, earth-mother. We went to bed. She says: "Sssst!"

Me: What?

She: You ever had an orgasm?

Me: Can't remember.

She: Liar. I mean during fucking. I never did. Women are
all liars about it, like Vicki Graham. She just pretends, to show
off, you know.

(Silence.)

She: Ever want babies?

Me: I dunno. Sort of. Not really.

She: I do.

(Silence.)

She: They don't let you, if you're poor. But here—

Me: I see. Well, good luck. How are you going to handle
the men?

She just laughed. Then she said with perfect certainty,
"Those babies'll love *me*, not their daddies." She nudged me.
"Hey, mad-head, Ude and Graham are going to take your pills
away from you in the morning."

"And who told them, you bloody traitor!" said I.

"Sssssh!" She looked around uneasily, then whispered, "I
did."

She added, "But I told you too, didn't I?"

• • •

Day six: I am set upon from behind, bound, and searched,
protesting indignantly. They slit the lining of my jacket (Cassie:
"Oh, don't take on so; I'll sew it up again!"), violate my leather
belt ("Hey, look, it's got pop-outs," says Alan), and pinch my
body-suit up and down (without me in it, of course). They

collect all the psychedelics. I cry, very very hard. They free my hands so I can blow my nose and I whack Cassie, who looks startled. Then they let me put on my body-suit and Victor Graham stands very impressively in front of me, hands out: "More."

"Me?" I said. "Me have anything more? I swear—"

Finally I unscrew my left shoe-heel and give them Cassie's headache medicine. Then I unscrew my right shoe-heel and hand over a glass vial. Victor starts to crush the thing, and this part of the scene is genuine, believe me; I yelled "Don't! Stop!"

Consternation.

I said, "That's lethal. It's a nerve poison, works right through the skin. You don't have to drink it. Victor! Just put it down. No, it's not bio-degradable, so you can't put it in the chemical toilet. Just leave it in the sun for a while. That'll ruin it. *But don't let anybody touch it.*"

Victor confers with John Ude, both of them gingerly handling the vial. Ude nods. I've told the truth. (And I have. What I did not tell them was how many more I've got hidden back at the old site.) I started to cry harder, which isn't difficult because I'm thinking of how damned unfair it is that I shall never hear again my melancholy Dowland: *semper Dowland, semper dolens.* Ever Dowland, ever doleful. No tee-hee-hee-quoth-she for him. I noticed through my tears that Nathalie appears to have formed some kind of alliance with John Ude, her moral impressiveness having proved unequal to Alan's muscles. The two intellectuals. The two bureaucrats. Tee-hee-hee in the mattress. They don't want to set me free, but that *is* foolish, as I tell them at great length, and I cry a lot harder, and even rock back and forth, which is nine parts fury, until Cassie says, "Oh stop it, hon, I'll fix your jacket. What were you going to do with those things, anyway? Kill yourself by an overdose?"

"No," said I. "I just feel humiliated." She put her arm around me, which is enough to make you feel an awful bemmon. She then promised to fix my jacket.

I gave them back the screwdriver.

Oh, it went like a charm!

John Ude, still uncontrollably curious, says to me on the last trek back to the old place: "Really, I cannot understand why you want to die."

"Neither can I," I said.

"Well, then?"

I said, "John Donne, John-John-with-your-britches-on, John-Whittington-turn-again-lord-mayor-of-London-Town, we *are* dead. We died the minute we crashed. Plague, toxic food, deficiency diseases, broken bones, infection, gangrene, cold, heat, and just plain starvation. I'm just a Trembler. My God, you're the ones who want to suffer: conquer and control, conquer and control, when you haven't even got stone spears. You're dead."

"For dead people, we're acting pretty brisk," says Ude, with The Smile. Haven't seen that for a while; Nathalie must've bucked him up quite a bit.

"It's one of the symptoms," I said. "Galvanism. Corpse jerking. Planning. Power. Inheritance. You know, survival. My genes shall conquer the world. That's death."

"Hear you were quite big in that power and planning stuff about fifteen years back," he says.

"Then you heard wrong. I walked out one day and gave it all up. Hideously ineffectual."

"Still—"

"For everything there is a time and a season under Heaven; now you ought to know that."

He keeps on smiling The Smile. No recognition.

I said, "You're not a historian of ideas."

"Clever," says he. "I wondered when you'd tumble to it. I was what you'd call a bureaucrat. That's why Nathalie and I get along. She says we think alike."

"Sure, after yesterday," said I. Ude halted.

"Don't push us," he said. "Don't you push us too much now."

"Then leave me alone," I said. "Just leave me alone and I'll have no reason to push anybody, huh?"

But they won't be able to leave me alone. I know. Not because of the child-bearing, because of the disagreement. The disagreement is what matters.

How far will I push them? To where? All the way?

•   •   •

Day seven: as lunatics or lemmings will, we dragged our glass-and-plastic bungalow, the only dwelling with a heater this side of God-knows-what, two kilometers to the stream, the travois

being its own light-but-stubborn bottom. It took all day. Too
tired to do anything else. Lying on the mattress outdoors,
Nathalie sketching in the dirt the plans of sanitary latrines
(downstream). Quickly goes in and washes and disinfects her
hands. No one has yet deliberately ingested one morsel of anything in this place; still we must have been breathing in and
swallowing a good deal, and no one's dead yet. We live on the
freeze-dried. How to test it out? A fruitless (sorry) question.

They asked me to sing. My memory was stuck on Dowland; I thought of "Flow, My Tears," "In Darkness Let Me
Dwell," "A Heart That's Broken"—well! This is not good
public relations. "Come All Ye Sons of Art"? Nothing with
polyphony. Finally I sang "Sweet Kate" with all the tee-hee-
hee. Taught Cassie, who has a good natural voice, to come in
on it, and added a few nasty Renaissance songs about jealousy
(dreadful people), "Farewell, Unkind," and finished with a
sudden burst of remembrance, swooping in great fake arcs,
those posh-velveteen melodies:

> Blue desert
> And you and I . . .

(Where on earth did I learn "The Desert Song"?)
Lori sang Gilbert and Sullivan and forgot the middles.
"Oh, you *can* sing!" cried Alan, in a burst of admiration (at
me, not at Lori; the mystic maiden can, of course, do anything).
Schubert! Of course. I said, "More tomorrow." But can I do
the eleven-note jumps upward on an o-umlaut? Never. Ah! Sea
songs and folk songs.
(Did I learn them in high school?)
Good night, court jester.

•   •   •

Day eight: the great womb robbery. The day started out well
enough, with me limping so badly (at least I tried to) that I was
excused work by John Ude, told, "Oh, that's too bad," by several others, and ended up playing cards with Lori (I mean the
bedsheet cards). For some reason nobody mentions she's never
expected to do any work, God knows why. She kept beating
me at Casino, while I rubbed my ankles.

"Are those orthopedic shoes?"

I said uh huh.

She yelled excitedly, "I've got the ten of diamonds!" and took in an eight of clubs and a two of hearts. (That's three points.) She looked at me sideways, then stuck her nose up in the air.

"So you want us to kill ourselves!" she said, with contempt.

I just made a face and threw up my hands.

"You think nobody'll find us?" she added, a little sharper.

"Oh, I was just talking," I said. She was counting up her winnings so far. She said, frowning, "You're a coward!" and put her cards down in a neat little pile, with a stone on top of it.

I said uh huh again.

"The one thing my Mummy and Daddy taught me when they got me from the crèche when I was seven," she said, still sharply, "was never to give up on anything. And never to be a coward." Five years of money, that's five years of enforced childishness. She started shuffling the cards in a very slow method invented by herself: put them in piles of three each, with a pebble on top, then take one off the top of each pile, then subtract every fourth card and put *them* on the bottom. I can't figure it. Daddy had set up a kind of awning with four stakes chopped from a tree and one of the sheets; we were sitting under this and watching the others sweat at the foundation of the communal house, about fifty meters away from the water and several meters above it on a slight elevation. Nathalie had suggested some kind of wooden rockers under the house, like the type used in Colonial New England: good for winds, for shifting ground, and floods. I don't know what they think they're going to insulate it with—wood shavings, chopped by hand?

Lori started to deal the cards. You have to pick each of them up with both hands and hold it taut: otherwise it drapes and you can see the other side. Managing a handful of them isn't easy. I said:

"Shall I tell your fortune?"

"Huh?" said she.

"Do you know how to read palms?"

She shook her head. "That's silly." She stuck out her hand, then giggled and drew it back.

"All right," she said, after a moment. "Go ahead. But I know what you'll say!"

"Hmm," I said, "do you now, little miss." That struck her as excruciating: Me, the gypsy. She put on an expression very like her mother's only far more exaggerated: eyes rolled up, corners of the mouth pulled down.

I said, "You have an immensely long life-line." (I cannot tell a life-line from a thumb.) "Here," I said at random. "You will die sometime in your eighty-ninth year. You will be well-known. Even famous. Extraordinary!"

"Known to how many?" said Lori quickly.

"Millions," I said (acting out vast surprise). "Your life-line is interrupted here by . . . by relative isolation for a period of years . . . not many years, perhaps eight or nine. And then there's a great blossoming of renown, almost as great as what I see at the end of your life."

"Well, obviously we're going to be saved," she said pedantically.

"So it would seem. Here" (I think I was somewhere in the middle of her palm) "is the line which indicates either children or good work, fruitful work. It branches four—five—no, many more times. But I don't know if that means children or work."

"Work," she said promptly. "I'm a musician."

"Oh," I said.

"Yes," (and she nodded); "I'm a composer."

"Are you? Think of that!"

"Well, I will be," she said. Then she added, "That's the same thing. But I'll tell you a secret—" (she all but whispered this, leaning over the piles of cards) "*I don't like commercial music.*"

"Oh," I said. What hearts did *I* wring when I was a child? Just a biological device, Nature keeping us old ones in the service of the young.

She said, frowning, "You look funny."

Then she added, without the slightest transition, "I like serial music. You know, the late twentieth-century stuff where it goes deedle deedle deedle deedle deedle deedle deedle deedle for half an hour and then it goes doodle just once, and you could die with excitement."

"Uh huh," I said.

"I've written one—well, half of one—composition." She stuck out her hand. "Go on."

I said, "You know, Lori, what I think your fortune means is that you will not only be famous for music, but also for having been rescued here. They'll probably call the place after you. They do things like that, you know."

"Of course," she said. "And everybody gets rescued. As my father was trying to tell you."

"John Ude was trying to tell me, I believe," I said.

"*My father!*" She stuck out her hand. "Go on."

"It's a musician's hand," I said shamelessly, "that's true. And the rest . . . well, I can't see much out of the ordinary except riches, of course . . . you know that . . . I think you will write a book about your experiences—*here*" (pointing) "but of course I can't tell whether that's a book or music. The wealth line increases at that point. And marriage—"

"I'll *never* get married."

"Yes, there's hardly anything. Though your love line is quite another thing. But who, of course, or even what, I can't tell."

"Artistic passion?" said she.

"Mm hm. And the rest . . . well, it doesn't tell us anything we don't know. Sensitive. Intellectual. But animal vitality, mustn't forget that. That's about it."

"Oh," she said. She was disappointed.

"It changes," I said, "almost day to day. Most people don't know that. Small changes, of course, nothing big. But that's all I can see today."

"You'll do it again in a week," said Lori decisively, beginning to deal her cards. It did not seem to occur to her that she was giving me orders. I pictured her giving orders to Alan-Bobby.

No.

She dealt the cards, a very finicky young woman, concentrating deeply.

Suddenly she said, "Are you really a coward?"

"No," I said.

"Yes you are," she said. "Pick up your cards. If you teach me to read palms, I'll read *your* palm. That'll tell us."

She won the next game, too.

We were well into our third and Lori was singing something from Gilbert and Sullivan about not telling him, her, or it, because etiquette didn't permit, and not even hinting, whispering, or pointing it out—yes, very apposite—and I was bored —when Alan shouted "Over here, everyone!" because he had the big voice. They had been slacking work for some time, with a lot of talk between Nathalie, the ex-professor, and Victor. (One to dig, two to chop, and two to carry either logs or dirt in the tool chest: Nathalie, Alan, Valeria—with the hand hatchet—Victor, Ude.) Symptoms of a conference.

"Bring your tent!" shouted Alan conscientiously.

So we did—rather, I did; Lori wouldn't touch it for fear that she might break out in hives. I told her while I was uprooting it (and not entirely out of compassion; she could be a real whiner when she chose) that she'd live to be eighty, name all the plants in the region, lose her allergies as she grew up, and end up writing the first book about Lori's Planet.

The court. Under another jury-rigged tent. After this my memories get a little muddled. Disturbance: ripples in a pond. I smiled mechanically. Won't be thought a good, reliable witness—

(*By whom?*)

reliable witness.

Victor's very big. *Very* polite. So you can't get at him, perhaps. Valeria was off to one side, with Cassie. Victrix patted the ground next to her invitingly and Lori stared carefully in another direction. Alan, awed, with his mouth open; John Ude peculiarly cool; and Nathalie grimly watching the ground.

Mister-not-Professor Ude said, "I call this meeting to order."

Oh. Oh my. Important.

"You're chairman?" I said. "Well! Who made you chairman?"

Nathalie: "I did."

That is, they both did. Things are going to be very interesting.

Victor: "That's a valid objection. I suggest we begin by selecting a chair."

Silence. Then Nathalie said wearily, "I nominate"—Guess Who?—well, he was nominated, seconded, and voted in. Almost unanimously.

John Ude: "Do you have any more objections?"

Me: "No."

(Almost unanimously means me and Lori, Lori because she wanted her father to be, and I abstained.)

"We have to talk about something very important," said Ude. "I mean having children."

Hand up, me. He recognized me—does this sound as crazy to you as it does to me?—and I said, "Priorities backwards. First we have to poison Lori."

"Huh?" she said; "you're crazy."

"Mr. Chairman," I said, "point of order. Is it necessary for us to pretend that we've never met before?"

He smiled. Oh, the universes tremble when John Ude smiles! He said, "I suppose we can afford to be somewhat more informal. In fact, I think it will be a very good thing. Please go ahead."

I said, "I'm only trying to suggest that before we start any babies, we'd better start finding out what we can eat around here."

(Lori, sotto voce, with a dig in the ribs, "Why'd you say poison?")

Cassie said, "Sure, why the baby?"

"I was joking," I said. "I meant she's allergic to so many things. She should be the last person to eat anything."

Nathalie: "Will you volunteer to be the first?"

"No," I said. "Will you?"

Nathalie got up, very angry. "We have food and water for five months and three weeks! Perhaps you'd like the rest of us to eat grass and leave it all to you?"

"I waive it," I said. "I leave it alone. Give me the broomstick and I'll go up to the head of the stream and drink the water without the purifier. If I start hurting, I'll kill myself."

"This is no time for joking." (John Ude)

I said, "I'm not joking. It's a genuine offer."

Silence.

"About the children," said Ude. "Mister Graham, as the oldest of us, has offered to donate his genetic material first."

Cassie giggled.

Nathalie glared at her. But Nathalie also sat down.

(Was Victor on a special diet, on the ship?)

I got up and ambled toward the stream. By all that's alive, a melodramatic "Stop!" and then "Stop her!" from John Ude, and here was Alan-Bobby running ahead of me, like some crazy postman with a Special Delivery (excuse me) and turning sheepishly to stand in front, his arms stretched out.

"All right," I said, "all right, I can go taste the river when you're asleep, can't I?" and I headed back toward the improvised council tent, feeling in my palm the pellet-gun. Reflex. Not here, not now. Back in the sleeve of the jacket you go.

How'd it get there?

Oh, I forgot to tell you. . . .

Between yesterday and today, when everyone was asleep, I went back to the old site and dug everything up. Including my pharmacopoeia. Left them lying on the ground with dreams of "The Desert Song" ringing in their ears. (I had mist-spray hypnotics in my underwear. I'm not *that* quiet.) I tiptoed off, anyway, felling Alan-Bobby as he sat up, probably talking in his sleep, with a swift squish to the nostrils and very daring, went off on the trudge to the old camp, where it took me forever to pry up that rock. I left in the dusk; I returned at the end of the dark: the sky ragged where the sun rises and sets, one patch of cloud red, red as blood, red as fury. I gave them each a last spray as I came, too. Except Lori. (She might be allergic.) She was wiggling and muttering uncomfortably to herself. Watched her face slowly settle itself and become clarified as the light grew and grew. Without getting anywhere—I mean the light—for hours and hours more.

"Hey, you better go back," says Alan.

"Oh." I sigh. "Okay." And go back, helpless.

Now I'm going to be first. I said, "Well, you'll have to wait until I'm off the pills. And then it sometimes takes a few months to restore fertility. And we *don't* want septuplets, so that's another couple of months."

"You're not taking any pills," said Nathalie.

"Because you've never seen me do it? Whew!" said I. (That last's a whistle.)

"What are you taking?" said Ude.

I made up a name.

"Then you don't," (he said, blinking slightly but looking steadily at me the while) "have to worry about multiple births. There haven't been any on that since '07. I don't see why you and Victor can't start now, if you like."

Victor said politely that he certainly wouldn't mind as long as I wouldn't mind.

I said I would mind.

"Why?" said Nathalie.

"Personal preference," said I.

"It's her religion!" said Cassie, a little indignantly. "You should respect a person's religion, you know."

"She's probably *left-handed*." This is Mrs. Graham, spitefully. Cassie obviously wasn't sure what "left-handed" meant; she leaned towards Mrs. Graham, who whispered to her.

Cassie colored to the roots of her hair—and her neckline (a sheet).

"In a month, if you don't mind," I said to Victor, with a sort of little bow. "When it'll do most good." Now he can't have liked that. But he looked unmoved and nodded his head. Polite. Calm. Great, handsome, hollow monument of a man. Perhaps he's run out of something. Perhaps he's going to be ill. Hypertensive or cardiac, I can almost smell it. Or some other fatality hanging in the air and nobody wants to talk about it in front of the daughter. Get him before he dies.

"Before that month, then," said John Ude, grinning in my direction, "Nathalie has suggested herself, and afterwards the other lady, Cassie. The—uh—persons involved can certainly find privacy almost anywhere, I suppose. Anyway, it's none of our business."

Cassie, who was folding the hem of her improvised dress under and over with her fingers, again and again, said:

"I'm going to be called by my full name. I don't like Cassie. That's only a professional name."

"Of course," said John Ude.

"Tell us," said Victor.

Alan looked blankly receptive.

"My name is Cassandra," said Cassie.

Nobody caught it. Lori said, "That's a nice name," (possibly to annoy her mother). I inhaled when I should've swallowed and for thirty seconds there until I stopped coughing John Ude was very tender and careful with his walking womb.

"Cassandra's always wanted children," he said pleasantly to me when I could breathe again. Nathalie was behind him, looking over his shoulder.

I tried to call him a son-of-a-prick and only croaked.

"Yes?" he said, very alert—but he always seems alert; it's part of the window-dressing.

"Listen," I whispered, just managing to speak. "I'll go away. Take the broomstick and send it back, very slow, so you can catch it. Go upstream—downstream—doesn't matter—try the water. Take no food. Just leave me."

"No!" said Nathalie.

"Why?" I coughed some more.

"If I've got to do it, you've got to do it," said Nathalie.

"You . . . don't have to." And I cleared my throat. At last.

"We'd better keep an eye on her," said Nathalie to John Ude.

I think I put my head in my hands. Suppose they found my gun? My things? Wait long enough and it won't matter. Although I can always do it. Anyone can do it. Easy enough to kill if it doesn't matter about being found out. Then perhaps they'd kill me, and it would be over, and that's all right.

But I'm afraid of waiting too long. Eroding. Purpose all gone. Slipping into no-decision, no-purpose; hard enough as it is. God knows. I think everyone loves it here because their choices are all made for them; we were never very comfortable with our fate in our own hands, were we? Better to act on the modern religion: an incarnation of the immortal germ-plasm. Nostalgia for the mud. Simplicities.

I said, "Cassandra!" and burst out laughing, coughing again.

"You're going mad," said Nathalie, with a certain satisfaction and she and John Ude stepped backwards so they could talk, I suppose, about *keeping an eye on me.*

And nobody knows. Nobody knows anything about anything.

"Aren't you going to play cards with me?" said Lori, suddenly turning up with the cards in a sort of bag she'd made out of a scarf of her mother's. It was bright, bright blue. Royal blue.

"Sure," I said. "Why not?" And did.

• • •

Day nine. I took my turn digging and carrying. I was watched, always by someone. Nathalie and Victor disappeared dutifully over the hill while the rest of us snored (presumably).

• • •

Day ten. Watched. They overestimate their perseverance. At bedtime—the sun still circling around the same eternal altitude —Nathalie talked angrily about tying me to something for the night so's I wouldn't disappear. I told her not to be a fool: anything she could tie, I could untie.

People were embarrassed.

• • •

Day eleven. Idiot labor. A Long House none of us will ever live to enjoy. The food goes faster this way. A midday siesta under the tent, all of us huddled together in the shadow. But it merely gets hotter and hotter until sunset.

The sun is not changing its position, not fast enough to be timed, anyway. The weather stays the same. No rain, but the stream keeps up. By some eerie common consent Valeria has become the cook—good for nothing else, I suppose. That is, she prepares the packets of freeze-dried and pours stream water into the purifier. No one dead yet.

The idyllic desert island. Odd how that started out "deserted" and ended up "desert." Hence the conventional sand and palm trees. No, "desert" once meant only wild.

That it is.

• • •

Day twelve. Victor's ill. He sat all day under the tent, dozing and taking some sort of pills. Angina, I'll be bound.

More hauling, more digging on that idiot building.

Early evening (when the sun stands at four o'clock above a particular hill; we are in a little valley with a close horizon): Flop. Flop. Flop. Flop. Valeria and Victor have already flopped. Discarded pill-bottle on the ground. Lori's being kept away, mostly by Alan, sometimes by Nathalie, who says that she ought to work for a change.

(Lori stuck out her tongue. I giggled.)

Victor looked unconcerned at this invasion of his privacy: or not concerned, rather.

Lori said carelessly, "Oh, Dad's had this before." Valeria is paying no attention to him or to any of us; she's asleep. I have

begun to be startled at anyone's coming up behind me, with a
kind of shrinking at the presence of the rest of them, but Victor Graham is magnificently vacant; doesn't care that there are
people around him.

We slept—we've gotten into the habit, it seems, of sleeping
in stages: part in the middle of the "afternoon," then a siege
before the dark, then a kind of premature wakefulness for a few
hours until the twilight begins and depresses everybody. I seem
to go to sleep faster than anyone, but I always wake a little earlier. Nervousness. I had my head by his knee.

Shocked awake.

Yawning. It wasn't anything, I thought.

Listening wakefully. Eyes open.

It's a little gasp from Victor Graham. He got up, holding (I
think) his left arm with his right, for I saw him pass over me,
and from that position on the ground, with my face down, it
was like feeling a cloud go over you at an enormous height;
I said he walked between us and over us, between two hills,
Equator-wards.

He stopped to retch.

All I have to do is lie here and pretend to sleep.

He's walking off between the hills. Going to die alone, I
suppose.

I got up carefully and picked my way to John Ude, put one
hand over his mouth, and with the other, pinched him.

"Ssssh!" I jerked my head at Victor. You must say for the
not-Professor that he takes things in quickly. We knew that
neither of us must wake Lori and that she's the lightest sleeper
of all because she hasn't worked.

"Where'd you put my stuff?" I whispered, off at the edge of
the group.

His wits are wandering. He had to go back and wake Nathalie. And all the time, you know, it was burning a hole in my
pocket, I mean my belt pop-out, the stuff he should be using; I was extraordinarily conscious of it sitting over my left
hip-bone.

He came back with Nathalie, and we ran. Victor had sat
down under one of the stumpy trees and was staring ahead of
him. Nathalie, fingers shaking, spread out on the dirt the stuff
they had confiscated from me and looked helplessly at Ude,

who was beginning to frame a question, but I had it out and the string around his arm, the stuff into the vein. These are collapsible, permanent syringes, foldups like accordion pleating.

Nathalie said, "Antisepsis—"

I said, "Lie down, you fool," to Victor, and he did. A little less livid, as the stuff got to him.

I said, "It's a stimulant. Can you swallow?"

"No," he said, still concentrating on the pain.

"You can," I said, selecting from the pile, "bite on this and breathe. It's a mind-bender; won't stop the pain, but it'll separate you from it. Takes the nastiness out of it."

He did. Nathalie bent over, but I shooed her away. "Do you want Lori?" I said.

"No."

"Your wife?"

"Won't come." He whispered, very carefully. The cyanotic grey was ebbing. I said:

"The stimulant is only temporary. I can give you more until we either run out of it or it wears you out, but I can't heal you. You may heal yourself if you lie very still."

He said, "Tell Lori—"

"What?" said Nathalie anxiously.

"Anything. Make it up."

I said, "Mister Graham has other things to do right now. We will tell Lori and Valeria that he thought of them, that his last words were of them, and that he loved them."

The dying man laughed. "Not—wife."

"But I can tell Lori, can't I?" I said.

He nodded, just a bit.

"Victor loves his daughter and gives the planet to her. He's proud of her and knows she'll do well. Okay?"

"Yes!" His color was stealing back, almost magical, but it puts a worse burden on the great arteries crowning the heart. I said, "I think you'd better go back and deal with the scene there. Both of you. When they wake up, you know; you can tell them whatever you like."

"I?" said Nathalie. "I'm supposed to be with him!" Victor's gaze was still so fixed that to get his attention you had to be right in front of him. Nathalie put herself in front of me, directly in his line of vision; she had the anxiety lines of the brows furrowed together, in that very expressive field of musculature above and around the human eyes. The eyes themselves, you know, show almost nothing.

John Ude said, "Perhaps I should stay—"

I said, "Are you afraid of Lori?" and then to Victor, "Who do you want to stay with you? Which of us?"

"You," he said.

"Of course. She knows the drugs," said John Ude with The Smile.

"You're not afraid," he said, "of me."

Silence.

"Leave that and that and that," I said, pointing. "Now get cracking! You've work to do."

"None of these is marked," said Ude finally, gathering up half my things. (He thought he had it all.)

"I know," I said. "I also sell knowledge." John Ude patted me on the shoulder: loathesome, loathesome!—said into my ear, "Good of you."

Victor said, with a smile, "Are you sorry? You know . . ."

"I think I am," I said. And almost was. Sorry for him, I mean. One thing dying people usually know, if they have any sense left, is what they want; and that is so rare in the human condition that it commands a certain kind of respect. Although I suppose they may know what they want only because there's so little left to choose from that the task's easy. It strips people down. And what I feel—or felt—about him, I don't know. An intense curiosity. Where he was going, where he came from, who he was. It's a world going out—though there are some worlds I know too well to care about, like Ude.

"I was poor," he said. "Didja know that?" I shook my head. Something of the old timbre back in his voice, still half a whisper. I could never find pulses in the wrist, so I put my fingertips on the great vein in his neck. He smiled. "Feels nice," he said. Then: "I worked on myself. Made myself good-looking, you know: clothes, accent, the works. Spent a lot on surgery; no whore could've done better."

He grasped my hand, then let his arm fall but still kept holding on to my hand, I think out of fear, though he wasn't feeling any pain; couldn't have talked that easily if he had.

He said, "I can satisfy anyone."

"Did you practice?"

He nodded. "Of course." What a way to spend a life. Here is the kernel of Victor Graham: I can satisfy anyone. Myself, I eat potatoes. Well? He must've read something in my face because he imprisoned my fingers more severely; thank God I don't wear rings. He said, "Do you despise me?"

"In comparison with *my* friends?" I said, and couldn't help it; I began to laugh. This pleased him.

Then I said, "I only wish it had been more fun for you."

"It was all right." The cyanotic tinge was coming back but he didn't seem to feel it. "Wasn't so easy the first few years, but when I met Val I knew I had it made. Worked like hell to get her, too."

"You took her name?"

"No. She's old-fashioned. I used to—was able to—order her around sometimes, then . . . think we flipped a coin . . . you know, I loved her but I can't remember now."

"And Lori?" I said.

"A beautiful child. Still a child. You'll look after her?"

"Of course."

"This is all for her," he said, with a stirring of the arm as if he would sweep it round him to indicate the horizon.

"She'll grow up better here," I said.

"Sure," he said without irony, "and her mother'll do some work. It'll do her good. Val'll live long." He sighed. He said, "You should take some of this. It's religious. I feel like a Christian."

"Instant religion? There's something like that in the trade name: Forgiveness without tears. Something. But I don't feel like forgiving anyone, you see. I'm nasty."

What I didn't say: how dull it can become after a while, these exaltations that leave nothing behind them. The headiness of anger. Perhaps I'm an addict. An anger addict. I said, "Victor, the analgesic will last for hours, but the stimulant's wearing off. I can give you more"—holding it up—"or you can fight it out alone, or there's this"—putting the glass ampoule by his free hand where his hand lay on the ground, that eternal mid-afternoon sun palely lighting it, the time just before the light becomes ruddy. In a few hours we would have our twilight.

"What's that?" he said. "The ultimate analgesic?"

I think that surprised me more than his use of "Christian." I said, "You clever man!"

He said, "If you hold my hand."

"Can't," I said. "It's a contact poison, works through the skin. You break the ampoule. If I held your hand I would run a considerable risk of being ultimately anesthetized myself."

"Death's your friend," he said.

I shook my head. "Never!"

"Don't want it," he said, trying to flick away the ampoule with his finger, so I rescued it—very carefully—and laid it to one side. Must remember where it is, too. Better still, pick it up and put it away in my belt. Which I did.

He said, "I haven't been much good to Val these last months." He was still looking straight ahead of him. He said, "I want to see the sun," so I turned him about with great care, Pole-wards—the sun was declining into what we had agreed to call the north, interrupted by a stumpy tree on the side of a hill. I moved him until he could see it, propping his head in my lap—he was a heavy man—I think leaving the poison with him would have been useless unless I'd put it in his hand; he was too feeble, for all his talking.

He said, "I'm going to die."

He was not that cyanotic. Perhaps the light concealed it, turning him rosy. This damned place has been looking stranger and stranger each morning, despite my trying not to see it that way—imagination? Like meeting a childhood friend: at first the resemblance is as clear as can be, and then after a quarter of an hour, you begin to wonder. I suppose you see all the other things time has laid down on the face.

He said, "Go away."

I didn't move. He was breathing with difficulty. I could hear his breath stop, catch, go on, then stop again, like an electric motor with a bad connection—too apt a comparison—catch a few times, go on, stop—

I think I was hypnotized by the tree's shadow as it crawled towards us, or the shifting motes of sun in it between the leaves, the sun having sunk behind the tree and each spot of light a camera obscura of the sun: round as a coin and twinkling.

He was trying very hard to breathe. No oxygen going to that brain. Then he stopped. Easy as pie. I knew Victor was still there, shut up inside himself, but the housing was shot. No good any more. He couldn't feel anything anyone could do to it. An eerie feeling, that heavy, motionless head in my lap; you never know how mobile people are (in sleep, in hypnosis, in the deepest, drugged state) until you feel them dead. "Dead weight" is the real thing. I know.

Two minutes.

Five. . . .

Gone. The last traces died out. Only the coral shell now; the thing making it had gone somewhere else. Or anyway, wasn't here. I let his head down on to the ground—he was staring straight up—and stretched, spinning about dizzily as if for all the world I could catch him as he flew off. Catch a sight of him. There's some complicated, biochemical reason for the loss of weight at death—though it feels the opposite—but if Victor in the shape of a butterfly was zipping off to better realms, I never saw him.

The sun still hung there, behind the tree. It won't set for an hour. I've been talking into my vocoder (back in the left-hand sleeve if anyone comes) all about this. Will put it back now. Go tell everyone else, ugh.

Peaceful for the first time here. My God, how peaceful. How quiet it is. Sinful to violate that quiet.

Inconvenient to me, anyway.

Sssst! Victor!

Bon voyage.

(There's some old play where that is sung to a sinking ship, more and more merrily as the ship goes down. "We hope you know how to swim," they say. Perhaps we all know how to swim, by instinct, the way newborns do. They do.)

God help us, a life after *this* one?

One's enough.

• • •

They found me, they said, asleep by the (dead) body. Nathalie was very angry. They shook me awake and I stumbled and yawned back to the others; Lori was crying next to her mother while Valeria said (pushing her daughter's head into her own lap, as if blinding her), "We want to remember him as he was." Amazing.

The sun gone, the twilight darkened. The Smudge comes out.

As we've named it.

•   •   •

Day thirteen. Time to try again. Victor was put in the earth but I wasn't allowed to help—I think I've become tapu. Either that or envy. (What an extraordinary idea, planting people in the ground as if you expected them to sprout! I think they should be left about to rot, day after day, so we'd get used to it and stop being afraid of it.) When the burial party came back and the shovel was passed to Nat for digging the latrine (some more) I went and sat at her feet. I was careful about my eyes because she might throw dirt at me with the shovel—on purpose or otherwise.

I didn't say anything.

"Well?" said Nathalie, dirt-streaked, the sweat darkening in patches on her black body-suit.

"Let me dig?" I said. She leaned on the shovel, looking down at me, then turned back to her work, making the dirt fly. She was extending the pit into a shallow channel which would later be lined with something; I'm not sure what they expected to do, maybe collect fertilizer. Standing, she was above me; if she'd been down in the pit, our heads would have been on the same level.

I said, "Just wanted to talk to you."

Then I said, "I envy you."

She stopped and looked at me, nonplussed.

"I mean," I said, "that it must be a great simplicity. Right? A good feeling. Not being a wretched, mixed-up mess like me. I mean to face the old problems instead of the new ones, to know what the solutions are. Even though it's so hard."

I said, "All right, I know I'm a trial to all of you."

Now I did not like the expression on Nathalie's face. I like to know what's coming, too. She threw down her shovel (which, hitting a projecting rock in the side of the pit, instantly un-hinged itself into two separate pieces) and stood there looking at me. I wondered if Nathalie were not perhaps the Spirit of Death around here: I mean hard work, looking to the future, planning about things, that sort of stuff. She said:

"You fool."

Then she said, "*Do you think I WANT to be here!*"

"Don't—I—" I said, leaning backward. If your legs are crossed, you can't get up unless you lean forward, so I was effectively tied in a knot; if I'd got up, it would've been right into Nathalie's face.

She said, "Oh God, you make me sick!"

I could roll sideways and get up.

"You," she said, but her voice had changed and her eyes were no longer all pupils, so I knew she was only going to talk and I could afford to stay there, to stay helpless; she said, "Oh, what do you know about it!"

I said, "I'm sorry." I looked meek. (And I was sorry, only none of them will take the cure, not one.)

She sank to her knees, but still leaning over me, which is something they teach them in government school, maybe; she said, "Do you know where I was going before I came here?"

I shook my head.

She sat down, sort of collapsed sideways. She said, "Well, I wasn't going to dig latrines. Or bear babies. Or plant crops."

(There are no crops.)

"I was going," she said, "to school. And not to learn how to lecture on music, little woman! Something quite different."

"Yes," I said.

"Do you? You can't. None of you can, not even Ude; he's a paper-pusher. I wasn't; I would've learned how to kill him with my bare hands, I would have learned to make explosives—yes, even here! I would've learned how to find the right stuff and make them—and when I was finished there wasn't one of you who would have dared to come within twenty meters of me, let me tell you—and Alan would be dead."

She pulled angrily at the grass before her, which may poison us.

"I'd love to see that other-fucker with a broken neck," she said.

I laughed—suddenly couldn't help it. She sprang to her feet. "Two minds with but a single thought," I said. She sat down: very slowly, but she sat down. Loosened a little.

Nathalie smiled.

"If only we had some—" said I.

"Plaster," she added, "and wax, we could—"

"Make a cast—"

"Of his—"

She laughed; in fact she roared, throwing her head back. Then she said:

"And a sperm bank." Very sober.

"There is that," I admitted.

A short silence.

"How was Victor?" I said.

"What?" said she. "D'you mean, was he fertile?" (They had looked at it from different viewpoints, apparently.)

She added sharply, "How is he? He's dead!"

I stared at the ground. Earth, grass, pebbles: could've been anywhere. Nathalie got up. "You see, one goes on," she said. "Unless one's afraid, like you. One learns that."

"Afraid?" I said.

"Yes." She strode to the pit, reached over the edge for the shovel, then straightened up and bent the thing until the handle clicked back together. With her left hand she pushed her hair behind her ears. "You're demoralized, like all civilians," she said. "You miss your luxuries."

She shoveled a spadeful of earth out on to the bank, tucked her hair behind her ears again (it always came loose and swung in her face), and leaned on the shovel: bitter, severe, very pleased with herself. She said:

"My parents were poorer than Cassie's. Did you know that? Of course not. But that's why you all need me, because I know how to fight. I didn't grow up in private, like that damn-fool little girl and I didn't grow up rich. I was in a youth group and I learned how to fight. You're bloody lucky you've got me."

I said, "You won a lot of scholarships, didn't you?" but she didn't like my guessing it and went back to digging, with her face set as if every bash at the dirt were at Alan-Bobby's backbone.

I said, "Survival—" and she said, "Survival's the name of the game. You'd better move; I'm switching to this side." So I did.

But for what? The sound of the digging stopped; Nathalie had straightened up and was looking at me again, the death's-head.

I had spoken out loud.

I said, "All right, all right, I didn't say it!" and scrambled to my feet. This is crazy comedy; one must, after all, do it sooner or later, and the madwoman in black is going to hit me with her shovel or fling it at my head because I want to get right in my soul before I die.

She said, "You walking cunt, I would like to kill you, too."

Her face is blanched to the color of paper; her eyes are black and white: all pupil. She's quite mad. If I shoot her, the others will come running. I said, "I'll dig," and she threw me the shovel, which did indeed almost hit me. I rapped the hinge to make sure it wouldn't fold up. Nathalie strode away over the freshly-turned dirt, head high, blazing, broadcasting hatred. "It suits you!" she cried, meaning (I suppose) that grave-digging was my proper occupation. (It used to be taboo, like executioners.) I dug at the channel—a little sloppily, for I haven't half her purpose—and you don't develop strength by being told off to play cards with Lori. They had, at least, the sense to put the latrine downstream, though the odd thing about this hole is that nobody is ever going to use it.

Did you know that hangmen were once taboo?

What do you know?

Do you know anything?

• • •
• • •
• • •

Who are you?

• • •

I should go back and erase all that silence; the vocoder makes a mark whenever I stop, like a punctuation mark but different; then it begins a new line. There must be too many of them. No, hell, let them stay. What happened later: we had our siesta; we dug some more; Lori asked me to sing and I did, the sun hanging in the sky, dropping no lower, remaining motionless over the same inky, fiery, spotted bush. Silhouettes. The same long shadows from dawn to dusk. I sang "Chu Chu Chu"; I sang "Love Is Splendid, Isn't It!"; I sang "What A Perfect Day This Has Been." Ude had a long conversation with Alan, who is becoming more and more authoritative and more and more pleased with himself. They spoke in low voices; I couldn't hear what they said. Making plans?

(We lay down to sleep.)

• • •

By writ and tort, by hullaballoo and brouhaha, I declare this tapedeck locked to all voice-prints but mine, locked *re* play-back, locked *re* printout, and may God have mercy on your soul.

So be it.

Day twenty. Eighteen. Nineteen? I can't remember. Too much going on. Managing people is a melancholy skill; it depends mostly on keeping your mouth shut.

The night after we'd buried Victor Graham I took off with the broom and the face-mask, making up a package of food, soap, a mattress, bits of plastic towelling, spare underwear, things like that, all tied up in a sheet with one set of corners tied above the other. I went upstream. I got up in the middle of the night and used up the last of my sleepydust, spraying them as if I'd been putting *Grow* on plants, tomato beds perhaps, stepping carefully between them as you would between your eggplants or your cantaloupe vines, then taking the broomstick low above the water, for the ground-effect leaves a trail: some crushed things don't rise and over bare earth there's a characteristic sort of smudge: loose stuff blown to both sides like a giant broom. So they might find me.

I went up two hundred and forty kilometers, until I hurt all over, until the river cut between sharper and sharper hills like glacial debris and glacial scaur: an old garbage-heap that glaciers push in front of them and leave behind when they retreat. Until the river went down between two hills and vanished, down into the ground.

I found a cave. The drop to the water: twenty meters, the other bank almost flat. A streamlet three fingers across rising in the loose rock-rubble in the back and making straight for the edge, with the necessary number of curlicues to avoid stones and hillocks. Beyond, a steep hill covered with thorny tangle, something new, like blackberry vines, and the cave not really a cave but an accidental hole-in-a-heap with boulders wedged together and stuff grown over the top. But very big, very solid boulders. The streamlet-bottom is pebbles, fine gravel. I put everything down and poked assiduously in the rubbish in back with the broomstick handle and even lit a fire with some of the litter found outside, thrusting burning stuff into the back of the cave in several places.

Nothing. No alarums and excursions, no nasty little dwellers with pincers, no alarmed rustlings, no sound, no motion.

So there's only people.

I'm about one-point-fifty meters tall; the cave is about one-point-sixty-five and I like that. Tall people can't stand upright here. I propped the broomstick against the drift of friable rock and harder pebbles at the back, put down my hobo's bundle, unrolled the mattress, and laid my things out. The extra underwear I'd put in the metal box I once used to store my music tapes; this is where the vocoder print-out will go (when I make a print-out). I guess we will bury it. There was room for my mattress at the edge, to one side of the little, bisecting stream: bed, running water, and I can hear in the directions I can't see. The streamlet makes almost no noise: too tiny. Wonderful for sanitation. And it didn't kill me. I had gone two hundred and forty kilometers, perhaps a hundred sixty as the crow flies (none here), and that's six or seven days' walking for exceedingly determined people.

And that is why I carried nine days' food.

• • •

But I lost track. I thought they'd gone away. I went out scouting with the broomstick and saw no one, not from the tops of the highest hills. I couldn't go too far or I'd lose my way back—until I thought of spreading some underwear under two rocks; you can see the white very far.

There was nobody coming, no black specks, no swaying in the bushes, not even three-quarters of the way down the river. It was altogether beautiful. But I couldn't go any closer. Wouldn't. Didn't want to. Didn't dare.

So I lost track.

• • •

They came in the afternoon. Putting one's head down close to the stream, you can just barely hear it talking, but I think

I screened out everything else with the river because I never heard them. I woke from a dream of talking very rationally to Cassie somewhere utterly indistinct and uncharacterized (so that it might have been equally easily back on the ship or in the middle of the Grand Canyon) and there she was, standing in silhouette in the door of the cave; I was mucking about in the floating layers between light sleep and lighter sleep when you become aware of your body and don't want to, like anesthetic: places in the mattress that weren't as thick as they should be. Stretching. Stiff back.

I said, "Why have you come for the water thingie? I left it."

I woke up.

Why didn't they come in? Because they couldn't see in, probably. I had thought Cassie was already inside, but as my vision came back I realized I'd only been asleep; everything's flat for a moment after you wake up.

I said, "How'd you find me?"

She said, "I want to talk to you. Can I come in?" Brave Cassandra!—whose shaky voice indicated something else was going on. Probably Alan-Bobby exploring the hillside. There are heavy scramblings overhead, something rather large and stupid moving about on the cave roof. Either he's proving himself for Lori or (more likely) they decided he was It. I propped the mattress (which is very thin and light) against the rock-rubble at the back of the cave; don't want to trip on it.

I said, "Good Lord, you didn't bring Lori, did you?"

"No, she's with Val." So it's Val now. I said, "I don't know what you're doing here and I don't know what you want of me. Go away."

She said, "Can't you come out for a minute?"

I let a moment go by. "All right," I said. I suppose one of us has to act in good faith that the other is in good faith, slender as such a chance may be. Let's test it. I put on my jacket, picked up a couple of rocks about the size of my hand. Circled close to the cave wall, on the side Cass was on so she couldn't see me, watching my feet carefully, and made it almost to the entrance without making too much noise. Which I hoped sounded like echoes, anyhow. Still in shadow. I threw one of the rocks across the cave and it made a very satisfactory, verisimilar sort of sound, falling in the loose shale over there, and there was a truly tremendous scramble from above, as Alan-Bobby the Megatherium dropped from the cave roof and rushed inside.

And bashed his head against the ceiling. He does not realize, I think, just how expendable the others consider him to be. On his hands and knees, shaking his head from side to side. Then he fell into the streamlet. He couldn't see very well, of course. And the others might not have told him to do this; he might be acting on his own. It's possible. I threw the other rock at the back of the cave and when he turned to follow the sound of where it landed—I think he was still dizzy—I had meant to give him a shot of something. I did. I really did. But there was no time. And I knew I must not let him touch me; then he'd know where I was. So I picked up another rock, picking up something in my head that wasn't mine, too, that I still don't know, and before he could get up, I hit him down and down again, just above the ear.

Concussion, at best.

So there's no going back.

"Alan?" said Cassie.

Nathalie, John, Cassie. If no Val. I kept quiet. Cassie stepped out of my view and there was some sort of parley out there, little whisperings and scufflings about.

"Hello in there!" said John Ude.

I said nothing, "What do you want" being a question that in this case seemed rather obvious.

"Hello?" he said.

I cried, "You've got the water-cycler, for God's sake, you've got it!"

He said, "But we want you back. We like your singing."

I said, "John, I only want to be by myself. I'll give you the broomstick; I can push it out."

"Alan?" said someone, a woman's voice.

"Hibernating," I said. "Out like a light. Your Hero bashed his head against the ceiling, which is very low. Showing his usual intelligence, which is likewise. If you'll stand away from the entrance, I'll push out the broomstick. No, I'll break it, that's better. Ruin it. Push out the pieces. That way nobody has it, you see?" There's probably someone else on the roof, but I can't see the shadow. If I were there myself, I'd wait until I saw somebody come out, then jump them, maybe push them off the edge. There's an old trick with a hat, but I haven't got a hat. My ears all on edge waiting to hear Alan-Bobby stir, wishing he would, wishing he wouldn't. I said, "Stand where I can see you."

Cassie moved into view in the cave opening on one side, Ude on the other.

"And . . . ?" (said I).

"Nath is ill," he said. "We left her back home." Back *home*! And Val and Nath and Cass—what a lot of intimacy has been developing in the last few days! I decided to believe him, or pretend that I believed him, or act as if I were pretending that I did believe him. If there's a fight, I might get broken. So I stepped into the sunlight at the mouth of the cave—but not quite out—until my eyes got accustomed to the light; it was a shock to see them looking so grubby, so angry. They must've been drinking river water on the long march up.

I said foolishly, "What've you been drinking?"

"The same as you," said John Ude, "see?" and he held up something that caught the sun and sparkled wonderfully. "Compass," he said. "Bet you didn't know. There's a magnetic field, all right. And you forgot that Nath was up this way before. We came overland." Then he yelled "Now!" and somebody dropped on me from above as he grabbed me, both together, Nathalie undoubtedly because it smelled like her, not that I'd ever noticed before. Fallen on sloppily, *thud!* with my face in the dust because I hadn't had the sense to duck, and thinking only it was so odd that I did know what Nathalie smelled like.

"Let her up," said Ude. Big man. "Cass, go get Alan." So I suppose Cassie went inside. I was not going to turn around to see; don't want to get my back to the edge. I heard her moving around tentatively in there. Looked up so very carefully, hugging the ground: the woman to one side, the man to the other. Two bureaucrats. Looking up makes me dizzy.

I started to cry. Because we never could be friends, I suppose. Cassie would be blinded by the dark, but not for long. There wasn't much time. He leaned over me, the silly way you do when you think you've got somebody down; he put his hands on his hips and with as much angry relish as if he'd been talking to the whole damned planet itself, he said, "You're mad. Did you know that? We're going to tie you to a tree with your hands behind so you can't get loose. We can never trust you again."

I pulled his feet out from under him. He sat, or went down backwards along the ledge (I don't know which) and I turned and shot in Nathalie's direction, not even seeing her, not knowing if it would miss her or not.

But she was awfully close.

Gas-guns don't make noise.

I shot at him without seeing him. Following my motion with my eyes a moment later to see him—I think he was hit in the knee or something—clutching one thigh and standing on the other foot. There was a great roar behind me, pebbles and boulders going over the edge down the bank. I shot him again, aiming this time, and—once he fell—kicked him down the slope. Another landslide.

There was no one on top of the cave, no one on the hill. I suppose Val really hadn't come. I felt even dizzier and waited on the empty ledge without standing up for Cass to come out with the broomstick, or discover Alan with his head beaten in and scream—and was he alive? And what would she do? And what would I do then?

She came out empty-handed. No, with a rock in one hand. Blood on it. She dropped it to the ground with exaggerated calm, wiped her hands on her sheet-made-into-a-dress, and sat down cross-legged on the bare earth, which she did with astonishing gracefulness. Something to do with having been a dancer once, I suppose. Anyway, Cassie hadn't wasted love on any of them.

"Well!" she said, peering over the edge, "you have been going it, haven't you? Someone ought to give you a medal." She licked her index finger, then tapped her own shoulder with her third finger. "Run home before it dries."

I said nothing.

She remarked conversationally, "The prof person said you'd be up here. You know, along the water somewhere. Frankly, you should have gone a lot farther away. A hell of a lot farther. That's what I would have done. I told them to let you alone."

I said, "Cassandra—"

She said, "I know, I know. If I had a baby, it would die. And if it didn't, I would die. Anyway, my Ma had me by Caesarean."

She said, "I could tell you all about it, the kind of anesthetic, the scars, the stitches. God knows I heard about it enough." She laughed. Swaggering Cassandra, the beautiful waitress, born to be a star, born to be a loser, doesn't know that hard births don't run in families. Not as simply as that.

"Oh damn them!" she said. "Damn them, don't they ever even come back to *look*?"

I shook my head.

She said, "What do we do now? Fight to the death? Like stupid Nathalie, who thought she was a man?" A social solecism Valeria Victrix would never have perpetrated, despite her being a Mrs. But in Cassie's terms Cassie is right, I suppose.

"Here," she said harshly, making me jump, "give me that," and reaching out in an absurdly unbalanced position, she had the gas-gun in her hand and was trying to get her fingers round it. It's a flat, half-shapeless piece, because it's designed to be hidden, and you have to know how to use it. I shut my eyes. "Careful!" Not like this.

"Give me that stuff," said Cassandra the brava. "Right now."

"What?" I said, opening my eyes.

"That stuff you're always carrying," she said sharply. "You've got it about you somewhere. You're too much of a coward to be without it." She turned red. "Trust you not to go around without carrying every kind of poison there is, you viper! Always wants a way out, doesn't she? Give it!"

So I did. I popped from my belt two pellets, which I put on the ground between us under those angry, angry eyes, two greenish-grey, extra-special, euphoric exits that looked just like Cassie's eyes. They fetched a great deal in the market once. And are fetching a great deal right now.

I said, "Please don't throw that down." I meant the gun. She put it more carefully down in the dust between us. I watched her pick up the pills. I think I was shaking. Something—not me—said, "Cassandra, I would be very pleased to share your company. Very grateful."

"I ought to poison your water," she said, "but I won't. I'll go do it somewhere else. What do you do? Swallow them?"

I nodded. She was showing off again, Cassie the 3-D Cat, Cassie the actress.

"Now you can go kill Lori," she said. She started to pick her way sideways over the hill, a little ageing in her imitation peplum or whatever it was. Then she stopped, and turned back, and smiled.

"Honored to share my company, huh?" she said. She added: "For how many years?"

Then she went away.

• • •

Alan-Bobby was dead. No pulse in his groin, no chest movement. I used the broomstick to haul Nathalie's and John Ude's bodies from the stream-bed, one at a time, and take them a good km or so downstream; they could rot there. Dead people are like sandbags but in odd shapes because they keep folding up, and because they were still warm; I kept getting irritated at them for flinging their arms and legs out like that and not helping me. I think that's characteristic. I left Alan alone, because I was tired, and decided to go downstream. From high enough (I was not stuck with the water now) you can see the river winding like a silver snake in the distance and the grey-green brush folded over on itself in hill after hill, each darker and stranger than the last, plum-colored at the horizon. League upon league. A rumpled, painted tablecloth where the glaciers had come down. I went down by the side of the stream this time and much straighter, leaving a snake of flattened vegetation over the hills. Watch it after you pass and you can see it slowly straighten up.

I had to go down.

Otherwise they might have to decide to come up to me.

• • •

No stops this time.

• • •

I left the broom by the stream and far enough away; nobody's going to steal it or break it or hit me over the head with it. I slept for a while; it was going to start greying-out soon. I ate the stuff I'd brought with me, a kind of candy bar and then something salty you mix with water and which I'd mixed and

carried in the plastic wrapping, but that had got all over itself
and on to my jacket pocket. Supposed to be soup, anyway, not
paste. I tried to wipe it off with the plastic but it was very uncomfortable: beginning to go stiff. When it dries, it'll fall off.
(Most of it.)

Then we sit.

Where is Val?

There are bushes, trees, the marks of feet. I can't smell the latrine. There are long, flattened smudges on the ground where
things have been dragged. Do I remember how to get to the
new camp?

Where's Cassie?

It all looks familiar, but then everything here looks familiar.
Follow the water (again). I kept it in sight, trying to hide behind bushes. There were more footprints, a kind of confused
scramble and crossing of marks, a place very much walked on.

I saw something white between the trees. That's not a natural color. A little closer: someone had tied a sheet to the edge
of the old bungalow, for a lean-to. Very sensible. But there's
nobody there. Doesn't seem to be anyone about.

Valeria came out of the bungalow, flapping a towel in her
hands as if to dry it or shake crumbs off it. Then she hung it
on one of the sticks that made up the lean-to. She stared into
the distance, almost as if she'd seen me, then turned and went
slowly back into the bungalow, only to come out again a moment later with another towel draped over her arm. Oddly: it
covered her hand. She walked idly forward, looking at nothing, short Val, old Val, her hair grey at the roots, not in her
royal-blue sari and her earrings now but in somebody's cast-off
khaki trousers and a white shirt. The curve of her back near
the neck is very much exaggerated by age; that's called "dowager's hump." Nothing balances on the spine quite as it used to
twenty years before. The opposite posture from what soldiers
used to do or at least were supposed to do.

She was perhaps nine meters from me, still without purpose,
still peering about, when I realized she had seen me from the
first. Must've. She was faking. The towel dropped and Val Victrix was holding a gun. Revolver, I think. She walked closer
and stopped at twice conversational distance. She looked as if
she had just noticed me. Then she said:

"You're not coming near my child!"

I said, "It's all right, Val. The others are coming. They're not using the broom because Nat's got a broken ankle."

"Oh, did you give it to her?" she said, enjoying herself. "And tell me why Nath would walk with a broken ankle?"

"And why they'd trust you alone?" she added. It was a revolver, no question. I said quickly:

"How is Lori? You know how much I care about Lori."

"I won't let you near her!"

"All right," I said. "My goodness."

Silence. Mrs. Graham is running out of melodramatic things to say. After a moment she remarked, "This has still got all its bullets, you know, sixteen of them," so if she were lying I might get her to use up the ammunition, but then again she might use it up in me.

She said, "When we took Lori from the crèche, she was such a little thing. And so beautiful, so tiny, but you wouldn't know that. You wouldn't know anything. No one does, not even my husband. That's right, even Victor. And you don't know how to live, my girl, you really don't. Take it from one who does."

Who hid that gun? Whose gun is it?

"It's tragic to think," said Mrs. Gee cheerfully, and by this I deduced that power was making her talky, "that when we die here, you'll never have lived but I will. Think of that."

I thought about it, conscientiously. No one has listened to this woman for weeks so that thing in her hand is a compulsory Ear; it means I must listen and she likes that. She went on:

"How much money do I have?"

None now, of course.

"You don't even know," (she said amused). "Well, I'll tell you. Six mill a month. Eurodollar. That puts me in the top one-tenth of the top one percentile, I believe. And I'm in the credit economy, too—I'm not a civilian, you know, not legally —and with a credit-level-one you can have anything you want in this world, anything at all."

This world? Goodness!

"Clothes? No!" (she went on) "Food? Service? No! That's just ordinary life. You grubby little people think 'Mrs. Graham' is foolish, don't you? And maybe you think it's foolish and strange and rich to buy a man and strange and foolish and rich

to buy a child, but one gets sick of renting people and even
sicker of renting pets—it's dull—and I don't enjoy politics and
there's one thing about bought people if you're wise: they stay
bought. You can't have it both ways but I can: the old *and* the
new."

It must be new money. The politesse isn't there. The taking
for granted. Or has she just gone a little batty these last few
weeks? She smiled. She said, "My friends think I'm quite eccentric, did you know that?"

Then she said, in an altered tone of voice, "I didn't buy Lori
for myself, you know. I thought I would but it didn't work out
like that. She was an awfully sick little thing; she needed money
like mine. That's why I chose her. Well, one reason. Do you
know how many operations that child's had? She was hooked
to a kidney machine when I first saw her and she needed a heart
implant. And dozens of things. They said the only things that
really worked were her central nervous system and her skeletal
muscles. The surgeon said she had actually become immunized
against herself in several ways; we almost didn't lick that one.
And I did it, I did all of it, I paid for it myself and every bit of
it on P.D. too so she wouldn't have to be there while they were
doing it to her! Otherwise it would have killed her. Even so I
think it might have had some bad effects; psychic displacement
can play hell with the mind if you're not careful. A sort of back-
lash, they say. But we had the best, the very best." She laughed.
"That child cost as much money as a small New England state.
Believe it. I don't quarrel with Cass, but to have a baby and call
yourself a mother—! One doesn't say such things, of course.
One doesn't quarrel. Not here. But having children . . ."

She looked at me, quite scornful and very happy, still holding the gun. She said:

"Victor fell in love with her. That was a good thing, of
course. A sick child—well, it does something to you. To have
her around. After a while. I love her too. It gets to you, you
know."

"Of course," I said.

She said, "I did it. I am the real mother here." Then she said,
"That's all I'm going to tell you about myself. I don't think
you'd understand the rest. It's very odd for me to be here with

all of you, but of course one tries to make do. To be polite. And of course you'll tell no one what I've told you."

"Of course not," I said, immensely relieved.

"Because I shall kill you right now," said Valeria Graham.

As if on cue, from back in the bungalow, came a faint "*Moth-errrrr!*"—but this ghastly screech, which we should not have been able to hear at all, is merely Lori's I-mean-business voice, the voice of a handsome tarsier or a pretty macaque monkey possessed by demons. Such an expensive life. Smiling tenderly (and just a little self-consciously dramatically) Valeria Graham motioned me away from the bungalow and farther into the trees. She put the forefinger of her free hand to her lips. Lori must not hear it. Lori must not find the body. We all know that child's preternatural hearing. Val is too close to me. I fell to the ground, roaring "*Lori! Help! Lori! Help!*" and trying to roll towards the mother. There's a shot *blam!* in here somewhere, and I can't hear a thing, deafened, grabbing her ankles, only I haven't got proper leverage and she won't fall all the way down. She gets on her knees, steadying herself with one hand, and points the gun a hand's-width from my face, happily ready to shoot me.

I grabbed the barrel and snapped it around so the gun was pointing at Mrs. Graham's white shirt—she didn't seem to understand that you must hold a gun rigidly, like an extension of your arm—and either the motion pulled the trigger or she pulled the trigger or something pulled the trigger or at any rate the little machine went off again.

She collapsed slowly sideways with only a very little blood in the front. A big slug like that makes one jump, first. Odd thing to see. They must've left the gun with her, for protection.

She never fired a gun before in her life.

Dead. Or near it. The revolver fallen on the ground. I picked it up and ran towards the bungalow. Lori is going from screeching to downright squealing; this is her you-must-attend-to-me-right-away-or-else voice. I sprinted the last few meters and fetched up breathless against the bungalow doorway. Couldn't see a thing at first and then even when I could there was no Lori, only an odd, dark shape showing on one of the bunks.

It was her back.

She was sitting up in the bunk, wrapped in one of her Mommy's royal-blue-and-gold saris, with Mommy's card deck made-from-sheets more or less on her knees and (I think) on the bed around her. Her legs were crossed. She leaned forward, putting one card on top of another somewhere in her lap. She said:

"I'm not coming outside; I don't care if it *is* healthy."

You must not shoot a Lori with a large-caliber revolver. It's not right. I shifted Mrs. Gee's gun to my left hand but quietly, quietly. You must not shoot an ebony-haired Lori.

"Hello," I said.

That impossible child did not even turn round. She only said:

"What an awful noise! What were you doing?"

"Target practice," I said.

"I wish you'd shoot Mother," said the Lori absently. There was a moment's silence. Then she added, "Mother keeps telling me I must be careful. Careful, careful. I'm tired of being careful. I think Mother is over-protective. Don't you agree?"

"No," I said.

"Oh, go away," said the Lori, "you're revolting" and she put a card on another card. I shot her in the back of the head. Did it with the gas gun, shrugging it from my sleeve, practically touching her hair. There is a kind of swooshing sound as the bullet explodes within. She slumped forward to one side, against the wall, her crossed legs keeping her half-upright. I thought I might gather up the cards and take them with me, but I didn't. No reason to, after all.

Felt nothing.

Odd, to feel nothing.

She might want the cards back. She might come for them.

I went outside and sat, thinking. Woke near dawn. It was like the first time I'd fled—only then they were all alive—and the problem was, what about the water-cycler? I mean this is what I had thought, under that awful heaven, more than a little dazed, trying to move about in the near-dark and not step on anyone—I mean didn't I have a moral right to take the water-recycler because they were trying to colonize, which would require them to drink the water raw, and here all I wanted was to starve comfortably to death? But they would be awfully mad if I took it, which might send them after me, though they might come after me anyway, and I could leave a note on playing cards: *Will send broomstick back walking speed*—but that'll give them my direction if this place has a magnetic field to make the compass gyro work and if not it'll get joggled and move off somewhere else. Or I could leave a sketch of a still: *Ord. wood fire deform plastic tumblers, water in here* (arrow). It wouldn't be poisonous. We'd been using boiling water in the tumblers over and over again.

I had thought a great deal about these things that night, on my knees, staring straight ahead, probably having breathed in some of the sleepygas I had puffed at the others. Very vague in the head. It occurred to me (then) that I could hold the water-cycler in my lap, but I would first have to unscrew the coupling to the storage tank; so I did and sat with the cycler in my lap on the broomstick, and fastened my belt around the cycler. Just fitted. (Now.)

What was the first trip. What you might call a rehearsal for the second. Much like the second.

Find the broom, stumbling in the dark, water-cycler cradled in one arm, harder this time because it's upstream, put on the dust-mask, flip *Go* and *Rise*, make the little toggles all *Manual*, and point Polewards. Silly to say North. Swing round, sending dust over everything (is it dryer than it was before?) and make a broad loop towards the Equator; you want to find bare rock because the mask is getting clogged and this time no forced-draught mist from the river, either. Over the hills and through the woods, dead dark blots against the ordinary darkness: these must be trees. (The first time I went carefully Equator-wards over the hill Victor had died on.) An old, old tune through my head, pre-Modern music:

We're off!
We're off!
We're off in a motor car!
There's fifty coppers
After us
And we don't know where we are!

How extraordinarily silly. Yet the first time there'd been joy in it. I went slowly at first, on account of the dark, and the cycler pushing its angles into me in the very worst places. The broom was going perhaps twenty-three kph. Nothing about the countryside changed and I was afraid I'd get lost because I wasn't riding right over the water (like the first time) so I turned left, refastening my belt around the cycler (this time).

Then I waited. (Both times. The first time I made a great loop Equator-wards, to find bare rock, not to leave a trail.)

One does see, really, in the dark. If you wait long enough. Not real dark, underground dark. But even in a bare night you can see if you wait long enough. Just don't look directly at things. You can even tell water from non-water.

So I knew it must be dawn. And speeded up a little—which lifted me a little, though it never goes far, not much above knee-high—and knew I was going towards the Pole, which is the opposite way from The Smudge this time of night. And when I realized it was indeed that greyish, crepuscular, eye-swarming, can't-see time, I checked the switches on the broom to make sure I had done it properly by feel the first time (both times).

The first time I had had the brilliant idea of riding over the water itself, following the stream up to wherever it began, for I would have to have water, and though the ground-effect makes a sort of immense trough in the water (a mist-shower which wets you all over and you have to take off your shoes and roll up your clothes to your knees; still it's like riding in air-and-water mixed) the second time I followed by the side of the stream and evened out a lot of the windings by staying on the rising bank because it didn't matter. I dragged my legs in the brush. And so on. And on. Endless twilight. Things swimming about greyly, like riding through an aquarium. Water to the eye. It got chillier and chillier. I've kept my watch; it can't tell time in the usual sense because one really doesn't give a damn about the standard day, but there are other uses: timing one's pulse, the length of the day, even the turning of the stars.

Aren't any. (Only planets.)

Ah, yes, there's one. I saw it prepare endlessly to rise; everything grew more distinct (but was all the same countryside:

little hills, brushy scrub, low trees) and after many hours, which I did not bother to time, and after I dozed, for I don't remember when the color came back to things, I saw our single star—I mean our sun—rise slowly but very visibly because at these latitudes its track around the sky is so low that it rises perceptibly sideways.

It got warmer.

The first time I'd pushed myself; second time no reason. I stopped whenever I began to nod. I stopped to relieve myself. I just stopped. Wading in the stream, sun dries your feet afterwards. Just sitting. Even without that preposterous object in my lap with its cubical-but-too-many-corners balancing act, one's bottom hurts, eventually, and one's back; it took hours and hours. All times the light was the same, the sun at the same height in the sky always; there were no bird sounds, no insect sounds, no animal sounds; it's all the same always, only around the rim of this enormous stage-set there is a spotlight that swings slowly around to my back.

The stream got deeper. The countryside got a little dryer and rockier.

And how I liked it! I haven't moved this fast in a long time. It unwinds like a highway, faster than funicular, faster than a bicycle, almost as fast as an electric car, it's like walking effortlessly, gliding on someone else's feet, like museum exhibits in which you sit in an armchair and are carried effortlessly past miniatures of subterranean cities, underwater farms, the interiors of fusion plants, the lunar mountains, observatories and colonies on Mars, on the solar planets, among the asteroids, even alien landscapes, imaginary landscapes.

Even

• • •

Well, it was pretty. It was pretty enough. It got rockier and more hilly. The ground sprouted patches of something new that eventually joined into a complete ground-cover: tangles and barbs like blackberry brambles (which meant I had to wear my shoes) and the right-hand bank of the stream got higher and higher. The stream grew narrower and deeper. As I said, it was like going from the hills of an ancient flood-plain (roundish and low, not the sharp crumple of a rock layer pushed up from below) into glacial debris and glacial scaur; what this is, really, is an old garbage-heap which the glaciers pushed in front of them like a land-scow and then left behind.

I say it resembles this.

But pretty. Very pretty. Water started to come down from here and there on the high bank, streamlets big as a finger, mere drip-drops, mistfalls that evaporated halfway to the surface of the river—these can't be rain-fed, not here—and the first and second time I was making silly pictures in my mind of jungled and trellised interior pipes, real ones of metal or baked porcelain (with flanges) which had been broken up by the glaciers, and that was why the water began indignantly seeping to the surface or springing up here and there. The air was very dry, though, all the same. There ought to be monkeys, orchids, brilliant birds, canoes full of native heroes. Both times I turned aside at a fairly big waterfall-let, maybe three fingers across, and steered with difficulty up the steep bank (the stick turns over if you try to send it up a too-steep grade).

This is my cave. Nice things: mattress, little bisecting stream, metal box, extra underwear, some food, the vocoder. And so on. Very nice.

Well, I told you all about that.

Inside is something very unpleasant, unless he's got up and walked away.

Oh, he hasn't.

I really didn't want to go in. I don't mean anything rational; it just kept turning me away.

I said, "Look here, it's *my* cave. You get out."

He was so dead. Like a statue: cold as marble but made of rubber and everything stiff and at strange angles, with this Godawful picture of death imprinted on it. I can't say I cared to look at him. And had to clean the cave floor, too.

The broom will never hold us both; he's too heavy. He's taking up a lot of room in my home, besides, and that's irritating. So finally I strapped him on the broom with my belt and tied him on, too, with strips of sheeting, and pointed the whole mess over the edge of the bank. The broomstick rolled end over end down the bank—I was afraid it would catch in a sidewise position and just lie there, pushing—but it wobbled upright like a live thing when it reached flatter ground (I thought I might have to go fix it) and began to ascend the other bank, a little drunkenly. His legs were catching in underbrush and making the thing jerk. But it smoothed out when it hit flat ground and up the hill and over the top, smoothly and efficiently, the way it's supposed to, and unless Alan-Bobby falls off (can't hold on; he's dead) it's off for a jaunt around the world, in the opposite direction to the sun.

So if Alan-Bobby is going West, then the sun is rising in the West and setting in the East or we are really near the South Pole and not the North Pole, and he's going East and the sun's going East-to-West.

Only names, only names.

On the way up I saw, lying among the bushes, Cassie's white peplum. I think Cassie was inside it.

Oh, yes, I forgot to tell you. . . .

I know she was; I saw her. Wanted to circle around her and didn't. She was lying on her back, limbs a little sprawled, staring at the sun, and something uncharacteristic in the air (for there are few breezes here) was moving some strands of her hair up and forward over her face, up and forward, over and over again. I've seen people who died using that stuff; they usually lie down and are happy long before the end. I wondered what would've happened to her if.

Please, I'd like to take another flight; this one doesn't fit my tour. Can't I have another flight? I want to get my hair done at the hotel.

Alan-Bobby has gone to see the world. Lori is playing cards in Heaven. I'm not alone yet, but when the broom wears out and crashes (where?), when he falls off, when the bodies rot with their own internal bacteria, when they're all gone, when Lori is dust and Valeria earth, when Alan-Bobby moulders and sinks into some other continent, when Nathalie and John are bones in water and then air and then nothing, then I'll be alone. When Cassie is only a white flag, a shred of artificial silk, bits of sheeting abraded to powder and sunk into the ground, a few fibers slowly settling into the ground around the roots of plants.

Then I'll be alone.

I'm alone.

• • •

Now I'll tell you about the first time. My four or five good days. When I woke up my watch had stopped; I must have slept long. It's the old-fashioned kind that winds itself up by the movements of your arm, which means that once a month you shake your arm vigorously, but I think the water had got to it. Ah, why didn't you buy one with a sealed power-source, as everyone told you to? (Because they're expensive.) Not that it mattered. I made a sun-dial from a thing like a twig, just stuck it in a patch of bare ground out in front of the cave. I'd fallen asleep before I'd marked where the sun went down (and comes up); so I had no landmark for it.

. . . thing *like* a twig.

They're succulents. This was a shock. I went out very carefully from the cave because I didn't want to fall and break some part of me as I'm very likely to do because my footing is never very good. I scrambled up the slope outside, trying not to touch anything in the rubbish. They looked like the downstream trees: low, silvery, a sort of grey-green. The "silvery" was probably hairs, like a cactus. I don't think any of us ever noticed. Succulents are water-conservers; they're relatives of cacti, and that should mean there's going to be a very hot summer. Or a very long summer. Or a dry summer. Or no winter.

What do these trees do in winter?

Answer: they walk to the Equator. Well, maybe they do. This is not in the least like New Jersey. I used to have a potted plant called Hen-and-Chickens, a little pot of it, and they felt just like this: tough, elastic pillows. But these are much flatter. There's no join between stem and branch, as if they didn't ever fall off the way deciduous leaves do, though from a short distance away they look wonderfully alike. I thought to myself that I should not touch anything—allergic poisons? Just plain poisons? No way to tell.

The light may be turning them grey, except at sunrise or sunset. It's a pale, whitish, Northern sunlight, the way I remember North Canada. Oddly wintry for such an outwardly amiable place; during the day the light is winter and the plants are tropical but it's dry, very dry; this does in a mild, subtle, discordant way what the night sky—which I am going to be careful never to see again—does so horribly, so insistently.

I don't want to look at The Smudge ever again.

From inside the cave one can see the ledge stretching about a meter to the edge of the cliff and then the lower bank, some twenty meters away, and more low, irregular hills beyond, close enough to enact a very satisfactory imitation of mountains. Deal with things a little at a time. It's a pretty landscape. An imitation or remembrance of mountains.

One thing at a time.

I went out and sat on the edge of the cliff, my feet dangling, chunking stones into the river. If I were a geologist (I mean a planetologist) I might've known what kind they were. There are no traces on either bank of the river's ever having been higher than it is now, so either it was at its height now and would go down later or it would never go down. Which is odd, when you think of the succulents. (Which grow right down to the bank and did downstream, too, as far as I remembered.) Which should be storing water but they're flat. Therefore they aren't storing water, at least not yet. So the river will rise or it'll rain or something before they stoke up for the drought. But the river's never been higher. So it won't ever rise. So the succulents don't know what they're doing.

I went back inside and arranged my calendar: a cleared place with one pebble *squat!* on the earth. Day One. Simple. I set up the water-cycler in the back of the cave, where the stream comes out of the rocks and I had a jolly time getting the tripod level. Then took the clothes out of the metal box and put my extra clothes on top, and the soap, and the food. Just a pair of shorts and a shirt, really, and an all-over undie. Had a fit of the giggles (Elaine On Desert Island—of which there are none on Earth that do not contain resort hotels—her 3-D viewer, her burning-glass, her resourcefulness, ages eight to twelve). I had to stay up until sunset so I could mark where sunset was—and wouldn't you know the blasted astronomical event happened right in back of the cave? So I had to climb the hill to get a decent look at it; it was either that or back right off the ledge. Then I ducked inside and went to sleep really quick. I didn't start a fire with my lighter, no need, though Elaine

had a pocket lighter. (Would've probably burned myself up.)
It was my little apartment. My little hotel. I had a dream full
of echoes; I was standing alone on an empty stage, under one
spotlight, singing with immense power and élan:

When I'm calling yoo-hoo-hoo-hoo-hoo-hoo-hoo

•   •   •

There was Pebble Two after Pebble One. When the sun was
over a particular fold in the hills, marked also by a tree on the
opposite bank, I put a pebble down. It's midday. In this thirty-
hour (?) day I sleep twice, once through the dusk, the night,
the dawn, once in the middle of the afternoon. It suits. I like
watching my little amphitheatre change, the shadows wheel
obediently around the trees, the sundial reach 270 degrees (or
thereabouts), everything begin to turn orange. I slept a lot and
sang a lot, the first time. I knew I wouldn't sleep more than
ten hours a night, more than two or three hours in the day.
I never used to have sleep enough, always had to get up for
something-or-other, I could never sleep long enough. Dreadful mornings shivering and cold, hours and hours to real waking time. Evenings when I lay in bed wakeful and desperate. I
always wanted to sleep 'til noon, sleep 'til one, then get up and
find it morning. Now I do. No standard time here. The sun
was no lower, the place it rose and the place it set no farther
apart. Pebble Three. Pebble Four.

Maybe it takes years for the summer solstice here.

Which was when I lost track.

•   •   •

Second time, I had to clean up, gather dried blood clinging-
to-dirt in my extra shirt and throw it over the ledge. Put the
mattress back where it'd been, put the water-recycler back up.
The first time I came here I said out loud, "I'm alone!" but the
second time makes this a very crowded little cave. Nothing to
do about it, only wait; they'll fade; they'll go away. I felt like an
interior decorator the first time, such glee.

(Why didn't I go back and circle around Cassie? Didn't,
though. Now I want to go back.)

One thing at a time.

I re-set my calendar. Filled the water-cycler again from the little stream in the cave; then put my shorts, my shirt, my all-over undie in a corner, folded up. Very neat. Pulled the mattress about and took some pebbles out from under it. I'll leave the other rocks and pebbles—I'll have to do something with them later. Boring otherwise.

And I talked all this out into the vocoder, ate, defecated into the stream (which takes an hour or so, busily running, to deal with it), woke, dozed, slept a lot. Fell asleep in the afternoon and had a long, inconclusive dream about Alan-Bobby in which he came back (in the dream) and we had a fight or anyway something was very boring and very wrong. Woke up stiff. The mattress feels harder this time.

I shall be bored to death long before I starve. The sun is up longer, if possible, or at least no less, and rising and setting no farther apart, so maybe it will be hotter. The daylight longer. Maybe there will be no night at all. I got very hungry (food all gone) and I think my stomach was preparing to eat itself, but if you've dieted, you know this quiets down after the first few days. I drank a lot of water (which I knew I would) and it didn't help (as I knew it wouldn't). On a diet you do everything you can to keep your spirits up. The neo-Christians had a way of coping with boredom by meditation but if you do that you're apt to get hallucinations instead. How interesting.

Just realized: I am fasting like a Desert Father, so in a few days I'll have hallucinations anyway. It is a driving, driving: to get food.

My cross is gone, you know? my cross is gone, my cross is gone, I can't wear it, O dammit, dammit, why didn't I keep it?

Well, let's get on with it.

• • •

It's boring. So boring. Pebble Three. I'll tell you about the neo-Christians; they're nobody. It was just an intellectual fad. We used to meet in somebody's attic in graduate school (I was thirty, L. B. was thirty-five) until a media rep got hold of it and then all of a sudden there were neo-Christians everywhere, like Amanita mushrooms. That's when I quit. Who wants to sit in an attic and argue about Descartes, anyway? It was only stealing ideas, but I suppose it'll go into the history books as "eclectic."

History is all fantasy.

It's boring. Starving is boring. I just went over everything I dictated to the vocoder, then decided to leave it as it was. What's the use of listening? All you hear is your own voice. I ought to rig up the machine to wake me in the middle of the night and whisper something shocking like, "We're going to get you!" In my voice, of course. Would if I had the tools.

I certainly have the time.

It is so boring that I am here and now going to write the history of the neo-Christian movement, which began with a classmate of mine named L. B. Hook (he played the tuba) and ended in spectacular persecutions, martyrs who shrieked their faith aloud in the flames, no no, we never got the chance, worse luck. It ended like everything else, just sort of petered out. Like dyeing your eyelashes a different color every week or regulating all your daily movements with a pocket watch according to the Leuter system of exercises. Other hobbies. Mixed with Zen, old Christianity, vegetarianism, archery, astrology, don't know what. Whatever.

No, I won't write it. No reason to. I'm sure that—presenting no threat to the Powers That Be—it's amply documented somewhere. (Actually I did talk out a long history of the whole business and then erased it. It took up perhaps half an hour. Passed the time. I can't tell now the difference between my politics at the time and my love affairs, between music and economics, or economics and metaphysics. I was drunk when L. B. and I went to the jeweler's to get our crosses made, you know, one of those little places that always exists: planting the flag of handmade pottery everywhere! The neo-Christian symbol was a cross inside a circle—that is, a quartered circle—which probably comes from some other iconography, but we always called it a cross. Had an awful time making the man understand what we wanted. I kept mine in memory of L. B. and getting drunk.

(And my attempting—drunk—to play the tuba.)

• • •

Dull. Oh God, dull. Trying hopelessly to push the sun along. If you scream, will that move it? I can't get through the next minute, I know I can't. Count your fingers one way and then back (nineteen), assigning them metaphysical values or pictures: house, book, Byzantine Empire, salvation, orthodoxy, burnt bacon, play, and so on. Do it backwards; can you remember them? Clock watching. Sun watching. The sun doesn't set directly in back of the cave but almost downstream. That's why I can see it rise.

I think the rising place and the setting place are moving closer together.

If it moves over *that bush*, I'll survive. If it hits the edge of *that tree*, I'll stay sane. Then I can leave work and go home. Block out the disc with one palm and count: seventy-five pulse beats for the bush, a hundred and fifty for the tree. If I didn't move my head or my hand or my arm and didn't get excited. I marked out elaborate divisions on the sun-dial, scratching them in the dirt, then threw the biggest rocks to the side of the cave. Much tidier. Thought I'd save the rest of them so it would leave me something to do, then with an absurd sense of utter defeat, sat down and cried.

I'm not afraid of death but there's nothing to do. Nothing, nothing, nothing.

I wept.

Had a brilliant idea: to recite all the poetry and prose I ever remembered into the vocoder, have it print-out. I'll have a library.

Didn't do it.

Sat and sat. Stopped being hungry for a while. I feel all right except that it's odd to swallow water as if it were food and feel that everything's *cleared up*, somehow, not that anything's happened to my vision. There used to be bulk cellulose you could buy for starving, i.e. dieting, but there's nothing to buy here. The withdrawal symptoms of a buying addict. A talking addict. A busy-ness addict. The sun says: Sloooooow Doooooooown.

Well, maybe (have to do something special to the vocoder to get it to do that, above).

If:
beef teriyaki
caramel sauce
vanilla cream
frenchfries
noodles with pork

bombe glacée
pressed seaweed sticks
Salt!
I forgot salt; I'm going to die for lack of salt.

• • •

A false alarm, of course. But I gave myself a jolt of adrenalin
that—you know—crying, trembling a lot, walking around,
wringing the hands—I do carry salt with me, for there are
places where it's very expensive, not a drug but terrestrial sea-
salt for gourmets. And there's more back at the bungalow.
There's food back there.

That frightened me. Made me hungry for food, even though
there are corpses back there. And hungry for the company
back there, too. (That's not exactly clear-headed.) I spread out
everything I owned, pop-outs from my belt, stuff in the jacket,
in my shoe-heels, et cetera, and marked in my mind what and
where, and then put it back. Must not, should not, cannot
take off anything for a moment. Must be with me, always.
Wished I had the broom. Still, I could walk it. Must've spent
about ten minutes taking all those drugs out and putting them
back again but I couldn't even get up; I was trembling. Heart
pounding. Very dizzy.

Did I put a pebble down? Can't remember. I put another,
which made four. Five. Six. Seven. Eight. Nine. Ten. Eleven.
Twelve. I don't think you can die from lack of salt all that fast.
Looked very nice. I made a circle of them, then scrambled
them up, then scrabbled about for a whole bunch of pebbles
and made on the floor—by laying them out neatly and carefully
—the picture of the quartered circle.

Too late for exploring. That was the idea: no food, no
broomstick. You're not supposed to change your mind. If I lie
still for a few minutes my head clears and I can talk connect-
edly, e.g. there's something trying to get into this cave or into
my head. No, not for real. But something.

Going to sleep now. Nothing will change.

• • •

Next day, don't know what day it is. Probably five. Who
cares. If history were not fantasy, then one could ask to be

remembered but history is fake and memories die when you do and only God (don't believe it) remembers. History always rewritten. Nobody will find this anyway or they'll have flippers so who cares.

Sign off.

• • •

Late afternoon: these were my politics: Communism and share-the-work. If you can't tell Communism from Socialism, Socialism from Anarchism, go away. The theory: a new class, even a new economy, developing within our mimicry of the old one, big business, big government, big labor, and all science, and out of it comes the real producers. A short chain formed from part of a long chain that's doubled back on itself. Look carefully or you won't see that much government is little government, much business little business, most labor little labor, but all science big science. Now.

The truth is, they don't need us.

Will we be killed off eventually as simply unnecessary? Or kept as house pets?

• • •

(Questions: What is "house pets." What is "eventually." What is "politics." What is "Communism." What is "economy." What is "mimicry." What is "labor." What is "business." What is "doubled." What is "theory." What is "class." What is "Anarchism." What is "Socialism." What is "producers."

(If you and your flippers get that far.)

• • •

Vocoder has made eighteen spaces, which I erased. If neither alien nor human, you're God. Who already knows. So I'm left talking to myself. Which is nothing and nobody.

• • •

I guess I'd better tell you about my politics because you're such nice people you might think I did something wrong but I didn't. I got into the Populars at about age twenty-six and spent about a year talking to University groups and various funded groups (these are the most vulnerable because the most parasitic) until in some inexplicable way the tide turned against us (although the media had never picked us up) and one night I heard a sound from the audience that doesn't need explaining any more than the shape of a chicken-hawk to a chicken, something I can only describe as a growing volume in the infra-bass as if the floor were preparing to rise and the walls come tumbling down, an ominous, slowly-rising roar that has nothing whatsoever to do with shouting or heckling; they're nothing. I stood listening to that fascinating sound until it occurred to me that they were after me—me, who had never harmed them! —and then I ran. I sprinted into the wings, smiled charmingly at the Fund officials (who were trying to grab me), twisted the pinky finger of one lady, stepped hard on the bare instep of another gentleman (but smiling, smiling all the time), dropped my over-tunic in the hall (bright red-and-green, far too distinctive) and took the fire-elevator to the third sub-basement, thus avoiding a long discussion with the fire marshals in the lobby in which you have to say for five minutes Gee, I'm sorry, I didn't know I wasn't supposed to do that (then you show them your I.D.), found the freight elevators locked, and finally staggered up three staircases, took an ordinary elevator to the street level, and walked inconspicuously out of the building. Don't know where all those sudden skills came from. It was fun in a way. But not the kind of thing you'd want to do twice.

I didn't even go home for two days but when I did, nothing happened.

Oh the jail, that was later, that was a lark. Four neo-Christians talking to some incredible aardvark like a real, live Civic Improvement Association in a city park during a summer windstorm that backed up a small, ornamental lake and flooded the place. We were rather perfunctorily arrested and locked in the storage shed used for the carousel in wintertime. Place damp and full of old picnic tables, which we sat on. And sang. And played dominoes. And took bets if the water would rise enough to float us away. I had to keep my feet on the tables because I was the only one wearing shoes and when the friendly police couple let us out to run to the public bathroom (ten meters away) I remember taking them off (the shoes) and leaving them on a table. Nobody touched them.

I've told this story a hundred times and people are always impressed and I am damned if I know why.

That enormous building I spoke in (or almost got killed in): the interior carpet-sprayed and wall-flocked in a certain extremely limited range of bright, stylized colors, everything flat and dry to the touch, neither cold nor hot, and you can't smell anything except the carpets (if they're new) or maybe the disinfectants blown through the air ducts at night. Brochures often describe the hologrammic numerals hanging in front of the doors in such buildings as "softly glowing"—which means they're in the same range of colors as everything else but the hall is dimmed a little so you can see them and they carry the intangibleness and non-tactility of the place to the point of driving you gaga. Books say it. Actors on TV say it. Everyone says it except people.

Yet the style of architecture is a good eighty years old. We are trapped in somebody's old dreams of Utopia, trapped outside what's really new. Modern Baroque is new: think of those non-civilian buildings we know about: great, opal-streaked globes, each with its separate stem, those sixty-four-square chessboards you find in Iowa, each grid half a mile on a side, spaghetti-clusters of transparent tubing for private homes or the same stuff, twenty times as big, built over rivers or waterfalls for factories. Nobody keeps us out. Nobody forbids us. You can even go in and get yourself a tour—only you'll never learn enough to go home and reproduce it yourself. If you had the tools. Which you don't.

My God, how naive we were. If somebody tried to bust us up, we must've been going in the right direction. I mean the Pops, the Pops, of course, not the other—and I knew it. (And the media never even touching us!)

Although the Civic Improvement Association was worse (or better?); anyway, they still thought they were *at the center*. You have to think that or die. Either you limit what you think about and who you think about (the commonest method) or you start raising a ruckus about being outside and wanting to get inside (then they try to kill you) or you say piously that God puts everybody on the inside (then they love you) or you become crazed in some way. Not insane but flawed deep down

somehow, like a badly-fired pot that breaks when you take it
out of the kiln and the cold air hits it. Desperate.

So I said Hey, if you're going to send mobs against me, I'll
change what I say; I'll say God puts everybody on the inside
—and anyway it's true and one must believe it—and I zipped
like lightning back to the edge of the board. The music (which
I like) and the audiences (which I don't) and the catching cold
(run out of Interferogen) and the too-much reading when I
travel (because I'm bored) and the paid corps of nitwits who
travel one day ahead of me so they can ask the identical, stupid
questions over and over, meanwhile (in between lectures) frantically changing their height, their weight, their coloring, their
faces, and their voices—everything but their minds.

Far, far away from the cutting edge of change.

God knows I'm private now. And on the periphery now. As
far from anything as one can get. Outside the outside of the
outside.

I dozed and dreamed. Thought I'd got my period. But I
seem to have gone anestrous, way off my regular schedule.
First time in my life. I guess I'm already too skinny; I'll be
amenorrheic forever.

A cheap vocoder could not spell that; "amenorrheic."

● ● ●

I've thought this through a hundred times; was going to erase
it. Didn't, though.

The sun's moved.

A blessing.

● ● ●

Morning. Dreamed near waking, something very confused and
vivid. It was about catching cold, but I don't remember what
the cold was supposed to be. Ears ringing with solitude. It's
so quiet that I seem to be at the center of a noise-factory:
gurgling innards, bellows in my chest, all sorts of scraping and
scratching of skin against clothes or pebbles moving. Even one
knee that clicks, I swear.

It's hotter. Though I should be putting out less heat because
of not eating. There was a thermometer back in the bungalow.

No. Sit still.

The old monks: "Sit in thy cell and thy cell will teach thee all things." Helps if you've got a cell in the middle of downtown San Francisco.

I feel a reluctance to speak into this machine. Because something is leaning over my shoulder. Is in here with me now. Is at the door. Is coming in. Is outside the cave. Which probably means I'm starting to go bananas.

Rest. For a while.

• • •

Well, I still can't think of death properly, can I, though I worked for more than a year in the terminal counseling end of a hospital in San Francisco. I mean death is what happens *in a hospital*, nobody just dies, for goodness' sakes, and if you want death there's no sense getting ready for it anywhere else than a hospital because you won't get it. You have to order it, like a special diet. And pray for it. And take medication for it. And consult with your doctors about it. And be in a hospital bed. Which is nonsense.

Wish I'd gotten rid of the food back at the bungalow.

(I tried to get up and my head swam; everything whirled.)

Anyway it's not so bad because the worst kind I ever saw were those whose lives had gone long before their bodies. The useless people. Screaming, "I don't want to die, I don't want to die!" the way children still scream at the allergist's, sometimes, having whispered to each other long, ancient, horror stories about "needles" (allergists don't use them). Clinging to money and power because there's nothing else. (A five-year-old boy screaming himself blue in the Allergy Room with everyone standing patiently at least two meters from him. He had shut his eyes in convulsive stubbornness; then I saw a doctor say, "All right, Stevie, we won't do it," and give him the shot. Opened his eyes and cried, "All right. Do it! Do it now!") The number of old hands I've held, saying: Dying is a task. (One wit answered, "Come and join me, then.")

Hello. Hello, old wit.

It never moves in stranger ways than when It moves inside us.

There'll be hallucinations about being rescued, I know: croaking thinly, "no, let me die!" (with immense dignity, of course) and I'm carried out to a shuttlecraft by great, coarse, strong, disgustingly healthy people in uniforms, with thick necks. Actually it would be a little awkward trying to explain what happened to the others.

You killed them. Why?

They were trying to kill me.

Why?

To prevent me.

From doing what?

Dying.

A shadow at the mouth of the cave. Wasn't. My mistake. I can't have gone hungry that long, it's only a few days; must be spooking myself.

Sleep some more.

• • •

I know, I know, I'm an awful stupe. We all knew, really. If the media ignored something as big as the Pops (and other such, as I found out later), it wasn't because we were dull; it's because we were dangerous. They would have publicized a miniature Sheboygan World Trade Tower made out of waffles and they did. Mind you, there doesn't have to be that much of a conspiracy if your social reflexes are automatic enough. Then I asked a friend to drift past the building where I'd (not) spoken and she said there was God's own amount of repair material going up to the forty-third floor: women with carpet-sprayers' guns, men with the other rig for the walls, bales of sheet plastic that you use to cover things you don't want colored, plyboard, furniture, even packages of searchlight lenses flown down on to the roof. My, my, my! And not a word of it anywhere. Now that's real censorship.

That's when I cut out. With no qualms.

I know, religion vs. politics (q.v.) the whole bit: saving people retail is O.K. but don't do it wholesale. My one original contribution to the whole business was a graffito that nobody would use although I thought it rather zippy myself: "*Money doesn't matter when/Control is somewhere else!*" (Although I saw it in the Auckland underground station years later so maybe it got somewhere. Or occurred to someone else, which isn't unlikely.)

I knew all those things. But never in my life did I make such an absolute, inflexible, and somehow automatic decision. And I stuck to it even though it wasn't (in some curious way) mine at all. I wasn't angry. I wasn't even afraid. I was, in fact, in some odd way, rather pleased with myself. I knew, of course, that the tide turning against us wasn't "inexplicable" but I didn't care as the others did; I only wondered how they did it, exactly. And who "they" were. And admired them. And thought I'd like to meet them, if I could, and find out what they were really up to.

Never will, of course.

And what will neo-Christianity do in the future? Will it mean anything? That does bother me.

It's a bore, a dreadful bore, being outside history.

• • •

Day Something. Dreams about Cassie. I woke up and actually saw her stand at the door of the cave. Then she vanished; I mean became again the patterns of rock and sun-spots-in-my-eyes I'd been making her out of. Hallucinations aren't just "seeing something"; they're a special case of perception in which you work a little harder, that's all.

Cassie. Every mind is its own galaxy. If I told Cassie I had wanted to be inside History, she'd say, "Oh, so you want to be *important*, do you?" I'm an awful snob. I must move around. Only starve to death a little sooner, that's all, but this sedentariness is enough to make you sick by itself. For a moment I had a violent craving for the broomstick, anything, car, helicopter, G.E.V., monorail, anything that lets you move, move, move. I'll go out; breaking a leg doesn't matter because it'll just speed things up. I can go out on my own front porch anyway, I should hope to kiss a pig. If I hold on to the wall.

Cassie. Go. Away. Please?

I'll be seeing her all day now, in flashes, out of the corner of my eye.

She's very polite. She went away.

I know you are wondering by now how I can do so much and keep talking all the time; what I have done is to tie a strip of cloth through the hook on the vocoder and hang the vocoder around my neck. It goes with me. So I will go out on the cave porch with it, and sit on the edge of the ledge and get the giggles about falling. This is it:

There is a low and impossible sun in the painted backdrop of the sky. So bleak. So empty. Might as well be unreal if I can't get into it. The color is as strange as anything I've ever seen, though part of that must be the light: pale, Northern sunlight that slides down these equivocal stems or what aren't really bushes—or trees—and ought to be somewhere in Death Valley National Park anyway, not within the Arctic Circle. River-noise is clear now (somebody behind the scenes just turned up a switch and thank you very much).

I like this place. It's nice.

I know Cassie is an hallucination because she doesn't move, just appears for an instant in that attitude in which I saw her last (arms and legs sprawled, staring straight up) but she appears vertically instead of horizontally because that's how she was in my field of vision then because I was looking at her from above. She's like a portable cut-out.

Hallucinations can be memories, too. If I tried I could hear in the noise of the river the sound of the rain on the old carousel shed in the park; I could invent the sound of a door slamming shut somewhere from time to time, irregularly, as the wind whipped about. (I tried to drink from out of an unboarded window and got my shoes wet in the puddle that'd blown in under it.) Or the sound of the audience that was going to kill me—you can't get that from actors, you know; it's inimitable—that one's easy if you start with the noise of river-water. Something very similar about the echoes, the undertones, the simultaneity of sources. I remember quite vividly standing on the platform and being able to see nothing but the light cage in the back of the hall, wondering if the bored-looking person in it would turn the lights off me and on to the audience because if you do that, they can sometimes be diverted into smashing the lights, at least for a while. But I guess she was paid not to. (Though they broke a lot of glassware anyway; at least the lenses were being replaced wholesale a day later.) I said, smiling, "I'm not the speaker"—or at least I became aware that I was in the middle of saying it—and then the floor of the room started to rise with the sheer volume of the sound and I walked off.

Don't know what happened to my friends.

Did the Pops start as three people in an attic? By the time it got to us it was a traveling symposium, which shows you it was past that stage or maybe was never in it, though some of the speakers were—God knows—bad enough to be idealistic amateurs.

Another graffito: "*I have just lost all my fingers to/The cutting edge of change.*"

I must've been the smallest minnow ever to slip through that kind of a net. If there was a net. When there's no real organization you don't need to catch anybody; just scare them sufficiently and the whole thing dissolves back into individuals.

No, Cassie. No. No. No. Go away.

She moved. She'll be talking next.

• • •

Thought I'd go down to the bungalow—surely I could find my way there and back, just follow the river—but I don't walk very well. It's a long way up to get up. Or something. Anyway, I got hideously light-headed, probably from having spent so much time sitting down. I will probably get scurvy or an ulcer. Cassie and I had a long talk (which I know is imaginary).

I don't remember a thing about it.

• • •

Things are for the best and if they aren't I certainly am not going to make a fuss about it. Not now. Like the time I was under anesthesia for a tooth implant and kept murmuring dreamily to myself, "I don't care what you do to *Me* so long as *I* am not here." (Which came out, they tell me, as something like "ff. . . . ff. . . . ff. . . .") It was such a relief. Then you come to, spitting blood and sick to your stomach.

Guess I really am starving. But not apathetic enough (yet) to stop talking. Never will, I guess. Everything's being sublimed into voice, sacrificed for voice; my voice will live on years and years after I die, thus proving that the rest of me was faintly comic at best, perhaps impossible, just an organic backup for conversation. Marvelous, marvelous conversation! The end of life.

And music's coming back. Bits of Handel this morning, swaying in the pine trees. I mean in memory, of course, I'm not that cracked.

Not yet.

• • •

My father dying in a hospital, years ago, under the loose, transparent folds of an oxygen tent, weakly grabbing my hand: "I don't want to die!" I said, "You won't." (An oxygen tube taped to his nose.)

But he knew.

There's a neo-Christian exercise for this sort of thing, which you are supposed to prepare for by taking a good stiff jog around the block, which under the circumstances is, I think, just a little bit impractical.

Must be some other ones.

I drink when I'm thirsty; when I'm tired I sleep. Everything's so close together here. I stand up and wait until my head clears, then straddle this hygienic little streamlet. Brilliant possibility: sitting in it and let the bladder go. A sort of ambulating bedpan, and without the usual plumber's attachment, too. It's warm enough to go naked. A scientist might be able to make up theories about this cave, but I can only look at it. Which I do, during breathing exercises (told you there were other ones). I've been standing up more—starving is overrated, doesn't get you that fast—and then a walk round the cave, then a rest, then two more walks. I am sitting cross-legged, talking this. There's no reason to collapse if you don't collapse. If I fell over the edge I'd even be able to get back (in an hour or so) so why not. Putting my legs over the edge of the ledge and hooting. Although the bungalow's certainly too far and I bet that food's rotten by now.

Why didn't I bring a mirror with me? Clever, perhaps, not to; I could hang it on some projection of rock or branch, let my face go into it, my identity, and be faceless forever more. And there's nothing to blow my nose in (except my fingers) because I can't catch cold, nobody to catch it from.

Starving doesn't drive you mad. But solitude does.

Morning. A morning. Studied the rock wall of the cave, extraordinarily beautiful and rich, such full arrangements of color and shape, such extremely crowded information. Fra Angelico painted on his knees. I really couldn't get over the textures (perception is abstraction), how little detail it takes to see them (though perhaps it's half memory), how they fit so. But then of course everything fits; it has to, if it didn't fit it couldn't exist, not on this world or any other. I fell to sniffling a little. Then I stopped because crying usually puts an end to this and if things got very good, maybe I could make the people come back: the edge of a naked plant-root, taking a shortcut for a moment out of the wall and haloed by the sun in all its little hairs, wet pebbles shining at the back of the cave where the stream comes through, rocks loudly declaring their own internal structure by their shape, by their color, by the places where they broke, and everything mutely going hallelujah on the gravity of transcendent gravity: the earth and rubbish piled up against it, the water dropping down with it, occasionally wobbling a stick (more gravity) or prying loose a few darkish grains of something. The eloquence of it. The mutual agreement of it. What to do if the elements fall to quarreling? I knew if I cried it would stop so I didn't. I just waited.

It went away.

(Thinking sentimentally: Sit in thy cell and thy cell will teach thee all things.)

Outside was afternoon. The round planet turning into the cone of its own shadow. A youth in the something of his something lying. (Can't remember.) This endless whirling that is taking us noplace, so you think they'd stop.

I wanted to stay up and watch the night sky but began to doze a bit on the ledge so I went back in. I guess the habits of sleeping were too strong.

So this should be not morning but the next morning. If I did part of it then. Must have because I say I went to sleep in the late afternoon and I remember that I did. But I can't find the break in the tape.

So dating things is no use.

• • •

Cassie. The only one I liked. The gossip we could have had. Even behind the mask of John Ude must have been something human, though if you will pardon my cynicism I doubt it, having had far too much to do with that type before.

But Cassie . . . !

The point is, when I cross over, will I meet only Victor? And do people who have died naturally, as we call it, go somewhere different or cross over in some different way than those who have died by violence? This is physically and metaphysically silly, the whole damned subject, but it does seem to have preoccupied people: different heavens in Scandinavian mythology, different hells in Dante, no heaven at all for the Greeks. Ghosts stuck in the place where they got strangled and so forth.

If those seven and I ever get together, the only thing they'll want to do to me will be kill me, and that will be rather difficult under the circumstances.

Eternity with Victor: could do worse.

But Cassie . . . I know I'm romanticizing something about my own life, or something that isn't in my own life. We always make such distinctions between those of us who are us and those of us who are tables and chairs and then some table turns up and *thinks* at you, criticizes you, talks to you, looks down on you.

Likes you.

Little twelve-year-old girls walking about with billions of dollars of improvements inside them. Like dolls with tape decks in a slot in the back.

Not that she felt that way, of course.

What were the Grahams like at home? An "At-Home," that is. Mr. and Mrs. Graham at home Tuesday next. But where? High, high up on Staten Island with a real, polarized city window from which you can see all the other private millionaires' spires and perhaps even the river? No, too small. They'd have an estate pitched on the ruins of what used to be Adirondack cattle country (with the farmland underneath now, not above) or way up in Northern Maine where nobody ever went anyhow, a real, honest-to-God estate with piles sunk into the marsh and a heli field. (New-money faddy, old-money relaxed. Some of each.) Royal-blue curtains over glass that doesn't always reveal the Maine tundra (that's old-money) but that doesn't always substitute some other three-dimensional scene either (too vulgar). Forty years of gold and royal blue, everything that Valeria wants and yet Victor's rather proud of himself, really (especially when he reaches the age at which she has to pay him and can take it easy), fond of his wife but absolutely crazy about Lori. Reverting to type. I think Val first chose royal blue to flatter herself and then dyed her hair to flatter the royal blue, stuck in it, so to speak, liking it. The eyes of the old are blue-hungry.

Alan-Bobby, totally harmless in most places to most people. Even, I suspect, running earnestly about the field, panting while solemnly playing *le futbol*.

And Sister Nathalie. Mirror-sister Nathalie. That vicious woman. I almost said to her once, aboard ship, "Wait a few years; you won't be so eager." But she was, desperate with her unbearable hatred of civilians, barely able to control herself until she could pass over into that other, real world.

What would she have done if there'd been no accident? If she'd got there—and trained—and flunked?

Become a music lecturer. Of course.

Cassie, Cassie, come out to play.

Come over for a chat.

I don't mind if you're rotting.

• • •

I stayed up last night to see The Smudge and locate sunrise, which is distinctly closer to sunset than it was. Plan: to kill myself on the exact, glorious day of the summer solstice but I won't know what day that is until several days afterward. Which makes things difficult. (Like the old recipe for nitroglycerine: stop heating one second before it explodes.)

There was a streak of light at the zenith, falling towards the Poleward horizon, looking mighty like a Patrol ship coming in for a landing but much too fast.

Then another.

And another. All over the sky. A meteor swarm. As if veils were being plucked off the stars moment by moment and they'd been there all along. I watched until we rotated out of whatever debris it was, then marked where the sun came up

(my position, nose on ground, where my feet were and where
—from that—the sun was behind the sundial). Then I slept. I
dreamed that a ship landed somewhere and sent a party that
tried to rescue me, me with cunning patience hiding in my cave
and shooting down every single one of them. Woke up with
some long and involved declaration—myself or person or persons unknown—fading in my hearing. It came back only when
I lay down again, just before I drifted off, i.e.:

*No use trying to rescue that one; can't you tell a corpse when
you see it?*

(I am elegantly self-satisfied. My fakery is working.)

She's been walking around dead for years.

• • •

Evening. Dawn. Morning? Can't tell.

• • •

I started to say something.

• • •
• • •
• • •

Oh yes. It's hotter. I feel fine. I've been sitting with my feet
in the stream—mustn't sit right in it or it backs up over
everything—and I can move well enough if I keep it slow. Or
lying on my stomach, playing with the water. Obese people in
clinics can starve painlessly for months and what do they have
that I don't have except some idiot in a pale-blue (ill-fitting)
coat who comes around every morning and says "Aha!" (?)
Only I'm not obese. Only I haven't gotten any skinnier. Only
I haven't looked because I don't want to know and I'm not
going to, either.

Whoever you
Whoever finds

• • •

Cassie's come. Doesn't do anything, just sits against the wall
(my favorite wall, too! the other's got big boulders sticking
out of it) with her arms folded and looks at me. I've put the
vocoder on whisper so she won't hear. Not that I expect she's

real; if I got up she'd probably rise in my field of vision like all hallucinations do—either stand up or float in the air—I have a talent for these things, always did; had to be careful with all those neo-Christian "exercises." Could never be hypnotized without drugs, though, probably a defense against my own imagination.

I said to her (smugly, I'm afraid), "I can't be hypnotized." Words in my mind: *You're schizoid.*

Insults! Insults from her.

We had a long—no, we didn't; that's an invention; I simply could not help looking at her because when you hallucinate or remember, that is your center of energy, I mean you're creating it. So you get fixed on it. And I watched her. Breathless. Not frightened. In suspense.

She did nothing.

I'll tell you how she went away; this isn't really visual, you see, it's a matter of conviction and what happened was the conviction went out of me and I knew I was looking at a memory. There was a pattern of roots and shadows and a ghost and a pattern of roots and shadows and a ghost. Then the memory goes. Nothing positive but it's not there and *of course* she picked that side—it's all rocks and shadows.

When they finally arrive, what will they all say to me?

I was very cross with her.

• • •

Day again. There's a philosophical problem here. Falling asleep, waking, hard or soft, hunger, eating, illness, feeling sex, running, being dizzy—why can't we remember them? They evaporate. Right now I can't remember a hot bath. About my tooth implant, I remember the office, the medical lady in the pale-green coat, what everyone said, what I thought under the anesthetic, and the extreme oddity of it, too, I remember that. But I can't remember the pain. There's only a warning muddle somewhere at the back of the experience, a faint haze of obfuscation. Now I know that physiologically, literally, it's still all there—all in my brain waiting to be waked up. I mean if you had the proper electrodes. But why can't *I* wake it up, dammit? The second time I had a tooth put in I didn't remember but my feet knew (they kept trying to turn around and walk me out of the office) and I suppose my body knew (I couldn't sleep the night before) but *I* didn't know. Until it began to happen again and then I wondered: how could I ever forget!

And then I forgot.

You know, I was very old-fashioned as a teenager; I really thought that a real physical letting-go (pleasure, anger, anything where I'd stop controlling myself—I called it "stop thinking") would absolutely bring the roof down around my ears, or if it didn't lead to instant death, disgrace, shatterment and horror, it would cure me rightaway of all my "problems" and I would never be unhappy again. Don't know where this came from; it must have been in the air because nobody ever told me in so many words, but we are still—maybe it's the price we pay for being so rich—a Puritanical people.

I was *so* disappointed!

Primary things—the stuff bodily experience is made of—just don't last.

Even music, beautiful music, hearing, that won't last unless you translate it into ideas, put it into your head, recreate it, drum it in. A weird business: grief without bodily pain, joy without bodily pleasure, emotion without flesh, idea-joy, idea-grief, but it makes you shiver and it makes you cry and it can be dreadful and wonderful and unbearable. And that's not the body making you feel (which of course it can); it's the body trying only to follow what you feel. To mean, not be. Which the body is not good at.

(For example, fucking. Why is it sometimes rememberable and sometimes not. And what do you remember? I think either a picture or an emotion but not the physical thing itself, not half an hour later, sometimes. Like a dried leaf. A dead rose. A taste that's gone. Actors practice sensory memory for years and even they have to turn it into something else. I mean put it into their heads, translate it into ideas.

(I can so vividly recall Marilyn, who must have drifted past that eighty-story building with terrific aplomb—as always—with her hands in her pockets—saying to me quietly, "it's not in the papers" right after "they're rebuilding the whole floor" with her usual, slightly hesitant way of speaking, as if she were apologizing for the triviality of what she was saying and yet always very passionate about it, and wrinkling her forehead in anxiety above those queer, huge, round, owl-like eyeglasses she always wore, looking at me with her magnified eyes as if to say: now we both know. And also: the world is falling apart.

(I also remember L. B. trying to get a contra-tuba—of all things—through the door of the attic where we were holding a neo-Christian meeting and not quite succeeding and finally sitting on the landing outside that very expensive attic, which was in a house made of real, restored wood (practically a national monument) with his large, delicate, slightly flushed ears sticking out—as always—and finally managing on that absurd, coiled, huge instrument to produce a dreadful, toneless, melancholy howl like that of a locomotive *in extremis,* as if the last nineteenth-century steam engine in the Smithsonian were finally expiring and telling everybody about it.

(I remember the third time we made love and how I decided it must be so very different because the room was different or I was just precisely drunk enough—though I wasn't drunk at all —or had eaten for once exactly the proper kind of dinner. He said it was because we had the contra-tuba in the room with us and that the contra-tuba, alone among all the instruments of the orchestra, had a soul. My memory of him is built up of many, many times after this, all made into one, just like the year I was speaking for the Populars and in just the same way: an intelligent, ruthless abstraction of *what mattered,* details plucked unhesitatingly from the real, unstable times and places and put together into a meaning, a mosaic, a symbol, an icon, because that's what mattered and that's how it mattered, and because I knew more than I ever have before or since just what mattered and what that meaning was.

(Meaning preserves things by isolating them, by taking them beyond themselves, making them transcendent, revealing their real insides by pointing beyond them.

(If we perceived everything, we would know nothing. There would be no pattern.

(But I don't remember hunger. I chose that because it fits intellectually. I don't feel it. Though I recall very clearly my rage when I was seven and told to eat my loathesome soup because little children were starving in . . . well, you pick a place. Alone in my gleeful rage among eleven well-behaved little boys and girls, it was I who pushed forward my bowl and said, in sly satisfaction, "Send it to them." How do you ship soup? When I was six there was the first real space travel, I mean instantaneously from one point to another; I remember this only because the whole topic was so profoundly uninteresting and we all had to sit still to hear about it. And I remember—at ten—remembering what a nump I'd been at six and wishing I had remembered all the right, glorious, proper, great things about that great day instead of the silly damn fool things I did remember: that Ruby Fossett beat up Charlie Washington for saying black people were the same as Indians and Indians had to come from India, so black people couldn't have come from Africa; that somebody called somebody else Slotface and knocked over my block bridge (accidentally); that at dinner I gave some vegetables I didn't like to Ruby Fossett who got rid of them in some awesome and mysterious way without eating them. But I knew Ruby Fossett was a magical person because she was seven and could stand on her head and had a big, beautiful, rusty-red 'fro, which was by far the most impressive hair I had ever seen. I do not, by the way, remember what the Day-care answered when I offered my slopping soup to be mailed to the starving children; I think he just imitated the Great Stone Face. Don't really remember Charlie's last name, either; it was something else. I think. And I don't remember what the Center looked like, even. I don't remember much.

(And Hunger's gone. Kachina-mask-dancing Hunger like a figure in a play, that I can imagine. Or a word in a dictionary with pronunciation marks over it. Or I hunger for righteousness, that's a metaphor. But I cannot even begin to imagine what I felt. Or that I felt at all; it's dropped out of the world. It's a hole. It's nothing.

(Not even nothing. Just the intellectual conviction that there ought to be a gap somewhere. Only that.)

So ideas stick. Meanings stick. Anything you can force inside your head and keep it there. Also emotion. Which shouldn't last but it does. My God, it lasts and lasts. Wish it didn't.

Old poem: when the bones are clean and the dead bones gone . . . but I'm getting it wrong. The Celts had three lasting things: Grass and Copper and Yew. The Germans had something else, some other story. Medieval Europe seems to have valorized such games: this number of lasting things, that number of changing things, so many wonderful things, so many sins, so many virtues.

I have Six Lasting Things: Valeria, Nathalie, Cassandra, John, Alan, and Lori.

Especially Lori.

• • •

There was a trial. Dreams merging into wakefulness, back to dreams again. I was very cross. They ranged themselves round the cave, knowing I was too weak, too tired, too starved, to get away. It wasn't fair. Big, dark shapes I couldn't see. When you first wake up you can't see clearly and everything's flat; that's when a coat hanging on a closet door becomes something huge standing over you, until you can see in depth again. It's the closeness that's threatening, right on your eyeballs. Things at the foot of the bed or right on the bed, but it's really a picture on the wall or a window curtain. When I'm badly off. When I'm tired. I couldn't see their faces. I sat up and thought I would go to the water purifier to wash my face but I couldn't. I was too tired. I lay down again—or stood up, I can't remember—anyway it was none of their business and I hadn't invited them.

I said, "Go away."

They just shifted a little.

John Ude said. . . .

Then Nathalie said . . . and Cassandra said . . . and Alan said. . . .

Then John Ude said again. . . .

I yelled, "You're always first, aren't you? You and the goddamn government! I bet you were a clerk. I bet you never got within five miles of anything real."

He said, *You know that I worked for the real government.*

"You are a damned, damned bully," I told him; "But who can you bully now? Who are you going to bully through eternity?"

You.

Silence.

I said, "All right, I'm a coward. Satisfied? I didn't have the guts to stand out against you in '25; I let myself be scared off. But what does it matter now? We're all here now, aren't we?

And there'll be others. And my religion is just as real and just as important as the other so don't you go tampering with that. Don't you go telling me I'm an escapist or something."

He said, *God is easier than guns.*

Silence. I don't believe him. It's just what he'd say. You can shoot a lot of things but you can't shoot down death. And if you capture a tank, what can you use it for except what a tank does? You can't plant a garden with it.

Coward, he said.

I said, "Oh go to hell." (Quickly, as if it were one word, the way you do. You know.)

Killer coward. But it was a worse word than that, somehow, I don't know what it was, and not John Ude who is only a mask. I looked at the people standing around my home, dressed as I had seen them last and with not a mark of death on them; there's no fogginess in this cave. It is from the big boulder on the left-hand side as you face out—counting clockwise—John, every inch The Professor, polishing his pipe on the edge of his now (rather ragged) jacket; Cassandra (who looks away from me, head averted as if she didn't want to talk to me in her white sheet or was ashamed or disliked me); and then Valeria, who stands with her arms clasped in front of her loosely but looking very severe; and beyond her (on the other side, none of them are standing in the sunlight) Nathalie—again separated from them all—disgusted, fiercely impatient with everyone, sitting with her knees under her chin, scowling and pitching pebbles at the cave floor. Then Lori, who's reading a big, illustrated storybook with a fairytale cover, a fairy godmother or something like that, and beyond her in the shadows, but somehow luminous, young, and very beautiful, standing with his arms folded across his chest, emotionless now, the one who called me a killer.

Killer coward, said Alan-Bobby for the second time.

I said, "I suppose you're in on this little kangaroo-court because I wasn't stuck on you, like Lori, and you didn't get to beat me up, like Nathalie, and I didn't praise the shit out of you, like the men, so I guess I just didn't kowtow enough to your beautiful, strong, masculine bod, huh?"

He said, *I had none.*

Silence.

I had the muscles of an ox, which always embarrassed me, I was not beautiful, I was stupid, and I knew nothing.

That's Alan-Bobby now, who is thinking or talking or somehow putting these words into my mind, standing angelically tall in the darkness of the cave (which should be too low for him; that's how he bashed his head) and somehow lighting himself up from inside, like a Christmas-tree candle. He is so lovely. He said:

We're dead. So we're wise. But still, you killed me. Is it allowed to kill fools?

You killed me, said Lori, uninterested, glancing up for a moment from her book.

And me, said Valeria with calm evenness, and I saw with surprise—no, really with astonishment—that although she could have—well, I suppose, being dead, you know—I mean she could have come back in her blue-and-gold Indian sari, her gold jewelry, anything she liked, but she hadn't. She was in trousers and blouse, just the way I'd last seen her. Her hair was grey at the roots.

She said, *You killed me. I was half-crazy then. Is it permitted to kill the crazy or the rich? Is it permitted to kill someone weak and old whom you could have disarmed?*

And me, said John Ude urbanely, pulling on his unlit pipe. *A reasonable man who could have been persuaded, a despairing man whose despair you never even saw, whose despair you might have helped, but you never saw it, whose despair you might have used, but you never tried.*

A fool who could have so easily been deceived, said Alan.

A fifty-year-old you could have knocked down, said Valeria.

Cassie said, *You ended my life, too*; she was in tears. Her face suddenly presenting itself to mine, the horrible weeping of suffering without control and without hope; I didn't want to look at it. So I put my hands over my eyes but even so they were all visible: Cassie rocked back and forth in pain; Lori read her book; Cass cried out loud, *Oh Nath, Nath, what has she done to me? I'm so lonely!* and fell to her knees, her chiton spreading out on the rock, her hair stirring about her face, one lock drifting up and back, up and back, and she throwing her arms out in a cross, as if quartering the circle she was part of, dropping her mouth open, staring outwards in the stupor of utter despair.

Nath got up. She stepped out of the circle—and oh, how that shocked me!—and lifted her blazing-white face, wringing her hands together but not at all like someone suffering; rather she was exercising the joints and the bones, locking her fingers together and pulling, like an athlete limbering up, like a violinist getting ready to play, like a fighter going into the ring. She said:

Starving? You've been starving all your life. What do you know about it, you with your petty religion and your baby's politics, thinking you could change the world! You are an arrogant, vile, unimportant woman.

Silence. They're all speaking at once. They're silent. They all have the same voices. They're running out of words.

You incompetent bitch, she said, *what else can you do but die? It's the only thing you're good at. Exiled to this place? It was made for you; if it hadn't existed, you would have created it. When you were born, there was no real place for you, no one was fond of you, not really, not of that real self only you knew, so you took the whole world on your back and put yourself in the center of it and said It's mine and said I'm going to get everything and I'm going to change everything. And when it didn't work you ran away, and when that didn't work you started starving yourself to death but slowly, slowly, with lectures you didn't like and friends you didn't know any more and when that didn't work you wanted to die but you wouldn't leave us alone, not you, you wanted company; so you killed Alan and you killed John and you killed Lori and you killed Cassie and you killed Val and you killed me.*

Look at yourself, she said. *Look at your fear. Look in my face and you'll see your own rage and your own deprivation. I know you. Do you think I don't know you?*

Look in the mirror.

They didn't fade. They got sharper and sharper, exactly as I had seen them last. They walked out of the cave without touching one another, as if they had no feelings for each other and no relation to each other: Val went first and John Ude second, then Alan, with none of his beauty left, and Nathalie, without any expression on her face, and then Cassie, with as commonplace a look as if nothing had happened. They stepped out into the sunshine and I think they may have turned to one side or the other on the little ledge that's in front of the cave, but I don't know. They just disappeared. Then Lori came, dragging her book, and her other hand in her father's: Victor Graham in his beautiful, blue dress-suit, not as he had looked when he died, but spruce, rich, handsome, even smiling. He looked free.

He said, "They do go on, don't they? But we all have something like that." Lori was intently shaking the dust off her fairy-tale book. He said, a little apologetically, "She likes that kind of thing. You know? And I'm told it's a good book. Come on, dear," and he started towards the entrance to the cave. I noticed with a kind of horror that he had to bend over because he was such a tall man; the roof was too low for him. At the threshold he stepped out as if he were going to continue walking right out into space, and as he began to dissolve in the sunshine—or I lost sight of him because my eyes weren't used to the dazzle outside—Lori tugged at his hand for a moment and turned back. She said something to me and then she went out with her father into that brilliancy I couldn't see, and was gone. I have never seen that child so well-mannered.

She smiled at me dutifully.

Then she said, "Thank you."

"For what?" I said. She looked surprised.

She said, "For killing me."

• • •

Nothing settled. Nothing! What's inside my head comes out, that's all. Don't think I believed in them, that they could get here, that they accused me, that six people could stand up inside this cave, that they levitated out the door, that I didn't form them from the cracks and striations in the walls, the dirt, boulders, bumps, lumps, shadows, that stuff.

Anyhow she was only being polite to please her father.

• • •

Afternoon. L. B. came to visit, much more realistically, by the way, sitting cross-legged against the side wall and shifting around uncomfortably, sticking his tongue out a little when the pebbles hurt his ass. There were even footprints coming in from the ledge outside, I mean places where his feet had disturbed the cave floor; at least for a while there were. I was so pleased to see him, so glad, but I didn't dare touch because I knew he'd go. So I asked him why didn't he bring the contra-tuba he'd left outside the cave.

He said, "Are you kidding? The silly thing's *enormous*. Think of all the ectoplasm it would take. Besides, you know I can't play it."

I got snide and made an improper suggestion about something else he couldn't play in his present state.

He blushed, mostly in his delicate ears, where you could always see it happen; he has wonderful ears, slightly transparent, that always reminded me of a bat's, they stick out like two silky signal flags; he said, "Oh dear, no, really you shouldn't," which is exactly the way L. B. has always talked.

I said, "Well, what are you doing now? Still preaching? Still teaching? Are you asleep somewhere and visiting me in your sleep?"

Silence. He looked at the floor. He seemed very unhappy. That twist of the head, putting his chin into the hollow of his collar-bone. Hunching up the shoulder. Rubbing his cheek and his shoulder as he always did when he suffered, ol' knobbly man, and now he's doing something else, something rather distressing; he looks up and there are tears running out of his wide blue eyes.

I cried, alarmed, "Elbee, are you *dead?*"

Silence. The erotic is going out of him like water out of a glass; once I saw someone nearly sever a finger when I was working in hospital and the color went out of his face like a column of mercury dropping; that doctor turned from brown to greyish-brown as if somebody'd pulled down a shade. L. B. is doing this, and he's getting flatter and flatter somehow, sharper and sharper, like an image that's alive but doesn't quite belong with its background. I don't like this.

He said, "Oh my dear, you've committed murder."

"Go away." (I said it again, totally shocked: "Go away!")

"But my dear, how can I love you if you've committed murder?"

I started to cry. "Yes," I said, "all right, you Christian, don't." I added, "You know it was self-defense!"

He merely looked at me.

"Of course it was, of course it was!" I said. "You saw it. I mean, if you're made of ectoplasm and all. I mean running into the brush yelling Colonize, Colonize, and all that. They were going to force me to have babies. I was going to be tied to a tree and raped, for goodness' sake. It was a mass-delusional system, L. B., you know what they're like, and anybody who doesn't agree has to be shut up somehow because it's too terrifying. So I ran away, but they wouldn't let it be; they came back after me to drag me back into that insanity and I killed them; I had to. I kept telling them we were all dead. You know that. And we were. I bet they had a lot more fun chasing me than they would have had by dying slowly in a few months. It gave them something to do. And I might remind you, old buddy, that several of those nice people were trying to kill me."

"Murderer," he said.

I started crying again. I said, "You get out of here, you father! You just get out of here! This is not your cave so you just haul ass!"

He said thoughtfully, "Murder. Pure murder. Don't you think? And for no reason. Just because those people annoyed you. You assumed, of course, that they ought to adapt to you; it never occurred to you that you ought to adapt to them. You simply didn't like them."

I couldn't talk.

He said, "Out of spite, really, I think. Don't you? A hidden wish. Anger. The chance to do what you'd always really wanted to do. I think what you always wanted, under the camaraderie, under the sociability, was the chance to be really and truly alone, autocratically alone, one might say. Arrogantly alone. Yes, that's right. You talk so much about there being no law here for the others, but I don't think you ever reflected truly that, after all, there was no law binding you, either, nothing to keep you from ultimately doing exactly what you wanted to do. And what was it? Why, to kill. One might look at the whole series of events as a series of provocations; you see, you pushed them to the point where they'd give you a pretext for murdering them and then when Nathalie nagged them into following you—it was she who did it, of course; if Nathalie had been more intelligent and a little less conventional, and hadn't needed people around to boss so much, I think she would have done exactly what you did—well, you're very like Nathalie, you know. Very like. Probably the only person in history to depopulate an entire planet so easily. Pocket genocide, one might call it. And for spite. For sheer nastiness and bad feeling. And for no other reason. So I can hardly love you now, can I?"

I got to my feet, although I was dizzy and shaking—oh, was I shaking!—and I cried, *You liar! You fake! Why are you here? Why'd you bother to come? You never loved me, never, never, you only pretended and then you fake things up because you know it wasn't like that and it's all just to destroy me!*

He said calmly, "That is true."

Then you're the killer! and I screamed, I really did. There was more argument running in and out of my ears, pro and contra, not a loud booming or even a sound but pure confusion until I couldn't tell if I were speaking or not or he was or not; it was all a tangle.

So I leaned over to hit him and fell on my face. I don't think falls can hurt me now, I'm too light. Anyway, there was a sort of cushiony, dreadful mess of arguing and pullings-apart and past lives all over the floor; I think that helped. And my own blood sounding in my ears. By looking up I could see L. B.'s face close to mine and though it was the same face, it wasn't, not really; it had become unchangeable, like a photograph. A photograph of a smile is a smile first but look at it too long and it comes apart into tics and muscular oddities; soon you can't even tell if it's a smile or not. The time element has been left out. L. B. was like that. I think he was gloating, but I couldn't tell. He might have been smiling. He might have been sad. He was going to do something very bad and it would make him happy. Then I knew it wasn't L. B.

He said, *God hates you.*

Now that's ridiculous. It's abominably silly and it would never cross L. B.'s mind, let alone his lips, except as a particularly comic, blasphemous horror. This is someone else.

I said carefully, "How do you know?"

He said with a sickly-sweet smile, "I know what you know."

I said, "But how, L. B.? How do you know? Are you my conscience?"

"Yes," he said, edging along the wall as if he wanted to get out of the cave without getting to his feet. "Yes, I'm your conscience."

"Come on, L. B.," I said. "You're not my conscience."

"I'm not your conscience."

"Tell me," I said in, I think, a kind of croak because everything was breaking up very fast now and oh, I had to be cunning or I would have to live with this monster for the rest of my life, for eternity, who knows, I said, "Tell me, tell me, where is L. B. right now?"

"Don't know," he said.

"Are you L. B.?" I said, and suddenly still, he assumed an even odder, intense kind of fixity—yet this one was totally human—like the moment when someone touches you on the shoulder from behind and you don't know who; you gather your forces internally, perhaps, or do what's called "holding your breath" though it's more like holding your mind, not thinking. The strict arrest. I'm not sure I want to find out who this is.

He said pathetically, "I try. I do try. Please believe me."

"Who are you?"

"You give me such an awful role to play. That's because you're such an awful person. You're most unfair."

"Now look here, you idiot—"

"Yes, I'm an idiot. *You're* an idiot! Making poor Elbee into your conscience and what a conscience! It's just like you. Of course he never loved you. Who could? You're not loveable. *I* don't love you. Nobody could ever love you. Why? Because you're bad, bad, bad, bad, bad—"

and was talking to myself. Had been. All along. Of course. Unmistakeably sincere. To think as badly of him as that!

But I am. I'm impossible. Dreadful. Totally wretched little bit of nothing. He should have dropped me long ago.

What I could have

Should have

Couldn't

Should have thought really

Really! Arrogant, solitary, secretly cruel, I am. I am. Used to say to myself Who isn't, who isn't, but it's not true. I've been unhumanly hungry and starved for years, as nasty as a starved rat. A cannibal. Wished they wouldn't be persuaded. And glad they weren't. Give it a good end, go out in a great big bang. End to stupid parties after lectures, people I didn't know, people I wanted to kick, trying to live without roots like an air plant, endless traveling with idiots, trying to pretend they're bright when I'd like to hit them and I like them when I don't and it doesn't matter when it does and I ought to love that hateful, ghastly bunch and oh Lord, what was I *doing* there, anyhow.

I rather enjoyed killing them off and I don't care. Except Cassie.

Alan-Bobby hit in the head with a rock, *good for him!* Nathalie shot? *Good for her!* John Ude shot, *good*. Lori, *fine*. Val, *best of all*. Goody good good for *them!* It's a game they understood inside-out and once I started playing I rather liked it because I'm not exactly an amateur, either, you understand, and it's all yummy self-assertion, all big adventure, isn't it, oh my, creeping about in the canebrake in our underdrawers, trying to pot each other.

No, I had to. I really had to.

But all the same I did. What "pocket genocide"? I guess so. Up to the elbows in blood. Poetry.

And now I have to live with this awful, awful woman, this dreadful, wretched, miserable woman, until she dies.

● ● ●

I cried myself to sleep—not real tears, silly, easy tears; the awful thing was that I couldn't stop, they're the kind that keep leaking out of you—and I called myself all sorts of insulting names. I fell asleep calling myself names. Dreamed we were back together at my place, all this sensuality a topography I couldn't describe to you, a sort of lovely pocket universe, and in the summer dawn (this really happened once) from some dingy, cement ledge outside our window:

SQUEEEEEEEECH!

Like a siren right under your pillow. The damnedest sound. The bed quaked. I thumped him in the ribs, said, "Bang on the wall." He said, I think sitting up, "What? What?"

I said, "Sparrows. Bang on the wall."

There was a nest in the air-conditioner. It was an old portable and made a beautiful bird's-nest, right between the ledge and the bottom of the exhaust cave, a lovely steady current of warm air. Tremendously attractive. If you'd been able to go outside, you'd have seen grass and twigs sticking up haphazardly from beneath the machine. Sparrows are messy builders. If you whop at them, they shut up for a couple of minutes, just enough to get back to sleep.

SQUEEEEE-HEEEEECH!

By then he was up. Quivering. He said, "Kill them."

I sat up. "Why? They're just babies."

"Babies? They're banshees."

"Look, the building people are coming in a week to close up the gap. They'll be flying and out by then. You don't want to murder a whole bunch of helpless little cutey baby birds, now do you?"

"Yes," he said.

I said, "Um . . . I know, but you can't take the unit out; I tried. Takes special tools. And you need a cable through the hook on top or the whole unit falls eighteen stories and murders someone."

The food factory was at it again. Oh God, it *was* awful.

I said, "Elbee, have respect for the sanctity of life."

"*Sparrows?*" he said.

And sparrows they were. Every sunrise the infants woke and screamed horror and starvation—you have no idea what that is like only a meter from your ear and no soundproofing—and opened their tiny, little, red beaks: *feed me! feed me!* (at about one hundred and sixty degrees' extension) and drove their desperate parents, who probably wanted to sleep as much as I did, out to exhaust themselves and ruin their health finding enough polluted insects to cram thrice its own weight each day into that insatiable scarlet gullet. There is nothing—I repeat, *nothing*—in the homeothermic realm uglier or stupider than a baby bird. And sparrows! The only flying species nobody's ever had to re-seed or protect or re-transport or do anything but discourage. If they'd been swallows or cranes or titmice, anything. Even grackles. But sparrows? They're taking over the world.

SQEEE-HEEEEE-HEEEEE-HEEEEEEEEECH!

"Oh God, have you been living with that?" he said.

I said yeah, well, at least they matured fast. Then he began to look as if he were getting dangerous ideas—dangerous to himself, I mean—like attempting to open the top of the window or unscrew the front of the conditioner and try to poke through the coils.

They did it again. He pounded on the wall. "Shut up, you bloody birdies!" Silence. We had slept two hours. I usually wadded the extra pillow over my head and managed somehow. L. B. shouted, "Filthy, lousy, bird-brained birds!" He was always accurate. And added, "Oh, why couldn't you have had the sense to be born fledermausen?"

We liked bats.

Then he said, "Oh hey, do you have a rubber hose? If we could pry some of the insulation off and run a hose through the edge—"

"And pipe them ten thousand worms?" I said. "Oh no. They'll stop in an hour, honestly."

He said, hopefully, "Boiling water?"

I shook my head. "I tried." The trick is to get at them when they're first nesting and repeatedly scare the living daylights out of them—birds are very emotional—until they get the idea there's a large, very irritable, dangerous mammal who comes with the site and they do, finally, go somewhere else. But once they've laid eggs, it's you or them. And I hate them. Nesting in my ear. Denouncing us. Making everything in your nervous system fire off all at once when you're peacefully asleep, as if you'd been electrocuted. We discussed various avicidal methods, each worse than the last, for the next hour until the clamor, no din, no—the *screams*—died down, and then we lay down again. I said, "Oh, what a mess there'll be when they clean out the window." And then (and I knew I was dreaming, but my dream continued to follow that scenario of twelve years ago) I prodded L. B.'s velvety-bony rib. He gave a sleepy, chuckling gasp: harpf. Hoopf.

"Hey," I said, "hey, Elbee, what would you do if it was people?"

Hapf. Sometimes he felt like a moose in bed: all antlers.

"Really," I said, "what?"

"Kill'm." Pwft.

"No, if it was people, if they bothered you more than that, if they really wanted to . . . to put you in jail forever or mess your life up or something, I don't mean kill you but something really bad, what would you do?"

An adult bird twittered softly outside: there, there, my lovely little red-funnel darlings, my yelling stomachs, my squally, pin-feathered dearies, my hope, my joy.

Damn them! Parental insanity.

I woke up.

• • •

Twelve years ago I'd gone to sleep and so missed the answer that way. A classic, textbook dream but so far, so very, very far, so unfortunately far away from any textbook at all.

I'll tell you the neo-Christian theory of love. The neo-Christian theory of love is this:

There is little of it. Use it where it's effective.

Then I started to cry again but too easy, just leaking out of my soul, almost comfy. Penance can't be like that. And then I thought of Nathalie, Alan, Val, & Co., all fledglings in a nest, all flopping about and squeeching like mad: oh feed, feed, feed! Agree! Agree! Agree!

I *am* arrogant. Dreams don't lie. Can't do it in a dream. It made me laugh. I'll never be properly guilty, can't be, it's too funny.

Feed me, feed me, feed me! (Am I one, too?)

Read me, read me, read me!

• • •

Marilyn came, not in a dream or vision, but just a fragrance I couldn't see beyond the edge of the ledge. Night. The Smudge rising. When there are no stars you see the sky differently: huge, immense, utter Nothing if there's any light, then flat and right against your eyes when it's black. You imagine walls, as if it were a room. She was visiting. You know? I imagined talking to her. Can't remember, except a general feeling it was all right. Marilyn talking silently, ever so eloquent gestures. Like the alphabet for the deaf with her hands but so beautifully tender: *One* and she opposed her right forefinger to the third finger of her left hand: *Two* and it was third finger to third finger; *Three* and it was fourth to the same third, left-hand finger; *Around* and she rotated both hands, fingers loosely half-curled like a shell; *Together* and she joined one palm to another, spread fingers to spread fingers, like mirror meeting mirror. Her lips moving. Head to one side, perhaps wry, perhaps smiling. Bending her head to take off her big glasses: behold naked Marilyn! She touched lightly the collar of her shirt: another difficult curve, this one half-closing, flatter, fingers together but thumb apart. What fine points she was making. I watched her until sunrise, slept, dreamed of L. B. playing in an orchestra (ah, but he played *le jass* on the side, L. B. skulking into magical romantic cellar at midnight with infra-tuba, plugging self into huge console in middle of smoke, tilting hat over face for *flics*, slurping beer, blowing tuba, making wicked and forbidden sounds from current in brain, sneer on face, hat tipping up and down, shoulders bouncing, nope, friend-o, I just do this for amps, great screams, *les cops!* and off we go into the night, no L. B. but only infra-tuba-with-legs and blushing ears going skrimble skramble down cobbled pavement into romantic darkness and falling flat on face) and when he took off his traditional, somber, musician's black tights with silver-sparkle round the wrists, neck, and ankles, and he said—peering at crotch level—"What is this?" and I "What is that?" and we cried out together, "Love!" and danced naked but very classically, until he got down on one knee and I went up on point on his unpadded thigh, bracing myself against his bony shoulder, doing an arabesque, and he said, "Must you?" and then he said, "Really, you'd better wake up; that hurts," and he added, "Why are you dreaming in French? It's not like you."

I woke up laughing.

• • •

Day. Day something. Something from Marilyn stays about, something from L. B. I'm dreadfully thin. I mean in the ordinary way, of course, not starving yet because starving takes too long, I think. It takes months. That's amazing. Can see not only my ribs, which I always could, more or less, but also the bones around my knees and my thighs have got all flappy. Arms, too. Does that signify anything? My thumb and middle finger meet round my upper arm. I sat in the water and thought: should I measure myself? (Being delightfully dirty; you can shit in the water, first of course sitting in it and backing it up, and eventually you'll be clean all by itself. I get dizzy standing.) Only maybe this is an hallucination, too: skinny legs, big knees, hanging belly, something left over from a newsreel. Well, I'm not swollen up. Can't remember what that's called, with the no-protein. Or is that only with children? Different when you're grown up.

I don't know.

A couple of times I tried to see my face in the water. I mean I think I did. But now doesn't matter, I'm just being, the most extraordinary freedom just to be behind your face and not cultivate it as if it were a house plant. "Cheeeeez!" Me at five, fidgeting in the holo studio, fancying the cameras are dental machines and I'm being terribly brave. Less boring than just waiting. Earlier today there was lots of music coming from all over, which was a terrific liberation; it's all been sealed up inside me till now and I doubt somebody strung up wires and speakers all over the cacti. You don't need them if you've a good memory. I went slowly to the ledge and hung my feet over, feeling like the Old Herb Lady who lives in the cave; it was coming from all around, in this strange place, like a vast, inhuman auditorium, Bach from the hills and bushes and when I looked into the blazing blue sky, Handel. Very appropriate.

The trumpet shall sound!

I wonder if they really believed that. Et cetera. The trumpet shall and we shall, et cetera. My singing must sound awfully squeaky and the vocoder isn't set for music; this will just be words. It was memory-music but I had no control over it, it just came, what I've lectured about for years and loved for years, like Saint Francis preaching to the birds (except sparrows); here I am playing music for silver-haired plants and alien hills. They all sat in rows and listened. From the organ (which? brain? kidney? lung?) Bach's Toccata and Fugue in D Minor, which if you don't know it, I'm sorry for you. A great, majestick, howling discord that grumbles down into the abyss and then insists its way stubbornly up again, bigger than a building, bigger than anything; to play it properly you'd need a speaker the size of a cathedral. A throat as big as the Mississippi. It played and played; everything I knew played until I wept, how can one not? If there's faith, there's music. They whisper:

Since by Man came death. . . .

(heh heh that leaves me out, even in the minor key, pianissimo)

Since by Man came death. . . .

(more insistent now, and heavier, but they still believe it)

BY MAN CAME ALSO! THE RE-SUR-RECTION!

(wups, fast and fortissimo and major; I think they mean it)

And they played and they sang and I wept, everything I ever knew, for Baroque music is keyed into Isaac Newton's kind of time; it's the energy of that new explosion of philosophic time: perspective, mathematics, instant velocity, the great clock, the great wheel, harmonies, the Great Godly Grid.

Then the bushes whispered in succulent German O my heart, my heart. Out of my big griefs. My little songs. Inching towards Einstein. Let me love, mother, let me lean on his bosom. I thought the frost-flowers on the windowpane meant Spring. . . .

Over here the Phoenix Reaction and God as Engineer. Over here entropy, suffering, death. And then the real Einstein, too complicated for me although I know what I'm supposed to like, Stravinsky and after; it makes my head ache, referring to things in all dimensions and sometimes backwards. And then it turns primitive, this is a bloody great dynamo and this a laboring flute. And then music-as-theatre. And round again. Round and round.

All the music in the world says all the things in the world—I mean the universe, of course—and that's everything there is.

So it all cancels out.

Sound the trumpet!

It is.

And let the listening hills rejoice.

They are.

I started up The Messiah but you have to be quite careful about *Every valley* because I'm near one and it might get ideas; I mean *shall be exalted* and there we go with an X-quake.

Well, if it all goes round, it's a spiral anyway—a four-dimensional one ("hyper-spiral") or like that theory of the four cosmi bongling into each other perpetually like ping-pong balls—matter with "forward" time, matter with "backward" time, antimatter with "forward time," antimatter with "backward" time, only I think that would take five dimensions (six?

seven? seventeen?) no, only three and Time, and you have to have ideal Ping-Pong balls because they never damp out. I like the older way better because I'm irresponsible: Forever and ever. Forever and ever.

Forever and ever!

Hallelujah, hallelujah, hallelujah, hallelujah, hallelujah, hallelujah, hallelujah, hallelujah! Forever and ever.

Quite a trick, for someone who doesn't believe in God.

Only Handel always makes me cry so. The people who walk in darkness, those who dwell in the land of the shadow of death, they all do a lot of crying.

• • •

Day. Sometime. I looked up and, you know, it wasn't surprising, there's another piece of my past come back; I am really not quite sure if this is another hallucination or only a memory, but by my knee at this moment there is a five-year-old little girl standing in grey trousers, red cloth shoes, and a blue cotton polo shirt. Wearing what the gilded youth of Empire would have worn on the playing fields a hundred and sixty years ago. More or less. She is the only child I ever knew who was named after an airport.

I said, "Kennedy?"

No answer. She died in a car crash years ago but Marilyn lived. Marilyn's her mother. Three months in hospital: broken ribs, a broken arm, concussion, two operations on her knees, broken bones in her face.

Kennedy died twenty minutes after the crash. She was unrecognizable. I mean they could tell who she was only by her size; there was another child, someone else's, in the car, and Marilyn had another daughter. The other child wasn't hurt, only bruised. The inflation bags didn't open for some reason: people thrown about the inside of a steel can. They had to cut the car open.

She's put her hand on my knee. But I can't feel it.

Silence. I said, "Kennedy, you were quite obnoxious when you were alive. You were a screamer. You used to steal my needle and scissors to fight beasts with when you visited. You lifted up your voice and complained and when I took them back, you kicked me."

Silence. She has no expression. Not grave, not gay. Interested, perhaps? No, she's only looking at me.

"Have you come to get me?" I said.

Silence. That same almost intent—yet not intent—gaze.

She must have something to tell me. Otherwise why come all that way? If she had lived two weeks longer she would have gone from daycare to school and she was rather proud of that because she was one of the very few children (the only elegance she could parade) who had a single mother and not eight mothers or five dads or a mix of mothers and dads or two dads or three mothers, and she was great friends with a little boy named Harold, who had a single father.

"Where's Harold?" I say to her.

Silence. She was anxious, rather obsessed with growing up, very fierce in defending her rights, and her death nearly killed her mother.

I tried. "Marilyn—"

She put her hand again on my knee and this time I felt it, a thrill, a fear, a warning, that insistent, communicating, hot-damp, little hand.

A gateway. A sign. A messenger. Though nothing's settled. Fill in all the standard things about living being dying and the questions making the answers, everyone's dying all the time, dying is life, &c., &c. But I still don't know anything.

This is not Kennedy, who is drifting towards the door of the cave without a backward glance at me, like the night Marilyn was brought into hospital and I kept seeing her standing between two rooms, a lit one and a dark one, but they were both empty. Turning softly and vaguely from one to the other, and both empty. I still don't understand that. I mean, both empty.

Kennedy was always so fierce in life: squinch lines around her eyes, thin mouth either distended or twisted, cheeks blown out with rage, sucked in for gloom. She was never still; you could never measure the proportions of her face.

I guess I ought to follow her out, throw myself over the cliff. Can't, though. I'd only roll down like an idiot or a thistle and get impaled on something; I can't jump any more. I've printed out most of this and put it in the tin box; I'm wearing the rest of it around my neck. Pushed the box into the back cave wall because it's going to fall soon. I mean in a few hundred years or so, sometime, it's clear it will.

The splendid sun out there, lighting up the world. The lit room. The empty room.

I will record a few last words, try to think of something significant, and since after that concert—everything's ringing still —there's not much else to do. I mean. I mean I will not. Since I don't care. Thank God it's over. Odd to look back and see how much should have been changed, but one forgets the everydayness of it and the reasons why; I don't suppose I did better with the room than most or worse or whatever. I mean if they make you rent it unfurnished, you see.

An afterlife: that would be nice, I suppose.

No. Better not.

Time. Time to go. Which way: instant, euphoric, religious, sleep, trancelike—really, nowadays you'd think one was shopping for couch covers. I think I'll leave them all behind, pity not to get to the real thing at last after all this trouble. I can muster up a jump. I can roll off the cliff, maybe bump my head, maybe die of thirst; lots of delirium, dirty my pants, interesting stuff, my whole past or something. The natural method.

I'm going to do a joke; I will put as the last words on this, Oh I see people in uniforms coming through the brush downstream; someone's coming to rescue me, Goddam.

And there they are! Coming through the brush—almost at the horizon, I think, but in white—people in white, as if they were the survey team for this tagged, unfurnished house—and they're following the line of the river. Six of them. Coming this way. What a damned nuisance, I will have to be alive again, how exasperating.

Bet you believed it.

Told you, joke.

Can't remember worrying about this. This dying. Can't remember. Why? Will put the print-out away, wait for the hill to bury it, and keep the vocoder. Such immense kindness from the hill. Nice hill. Nice sun (setting behind a bush someplace). So friendly, all this strange world, really. Walls. Floor. Astonishingly put together.

● ● ●

I've done it. But kept the vocoder. And I have to be near the box or you won't find it. Whoever you are. It's the loneliness, really. Marilyn still alive somewhere, that's the ghastly thing.

I'll do it the instant way, I suppose, just to be finished with it. Get it all over, all that dying. Long dying: long, long dying, forty-two years, that's too much and I really *wish*

● ● ●

If only I can get into it right, fit right. You know. I've got the ampoule in my hand, only have to break it. Skin contact.

Death, thou shalt die
The City of Dreadful Night
Eternity as a bath house full of spiders (but he was nuts)
The Celestial City
Gehenna
History is a nightmare from which humanity longs to awaken
Death is not part of life; death is not lived through (I'll buy that)

Got this thing in my hand. O.K.

● ● ●

well it's time

ON STRIKE AGAINST GOD

Author's Note

My apologies to friends whose houses, dogs, gardens, mannerisms, clothing, and landscapes I have stolen for this book.

I have also stolen literary quotations. "Indefinable rapture" comes from Mary Ellmann's *Thinking About Women* (Harcourt Brace, Jovanovich, New York, 1968, p. 95). The various quotes from literary women are as follows: "How are we fallen! fallen by mistaken rules"— Anne, Countess of Winchilsea; "Women live like Bats or Owls, labour like Beasts, and die like Worms"—Margaret Cavendish, Duchess of Newcastle, both quoted by Virginia Woolf in *A Room of One's Own* (Harcourt, Brace, & World, New York, 1957, pp. 62 and 64). "Anyone may blame me who likes" is the beginning of the famous feminist outburst in Charlotte Brontë's *Jane Eyre*; "How good it must be to be a man when you want to travel," is quoted by Tillie Olsen from Rebecca Harding Davis's letter to a friend in Olsen's biographical essay on Davis in *Life in the Iron Mills* (The Feminist Press, Old Westbury, New York, 1972, p. 101). "John laughs at me but one expects that in marriage" occurs in Charlotte Perkins Gilman's *The Yellow Wallpaper* (The Feminist Press, Old Westbury, New York, 1973, p. 6). "It had all been a therapeutic lie. The mind was powerless to save her. Only a man—" is part of Mary McCarthy's story, "Ghostly Father, I Confess" in *The Company She Keeps* (Harcourt, Brace & World, New York, 1942, p. 302). The last quotation, "I/Revolve in my/Sheath of impossibles—" is part of the eleventh stanza of "Purdah" in Sylvia Plath's *Winter Trees* (Harper & Row, New York, 1972, p. 41).

Some of the above have undergone minor revisions, but there are no major ones.

For those interested, the strike referred to in the title is the shirtwaist-makers' strike of 1909–1910 which occurred in New York and Philadelphia. It was the first general strike of its kind and the first large strike of women workers in this country. It involved between ten and twenty thousand working women, most between the ages of sixteen and twenty-five. They held out for thirteen weeks in midwinter. One magistrate charged a striker: "You are on strike against God and Nature, whose prime law it is that man [sic] shall earn his bread in the sweat of his brow. You are on strike against God." Details may be found in Eleanor Flexner's *Century of Struggle* (Atheneum, New York, 1970, pp. 241–243).

"YOU ARE on strike against God"—said by a nineteenth-century American judge to a group of women workers from a textile mill. He was right, too, and I don't wonder at him. What I do wonder is where did they get the nerve to defy God? Because you'd think something would interfere with them, give them nervous headaches, hit them, muddle them, nag at them (at the very least) and prohibit them from daring to do it, just as something interferes with me, too, tries to keep me away from certain regions. As I write this the cold March rain is turning the new growth of the trees and bushes an intenser yellow and red, a sort of phantom fall in the tangle of weeds and bramble outside my window. But something doesn't want me to think about that. It's too beautiful. I once had a friend called Rose, whom I'd known for years, who lived in a slum that no matter how she painted the walls, it still looked rotten. The last time I ever saw her was just before I started teaching; I was twenty-nine. I went to visit her in East New York (Brooklyn) where she still lived with her mother and we talked, as we always did, about art and about the college professor she'd been in love with for years, a man much older than she. Rose and I went to high school together. It's this long-drawn-out business of interpreting his glances, his casual remarks, how he shakes her hand. She's got it all elaborately figured out. When I visited her she was putting away her three suits, her two scarves, her one sweater, her two changes of junk jewelry—all Rose has. She lays it out exquisitely in her bureau drawers and enjoys the sensation of living light. It's cheap but she takes endless time choosing it and laundering or cleaning it. (She works as an accountant, but not often, so she hasn't much money.) Whenever Rose decides to renounce the world she feels so good that she goes out to the movies and calls friends that very night. When I was there her mother had the TV on in the living room of that very little house—they live in a section of dilapidated clapboard houses, iron gates over all the storefronts at night, lots of weeds. Her mother's great pride was a pink, plastic tablecloth and matching plastic curtains in the living room, a vinyl-topped table for the

309

TV. Rose had just repainted her own room with quick-drying paint; she was arranging her clothes, she who never goes out (hardly) and telling me in great detail about her fantastically complicated, draining, difficult, unhappy love affair with this man, which would be consummated (I suppose) in about twenty years when he was seventy and she almost fifty. She's very, very fat and good-looking, with a fat woman's strange and awesome smoothness, her monumental (and fake) physical serenity.

I said, "I'm in love, I'm in love again. Rose, did you hear me?"

She went on talking, folding and re-folding her clothes, turning toward me her witty, careful, pointed glance, so imitative of happiness. She knew I didn't mean it. At that time I didn't, and I don't know why I said it. Rose was preparing to leave the world again, which meant she would be very unhappy in a week or so. She didn't even listen to me. She was telling me how her mother had once seen her walking in front of a speeding car when she was a child and hadn't warned her.

I left her wallpapering her much-loved, much-tended little corner of hell.

Not really being in love then. Heavens, no. Not even thinking about it. Without love there's nothing to bring into focus what's outside oneself, like (let us say) the soul of things non-human as manifested in the quiet clearness of a hillside in late winter, the place I live now, from the yellow grass-stems to the pebbles to the cut made for the road to pass through—all this in the misty graying-out of the Pennsylvania hills, the regular, rocking line of the ancient flood-plain, the occasional fountains of yellow-green where the willows are coming alive, red where it's some kind of bush, all these harmless, twiggy nerve-centers, the animate part of the great World Soul. Harmless until now, anyway. Landscape has a dangerous and deceiving repose, unlike cats or dogs who have eyes with which they can (gulp!) look right at you and sometimes do just that, as if they were persons, looking out of their own consciousness into yours and embarrassing and aweing you. Wild animals are only mobile bits of landscape. Until you learn better, you think that a landscaped world can't hurt you or please you, you needn't bother about its soul, you needn't be wary of its good looks.

Until you learn better.

I went out one night last August to look for my friend Jean, who's a graduate student in Classics here. The small town I work in (I teach English) has a collegiate appendix stuck on one end, two small streets on the hill down from the University, and in the more important block, the one restaurant that stays open throughout August, even after summer school has closed, the kind of place that's called Joe's, Charlie's, or Kent's; you know what I mean. Earlier in the evening there had been clouds sailing across the moon, up there in that deep inky-blue; so it was obvious to everyone that it was going to get much warmer or much colder by morning. I passed the melancholy parking meters (unused now), the pizza carry-out, the electronics parts store (closed), the laundry, the drugstore, the Indian boutique, the piano somebody has stuck on a sturdy pole and painted aluminum-color to advertise a private house that sells pianos—this looks very odd under the street lights and is really the damnedest thing I have ever seen. I'm going to look for Jean, the Twenty-Six Year Old Wonder: the eternal shield of her large sunglasses, her absurdly romantic long dresses (mauve or purple), her beautiful, square, pale, Swedish face, the tough muscles in her arms from three months on crutches (after a skiing accident in which she smashed her kneecap).

But she wasn't there. Nobody was, I mean nobody I know. There was someone I'd met at a faculty cocktail party, if you can call it met, but I ignored him because I really had thought that Jean would be there, or somebody. And I might have seen him in a play, not met him, I mean he might have been one of the Community Players; that's embarrassing. So I jumped when that fellow came over right after I'd sat down, I mean the unfriend, smiling suavely and saying, "Waiting for someone?" And what can you say when you jumped, when you thought you didn't know him, when you *don't* know him, not really? Are you going to turn down the chance? That's a lovely way to end up with no chances at all. And I'm thirty-eight. He frowned and said uneasily, "Um, can I sit down?" I'm not going to be mean. Four years ago—but it's different now—four years ago was my Israeli graduate student whom I picked up here out of sheer desperation right after I'd moved here (from another college five hundred miles away), sheer desperate loneliness (and because I knew I had to learn how to pick up men in bars)—he approved of my not wanting car doors opened for me like most demanding American women (but none of that pierced my ghastly haze of distress) and told me his views on America and the politics of campus revolution and what he was studying and why and what I should be studying and why. I said yes, yes, yes, oh yes, not even telling him I was a teacher, gibbering like anything out of sheer terror at existence (I had just got divorced, too) and later blew up at him when he tried to kiss me "because you're so understanding." Because it was a fake. Because he wasn't there. Because I wasn't there. Because he didn't know that I knew that he didn't know what I knew and didn't want to know.

Yes, dear, oh yes yes yes.

Why do men shred napkins? Three out of four napkin-shredders (rough estimate) are male. Female napkin-shredders are really napkin-strippers, i.e., they tear napkins into little strips, not shreds. But men who tear napkins tear them to shreds.

My new napkin-shredder sat down, a little dark fellow in Bermuda shorts and knee socks, and Goddamnit there went his hand out for the very first napkin. Blindly, appetitively seeking. Do you think I could ask him? Do you think I could say: Please, why are you tearing that there napkin into shred-type pieces? (Or pieces-type shreds, possibly.) Why? Why? Why? Oh, put your hands in your lap and leave the napkin alone!

Now, now, he's as nervous as you are, dear.

I said, "Your napkin—"

"What?" he said, alarmed.

I shook my head to indicate it was nothing. First we'll talk about the weather, that's number one, and then I'll listen appreciatively to his account of how hard it is to keep up a suburban home, that's number two, and then he'll complain about the number of students he's got, that's number three, and then he'll tell me something complimentary about my looks, that's number four, and then he'll finally get to talk about His Work.

"I've got an article coming out next May in the *Journal of the Criticism of Criticism*," he said.

"Oh, congratulations!" I said. "It's such a fine place. They don't keep you waiting, do they? Like *Parameter Studies*."

(My analyst and I often discussed—years ago—my compulsion to always have the last word with men. We worked on it for months but we never got anywhere.)

"They didn't keep *me* waiting," says Napkin Shredder (thus neatly dodging any mention by me of my seven articles in *Parameter*); "Perhaps you saw my articles there—the imagery of the nostril in Rilke?"

I made myself look frail and little. "Oh, no," I said. "I just can't keep up, you know."

(So far, so good.)

He then told me what his article in C of C was about and how he was going to make it into a book, none of which I particularly wanted to hear—nor did I want to talk about mine, which I also find extremely boring, why inflict it on strangers? —but it's a sign they like you, so I listened attentively, from time to time saying "Mm" and "Mm hm" and watching the front window of the restaurant in the hope that Jean might walk by. *Why are you telling me all this?*—but that's a line for the movies. Besides I know why. And, as usual, the burden of maturity, compassion, consideration, understanding, tolerance, etc. etc. is on me. Again.

"Oh my, really?" I said. (I don't know at what.) He beamed. He began to tell me about a grant he was going to get. He told me this in a confidential way (leaning very close across the table) and I thought in a confused fashion—or my manners must have been slipping—or I'd been watching the front window too long—anyway, one ought to help, oughtn't one?—so I answered without thinking (my analyst and I worked on this too but we didn't get anywhere):

"Don't do it. Just don't do it. They make you work too hard for your money. I know; I've gotten grants from them twice."

There was a strained silence. Perhaps I'd discouraged him. He told me the names of his last four articles, which had been published in various places; he told me where, and then he told me what the editors had said about them (the articles). He was talking with that edge in his voice that means I've provoked something or done something impolite or failed to do something I should've done; you are supposed to show an intelligent interest, aren't you? You're supposed to encourage. So I analyzed the strengths of all those separate editors and

journals and praised all of them; I said I admired him and it was
really something to get into those journals, as I very well knew.

"I often wonder why women have careers," said Shredded
Napkin suddenly, showing his teeth. I don't think he can possibly be saying what I think he's saying. He isn't, of course.
Never mind. I'll stand this because Reality is dishing it out
and I suppose I ought to learn to adjust to it. Besides, he may
be sincere. There is a human being in there. At least he isn't
telling me about something he read in the paper on women's
liberation and then laughing at it.

"Oh goodness, I don't know, the same thing that makes a
man decide, I suppose," I said, trying to look bland and disarming. "Cheers."

"Cheers," he said. The drinks had come. He opened his
mouth to say something and then appeared to relent; he traced
circles with his forefinger on the table. Then he said, leaning
forward:

"You're strange animals, you women intellectuals," he said.
"Tell me: what's it like to be a woman?"

I took my rifle from behind my chair and shot him dead.
"It's like that," I said. No, of course I didn't. Shredder is only
trying to be nice; he would really like me best with a fever of
102 and laryngitis, but then he's not like everybody, is he? Or
does he say what they only think? It's not worth it, hating, and
I am going to be mature and realistic and not care, not care.
Not any more.

"At least you're still—uh—decorative!" he said, winking.

Don't care. Don't care.

I said quickly, "Oh my, I've got to go," and he looked disappointed. He's beginning to like me. I am a better and better
audience as I get numbed, and although I've played this game
of Impress You before (and won it, too—though I don't like
either of the prizes; winning is too much like losing) I'm too
tired to go on playing tonight. Will he insist on taking me
home? Will he ask me out? Will he fight over the bill? Will he
start making remarks about women being this or that, or tell
me I'm a good woman because I'm not competitive?

Oh why is it such awful work?

Shredder (coloring like a schoolboy) says he hopes I won't
laugh but he has a few—uh—odd hobbies besides his work;

he's always been tremendously interested in science, you know (he tosses off a frivolous reference to C. P. Snow and the "two cultures") and would I (he says, shyly) like to hear a lecture next Thursday on the isomeric structure of polylaminates? As I would, actually, but not with him. (His ears turned pink and he looked suddenly rather nice. But will it last?) I don't want to make a bafflefield—sorry, battlefield—of my private life. Baffle-fiend! Goodbye, Mr. Bafflefiend. I will leave Shredder and go look for a Good, Gentle-but-Firm, Understanding, Virile Man. That's what my psychoanalyst used to keep telling me to do. To avoid quarreling I let Shredder pay for the drinks (a bargain for him but not for me); to avoid endless squabbling insisten-cies I let him walk me around the corner to what I said was my home; and to duck the usual unpleasant scene ("What's the matter with you? Don't you like men?") gave him my—entirely fictious—telephone number. I waited inside the building un-til he'd vanished uphill and then slipped out into the street and started off in the opposite direction. Spoiled, spoiled. All spoiled. My psychoanalyst (who has in reality been dead for a decade) came out of the clouds and swooped at me as I trudged home, great claws at the ready, batwings black against the moon, dripping phosphorescent slime. Etcetera. (All the way from New York.)

You will never get married!

All right, all right, Count Draculule.

You fear fulfillment.

Buzz off, knot-head.

Your attitude toward your femininity is ambivalent. You hope and yet you fear. You attract men, but you drive them away. What a tangle is here!

I giggled.

You do not like men, Esther. You have penis envy.

They have humanity envy. They don't like me.

Come now, men are attracted to you, aren't they?

That's not what I said, kiddo.

He comes back every once in a while, very stern and severe; then he goes back up into a cloud to clean his fangs. We get along. After a while you tame your interior monsters, it's only natural. I don't mean that it ever stops; but it stops mattering. I trudged down the hill and up the hill to home (then up the stairs). My kitchen is always a greeting; I don't know why. I don't like to cook. Yet my apartment always strikes me—after each small absence—as something I've created myself, with my own two hands, something solid and colorful and nice, like an analogue of myself. It greets me. You can see that this is going to require an awful lot of (naturalistic) padding while I walk home, climb steps, sleep, or go from one room to another. But in recompense I will tell you what I was thinking all the way home in that chilly, fragrant, August night: I was thinking that I felt sexually dead, that I was perpetually tired, that my body was cold and self-contained, that I had been so for eleven years, ever since my divorce, and that nothing I had done or could do or would ever be able to do would ever bring me back to life. I didn't like that. Not that it was a tragic feeling; it was only something mildly astonishing (in the middle of all the things I do like and enjoy). It amazed me. As I threw the windows open to the night I thought that at least I had fed my showy, neurotic, insecure, exhibitionistic personality to the full over the last few years, that in this one way (and many others) I was very happy, I enjoyed myself tremendously, but there was something else I didn't have, another way in which I was deprived. Yet a mild feeling, believe me. At least so far.

I'll tell you something: my psychoanalyst (I mean the real one) used to ride around Manhattan on a motorcycle. It was his one eccentricity. I think he was secretly proud of it. Whenever patients in our group (what a word, *patients*) got audibly worried about this rather dangerous habit, he would (I think) be secretly delighted; he would beam without apparently being aware of how pleased he was, and then this tall, balding businessman would say, "O let us analyze your anxiety." He never analyzed his own liking for the motorcycle. He was thrown from it in a collision with an automobile and died in the street, leaving behind a widow (badly provided for) and two small children. He was younger than I am now. You may gather that I didn't entirely like the man and that's true—but when he comes zooping down from his black cloud, fangs aquiver, I think of his death and it warms me. It pleases me. The man was such a fool. I try to make myself sorry by thinking of his wife and children—there's his poor wife, compelled to believe all that nonsense, yes, and live it too (don't tell me she never sneaked a peek in Freud, just to see). Did she have the wrong kind of orgasm? Did she succeed in renouncing her masculine protest? Hypocritically I try to make myself cry, thinking that I should feel sorry for anyone in such an accident, all that blood over the street, etc., the twisted motorcycle, etc. Then I'm not pleased. Then I have a very different reaction.

Snoork! I laugh.

To be sexually dead. . . .

Well, people pretend to be better than they are. That used to mean frigid, but now it means something else. The truth that's never told today about sex is that you aren't good at it, that you don't like it, that you haven't got much. That you're at sea and unhappy. When I was married I never lay back and opened my knees without feeling (with a sinking of the heart, an inexpressible anguish) "Here we go again," a phrase I couldn't explain to my analyst and can't now. I think it was because my thighs hurt. I did get some mild pleasure out of the whole business, I don't want to misrepresent that, but not much; I could never get my feet down on the bed when I put my knees up (my tendons were too tight) so after a few minutes my knees and thighs would begin to hurt; then they'd hurt a lot and if I turned over and we did it the other way my face would get pushed into the mattress and I didn't like that. I couldn't move at all that way. And if I sat on top it was lonely and I couldn't relax and I knew I was supposed to relax (all the books said it) because if I pushed or tried to take control, then I wouldn't come. But my husband never seemed to know what to do. *To be made love to*—that was the point. Only I was no good at it.

What I cannot convey is the intense confusion I felt when I tried even to think about it.

Cures: my analyst told me not to try for orgasm at all, so I knew I was wrong to be hung up about it because it wasn't important; or rather it was so important that you had to treat it as if it wasn't important (or you would never have it); so for a long time I could never think of myself sexually at all without intense confusion (as I've said) and great personal pain.

Have masochistic fantasies—but that's much too close to real life.

Pretend you're a man—I did that when I was fourteen. But that's forbidden (and impossible). I used to daydream (twenty-four years ago, can you believe it was so long? I can't) that I was a man making love with another man. Which still strikes me as fairly bizarre, if you start thinking about the transformations of identity involved. I told my analyst.

He: In this—ah—daydream, are you the active or the passive partner?

Me: What?

He: (patiently) Psychology knows that in homosexual pairs, one man is always the active partner in love-making and the other man is always passive. Now which do you imagine yourself being?

But here an abyss opened beneath my feet. I still am not really sure why. The truth is that I felt the coming battle without being able to name a thing about it; was it that I wanted to say one thing and would be made to say another? Or ought to say another? Or must say one thing and must not say it at the same time? I didn't know. I knew one thing only and that was crystal-clear: *I was going to lose.* So it was with the simultaneous sense of sneaking home safe and yet being intolerably —oh, just intolerably! coerced—that I replied very haltingly:

Me: (blush) Um . . . passive. The passive one.

He: (delighted) Ah! So you really are the woman, you see.

Which is not so. It's just not so.

"You know," said my analyst, "there's no reason you can't tell your husband what you'd like him to do to you. Women ought to be aggressive in bed."

Me: Lost again. I always lose. (But I didn't say it. I smiled a sick, feeble, little smile and agreed.)

What else could I do?

I remembered summer camp at the age of twelve when I necked with my best friend (we all did) but wouldn't touch her breasts because I was too embarrassed. The next summer everyone had apparently forgotten what we had done the summer before. (A point of peculiar integration from which everything has gone most definitely down-hill.)

I desired my husband—but it didn't work. I experience the same muddle-headedness when I try to remember *what* didn't work. I have no words for it.

Having a heart-felt crush on beautiful, gentle, helpless, intelligent Danny Kaye at age twelve and a half. I seem to be going through the right phases at the right times. Still, I keep wanting to rescue him from things. Can that be right? (Is it sadism?)

The best solution (and the one I pursued after my divorce): Not to think about it at all.

Jean dropped over for breakfast the next morning, which was Sunday, bringing with her black cherry ice cream and bacon, both of which we ate. This is an honor; she seldom spends money for luxuries because she lives on a fellowship in a co-op downtown. Sat around the kitchen, loath to leave (the most crucial room in the house), drinking endless cups of tea until the memory of the black cherry ice cream became unpleasantly dim. There was a wonderful surfeit of odds and ends on the table. I had been trying to plan the day's affairs to avoid the premise that I had absolutely nothing left to do, for a three-months' vacation (my vacation, an academic one) is like the jungles in H. Rider Haggard: first your little traveling party goes through the harmless fringes of the first few days, everything looking only mildly sinister; then there's the thickening growth and the awful feeling that it'll never end, and then you start losing people—beating the bushes for them, holloa-ing for them (but it's no use)—and finally all those early glimpses of prehistoric monsters and strange footprints (or arrows or axe-heads buried in tree-trunks) pay off, so to speak; I mean that your camp is attacked in the brief tropical dawn by Beast Men or a Phagocytus Giganticus who eats the native guide, the heroine's father (a scientist), his assistant, and all the maps, leaving our heroine alone in the jungle she now knows contains almost two months more of vacation and nothing whatever to do. There I was. With the hope that I could eventually walk in a sort of trance to the foot-hills (I mean that you will get used to it) and begin to climb. But my apartment's been burnished to a high gloss (including cutting fuzz off the rug with a nail scissor, honest) and I've also decided not to move to another apartment. The dinosaur's eaten the map.

I told all this to Jean.

"Look!" she said, and she drew three interlocking circles on her napkin (like the beer ad).

"Mimetic," she said. "Didactic. Romantic." And went off into something I couldn't follow.

"This morning I dreamed I saw Death at the foot of my bed," she said. "He was reading a newspaper. Hiding his face in it. Banal, really."

"Work is a real blessing," she said. (She's right.)

I stirred my tea. I played with my food. Brightening up, she told me how the cooperative's dog had caught a rattlesnake: courageously biting it in two although it made him vomit. So-and-so had made noodle pudding. So-and-so was trying to fix the phonograph. It's a loose practical association, nothing very striking; I mean you must not think of it as any close, mystical, hippie-dippy sort of thing because it's not. Jean studies mathematics for fun, makes her own clothes as a recreation, can do anything, is ferociously private. Stupid Philpotts (the cooperative's dog) is a cross between an Afghan and an English sheepdog; first he chases the sheep, then he knits them into sweaters. I couldn't stop laughing. Jean, whose arrogance toward other people is often terrifying, was staring dreamily ahead, one hand curled in her lap. Stupid Philpotts (she told me) is large and skinny and covered with immense amounts of curly white hair (which quite conceals his face); if you lift the hair, you see his beautiful, intelligent, long-lashed eyes, which gleam at you like lovely jewels. He was missing for eight days last winter and came back with ice-balls the size of golf-balls frozen into his hair. And diarrhea from eating garbage.

"Those damned bastards," said my friend, thinking of something else entirely.

In the summer, in my apartment, you can always go into the living room and look over the hills. Actually you can do it in winter, too, because the setting sun—in the course of one year—describes an arc that stretches from the Southernmost window of the living room (in December) to the Northernmost end of the study window (in June). You can watch the sunset every day of the year through my enormous windows. Overhead the third-floor tenants were walking about, a nuisance that somewhat dilutes the pleasure I take in my windows. Jean sat here exactly eight months ago, basting the lining of a coat; she often hauls her sewing around with her.

But don't think of this as anything domestic or feminine in the ordinary sense; Jean's sewing is part of her perfectionism. It's armor plate.

"Those—!" she said again. Some teacher of hers (she told me) making passes at her in spite of her saying no; some teacher's wife (at another time) badmouthing women graduate students with that venomous sweetness that shows you how very "feminine" the woman is—she can't get angry openly, not even at another woman. Pathetic and awful, both of them. And the men in the collective not wanting to do certain kinds of work.

"Men run the world," said Jean. "Men are people; therefore people run the world."

"Evil people," I said. "Are you a man-hater?"

"Don't be silly" (absent-mindedly).

Am I a man-hater? Man-haters are evil, sick freaks who ought to be locked up and treated until they change their ideas. If you think (under those conditions) that I'm going to admit *anything*, you're nuts. Let's just say that I don't like to sit still and smile a lot. And I would rather not hate anyone (virtuous me!); that is, I would rather there was no reason for it.

"Jean," I said, "did I ever tell you about my friend Shirley?" (Shirl the Girl who went into an expensive private mental hospital in New York and came out insisting *she had to wear stockings* or they'd get her again. "You gotta conform," she'd said to me grimly.)

"Yes. Many times."

"Oh," I said, shaping the O sound very purely (but silently) with my lips. Playing. Bored.

"I would rather not hate anyone," said Jean, pausing in her work (she had brought a pair of white gabardine slacks with her, to hem by hand). The Duchess Look: objective, dispassionate, not pleased. I told you that last night was very clear, active, and cold; now huge black clouds are rising on the Southwestern horizon, the place our weather comes from through a pass in the hills. Leaves, twigs, and bits of detritus are being blown all over the place. The light's turning green. I went about shutting windows and wondering if the rain-gutter would fall into the garden again—not that we have a real garden, I'm talking about the rather elementary piece of lawn the landlady pays the boy next door to mow once in a while and our two unkempt forsythia bushes. The house is old, and besides providing a sounding-board for footsteps, it has trouble with some of its trim. Jean and I sat and watched the faraway part of the town (in the valley) disappear under rain; there was a *crack!* and you could see the streets darkening one by one. Sound of machine-gun fire or round-shot in buckets. Myriads of dashes on the screens first, then on the windowpanes. Pockmarks on the porch roof. Then with another rattling slam the windows became invisible and the whole house ran with water, a real summer storm. The air in the living room was already getting stuffy. Stupid Philpotts (said Jean) would be hiding under somebody's bed now, although what all this meant to him, deep in his doggy mind, nobody could tell.

"Ah! *he* knows," said I. Jean giggled. She fiddled with my radio and then turned it off. Our storm withdrew down the valley and along the lake, grumbling and muttering. Eight minutes after it had begun we opened the windows; the temperature had dropped fifteen degrees during the rain, but the sun was coming out, straight overhead and very hot. It was noon. No, it was high noon, sun-time. I don't know if a clearing storm can ever be followed by a rise in temperature unless it's hot beforehand, but that's what happened. Summer was back again. Proper August: humid air and puddles. I looked at Jean again, wanting to say something-or-other and expecting she'd be back at her work, but she was looking past me, the Duchess look gone from her face, all the cynicism gone, the laziness, the bitterness. Through my bedroom window, where the sun rises in December, through the Southeastern window just opposite the direction of the departing storm, was a double rainbow which the Australians call mother and daughter. So rare, so lovely. Everything a vivid emerald green in which the mailbox on the corner shone like 1940's lipstick. Those strange, aniline hues you never see anywhere in nature, and at the earthly end (guaranteed or your money back) King Solomon's Mines. (I'm in the foothills at last.) It's not possible to stay unhappy. I took Jean's hand and we waltzed clumsily around the room. We said, "Isn't it lovely?" as people do, but we really meant more than we could say: this double rainbow, a completely circular ice-bow on Cape Cod, a seagull against the sun, cherry trees in the Brooklyn Botanical Gardens, being wheeled there when I was a child, times like these.

We meant: It's a sign.

Even if it were permissible to hate men, I don't think I would. You can hate some of the men all of the time and you can hate all of the men some of the time. Tell the truth or bust! (We shall not bust.) I remember walking down the city streets years ago and being suddenly amazed into a stab of love and admiration for my beautiful, gentle husband with whom (as I told you) I could not make love. Why did we ever separate? Something must have shown on my face, for people stared. I remember being endlessly sick to death of this world which isn't mine and won't be for at least a hundred years; you'd be surprised how I can go through almost a whole day thinking I live here and then some ad or something comes along and gives me a nudge—just reminding me that not only do I not have a right to be here; I don't even exist. Since I crawled into this particular ivory tower it has not been better, hearing about the typical new man in the department and his work and his pay and his schedule and his wife and his children (me? my department), well that's only comedy, but what goes right to my heart is the endless smiling of the secretaries where I work, the endless anxiety to please. The anxiety. Like my husband, coming home on the bus with me from my shrink and blurting out, "There's only you and me, what does he mean, *the* marriage!"

Still, sex was no good with him. Seeing a double rainbow with Jean and waltzing around the room (clumsily but solemnly) has somehow enabled me to remember that sex with my husband was in fact very bad, the badness of it being (as I remember) a good measure of the truly vast number of things I could not—then—manage to remember. Or rather, I labored so conscientiously to remember to forget them; if only I'd had a worse memory! But I didn't. I am a good, earless, eyeless girl who walks past construction workers without hearing or seeing anything and the last time I hung upside-down by my knees from the top of the jungle gym I was five years old. I wonder what I made of that upside-down world. Already dainty and good, not liking to have smudges on my dress (when I remembered) and setting my dolls to school like my elementary-school

teacher aunt, dressing them in appropriate costumes for the
season (which practice I continue with myself, by the way),
and spending a lot of time fussing over which of them was the
tallest and which the shortest because they had to be put in
a row of graduated height for school. I wrapped up my best
doll and took her downstairs once to see a hailstorm. But I
got dirty, too. And I liked the world upside-down (having bat
blood) and longed fiercely to get up in the clouds, which you
could only do if they were "down"—i.e. hanging on the jungle
gym. I would swing my way absentmindedly to the top like a
monkey and then hang there, stern and sensible, full of cosmic
awe. There's a picture of this dead little five-year-old woman
looking at the inside of her first post office, rows and rows
of post-office boxes right up to the ceiling; she's hanging on
to the knobs of two of them with an indecipherable—perhaps
stunned—expression. I'm looking at a jail. The Rose-Growers'
Association gardens where we went every week-end was my
mother; my father was the post office (because he worked in
an office); I myself was the stone lion outside the post office.
There's a picture of me sitting astride it, looking uncomfortable and exalted. In the earliest family snapshot of all (I mean
after the wet-lump stage, which does not show personality, at
least in a kodak) I am peeking dramatically around the corner
of a city fire hydrant, my face smeared beautifully all over with
chocolate ice cream. It all looks so good: don't give a damn
about anybody and having a good time. I am told that these
short people are still alive somewhere, possibly inside the great,
grand palimpsest of Me, and somewhere at the center (like
a kernel in a nut) the archaic idol, all red wrinkles, who got
wrapped screaming in a blanket (covering her enlarged vulva—
this is true, you know, for a few days after birth) who sucked in
foodstuff at one end and squirted product-stuff out the other,
like a sea-anemone. But this I don't believe. You're supposed
to break your teeth on this archaic center if you bite too deeply
into things—but I find the howler monkey, the wanter, the
hater, the screamer, far too modern and present to think of her
as the leftovers from a baby. And who could call a wet lump
she? You might as well call it Irving. What has truly never left
me is the post office boxes (which I rather liked; they certainly
looked powerful and important) and the jungle gym. Witches

do everything upside-down and backwards; they go in where they should go out, and out when they should go in. Or flat. Like all women. So get used to seeing everything upside-down as you read this.

But the name is bad. The name is awful. I mean that everyone I've met, everyone I know well (unless they're lying, as I always am in a social situation—you don't think I want to get locked up, do you?)—anyway, every female friend of mine seems to have accepted in some sense that she is a woman, has decided All right, I am a woman; rolls that name "woman" over and over on her tongue, trying to figure out what it means, looks at herself in a full-length mirror, trying to understand, "Is that what they mean by Woman?" They're ladies. They're pretty. They're quiet and cheerful. They want a better deal, maybe, but they're easy-going, they have a certain serenity, they're *women*. Perhaps they've lost something, perhaps they've hidden something. When they were sixteen they could say, "I'm a *girl*, aren't I?" and not be stupefied, stunned, confused, and utterly defeated by the irrelevant idiocy of the whole proceeding.

I'm not a woman. Never, never. Never was, never will be. I'm a something-else. My breasts are a something-else's breasts. My (really rather spiffy) behind is a something-else's behind. My something-else's face with its prophetic thin bones, its big sunken eyes, my long long-bones, my stretched-out hands and feet, my hunched-over posture, all belong to a something-else. I have a something-else's uterus, and a clitoris (which is not a woman's because nobody ever mentioned it while I was growing up) and something-else's straight, short hair, and every twenty-five days blood comes out of my something-else's vagina, which is a something-else doing its bodily housekeeping. This something-else has wormed its way into a university teaching job by a series of impersonations which never ceases to amaze me; for example, it wears stockings. It smiles pleasantly when it's called an honorary male. It hums a tune when it's told that it thinks like a man. If I ever deliver from between my smooth, slightly marbled something-else thighs a daughter, that daughter will be a something-else until unspeakable people (like my parents—or yours) get hold of it. I might even do bad things to it myself, for which I hope I will weep blood and be reincarnated as a house plant. I do not want a better deal. I do not want to make a deal at all. *I want it all.* They got to my mother and made her a woman, but they won't get me.

Something-elses of the world, unite!

Do you think Jean is—might be—a something-else?

Sally, Louise, Jean, and I were watching a bad movie on TV. Behold a handsome, virile, football-player actor pretending to be an eminent scientist. It was one of those movies in which a computer takes over the world and you jolly well wish it would—anything's better than the people. I notice that the Amurricans are all glamorous mesomorphs under thirty-five but the Rooshians are fat and middle-aged. So I'm in trouble with art, too. Sally and Louise are visiting—old acquaintances of Jean's, not really friends, for they're much older than she is (she's twenty-six)—with a dog named Lady who barely got into the apartment before she zipped frantically under the sofa and stayed there for the entire visit, at the end of which she came out very stiff and stretching herself as if she'd had rheumatism. Lady's afraid of new places. Lady, I was told, is a Belgian sheepdog with a tendency to herd strange children— that's funny to tell about if nobody takes you to court over it; nor is it funny or pleasant for the children who have their heels nipped, I imagine.

What are Sally and Louise like?

Well, they look like—well, like anybody. They aren't glamorous. From a distance they look young (that's the blue jeans); but they're grown women in their late thirties, even as you and I; Jean knew them when they were English teachers here. I don't know them. Louise is the chunky one who wears huge, fashion-model sunglasses and tried very patiently to coax Lady out from under my sofa (Lady growled and retreated). Sally is the skinny one and talks a lot. If she weren't so friendly and civilized, one feels, she'd be into your refrigerator instantly, or examining your drapes for blister rust or your cupboards for teacup blight. Not that she's pushy; she's just interested. Truth to tell, Louise is not so plump nor is Sally so skinny; it's only that there's little to say about women who don't project themselves dramatically by way of makeup or dress. And there was the weariness of their eight-hour drive from Virginia. In both ways totally unlike my friend Jean, who was being very WASP college-girl fresh and beautiful: her hair caught back by a green ribbon, her bell-bottomed green pants, a man's white shirt tied together in front. All of us, I think, had the academic drabness in which everything has run to voice, so I remember Sally's quick, brilliant, insistent hammer-blows (the voice of a short woman who's on her way to becoming a time-bomb because nobody ever takes her seriously) and from time to time Louise's slow, deeper, ironic, Southern interruptions, one hand going down to rub the dog's nose. Lady didn't say a word. And Jean is always just Jean.

What did we talk about?

I don't remember. We talked so hard and sat so still that I got cramps in my knees. We had too many cups of tea and then didn't want to leave the table to go to the bathroom because we didn't want to stop talking. You will think we talked of revolution but we didn't. Nor did we talk of our own souls. Nor of sewing. Nor of babies. Nor of departmental intrigue. It was politics if by politics you mean the laboratory talk that characters in bad movies are perpetually trying to convey (unsuccessfully) when they Wrinkle Their Wee Brows and say (valiantly—dutifully—after all, *they* didn't write it) "But, Doctor, doesn't that violate Finagle's Constant?" I staggered to the bathroom, released floods of tea, and returned to the kitchen to talk. It was professional talk. It left me grey-faced and with such concentration that I began to develop a headache. We talked about Mary Ann Evans' loss of faith, about Emily Brontë's isolation, about Charlotte Brontë's blinding cloud, about the split in Virginia Woolf's head and the split in her economic situation. We talked about Lady Murasaki, who wrote in a form that no respectable man would touch, Hroswit, a little name whose plays "may perhaps amuse myself," Miss Austen, who had no more expression in society than a firescreen or a poker. They did not all write letters, write memoirs, or go on the stage. Sappho—only an ambiguous, somewhat disagreeable name. Corinna? The teacher of Pindar. Olive Schreiner, growing up on the veldt, wrote one book, married happily, and never wrote another. Kate Chopin wrote a scandalous book and never wrote another. (Jean has written nothing.) There was M-ry Sh-ll-y who wrote you know what

and Ch-rl-tt- P-rk-ns G-lm-n, who wrote one superb horror
story and lots of sludge (was it sludge?), and Ph-ll-s Wh--tl-y
who was black and wrote eighteenth century odes (but it was
the eighteenth century) and Mrs. -nn R-dcl-ff- who wrote silly
novels and M-rg-r-t C-v-nd-sh and Mrs. -d-n S--thw-rth and
Mrs. G--rg- Sh-ld-n and (Miss?) G--rg-tt- H-y-r and B-rb-r-
C-rtl-nd and the legion of those, who writing, write not, like
the dead Miss B--l-y of the poem who was seduced into bad
practices (fudging her endings) and hanged herself in her garter. The sun was going down. I was blind and stiff. It's at this
point that the computer (which has run amok and eaten Los
Angeles) is defeated by some scientifically transcendent version of pulling out the plug; the furniture stood round us unknowing (though we had just pulled out the plug) and Lady,
who got restless when people talked at such length because
she couldn't understand it, stuck her head out from under
the couch, looking for things to herd. We had talked for six
hours, from one in the afternoon until seven; I had at that
moment an impression of our act of creation so strong, so
sharp, so extraordinarily vivid, that I could not believe all our
talking hadn't led to something more tangible—mightn't you
expect (at least) a little blue pyramid sitting in the middle of
the floor? But there wasn't anything. I had a terrible shock,
something so profound that I couldn't even tell what it was;
for nothing had changed—the sun sank, the light breeze blew
through my enormous open windows. The view over the hills
was as splendid as ever. I looked for the cause in Lady, who
had eased herself stiffly out from under the sofa with a plain-
tive whine of discomfort, I looked at the lamps, the tables, my
floor-to-ceiling bookcase, my white walls, my blue rug and
red curtains, my black-framed pictures of roses and robots.
But nothing has exploded, or changed color, or turned upside down, or is speaking in verse. Nor had the wall opened
to reveal a world-wide, three-dimensional, true-view television set playing for the enlightenment of the human race and
our especial enjoyment, a correct, truly scientific (this time)
film about a runaway computer in Los Angeles in which all
the important roles were played by grey-haired, middle-aged
women. That would violate everything. (The other way only
we are violated.) Perhaps in the days of the Great Goddess

(before everything went wrong) creation was both voluntary and involuntary, in the mind and in the body, so to bear the stars and planets—indeed, the whole universe—She had not only to grunt and sweat with the contractions of Her mind, but think profoundly, rationally, and heavily with Her womb.

Then the spontaneous remission. The healing. The Goddess's kindly and impatient gift. I started thinking again and the first thought was very embarrassing: I realized I had been staring very rudely at Jean, who was sitting in front of the window and whose breasts were silhouetted through her blouse by the late afternoon sun. I tried to tell all this to the others, but I think they were only amused. "We're brilliant," I said. "We're the great ones." (I meant: what those others say about us isn't true.)

"Sure," said Louise.

I wanted to say to Jean, I'm embarrassed because I saw the outline of your breasts and you're running around without a bra. But my head hurt.

"I'm dying of hunger," said Sally. "Let's go out."

(You see, we're the real people. We're the best. I don't mean that we're "as good as men" or that "everyone is equal" or that "people should be judged as individuals." I'm not referring to those others out there at all. It's a question of what's put at the center. See Copernicus and Galileo. I know you know all this, but indulge me. Listen to me. The roof has just come off the world and here is the Sun, who took Her broad, matron's face down behind the last, the Westernmost hill, and here is baby Night, who's leaning Her elbows on the cool sill of the East. She carries a fishing rod so that She can dangle the bright bob of setting Venus over the brow of the Sun. Something has vanished from the top of the sky, some lid or lens or fishbowl that's been closed oppressively over my head as long as I can remember and nobody ever even remarked upon it or criticized it or took the trouble to suggest that it might not be a good thing, that it might even be better if it were removed. I trailed after Jean to the door, thinking that I was making some other decision, too, but something I didn't understand, and that it was unsettling to feel voluntary action taking place in a region you can't even reach. Anyway, it's just one of my fantasies. And it doesn't matter. Not that it's something in me; it's only something strange in the way the world is put together, something about the way foundations of the world are arranged.

(But what is "it?"

(I don't know.)

My fantasies. Oh lord, my fantasies. The human bat fantasy about mating in mid-air. The Super-Woman fantasy (before the comic book). The hermit fantasy. The Theda Bara fantasy. The disguised lady as reckless hero fantasy (Zorra). I have a million of 'em. One of us who is writing this (we're a committee) was told by her mother that she was named Joan after Juana la Loca or Craz Joanna, a poor Spanish Queen bereft of her wits who followed her husband's embalmed corpse around An-da-lu-*thee*-ya etc. for eighteen years. It's in the encyclopedia. Now this is a hell of a thing to put on your daughter. I found out last week that her real namesake was in fact the spiritual leader of the entire Western World and somebody who scared everyone so much they had to rearrange the succession of Popes (with two years left unaccounted for and one Pope John), efface her from the history books for four hundred years, and demand a physical examination of every candidate for the Papacy thereafter, lest they again get stuck with a woman (Brand X). I mean, of course, Pope Joan—or John VIII, Joannes in Latin. Not to mention the saint who came after her, which makes this particular name very powerful indeed.*

That poor mother was deceived. She had become abject.

It is very important, Boadicea, Tomyris, Cartismandua, Artemisia, Corinna, Eva, Mrs. Georgie Sheldon, *to find out for whom you were named.*

Queen Esther, my namesake, got down on her knees to save her people, which is no great shakes, but Ruth—whose name means Compassion—said Whither thou goest, I will go too.

To her mother-in-law.

Big news for all the Esthers and Stellas in the audience —your name means "star." Forget Hollywood. Stars, like women, are mythologized out of all reality. For example, the temperature at the core of Y Cygni, a young blue-violet star of impeccable background (the main sequence), is thirty-two

*d. 855, anathematized *1601*. Oops.

million degrees Centigrade. This is also Epsilon Aurigae, that big, cool, unwieldy red giant, whose average temperature is a bare seven hundred degrees C but whose outer edges are as big around as the orbit of Uranus. And the neutron stars, denser than white dwarfs (20,000 times the density of water) and those even more collapsed but poetical persons who are supposed to disappear entirely from the known universe, at least to the eye (their immense gravitational fields trap the light trying to escape from their surfaces) but who remain at the center of an unexplained attraction—the disturbing center at a lot of nothing, you might say. Sylvia did this once or twice. If you're really ambitious, you might try to be a nova, which (says George Gamow in *The Life and Death of the Sun*, Mentor, 1959):

will blast into an intensity surpassing that of its normal state by a factor of several hundreds of thousands and, in some cases, even of several billions.

(p. 155)

Or

an essentially different class of stellar explosions [with a] *maximum luminosity on the average 10,000 times greater than that of ordinary novae and exceeding by a factor of several billions the luminosity of our Sun.*

(p. 157)

This part of the book is full of italics; I think even the author got scared. Moreover, a supernova is visible from Earth every three centuries and we're about due for one. Just think: *You might be it.*

Did you hear that, Marilyn? Did you hear that, Natalie, Darlene, Shirley, Cheryl, Barbara, Dorine, Lori, Hollis, Debbi? Did you hear that, starlets? You needn't kneel to Ahasuerus. You needn't be a burnt offering like poor Joan. Practice the Phoenix Reaction and rise perpetually from your own ashes! —even as does our own quiet little Sun, cozy hearthlet that it is, mellow and mild as a cheese, with its external temperature of 6000 degrees Centigrade (just enough to warm your hands

at) and its perhaps rather dismaying interior, whose temperature may range anywhere—in degrees Centigrade—from fifteen to twenty-one million. The sun's in its teens, fifteen to
twenty-one. The really attractive years. The pretty period.

And that, says *my* bible, is what they mean by my name.
That's an Esther. That's me.

Jean and I went to a party. It was given by Jean's parents, with
Jean acting as a social slavey along with her younger sister,
her younger brother being exempt and her older sister having
married a tree manufacturer in Oregon—sorry, a lumber manufacturer. (Only God can make a tree and She seldom tries,
nowadays.) It was mostly academic people, friends of Jean's
parents, who are both biologists at the university agricultural
and veterinary school, her father a full professor, well-paid,
her mother a part-time researcher, unpaid. (Their work is far
too esoteric for me to understand, let alone explain.) The first
thing that happened at this party was that someone started
a contest between the men and the women—there was one
way in which women were physically superior to men, which
involved standing two feet from a wall, putting your forehead
against it, and then trying to raise a chair. It was something to
do with leverage. Whatever the damned thing was, I wouldn't
do it. They coaxed me but I wouldn't. "Aren't you interested
in the differences between men and women?" they said. I said I
thought we ought to judge people as individuals. What I really
wanted to say was that if we were having a contest of physical
abilities, I'd like to see some of the men give birth, but if you
do that (I mean say it, not do it) you spend the rest of the evening fending off some extremely respectable character (sometimes, but not always, from the Middle East) who has been
looking all his life for a free, independent woman to Talk Dirty
With. Jean's parents had made her put on stockings so she was
scratching herself as ungracefully as possible whenever anyone
looked at her. She was sulky. The talk next turned to push-ups,
which the men got very excited about (but I can't do push-ups
either) and then to the more usual things, like weather, so it
appeared that we might be getting out of the woods, but then
somebody leaned across the coffee table (dropping ashes on
the family's expensive but sturdy-and-practical rug—why is it

that the only aesthetic people in science are the physicists?) and remarked, looking rather pointedly at me:

"I hear someone's giving a paper on menstruation at the next MLA." The MLA is the Modern Language Association, a sort of English-teacher monopoly.

O giggle giggle giggle (all over the room).

Probably a eunuch, said I. Aloud I said:

"Come on, you're just making that up to tease me."

"Oh, no," he said. "Honestly. I wondered what you thought about it."

"Be serious," said I, brightly.

"But I am!" And he writhed a little, like Uriah Heep. "I want to know your opinion of it."

I wanted to say that I could hardly have an opinion of it, not having read the blasted thing, but something took it out of my hands.

"Why are you telling me this?" I said.

He winked gallantly.

I went to the bathroom.

Twenty minutes later when I figured it would all be over, I came out. I was right; they were talking about chowders or clowders or fish parts or something. The trick of doing this is to insinuate yourself carefully into the group by stages in a dimmed-down sort of way so that the inevitable liberal in the group can't come up and apologize for the bad behavior of the first nut, because then you have the problem of whether or not to dress him down for not having come to your aid earlier, whereupon he gets a little snappish and says he thought that a woman fighting her own battles was what women's liberation was all about. Another way to avoid this is to eat a lot. I saw that Jean was attempting to slouch as disgustedly as possible in the kitchen (stomach out) because she does not like her father's friends. Her parents have very good, unimaginative food at their parties, which is a relief after you've been exposed to a lot of bad attempts at curry, or the kinds of things graduate students do under the romantic impression that nobody's ever cooked before. Jean's mother has a maid who comes in every day to clean up and everyone in the family (but Jean) thinks the maid is a very serious cross to bear because she talks a lot. I suspect the maid has crosses of her own. (She's white

hill-people with bad legs: varicose veins and swollen ankles.)
Jean's mother stayed home with her four children until the
youngest was eleven, as was only right (she said); then when
she went out to work after eighteen years she had, of course,
to get household help. "My mother has too much energy,"
says Jean. There was the usual nervous discussion about Them
(Blacks, who else?) in which Jean's father maintained with desperate, unhappy passion that They were better off than Black
people in other parts of the world and the whole company
(including me, I am sorry to say) jeered at him most cruelly;
Jean's father is a kind of eccentric knickknack in his friends'
eyes. They're liberals and they won't stand for anything biased
or unfair. I have in me a demon who had slept all through the
previous really rather personally painful exchange (I mean the
MLA article) and which was now beginning to wake up—to
keep it down I started talking with my female neighbor about
the clothes you can't buy for summer any more, and the old
trolley-cars (which we both remembered) with the woven sides
that went half-way up. My mother's summer shoes used to be
similarly woven, with some sort of holes in the straw-y fabric,
and her rayon dress (the first synthetic) also had little patterns
of holes. I used to think summer was made of little patterns of
refreshingly aerated holes. Also putting away the winter drapes,
if you remember, and the rug, and putting slipcovers on the
furniture, although I do not know why anyone ever did or (for
that matter) stopped. Mysterious. I love women—I mean I just
decided that, talking to her; I mean women don't come up to
you and go sneerk, sneerk, menstruation ha ha. You can have
a simple, lovely conversation about 100% polyester double knit
and what do they *think* they're selling for summer fabrics these
days!—it's like astronomy, like zoology, like poetry—without
taking your life in your hands, as I seem to do every time I
talk to a man. The men, by the way, were deep in international
politics (of a rather amateur kind) at the other end of the table.
The one Continental thing Jean's parents do is to serve a good
deal of wine with their formal meals, so I think my neighbor
was getting a little zonked; she was telling about how it had
been, going to a woman's college twenty years ago, that if you
wanted to be a scholar you had to wear lisle stockings, Ox-
fords, and mannish suits or nobody would take you seriously.

Wasn't it wonderful now (she said) that we could all be *femi-nine?* She said this over and over, like a life-raft. I said Yeah, I guess. Faculty wives (she teaches part-time—freshman courses) tend to dress for parties like a rather weird version of TV talk-show hostesses, as if they had tried but hadn't got it quite right —and this nice lady, my table-mate, was wearing a long red silk skirt slit up one knee and a white organdie blouse with ruffles down the front of it. Dangling ivory earrings, I believe. Very strange. I mean all those things that glittered and all that stuff *put* on her (on her face) and inside all that the real face, looking sad. She said *she* wasn't a woman's-libber, she wouldn't burn her bra, but with such a frightened look that I wanted to put my arms around her. Blonde hair carefully combed down her back (dyed). Not what you'd call freely blowing in the breeze, exactly (like in the ads) but that was the idea, I suppose. "Oh, that never happened," I said. "That was invented by the news-papers." (And this is so.) Then she began to tell me what a rotten life she had—at every faculty party there's a faculty wife who ends up with me in a corner, crying over what a rotten life she's had (but it's always a different woman)—and then when I started talking about babysitters, free time, husbands doing housework, etc., she said: "I have a very rich life. I love my hus-band and children," and retreated into the fruit salad. "What a beautiful child Jean is!" said my neighbor. "You know," she went on, "family life is not dying, as they say," and here, in an assumed tone of immense superiority, started to talk about how her children needed her because they were fifteen and sev-enteen respectively. "Yes, dear," I said; "Isn't the salad nice?" (Sometimes they begin crying at this stage.)

Don't imagine, she said, *don't imagine that anything I've told you indicates—is—the slightest—shows that I'm—means shows the slightest—*

"What are you two gabbing about!" cries her husband with uncharacteristic heartiness and jollity from the other end of the table.

"Patterns," I said.

"I think," said my neighbor, her chin *very* high in the air (and still spiffed, I am glad to say) "that women who've never married and never had children have missed out on the central experiences of life. They are emotionally crippled."

Now what am I supposed to say to that? I ask you. That women who've never won the Nobel Peace Prize have also experienced a serious deprivation? It's like taking candy from a baby; the poor thing isn't allowed to get angry, only catty. I said, "That's rude and silly," and helped her to mashed potatoes.

"*You* wouldn't know," said she, with a smirk.

"It's rude, Lily," I said in a considerably louder voice, "and if you go on in this way, I shall have to consider that you are both very foolish and very drunk. Eat your potatoes." Scenes bother ladies, you know. Also she thought her husband might be listening in. Do you know who her husband is?

The liberal!

"Phooey," said Lily dimly, into her plate. (Oh dear, but she had had a lot to drink!) "*You* can't catch a man."

"That's why I'll never be abandoned," said I. Fortunately she did not hear me. Did I say taking candy from babies? Rather, eating babies, killing babies, abandoning babies. So sad, so easy.

Something is changing within me. Did I mention my demon? It goes to sleep at its post sometimes, but it was back now and now I didn't mind it; when we got up for dessert and coffee in the living room (and then the screened-in back porch, for it was a hot night and everybody was sweating from having eaten so much) I decided I liked my demon. It has possibilities. Conscientious clawlets out, a-lert and a-ware, prowldy, prowldy, woman's best friend. Maybe I was a little drunk myself. Something in the back of my mind kept coming up insistently and I kept irritatedly shoving it away; I don't want to think of that now. Did you know that the Liberal is a tall, athletic type with everything except a straight backbone and the original Hartyhar is ginger-moustached, older, shorter, redder, a little plump as if he were going to burst his clothes, which are imitation British? He's one of those academic men who imitate English dress under the impression that—well, I don't know under what impression. It's idiotic, especially in summer. They're not such big deals; they're just fools. Oh, I know they're fools; I've always known. Stay with me, demon. Somebody started a discussion about the mayor we're all going to elect in the fall because we're politically conscientious (though his winning certainly won't change my life). I was asked what my politics were.

"Menstruation," I said, with a bit of a snarl.

"Oh come, come, come," says slick-and-suave, "I really do apologize for that, you know." (But he never looks sincere, no matter what he says; he always looks greasy and lying.)

"My politics," said I in a glorious burst of idiot demonhood, "and that of every other woman in this room, is waiting to see what you men are going to inflict on us next. That's my politics."

"Well, you can't get along without us, now can you?" says piggy, with a little complacent chuckle. This is my cue to back off fast-fast-fast—and Jean was looking at me from inside the living room—was it warningly? I couldn't tell. She was too far away to be anything but sibylline. I said crossly that they could all go stuff themselves into Fish Lake; it would be a great relief to me.

He twinkled at me. "Disappointed in love," he said.

I think he thought that I thought that he thought that I thought I was flirting. This is unbearable. I'm absolutely paralyzed.

"I can see that you like spirited wenches," said the obedient puppet who lives inside me.

Everybody roared appreciatively.

"What you don't understand," said our fake Briton (why do they always say this?) "is that I'm not against the women's liberation movement. I believe in equal pay for equal work. But surely you ladies don't need equality when you can wrap us around your little fingers, now do you?"

The Liberal was looking at me with his eyes shining, as if I were going to stand up and sing Die Walküre. Afterwards he will come up to me and say in a *very* low voice that he thinks I was *very* brave.

"Leave me alone," I said leadenly. I should never have started.

"Ah, but that's just what we don't want to do!" cried piggy. "We love you. What bothers us is that you're so oversensitive, so humorless, of course that's the lunatic fringe of the movement—I bet you thought I didn't know anything about the movement, didn't you!—but seriously, you've got to admit that women have free choice. Most women do exactly what they want."

"Just think," said someone else, "how much good the women of this community have done lobbying for a new school."

The demon got up. The demon said Fool. To think you can eat their food and not talk to them. To think you can take their money and not be afraid of them. To think you can depend on their company and not suffer from them.

Well, of course, you can't expect people to rearrange their minds in five minutes. And I'm not good at this. And I don't want to do it. It's a bore, anyway. Unfortunately I know what will happen if we keep on; I'll say that if we are going to talk about these things, let us please talk about them seriously and our fake Britisher will say that he always takes pretty girls seriously and then I'll say Why don't you cut off your testicles and shove them down your throat? and then I'll lose my job and then I'll commit suicide. I once hit a man with a book but that was at a feminist meeting and anyway I didn't hit him really, because he dodged. I have never learned the feminine way of cutting a man down to size, although I can imagine how to do it, but truth to tell, that would go against what I believe, that men must live up to such awful things.

Dead silence. Everybody's waiting. What do you do after you blow up, nitwit? I could already hear them twittering, "Didn't you notice? She's unbalanced." There's a solution to this problem. The solution is to be defeated over and over and over again, to always give in; if you always give in (gracefully) then you're a wonderful girl. I am terribly unhappy. I smiled and got up, and I made my way out in that ghastly way you must after a defeat, while Piggy-brit said something or other which I didn't even hear, thank God. Like being eight again on the playground; I will *not* let them see me cry. I walked through the living room and out the front door; after all, I can go back in another twenty minutes. I can ask to help Jean in the kitchen, to avoid all those others. My mother used to tell me not to hurt people's feelings, but what do you do if they hurt yours? But it's my own fault. The worst thing is that you can't kill that kind of man; I imagined very vividly hitting him with a plate or the punchbowl. Then I imagined pulling

his ear off with my fist. I called him a shit-head and a stupid,
filthy prick. I knocked him down. After I had sort-of hit the
man with the book, I had trembled all day and cried. You can't
kill them; they grow up again in your nightmares like vines. I
thought I would feel better if I stepped out on the lawn and
smelled the good night air, which doesn't care that I'm crazy.
Somewhere there is a book that says you ought to cry buckets
of tears over yourself and love yourself with a passion and wrap
your arms around yourself; only then will you be happy and
free. That's a good book. I stood inhaling the scent of the ever-
blooming roses on the corner of the lawn and thinking that I
was feeling better already. God, had I been a liar when I'd said
we ought to judge people as individuals? Of course not! I'd
had a bad analyst—well, there's no guarantee. I'd had a nice,
crazy, bruised husband. Well, he'd had a bad family. There's no
reason to spend time with people you don't like. Jean doesn't
like her father's friends, either (her mother is very quiet and
doesn't initiate social things much). I said to my demon that
there are, after all, nice people and nasty people, and the art of
life is to cultivate the former and avoid the latter. That not all
men are piggy, only some; that not all men belittle me, only
some; that not all men get mad if you won't let them play
Chivalry, only some; that not all men write books in which
women are idiots, only most; that not all men pull rank on
me, only some; that not all men pinch their secretaries' asses,
only some; that not all men make obscene remarks to me in
the street, only some; that not all men make more money than
I do, only some; that not all men make more money than all
women, only most; that not all men are rapists, only some;
that not all men are promiscuous killers, only some; that not
all men control Congress, the Presidency, the police, the army,
industry, agriculture, law, science, medicine, architecture, and
local government, only some.

I sat down on the lawn and wept. I rocked back and forth.
One of those awful drunk downs. (Only I was sober.) I
wouldn't mind living in a private world and only seeing my
women friends, but all my women friends live in the middle
of a kind of endless soap opera: does he love me, does he like
me, why did he say that, what did he mean, he didn't call me,
I want a permanent relationship but he says we shouldn't

commit ourselves, his feelings are changing towards me, ought
I to sleep with him, what did he mean by that, sex is getting
worse, sex is getting better, do you think he's unstable, I'm
demanding too much, I don't think I'm satisfying his needs,
he says he has to work—crisis after crisis and none of it leading
anywhere, round and round until it would exasperate a saint
and it's no wonder their men leave them. It's so unutterably
boring. I cannot get into this swamp or I will never get out;
and if I start crying again I'll remember that I have no one to
love, and if anyone treats me like that again, I'll kill him. Only
I mustn't because they'll punish me. Certain sorrows have a
chill under them, a warning-off from something much worse
that tells you you'd better leave certain things unexplored and
unexplained, and it would be best of all if you couldn't see it,
if you were blind. But how do you blind yourself once you see
enough to know that you ought to blind yourself?

It was at this point that I heard behind me a formal, balanced sentence, an Ivy Compton-Burnett sentence, hanging in
the air in front of the house. The kind of thing written in letters
of fire over the portals of the Atreidae. Such language! It was
in Jean's voice. It was elegant, calm, and very loud. The words
"stupid prick" recurred several times.

She came up behind me in a great rush and flung her arms
about me. It occurred to me that although we'd shaken hands
and made those rather formal, ritualized cheek-kissings that
one does, otherwise we'd never touched before. It was a bit
startling. Also she's bigger than I am.

"Oh you good girl!" she cried. "Oh you splendid good girl!"
She added, more conversationally, "Did you hear what I said?"

"But your mother—" I said. "Your father—"

"That!" said this unbelieving Valkyrie with scorn, and hugging me as if I had acted like a heroine, which you and I know
I most certainly had not. "Look, Esther, I don't have to come
here. If they want to keep up the family pride by having me
visit once in a while, they treat me right. Otherwise I stay
away." She laughed.

"A secret ally," I said.

"Oh," she said, "you should have seen their faces when I
told them you were right!"

Her last words, she said, before she had informed the whole
company that they were a bunch of cowards. ("You don't know

the effect that has on the liberal types," she added, making a face.) Jean is an aristocrat who believes in good people and bad people (mostly the latter) but not in class warfare; I reminded her of this.

"Exactly," she said comfortably. "They're bad. They deserve to be told so. Besides, I already have my money for next year. My last year."

"You can cope and I can't," I said. Then I said, "I thought you weren't a feminist. Not really."

"I'm not," said Jean, squatting on the lawn and smiling at me. "I'm a me-ist."

"Let us," she added, with a look at the house and in a tone of profound disgust, "go somewhere else, for heaven's sake."

We went to Joe's and had a beer and French fries, sitting so we didn't have to face the television set directly. It went from a Western to a hockey game to a fight. Then Olga Korbut, the Russian gymnast who is only 4′ 10″ high, came on and started doing beautiful and impossible back-flips; but just then one of the men from Jean's co-op waved to us and came over. He began talking earnestly about Jean's commitment to social revolution and Jean said lightly, "Oh, you'd be amazed at the number of things I'm not committed to," but he wasn't going to take it as a joke—which (unfortunately) reminds me of all the circumstances under which I have behaved in exactly the same way. He said again that he hadn't seen any evidence of Jean's being politically committed, and she said furiously that the next time she came out of the library with a fifteen-pound foreign-language dictionary, she'd drop her commitment on his foot. He said, "You're selfish." (Some of the things Jean is not entirely committed to in his opinion: Communism, Third World peoples, the workers, ecology, and organic foods. The one thing she is absolutely not committed to: white middle-class young men who suffer.)

I gathered X's shirt-front in one hand and brought us nose to nose. Oh I had cool! I said the following, which I am going to quote you in full because I am proud of it, very proud of it indeed, and it embarrassed him. Radicals shouldn't be embarrassed. It went like this:

"You a radical? Bullshit. Radicals are people who fight their own oppression. People who fight other people's oppression are liberals or worse. Radicalism is being pushed to the wall. Would you dare to tell Sawyer" (a Black acquaintance of his) "that he's selfish because he's committed to himself? Yet you tell us. Do you dare to tell a little country with bombs being dropped on it that it's selfish? Yet you dare to tell us. You're white, male, and middle-class—what can you do for the revolution except commit suicide? When the sharks start swimming around our raft, *you're* gonna get Daddy to send a helicopter for you; you could shave your beard and cut your hair and in five minutes go right back to the enemy. Can Jean cut off her breasts? Don't say it, pure soul. You a revolutionary! You just want to purge your sins. If you're still a revolutionary in ten years I'll eat this tablecloth."

Isn't that stunning? (Even if it wasn't *quite* as good as that.) Then I added, for the poor thing looked as if it might speak, "No, don't say it. Go away gracefully. Anything either of us does now is bound to be embarrassing."

He said that we couldn't make him leave because he had a right to be there, so I said *we'd* leave, but on second thought we didn't want to leave, so he'd better go because if he didn't I could do all sorts of unpleasant things, like shouting in my trained teacher-voice (current suburban children can't speak above a whisper), or wringing his nose (which hurts awfully and looks silly into the bargain), or yanking at his ears, or throwing water all over him, or hitting him, which I might not be good at but oh, would it be embarrassing. He got up.

"No," I said seriously. "Don't say it. Think again."

He went away.

I felt sorry for him. It's that tender, humane compassion you feel right after you've beaten the absolute shit out of somebody. I suppose if he feels so bad somebody must be doing *something* to him, but this, of course, is exactly what our walking Jesus Christs never admit. I could have mentioned this is my magnificent rhetorical performance, but it's a fact I cleverly concealed out of sheer brilliance.

Why does Jean look now as I looked before? Why did I look then as she looks now?

"Jean, dear," said I, "tell me about God," for religion is the one thing we really have in common. Jean's religion is this: that somewhere (or rather, everywhere) in the universe there is a fourth dimension, and that dimension is the dimension of laughter. Eskimos, finding themselves stuck in a blizzard for the fifth day, foodless, on a piece of ice insecurely fastened to the mainland, burst out laughing when that piece of ice finally moves out to sea, thus dooming them (the Eskimos or whoever they really are) to a slow, painful, and horrible death. They laugh because it's funny; Jean and I understand that. On the Day of Judgment, Jean says, when we all file past God to be judged, He will lean down and whisper into our ears the ultimately awful joke, the ghastly truth, something so true and yet so humiliating, so humiliating and yet so funny, that we will groan and rock back and forth and blush down to the bone. "I'll never do it again," (we'll say) "never, never. Oh, I feel awful." Then they'll let you into Heaven. There will be long lines of sinners giggling and snurfing and bending double with shame.

"What will Christ do during all this?" I said.

Jean said Christ was a liberal and would stand around looking sort of upset and helpless, saying, "Oh, Dad, don't."

I've talked of God as She. Perhaps it's the He-God who repeats the joke. The She-God *is* the joke.

But Jean had a toothache, a mental toothache. She didn't want to stay. It's a dreary subject, whom you outrank and who outranks you, and I pull rank on him and she pulls rank on them, and this plane leaves for Bergen-Belsen in fifteen minutes, not that we really murder each other, Heavens to Betsy, no, not yet.

Jean didn't like Joe's any more.

Leaning her silly, beautiful, drunken head on my shoulder, she said, "Oh, Esther, I don't want to be a feminist. I don't enjoy it. It's no fun."

"I know," I said. "I don't either." People think you *decide* to be a "radical," for God's sake, like deciding to be a librarian or a ship's chandler. You "make up your mind," you "commit yourself" (sounds like a mental hospital, doesn't it?).

I said Don't worry, we could be buried together and have engraved on our tombstone the awful truth, which some day somebody will understand:

WE WUZ PUSHED.

*

Many years ago, when I thought there was no future in being a woman, I awoke from a very bad dream and went into the bathroom, only to find that I had just got my period. I was living in a small New York apartment then, so there was barely room for me in the bathroom, what with the stockings hung over the railing of the bathtub and the extra towels hanging on the hooks I'd pounded into the wall myself. I stared at that haggard 2 A.M. face in the mirror and had an (imaginary) conversation with my uterus. You must imagine my uterus as being very matter-of-fact and down-to-earth and speaking with a Brooklyn accent (I grew up there).

LITTLE VOICE FROM DOWN BELOW: Look, I'm not doing anything. Whaddaya want from me anyway?

I lit a cigarette from the pack I kept on top of the toilet tank. (I used to smoke a lot in those days.)

LITTLE VOICE: If you're mucked up in the head, that's not my fault. I'm just doing the spring cleaning. You clean out the apartment once a week, right? So I'm doing it once a month. If you wanna be fertile, there's certain ways you gotta pay. It's like income tax. Don't blame me.

Silence. I smoked and brooded.

LITTLE VOICE: I want a hot water bottle.

So I got the sensible little thing its hot water bottle, and I went back to bed and fell asleep.

I accompanied Jean for days, looking sideways at her and admiring her romantic profile, her keen eyes, the large, fake, railroad-engineer's cap she wore in imitation of a famous French movie star in a famous French movie. I followed my shield-maiden all over campus as we rambled through libraries and gardens. I wanted to open doors for her. I do think Jean is one of the seven wonders of the world. My shrink once told me that I would stop envying and resenting men when I had made a satisfactory heterosexual adjustment, but I think he got it backwards. We had an awful fight about it. Jean and I sat in the hidden garden behind the art museum and told each other horror stories.

". . . and, as any connoisseur of the subject might imagine, a disembodied Hand came creeping round the bed-curtains like a large, uncomfortable spider. Lady Letitia screamed—"

"—and screamed—" (said I).

"—and screamed—but not very loud because I have to finish the story. The Earl, awakened by he knew not what formless bodings, stumbled out of his room and down the great staircase—"

"—but quietly, because you don't want to wake anyone else up—"

"—where he was found dead the next morning, a look of nameless terror stamped upon his perfect British features. Meanwhile, back in the pantry, a slithering, rugose tentacle investigated ranks upon ranks of jelly-jars. Could the pet octopus have got loose? Alas, it seemed not likely since—"

Oh, the numbers and numbers of slithering, rugose tentacles I've met in my time! And the squamous abominations and nameless cravings from beyond the stars and accursed heaps of slime in ancient, foetid cellars, and the opened crypts lit by hellishly smoking torches whose filthy punk (that's wood, lunkhead) give out an odor of the charnel house whilst succubi vanish into mouseholes in the fourth dimension (located in old New England attics) and strange figures celebrate blasphemous rites with unspeakable howlings and shocking sacrifices to nameless eidolons of hideous basalt mounted on . . . well, on Singer sewing machines, I suppose. And my eyelids sink in a luxurious, lovely droop. Why are horrors always nameless? Does that make them worse? It certainly puts you to sleep faster. The names things do have to put up with sometimes—for instance this secret garden (hidden behind the old museum, which was some trustee's mansion in 1875) is called the Emily M. Mapleson Planting after the lady who left it as a bequest to our institution. Poor woman! I would have called it Emily's Garden. For some reason every flower in it is white; at different times of the year different white blooms are potted in (though I've never caught anyone doing it; perhaps Ms. Mapleson endowed it with elves, too). Emily's Garden is completely hidden from the outside view by a dense stand of evergreens; inside are two stone benches, and in the middle of the flower beds a plaque with the name I've mentioned and a rather lumpish bronze faun with silly teeth. The whole thing is no more than fifteen feet across. At this time of year, in mid-August, very little is flowering; there's a lot of groundcover, small white blossoms (like Baby's-breath or Sweet William), with swaying Cosmos just inside the borders and a lot of dishevelled Phlox in the middle, shedding like mad. Someone has put a few Shasta daisies (which are—or look—greenish in the shade) behind the benches. It's not yet time for the Aster family and last week's white snapdragons have failed and been taken away to mourn themselves. Late summer is a difficult time for gardens because so little happens. Jean has got to "a terrible slithering splash in the old attic" and I tell her for Heaven's sake, how can you splash in an attic?

"In the cellar," she says. "Besides, they keep an old washing machine in the attic." Helpless laughter from both of us at the idea of the Lurker from the Stars bobbling about in the family laundry. I ask her will she finish the thing off, for goodness' sake.

"All right, a great number of shots rang out and everyone dropped dead. The end," said Jean.

It was very quiet in Emily's Garden. Flowers make no noise. Beautiful little plant genitals swaying in the breeze and surrounded by vast evergreens; earlier in the year yellow hemlock-pollen had drifted on to the spring flowers, the ground, the benches. Even the now-disgraced snapdragon bells made no noise. I was trying to concretize all this "blasphemous," "rugose," "nameless" stuff in the person of a clump of hysterical Phlox at my feet, each plant looking like a mad prima donna: Ophelia, perhaps, scattering used-looking white flowers in all directions. Phlox blossoms are insecurely fastened to their stems at best, so the flower-spire always gives the impression of letting its hair down. Phlossoms. The phlossoming Phlox. The phantasy of the phlooms of the Phlox.

I looked up into Jean's face, about to tell her about the Phlooms of the Phlox, but I was dazzled. Absolutely dazzled. All this happened before I had words for it, before I could even identify it; I felt the blow, the astonishment, the thing-in-itself. Something transmitted, something endured with a gasp. Unspeakable. Unnameable.

Elves got your tongue? said the swaying white Cosmos.

"'Rugose' only means 'red,'" I said to Jean.

She agreed.

It's all right as long as it's nonsense, just fantasy. I'll understand in a moment. It's ridiculous to say that I'm in love with

Jean, because Jean is a woman, and besides she exasperates me too much for that. I know her far too well. It's all fantasy and admiration, just as the blooms in Emily M. Mapleson's Planting are not Lucia di Lammermoor (a heroine of the patriarchy who went mad when deprived of her lover, stabbed her husband—with the overhand, or opera grip, not the proper underhanded tennis-racket one—and died, presumably from too many high C's). How can I giggle about Lucia and yet not be able to keep my eyes off Jean? It's all right if it doesn't mean anything. The memory of seeing her breasts silhouetted beneath her blouse went through me, went right through me, with such a pang that the horizon ducked as if I'd tried to hit it—ducked like a boxer while I clung to Emily M. Mapleson's cement bench because I was falling down. There's no excuse for it. I must make my heterosexual adjustment, as Count Dracula told me when together we chased the Big O, that squamous, rugose, slithery little man with his techniques and his systems and his instructions about what "wives" do for "husbands" and what "husbands" do to "wives"—what did he think *we* were doing, running after love with a butterfly net?

It's all right if I don't mean it. If I never tell Jean. If I never tell anybody. If I do nothing.

I accepted it on those terms.

What you do sordidly, in cellars.

"What?" said Jean. It seems that I had spoken aloud. She then informed me that she had already finished that silly horror story. I decided I must babble of something so that she would think I was behaving normally, while the sun shot arrows through my bones—although I do not look like a truck driver with a duck-tail haircut, do I?—while my sex radiated lust to the palms of my hands, the soles of my feet, my lips (inside), my clumsy, eager breasts, while they radiated it back to between my legs and I very obligingly thought I was going to die.

What is lust?

A permission of the will.

Jean began to talk about tenth-century Icelandic proper names—but that's all I heard, for she was walking in front of me and I watched her tapering back fit into the vase of her behind as if I'd never seen such a miracle before—which I hadn't, because I swear on my foremothers' bones that this is the first

time since the age of twelve that I'd even thought of such a
thing. And who doesn't, at twelve?

Count Dracula told me I was blocked. He told me I must
Try. How to Feel Lustful Against Your Will. He never told me
how it goes in waves from your belly up to your chest, and
then into your head, and then down again; when I felt nothing above the belly-button he seemed to think that was A-OK
—the Lurker in *his* Attic was "genital insufficiency," which the
ladies seemed prone to (said Count D.), the poor ladies who
wanted a lot of all-over skin contact, he with his screwdriver or
power-lathe approach.

"Are you sure you're all right?" said my suspicious friend,
turning around and frowning with concern. "You look funny."
Telepathy? Two can play at that game.

I told her I was very, very depressed. About the snapdragons.

We both screamed with laughter. I thought I could risk a
look at her again, blazing with beauty with her Swedish chin
and her beautiful behind, but again it happened: the pang, the
blow, the astonishment.

Why, oh why didn't anyone tell me?

"Jean," I said, tottering at my own daring (but I won't tell
her, oh no, not in a million years), "do you think one ought to
go to bed with one's friends?" She looked at me with her wry
look—beautiful, of course, for everything my friend Jean does
is beautiful. And intelligent.

"With who else?" she said drily. "One's enemies?"

I tried to be a good girl, honest I did. I looked in the mirror
and told myself I was bad. (This worked at the age of five, why
not now?) But the self in the mirror loved me and laughed and
blew kisses. I went about, cheerfully bawling popular songs in
a very graceless manner; I sang "All Of Me, Why Not Take All
Of Me" and "Love Is A Many Splendored Thing." I sang a
bad country-and-western ballad with lots of twangy accompa-
niment between the lines, like this:

Ah hev a never-endin' luv fer yew,	(bloing, bloing)
And mah never-endin' luv is trew.	(bloing, bloing)
Ah luv yew so, whut kin ah dew?	(more bloing)
Ah hev a never-endin' luv fer yew.	(final bloing)

I'm lean, moody, prophetic. I'm aging well. (That's what the mirror tells me.) I want very much to sit in Jean's lap. Count Dracula and I have a long conversation about what is happening to me:

COUNT D: Now, Esther, let us discuss your perwersion.

ME: Sir, sirrah, ober-leutnant, sturmbannsfuehrer, wherefore is it that you speak with a Viennese-Polish accent, whilst you are as Amurrican-born as you or I? Could it be that you have been reading too much Freud?

COUNT: No diwersionary tactics, Miss Frood. We must nip this abnormality in the bud before it flowers into something orbful. Do you realize that your present daydreams and style of life might lead to—gasp!—Lesbianism?

ME: Oh sirrah, tee hee, haw haw, you jest.

COUNT: I do not, indeed. What will you do when you are pointed at by The Phallic Phinger of Scorn? When your vile secret is exposed and your landlady throws you out of her apartment? When you lose your job? When rocks and sneers are thrown at you in the street?

ME: Who's going to tell them? You? I'll bust you in the fangs.

COUNT (complacently): Mordre wol out.

ME (mockingly): God will pun-ish.

COUNT: But seriously, Esther, don't you realize that your sexual desire for women is merely an outpouring of your repressed and sublimated desire for Mommy? How can I stand to think of my dear little girl, who might have a repressed (and therefore normal) desire for Daddy if she so chose—missing out on all the good things of life? You too could have a baby—

ME (aside): Little does he know that I could have a baby anyway.

COUNT: You could have a home in the suburbs, a floor to wax, a dear hubby all your own, a washing machine, a ouija board—

ME (sotto voce): I think I *will* have a baby.

COUNT (unheeding): Of course I know you have an automobile already, Esther, but think what an old, cheap automobile it is. It's the wrong make. You could have a nice, new, expensive automobile if you were heterosexual, especially if you were heterosexual with the right sort of man, i.e. men who

have high salaries, like stock exchange brokers. Men make so
much more money than women do. Think, Esther! all this and
penis, too. But you prefer squalid, inconclusive embraces in
basements, disgusting scenes with big, fat, low-income women
in ducktail haircuts—

ME: What's wrong with being big and fat and having a
ducktail haircut? What's good for Marlon Brando is good for
the nation!

COUNT: Yes, you prefer doing things like in *Esquire* or
Playboy—only backwards—all this instead of mending your
hubby's sox and seeing the love shine thru his eyes.

(He thinks for a minute. This business about *Esquire* and
Playboy is obviously not getting to me, perhaps because it has
nothing to do with me. He thinks that I think that he thinks
that I think that I *really do* read girlie magazines. Then he finds
it.)

COUNT: Esther, have I ever lied to you?

ME: Yes.

COUNT: Then listen to me now. Don't you realize that your
desire for women is merely a repressed and sublimated desire
for men? If you could get men, you wouldn't want women and
we could forget all about this dreadful nonsense. You're not a
real homosexual. Real homosexuals have horns. Your pseudo-
homosexual desire for your friend springs from an insist complex whereby the great mother-figure stands at the doorway of
your libido, making nasty, negative gestures and warning you
back from the promised land of your father's womb.

ME: My father's—?

COUNT: If only you were able to realize that the penis is
equivalent to the breast and the breast to the penis, you would
understand that the great reality of normal sexual intercourse
(which includes fellatio) lies in its ability to simultaneously allow the male to express his own maleness and the female to
possess the male's maleness through her passive receptivity of
his penis, thus transcending her own receptivity-oriented passivity (or passivity-oriented receptivity) and for the moment
making the two one. And that one is the husband. People who
suck each other off with their mouths or fingers are evading
this great, primordial identity crisis (in which everybody becomes male) and remaining their sexually undifferentiated,

irresponsible, pathologically pleasure-seeking selves. How do they know what kind of shampoo to use? What kind of deodorant? What color of comb? In such terrible cases a male might put on a flowered Band-aid or a female a shirt that buttons from left to right instead of from right to left. I might wake up one morning and find that my wife had bought for my birthday a belt with daisies embossed upon it. The heavens would fall!

ME: That is a better birthday present than strychnine, Count D., which otherwise your poor wife might assuredly get for you. Count D., Count D., I hereby dub thee not Count Dracula but Cunt Dracula. Come back, oh D., to the womb, come back to the head, come back to the cunt and fingers and feet which once called thee forth. You died long ago in reality; so what is not-me I hereby reject and throw out with the weekly garbage; what is me I re-appropriate.

Go away.

HIS PARTING SHOT: Esther, you are *bad* (because you don't like men).

Ah! that's a weak spot. I don't. But if what I feel for Jean is a substitute, then I had better never meet the real thing because I would certainly die from it. As it is, every time I have to wipe myself after going to the bathroom I bend double. Years ago, after our group therapy time was over, we would go to a coffee shop in the East seventies of Manhattan, a district full of embassies, of private schools, of luxury high-rise apartment buildings, one of the most expensive neighborhoods in any city in the world. Here Dr. D. had his office, despite the cost (for which we middle-class white people paid, even though we loathed writing copy for catalogs or putting out industrial newsletters) so every Thursday night after the post-mortem we would go and have "coffee"—this means hamburgers, pastries, late dinners for some, what-have-you. I liked these gatherings. I didn't like the sessions themselves; no matter how they went I didn't want to be there. Every week the woman who was afraid of staircases came in to report that she had gone up and down two steps or she hadn't and we commended her or blamed her; every week the man whose marriage was breaking up came in and told us how he was "working at the relationship" and we said Good for you. And every week for three years a little voice

inside me said *Get out of here!* although I could never explain it.
I liked the people. It was like that book on the power of positive thinking: *Every day in every way I am getting better and better.* There seemed to be no way to measure anything except by the book. Sometimes people in psychoanalysis were really cured and got normal—although there was no way for them to tell when they were normal, the doctor told them, I guess—and then (presumably) you just stopped coming because you Measured Up. Nowadays "relationship" is a euphemism for fucking or having a love affair, but then it meant something different, something grim, hard, central, and unrewarding, something you had to do anyway, whether you wanted to or not. You had to *work* at it. My husband, to the intuitive marrow of his bones, knew it was bad.

"How do you know when you're happy?" I said once.

They said impatiently that they weren't talking about that and besides of course you knew. The doctor added that a bag of heroin could make you ecstatically happy, if you wanted to function at such a low level. That sounded fine to me and I thought about it quite seriously, but in the end was scared away by the law (and my own inexperience).

I liked the coffee shop; that was where we really talked.

One night a new patient showed up: a cute ugly woman with a huge hooked nose and a receding chin who knew (she said) that if she'd only been born beautiful, she wouldn't have any "problems." Beauty was what mattered in this world.

"Oh, no, it's not important," we said with one voice—imagine, we in our high heels, nylons, girdles, wigs, padded brassieres, make-up, false eyelashes, painted fingernails, tipped and permanent-waved hair, and costume jewelry!

I never came back. Oh not melodramatically, not like that, but within a few months. It was an odd kind of religious cult like the Flat-Earth people or the Shakers; in a hundred years they will still be sitting around the coffee shop (it will still be 1963, it will still be the most expensive part of the world) waiting for the tooth fairy to zap down from the ceiling and endow them with the suburban substitute for bliss. Just as the suburbs are a bad imitation of the country and I and my husband were bad imitations of—well, would you believe angels? I do not mean to make light of the suffering, which was real enough and which at least brought us all face-to-face with something real, whatever it was and however frightening it might have been—but oh the muddle, the mystification, the nonsense, the earnestness, the silliness of the whole wretched business! It was without dignity, courage, or sense. It helped with some things —the gross things—if there'd been no return at all, how could the doctor have stayed in business?—but all the same it reminds me of nothing so much as Ravel's "Bolero," which is the middle-brow substitute for music, that ghastly mock-Spanish piece you hear on every Muzak-bedongled elevator; it and the elevator and the people in the elevator go round and round to infinity without ever getting anywhere, like a snake eating its own tail.

I hope somewhere they've all gotten out of 1963 and are thinking the same things about me.

I used to go home futilely to my sad, mad (but never bad) husband—who knew his own sickness too well to meddle with it—and admire his broad, knotted back, the muscles in his shoulders and arms, his lovely vulnerable belly, that pelvic crease of Greek sculpture that comes out in a man only when he stands on one leg, his funny little round-flat ass, his rubbable, bristly chin, that indescribable line from rib to hip, so subtle and so different from a woman's. Men have straight knees and elbows; women's go in. He would stand—wistful and banana-flowered—and I'd say tiredly over and over again (to an absent Dr. D.) that I had no troubles with sex, only with men, and that my trouble with men did not come from what was between their legs but from what was between their ears. My husband envied me my brain, that Bear of Little Brain. But I cannot think of myself as the Nut Brown Maid or the Pretty Lady, truly I can't. And we only multiplied each other's angry clinging, he and I.

An awful thought:

What if Jean . . . won't?

I had two dreams that night and woke up scared; in one I was falling—nothing to see, just the sensation—and somebody giggled and told me, "You're in free fall." In the other I was very sick, being taken to the hospital on a stretcher and feeling so awful that I started to pray to get well, but that made me feel more helpless; so I prayed only that She might grant me endurance. That's all. "Give me my Self," I said. Then I woke up, with a sense of the dream over and (along with the fading of the dream) the sense of something being over for good. That's all the guilt I ever felt. I think I had it out somehow that night; it's like going through an electric fence where the worst point is just before you touch it and your nerves jump, but once you go through, it's O.K. I thought in my innocence: *Now I can be friends with men.*

Another marvelous discovery, in one of my waking periods at about 4 A.M., a vision of the local Howard Johnson's (East of the campus, on the superhighway) full of healthy, comely young women. *There are others besides Jean!* For the first time in my life I felt free. In fact, I felt perfectly wonderful.

So I went happily back to sleep.

Jean came over for breakfast the next day, bringing some inferior lox, which is the only kind you can get in a small town like this. We ate it and made a face. I was wildly excited. I finally got up and did an imitation of Jean's last—latest?—boyfriend who was somewhere in Canada slaving away at a doctoral thesis.

"Absent lovers are the best kind," she said.

I can't wait. Can you?

The trouble is, if I make a pass at Jean or tell her anything, she'll just push me away. It'll ruin our friendship. And suppose she tells someone? (Though I don't think she'd do that.) It would be awful to have to have such suspicions. My kitchen had never seemed friendlier. We sat and talked about one thing and another—she was telling me nasty, funny stories about her professors (my colleagues!) and I had to decide there was nothing I could tell Jean, even though I'm looking over her shoulder at her math textbook (a course she's taking just for fun). I've pulled my kitchen chair so close that I can smell her, which makes me want to cry.

I will have to keep it a secret.

Unhappy. Miserably unhappy. Why? Because people do not do things like that in reality. Reality doesn't allow it. In books or movies or maybe newspapers, yes, but real life is not like that, and in real life if I were to throw my arms around my friend and kiss her, she would only wonder at my madness; she'd say,

"Esther, stop it!" very sharply, and the heavens would re-form; reality—in which, by the way, I have as considerable a stake as anyone else—would simply remain itself. If I ever try anything I will be struck dead from on high anyway. (Some of the other things real people just don't do, according to my family: get divorced, become drug addicts, murder someone, kill their children, kill themselves, expose themselves in subways, get raped, fail in business, go mad.) So I can't do it. Of course I can't.

Clumsily I put my arms around her, twice-clumsily I kissed her on the neck, saying hoarsely, "I love you." (Which was something of an over-simplification, but how are you going to explain it all?)

She went on reading.

She blushed delicately under me, like a landscape, I mean her neck, she just turned red, it was amazing.

Reality tore itself in two, from top to bottom.

"Jean," said I, not believing my ears and eyes, "do you really—" but I guess she did! because she continued to pretend to read, only reddened like a tide, a forest, an entire planet. You don't ask the whole world if it's really doing what it's doing. I felt her skin get hot under my mouth. She closed her book deliberately, turned to me, and put her arms around me. *People* get divorced, *people* kill, *people* go mad. Saying I loved her might not have been so untrue, really—well, here was something worth dying for! When I think of those times that I did it to oblige, or because it was my duty, or to get affection, or because I couldn't refuse, I am ashamed. When I say "dying for" I mean the poems and the stories, the jokes, the obsessions, the terror, the wonder. I am dreadfully ashamed of my past.

We sat back and looked at each other (frightened) at the same moment. Not because it was wrong but because it was an overcharge, like the copper wire you unwittingly overload and it's going urp! help! eek! aargh! oop! (in Wire) and you don't even know why the poor thing is jumping and twitching so. Better if calmer. Men think that once you admit your desire you have to fall down and fuck on the floor right-away, but women know better; I helped her to some inferior lox and A & P cream cheese and she did the same for me. We munched away at our bagels together. Suddenly she laughed and choked on hers.

"Shame on you," she said, "making love to someone you've known for only three years!"

I said, "Well, I can't get you pregnant, can I?" feeling very daring.

We laughed until we cried, partly out of nervousness. We were both (I think) rather wary of touching each other again. So much more is at stake now. Jean went back to explaining her book, only she reached out now and again and stroked my hand. I was blind, deaf, overwhelmed. I kept wanting to put my fingers through the central hole of the last bagel because it struck me as such an extraordinarily good joke; there was a sort of divine giggle somewhere in the room.

"You don't mind?" I cried suddenly.

She caressed my hand again. The nearest part of Jean to me (once she sat back and continued reading) was her foot, for she had crossed her legs and one foot kept advancing toward me and then retreating. Now feet are not as compromising as hands and not so close to the person, so I grasped Jean's individual, very expressive foot and admired her arch, which is so much higher than mine. I was terrified. (She looked pleased and a little embarrassed.) I explained about feet and that I was not a foot-fetishist, really, but hands were too vivid for me right then, so she let me hold on to her ankle; I kept imagining that she would change her mind at any moment, that she was merely being charitable, that she was intimidated, that she'd "mind."

I know too well what can really be going on when women are silent.

We talked about how everybody was bisexual, and how this was only the natural result of a friendship, and how we had better take our time, and then—like virgins—began to whisper, "When did you first—?" and "When did you—?" "I knew instantly by the way you looked at me," she said, and I turned red from head to foot at the thought of being so transparent, in veils and waves of heat.

Jean "screwed" the last bagel with her forefinger, looking very severe and haughty.

I gingerly picked up the ends of her dark hair, where they lay on her shoulder. It was like picking up something living, with nerves in it, and it used to annoy me when men told me I should grow my hair. Though I would never tell anyone what to do.

"I have to go," she said.

Relief.

"My job," she said. "You know." (She has a part-time job at the University library, checking out books or something.)

"You won't—" I said.

"I'll tell *everyone*," said my friend, making a face, and I was really ashamed. I knew and she knew—and she knew that I knew—that really it was too much and we'd better both re-cover a little. Better to be calmer. She said she would come that night—no, tomorrow night, but tonight come down to the co-op and help bake a cake if I wanted—she would turn up tomorrow night with some pot.

"It hurts my tonsils," I said. (But the idea was to keep from getting scared or anxious.) "Poor little thing," she said, and then bent down and kissed me on the mouth for a few sec-onds. Oh dear. They never tell you your clitoris is connected right to your stomach. I was terribly frightened that sex would be just as bad with her as it had always been with a man but at the same time I didn't care because it was such a glorious opportunity to fail, you see. I didn't really care. (I think I had better stop saying "really.") But if it turned out badly, what would I do then? I kissed her back on her velvety cheek. Wom-en's faces are covered with fine, almost invisible down. I said to myself that whatever happened, we'd still be friends, but I knew that was the talk of a fool; I didn't want to be friends. I didn't actually know what I wanted, being too much involved in her individual odor, and the smoothness of her skin, and her heavy, utterly lovely behind, to care about what had not yet happened. I kissed Jean on the cheek and said a trembly good-bye.

And staggered to the bedroom, kicked off my shoes me-chanically, sat down on the bed. Pulled the curtains to, pulled down my pants, reached in the bottom drawer of the bureau for the vibrator.

A little voice cried, *You'll wear yourself out!*

But ah, that was impossible.

*

I didn't go to the co-op that night because my soul was already
in too many pieces. Spent that day and the next wandering
around: gardens, swine pens, the lamb barns with the lambies
and their mommas (I was sobbing a little at everything because
it was all so sweet). Just up and down the usual goldgreen lawns
and under the lovely trees with their dark-goldgreen shadows,
and some day we will all go to the great Multiversity in the
sky. Beamed at all the men in the street. By 6 P.M. was convinced she wouldn't come, but every time I heard footsteps on
the stairs I jumped. Something about keeping windows open
(in the summertime) makes electric light very bright indoors.
When she did come I was in the living room dusting the tables and didn't even hear her knock until she repeated it (Jean
almost beats doors down). I had the weirdest fancy that Rose
(you remember Rose; she's buried way back on page 1) was
sitting in the shadows outside the lit circle of the living-room
lamp. I walked from the dark room into the lit one, a progress
to which all creation moves, one of those moments in which
the shape of your house or your life takes on all the meaning
in the world. I opened the door with no nerves at all, and
Jean waved a bottle of wine at me. She's old-fashioned, she's
decided, and doesn't like pot. It felt like any other visit. What's
the etiquette for this sort of thing? I haven't tried to get drunk
for love-making in years, but this is going right back to adolescence, so we solemnly took two glasses of medicine (feh) and
then I ruined it by remembering a pound of ice cream I had
in the freezer, which of course we had to share, more or less.

"I can't make love; I'm too full," said she.

I stroked her hand, then her arm. I put my arm around her
and kissed her on the cheek.

"Do you want to?" I said. She nodded. We went into
the living room and carefully pulled the curtains shut, then
dragged a quilt from the bedroom. There isn't enough room
on a single bed; besides, I like to feel that my whole house
is my home. We put the wine on the floor near the quilt and
lay on our stomachs, fully clothed. There is this impalpable
barrier between everyday life and sex, perhaps to be connected up with that lack of etiquette I spoke of before; anyway there's some sort of gap you have to jump with your eyes

shut, holding your nose (so to speak) as if you were jumping into water. I remembered, with fear of exactly what, I can't specify—that Jean is, after all, twelve years younger than me. Before we brought in the quilt I had trotted into the bedroom and brought out my vibrator, hiding it shyly between the couch cushions because it is really a gross little object, about eight inches long, made of white plastic and shaped like a spaceship. Contrary to popular belief, most women use vibrators on their outsides, not their insides. Unfortunately the batteries are wearing out and instead of going bzzzz it just rattles—the truth is I'm afraid Jean will find it repulsive or possibly that she will find me repulsive. She's down to her slip by now. I've always assumed I was reasonably good-looking—to men—but why should a woman have the same standards? Jean has finally taken off her clothes and so have I; to me she looks beautiful but very oddly shaped; I suppose there's the unconscious conviction that one of us has to be a man and it certainly isn't me. Jean says she wants to put a record on the hi-fi but I don't because it's too distracting. So she bursts into angry tears. I put my arms around her and rock her back and forth, which kept me from looking at her, so although she might have still looked odd (it was wearing off) she felt beautiful. Who doesn't look odd? Men look odd. God looks odd. We smooched a little, then put a record on the player (I don't remember what. Baroque?); then lay down and necked a little more, less timidly. I love Jean. She's a vast amount of pinkness—fields and forests—but with my eyes closed it feels more to scale and it's nice. The way you measure the genuineness and goodness of an experience is this: what does it do to reading an ordinary magazine? If *Life* looks inexplicably silly to you, then life is doing its stuff. This is what I use myself and I recommend it (undoubtedly there are other tests). My friend is snowfields and mountains. Another world. Her odor (everyone has a particular, own smell) is a complicated key, one among millions. I don't understand her. For example, I don't know why she's still upset now—so I said, "Oh, phooey, turn over and I'll give you a back rub." Phooeys we doubt ever got phoooeyed. She lay mistrustfully on her stomach and I knelt between her legs, gaily pounding away at her shoulder blades, very professional though I don't know a massage from a message. So soft, so soft. Back-rubs are sneaky, low-level trickery because there's something in our mammalian ancestry that signals Good good good when your back is rubbed and you wouldn't dream of not being trustful (like scratching a dog's ear or rubbing under a cat's chin). It's taking advantage. After I had busily kneaded her shoulders for a while, I sneaked down to the small of her back and started kissing her neck; she said, "This isn't fun for you, Esther, is it?"

"Oh no, not a bit," I lied. And slid down to the rose between her legs. That's exactly what it is. Amazing. (Medieval stories.) I have the advantage of knowing where everything is and more or less how to do it. And feeling the strangest sympathetic pangs. Besides, you cannot bite men's backsides because they haven't any. Jean began to breathe hard, which made me want to cry; I kissed her on the neck where I know that sensitive place. To be the cause of so much pleasure to someone else!—as the book says, *to make a difference*. I knew that when Jean came, I would burst into tears.

"No—wait a minute—stop!" she said, rolling on her side and angrily pushing me away. She's very fair-skinned. From neck to groin my friend was covered with pale-red spots like an interesting variety of measles; I had never seen what the book calls "the sex rash" before. You know, just before climax. Utterly fascinating. You can only see it on very fair-skinned women and Jean is the eighteenth-century Irish ideal: dead-white skin, blue eyes, black hair. "Stop," she said. "I can't feel anything," she said. Wild roses and milk. The first time I came with a man (fooled you, didn't I? I bet you thought I never came with a man) I shouted "I can't! I can't get there, God damn it!" and proceeded to go into internal waves that surprised me because I thought you lost your mind when you did it. And there I was, thinking away as usual.

"Oh, Jean!" I said. She stalked angrily into the kitchen—to the window that was hidden (thank Heaven) by the branch of a tree—she drank a glass of water and came back into the living room. For those of you I am confusing by the "internal" in "internal waves" (above) I will tell you my own, recently-developed theory of sexuality, proven by years of experimental masturbating: i.e. you feel your climax most whenever you are being most stimulated. This opens surprising fields of research to those of us with suckling infants or three hands or other situations like that. Honest.

"I guess I can't," said Jean. "Or I don't want to. I mean I do want to but I suppose I can't—can I—if I'm behaving like this."

"If you don't want one, I don't want one," said I promptly. I thought *Behave any way you like. Stand on your head. Keep your clothes on. Make it with the electric toaster.* If I had to choose between always pleasing her but never myself and always pleasing myself but never her—well, I'd choose the former. At least for a while. I can always please myself afterwards. An orgasm is an orgasm, but how often is there a Jean?

"Never mind," she mumbled. "I never come with anyone."

Now this is really surprising, considering how many men she's been with. I suppose this is the time to whip out the vibrator and attack her with it, but somehow I have doubts about the whole proceeding. I think we began this wrong.

I tell her so. There should be no failure and no success.

Blushing very deeply, she asked me if she could do something. I said yes, of course. She averted her face and moved my hand on to her rose (sorry to be so kvetchily sentimental).

"Let me—ah—um—do it myself."

"Oh my goodness yes, is *that* all!" I cried. Trying to memorize the motion, an odd sort of diagonal one. Jean seems to like things done lightly.

She came in the usual way about three minutes later, not very satisfactorily, it seemed to me. She said I couldn't put my mouth down there because she hadn't had a bath for days. I said that sounded reasonable to me, although we might be wrong. She said her wrist hurt, and rubbed it. Then I lay down and Jean gave *me* a back rub and I was hung up on the edge of it forever. Finally, with not much satisfaction, I flipped over.

"That was awful!" said Jean, sitting up, tears in her eyes.

"Well," said I reasonably, "you know what they say in Swedish movies about the first time."

"What do they say in Swedish movies?" (rather sharply)

"Oh, dear, I don't know."

We sat for a while, had a glass of wine, and then began to cuddle. The formalities were over. (Thank goodness.) She kissed me and whispered to me that I was beautiful. I blew in

her ears. I fulfilled a daydream of twenty years' standing and
nibbled along her hairline, under her temples and around her
ears. We lay on the quilt and got mildly potted, feeling—as is
usual, I think, with people who take off their clothes—that
nudity is the only pleasant state. The living room was a garden. We locked big toes and had a toe fight, then began to
throw couch pillows at each other, but stopped guiltily when
we knocked over my floor lamp.

"My big toes are bigger than your big toes!" hissed Jean,
raking her toenails up and down my back.

"Ooooo!" I said. "Oo, I like that."

"She likes that muchly," said Jean.

Now what is the trouble? That sex doesn't commit you to
anything, in spite of our tradition about it? That love doesn't
give you a code of behavior? I think so. She could go away now
and never come back. I saw already what the pattern of my love
affair would be—worrying each time she was away, relieved
each time she came back—or does that mean that Jean and I
don't really love each other? Anyway, it's awful.

Jean got up and said Oh feh, she had to go. She put on her
clothes regretfully and I put on mine; we rooted in the ice-
cream container for the rest of the ice cream (Hail, Hearth and
Home! Hail, O Great Food Goddess!). Then Jean went to the
door. We said in unison:

"When will I see you again?"

A great relief, after years of being the only one to say it!
I can't come to see her because of the co-op gang and Stupid Philpotts (though we could tie him to a peg on the back
lawn if we had to) but there wouldn't be enough privacy in
the co-op, though Jean has brought men there many times
before. There's a difference. She kissed me on the edge of the
chin and I watched her as she went downstairs, swaying like a
snake standing on its tail. The Snake of Wisdom? Something
embodied. Jean will surprise me some day and perhaps not
nicely; there's the chill of finding out that I didn't know her as
well as I thought, that there's something in her sexuality, even,
that I didn't know about. Though I like it that she never came
with a man, I love it that she came with me, however awkwardly, and I will love it no matter what she uses: my hand, her
own hand, my glass paperweight with the private snowstorm

over the New England Church (with the spire, kiddies). As the real Jean waned, the mythical part of Jean came back into my kitchen, flooding the waxed floor and the refrigerator and the little study I'd fixed up in the kitchen around the corner of the L; I tasted Jean, saw Jean, thought Jean, breathed Jean. The Jean I can keep in my head.

Bonny, bonny Jean.

George Eliot never ended her books properly. There's so little for heroines to do; they can fall in love, they can die. As the story begins, you wonder whether the heroine will be happy, but by the middle of it you're beginning to wonder if she will be good. Such is George Eliot's sleight-of-hand, i.e. cheating. We still think this way a hundred years later. I've been reading wretched-housewife novels written by women and they all end the same way; either the awful husband has a mysterious change of heart (off-stage) on the last page but one or the wife thinks: Yes, but I really loved him so it was all right. You would not believe the suffering and wretchedness in these books. (And one of the characters is called Sophia, too, which means Wisdom.) I spent two Jean-less days reading these books and making marginal notes for some article or other I was going to do next winter if I ever got around to it, and then, like the heroines of these stories, I had a great "realization," a pious illumination (they're always having these, like their children really love them or they adore housework or they are really happy even though their husband ties them to a newel post and beats them with a goldfish). Progressing by a series of flat denials of the evidence. My pious illumination was that I did not want to do the article. But everything in print is sacred, as we all know, including this sentence. All words are sacred. (Unless written by a computer, in which case the *computer* is sacred.) Some astonishing things are sacred, really; thus we have the Pain Goddess and the Sleeping-late-in-the-morning Goddess, the Trip Troll (who makes the transmission fall out of your car fifteen miles from your destination), and the Mayonnaise Diety, who presides over gourmet cooking. Love is like sleeping late in the morning; you dive down through layer after transparent layer, utterly content, farther and farther until you reach the sea floor. But it's bottomless.

Waiting for Jean is pleasant: one anticipates her arrival.

Waiting for Jean is useful: perceptions are sharpened.

Waiting for Jean is educational: it teaches you that even good things must be waited for.

Waiting for Jean is fortunate: that she will come at all makes you feel blessed.

Waiting for Jean is exasperating: I can't wait much longer.

On the superhighway at night, doing sixty-five in my old rattletrap; the wet, cloverleaf roads twist and turn under the city lights like shining black snakes. It's just rained: brilliance and darkness. I'm coming home from the art museum in a town sixty miles away.

The world belongs to me. I have a right to be here.

Two days later, by mutual agreement, Jean came "just to visit." She came trotting up my stairs—or rather, dragging behind her the stately hem of a long, mauve-paisley dress. She always puts on long skirts and her shades when she wants to go in disguise. I sat with my feet curled under me, timid as a mouse, on my corner of the couch (where I was prepared to sit until Doomsday, if necessary) while Jean retailed gossip. Her gossip has one extraordinarily redeeming feature: she makes it all up. None of it is ever true. In the middle of an impossible detail about something the Dean's wife had said to the salesgirl, she looked at me long and hard and then narrowed her eyes, for I had cleverly drawn the curtains *before* she came. Just in case.

Then she took off her sunglasses and smiled at me, so that tears rose to my eyes. She unhooked her dress (home-made so no zipper) and let it drop to the floor, then with crossed arms shucked her slip and did a little victorious dance around the room, waving the slip in the air. We took off all our clothes, very soberly, and then had a cup of tea, sitting politely on the couch, naked; I went into the kitchen to fetch it in my bathrobe. We looked each other over and I showed Jean the mole on my hip; so she lifted her hair and showed me the freckles on the back of her neck. We compared our "figures" like little girls. We sat on the two ends of the couch, our knees up, feet to feet, and talked about the ecstasies and horrors of growing breasts at twelve, of bouncing when you ran, of having hairy

legs, of being too tall, too short, too fat, too thin. There is this
business where you think people end at the neck; then gradually as you talk, as we talked, as we reconstituted ourselves
in our own eyes—how well we became our bodies! how we
moved out into them. I understood that she felt her own ribs
rise and fall with her breathing, that her abdomen went all the
way into her head, that when she sat, she felt it, I mean she felt
it in herself, just as I did. Until she looked—as she had felt to
me before—all of one piece. Why is it impossible to talk about
women without making puns? When you fuck someone, you
are fucking with their eyes, too, with their hair, with their temples, their minds, their fingers' ends. (If we didn't wear clothes
all the time we'd see personality all over, not just the face.)
We sat side by side, holding hands and quite naked; then Jean
put her arms around me and it felt so good that it made me
stammer. Such astonishing softness and everything shaped just
right, as if thirty years ago we had been interrupted and were
only now resuming. I'd been worried, but it turns out to fit
some exact shape in your head that you never knew you had,
fits it with the perfection of a Swiss watch. As close as we blurry
human beings can ever come to instinct. I had been worried
about Jean, as I said, but now I didn't care, although I think
she disliked the awkwardness of having to break apart in order
to get up and go into the bedroom. I stroked her back to let
her know I would do anything for her, set fire to the rug if she
wanted, lean out the window in my skeleton, make a gift to
her of all my insides, my pulsations, the electricity in my hair,
the marrow of my bones. That's what they mean when they
say your bowels yearn; something tries to move out through
your skin. We lay down on the bed in each other's embrace
but didn't do much; only I tried to explain how lovely it was
for her to have long hair. She stopped me. "I don't mean to
be sexist about it," I said; "It's just fortunate." It came to me
as an inspiration, an astonishingly fine and surprising idea, that
we should fuck each other now, for the excitement (although
spread all over) did seem to be centering in one particular place
and I was so beside myself with aching that I thought she must
be too. And I must say the only disadvantage to its being Jean
was that there weren't more arms. Anyway at the end you don't
care if you are fucking a rhinoceros; you just want to go on and

do it. She half did it and I half did it, moving against her hand, and because Jean knows what a woman feels she didn't stop at that moment but a little after, as soon as I had stopped. Then she said, "Hey, I took a bath this time," so I slid down and very cleverly (I read this in a book) sucked at her, this being something I would never think up all by myself because you can't very well practice on yourself, now can you? And we tried a little of this and a little of that, Jean being as inexperienced this way as myself, until we ended sitting up in bed with Jean in front of me, my left arm around her waist and my right hand between her legs, a very beautiful, statuesque pose. I think the other takes practice. She came once a little bit but told me to keep on, which I did; she came again, awesomely. Like someone who's speaking in tongues, crying out, seeing visions.

"I'm noisy," she said. "I'm sluttish."

"Oh, do it again," I cried admiringly, "do it again!"

"Don't want to," said Jean.

"I hope I feel like an armchair," I said. I think what I always missed about men was breasts. Jean's are the usual shape—don't laugh, I mean they're not conical, the way some of us are—round enough, small enough; pulled down by gravity to be fuller underneath. She has one oddity; light circlets of hairs round her aureoles. Dreadfully sexy. How odd, to carry these empty milk cartons in front of us for sixty years, whether we use them or not. I think my own body has imperceptibly got to be some kind of standard for me; yet it was fascinating to see her so different. Not a line of her was imperfect. My bowels yearned with gratitude because I wanted to give her something, not for any reason, but for my own relief, for something that wanted to transfer itself out of me. My true love hath my heart and I have hers. Nothing I can name. This may simply have been a second grand idea that we should do it again, but at this point Jean got up and went into the bathroom in my sleazy pink rayon kimono (this is not my bathrobe because I own both).

"Madama Butterfly," I said.

When she came back, she sat down on the bed and started putting on her shoes. I said, "You're not going!"

She gave me a look which I recognized, having once been on the other side of the fence myself.

"I'm not?"

"Oh, of course you are," I said, "but please, please, don't. Please stay."

"I want to think about it," said my friend. She began to put on her underwear. This is the part of the movie or TV special where he speaks to her authoritatively and she obeys, or he tells her how she's got to be honest, so she bursts into tears and reveals her problem, which he then solves. But you and I know better; I'm not going to give Jean an excuse to pick a quarrel with me. And I didn't even try to look forlorn and waif-like; I was much too happy. And I could think of nothing except her. I begged her to wait until I had dressed so I could accompany her to the door, so she did. And I did. We both got decent. Standing at the door with no premonitions, waving goodbye as if we'd been having a late tea, with our clothes on all the time, quite respectably, in as false a position as possible. I saw her descend the stairs, me shutting my own door before she reached the bottom and went into the street. There would be something too final about the other way. I sat at the kitchen table, not to think (there was nothing to think about) but only to feel her all over my skin, to wonder what had gone wrong, how long it would take to set right. Twenty minutes later the phone rang.

"Hello?" I said, wondering who on earth could be calling now.

"Jean here," said she (a habit she'd picked up on a visit to England two summers before. Jean is a sponge to other people's mannerisms).

"Oh, *Jean*!" said I, pleased.

"I forgot to say goodbye."

"You what?" I said.

"Goodbye," she said distinctly.

And she hung up.

I let a day go by. I didn't do anything because I knew what would happen if I did. It came—I called the co-operative and they said she'd left the day before with all her possessions. Her family didn't know where she was. I said, "You don't *know*?" over the telephone, trying to make them feel as guilty as possible. That's it. This is the painful part. I'm subject to thinking

that I've invented things, so for a while the thought kept coming back to me that I'd invented the whole love affair, though
that isn't possible, and then the idea that unrequited love is
ghastly because it turns into a cult or phantasmagoria, something poisonous, too private a puppet show to exist. I wanted
to call the family and tell them I was her wife (or husband) but
I didn't think they'd enjoy that. Then I called the co-op again
and got the same message—they very obligingly provided me
with a second person to talk to, so nobody knew I had called
twice. Like calling the weather on the telephone. Nothing but
machines left between people. Telephones, taxis, letters, the
discarded automata of the modern love affair. I thought perhaps I'd made the whole thing up. This is an awful despair.
After the first shock you think, "Well, *that's* over," but what
do you do then? The news that kills is the news that makes
everything else impossible; you can't sleep or go out or read
or watch TV because you can no longer enjoy anything; I had
never before realized what a substratum of pure pleasure there
is in just going to sleep, for instance. Just eating. All spoiled
now.

And I can't tell anyone. I can never tell anyone.

I decided to take a walk, thinking that perhaps I might meet
Jean, but I faltered at the bottom of the stairs. Stood for a while
on the last step. What a push it takes to get out of the house!
Having only imagined it would be—somehow—worse than
anything—better to be unhappy—so I forced myself out into a
world where everything was lovely (there was a full moon) like
a Jean who said "I didn't really mean it, you know" from every
black bush, from every gilded housefront. It was a beautiful and
horrible sight. I thought of going back to my apartment and
writing to Sally and Louise, but they weren't friends. I didn't
know them well enough. Besides, what could I ask from them?
If I went to visit friends (and I do have other friends) I would
have to tell them I'd had a love affair with a man who'd fucked
and run; then they'd say, "Oh well, men do that," and I'd say it
wasn't like that, we were old friends; so they'd say "Why did he
leave?" Because he was a homosexual? Then (they'd say) I was
well rid of him and if I kept on grieving I was a fool. There's no
equivalent and I can't tell the truth. With each step it got worse,
as if I were walking through molasses, my nerves all exposed,

what will I do if I meet anyone? (Spies.) So I went back home, hastening all the way. Though I have no home, really. And remembered my past "depressions" when I'd thrown a screen out the window in the powerful, vague fear that otherwise it would be me. All long, long ago, sadly. The rule now is for the wounded to recite, like Scarlett, oh tomorrow will be another day. I can't get back to my old symbolic craziness. I wished for Count Draculule, but he's dead; all my imaginary monsters are dead. It occurred to me that if Jean had called while I was out, I wouldn't have been able to hear the phone ring, so I ran the last block and up the stairs.

It was quiet. Everything was exactly the same. Everything was just as I had left it: the gleaming refrigerator, the red-and-blue curtains, vinyl table, cupboards, white sink. I thought it would have changed somehow. Oh, the dreariness of that place! I tried to persuade myself that there was still some enjoyment to be got out of it, but it looked dreadful. Nothing there. Nothing elsewhere; my other rooms were equally intolerable. Ditto the outside. People always tell you you'll get over things (and they're right) but what do you do while you're getting over it? The old joke: your wife is buried, you weep on her grave, your friends tell you in a year you'll forget it, you'll go out, meet someone else, get married again. "But what'll I do *tonight*?" I first heard this told about an Italian and it was supposed to show how sex-crazy Italians were (I think), Italian men anyhow, but you know what I mean. In graduate school I'd envied the cats who came into my back yard and rubbed their fat, whiskery faces on the stems of the lilac bush. They had it easy. I lay down on the couch because it hurts less in the horizontal (the old lesson of a seasoned veteran of grief) and I thought I would begin a letter to Sally—no, Louise; Louise looked kinder. But what can you say except "Help me?" They won't fly up here to be my lover. I could be cunning and tell them Mommy and Daddy never loved me. Mummy loved me but she died (weak giggle). I got up to write some sort of letter to them, but realized I hadn't any idea how to begin. Jesus, I didn't want to write anybody. I wanted to feel better is all. Once years and years ago I tried getting drunk when I was miserable; I only became drunk and miserable. What is so astonishing is to realize that not only the people who love you but also husbands and wives, I mean people bound together by a legal tie as real and impersonal as the one that keeps me in classes and pays my salary every month, even these people can just disappear like soap bubbles. And do. But my money will keep coming in every month. That's why money is more reliable than love—people become misers this way. I thought of my work and therefore, grief-drunk, sat down to work; I dusted books and looked through some magazine articles I'd kept to throw away duplicates. I couldn't do anything less routine than that. There's always work to do. Jean called work a blessing.

I sat down at the kitchen table, leaned my face and arms on the cold plastic tablecloth (but it's pretty, it is, it's an unusual deep, pleasant red) and began to weep. No more can I sing: I love my kitchen, my kitchen loves me. There's nothing so awful as being (coming) alive.

They call this mourning, that is: grief work.

George Eliot depicts suffering very well: her heroines just sit in a room and hurt. They don't have the money to do anything else. In lousy novels heroines with broken hearts plunge into "a mad round of dissipation" about which I have only one question, i.e. where do you find it. One academic party A.J. (After Jean) and I was out the door after ten minutes with "a bad headache." You can drive around a lot but a beat-up old station wagon is no Duesenberg (*The Green Hat*, 1920's). Ah! they smoke cigarettes, too, in those books. I called writer friends in Watertown, N.Y., in whose house I've always felt at home, and asked for permission to visit them; I was going to stop over in New York City.

Fine, they said.

My New York friend—only one of them but the one to the purpose, for I wasn't going to see any of those people left over from college, i.e. the amateur Thespian who'd married and moved into the suburbs and who did nothing now but pick up after an immensely destructive two-year-old, or the thirty-year-old insecure spinster who worked for an opera magazine and thought marriage would solve everything, or the Phi Beta Kappa poet who works at a secretarial job, getting drunk on week-ends and wishing she were back at school—as I said, my real, live friend is a gay man a few years older than me. We met after a ballet matinée which I had sat through in such complete, implacable, hostile silence that I had caused several of the people around me to become acutely nervous, at least I certainly hope so. High art doesn't neutralize misery, far from it. And ballet combines obsessively romantic, heterosexual love stories with athletics and you-know-what. (Rose and I after *Swan Lake*, crying into our coffee.) It's ridiculous. I met Stevie at an expensive chain restaurant place on West Eighth that serves nothing but French crèpes; you know, fake wooden beams, fancy Breton costumes on the waitresses, the menu hand-calligraphed in two languages, and right out in the middle of the room (where you could watch the crèpes being made) a large griddle with the fake ménagère of this fake tavern and vats of the stuff they put into their pancakes: spinach, cheese, ham, chestnuts, whipped cream, jam, all that. It's not bad food, really. I was in love with Stevie years and years ago, when I was twenty-one and believed that dreams came true. Thinking of those days—there was my old friend Rose (remember her?), there were splendid pink sunsets in mid-winter when I was coming to group therapy, or summer evenings with the dirty air turning a delicate rose and blue and the trees on Park Avenue (almost dead of the dust) smelling fresh, but only when you were very close to them.

Stevie's a good friend now: willful, tense, hard-working, good to lots of people, extraordinarily well-informed and well-read. He could no more live where I do than a fish could migrate to Death Valley. I saw him before he saw me, and waved; catching sight of me, he patted the place setting opposite him, meaning of course that I should approach and sit down. He beamed at me. He was wearing one of those dreadfully recherché things he loves; this time it was a rhinestone pin in the shape of a pair of kissing lips. Stuck on a fish-net shirt. Which, with leather shorts and sandals, and a Viking beard, gives you some idea why Stevie would be stoned to death in (say) Watertown, N.Y. I sat down and we made nice and kissed each other and exclaimed a lot, and asked about everybody's friends and relations, like the people in *Pooh*. I complimented him on his beard, which had squared off since the last time I'd seen him. I had suddenly and very intensely the feeling that Stevie is smarter than I, braver, stronger, better, more knowing; I admired him and feared him.

I was going to tell him about Jean.

He ordered spinach-and-cheese. I got greedy and ordered chestnuts and whipped cream.

"Well, love, how's the world been treating you?" he said.

I got shy. I described in melodramatic detail the headaches of marking papers, summer cleaning, getting the car fixed, my academic-ugly neighbors.

"Ah, you're a New Yorker at heart," he said.

I told him it wasn't so bad being away if you stayed glued to the TV. We both snickered. I told him my survivor's instincts had become atrophied after such a long time away; I wouldn't be able to function any more. He laughed and shook his head. Then I began hesitantly to tell him that I'd had a bad love affair, using phrases like "the person" or "the other person." It occurred to me that I could even use Jean's real name because people would confuse it with Gene, a man's name.

Finally he said, "Darling Esther, this fellow is *no good*." He had rested his chin in his hands, listening intently.

"He's not a fellow," I said, confused. "He's my best friend."

He tsked and demurred. He smiled and a wry look came into his face. "Would *I* like him?" he said. We'd had a running joke for years about the similarities of our taste in men. I looked down. Red-alerts everywhere. Don't say it; he won't like it. But why not?

"It's a woman," I said.

Stevie said nothing. I guess he's thunderstruck. Surprised, anyway. Despite (or because of) the china collection, his affectation of hating politics, his desire to be a nineteenth-century Russian aristocrat, the rhinestone pins, etc., Stevie is a very good-looking man, and sitting here, trying to cover my embarrassment or my stiffness at his embarrassment or his embarrassment—I feel an eerie return of that love of ten years ago. How I had liked him! (I like him still.) I wanted him because he was unattainable—that was the official version. No. I liked him because he was on my side.

He looked up, his face closed. He said:

"When one gets to a certain age, there's the desire to experiment. You know, to try everything." A year ago I would have agreed.

"No," I said.

Opportunely, the food came.

It was disapproval; it was also a kind of shrinking. Perhaps he wants straight friends. I don't know. When I first met him I was shy, amazed, and very put off, but Stevie doesn't mind middle-class people who are put off; he thrives on it; I've seen him handle roomfuls of middle-class people who disapprove of him and do it so well that everybody went away glowing with conscious virtue. But now I've done something wrong.

We ate silently.

Then he said, rather affected all of a sudden, for Stevie can turn himself inside out like a glove:

"Dear me, this *is* a surprise!"

I began to explain that I had tried to be good but I just couldn't take men any more. Straight men, that is. He said, making a face:

"Oh, I see. Lady's lib."

Now I've asked him before not to call it that. This is Stevie's malicious side: get-away-from-me-or-I'll-scratch. The next step is for me to remember that he's suffered worse than I, that he has been—or could be—beaten up in public, that he could be killed, that nothing I've gone through can hold a candle to what he has. Things always go well after this stage.

"Don't use that word," I said. "It's belittling."

His eyes narrowed. He's going to drawl. He put his chin in his hands, and leaning his elbows on the fake fancy oak of the restaurant table, said deliberately:

"Little Esther's going in for the militant marching and chowder society. You're losing your sense of humor, dear."

I stared.

He said, "You're not gay. You're just being programmatic. For Lady's Lib."

"Women are oppressed," said I suddenly. (What can one say?)

"Oppressed!" cried this sudden stranger in a cracked voice. "You don't know what the word means, darling! Oppression in your happy, sheltered little life?"

He said I was a parasitic, self-indulgent, petty, stupid, bourgeois *woman*.

He said I should try being beaten up by the police.

"Breeders!" he muttered, the color coming back into his face. Breeders is Stevie's term of contempt for the straights.

I told him—but I didn't. I said, "Oh, never mind." The restaurant cuckoo clock struck five. A Bavarian cuckoo clock of carved wood, the wrong thing in the wrong place.

The whole quarrel had taken three and a half minutes.

I left my food—and with wonderful, unconscious cunning, also the check—and hailed a taxi. Leaning my head out the window to refresh myself with the gasoline fumes. Getting my breeder's body sick. I know I can't tell my writer friends about Jean but I'll tell them about feminism because that cuts across everything. When I was seven years old I had a best friend called Yolanda who was Black; I didn't know what being Black meant and I certainly didn't know what being a homosexual meant, but I jolly well knew what being a girl meant. In a then-current Fred Astaire movie called "Yolanda and the Thief" the thief (who was probably Fred Astaire, thinking back on it) danced over the skyline of New York while Yolanda watched him. When Yolanda and I grew up (we planned it that way) we would do the movie over again, only this time it would be Yolanda and me dancing over the tall buildings. Yolanda not only had a wonderful name, she was very independent; she got a quarter from her father every week for mopping the bathroom floor. I tried that but my parents wouldn't let me. They preferred to give me things.

I—the old me who's just got Stevie so mad at her—began to cry in the taxi. It's all such a tiresome puddle of failure. There's this horrible insistence (just as if somebody were riding in the cab next to me and nagging me) that I ought to understand Stevie, that I ought to make allowances, that I've behaved badly, that I'm selfish. I thought of asking the cab-driver to take me to a gay bar, but was interfered with by a memory from a book: woman asks cabbie to take her "where women go." He says "Right, lady," and lets her off at the Y.W.C.A. Years ago a painter friend of mine was stopped on Eighth Street by a small, dark foreign man with a monobrow who hissed at him from behind one hand, "Where are the secret places?" My friend, of course, did not know. As he said: If you can't make it with the people you know—

Then what?

Anyway it's got nothing to do with me; I'm not a Lesbian. Lesbians. Lez-bee-yuns. Les beans. Les human-beans?

I'm a Jean-ist.

A nasty little tune I couldn't place followed me into the cab, to my hotel, through the Metropolitan Museum the next day, out to the airport, like a snail leaving disgusting little tracks on the European paintings, the Middle Eastern carpets, the fancy airport luncheon, the jets taking off, everything I am supposed to enjoy. It was about somebody looking for a job in the last century and never getting one because (here the refrain would come in):

> I asked the reason why.
> He said, Now don't you see that sign?
> *No Irish need apply.*

Though it was about a man looking for a job, not a woman. Always a man.

Pain is boring. That's the worst of it. I cried so much in those two days that I had to put on dark glasses in self-defense. I won't bother you with the details: the sobbing in the public rest room, the haughty, injured look you put on to conceal the fact that you've been crying. I flew up to—sounds very sophisticated, doesn't it?—but my plane was a tiny one of a line I won't mention, a sort of flying Toonerville Trolley that carries baby chicks and live lobsters as often as people (and airmail) and sits out on the field as if in flat denial of the laws of aerodynamics: You mean I'm going to fly in *that*? Half the stops are made in ports that don't have central towers or ground-to-air radio; you just come in for a good look and take the chance that nobody else wants to land on the same patch of grass. I found myself next to a little old Italian lady who was carrying vast quantities of bundles: bread, salami, cheese, wool, sausages, sweaters, God knows what. It seems this was stuff her relatives had given her. She explained in bad English that she'd come in on the morning plane and was going back on the afternoon one. We spread her bundles on the seats behind us (Toonerville is

never full) and then I hid behind a book. The affront of all that
upstate New York scenery—blue sky, white clouds, mountain-
colored mountains (as the Chinese say). Promises, promises. A
young unmarried couple (no ring) across the aisle was reading
a copy of *Life* magazine, sort of leafing through it and looking
at the pictures. They were working-class Appalachia, I suspect,
covering bad nutrition and lack of means with lots of make-up
in her case and lots of self-assertiveness in his. She wore a bee-
hive hairdo and sneakers with her pink dress, he, some sort of
sleazy, green rayon suit. She looked around the plane slowly
and wonderingly (it was almost empty except for us and a family in back), apparently rather bored, and said:

"I bet this next election will be different because—" (here
she named a current government scandal).

"No it won't," he said. "Why should it? It won't be. That's
full of crap." And he went back to reading. She looked around
again, a little desperately—it's not boredom, just the last-ditch,
lip-wetting, oh what shall I do now. They leafed through the
pictures.

"Oh hey," she said, "look at that. Isn't that weird? It says
we're all descended from fish. Just imagine, a million years ago
your great-great-great-grandaddy was a fish." I thought this
rather imaginative. He twitched the magazine page out of her
fingers, saying sharply:

"Jesus, you'd believe anything."

Again the glance round, to hide her embarrassment. She
was radiating dumbness in all directions. We all know that self-
deprecating uh-oh I put my foot in it. She got stupider and
prettier as I watched (from behind my book). Finally she wet
her lips and with an exaggeratedly casual air, slipped her arm
under his and made a little kissing face at him. This he liked. So
they began to neck. Imagine forty years of this. Think how girls
like that idealize men who "act like gentlemen." I attempted
to disappear into my seat and meditated why beautiful always
means expensive, why in order to be "naturally beautiful" you
need the clever haircut, the skin conditioner, the good diet, the
cod liver oil, the dental work, the fashionably-fitting clothes,
the expensive shampoo, the medical bills, the exercise. Always
money. The voices of my inarticulate, radical young students
are full of money.

Then I thought of Jean, who radiates not only money but a frightening personal force, a truly terrifying, unconscious determination—she thinks everybody has it. I drifted away, pleased at first, then remembered she didn't want me. Bad.

I was rescued by a thunderstorm, water shivering across the windows and blue glare you wouldn't believe. The plane dropped twenty feet and left our stomachs on the ceiling. The pilot (chuckling on the intercom) told us he'd gotten careless, heh heh, and it was only a little local storm heh heh and we'd be out of it in a minute and into Watertown. Wow, a joke, right?

It got better but not much; there was a bad, bumpy descent and I began to get airsick.

The pilot is amused. Someone has placed that abominable young couple right in my way when we all know such scenes of mutual neurosis and degradation are few and far between in this our free, modern, sexually liberated land.

Is somebody trying to tell me something?

Hugh and Ellen Selby live in Watertown, N.Y., near the Canadian border, in a vast, rambling Charles Addams mansion —there is a story that a leak in the roof once had to be repaired by helicopter. Their place has been a mecca for their friends for years. The Selbys, because they are writers, know what nobody else does: I mean, why writers need quiet, why they keep odd hours, why people can't always stay where they're born, why publishers are no good at all, why sitting still and thinking is hard work. He edits various kinds of specialized technical books; she writes children's fantasies, very good ones. Ellen grew up in Kansas, in some Fundamentalist sect (which I never got quite straight)—no cards, no dancing, no movies, no make-up, no drinking. She takes children and what children read very seriously. Hugh comes from a more ordinary small town but when asked about it he will only giggle and light wooden matches with his feet (honest); but I understand that they both left their respective homes as soon as they could. Ellen is the steady one; Hugh is short, fat, and wears old-fashioned striped bathing suits in the summer, over which his uncut grey beard floats like Spanish moss. The Selbys, in addition to planting the delphiniums in their front yard in a

hammer-and-sickle pattern, have inside their house a vast por-
trait of Grandfather Mao—this is a joke but the neighbors can't
be trusted to understand it.

Ellen cooks—plainly but well. Hugh has water-fights and
greenpea-fights in restaurants (sometimes).

There are in the Selby mansion four fireplaces, a tank of
tropical fish, statuettes of monsters from outer space, a living
room thirty feet by thirty feet, and a miscellaneous collection
of Victorian plush furniture: green and rose-red are the pre-
dominant colors.

Some of the furniture is falling apart.

You find manuscripts everywhere, sometimes even in the
(separate) garage.

My friends' one fault is that they don't believe names run in
cycles and that the name of their infant daughter—Anya—is
part of the new wave of fashion after Sherri, Debbi, Dee, and
Leslie. Little Ivan, little Anya, little Tobias, are the names of
the future. The Selbys think they picked out their daughter's
name all by themselves.

Aside from that, it's the best of all possible worlds.

I took a taxi from the airport and walked in; Ellen was in the
kitchen. When she heard me, she came out and put her arms
around me.

"Mm," I said. "What do I smell?" (Something cooking, that
is.) My insides know that the Selbys are my real momma and
poppa. They themselves often mention young writers who
want to be adopted by them, but I've never presumed so far. I
went out at Ellen's direction into the back yard to get lettuce
from the kitchen garden. I'm such a bad cook—or rather a
non-cook (I often get interested in reading and let the food
burn) that I eat well only when at friends' houses. Years ago
I used to be very embarrassed at the awkwardness of my first
hour with the Selbys, each time I visited—I used to think it was
my fault—but now we all seem to accept it. It's one of those
things that happens with friends one sees only twice a year.

I gave Ellen the lettuce to wash—she insists she knows
where everything is and I'd only be in the way—and watched
while she chopped it into the salad. Ellen is forty-five and trim
rather than pretty; nonetheless her gestures and attitudes have

that extraordinary interest or glamor or beauty or what-have-you that some people radiate. One might call it authority or one might call it love. I don't mean that I love Ellen in the ordinary way or that I'm sexually attracted to her. I mean she's a blessing.

Hugh is a mad, plump owl (his round glasses) who hangs from ceilings, wiggling his bare toes. (He has actually been known to do this when parties occur in houses with exposed beams.)

Ellen took clothes out of the washer and put them in the dryer. She let me help her set the dinner table in the next room: i.e. she handed me the dishes and I took them in. The Selbys have a dinner table that seats fourteen, though there are seldom that many people in the house at one time.

"No, four," said Ellen.

"Anya?" I said. (Anya is two months old.)

"Somebody else," she said. She went down into the cellar for canned goods and preserves. (She puts up preserves, too.)

Just before dinner Hugh descended from the higher regions of the house, glasses and all, and started poking into the oven (after saying hello to me, of course). Letters and packages were scattered all over the kitchen; he started opening some of them and making interested noises: chuckles, mimed disbelief, sounds of wonder. I took paper napkins into the dining room and laid them in a heap on the table. (The Selbys are not formal.) We trooped into the dining room, where Ellen had laid out everything on those heat-proof pads.

The bell rang.

"There she is," said Ellen. She and Hugh looked guardedly at each other; they had apparently been trapped into having dinner with someone they didn't like. We don't want that one here. I saw "that one" in the old pier glass opposite the coat rack in the hall—a series of blue-and-white reflections spotted and stained by the leprosy of the old glass—and then I saw her come in through the kitchen.

"Leslie," said Ellen. "This is Esther."

"Esther, Leslie," said Hugh, satisfied.

Leslie was a tall twenty-two-year-old with long fair hair like Alice Liddell's, long legs in impeccable, flared white trousers, white wedgies, and a blue, clinging, frilly nylon tank top that kept pulling up above her belly-button. I had never seen such expensive clothes. She was an ex-student from Richmond, Va. who "wrote" and who had come to Watertown only God knows why; she had taken a small house outside of town, she said. As she ate her salad, she kept pulling languidly at the tank top to get it to meet her trousers, but you could see that this was only a gesture; her heart wasn't in it.

Ellen helped her to some canned paté.

"Merci," said Leslie, with an impeccable accent. I had a sudden yen to announce that I could understand only Yiddish. Leslie talked for a while about her family's maid in Richmond and how the maid was phobic about snakes in the garden but had to go there every day to get flowers for the dinner table.

They had a wonderful dog named Champion, a malemute who had to stay indoors in the air-conditioning most of the year. Leslie went right on, all about Mother and Father and the maid and the cook. She thought her own girlhood was fascinating.

Leslie had been the most beautiful girl in Richmond.

Ellen was getting annoyed at being addressed in snippets of French, I could tell. The way she shows it is that she gets very steady, very controlled, and her voice becomes perfectly civil.

Leslie said, "Georgie and I think we'll go to Greece this fall. When I go back home in September, I'll just have to leave, you know. I couldn't stand the winter." She started talking about this island they'd gone to the year before which nobody else had discovered yet; you had to get there by water-taxi. Georgie (she explained) was Georgette, the teacher Leslie had been living with ever since she'd graduated from the University of South Florida. Georgie had an awful lot of money. But the owner of the apartment building where she and Georgie lived in Richmond wouldn't let them take Titi to the swimming pool on the roof. Wasn't that awful? Titi was a silver Siamese with marvelous blue eyes. Their building had a swimming pool, a boutique, a doorman, a sauna, a private TV system, and a quartz solarium. Their apartment had eight rooms. Leslie started to talk about a science fiction story she was going to write (about "a girl of the future") but at this point Ellen remembered something she had to go get in the kitchen. (Or the attic or the cellar). I excused myself and followed her. Ellen, of course, was not looking for anything but simply standing over the kitchen table and trying to control her temper.

"That—that *girl* never writes anything!" said Ellen.

"Look on the bright side," I said. "If she did, you'd have to read it."

"They live in two rooms," said Ellen vehemently, "she and that—that teacher of hers." (Georgie, it turned out, was a solid, middle-aged former Bostonian who had maddened Ellen by coming up once to visit her protegée and lecturing the Selbys about literature for two and one half hours by the clock. I assumed it was the usual collision of bad academic with real writer.)

"Do you think they're—" I said, embarrassed.

"I don't care," said Ellen. "I don't want to know. It's bad enough as it is." I remembered another young writer friend (male) who had come into Ellen's kitchen three winters before, having returned from his first European tour, and said, "Ellen, darling, I've found out the most astonishing thing about myself," while both Ellen and Hugh listened with weary patience, everybody else but the young writer having guessed it all long ago.

They don't really understand, of course.

We went back to the dining room and finished dinner—plain, fine food. Leslie didn't eat much; she never ate much. After the cherry pie she jumped up (did she know what we wanted of her?) and said she had to go, she'd almost forgotten, she was so sorry but she had to meet somebody who had a motorcycle. He was going to take her some place for a drink. I regarded Alice Liddell's pretty Anglo-Saxon face, her marvelous blue eyes, and foresaw the day when she'd burst into tears in the Selbys' living room, begging them, "How can I change!"

She went out, and three carefully-scheduled minutes later Hugh whooped. (Out of hearing, I suppose.) He told me that when they'd first met, she'd asked him his name and he'd said, "Just call me Hugh," whereupon she'd said, bewildered, "But what's your name?" He fluffed his beard with his fingers like actors in Chinese opera do to indicate rage. He blew into it, too.

We took our coffee into the living room, in front of the empty fireplace (summer nights near the Canadian border can be cold) and Ellen began to talk about the current ruin of the world in general and New York State in particular. Since the last time I'd seen her she'd become passionately involved in ecology—not the organic foods kind, the all-over kind. I know that bitter, hopeless desperation—the petitions, the radio appeals, the placards, the letter campaigns, the demonstrations. It's like trying to move a locomotive with your bare hands. Hugh nodded amiably and vanished upstairs to edit something; I yelled after him, "But Hugh—what does an editor *do*?" He chuckled. Ellen talked, hunched over, her hands trembling with continual anger; swamps were being drained all over the country, forests were being covered with asphalt, fish and algae were being killed. I said, "I know how you feel. There's something—"

"Tomorrow," I said. "I'll tell you tomorrow."

The Selbys' guest room is on their third floor, with a tiny mirror tacked to one wall, an old farm sink (iron) from which you can get cold water only, and the real bathroom a long flight of stairs down. I took a good look at my face in the bathroom mirror that night because I knew I wouldn't get to see it again until morning (would it change? I wonder!). I have a melancholy Jewish face, big-featured, lean, and hungry. A prophet's face. In some novel somewhere there's a Jewish character, a big fat man who fled Germany in the late 30's and who says Why travel? Wait, and they'll chase you around the world.

I kept the subject successfully at bay for most of the next day. Hugh and Ellen worked in the afternoon, so after browsing in their library, I walked into town to visit the local florist (who sold mostly garden plants—tomatoes, started green peppers, that sort of thing) and then on to the five-and-ten, browsing through the drugstore magazines, having a soda, and so on. There aren't many possibilities in Watertown. I had lunch in a hamburger place (gummy cottage cheese, tired fruit) and walked back to the Selbys', scuffing my feet in the dust at the side of the highway watching the white Queen Anne's Lace which blossoms everywhere at this time of year. Wild carrot.

I knew I would have to tell Ellen. Otherwise why be friends? I mean if it's not to be unreal.

There was another guest for dinner.

For a moment I thought it might be Leslie's friend who'd taken her out the night before—there was a motorcycle outside the house—but anyway inside it there was a friend of the Selbys called Carl, and I will call him Carl Muchomacho. This may be unfair. I remembered a satire he'd written in which there was (presented with unique completeness) the fantasy woman of a certain kind of freak male: I mean the sexy, earthy chick who loves motorcycles (because she has orgasms on them), who makes pottery, who balls all the time, who isn't uptight about anything, and who never gets pregnant. So Muchomacho is a satirical name. Carl has an attractive swagger, a pleasant, lean face, a dark moustache, and what is called a sense of humor.

But I wasn't in the right mood.

When I came in he got to his feet (he'd been having a drink with Hugh) and—with a flourish—offered me one of the old, plushy, green, Victorian chairs. They're hard things to push across a rug, by which I gather that Muchomacho was turning his sense of humor against himself. I said:

"Oooh, thanks, but I didn't know you were into that sort of thing."

"What sort of thing?" said he.

"Gallantry," I said.

"Well, I hope you were pleasantly surprised," says Carl, rocking back and forth a little on the balls of his feet. He's one of those restless, springy types who can never stand still.

"Surprised, anyway," I said. He smiled. The conversation is picking up. Here is a witty lady with whom he can fence. He said, "You don't dig it?"

"Well, no, not really," I said.

"Why not?"

"Oh, never mind," I said. "It's not worth—I don't want to talk about it all *this* much!" And I laughed. Hugh and Ellen exchanged happy glances of marital complicity: See-it's-working-out-I-told-you-she'd-like-him.

"But why not?" said Muchomacho, sincerely interested.

"It's not important," I said, so he supplied what my modesty would not or could not; he said:

"You mean you don't want to be a lady?" (smiling)

"That's right," I said. He looked interested and expectant. I squashed the suspicion that he and the Selbys were putting me on. I really don't think so.

"Well then," said Carl logically, "how *do* you want to be treated? Would you rather I ignored you? Or pulled the chair out from under you?" Hugh chuckled. Witty Hugh.

"Don't be silly," I said, controlling myself and trying not to sound like a governess; "Just treat me—well, decently. Like anyone."

"Like Hugh?" said clever Muchomacho. ("Please!" exclaimed Hugh happily.) Ellen looked as calm as if nothing were happening. I said, a little sharply:

"I'll tell you, the one thing I do not want to do is continue this discussion all through dinner." This time Ellen looked up.

"Sorry, but I didn't start it," said Carl pleasantly.

I got up, excused myself with a smile, and went to the bathroom. I figured that five minutes later they'd be talking about something else and so they were; then I got sneaky and introduced the topic of food additives so we had ecology all through dinner. Everybody listened respectfully. Carl, I am quite sure, did not care for the topic, but he honored it. After dessert we all moved back into the living room while Hugh started a fire in the fireplace; then Carl Muchomacho came over and stood at the back of my chair, saying lightly:

"At the risk of incurring your savage, feminist wrath, can I ask you out with me tonight?"

"Huh?" I said (and jumped).

"Can I take you out and show you a good time?" he said, adding, "I'm really harmless, you know."

"Oh, thanks," I said, "but—" (trailed off, trying to think of an excuse. I just washed my hair?).

"Frankly, I feel rotten," I said. "I don't want to go anywhere or do anything; I just want to sit."

"You can sit on my motorcycle," he said.

"I don't feel up to it," I said.

"Come on," he said, "It'll do you good. Get a little wind in your hair." The Selbys glanced at each other again. They too seemed to think it would do me good. I shook my head. Carl shrugged. We did not go on to have one of those endless arguments about whether sitting on a motorcycle is the same thing as sitting at home and when I said I didn't want to do anything, what did I mean by "do" and what does "mean" mean. Perhaps he's just getting too old to be persistent. He turned to Hugh, saying "See? I do treat you two alike," and proposed they go out somewhere to have a beer.

Which they did. (Though he didn't promise to show Hugh a good time.) Ellen said nothing but she looked at me disapprovingly.

I said, "Ellen, I just can't face it. Not again." (Which was only a small lie.) Then I burst into tears. They were unsympathetic, angry tears and they didn't get me any approval.

I can't tell her.

She said dryly that Carl was a good friend of theirs.

I said wasn't I?

She said softly and exasperatedly, "Oh, Esther!"

"Never mind," I said; "I'll call him tomorrow." (That's what dating's all about; it's to please your Mother. Darling, he looked like such a nice boy. But he's impotent, Mother.)

"You've changed," said Ellen gravely.

I said that yes, I had; I'd gotten a lot into feminism since I'd seen her last. Ellen knows better than to believe in bra-burners; she thought for a minute and then said carefully, "I suppose I've always been a feminist. You know, where I grew up it was impossible for a woman to have a career at all; she could only be a wife and mother, but here I am with both."

I said Yes, wasn't that wonderful.

She smiled.

"And Hugh does half the housework," I said, "and takes care of the baby." (Anya was at the baby-sitter's because I was there.) "Ah! that's unusual."

"He helps," said Ellen. Then she said, "I don't mind doing it." They all start out by assuming you mean somebody else: third-world women, welfare mothers, Fundamentalist Baptists, Martians. We went through all that. I told her that I meant us both, that I wouldn't have my job at all if I hadn't been twice as good as my colleagues.

"Make the world safe for mediocrity," I said.

She said she didn't care to know mediocre people and she certainly hoped I didn't.

I said, "That's not the point." (But I didn't know what was the point, not then.) I said, "Ellen, when you were with your first husband, when you were trying to write and had two children, wouldn't day care have helped? You couldn't have afforded a baby sitter then. And wouldn't it have helped if your family and the clergyman and all those people hadn't tried to shove you right back into your old place? I mean if they thought it was O.K.? My God, you lost your voice for two years."

"That's Fundamentalism," she said.

"Oh no it's not," I said, "look at TV, look at the magazines, look how convenient it is to have a wife, look at the ads."

"Esther, no one I respect believes what they see on TV or in the ads! For goodness' sakes, neither do you."

I said ha ha the things we took least seriously might affect us the most (T.S. Eliot). Clincher.

"Besides," I added, "you told me once you had to get up at 5 A.M. for four years to write because there wasn't any other time."

"If one wants something, one makes sacrifices," said she.

I asked if Hugh had made sacrifices.

"We are different people," said Ellen.

She added, "He may have made other kinds of sacrifices. I'm not going to defend him to you, Esther. The point is that we have to make our individual choices and lead our lives, man or woman, and everybody suffers one way or another. Life is compromise. And that's something none of us can evade. Whether man or woman."

I said furiously that I'd had quite enough of all this literary book club tragic-sense-of-life as an excuse for other people's privileges.

"You're bitter!" said she.

"Sure," I said. "Malcolm no-name saw his daddy killed before his eyes at the age of four and that's political; but I see my mother making a dish-rag of herself every day for thirty years and that's personal."

Ellen said my mother was responsible for that, if it was true, and we didn't have to repeat our mothers' mistakes.

I said didn't we just!

She said, "I've seen you over-reacting to all sorts of trivial, harmless things. If your ideas—"

"It's not trivial or harmless. It happens too often. It's just part of the whole damn thing. And don't tell me he didn't do anything that bad, I know he didn't, but the code of manners is only a symptom of the whole damn thing."

A long silence.

"As far as I can see," said Ellen steadily, "you want people to treat you according to some strange and special code of behavior that only you understand. That's hardly rational, Esther." She was looking down at her hands. As far as Ellen is concerned, this whole subject is finished because Ellen is Superwoman; if Ellen's responsible for everything, that's because it's her choice; Ellen still exists on five hours' sleep a night. I said nothing of this, only that I wasn't alone in my beliefs. I wasn't a Saucerian or an occultism nut, and I guessed it was the old argument about the cup being half empty or half full. We'd never settle it. Anyway, George Bernard Shaw said there is no great art without some fanaticism behind it, so I was starting ahead of the game, right? Her, too. Look at her and ecology.

Ellen said very quietly and distinctly, "I am not a fanatic."

I said, "No, no, I don't *mean* that." But she said again: "I am not a fanatic."

"Oh well, all fanaticism means," (said I) "is a truth somebody else won't accept. So we're both fanatics."

Ellen's anger only makes her more controlled. She changed the subject. Far be it from me to suppose she picks her beliefs for their acceptability to her husband's friends. She told me about a mutual acquaintance of ours who had become—God save us!—a Satanist and had sacrificed goats in the back of occult bookstores.

"Where on earth did he get the goats?" I said.

Ellen said it wasn't funny; he'd ended up in a mental hospital.

"You meet the best people there," I said.

"Esther, he's in a *mental hospital*." Not understanding my lack of understanding of her understanding of my understanding. I said I was sorry; I hadn't meant to be flip.

"Look, Ellen," I said, "I feel as if I'd been flayed, I mean I'm all nerves. I never should've come. I'll go tomorrow and call back in a few months. When I'm human again."

She said, looking right at me, "If this new belief of yours has such a bad effect on your relations with others, I think you ought to re-examine your belief."

(Years ago, when I was in group therapy, I wore "Bohemian" clothes: cheap Indian-print shifts, cheap Mexican dresses, lots of color, big old copper jewelry. This was long before such things became fashionable. The group didn't like the way I dressed; they said I only did it to get attention. They said, "You're trying to be different." This was also the standard explanation for juvenile delinquency that year. I said I dressed that way because I liked it and not because I wanted attention, because I did get gawked at and teased in the street, and that I definitely did not enjoy.

(They smiled.

(They said Oh, so you don't like looking different?

(I said I didn't like being teased.

(*Then why*, said they triumphantly, *do you dress the way you do?*)

I said good-night and went upstairs. My friend Ellen with her endless work and her earnest assurances to an interviewer last year that *her* children always took preference over her work in emergencies (Hugh is a hit-and-run father) and that she hoped more and more women would experience the fulfillment of both work and motherhood. "No one must go beyond me," she said. Do you know the last time the percentage of women in the professions and women Ph.D.'s and women entering colleges was as high as it is today?

In nineteen-twenty, that's when.

And you'd think friends—but Carl is her friend; the truth is that she prefers Carl to me.

There's this club, you see. But they won't let you in. So you cry in a corner for the rest of your life or you change your ways and feel rotten because it isn't you, or you go looking for another club. But this club is the world. There's only one.

"Why do you people go where you're not wanted?"

"Why do *you* go where you're not wanted? *I* don't want you." (My maternal uncle, at a resort that didn't like Jews.)

If Jean had stayed with me I wouldn't have cared, but now I must put on my putrid ankle sox and my cheerleader button because there's no right of private judgment and you can't think of yourself; you have to be thought. By others. Why did Ellen forget the classic exchange? I mean the one where they say But aren't you for human liberation? and you say Women's liberation is for women, not men, and they say You're selfish. First you have to liberate the children (because they're the future) and then you have to liberate the men (because they've been so deformed by the system) and then if there's any liberation left you can take it into the kitchen and eat it.

Oh, I must be bad. I'm hostile. I'm bitter. I'm hideously wicked. I must be crazy or I wouldn't suffer so. Taking things personally—! (Persons shouldn't take things personally.) I stood in my traveling pajamas over the iron sink, brushing my teeth and crying—how could she, how *could* she!—and when I straightened up, somebody else looked out at me from the tiny mirror tacked to the wall.

Who is that marvelous woman!

I was so pleased, she's so cute, with toothpaste around her mouth like a five-year-old. I like her, really. She's Esther who loves everything systematic and neat but it's all moonshine; she has elaborate schemes for traveling with a traveling iron and a collapsible miniature ironing board (which is too heavy to carry), and a traveling sewing case (which is *very* small), and traveling clothes which don't need ironing (so why take the iron!), and shoe-trees made of plastic so they'll be light, and a collapsible toothbrush with a marvelous plastic case, and air-mail stamps which she never uses.

Wonderful, silly Esther.

So my reflection comforted me and blew me stars and kisses. I thought of Jean—who'd left me—and Ellen—who hated me—and my own crazy nastiness, which is that I don't like men and I'm giving up on them and I don't care about them so I'm a monster and God will strike me dead. Sleeping with women is all right if it's just play, but you must never let it interfere with your real work, which is sleeping with men.

The mirror didn't believe it.

So I slipped into triumph in spite of everything, like an Eskimo lady in a nine-days' blizzard on an ice-floe. And very humble (but giggling) I went to bed.

I pray that She my soul may keep. (snf)

Thinking how nice it was to be horizontal when you're tired, and that after a non-committal, guilty, bland breakfast with the Selbys, after my rather lame excuses about catching a virus or not feeling well or something, after Hugh drives me to the airport and they say "Goodbye" and I say "Goodbye" and after I write a very nasty letter to my New York glamorous media friends who think bisexuality is groovy (but only for women and only if you're married and only if you like men better) there is something else I must do, an option Ellen didn't think of.

What do you do when the club won't let you in, when there's no other, and when you won't (or can't) change? Simple.

You blow the club up.

(The mystery of courage. The mystery of enjoyment. One moves incurably into the future but there is no future; it has to be created. So it all ends up totally unsupported, self-caused, that symbol of eternity, The Snake Biting Its Own Tail. I'm strong because I have a future; I have a future because I willed it; I willed it because I'm strong. Unsupported.

> (Ezekiel saw the wheel
> (Way up in the middle of the air—
> (O Ezekiel saw the wheel
> (Way in the middle of the air!
>
> (Now the big wheel runs by faith
> (And the little wheel runs by the grace of God—

(The above made up by professional hope experts, you might say, because willful, voluntary, intentional hope was the only kind they had in anything like long supply. Faith is not, contrary to the usual ideas, something that turns out to be right or wrong, like a gambler's bet; it's an act, an intention, a project, something that makes you, in leaping into the future, go so far, far, far ahead that you shoot clean out of Time and right into Eternity, which is not the end of time or a whole lot of time or unending time, but timelessness, that old Eternal Now. So that you end up living not in the future (in your intentional "act of faith") but in the present. After all.

(Courage is *willful* hope.)

Summer is dying. The airfield's still rank with Queen Anne's lace—its flowers look like white parasols—but the goldenrod's coming out too, and even a few blue asters, which means the beginning of the end. On a sunny afternoon you know summer will last forever, all that iridescent blue and green, but the nights are colder now. Three hours after sunset you can smell autumn. The pilot came in by sight after circling our cow pasture (we don't have ground-to-air communication here either) and I walked to my battered old heap in the parking lot. Home along the roads I know so well: butter-and-eggs (that's like tiny, yellow-and-white snapdragons), purple chicory, which I've heard called corn flowers or flax flowers, and the very few last (battered but game) black-eyed Susans. Everything was growing up through the hay like hair. We'll have hot weather again before October. I went through the town and up the hill, parking in my old place at the top, which is so awful to get into in winter because of the ice, and then hauled my suitcase upstairs, picking up on the way a note my landlady had slipped under my door. I forgot to pay the rent before I left. I opened the windows, disconnected the timer from the living-room lamp, ran water in both sinks until the faucets stopped spitting at me, all the things you have to do when you come back. You know. I was putting clothes away with one hand (mostly the laundry bag which hangs on the inside of the bedroom closet) and carrying the note in the other, with that unaccountable, feverish efficiency that comes over me whenever I come home and have to get everything put away and fixed up again. My suitcase gaped open on the bed and I kept having to step over a pair of shoes. The note said:

". . . how you buy a gun. You giggle a lot and tell the clerk your boy friend wants you to go hunting with him so you have to get a hunting rifle. You say Oh gee he told me to ask *you*; he said you'd know—"

I started again:

Dearest Esther,

Now I'm in town and you're not. I'm at 14 Tighe Street, number in the book under Anderson. Sorry I got scared and ran away. I went to Boston, to some friends, and learned a lot. Then I came back and just messed around. Do you remember three years ago, after the bomb scare, the University was going to keep lists of students who took suspicious books out of the University library? But the best bomb handbook turned out to be the Encyclopedia Britannica.

This is how you buy a gun. You giggle a lot and tell the clerk your boy friend wants you to go hunting with him so you have to get a hunting rifle. You say Oh gee he told me to ask *you*; he said you'd know everything. Then you keep your ears open. You'll pay too much the first time but that's O.K. Don't try to pretend you had it all written down on a piece of paper but lost it; they'll only send you out to get your instructions again. I know. And remember: *you're only a girl.*

As soon as your lights stop going on and off so regularly, I'll know you're back. I'll call or you call me; I want to talk to you.

Love,
Jean.

P.S. I hope you're not mad at me.
P.P.S. I keep Brown Bess in her wrappings in the kitchen. I can take her apart, clean her, put her back together again, load and unload her, and pot a tin can at fifty feet. When nobody's around I talk to her because I love her. I call her Blunderbess.
P.P.P.S. I love you, too.

I re-read Jean's letter. I read it until it didn't make sense any more. I brewed myself a cup of tea, then threw the tea in the sink. I don't want to go through that again, whether she loves me or doesn't love me, whatever "love" means. It's all spoilt. When I was very young—I mean eighteen years ago—I fell in love with a man who didn't know how to drive a car properly; when we hit a patch of ice on the roadway once, he steered against the skid and we went half-way across the road in a sort of figure-eight; he told me complacently that this was the right thing to do and I knew it wasn't but I didn't care because I adored him. Twenty-five years ago we had parties to which the boys didn't come, or if they did they wouldn't dance or talk or do anything. Twenty years ago I went to college and began to recognize that I was invisible; having dressed for a date (dates were absolutely crucial then) in my low heels, my nylons, my garter belt, my horsehair petticoat, my cotton petticoat, my taffeta skirt, my knit jersey blouse, my circle pin, my gold ear-rings, my charm bracelet, my waist-cincher, my lipstick, my lit-tle bit of eye-shadow, my heavy faille coat, my nail polish, my mohair scarf, and my gloves, I went into the dormitory garden to wait for him. The garden was full of late spring flowers. I had already admired myself in the full-length mirror on the back of my closet door—and that was very nice indeed, prov-ing that I could look good—but standing between the stone walls on the stone-flagged walk, watching the flowers grow ever lighter and more disembodied in the blue twilight—and sitting on the stone bench under the Gothic arches and all that ivy—and we were supposed to get A's and use the library —we were supposed to write papers—we were supposed to be *scholars*—I wanted to take off all my clothes and step out of my underwear. And then take off my hair and fingernails and my face and my flesh and finally my very bones. Just to step out of it. All the way out of it.

My date said, "There you are!"

If I was dying, my mother'd give me a cup of tea. So many times we've sat in the kitchen and fiddled with the tea things and talked inconsequential nonsense; then Daddy came home and admired us both, carefully urging Mother not to be so afraid of so many things, and Mother said she felt better and would go put on something nice.

But never did. Out of some furious, sullen instinct, she never did. She'd always ruin the effect somehow. And about most middle-aged women, don't they always ruin the effect somehow—too childish, too drab, too careful, too flamboy-ant, too frumpish, too expensive, too something? A genuine Picasso on which someone has scrawled at the bottom, "This is a fake"—or even more cleverly, "This is *not* a fake!"—so of course it's a double fake.

Did I tell you that my mother was the child of immigrant parents and that she taught herself to read English before she went to school? She never worked (I mean outside the house) so she had lots of time to make up fairy tales for me. They always began, "There was a little girl who—" I was immensely flattered. In her middle age she got fat, as if on purpose, gave up reading anything but historical novels because she said she couldn't understand what was written nowadays ("my poor brain"). She died at seventy, keeping to the end her invincible stupidity and her defiant, uncanny, extraordinarily thorough bad taste. That woman could make a shroud look tacky. I wish she'd come back and show me so we could have a good talk about it.

My father, about whom I'm sure you've been wondering, was a nice, ordinary man who did not have that intuitive understanding of feminine psychology always attributed to nice men in novels written by nice women for nice women. He didn't believe in the pretty, mindless muffin who's the style now—that wasn't in his time and it would have offended his sense of propriety anyway—nor did he believe in the busty roll-in-the-hay type (which was the thing in my teens)—to tell you the truth, I don't know what type of woman he did believe in. He used to read Sunday newspaper editorials about science (he thought of himself as an Informed Layman) although he tended to enjoy the physics most and to be skeptical about psychology. He praised and encouraged my mother, rather (I'm afraid) on the assumption that she was a kind of invalid, trying to cure her of her phobias, her daydreams, her distaste for people at parties, her insistence that she was stupid, her sleeping eleven hours a night, her love of gardens, her fairytales, her disbelief in science, her inability to learn to drive a car. He once remarked to me that he'd married her because she was "different"—then I suppose he had to change her back again. Or maybe he got more difference than he'd bargained for. I don't know. It's hard to tell what he thought of women because he always spoke of us with great formal deference.

"What Man can conceive, Man can achieve!" my father would exclaim, looking up from his Sunday-supplement article or his book of popular science.

My mother once confided in me that she didn't believe in atoms. I asked her what the world was made of, then. She thought for a minute.

"Elves," she said.

If she came back into my kitchen now, severely silly, dumpy and deliberately dowdy in her grave-clothes, how could I explain to her that it wasn't all her fault, after all? What could I say to her?

"Mama, how good it is to see you! What's it like being dead? Never mind, I know. Come have a cup of tea." We putter about. I put on the kettle. I gossip and chatter a little. I apologize for going over to Daddy's side when I was in my teens; after all, what else could I do? I was terrified he would think of me as he thought of her. Besides, the world isn't made of elves, not really. She cries a little. Then she shrugs. I say, "Mama, I'm going to tell you a fairy tale.

"It's about a middle-aged scientist who was also a politician and an army officer and a revolutionary and a judge and in Congress and a genius mathematician and a poet. And she—"

Why bother, why bother. I want the matriarchy. I want it so badly I can taste it. I *should* put a rug on the bedroom floor (which is all bare wood); I *shouldn't* have these thoughts. There's an actor on the Late Late Show I'm in love with—is that going to be my love life for the next thirty years, watching 1:30 A.M. TV? Suppose he wears out. Suppose I don't like him any more. Suppose they show other things. O idiocy! "Sorry I got scared and ran away." So you pick yourself up as if nothing had happened. Easy to say!

I don't want her.

I went about my business for the next two days, and if you're wondering about what I'm going to feel when Jean turns up, well so am I.

I spent my time in the library, picking out obscure references to memoirs written by bad ladies two hundred years ago and novels by worse ladies who, though personally blameless, wrote bad books. *A Romance of the Pyrenees, Marianna*, or *The Puritan's Daughter*. Weird, icky stuff. I've lost my awe of the library completely: this vast, defunct megalith over which we little mammals wander, nipping and chewing bits of its skin. I rip away at a little pocket: some authoress who wrote five romances (five!) under the pseudonym *By A Lady*. Domestic sentiments. Gothic castles. Purity. If only I can reduce this pulp to pulp and spread it out into some kind of shape. Dead voices, haunting and terrible: *I want. I need. I hope. I believe.* Where'd they live? Who did their cooking? Did they expect to get pregnant every year? (See Mrs. Defoe's journal.) The

awful constriction, the huge skirts. Mrs. Pepys's dress allowance ("the poor wretch" her husband called her). "How are
we fall'n, fall'n by mistaken rules!" "Women live like Bats or
Owls, labour like Beasts, and die like Worms." "Anyone may
blame me who likes." "How good it must be to be a man when
you want to travel." "John laughs at me, but one expects that
in marriage." "It had all been a therapeutic lie. The mind was
powerless to save her. Only a man. . . ." "I/Revolve in my/
Sheath of impossibles—"

Scholars don't usually sit gasping and sobbing in corners of
the library stacks.

But they should. They should.

In my dream the Tooth Fairy stood at the foot of my bed,
wearing an airy, blue, nylon net gown and glittering rhinestone jewelry, with a little rhinestone coronet on her head. Her
magic wand was star-topped and she looked just like a Tooth
Fairy should. She was going to give me three wishes.

But I woke up.

Bad weather brought Jean. A cold and blowy day with bursts
of rain, a premature autumn. Her umbrella made a puddle
on the landing outside my door. Tragic. Dark-eyed. Hands in
raincoat pockets.

She smiled sweetly.

She said, "Ick, what weather." I had to let her in. She shed
her coat, her umbrella, her packages, and her boots outside,
then came into my kitchen. She was no answer to anything.
She said, "Do you want to—?"

"No," I said.

"Do you want to sit in the living room?"

We sat in the living room and Jean gave me a look that said
So you're not a Lesbian any more, are you?

I said aloud, "That's not—" and then nothing.

"Shall I tell you about Betty Botter?" she said. "You know:
'Betty Botter bought a bit of bitter butter. Said Betty Botter,
This bit of bitter butter, It will make my batter bitter. So Betty
Botter bought a bit of better butter and it made her batter
better.'"

"What on earth—" I said.

"Blenderblunder. Betsy Batter. Batterburger. My rifle. She's in your kitchen, all wrapped up."

I said, "Who were you staying with in Boston?"

"Other Lesbians," said Jean comfortably.

Now I had done something terrible the day before that I haven't told you: I had been attracted to somebody else. I had been walking towards the library when I saw this twenty-year-old coming the other way in hip-hugger jeans and a funny little knitted top that left her bare from her ribs to her belly button. A silly, ruffled sort of blouse. That's what I saw first. Then I thought *Isn't she cold?* (It was raining.) Then I just knew there was nothing so interesting in the world as that midriff; my palms yearned for it. I wanted every little girl in the world.

That's different, that's very different. That's being a you-know-what.

She said, "'Tis with our judgments as our watches; none/ Goes just alike but each believes her own."

"You're mad," I said. Dumb with rage. Her absolutely inexplicable cheerfulness.

"I got you a present," she said, hauling a little brown-paper package from somewhere in her jeans (I don't see how she could have avoided sitting on it). Generously she held it out to me. "Go on," she said.

So I took it and untied the string (some present—brown paper and string!) and unwrapped it, holding in my hand a little white box. A dead mouse? A snakeskin? A bird's skull? These would be just Jean's style. Or, more conventionally, a flea-market ring, or the female symbol with the equals sign or the clenched fist, all done in lousy embroidery.

It was a watch sitting on a folded bit of paper. It wasn't cheap; I know the kind. I don't mean jewelry-expensive, but a good one. Perhaps twenty-five dollars. An awful lot, for her.

"You always say you lose the expensive ones," said Jean the liar, "so I got you a bad one. Here." And the bit of paper—unfolded—turned out to be an advertisement for a watch set about with diamonds, with a silly lady in false eyelashes, false hair, false everything. She was wearing a Jean Harlow slip—dress, I mean—and looking adoringly into the eyes of a handsome, shadowy man whose features you could hardly make out because he was the one giving the two-thousand dollar watch; and I suppose if you have that kind of money to buy ladies (or to buy ladies presents with), you don't need a face.

Something awful is happening. Rising. I don't think I can live through it. Also the ad is making me laugh. (I mean why not eat diamonds if you want to possess them? Only they'd come out the other end in a couple of days, wouldn't they?) Jean's watch has nice, big numbers I can read and no diamonds. I started putting her present on the white strip left on my wrist by my old watch, but something terrible was happening to the room. I've had an awful shock. Like a poor worm with a pin through it. And I wish to God Jean were somewhere else. Seeing her through what they call "scalding" tears, screaming tears, hurting dreadfully.

I wept, I wept, crying against her shoulder, nasty bilious tears, aching tears; don't ever let anyone tell you it's easy. And they didn't ease me. Is it like having convulsions? I didn't want to be touched, but I did; so she put her arms around me, say- ing "There, there" and "Now, now" and I put mine about her, feeling the shock of allowing it all to happen, knowing I could trust her. We held each other until I stopped crying; then I said, "I want to make love right now."

She said, "Your face is all runny," wiping it with a kleenex. Then she said, "I know, but you won't come; you'll just keep having these tremendous surges of feeling. It's too distracting."

"Huh!" I said sulkily, blowing my nose. To cheer me up, she told me about a letter some poor woman had written in a newspaper advice column, asking about how could she do away with her terrible deformity because she had this secret shame, this awful thing she couldn't let anybody know: *that she had little hairs around the aureoles of her breasts.* This, of course, is exactly what Jean has. Jean thought the letter very funny, but I turned away, groaned, wrapped my arms around my stomach—a pang of desire so keen I could barely sit up. Jean roared, which is exactly what you'd expect from a heart- less, sadistic Lesbian. They all chew tobacco and cuss like truck drivers. Next thing, she'll be putting out lit cigarettes on my breasts, just like a character in a book I read by C.S. Lewis who (after all) must know. She put her arms around me and gave me a fluttery kiss, such a close one, such a loving one, such a just-light-enough one that I began to understand pornography. Do you? I said, "Help, I can't wait!" so good-natured Jean pulled the curtains to and made love to me on the living room rug. We—uh—"did things," we—uh—"endured" and we—mm—"with our"—

See?

I trembled from head to foot, I really did. I didn't lift a finger, just like all those ladies in peignoirs in vampire movies. I have never been so utterly abandoned in all my life. Or so sorry when I came. (She was wrong about that.) After the third orgasm—three, count 'em, three!—but that's nothing, for a woman—I was content to lie there and throb, admiring beautiful Jean, who now wanted the same things done to her, now that I was spryer and she more languid, another kind of pleasure. So I did, trying not to laugh at the persistent memory of that poor woman so tormented by her shameful deformity that she had to write a newpaper about it. Sex, when it's good (but how often is it that?) is like nothing on earth. So silly, so grand. So indecent, so matter-of-fact.

Much later I said, peering through the curtains, "It's stopped raining. Nasty, though."

Jean said, "Get dressed and come into the kitchen, O.K.? I want to show you Blunderbess."

She added, "You ought to learn how to shoot."

The next day I was as paranoid as ever, smiling nervously at the men in the library, trying to keep my eyes off the women. I-know-they're-all-laughing-at-me-because-even-if-they-aren't-I-deserve-it.

Sex doesn't last.

That night I had a conversation with the Tooth Fairy. She came and sat down on the end of my bed, looking very benevolent, spreading out her blue nylon net skirts, and recalling to me (even in the middle of my dream) where I had seen her before—she was somebody I saw in a live stage show when I was eight and I'd swear it was the Ice Follies because I remember her in ice skates.

THE TOOTH FAIRY: Good evening, dear child. I am here to help you.

ME: Mmmmpf! What?

THE FAIRY: Tell me what you want and I shall get it for you.

ME: Thanks but no thanks ha ha. (My standards of wit are pretty lousy in dreams.)

THE FAIRY: Shall I restore to you your lost heterosexuality, so that you may once again adore on the Late Late Show handsome actors such as Buster Crabbe, Dirk Bogarde, James Mason, and Christopher Lee?—leaving it to you to determine what common characteristics (if any) animate this rather peculiar list because, my dear, (to be perfectly frank) you have the damnedest tastes I ever saw.

ME: Not on your life.

THE FAIRY: Shall I give you the gift of sixty million dollars?

ME: You haven't got it.

THE FAIRY: Shall I give you the gift of being attracted to real men?

ME (sitting straight up in bed, in terror): No, no, no, no, no!

THE FAIRY (crossing one leg over the other, thus revealing that she was indeed wearing ice skates, great big clumpy white ones): Well, what *do* you want, for goodness sakes! Don't be difficult. Tell me your heart's desire.

There was a long, puzzled silence in my by now very symbolic bedroom. What do I want? Health? Riches? Fame? Beauty? Travel? Success? The Respect Of My Colleagues? Do I want to become a saint? (God forbid.) I've wanted all those things in my time. Like the news of the day that runs round and round the top of that building on forty-second street in New York, so little sneaky tags and proverbs ran over the ceiling, now in neon lights, now in electric light-bulbs: It is better to marry than to have a career, Somebody lovely has just passed by, Always give Daddy the biggest piece of steak, It is Woman's job to keep the stars in their courses. None of this helps, of course.

I said, "My dearest desire—"

I said, "Some time in my life—"

I said, "What I really want—"

I said, "I want to kill someone."

Then I amended it. Not a woman. Certainly not a child, not of either sex.

I said: *I want to be able to kill a man.*

*

I said to Jean, "Why is wanting to be able to kill a man so bizarre? *Men* kill men. Watch TV. Men kill *women* on TV."

"Monopolistic practices," said Jean.

We were in her back yard, standing in the premature autumn leaves, shooting at tin cans. I hoped the neighborhood cats would have sense enough to be warned off by the noise, unlike the two-legged kind of cat, who is so often attracted by sounds like that. No rabbits, either. Just tin cans. I once ran over a dog with my car—not meaning to, of course—I was driving into the sunset and hardly saw him until he was right in front of me. I slowed down to twenty and he went right between the wheels; I felt him bumping against the floorboards (and heard him yelping) but he limped away fast, so perhaps he wasn't killed. It was an awful, hateful thing, worse in some ways than hurting a human being because animals can have no intentions toward you. Not real ones.

Bam! Jean is patiently trying to correct a tendency she has to pull to one side. Inherited from archery practice, probably. A strange, respectably dressed Professorial type appeared in the gap in the front hedge only half an hour ago, saying, amused— as if it were any of his business!—"What are you girls doing?" (As I told you, I'm thirty-eight.)

Jean had swung the gun round, quite coldly. And pulled back the safety catch. "Get out!" He turned pale and backed away, vanished behind the hedge. As if it were his business, you know, as if everything women did was naturally his business.

Against the wire fence at the back of the yard one early maple sapling flames up—pure scarlet. Such useless rage. I used to think I felt like a failure because I was neurotic, because I was over-sensitive, because I'd had a bad childhood (who hasn't), because I lacked that seventh outermost layer of skin that everyone is supposed to have; I said it was the price I paid for being an intellectual. I cried over it. I used to hate you so; I used to dream of killing you over and over again. I used to wonder, with an awe beyond all jealousy, what it was you had that protected you so, that made Rose fall in love with you (over and over again!), what peace, what blessing, what infinite favor in the eyes of God.

Bam!

Jean is, I suspect, holding it.

Bam!

(Any sensible rabbit would have fled long ago. The tin can jerks mechanically.)

"I'm pulling to the left," Jean says.

"Oh Jean, *symbols!*"

There's no sillier activity, practically speaking (or so it seems to me) than shooting tin cans in one's own back yard. Tin cans aren't alive. I don't want to get tin cans out of my way. Yet if men take to it like ducks to water (as a sign of the position in life to which it has pleased God to call them) I think I will practice anyway. I have been shooting all afternoon; my back hurts, my elbows hurt, my skirt's damp and stained from the leaves. Even long, lovely Indian skirts won't do for this sort of activity; first you "break" it, then you eject the used cartridge, then you put it back together again (like a stapler, see?), then you flop down on your stomach, then you push off the whatchamacallit (safety catch), then you brace it against your shoulder, which is going to hurt like blooming blazes before the day is over.

The Tooth Fairy floats down out of the crowded gray heaven, flops on a pile of leaves, and remains there, so shocked as to be nearly invisible. She watches us, bereft of words.

"Jean," I said, "what d'you do with a man you've shot?"

"Leave him alone, dear; he's not much good dead. Nobody is."

"Would you bring him back to life?"

"Dunno. Maybe. Maybe not. I'd probably have to shoot him again."

Bam!

Jean says angrily, "Oh damn, this blasted Bettybop's doing the Charleston. I'm tired." She sits up. "Will you do my shoulders?" So I kneel over her, trying to make like a backrub the best I can, and composing in my mind the following letter to my ex-friend Rose (see p. 1 paragraph 1) which I will entrust to the Tooth Fairy to deliver when it is finished:

Dear Rose,

How are you? Do you still commit psychic incest with persons bigger, brighter, stronger, richer, more successful, and in every way better than yourself? Do you look for hours at lipsticks in store windows? Are you beautiful?

My friend and I have just finished viciously murdering 4 rabbits, 3 tree stumps, 8 pieces of paper, and 6 unwary cats with a rifle called Bloodyborebingle. It is a bloody bore (bingle). It sings magically when we take it out of its wrappings and howls every time we shoot it. It wants blood. It wants us to shoot MEN and hang their stuffed intestines on our wall. My friend and I spit on the ground and cuss a lot. We have cut our hair. We flex our muscles in public and wear leather jackets. Are we revolting? You bet!

The weather here is fine. Winter is coming. Soon it will be too dark to shoot most of the time, so I am concentrating on reading, though frankly there isn't much I can stand, so I am sticking to the diary of Mrs. Daniel Defoe. Mrs. Daniel Defoe is not to be confused with Mr. Daniel Defoe; he has the names and is the man, so don't get them mixed up. I am also writing my own history, which is about how an unstable (tho' pretty) young girl beset by Indefinable Rapture can be corrupted (due to the lack of proper guidance) into a hopeless, happy, neurotic feminist militant invert. You may not know what "invert" means so you had better look it up. It is actually a word used to describe sugar and is synonymous with levulose or dextrose, I forgot which. My story is a warning to all parents, all children, and all psychiatrists.

Do you still fear to dress in velvet because it is sensuous?

Do you still think Shakespeare is all about fathers and daughters?

Do you still think your breasts are ugly?

I have beautiful breasts but you would not like them, so don't visit. The weather here's too bracing.

> Surrealistically yours,
> Esther.

P.S. We are on strike against God.

TOOTH FAIRY: I refuse to deliver that ghastly, obscene communication.

ME (coarsely): Buzz off! You were undoubtedly demoted from Fairy Godmother because of sheer incompetence.

TOOTH FAIRY (spitting on her ice skate blades): Never!
Never!

ME: Off! Or I will have you sent back to painting golden-
rods.

Jean said, "What are you whispering about?"

"I'm creating," I said.

"Would you stop creating and put your rugose tentacle here,
eh?" said Jean, indicating her shoulder under her collar. "It
hurts." She's begun to purr.

I said, "Jean, I am willing to come out, but not in the back
yard under the eyes of the neighbors."

"Then let's go in," she said.

The amazing peacefulness, the astonishing lack of anger, the
sweetness and balm of being at last on the right side of power.

You'll meet us. I'll tell you that the invisible stars I talked about
earlier are called Black Holes—but that's too-heavy symbolism;
we think I'll keep that to ourselves.

You're Stevie. I'll write you. We're still old friends, at least
for a while. Are your friends like you? Are your lovers like you?
I just don't know. (I must write Sally and Louise, too, but at
greater length.)

You can't recognize us in a crowd. Don't try.

You think Jean and I will go away like ladies and live in the
country with Stupid Philpotts and the cats. We won't.

You think we're not middle-aged. You think we're not old.

You even think we're not married. (We might be, even to
you.)

Worst of all, you think we're still furiously angry at you, that
we need you, that we hate you, that we scrabble desperately
at your sleeve, crying "Let me go! Let me go!" We've seen
you smirk a little over this, sometimes in public and sometimes
secretly in the mirror when you thought no one was looking.
You're right, because there is an Esther who still hates and
needs you but she never liked you (that was the giveaway) and
every day she fades a little more. She cared horribly when you
said guns were penises so she couldn't have one, that pens were
penises so she couldn't have one, that checkbooks were penises so she couldn't have one, that minds were penises so she

couldn't have one. (It astonishes all of us, this monopoly on symbols.)

When I smile flatteringly at you, we're a liar.

When we hate and need you, I'm dangerous.

When they become indifferent, run for your life.

At this point some hapless liberal sees the end-papers approaching and has started looking frantically for the Reconciliation Scene. It (the liberal) is either cursing itself for having got entrapped in what started as a perfectly harmless story of love, poignancy, tragedy, self-hatred, and death, or—rather smugly —is disapproving of me for not possessing Shakespeare's magnificent gift of reconciliation which (if you translate it) means that at this point I must (1) meet a wonderful, ideal man and fall in love with him, or (2) kill myself.

You write it.

The way to do it is this: (1) give up your job, (2) become impotent, (3) go on Welfare, (4) crawl on your hands and knees both to the Welfare people and your sex partners, and (5) just for the hell of it, turn Black.

Now you can write a *perfectly beautiful* reconciliation scene.

You are the liberal who might concede (if pushed into a corner and yelled at by twenty angry radicals) that morality does indeed begin at the mouth of a gun (though you'd add quickly, "It doesn't end there") but do you realize what does end at the mouth of a gun? Fear. Frustration. Self-hate. Everything romantic. (This depends, of course, on being at the proper end of the gun.)

You are the teenage male student who comes to us saying O teachur teachur why teachest not thou Conan the Conqueror, Brak the Barbarian, and Douglas the Dilettante, they are mightye of thewe and arme, O teachur, teach yon mighty heroes of olde, pray pray. To which we answer, Sirrah student thou jestest tee hee ho ho what interest hath a Woman of Reason in yon crappe? To which thou sayest, That is not crappe, O blind teachur, but Great Art and Universale; it is all about Myghty Male Feats and Being an Hero, appealing alike to yonge and old, hye and lowe, Blakke and Whyt. To which we reply Buzz off, thou Twerp, thou hast of sexism and acne a galloping case feh feh.

You—oh, what a *nuisance* you are!—will some day soon see
us on TV asked at a demonstration, or someone like me until
she turns round (you can't pick them out of a crowd)—

Interviewer: Who are you?

We (smiling): Oh, somebody. A woman.

Interviewer (he's getting insistent): But what's your name?

And we'll say very lightly and quickly: My name is Legion.

My father once taught me to shoot the same way he taught
me to play chess—badly, so he could beat me. He showed me
Fool's Mate (so I could avoid it, he said) and then insisted that
I play before I'd even memorized what the pieces were supposed to do, before I felt comfortable with them. He then gave
me Fool's Mate twice.

I'm a quick learner. We all are. We never played again. Just
as we never shot again. Just as we never challenged him again.

Until now.

Jean went to New Zealand. She got her degree, got a job there,
and left.

I went to my first Lesbian bar.

It's a gloomy place converted from an old garage and has
been bombed twice, not by bigots but by the Mafia, who run
the other gay bar in town. They did it late at night when there
was nobody in it, which was thoughtful of them, sort of.

I met a big, fat, low-income woman with a ducktail haircut.

I *really do* object to the low income and so does she.

I was introduced to her by a nervous, wide-eyed, twenty-
year-old who'd never finished high school and who told me
a long, complicated story (cracking gum) about an English
teacher who accused her of plagiarism when she was writing an
essay about religion, which she felt very keenly because at the
time she'd been planning to become a nun. When she found
out what I did for a living ("An English teacher!" she said in
dismay) she was very kind anyway; she insisted on playing a
game of TV ping pong with me and then took me around
and introduced me gravely to everyone in the bar. I ended
up sitting next to the big, fat, &c., with whom I cried a little,
about Jean's leaving, but then I perked up when she asked me
to dance. I felt like an awful fool, dancing, because I hadn't

done it since I was twelve in summer camp (and then we only learned to rhumba, for some peculiar reason) but she felt so good. So lovely and blessed, as upholstered people do. Which surprised me. So we wandered around the floor for a bit and then went to my place because a converted garage with dim lights is pretty depressing (she said it first) and I cried some more.

She showed me her great lavender hat (a cap with a visor) and told me what it's like to drive a taxi. I cheered up.

We made love, nervously.

You know, I am an awful snob. Or I have been an awful snob, but if it's possible to be miserable once and then not, one doesn't have to stay a snob, either.

It was all you, you, you (poor you!), secret guerilla warfare and I won't let you play on my affections; I'm allowed to joke about it but only on my back, this wicked, deadly, ghastly, losing, murderous folly you so genially, so cheerfully, and so jokingly insist on.

But there's another you. Are you out there? Can you hear me? We're going to meet a dozen times a day. You'll be in my c.r. group and you'll say you can't stand Lesbians, Lesbians are terrible, they're horrible, and I'll say (in a small voice, trying not to crawl under the sofa), "But I'm a Lesbian," and you'll say, "Oh," so much in an "Oh," so many worlds in an "Oh."

We'll joke across a store-counter, eyes meeting, across a mimeo machine, talk haltingly in a laundromat, saying, "Yes, I didn't think it would go up to eighty today," or "Yes, it's awful to drive in snow," meaning, "Yes, I know." Women who'd hate me if you knew; you don't want to hear about libbers and you certainly don't want to hear about the other thing, either, but still there's that amazing bond, following each other around the office tentatively, primitive Democracy, bits of words exchanged in the margins of Serious, Important, Public Life, little sympathies, women with silly gestures, women with self-deprecating laughs, women with too many smiles, women who wear white gloves, and under it all the most amazing toughness.

Once a week I get an airmail letter with an efflorescent stamp, a koala bear or a rhododendron, New Zealand, of all places.

Students who follow me with slitted eyes, with their private journals, with handkerchiefs balled in their fists, because they must talk all about Charlotte Brontë or die.

You're alone. You've had a bad time. You'd rather not talk to anyone, it's much safer, and yet somehow—imprudently—you do, every chance you get. You say the most amazing things to virtual strangers. You know whom you can trust.

You say nasty things about women and laugh, get tense and furious in the presence of women intellectuals, career women, man-haters, unChristian harpies.

You give me cookies and tea anyway because I look like a nice lady and you don't know it but you're right; I am a nice lady.

You have wonderful memories: a hat with a striped ribbon at age eight, waving at a troop train in World War One, being carried in a parade holding a sign that said Votes for Women, having to wear knickers and being forbidden to play with the neighbor cat, a baleful Persian tom with green eyes, whom you loved.

You breed cats. You ride. You fix cars. You can't stand my mother. Sometimes you are my mother. You write awful stories in my classes about women who work in factories (you know less than nothing about them) and whose husbands beat them and who are simple and elemental and who forgive everyone, and in the middle of these stale and dreadful fictions you put your own frightening, beautiful, terrible, vivid dreams.

You're Rose.

You go quietly mad in little backwaters, worry about your kids, tell everybody what's wrong with today's children, hate your mother, mutter aloud in department stores, say awful things in public to my friend's crippled daughter, drag yourself out at thirteen (one leg in a brace) to learn to ride horses. You're the radical so ready to destroy yourself that you intimidate me. You write letters to local papers in which you condemn all the working women in the world, all the Black people in the world, all the pot-smoking students, and all the radicals who would defile the promise of America, and you sign them, "A Christian American Anti-hippie Mother."

What can I say to you? You're more various than that. How can I love you properly? How can I praise you properly? How can I make love to you properly? How can I tell you never to kill for pleasure, never to kill for sport, never to kill for cruelty, but above all, don't play fair, because when they invite you in, remember: we aren't playing.

You teach introductory University biology, cry "Pull yourself togethah!" to your less-than-Spartan friends, and charge up mountains at forty-three, working like ten women, carrying a baby while you teach five classes, running a farm, dyeing your stiff British hair, and intimidating everyone with that upper-class British voice in which you tell us all—so thrillingly—to be Strong.

You live on unemployment, keeping gas money in a cut-off milk carton in the front of your car, fixing four or five cars for a hobby, getting full of grease most of the time, wearing your hair curled above your square jaw like Anna Magnani, whom you say you look like (and you do), and spending brow-knotted hours braiding macramé plant holders for geraniums.

You smile a lot and retreat a lot and discover strange things about mesons, very quiet, very shy, always losing things out of the pocket of your lab coat, deferential to your husband, deferential to everybody, always looking as if you had just said, "What?"

You're my Polish grandmother, bad-tempered and selfish, an immigrant at seventeen to a country that was not paved with gold after all, throwing dishware at your two daughters in a rage until they hid out of range on the porch roof, yet calmly taking a hot iron away from a crazy countrywoman, saying, "Sophie, dolling, you don't mean it. Give me the iron."

You're my friend Carolellen, who dressed as a Russian Maiden in summer camp when we had the costume party, fascinated by lipsticks and blue-tinted stockings at twelve, short-tempered, crying once because you thought somebody was letting a pet salamander die (you were so theatrical about that!), not wanting to hear about sexual intercourse from the camp counselor because you knew married people just felt each other up, and falling in love with your cousin who, to my mind, resembled a long, lanky, newt, but insisting that sex had nothing to do with it; it was his beautiful soul.

You write me letters about my books, saying, "Do you know what it's like to find yourself in literature only as a bad

metaphor?" and you sign them "Empress of the Universe" and
"A Reader" and "A Struggling Poet" and "A Married Woman."
You say, "I liked your book and am sending it to my daughter,
who is a telephone lineman in Florida."

Hello. Hello, out there. Have you met Jean in New Zealand? Did you meet somebody you thought might be Jean?
That's enough. Did you think you had no allies? What I want
to say is, there are all of us; what I want to say is, we're all in
it together; what I want to say is, it's not just me, though I'm
waving, too; I've hung my red petticoat out on a stick and I'm
signalling like mad, I'm trying to be seen, too. But there are
more of us.

You once sent me a poem. I have an awful feeling you may
send me thousands of poems. I can't read them. I'll have to
put them in my waterbed. (I haven't got a waterbed.) I'll have
to feed them to my camel. (I haven't got a camel.) It's too
many poems for one woman to read, but we should all trade
poems, we should all talk like mad and whoop and dance like
mad, traveling in caravans and on camel-back (great, gorgeous,
sneery eyes, haven't they?) and elephant-howdah and submarine and hot-air balloon and canoes and unicycles and just plain
shanks' mare towards that Great Goddess–Thanksgiving Dinner in the sky; Jean can rough-house with Stupid Philpotts and
tie his hair back with a red ribbon and then roll up her sleeves
and make her batter better.

We must all get some better butter; that will make our batter
better.

The shirtwaist workers who went on strike started just by
going on strike, but then they discovered things; they discovered picketing and unity and museums and *Les Miserables*
and Marx and journalism and racism* and parks and love and
work and how to cook and each other. I like to think they had
fights about whether trade unionism meant feminism and feminism meant Lesbianism and Lesbianism meant trade unionism
and so forth.

So hello. It's beginning. I don't care who you sleep with. I
really don't, you know, as long as you love me. As long as I can
love all of you. Honk if you love us. Float a ribbon, a child's

---

*Well, they *began* to. Some of them. Sort of.

balloon, a philodendron, your own hair, out the car window. Let's be for us. For goodness' sakes, let's not be against us. Somebody (female?) scrawled on a wall at the Sorbonne the most sensible comment of the twentieth century and it must have been a woman; I will bet a postage stamp (with a koala on it) that it was a woman.* She looked around her and she knitted her brow** and then she wrote what I think we should all follow, not to excess, of course,*** but to excess, because the Road to Excess leads absolutely everywhere, William Blake, q.v. (who was sort of one of us but not nearly enough, not to excess, not to wisdom).****

She wrote:

Let's be reasonable. Let's demand the impossible.*****

*I do not have in my possession at the moment a postage stamp with a koala bear on it. I do have, however, a postage stamp with a picture of the New Zealand rhododendron on it (stylized). I'll bet that one.
**Actually she may not have done this; she may simply have written it. You don't have to make a face, though it helps.
***Heavens, no.
****He proposed to his wife, one hot summer's day, that they take off their flesh and sit in the garden in their bones. She did better. She knew better. She sat in the garden in her naked soul.
*****Right!
******A foot note without a referent.
*******Another.
********And another. By far the best kind.
*********Yet another.
**********A perfectly blank footnote.
***********This one is special. It's for Jean.
************This one is *very* special. It ends the book. It is for you.

THE COMPLETE
ALYX STORIES

Bluestocking

THIS IS the tale of a voyage that is of interest only as it concerns the doings of one small, gray-eyed woman. Small women exist in plenty—so do those with gray eyes—but this woman was among the wisest of a sex that is surpassingly wise. There is no surprise in that (or should not be) for it is common knowledge that Woman was created fully a quarter of an hour before Man, and has kept that advantage to this very day. Indeed, legend has it that the first man, Leh, was fashioned from the sixth finger of the left hand of the first woman, Loh, and that is why women have only five fingers on the left hand. The lady with whom we concern ourselves in this story had all her six fingers, and what is more, they all worked.

In the seventh year before the time of which we speak, this woman, a neat, level-browed, governessy person called Alyx, had come to the City of Ourdh as part of a religious delegation from the hills intended to convert the dissolute citizens to the ways of virtue and the one true God, a Bang tree of awful majesty. But Alyx, a young woman of an intellectual bent, had not been in Ourdh two months when she decided that the religion of Yp (as the hill god was called) was a disastrous piece of nonsense, and that deceiving a young woman in matters of such importance was a piece of thoughtlessness for which it would take some weeks of hard, concentrated thought to think up a proper reprisal. In due time the police chased Alyx's coreligionists down the Street of Heaven and Hell and out the swamp gate to be bitten by the mosquitoes that lie in wait among the reeds, and Alyx—with a shrug of contempt—took up a modest living as pick-lock, a profession that gratified her sense of subtlety. It provided her with a living, a craft and a society. Much of the wealth of this richest and vilest of cities stuck to her fingers but most of it dropped off again, for she was not much awed by the things of this world. Going their legal or illegal ways in this seventh year after her arrival, citizens of Ourdh saw only a woman with short, black hair and a sprinkling of freckles across her milky nose; but Alyx had ambitions of becoming a Destiny. She was thirty (a dangerous time for men and women alike) when this story begins. Yp moved in his mysterious ways, Alyx entered the employ of the Lady Edarra, and Ourdh saw neither of them again—for a while.

Alyx was walking with a friend down the Street of Conspicuous Display one sultry summer's morning when she perceived a young woman, dressed like a jeweler's tray and surmounted with a great coil of red hair, waving to her from the table of a wayside garden-terrace.

"Wonderful are the ways of Yp," she remarked, for although she no longer accorded that deity any respect, yet her habits of speech remained. "There sits a red-headed young woman of no more than seventeen years and with the best skin imaginable, and yet she powders her face."

"Wonderful indeed," said her friend. Then he raised one finger and went his way, a discretion much admired in Ourdh. The young lady, who had been drumming her fingers on the tabletop and frowning like a fury, waved again and stamped one foot.

"I want to talk to you," she said sharply. "Can't you hear me?"

"I have six ears," said Alyx, the courteous reply in such a situation. She sat down and the waiter handed her the bill of fare.

"You are not listening to me," said the lady.

"I do not listen with my eyes," said Alyx.

"Those who do not listen with their eyes as well as their ears," said the lady sharply, "can be made to regret it!"

"Those," said Alyx, "who on a fine summer's morning threaten their fellow-creatures in any way, absurdly or otherwise, both mar the serenity of the day and break the peace of Yp, who," she said, "is mighty."

"You are impossible!" cried the lady. "Impossible!" and she bounced up and down in her seat with rage, fixing her fierce brown eyes on Alyx. "Death!" she cried. "Death and bones!" and that was a ridiculous thing to say at eleven in the morning by the side of the most wealthy and luxurious street in Ourdh, for such a street is one of the pleasantest places in the world if you do not watch the beggars. The lady, insensible to all this bounty, jumped to her feet and glared at the little picklock; then, composing herself with an effort (she clenched both hands and gritted her teeth like a person in the worst throes of marsh fever), she said—calmly—

"I want to leave Ourdh."

"Many do," said Alyx, courteously.

"I require a companion."

"A lady's maid?" suggested Alyx. The lady jumped once in her seat as if her anger must have an outlet somehow; then she clenched her hands and gritted her teeth with doubled vigor.

"I must have protection," she snapped.

"Ah?"

"I'll pay!" (This was almost a shriek.)

"How?" said Alyx, who had her doubts.

"None of your business," said the lady.

"If I'm to serve you, everything's my business. Tell me. All right, how much?"

The lady named a figure, reluctantly.

"Not enough," said Alyx. "Particularly not knowing how. Or why. And why protection? From whom? When?" The lady jumped to her feet. "By water?" continued Alyx imperturbably. "By land? On foot? How far? You must understand, little one—"

"*Little one!*" cried the lady, her mouth dropping open. "*Little one!*"

"If you and I are to do business—"

"I'll have you thrashed—" gasped the lady, out of breath, "I'll have you so—"

"And let the world know your plans?" said Alyx, leaning forward with one hand under her chin. The lady stared, and bit her lip, and backed up, and then she hastily grabbed her skirts as if they were sacks of potatoes and ran off, ribbons fluttering behind her. *Wine-colored ribbons*, thought Alyx, *with red hair; that's clever.* She ordered brandy and filled her glass, peering curiously into it where the hot midmorning sun of Ourdh suffused into a winy glow, a sparkling, trembling, streaky mass of floating brightness. *To* (she said to herself with immense good humor) *all the young ladies in the world.* "And," she added softly, "great quantities of money."

At night Ourdh is a suburb of the Pit, or that steamy, muddy bank where the gods kneel eternally, making man; though the

lights of the city never show fairer than then. At night the rich
wake up and the poor sink into a distressed sleep, and everyone takes to the flat, white-washed roofs. Under the light of
gold lamps the wealthy converse, sliding across one another,
silky but never vulgar; at night Ya, the courtesan with the gold
breasts (very good for the jaded taste) and Garh the pirate, red-
bearded, with his carefully cultivated stoop, and many many
others, all ascend the broad, white steps to someone's roof.
Each step carries a lamp, each lamp sheds a blurry radiance
on a tray, each tray is crowded with sticky, pleated, salt, sweet
. . . Alyx ascended, dreaming of snow. She was there on business. Indeed the sky was overcast that night, but a downpour
would not drive the guests indoors; a striped silk awning with
gold fringes would be unrolled over their heads, and while the
fringes became matted and wet and water spouted into the
garden below, ladies would put out their hands (or their heads
—but that took a brave lady on account of the coiffure) outside the awning and squeal as they were soaked by the warm,
mild, neutral rain of Ourdh. Thunder was another matter. Alyx
remembered hill storms with gravel hissing down the gullies of
streams and paths turned to cold mud. She met the dowager in
charge and that ponderous lady said:

"Here she is."

It was Edarra, sulky and seventeen, knotting a silk handkerchief in a wet wad in her hand and wearing a sparkling blue-
and-green bib.

"That's the necklace," said the dowager. "Don't let it out of
your sight."

"I see," said Alyx, passing her hand over her eyes.

When they were left alone, Edarra fastened her fierce eyes on
Alyx and hissed, "Traitor!"

"What for?" said Alyx.

"Traitor! Traitor! Traitor!" shouted the girl. The nearest
guests turned to listen and then turned away, bored.

"You grow dull," said Alyx, and she leaned lightly on the
roof-rail to watch the company. There was the sound of angry
stirrings and rustlings behind her. Then the girl said in a low
voice (between her teeth), "Tonight someone is going to steal
this necklace."

Alyx said nothing. Ya floated by with her metal breasts gleaming in the lamplight; behind her, Peng the jeweler.

"I'll get seven hundred ounces of gold for it!"

"Ah?" said Alyx.

"You've spoiled it," snapped the girl. Together they watched the guests, red and green, silk on silk like oil on water, the high-crowned hats and earrings glistening, the bracelets sparkling like a school of underwater fish. Up came the dowager accompanied by a landlord of the richest and largest sort, a gentleman bridegroom who had buried three previous wives and would now have the privilege of burying the Lady Edarra —though to hear him tell it, the first had died of overeating, the second of drinking and the third of a complexion-cleanser she had brewed herself. Nothing questionable in *that*. He smiled and took Edarra's upper arm between his thumb and finger. He said, "Well, little girl." She stared at him. "Don't be defiant," he said. "You're going to be rich." The dowager bridled. "I mean—even richer," he said with a smile. The mother and the bridegroom talked business for a few minutes, neither watching the girl; then they turned abruptly and disappeared into the mixing, moving company, some of whom were leaning over the rail screaming at those in the garden below, and some of whom were slipping and sitting down involuntarily in thirty-five pounds of cherries that had just been accidentally overturned onto the floor.

"So that's why you want to run away," said Alyx. The Lady Edarra was staring straight ahead of her, big tears rolling silently down her cheeks. "Mind your business," she said.

"Mind yours," said Alyx softly, "and do not insult me, for I get rather hard then." She laughed and fingered the necklace, which was big and gaudy and made of stones the size of a thumb. "What would you do," she said, "if I told you yes?"

"You're impossible!" said Edarra, looking up and sobbing.

"Praised be Yp that I exist then," said Alyx, "for I do ask you if your offer is open. Now that I see your necklace more plainly, I incline towards accepting it—whoever you hired was cheating you, by the way; you can get twice again as much—though that gentleman we saw just now has something to do with my decision." She paused. "Well?"

Edarra said nothing, her mouth open.

"Well, speak!"

"No," said Edarra.

"Mind you," said Alyx wryly, "you still have to find someone to travel with, and I wouldn't trust the man you hired—probably hired—for five minutes in a room with twenty other people. Make your choice. I'll go with you as long and as far as you want, anywhere you want."

"Well," said Edarra, "yes."

"Good," said Alyx. "I'll take two-thirds."

"No!" cried Edarra, scandalized.

"Two-thirds," said Alyx, shaking her head. "It has to be worth my while. Both the gentleman you hired to steal your necklace—and your mother—and your husband-to-be—and heaven alone knows who else—will be after us before the evening is out. Maybe. At any rate, I want to be safe when I come back."

"Will the money—?" said Edarra.

"Money does all things," said Alyx, "and I have long wanted to return to this city, this paradise, this—swamp!—with that which makes power! Come," and she leapt onto the roof-rail and from there into the garden, landing feet first in the loam and ruining a bed of strawberries. Edarra dropped beside her, all of a heap and panting.

"Kill one, kill all, kill devil!" said Alyx gleefully. Edarra grabbed her arm. Taking the lady by the crook of her elbow, Alyx began to run, while behind them the fashionable merriment of Ourdh (the guests were pouring wine down each other's backs) grew fainter and fainter and finally died away.

They sold the necklace at the waterfront shack that smelt of tar and sewage (Edarra grew ill and had to wait outside), and with the money Alyx bought two short swords, a dagger, a blanket, and a round cheese. She walked along the harbor carving pieces out of the cheese with the dagger and eating them off the point. Opposite a fishing boat, a square-sailed, slovenly tramp, she stopped and pointed with cheese and dagger both.

"That's ours," said she. (For the harbor streets were very quiet.)

"Oh, *no*!"

"Yes," said Alyx, "that mess," and from the slimy timbers of the quay she leapt onto the deck. "It's empty," she said.

"No," said Edarra, "I won't go," and from the landward side of the city thunder rumbled and a few drops of rain fell in the darkness, warm, like the wind.

"It's going to rain," said Alyx. "Get aboard."

"No," said the girl. Alyx's face appeared in the bow of the boat, a white spot scarcely distinguishable from the sky; she stood in the bow as the boat rocked to and fro in the wash of the tide. A light across the street, that shone in the window of a waterfront café, went out.

"Oh!" gasped Edarra, terrified, "give me my money!" A leather bag fell in the dust at her feet. "I'm going back," she said, "I'm never going to set foot in that thing. It's disgusting. It's not ladylike."

"No," said Alyx.

"It's *dirty*!" cried Edarra. Without a word, Alyx disappeared into the darkness. Above, where the clouds bred from the marshes roofed the sky, the obscurity deepened and the sound of rain drumming on the roofs of the town advanced steadily, three streets away, then two . . . a sharp gust of wind blew bits of paper and the indefinable trash of the seaside upwards in an unseen spiral. Out over the sea Edarra could hear the universal sound of rain on water, like the shaking of dried peas in a sheet of paper but softer and more blurred, as acres of the surface of the sea dimpled with innumerable little pockmarks. . . .

"I thought you'd come," said Alyx. "Shall we begin?"

Ourdh stretches several miles southward down the coast of the sea, finally dwindling to a string of little towns; at one of these they stopped and provided for themselves, laying in a store of food and a first-aid kit of dragon's teeth and ginger root, for one never knows what may happen in a sea voyage. They also bought resin; Edarra was forced to caulk the ship under fear of being called soft and lazy, and she did it, although she did not speak. She did not speak at all. She boiled the fish over a fire laid in the brass firebox and fanned the smoke and choked, but she never said a word. She did what she was told in silence. Every day bitterer, she kicked the stove and scrubbed the floor, tearing her fingernails, wearing out her skirt; she swore to herself, but without a word, so that when one night she kicked Alyx with her foot, it was an occasion.

"Where are we going?" said Edarra in the dark, with violent impatience. She had been brooding over the question for several weeks and her voice carried a remarkable quality of concentration; she prodded Alyx with her big toe and repeated, "I said, where are we going?"

"Morning," said Alyx. She was asleep, for it was the middle of the night; they took watches above. "In the morning," she said. Part of it was sleep and part was demoralization; although reserved, she was friendly and Edarra was ruining her nerves.

"Oh!" exclaimed the lady between clenched teeth, and Alyx shifted in her sleep. "When will we buy some decent *food*?" demanded the lady vehemently. "When? When?"

Alyx sat bolt upright. "Go to sleep!" she shouted, under the hallucinatory impression that it was she who was awake and working. She dreamed of nothing but work now. In the dark Edarra stamped up and down. "Oh, wake up!" she cried, "for goodness' sakes!"

"What do you want?" said Alyx.

"Where are we going?" said Edarra. "Are we going to some miserable little fishing village? Are we? Well, are we?"

"Yes," said Alyx.

"Why!" demanded the lady.

"To match your character."

With a scream of rage, the Lady Edarra threw herself on her preserver and they bumped heads for a few minutes, but the battle—although violent—was conducted entirely in the dark and they were tangled up almost completely in the beds, which were nothing but blankets laid on the bare boards and not the only reason that the lady's brown eyes were turning a permanent, baleful black.

"Let me up, you're strangling me!" cried the lady, and when Alyx managed to light the lamp, bruising her shins against some of the furniture, Edarra was seen to be wrestling with a blanket, which she threw across the cabin. The cabin was five feet across.

"If you do that again, madam," said Alyx, "I'm going to knock your head against the floor!" The lady swept her hair back from her brow with the air of a princess. She was trembling. "Huh!" she said, in the voice of one so angry that she does not dare to say anything. "Really," she said, on the verge of tears.

"Yes, really," said Alyx, "really" (finding some satisfaction in the word), "really go above. We're drifting." The lady sat in her corner, her face white, clenching her hands together as if she held a burning chip from the stove. "No," she said.

"Eh, madam?" said Alyx.

"I won't do anything," said Edarra unsteadily, her eyes glittering. "You can do everything. You want to, anyway."

"Now look here—" said Alyx grimly, advancing on the girl, but whether she thought better of it or whether she heard or smelt something (for after weeks of water, sailors—or so they say—develop a certain intuition for such things), she only threw her blanket over her shoulder and said, "Suit yourself." Then she went on deck. Her face was unnaturally composed.

"Heaven witness my self-control," she said, not raising her voice but in a conversational tone that somewhat belied her facial expression. "Witness it. See it. Reward it. May the messenger of Yp—in whom I do not believe—write in that parchment leaf that holds all the records of the world that I, provoked beyond human endurance, tormented, kicked in the midst of sleep, treated like the off-scourings of a filthy, cheap, sour-beer-producing brewery—"

Then she saw the sea monster.

Opinion concerning sea monsters varies in Ourdh and the surrounding hills, the citizens holding monsters to be the souls of the wicked dead forever ranging the pastureless wastes of ocean to waylay the living and force them into watery graves, and the hill people scouting this blasphemous view and maintaining that sea monsters are legitimate creations of the great god Yp, sent to murder travelers as an illustration of the majesty, the might and the unpredictability of that most inexplicable of deities. But the end result is much the same. Alyx had seen the bulbous face and coarse whiskers of the creature in a drawing hanging in the Silver Eel on the waterfront of Ourdh (the original—stuffed—had been stolen in some prehistoric time, according to the proprietor), and she had shuddered. She had thought, *Perhaps it is just an animal*, but even so it was not pleasant. Now in the moonlight that turned the ocean to a ball of silver waters in the midst of which bobbed the tiny ship, very very far from anyone or anything, she saw the surface part in a rain of sparkling drops and the huge, wicked, twisted face of the creature, so like and unlike a man's, rise like a shadowy demon from the dark, bright water. It held its baby to its breast, a nauseating parody of human-kind. Behind her she heard Edarra choke, for that lady had followed her onto the deck. Alyx forced her unwilling feet to the rail and leaned over, stretching out one shaking hand. She said:

> "By the tetragrammaton of dread,
> "By the seven names of God.
> "Begone and trouble us no more!"

Which was very brave of her because she did not believe in charms. But it had to be said directly to the monster's face, and say it she did.

The monster barked like a dog.

Edarra screamed. With an arm suddenly nerved to steel, the thief snatched a fishing spear from its place in the stern and braced one knee against the rail; she leaned into the creature's very mouth and threw her harpoon. It entered below the pink harelip and blood gushed as the thing trumpeted and thrashed; black under the moonlight, the blood billowed along the waves, the water closed over the apparition, ripples spread and rocked the boat, and died, and Alyx slid weakly onto the deck.

There was silence for a while. Then she said, "It's only an animal," and she made the mark of Yp on her forehead to atone for having killed something without the spur of overmastering necessity. She had not made the gesture for years. Edarra, who was huddled in a heap against the mast, moved. "It's gone," said Alyx. She got to her feet and took the rudder of the boat, a long shaft that swung at the stern. The girl moved again, shivering.

"It was an animal," said Alyx with finality, "that's all."

The next morning Alyx took out the two short swords and told Edarra she would have to learn to use them.

"No," said Edarra.

"Yes," said Alyx. While the wind held, they fenced up and down the deck, Edarra scrambling resentfully. Alyx pressed her hard and assured her that she would have to do this every day.

"You'll have to cut your hair, too," she added, for no particular reason.

"Never!" gasped the other, dodging.

"Oh, yes, you will!" and she grasped the red braid and yanked; one flash of the blade—

Now it may have been the sea air—or the loss of her red tresses—or the collision with a character so different from those she was accustomed to, but from this morning on it became clear that something was exerting a humanizing influence on the young woman. She was quieter, even (on occasion) dreamy; she turned to her work without complaint, and after a deserved ducking in the sea had caused her hair to break out in short curls, she took to leaning over the side of the boat and watching herself in the water, with meditative pleasure. Her skin, that the pick-lock had first noticed as fine, grew even finer with the passage of the days, and she turned a delicate ivory color, like a half-baked biscuit, that Alyx could not help but notice. But she did not like it. Often in the watches of the night she would say aloud:

"Very well, I am thirty—" (Thus she would soliloquize.) "But what, O Yp, is thirty? Thrice ten. Twice fifteen. Women marry at forty. In ten years I will be forty—"

And so on. From these apostrophizations she returned uncomfortable, ugly, old and with a bad conscience. She had a conscience, though it was not active in the usual directions. One morning, after these nightly wrestlings, the girl was leaning over the rail of the boat, her hair dangling about her face, watching the fish in the water and her own reflection. Occasionally she yawned, opening her pink mouth and shutting her eyes; all this Alyx watched surreptitiously. She felt uncomfortable. All morning the heat had been intense and mirages of ships and gulls and unidentified objects had danced on the horizon, breaking up eventually into clumps of seaweed or floating bits of wood.

"Shall I catch a fish?" said Edarra, who occasionally spoke now.

"Yes—no—" said Alyx, who held the rudder.

"Well, shall I or shan't I?" said Edarra tolerantly.

"Yes," said Alyx, "if you—" and swung the rudder hard. All morning she had been watching black, wriggling shapes that turned out to be nothing; now she thought she saw something across the glittering water. *One thing we shall both get out of this*, she thought, *is a permanent squint.* The shape moved closer, resolving itself into several verticals and a horizontal; it danced and streaked maddeningly. Alyx shaded her eyes.

"Edarra," she said quietly, "get the swords. Hand me one and the dagger."

"What?" said Edarra, dropping a fishing line she had begun to pick up.

"Three men in a sloop," said Alyx. "Back up against the mast and put the blade behind you."

"But they might not—" said Edarra with unexpected spirit.

"And they might," said Alyx grimly, "they just might."

Now in Ourdh there is a common saying that if you have not strength, there are three things which will serve as well: deceit, surprise and speed. These are women's natural weapons. Therefore when the three rascals—and rascals they were or appearances lied—reached the boat, the square sail was furled and the two women, like castaways, were sitting idly against the mast while the boat bobbed in the oily swell. This was to render the rudder useless and keep the craft from slewing round at a sudden change in the wind. Alyx saw with joy that two of the three were fat and all were dirty; *too vain*, she thought, *to keep in trim or take precautions.* She gathered in her right hand the strands of the fishing net stretched inconspicuously over the deck.

"Who does your laundry?" she said, getting up slowly. She hated personal uncleanliness. Edarra rose to one side of her.

"You will," said the midmost. They smiled broadly. When the first set foot in the net, Alyx jerked it up hard, bringing him to the deck in a tangle of fishing lines; at the same instant with her left hand—and the left hand of this daughter of Loh carried all its six fingers—she threw the dagger (which had previously been used for nothing bloodier than cleaning fish) and caught the second interloper squarely in the stomach. He sat down, hard, and was no further trouble. The first, who had gotten to his feet, closed with her in a ringing of steel that was loud on that tiny deck; for ninety seconds by the clock he forced her back towards the opposite rail; then in a burst of speed she took him under his guard at a pitch of the ship and slashed his sword wrist, disarming him. But her thrust carried her too far and she fell; grasping his wounded wrist with his other hand, he launched himself at her, and Alyx—planting both knees against his chest—helped him into the sea. He took a piece of the rail with him. By the sound of it, he could not swim. She stood over the rail, gripping her blade until he vanished for the last time. It was over that quickly. Then she perceived Edarra standing over the third man, sword in hand, an incredulous, pleased expression on her face. Blood holds no terrors for a child of Ourdh, unfortunately.

"Look what I did!" said the little lady.

"Must you look so pleased?" said Alyx, sharply. The morning's washing hung on the opposite rail to dry. So quiet had the sea and sky been that it had not budged an inch. The gentleman with the dagger sat against it, staring.

"If you're so hardy," said Alyx, "take that out."

"Do I have to?" said the little girl, uneasily.

"I suppose not," said Alyx, and she put one foot against the dead man's chest, her grip on the knife and her eyes averted; the two parted company and he went over the side in one motion. Edarra turned a little red; she hung her head and remarked, "You're splendid."

"You're a savage," said Alyx.

"But why!" cried Edarra indignantly. "All I said was—"

"Wash up," said Alyx, "and get rid of the other one; he's yours."

"I said you were splendid and I don't see why that's—"

"And set the sail," added the six-fingered pick-lock. She lay down, closed her eyes, and fell asleep.

Now it was Alyx who did not speak and Edarra who did; she said, "Good morning," she said, "Why do fish have scales?" she said, "I *like* shrimp; they look funny," and she said (once), "I like you," matter-of-factly, as if she had been thinking about the question and had just then settled it. One afternoon they were eating fish in the cabin—"fish" is a cold, unpleasant, slimy word, but sea trout baked in clay with onion, shrimp and white wine is something else again—when Edarra said:

"What was it like when you lived in the hills?" She said it right out of the blue, like that.

"What?" said Alyx.

"Were you happy?" said Edarra.

"I prefer not to discuss it."

"All right, *madam*," and the girl swept up to the deck with her plate and glass. It isn't easy climbing a rope ladder with a glass (balanced on a plate) in one hand, but she did it without thinking, which shows how accustomed she had become to the ship and how far this tale has advanced. Alyx sat moodily poking at her dinner (which had turned back to slime as far as she was concerned) when she smelled something char and gave a cursory poke into the firebox next to her with a metal broom they kept for the purpose. This ancient firebox served them as a stove. Now it may have been age, or the carelessness of the previous owner, or just the venomous hatred of inanimate objects for mankind (the religion of Yp stresses this point with great fervor), but the truth of the matter was that the firebox had begun to come apart at the back, and a few flaming chips had fallen on the wooden floor of the cabin. Moreover, while Alyx poked among the coals in the box, its door hanging open, the left front leg of the creature crumpled and the box itself sagged forward, the coals inside sliding dangerously. Alyx exclaimed and hastily shut the door. She turned and looked for the lock with which to fasten the door more securely, and thus it was that until she turned back again and stood up, she did not see what mischief was going on at the other side. The floor, to the glory of Yp, was smoking in half a dozen places. Stepping carefully, Alyx picked up the pail of seawater kept always ready in a corner of the cabin and emptied it onto the smoldering floor, but at that instant—so diabolical are the souls of machines —the second front leg of the box followed the first and the brass door burst open, spewing burning coals the length of the cabin. Ordinarily not even a heavy sea could scatter the fire, for the door was too far above the bed on which the wood rested and the monster's legs were bolted to the floor. But now the boards caught not in half a dozen but in half a hundred places. Alyx shouted for water and grabbed a towel, while a pile of folded blankets against the wall curled and turned black; the cabin was filled with the odor of burning hair. Alyx beat at the blankets and the fire found a cupboard next to them, crept under the door and caught in a sack of sprouting potatoes, which refused to burn. Flour was packed next to them. "Edarra!" yelled Alyx. She overturned a rack of wine, smashing it against the floor regardless of the broken glass; it checked the flames while she beat at the cupboard; then the fire turned and leapt at the opposite wall. It flamed up for an instant in a straw mat hung against the wall, creeping upward, eating down through the planks of the floor, searching out cracks under the cupboard door, roundabout. The potatoes, dried by the heat, began to wither sullenly; their canvas sacking crumbled and turned black. Edarra had just come tumbling into the cabin, horrified, and Alyx was choking on the smoke of canvas sacking and green, smoking sprouts, when the fire reached the stored flour. There was a concussive bellow and a blast of air that sent Alyx staggering into the stove; white flame billowed from the corner that had held the cupboard. Alyx was burned on one side from knee to ankle and knocked against the wall; she fell, full-length.

When she came to herself, she was half lying in dirty seawater and the fire was gone. Across the cabin Edarra was struggling with a water demon, stuffing half-burnt blankets and clothes and sacks of potatoes against an incorrigible waterspout that knocked her about and burst into the cabin in erratic gouts, making tides in the water that shifted sluggishly from one side of the floor to the other as the ship rolled.

"Help me!" she cried. Alyx got up. Shakily she staggered across the cabin and together they leaned their weight on the pile of stuffs jammed into the hole.

"It's not big," gasped the girl, "I made it with a sword. Just under the waterline."

"Stay here," said Alyx. Leaning against the wall, she made her way to the cold firebox. Two bolts held it to the floor. "No good there," she said. With the same exasperating slowness, she hauled herself up the ladder and stood uncertainly on the deck. She lowered the sail, cutting her fingers, and dragged it to the stern, pushing all loose gear on top of it. Dropping down through the hatch again, she shifted coils of rope and stores of food to the stern; patiently fumbling, she unbolted the fire-box from the floor. The waterspout had lessened. Finally, when Alyx had pushed the metal box end over end against the op-posite wall of the cabin, the water demon seemed to lose his exuberance. He drooped and almost died. With a letting-out of breath, Edarra released the mass pressed against the hole: blankets, sacks, shoes, potatoes, all slid to the stern. The water stopped. Alyx, who seemed for the first time to feel a brand against the calf of her left leg and needles in her hand where she had burnt herself unbolting the stove, sat leaning against the wall, too weary to move. She saw the cabin through a milky mist. Ballooning and shrinking above her hung Edarra's face, dirty with charred wood and sea slime; the girl said:

"What shall I do now?"

"Nail boards," said Alyx slowly.

"Yes, then?" urged the girl.

"Pitch," said Alyx. "Bail it out."

"You mean the boat will pitch?" said Edarra, frowning in puzzlement. In answer Alyx shook her head and raised one hand out of the water to point to the storage place on deck, but the air drove the needles deeper into her fingers and dis-tracted her mind. She said, "Fix," and leaned back against the wall, but as she was sitting against it already, her movement only caused her to turn, with a slow, natural easiness, and slide unconscious into the dirty water that ran tidally this way and that within the blackened, sour-reeking, littered cabin.

Alyx groaned. Behind her eyelids she was reliving one of the small contretemps of her life: lying indoors ill and badly hurt, with the sun rising out of doors, thinking that she was dy-ing and hearing the birds sing. She opened her eyes. The sun shone, the waves sang, there was the little girl watching her. The sun was level with the sea and the first airs of evening stole across the deck.

Alyx tried to say, "What happened?" and managed only to croak. Edarra sat down, all of a flop.

"You're *talking*!" she exclaimed with vast relief. Alyx stirred, looking about her, tried to rise and thought better of it. She discovered lumps of bandage on her hand and her leg; she picked at them feebly with her free hand, for they struck her somehow as irrelevant. Then she stopped.

"I'm alive," she said hoarsely, "for Yp likes to think he looks after me, the bastard."

"I don't know about *that*," said Edarra, laughing. "My!" She knelt on the deck, with her hair streaming behind her like a ship's figurehead come to life; she said, "I fixed everything. I pulled you up here. I fixed the boat, though I had to hang by my knees. I pitched it." She exhibited her arms, daubed to the elbow. "Look," she said. Then she added, with a catch in her voice, "I thought you might die."

"I might yet," said Alyx. The sun dipped into the sea. "Long-leggedy thing," she said in a hoarse whisper, "get me some food."

"Here." Edarra rummaged for a moment and held out a piece of bread, part of the ragbag loosened on deck during the late catastrophe. The pick-lock ate, lying back. The sun danced up and down in her eyes, above the deck, below the deck, above the deck. . . .

"Creature," said Alyx, "I had a daughter."

"Where is she?" said Edarra.

Silence.

"Praying," said Alyx at last. "Damning me."

"I'm sorry," said Edarra.

"But you," said Alyx, "are—" and she stopped blankly. She said, "You—"

"Me what?" said Edarra.

"Are here," said Alyx, and with a bone-cracking yawn, letting the crust fall from her fingers, she fell asleep.

At length the time came (all things must end and Alyx's burns had already healed to barely visible scars—one looking closely at her could see many such faint marks on her back, her arms, her sides, the bodily record of the last rather difficult seven years) when Alyx, emptying overboard the breakfast scraps, gave a yell so loud and triumphant that she inadvertently lost hold of the garbage bucket and it fell into the sea.

"What is it?" said Edarra, startled. Her friend was gripping the rail with both hands and staring over the sea with a look that Edarra did not understand in the least, for Alyx had been closemouthed on some subjects in the girl's education.

"I am thinking," said Alyx.

"Oh!" shrieked Edarra, "land! Land!" and she capered about the deck, whirling and clapping her hands. "I can change my dress!" she cried. "Just think! We can eat fresh food! Just think!"

"I was not," said Alyx, "thinking about that." Edarra came up to her and looked curiously into her eyes, which had gone as deep and as gray as the sea on a gray day; she said, "Well, what are you thinking about?"

"Something not fit for your ears," said Alyx. The little girl's eyes narrowed. "Oh," she said pointedly. Alyx ducked past her for the hatch, but Edarra sprinted ahead and straddled it, arms wide.

"I want to hear it," she said.

"That's a foolish attitude," said Alyx. "You'll lose your balance."

"Tell me."

"Come, get away."

The girl sprang forward like a red-headed fury, seizing her friend by the hair with both hands. "If it's not fit for my ears, I want to hear it!" she cried.

Alyx dodged around her and dropped below, to retrieve from storage her severe, decent, formal black clothes, fit for a business call. When she reappeared, tossing the clothes on deck, Edarra had a short sword in her right hand and was guarding the hatch very exuberantly.

"Don't be foolish," said Alyx crossly.

"I'll kill you if you don't tell me," remarked Edarra.

"Little one," said Alyx, "the stain of ideals remains on the imagination long after the ideals themselves vanish. Therefore I will tell you nothing."

"Raahh!" said Edarra, in her throat.

"It wouldn't be proper," added Alyx primly, "if you don't know about it, so much the better," and she turned away to sort her clothes. Edarra pinked her in a formal, black shoe.

"Stop it!" snapped Alyx.

"Never!" cried the girl wildly, her eyes flashing. She lunged and feinted and her friend, standing still, wove (with the injured boot) a net of defense as invisible as the cloak that enveloped Aule the Messenger. Edarra, her chest heaving, managed to say, "I'm tired."

"Then stop," said Alyx.

Edarra stopped.

"Do I remind you of your little baby girl?" she said.

Alyx said nothing.

"I'm not a little baby girl," said Edarra. "I'm eighteen now and I know more than you think. Did I ever tell you about my first suitor and the cook and the cat?"

"No," said Alyx, busy sorting.

"The cook let the cat in," said Edarra, "though she shouldn't have, and so when I was sitting on my suitor's lap and I had one arm around his neck and the other arm on the arm of the chair, he said, 'Darling, where is your *other* little hand?'"

"Mm hm," said Alyx.

"It was the cat, walking across his lap! But he could only feel one of my hands so he thought—" but here, seeing that Alyx was not listening, Edarra shouted a word used remarkably seldom in Ourdh and for very good reason. Alyx looked up in surprise. Ten feet away (as far away as she could get), Edarra was lying on the planks, sobbing. Alyx went over to her and knelt down, leaning back on her heels. Above, the first sea birds of the trip—sea birds always live near land—circled and cried in a hard, hungry mew like a herd of aerial cats.

"Someone's coming," said Alyx.

"Don't care." This was Edarra on the deck, muffled. Alyx reached out and began to stroke the girl's disordered hair, braiding it with her fingers, twisting it round her wrist and slipping her hand through it and out again.

"Someone's in a fishing smack coming this way," said Alyx.

Edarra burst into tears.

"Now, now, now!" said Alyx, "why that? Come!" and she tried to lift the girl up, but Edarra held stubbornly to the deck.

"What's the matter?" said Alyx.

"You!" cried Edarra, bouncing bolt upright. "You; you treat me like a baby."

"You are a baby," said Alyx.

"How'm I ever going to stop if you treat me like one?" shouted the girl. Alyx got up and padded over to her new clothes, her face thoughtful. She slipped into a sleeveless black shift and belted it; it came to just above the knee. Then she took a comb from the pocket and began to comb out her straight, silky black hair. "I was remembering," she said.

"What?" said Edarra.

"Things."

"Don't make fun of me." Alyx stood for a moment, one blue-green earring on her ear and the other in her fingers. She smiled at the innocence of this red-headed daughter of the wickedest city on earth; she saw her own youth over again (though she had been unnaturally knowing almost from birth), and so she smiled, with rare sweetness.

"I'll tell you," she whispered conspiratorially, dropping to her knees beside Edarra, "I was remembering a man."

"Oh!" said Edarra.

"I remembered," said Alyx, "one week in spring when the night sky above Ourdh was hung as brilliantly with stars as the jewelers' trays on the Street of a Thousand Follies. Ah! what a man. A big Northman with hair like yours and a gold-red beard —God, what a beard!—Fafnir—no, Fafh—well, something ridiculous. But he was far from ridiculous. He was amazing."

Edarra said nothing, rapt.

"He was strong," said Alyx, laughing, "and hairy, beautifully hairy. And willful! I said to him, 'Man, if you must follow your eyes into every whorehouse—' And we fought! At a place called the Silver Fish. Overturned tables. What a fuss! And a week later," (she shrugged ruefully) "gone. There it is. And I can't even remember his name."

"Is that sad?" said Edarra.

"I don't think so," said Alyx. "After all, I remember his beard," and she smiled wickedly. "There's a man in that boat," she said, "and that boat comes from a fishing village of maybe ten, maybe twelve families. That symbol painted on the side of the boat—I can make it out; perhaps you can't; it's a red cross on a blue circle—indicates a single man. Now the chances of there being two single men between the ages of eighteen and forty in a village of twelve families is not—"

"A man!" exploded Edarra, "that's why you're primping like a hen. Can I wear your clothes? Mine are full of salt," and she buried herself in the piled wearables on deck, humming, dragged out a brush and began to brush her hair. She lay flat on her stomach, catching her underlip between her teeth, saying over and over "Oh—oh—oh—"

"Look here," said Alyx, back at the rudder, "before you get too free, let me tell you: there are rules."

"I'm going to wear this white thing," said Edarra busily.

"Married men are not considered proper. It's too acquisitive. If I know you, you'll want to get married inside three weeks, but you must remember—"

"My shoes don't fit!" wailed Edarra, hopping about with one shoe on and one off.

"Horrid," said Alyx briefly.

"My feet have gotten bigger," said Edarra, plumping down beside her. "Do you think they spread when I go barefoot? Do you think that's ladylike? Do you think—"

"For the sake of peace, be quiet!" said Alyx. Her whole attention was taken up by what was far off on the sea; she nudged Edarra and the girl sat still, only emitting little explosions of breath as she tried to fit her feet into her old shoes. At last she gave up and sat—quite motionless—with her hands in her lap.

"There's only one man there," said Alyx.

"He's probably too young for you." (Alyx's mouth twitched.)

"Well?" added Edarra plaintively.

"Well what?"

"Well," said Edarra, embarrassed, "I hope you don't mind."

"Oh! I don't mind," said Alyx.

"I suppose," said Edarra helpfully, "that it'll be dull for you, won't it?"

"I can find some old grandfather," said Alyx.

Edarra blushed.

"And I can always cook," added the pick-lock.

"You must be a *good* cook."

"I am."

"That's nice. You remind me of a cat we once had, a very fierce, black, female cat who was a *very* good mother," (she choked and continued hurriedly) "she was a ripping fighter, too, and we just couldn't keep her in the house whenever she —uh—"

"Yes?" said Alyx.

"Wanted to get out," said Edarra feebly. She giggled. "And she always came back pr—I mean—"

"Yes?"

"She was a popular cat."

"Ah," said Alyx, "but old, no doubt."

"Yes," said Edarra unhappily. "Look here," she added quickly, "I hope you understand that I like you and I esteem you and it's not that I want to cut you out, but I *am* younger and you can't expect—" Alyx raised one hand. She was laughing. Her hair blew about her face like a skein of black silk. Her gray eyes glowed.

"Great are the ways of Yp," she said, "and some men prefer the ways of experience. Very odd of them, no doubt, but lucky for some of us. I have been told—but never mind. Infatuated men are bad judges. Besides, maid, if you look out across the water you will see a ship much closer than it was before, and in that ship a young man. Such is life. But if you look more carefully and shade your red, red brows, you will perceive—" and here she poked Edarra with her toe—"that surprise and mercy share the world between them. Yp is generous." She tweaked Edarra by the nose.

"Praise God, maid, there be two of them!"

So they waved, Edarra scarcely restraining herself from jumping into the sea and swimming to the other craft, Alyx with full sweeps of the arm, standing both at the stern of their stolen fishing boat on that late summer's morning while the fishermen in the other boat wondered—and disbelieved—and then believed—while behind all rose the green land in the distance and the sky was blue as blue. Perhaps it was the thought of her fifteen hundred ounces of gold stowed belowdecks, or perhaps it was an intimation of the extraordinary future, or perhaps it was only her own queer nature, but in the sunlight Alyx's eyes had a strange look, like those of Loh, the first woman, who had kept her own counsel at the very moment of creation, only looking about her with an immediate, intense, serpentine curiosity, already planning secret plans and guessing at who knows what unguessable mysteries. . . .

("You old villain!" whispered Edarra, "we made it!")

But that's another story.

I Thought She Was Afeard Till
She Stroked My Beard

MANY YEARS AGO, long before the world got into the state it is in today, young women were supposed to obey their husbands; but nobody knows if they did or not. In those days they wore their hair piled foot upon foot on top of their heads. Along with such weights they would also carry water in two buckets at the ends of a long pole; this often makes you slip. One did; but she kept her mouth shut. She put the buckets down on the ground and with two sideward kicks—like two dance steps, flirt with the left foot, flirt with the right—she emptied the both of them. She watched the water settle into the ground. Then she swung the pole upon her shoulder and carried them home. She was only just seventeen. Her husband had made her do it. She swung the farm door open with her shoulder and said:

SHE: Here is your damned water.

HE: Where?

SHE: It is beneath my social class to do it and you know it.

HE: You have no social class; only I do, because I am a man.

SHE: *I* wouldn't do it if you were a—

(Here follows something very unpleasant.)

HE: Woman, go back with those pails. Someone is coming tonight.

SHE: Who?

HE: That's not your business.

SHE: Smugglers.

HE: Go!

SHE: Go to hell.

Perhaps he was somewhat afraid of his tough little wife. She watched him from the stairs or the doorway, always with unvarying hatred; that is what comes of marrying a wild hill girl without a proper education. Beatings made her sullen. She went to the water and back, dissecting him every step of the way, separating blond hair from blond hair and cracking and sorting his long limbs. She loved that. She filled the

437

farm water barrel, rooted the maidservant out of the hay and slapped her, and went indoors with her head full of pirates. She spun, she sewed, she shelled, ground, washed, dusted, swept, built fires all that day and once, so full of her thoughts was she that she savagely wrung and broke the neck of an already dead chicken.

Near certain towns, if you walk down to the beach at night, you may see a very queer sight: lights springing up like drifting insects over the water and others answering from the land, and then something bobbing over the black waves to a blacker huddle drawn up at the very margin of the sand. They are at their revenues. The young wife watched her husband sweat in the kitchen. It made her gay to see him bargain so desperately and lose. The maid complained that one of the men had tried to do something indecent to her. Her mistress watched silently from the shadows near the big hearth and more and more of what she saw was to her liking. When the last man was gone she sent the maid to bed, and while collecting and cleaning the glasses and the plates like a proper wife, she said:

"They rooked you, didn't they!"

"Hold your tongue," said her husband over his shoulder. He was laboriously figuring his book of accounts with strings of circles and crosses and licking his finger to turn the page.

"The big one," she said, "what's his name?"

"What's it to you?" he said sharply. She stood drying her hands in a towel and looking at him. She took off her apron, her jacket and her rings; then she pulled the pins out of her black hair. It fell below her waist and she stood for the last time in this history within a straight black cloud.

She dropped a cup from her fingers, smiling at him as it smashed. They say actions speak louder. He jumped to his feet; he cried, "What are you doing!" again and again in the silent kitchen; he shook her until her teeth rattled.

"Leaving you," she said.

He struck her. She got up, holding her jaw. She said, "You don't see anything. You don't know anything."

"Get upstairs," he said.

"You're an animal," she cried, "you're a fool," and she twisted about as he grasped her wrist, trying to free herself. They insist, these women, on crying, on making demands, and

on disagreeing about everything. They fight from one side of
the room to the other. She bit his hand and he howled and
brought it down on the side of her head. He called her a little
whore. He stood blocking the doorway and glowered, nursing
his hand. Her head was spinning. She leaned against the wall
and held her head in both hands. Then she said:

"So you won't let me go."

He said nothing.

"You can't keep me," she said, and then she laughed; "no,
no, you can't," she added, shaking her head, "you just can't."
She looked before her and smiled absently, turning this fact
over and over. Her husband was rubbing his knuckles.

"What do you think you're up to," he muttered.

"If you lock me up, I can't work," said his wife and then, with
the knife she had used for the past half year to pare vegetables,
this woman began to saw at her length of hair. She took the
whole sheaf in one hand and hacked at it. Her husband started
forward. She stood arrested with her hands involved in her
hair, regarding him seriously, while without taking his eyes off
her, running the tip of his tongue across his teeth, he groped
behind the door—he knew there is one thing you can always
do. His wife changed color. Her hands dropped with a tumbled rush of hair, she moved slowly to one side, and when he
took out from behind the door the length of braided hide he
used to herd cattle, when he swung it high in the air and down
in a snapping arc to where she—not where she was; where she
had been—this extraordinary young woman had leapt half the
distance between them and wrested the stock of the whip from
him a foot from his hand. He was off balance and fell; with a
vicious grimace she brought the stock down short and hard on
the top of his head. She had all her wits about her as she stood
over him.

But she didn't believe it. She leaned over him, her cut black
hair swinging over her face; she called him a liar; she told him
he wasn't bleeding. Slowly she straightened up, with a swagger, with a certain awe. *Good lord!* she thought, looking at her
hands. She slapped him, called his name impatiently, but when
the fallen man moved a little—or she fancied he did—a thrill
ran up her spine to the top of her head, a kind of soundless
chill, and snatching the vegetable knife from the floor where

she had dropped it, she sprang like an arrow from the bow into the night that waited, all around the house, to devour.

Trees do not pull up their roots and walk abroad, nor is the night ringed with eyes. Stones can't speak. Novelty tosses the world upside down, however. She was terrified, exalted, and helpless with laughter. The trees on either side of the path saw her appear for an instant out of the darkness, wild with hurry, straining like a statue. Then she zigzagged between the tree trunks and flashed over the lip of the cliff into the sea.

In all the wide headland there was no light. The ship still rode at anchor, but far out, and clinging to the line where the water met the air like a limpet or a moray eel under a rock, she saw a trail of yellow points appear on the face of the sea: one, two, three, four. They had finished their business. Hasty and out of breath, she dove under the shadow of that black hull, and treading the shifting seas that fetched her up now and again against the ship's side that was too flat and hard to grasp, she listened to the noises overhead: creaking, groans, voices, the sound of feet. Everything was hollow and loud, mixed with the gurgle of the ripples. She thought, *I am going to give them a surprise*. She felt something form within her, something queer, dark, and hard, like the strangeness of strange customs, or the blackened face of the goddess Chance, whose image set up at crossroads looks three ways at once to signify the crossing of influences. Silently this young woman took off her leather belt and wrapped the buckleless end around her right hand. With her left she struck out for the ship's rope ladder, sinking into the water under a mass of bubbles and crosscurrents eddying like hairs drawn across the surface. She rose some ten feet farther on. Dripping seawater like one come back from the dead, with eighteen inches of leather crowned with a heavy brass buckle in her right hand, her left gripping the rope and her knife between her teeth (where else?) she began to climb.

The watch—who saw her first—saw somebody entirely undistinguished. She was wringing the water out of her skirt. She sprang erect as she caught sight of him, burying both hands in the heavy folds of her dress.

"We-ell!" said he.

She said nothing, only crouched down a little by the rail. The leather belt, hidden in her right—her stronger—hand began to stir. He came closer—he stared—he leaned forward—he

tapped his teeth with his forefinger. "Eh, a pussycat!" he said.
She didn't move. He stepped back a pace, clapped his hands
and shouted; and all at once she was surrounded by men who
had come crack! out of nothing, sprung in from the right, from
the left, shot up from the deck as if on springs, even tumbling
down out of the air. She did not know if she liked it.

"Look!" said the watch, grinning as if he had made her up.

Perhaps they had never seen a woman before, or perhaps
they had never seen one bare-armed, or with her hair cut off,
or sopping wet. They stared as if they hadn't. One whistled, indrawn between his teeth, long and low. "What does she want?"
said someone. The watch took hold of her arm and the sailor
who had whistled raised both hands over his head and clasped
them, at which the crowd laughed.

"She thinks we're hot!"

"She wants some, don't you, honey?"

"Ooh, kiss me, kiss me, dearie!"

"I want the captain!" she managed to get out. All around
crowded men's faces: some old, some young, all very peculiar
to her eyes with their unaccustomed whiskers, their chins, their
noses, their loose collars. It occurred to her that she did not
like them a bit. She did not exactly think they were behaving
badly, as she was not sure how they ought to behave, but they
reminded her uncannily of her husband, of whom she was no
longer at all afraid. So when the nearest winked and reached
out two hands even huger than the shadow of hands cast on
the deck boards, she kicked him excruciatingly in the left knee
(he fell down), the watch got the belt buckle round in a circle from underneath (up, always up, especially if you're short),
which gave him a cut across the cheek and a black eye; this
leaves her left hand still armed and her teeth, which she used.
It's good to be able to do several things at once. Forward,
halfway from horizon to zenith, still and clear above the black
mass of the rigging and the highest mast, burned the constellation of the Hunter, and under that—by way of descent
down a monumental fellow who had just that moment sprung
on board—frothed and foamed a truly fabulous black beard.
She had just unkindly set someone howling by trampling on
a tender part (they were in good spirits, most of them, and
fighting one another in a heap; she never did admit later to all
the things she did in that melee) when the beard bent down

over her, curled and glossy as a piece of the sea. Children never could resist that beard. Big one looked at little one. Little one looked at big one. Stars shone over his head. He recognized her at once, of course, and her look, and the pummeling she had left behind her, and the cracked knee, and all the rest of it. "So," he said, "you're a fighter, are you!" He took her hands in his and crushed them, good and hard; she smiled brilliantly, involuntarily.

When she fenced with him (she insisted on fencing with him) she worked with a hard, dry persistence that surprised him. "Well, I have got your—and you have got my teaching," he said philosophically at first, "whatever you may want with *that*," but on the second day out she slipped on soapsuds on the tilting deck ("Give it up, girl, give it up!"), grabbed the fellow who was scrubbing away by the ankles, and brought him down—screaming—on top of the captain. Blackbeard was not surprised that she had tried to do this, but he was very surprised that she had actually brought it off. "Get up," he told her (she was sitting where she fell and grinning). She pulled up her stockings. He chose for her a heavier and longer blade, almost as tall as she ("Huh!" she said, "it's about time"), and held out the blade and the scabbard, one in each hand, both at the same time. She took them, one in each hand, both at the same time.

"By God, you're ambidextrous!" he exclaimed.

"Come on!" she said.

That was a blade that was a blade! She spent the night more or less tangled up in it, as she never yet had with him. Things were still unsettled between them. Thus she slept alone in his bed, in his cabin; thus she woke alone, figuring she still had the best of it. Thus she spurned a heap of his possessions with her foot (the fact that she did not clean the place up in womanly fashion put him to great distress), writhed, stretched, turned over and jumped as a crash came from outside. There was a shuttered window above the bed that gave on the deck. Someone—here she slipped on her shift and swung open the shutter—was bubbling, shouting, singing, sending mountains of water lolloping across the boards. Someone (here she leaned out and twisted her head about to see) naked to the waist in a barrel was taking a bath. Like Poseidon. He turned, presenting her with the black patches under his armpits streaming water, with his hair and beard running like black ink.

"Hallooo!" he roared. She grunted and drew back, closing the shutter. She had made no motion to get dressed when he came in, but lay with her arms under her head. He stood in the doorway, tucking his shirt into his trousers; then this cunning man said, "I came to get something" (looking at her sidewise), and diffidently carried his wet, tightly curled beard past her into a corner of the cabin. He knelt down and burrowed diligently.

"Get what?" said she. He didn't answer. He was rummaging in a chest he had dragged from the wall; now he took out of it—with great tenderness and care—a woman's nightdress, worked all in white lace, which he held up to her, saying:

"Do you want this?"

"No," she said, and meant it.

"But it's expensive," he said earnestly, "it is, look," and coming over to sit on the edge of the bed, he showed the dress to her, for the truth was it was so expensive that he hadn't meant to give it to her at all, and only offered it out of—well, out of—

"I don't want it," she said, a little sharply.

"Do you like jewelry?" he suggested hopefully. He had not got thoroughly dried and water was dripping unobtrusively from the ends of his hair onto the bed; he sat patiently holding the nightgown out by the sleeves to show it off. He said ingenuously, "Why don't you try it on?"

Silence.

"It would look good on you," he said. She said nothing. He laid down the nightgown and looked at her, bemused and wondering; then he reached out and tenderly touched her hair where it hung down to the point of her small, grim jaw.

"My, aren't you little," he said.

She laughed. Perhaps it was being called little, or perhaps it was being touched so very lightly, but this farm girl threw back her head and laughed until she cried, as the saying is, and then:

"Tcha! It's a bargain, isn't it!" said this cynical girl. He lowered himself onto the floor on his heels; then tenderly folded the nightgown into a lacy bundle, which he smoothed, troubled.

"No, give it to me," she demanded sharply. He looked up, surprised.

"Give it!" she repeated, and scrambling across the bed she snatched it out of his hands, stripped off her shift, and slid the gown over her bare skin. She was compact but not stocky and the dress became her; she walked about the cabin, admiring her sleeves, carrying the train over one arm while he sat back on his heels and blinked at her.

"Well," she said philosophically, "come on." He was not at all pleased. He rose (her eyes followed him), towering over her, his arms folded. He looked at the nightgown, at the train she held, at her arched neck (she had to look up to meet his gaze), at her free arm curved to her throat in a gesture of totally unconscious femininity. He had been thinking, a process that with him was slow but often profound; now he said solemnly:

"Woman, what man have you ever been with before?"

"Oh!" said she startled, "my husband," and backed off a little.

"And where is he?"

"Dead." She could not help a grin.

"How?" She held up a fist. Blackbeard sighed heavily.

Throwing the loose bedclothes onto the bed, he strode to his precious chest (she padded inquisitively behind him), dropped heavily to his knees, and came up with a heap of merchandise: bottles, rings, jingles, coins, scarves, handkerchiefs, boots, toys, half of which he put back. Then, catching her by one arm, he threw her over his shoulder in a somewhat casual or moody fashion (the breath was knocked out of her) and carried her to the center of the cabin, where he dropped her—half next to and half over a small table, the only other part of the cabin's furnishings besides the bed. She was trembling all over. With the same kind of solemn preoccupation he dumped his merchandise on the table, sorted out a bottle and two glasses, a bracelet, which he put on her arm, earrings similarly, and a few other things that he studied and then placed on the floor. She was amazed to see that there were tears in his eyes.

"Now, why don't you fight me!" he said emotionally.

She looked at the table, then at her hands.

"Ah!" he said, sighing again, pouring out a glassful and gulping it, drumming the glass on the table. He shook his head. He held out his arms and she circled the table carefully, taking his hands, embarrassed to look him in the face. "Come," he said, "up here," patting his knees, so she climbed awkwardly onto his lap, still considerably wary. He poured out another glass and put it in her hand. He sighed, and put nothing into words; only she felt on her back what felt like a hand and arched a little—like a cat—with pleasure; then she stirred on his knees to settle herself and immediately froze. He did nothing. He was looking into the distance, into nothing. He might have been remembering his past. She put one arm around his neck to steady herself, but her arm felt his neck most exquisitely and she did not like that, so she gave it up and put one hand on his shoulder. Then she could not help but feel his shoulder. It was quite provoking. He mused into the distance. Sitting on his lap, she could feel his breath stirring about her bare face, about her neck—she turned to look at him and shut her eyes; she thought, *What am I doing?* and the blood came to her face harder and harder until her cheeks blazed. She felt him sigh, felt that sigh travel from her side to her stomach to the back of her head, and with a soft, hopeless, exasperated cry ("I don't expect to enjoy this!") she turned and sank, both hands first-most, into Blackbeard's oceanic beard.

And he, the villain, was even willing to cooperate.

Time passes, even (as they say) on the sea. What with moping about while he visited farmhouses and villages, watching the stars wheel and change overhead as they crept down the coast, with time making and unmaking the days, bringing dinnertime (as it does) and time to get up and what-not—Well, there you are. She spent her time learning to play cards. But gambling and prophecy are very closely allied—in fact they are one thing—and when he saw his woman squatting on deck on the balls of her feet, a sliver of wood in her teeth, dealing out the cards to tell fortunes (cards and money appeared in the East at exactly the same time in the old days) he thought —or thought he saw—or recollected—that goddess who was driven out by the other gods when the world was made and who hangs about still on the fringes of things (at crossroads, at the entrance to towns) to throw a little shady trouble into life and set up a few crosscurrents and undercurrents of her own in what ought to be a regular and predictable business. She herself did not believe in gods and goddesses. She told the fortunes of the crew quite obligingly, as he had taught her, but was much more interested in learning the probabilities of the appearance of any particular card in one of the five suits*—she had begun to evolve what she thought was a rather elegant little theory—when late one day he told her, "Look, I am going into a town tonight, but you can't come." They were lying anchored on the coast, facing west, just too far away to see the lights at night. She said, "Wha'?"

"I am going to town tonight," he said (he was a very patient man) "and you can't come."

"Why not?" said the woman. She threw down her cards and stood up, facing into the sunset. The pupils of her eyes shrank to pinpoints. To her he was a big, blind rock, a kind of outline; she said again, "Why not?" and her whole face lifted and became sharper as one's face does when one stares against the sun.

"Because you can't," he said. She bent to pick up her cards as if she had made some mistake in listening, but there he was saying, "I won't be able to take care of you."

"You won't have to," said she. He shook his head. "You won't come."

"Of course I'll come," she said.

"You won't," said he.

"The devil I won't!" said she.

He put both arms on her shoulders, powerfully, seriously, with utmost heaviness and she pulled away at once, at once transformed into a mystery with a closed face; she stared at him without expression, shifting her cards from hand to hand. He said, "Look, my girl—" and for this got the entire fortunes of the whole world for the next twenty centuries right in his face.

"Well, well," he said, "I see," ponderously, "I see," and stalked away down the curve of the ship, thus passing around the cabin, into the darkening eastern sky, and out of the picture.

But she did go with him. She appeared, dripping wet and triumphantly smiling, at the door of the little place of business he had chosen to discuss business in and walked directly to his table, raising two fingers in greeting, a gesture that had taken her fancy when she saw it done by someone in the street. She then uttered a word Blackbeard thought she did

*ones, tens, hundreds, myriads, tens of myriads

not understand (she did). She looked with interest around the room—at the smoke from the torches—and the patrons—and a Great Horned Owl somewhat the worse for wear that had been chained by one leg to the bar (an ancient invention)—and the stuffed blowfish that hung from the ceiling on a string: lazy, consumptive, puffed-up, with half its spines broken off. Then she sat down.

"Huh!" she said, dismissing the tavern. Blackbeard was losing his temper. His face suffused with blood, he put both enormous fists on the table to emphasize that fact; she nodded civilly, leaned back on her part of the wall (causing the bench to rock), crossed her knees, and swung one foot back and forth, back and forth, under the noses of both gentlemen. It was not exactly rude but it was certainly disconcerting.

"You. Get out," said the other gentleman.

"I'm not dry yet," said she in a soft, reasonable voice, like a bravo trying to pick a quarrel, and she laid both arms across the table, where they left two dark stains. She stared him in the face as if trying to memorize it—hard enough with a man who made it his business to look like nobody in particular—and the *other gentleman* was about to rise and was reaching for something or other under the table when her gentleman said:

"She's crazy." He cleared his throat. "You sit down," he said. "My apologies. *You* behave," and social stability thus reestablished, they plunged into a discussion she understood pretty well but did not pay much attention to, as she was too busy looking about. The owl blinked, turned his head completely around, and stood on one foot. The blowfish rotated lazily. Across the room stood a row of casks and a mortared wall; next to that a face in the dimness—a handsome face—that smiled at her across the serried tables. She smiled back, a villainous smile full of saltpeter, a wise, nasty, irresponsible, troublemaking smile, at which the handsome face winked. She laughed out loud.

"Shut up," said Blackbeard, not turning round.

He was in a tight place.

She watched him insist and prevaricate and sweat, building all kinds of earnest, openhearted, irresistible arguments with the gestures of his big hands, trying to bully the insignificant other gentleman—and failing—and not knowing it—until finally at the same moment the owl screeched like a rusty file, a singer at the end of the bar burst into wailing quartertones, and Blackbeard—wiping his forehead—said, "All right."

"No, dammit," she cried, "you're ten percent off!"

He slapped her. The other gentleman cleared his throat.

"All right," Blackbeard repeated. The other man nodded. Finishing his wine, drawing on his gloves, already a little bored perhaps, he turned and left. In his place, as if by a compensation of nature, there suddenly appeared, jackrabbited between the tables, the handsome young owner of the face who was not so handsome at close range but dressed fit to kill all the same with a gold earring, a red scarf tucked into his shirt, and a satanic resemblance to her late husband. She looked rapidly from one man to the other, almost malevolently; then she stood rigid, staring at the floor.

"*Well, baby*," said the intruder.

Blackbeard turned his back on his girl.

The intruder took hold of her by the nape of the neck but she did not move; he talked to her in a low voice; finally she blurted out, "Oh yes! Go on!" (fixing her eyes on the progress of Blackbeard's monolithic back towards the door) and stumbled aside as the latter all but vaulted over a table to retrieve his lost property. She followed him, her head bent, violently flushed. Two streets off he stopped, saying, "Look, my dear, can I please not take you ashore again?" but she would not answer, no, not a word, and all this time the singer back at the tavern was singing away about the Princess Oriana who traveled to meet her betrothed but was stolen by bandits, and how she prayed, and how the bandits cursed, and how she begged to be returned to her prince, and how the bandits said, "Not likely," and how she finally ended it all by jumping into the Bosphorus—in short, art in the good old style with plenty of solid vocal technique, a truly Oriental expressiveness, and innumerable verses.

(She always remembered the incident and maintained for the rest of her life that small producers should combine in trading with middlemen so as not to lower prices by competing against each other.)

In the first, faint hint of dawn, as Blackbeard lay snoring and damp in the bedclothes, his beard spread out like a fan, his woman prodded him in the ribs with the handle of his sword; she said, "Wake up! Something's happening.

"I am," she added. She watched him as he tried to sit up, tangled in the sheets, pale, enormous, the black hair on his chest forming with unusual distinctness the shape of a flying eagle. "Wha'?" he said.

"I am," she repeated. Still half asleep, he held out his arms to her, indicating that she might happen all over the place, might happen now, particularly in bed, *he* did not care. "*Wake up!*" she said. He nearly leapt out of bed, but then perceived her standing leaning on his sword, the corners of her mouth turned down. No one was being killed. He blinked, shivered, and shook his head. "Don't do that," he said thickly. She let the sword fall with a clatter. He winced.

"I'm going away," she said very distinctly, "that's all," and thrusting her face near his, she seized him by the arms and shook him violently, leaping back when he vaulted out of the bed and whirling around with one hand on the table—ready to throw it. That made him smile. He sat down and scratched his chest, giving himself every now and then a kind of shake to wake himself up, until he could look at her directly in the eyes and ask:

"Haven't I treated you well?"

She said nothing. He dangled one arm between his knees moodily and rubbed the back of his neck with the other, so enormous, so perfect, so relaxed, and in every way so like real life that she could only shrug and fold her arms across her breast. He examined his feet and rubbed, for comfort, the ankle and the arch, the heel and the instep, stretching his feet, stretching his back, rubbing his fingers over and over and over.

"Damn it, I am cleverer than you!" she exclaimed.

He sighed, meaning perhaps "no," meaning perhaps "I suppose so"; he said, "You've been up all night, haven't you?" and then he said, "My dear, you must understand—" but at that moment a terrific battering shook the ship, propelling the master of it outside, naked as he was, from which position he locked his woman in.

(In those days craft were high, square and slow, like barrels or boxes put out to sea; but everything is relative, and as they crept up on each other, throwing fits every now and again

when headed into the wind, creaking and straining at every
joist, ships bore skippers who remembered craft braced with
twisted rope from stem to stern, craft manned exclusively by
rowers, above all craft that invariably—or usually—sank, and
they enjoyed the keen sensation of modernity while standing
on a deck large enough for a party of ten to dine on comfortably and steering by use of a rudder that no longer required a
pole for leverage or broke a man's wrist. Things were getting
better. With great skill a man could sail as fast as other men
could run. Still, in this infancy of the world, one ship wallowed
after another; like cunning sloths one feebly stole up on another; and when they closed—without fire (do you want us to
burn ourselves *up*?)—the toothless, ineffectual creatures clung
together, sawing dully at each other's grappling ropes, until the
fellows over there got over here or the fellows over here got
over there and then—on a slippery floor humped like the back
of an elephant and just about as small, amid rails, boxes, pots,
peaks, tar, slants, steps, ropes, coils, masts, falls, chests, sails
and God knows what—they hacked at each other until most of
them died. That they did very efficiently.

And the sea was full of robbers.)

Left alone, she moved passively with the motion of the ship;
then she picked up very slowly and looked into very slowly the
hand mirror he had taken for her out of his chest, brass-backed
and decorated with metal rose-wreaths, the kind of object she
had never in her life seen before. There she was, oddly tilted,
looking out of the mirror, and behind her the room as if seen
from above, as if one could climb down into the mirror to
those odd objects, bright and reversed, as if one could fall into
the mirror, become tiny, clamber away, and looking back see
one's own enormous eyes staring out of a window set high
in the wall. Women do not always look in mirrors to admire
themselves, popular belief to the contrary. Sometimes they
look only to slip off their rings and their bracelets, to pluck off
their earrings, to unfasten their necklaces, to drop their brilliant
gowns, to take the color off their faces until the bones stand
out like spears and to wipe the hues from around their eyes
until they can look and look at merely naked human faces, at
eyes no longer brilliant and aqueous like the eyes of angels or
goddesses but hard and small as human eyes are, little control

points that are always a little disquieting, always a little peculiar, because they are not meant to be looked at but to look, and then—with a shudder, a shiver—to recover themselves and once again to shimmer, to glow. But some don't care. This one stumbled away, dropped the mirror, fell over the table (she passed her hand over her eyes) and grasped—more by feeling than by sight—the handle of the sword he had given her, thirty or forty—or was it seventy?—years before. The blade had not yet the ironical motto it was to bear some years later: *Good Manners Are Not Enough*, but she lifted it high all the same, and grasping with her left hand the bronze chain Blackbeard used to fasten his treasure chest, broke the lock of the door in one blow.

Such was the strength of iron in the old days.

There is talent and then there is the other thing. Blackbeard had never seen the other thing. He found her after the battle was over with her foot planted on the back of a dead enemy, trying to free the sword he had given her. She did so in one jerky pull and rolled the man overboard with her foot without bothering about him further; she was looking at an ornamented dagger in her left hand, a beautiful weapon with a jeweled handle and a slender blade engraved with scrolls and leaves. She admired it very much. She held it out to him, saying, "Isn't that a beauty?" There was a long gash on her left arm, the result of trying to stop a downward blow with nothing but the bronze chain wrapped around her knuckles. The chain was gone; she had only used it as long as it had surprise value and had lost it somewhere, somehow (she did not quite remember how). He took the dagger and she sat down suddenly on the deck, dropping the sword and running both hands over her hair to smooth it again and again, unaware that her palms left long red streaks. The deck looked as if a tribe of monkeys had been painting on it or as if everyone—living and dead—had smeared himself ritually with red paint. The sun was coming up. He sat down next to her, too winded to speak. With the intent watchfulness (but this will be a millennium or two later) of someone focusing the lens of a microscope, with the noble, arrogant carriage of a tennis star, she looked first around the deck—and then at him—and then straight up into the blue sky.

"So," she said, and shut her eyes.

He put his arm around her; he wiped her face. He stroked the nape of her neck and then her shoulder, but now his woman began to laugh, more and more, leaning against him and laughing and laughing until she was convulsed and he thought she had gone out of her mind. "What the devil!" he cried, almost weeping, "what the devil!" She stopped at that place in the scale where a woman's laughter turns into a shriek; her shoulders shook spasmodically but soon she controlled that too. He thought she might be hysterical so he said, "Are you frightened? You won't have to go through this again."

"No?" she said.

"Never."

"Well," she said, "perhaps I will all the same," and in pure good humor she put her arms about his neck. There were tears in her eyes—perhaps they were tears of laughter—and in the light of the rising sun the deck showed ever more ruddy and grotesque. *What a mess*, she thought. She said, "It's all right; don't you worry," which was, all in all and in the light of things, a fairly kind goodbye.

"Why the devil," she said with sudden interest, "don't doctors cut up the bodies of dead people in the schools to find out how they're put together?"

But he didn't know.

Six weeks later she arrived—alone—at that queen among cities, that moon among stars, that noble, despicable, profound, simple-minded and altogether exasperating capital of the world: Ourdh. Some of us know it. She materialized so quietly and expertly out of the dark that the gatekeeper found himself looking into her face without the slightest warning: a young, gray-eyed countrywoman, silent, shadowy, self-assured. She was hugely amused. "My name," she said, "is Alyx."

"Never heard of it," said the gatekeeper, a little annoyed.

"Good heavens," said Alyx, "not yet," and vanished through the gate before he could admit her, with the curious slight smile one sees on the lips of very old statues: inexpressive, simple, classic.

She was to become a classic, in time.

But that's another story.

The Barbarian

ALYX, THE gray-eyed, the silent woman. Wit, arm, kill-quick for hire, she watched the strange man thread his way through the tables and the smoke toward her. This was in Ourdh, where all things are possible. He stopped at the table where she sat alone and with a certain indefinable gallantry, not pleasant but perhaps its exact opposite, he said:

"A woman—here?"

"You're looking at one," said Alyx dryly, for she did not like his tone. It occurred to her that she had seen him before—though he was not so fat then, no, not quite so fat—and then it occurred to her that the time of their last meeting had almost certainly been in the hills when she was four or five years old. That was thirty years ago. So she watched him very narrowly as he eased himself into the seat opposite, watched him as he drummed his fingers in a lively tune on the tabletop, and paid him close attention when he tapped one of the marine decorations that hung from the ceiling (a stuffed blowfish, all spikes and parchment, that moved lazily to and fro in a wandering current of air) and made it bob. He smiled, the flesh around his eyes straining into folds.

"I know you," he said. "A raw country girl fresh from the hills who betrayed an entire religious delegation to the police some ten years ago. You settled down as a pick-lock. You made a good thing of it. You expanded your profession to include a few more difficult items and you did a few things that turned heads hereabouts. You were not unknown, even then. Then you vanished for a season and reappeared as a fairly rich woman. But that didn't last, unfortunately."

"Didn't have to," said Alyx.

"Didn't last," repeated the fat man imperturbably, with a lazy shake of the head. "No, no, it didn't last. And now," (he pronounced the "now" with peculiar relish) "you are getting old."

"Old enough," said Alyx, amused.

"Old," said he, "old. Still neat, still tough, still small. But old. You're thinking of settling down."

"Not exactly."

"Children?"

She shrugged, retiring a little into the shadow. The fat man did not appear to notice.

"It's been done," she said.

"You may die in childbirth," said he, "at your age."

"That, too, has been done."

She stirred a little, and in a moment a short-handled Southern dagger, the kind carried unobtrusively in sleeves or shoes, appeared with its point buried in the tabletop, vibrating ever so gently.

"It is true," said she, "that I am growing old. My hair is threaded with white. I am developing a chunky look around the waist that does not exactly please me, though I was never a ballet-girl." She grinned at him in the semi-darkness. "Another thing," she said softly, "that I develop with age is a certain lack of patience. If you do not stop making personal remarks and taking up my time—which is valuable—I shall throw you across the room."

"I would not, if I were you," he said.

"You could not."

The fat man began to heave with laughter. He heaved until he choked. Then he said, gasping, "I beg your pardon." Tears ran down his face.

"Go on," said Alyx. He leaned across the table, smiling, his fingers mated tip to tip, his eyes little pits of shadow in his face.

"I come to make you rich," he said.

"You can do more than that," said she steadily. A quarrel broke out across the room between a soldier and a girl he had picked up for the night; the fat man talked through it, or rather under it, never taking his eyes off her face.

"Ah!" he said, "you remember when you saw me last and you assume that a man who can live thirty years without growing older must have more to give—if he wishes—than a handful of gold coins. You are right. I can make you live long. I can insure your happiness. I can determine the sex of your children. I can cure all diseases. I can even" (and here he lowered his voice) "turn this table, or this building, or this whole city to pure gold, if I wish it."

"Can anyone do that?" said Alyx, with the faintest whisper of mockery.

"I can," he said. "Come outside and let us talk. Let me show you a few of the things I can do. I have some business here in the city that I must attend to myself and I need a guide and an assistant. That will be you."

"If you can turn the city into gold," said Alyx just as softly, "can you turn gold into a city?"

"Anyone can do that," he said, laughing: "come along," so they rose and made their way into the cold outside air—it was a clear night in early spring—and at a corner of the street where the moon shone down on the walls and the pits in the road, they stopped.

"Watch," said he.

On his outstretched palm was a small black box. He shook it, turning it this way and that, but it remained wholly featureless. Then he held it out to her and, as she took it in her hand, it began to glow until it became like a piece of glass lit up from the inside. There in the middle of it was her man, with his tough, friendly, young-old face and his hair a little gray, like hers. He smiled at her, his lips moving soundlessly. She threw the cube into the air a few times, held it to the side of her face, shook it, and then dropped it on the ground, grinding it under her heel. It remained unhurt.

She picked it up and held it out to him, thinking:

Not metal, very light. And warm. A toy? Wouldn't break, though. Must be some sort of small machine, though God knows who made it and of what. It follows thoughts! Marvelous. But magic? Bah! Never believed in it before; why now? Besides, this thing too sensible; magic is elaborate, undependable, useless. I'll tell him—but then it occurred to her that someone had gone to a good deal of trouble to impress her when a little bit of credit might have done just as well. And this man walked with an almighty confidence through the streets for someone who was unarmed. And those thirty years—so she said very politely:

"It's magic!"

He chuckled and pocketed the cube.

"You're a little savage," he said, "but your examination of it was most logical. I like you. Look! I am an old magician.

There is a spirit in that box and there are more spirits under my control than you can possibly imagine. I am like a man living among monkeys. There are things spirits cannot do—or things I choose to do myself, take it any way you will. So I pick one of the monkeys who seems brighter than the rest and train it. I pick you. What do you say?"

"All right," said Alyx.

"Calm enough!" he chuckled. "Calm enough! Good. What's your motive?"

"Curiosity," said Alyx. "It's a monkeylike trait." He chuckled again; his flesh choked it and the noise came out in a high, muffled scream.

"And what if I bite you," said Alyx, "like a monkey?"

"No, little one," he answered gaily, "you won't. You may be sure of that." He held out his hand, still shaking with mirth. In the palm lay a kind of blunt knife which he pointed at one of the whitewashed walls that lined the street. The edges of the wall burst into silent smoke, the whole section trembled and slid, and in an instant it had vanished, vanished as completely as if it had never existed, except for a sullen glow at the raw edges of brick and a pervasive smell of burning. Alyx swallowed.

"It's quiet, for magic," she said softly. "Have you ever used it on men?"

"On armies, little one."

So the monkey went to work for him. There seemed as yet to be no harm in it. The little streets admired his generosity and the big ones his good humor; while those too high for money or flattery he won by a catholic ability that was—so the little picklock thought—remarkable in one so stupid. For about his stupidity there could be no doubt. She smelled it. It offended her. It made her twitch in her sleep, like a ferret. There was in this woman—well hidden away—an anomalous streak of quiet humanity that abhorred him, that set her teeth on edge at the thought of him, though she could not have put into words just what was the matter. *For stupidity*, she thought, *is hardly—is not exactly—*

Four months later they broke into the governor's villa. She thought she might at last find out what this man was after besides pleasure jaunts around the town. Moreover, breaking and entering always gave her the keenest pleasure; and doing so "for nothing" (as he said) tickled her fancy immensely. The power in gold and silver that attracts thieves was banal, in this thief's opinion, but to stand in the shadows of a sleeping house, absolutely silent, with no object at all in view and with the knowledge that if you are found you will probably have your throat cut—! She began to think better of him. This dilettante passion for the craft, this reckless silliness seemed to her as worthy as the love of a piece of magnetite for the North and South poles—the "faithful stone" they call it in Ourdh.

"Who'll come with us?" she asked, wondering for the fiftieth time where the devil he went when he was not with her, whom he knew, where he lived, and what that persistently bland expression on his face could possibly mean.

"No one," he said calmly.

"What are we looking for?"

"Nothing."

"Do you ever do anything for a reason?"

"Never." And he chuckled.

And then, "Why are you so fat?" demanded Alyx, halfway out of her own door, half into the shadows. She had recently settled in a poor quarter of the town, partly out of laziness, partly out of necessity. The shadows playing in the hollows of her face, the expression of her eyes veiled, she said it again, "Why are you so goddamned fat!" He laughed until he wheezed.

"The barbarian mind!" he cried, lumbering after her in high good humor, "Oh—oh, my dear!—oh, what freshness!" She thought:

That's it! and then

The fool doesn't even know I hate him.

But neither had she known, until that very moment.

They scaled the northeast garden wall of the villa and crept along the top of it without descending, for the governor kept dogs. Alyx, who could walk a taut rope like a circus performer, went quietly. The fat man giggled. She swung herself up to the nearest window and hung there by one arm and a toehold for fifteen mortal minutes while she sawed through the metal hinge of the shutter with a file. Once inside the building (he had to be pulled through the window) she took him by the collar with uncanny accuracy, considering that the inside of the villa was stone dark. "Shut up!" she said, with considerable emphasis.

"Oh?" he whispered.

"I'm in charge here," she said, releasing him with a jerk, and melted into the blackness not two feet away, moving swiftly along the corridor wall. Her fingers brushed lightly alongside her, like a creeping animal: stone, stone, a gap, warm air rising . . . In the dark she felt wolfish, her lips skinned back over her teeth; like another species she made her way with hands and ears. Through them the villa sighed and rustled in its sleep. She put the tips of the fingers of her free hand on the back of the fat man's neck, guiding him with the faintest of touches through the turns of the corridor. They crossed an empty space where two halls met; they retreated noiselessly into a room where a sleeper lay breathing against a dimly lit window, while someone passed in the corridor outside. When the steps faltered for a moment, the fat man gasped and Alyx wrung his wrist, hard. There was a cough from the corridor, the sleeper in the room stirred and murmured, and the steps passed on. They crept back to the hall. Then he told her where he wanted to go.

"What!" She had pulled away, astonished, with a reckless hiss of indrawn breath. Methodically he began poking her in the side and giving her little pushes with his other hand— she moving away, outraged—but all in silence. In the distant reaches of the building something fell—or someone spoke —and without thinking, they waited silently until the sounds had faded away. He resumed his continual prodding. Alyx, her teeth on edge, began to creep forward, passing a cat that sat outlined in the vague light from a window, perfectly unconcerned with them and rubbing its paws against its face, past a door whose cracks shone yellow, past ghostly staircases that opened up in vast wells of darkness, breathing a faint, far updraft, their steps rustling and creaking. They were approaching the governor's nursery. The fat man watched without any visible horror—or any interest, for that matter—while Alyx disarmed the first guard, stalking him as if he were a sparrow, then the one strong pressure on the blood vessel at the back of the neck (all with no noise except the man's own breathing; she was quiet as a shadow). Now he was trussed up, conscious and glaring, quite unable to move. The second guard was asleep in his chair. The third Alyx decoyed out the anteroom by a thrown pebble (she had picked up several in the street). She was three motionless feet away from him as he stooped to examine it; he never straightened up. The fourth guard (he was in the anteroom, in a feeble glow that stole through the hangings of the nursery beyond) turned to greet his friend —or so thought—and then Alyx judged she could risk a little speech. She said thoughtfully, in a low voice, "That's dangerous, on the back of the head."

"Don't let it bother you," said the fat man. Through the parting of the hangings they could see the nurse, asleep on her couch with her arms bare and their golden circlets gleaming in the lamplight, the black slave in a profound huddle of darkness at the farther door, and a shining, tented basket—the royal baby's royal house. The baby was asleep. Alyx stepped inside —motioning the fat man away from the lamp—and picked the governor's daughter out of her gilt cradle. She went round the apartment with the baby in one arm, bolting both doors and closing the hangings, draping the fat man in a guard's cloak and turning down the lamp so that a bare glimmer of light reached the farthest walls.

"Now you've seen it," she said, "shall we go?"

He shook his head. He was watching her curiously, his head tilted to one side. He smiled at her. The baby woke up and began to chuckle at finding herself carried about; she grabbed at Alyx's mouth and jumped up and down, bending in the middle like a sort of pocket-compass or enthusiastic spring. The woman lifted her head to avoid the baby's fingers and began to soothe her, rocking her in her arms. "Good Lord, she's cross-eyed," said Alyx. The nurse and her slave slept on, wrapped in the profoundest unconsciousness. Humming a little, soft tune to the governor's daughter, Alyx walked her about the room, humming and rocking, rocking and humming, until the baby yawned.

"Better go," said Alyx.

"No," said the fat man.

"Better," said Alyx again. "One cry and the nurse—"

"Kill the nurse," said the fat man.

"The slave—"

"He's dead." Alyx started, rousing the baby. The slave still slept by the door, blacker than the blackness, but under him oozed something darker still in the twilight flame of the lamp. "You did that?" whispered Alyx, hushed. She had not seen him move. He took something dark and hollow, like the shell of a nut, from the palm of his hand and laid it next to the baby's cradle; with a shiver half of awe and half of distaste Alyx put the richest and most fortunate daughter of Ourdh back into her gilt cradle. Then she said:

"Now we'll go."

"But I have not what I came for," said the fat man.

"And what is that?"

"The baby."

"Do you mean to steal her?" said Alyx curiously.

"No," said he, "I mean for you to kill her."

The woman stared. In sleep the governor's daughter's nurse stirred; then she sat bolt upright, said something incomprehensible in a loud voice, and fell back to her couch, still deep in sleep. So astonished was the picklock that she did not move. She only looked at the fat man. Then she sat by the cradle and rocked it mechanically with one hand while she looked at him.

"What on earth for?" she said at length. He smiled. He seemed as easy as if he were discussing her wages or the price of pigs; he sat down opposite her and he too rocked the cradle, looking on the burden it contained with a benevolent, amused interest. If the nurse had woken up at that moment, she might have thought she saw the governor and his wife, two loving parents who had come to visit their child by lamplight. The fat man said:

"Must you know?"

"I must," said Alyx.

"Then I will tell you," said the fat man, "not because you must, but because I choose. This little six-months morsel is going to grow up."

"Most of us do," said Alyx, still astonished.

"She will become a queen," the fat man went on, "and a surprisingly wicked woman for one who now looks so innocent. She will be the death of more than one child and more than one slave. In plain fact, she will be a horror to the world. This I know."

"I believe you," said Alyx, shaken.

"Then kill her," said the fat man. But still the picklock did not stir. The baby in her cradle snored, as infants sometimes do, as if to prove the fat man's opinion of her by showing a surprising precocity; still the picklock did not move, but stared at the man across the cradle as if he were a novel work of nature.

"I ask you to kill her," said he again.

"In twenty years," said she, "when she has become so very wicked."

"Woman, are you deaf? I told you—"

"In twenty years!" In the feeble light from the lamp she appeared pale, as if with rage or terror. He leaned deliberately across the cradle, closing his hand around the shell or round-shot or unidentifiable object he had dropped there a moment before; he said very deliberately:

"In twenty years you will be dead."

"Then do it yourself," said Alyx softly, pointing at the object in his hand, "unless you had only one?"

"I had only one."

"Ah, well then," she said, "here!" and she held out to him across the sleeping baby the handle of her dagger, for she had divined something about this man in the months they had known each other; and when he made no move to take the blade, she nudged his hand with the handle.

"You don't like things like this, do you?" she said.

"Do as I say, woman!" he whispered. She pushed the handle into his palm. She stood up and poked him deliberately with it, watching him tremble and sweat; she had never seen him so much at a loss. She moved round the cradle, smiling and stretching out her arm seductively. "Do as I say!" he cried.

"Softly, softly."

"You're a sentimental fool!"

"Am I?" she said. "Whatever I do, I must feel; I can't just twiddle my fingers like you, can I?"

"Ape!"

"You chose me for it."

"*Do as I say!*"

"Sh! You will wake the nurse." For a moment both stood silent, listening to the baby's all-but-soundless breathing and the rustling of the nurse's sheets. Then he said, "Woman, your life is in my hands."

"Is it?" said she.

"*I want your obedience!*"

"Oh no," she said softly, "I know what you want. You want importance because you have none; you want to swallow up another soul. You want to make me fear you and I think you can succeed, but I think also that I can teach you the difference between fear and respect. Shall I?"

"Take care!" he gasped.

"Why?" she said. "Lest you kill me?"

"There are other ways," he said, and he drew himself up, but here the picklock spat in his face. He let out a strangled wheeze and lurched backwards, stumbling against the curtains. Behind her Alyx heard a faint cry; she whirled about to see the governor's nurse sitting up in bed, her eyes wide open.

"Madam, quietly, quietly," said Alyx, "for God's sake!"

The governor's nurse opened her mouth.

"I have done no harm," said Alyx passionately, "I swear it!" But the governor's nurse took a breath with the clear intention to scream, a hearty, healthy, full-bodied scream like the sort picklocks hear in nightmares. In the second of the governor's nurse's shuddering inhalation—in that split second that would mean unmentionably unpleasant things for Alyx, as Ourdh was not a kind city—Alyx considered launching herself at the woman, but the cradle was between. It would be too late. The house would be roused in twenty seconds. She could never make it to a door—or a window—not even to the garden, where the governor's hounds could drag down a stranger in two steps. All these thoughts flashed through the picklock's mind as she saw the governor's nurse inhale with that familiar, hideous violence; her knife was still in her hand; with the smooth simplicity of habit it slid through her fingers and sped across the room to bury itself in the governor's nurse's neck, just above the collarbone in that tender hollow Ourdhian poets love to sing. The woman's open-mouthed expression froze on her face; with an "uh!" of surprise she fell forward, her arms hanging limp over the edge of the couch. A noise came from her throat. The knife had opened a major pulse, and in the blood's slow, powerful, rhythmic tides across sheet and slippers and floor Alyx could discern a horrid similarity to the posture and appearance of the black slave. One was hers, one was the fat man's. She turned and hurried through the curtains into the anteroom, only noting that the soldier blindfolded and bound in the corner had managed patiently to work loose the thongs around two of his fingers with his teeth. He must have been at it all this time. Outside in the hall the darkness of the house was as undisturbed as if the nursery were that very Well of Peace whence the gods first drew (as the saying is) the dawn and the color—but nothing else—for the eyes of women. On the wall someone had written in faintly shining stuff, like snail-slime, the single word *Fever*.

But the fat man was gone.

Her man was raving and laughing on the floor when she got home. She could not control him—she could only sit with her hands over her face and shudder—so at length she locked him in and gave the key to the old woman who owned the house, saying, "My husband drinks too much. He was perfectly sober when I left earlier this evening and now look at him. Don't let him out."

Then she stood stock-still for a moment, trembling and thinking: of the fat man's distaste for walking, of his wheezing, his breathlessness, of his vanity that surely would have led him to show her any magic vehicle he had that took him to whatever he called home. He must have walked. She had seen him go out the north gate a hundred times.

She began to run.

To the south Ourdh is built above marshes that will engulf anyone or anything unwary enough to try to cross them, but to the north the city peters out into sand dunes fringing the seacoast and a fine monotony of rocky hills that rise to a countryside of sandy scrub, stunted trees and what must surely be the poorest farms in the world. Ourdh believes that these farmers dream incessantly of robbing travelers, so nobody goes there, all the fashionable world frequenting the great north road that loops a good fifty miles to avoid this region. Even without its stories the world would have no reason to go here; there is

nothing to see but dunes and weeds and now and then a shack
(or more properly speaking, a hut) resting on an outcropping
of rock or nesting right on the sand like a toy boat in a basin.
There is only one landmark in the whole place—an old tower
hardly even fit for a wizard—and that was abandoned nobody
knows how long ago, though it is only twenty minutes' walk
from the city gates. Thus it was natural that Alyx (as she ran,
her heart pounding in her side) did not notice the stars, or the
warm night-wind that stirred the leaves of the trees, or indeed
the very path under her feet; though she knew all the paths for
twenty-five miles around. Her whole mind was on that tower.
She felt its stones stick in her throat. On her right and left the
country flew by, but she seemed not to move; at last, panting and trembling, she crept through a nest of tree-trunks no
thicker than her wrist (they were very old and very tough) and
sure enough, there it was. There was a light shining halfway
between bottom and top. Then someone looked out, like a
cautious householder out of an attic, and the light went out.

Ah! thought she, and moved into the cover of the trees. The
light—which had vanished—now reappeared a story higher
and so on, higher and higher, until it reached the top. It wobbled a little, as if held in the hand. So this was his country seat!
Silently and with great care, she made her way from one pool
of shadow to another. One hundred feet from the tower she
circled it and approached it from the northern side. A finger of
the sea cut in very close to the base of the building (it had been
slowly falling into the water for many years) and in this she first
waded and then swam, disturbing the faint, cold radiance of
the starlight in the placid ripples. There was no moon. Under
the very walls of the tower she stopped and listened; in the
darkness under the sea she felt along the rocks; then, expelling
her breath and kicking upwards, she rushed head-down; the
water closed round, the stone rushed past and she struggled
up into the air. She was inside the walls.

And so is he, she thought. For somebody had cleaned the
place up. What she remembered as choked with stone rubbish
(she had used the place for purposes of her own a few years
back) was bare and neat and clean; all was square, all was orderly, and someone had cut stone steps from the level of the
water to the most beautifully precise archway in the world. But

of course she should not have been able to see any of this at all.
The place should have been in absolute darkness. Instead, on
either side of the arch was a dim glow, with a narrow beam of
light going between them; she could see dancing in it the dust-
motes that are never absent from this earth, not even from air
that has lain quiet within the rock of a wizard's mansion for
uncountable years. Up to her neck in the ocean, this barbarian
woman then stood very quietly and thoughtfully for several
minutes. Then she dove down into the sea again, and when
she came up her knotted cloak was full of the tiny crabs that
cling to the rocks along the seacoast of Ourdh. One she killed
and the others she suspended captive in the sea; bits of the
blood and flesh of the first she smeared carefully below the two
sources of that narrow beam of light; then she crept back into
the sea and loosed the others at the very bottom step, diving
underwater as the first of the hurrying little creatures reached
the arch. There was a brilliant flash of light, then another, and
then darkness. Alyx waited. Hoisting herself out of the water,
she walked through the arch—not quickly, but not without
nervousness. The crabs were pushing and quarreling over their
dead cousin. Several climbed over the sources of the beam,
pulling, she thought, *the crabs over his eyes*. However he saw, he
had seen nothing. The first alarm had been sprung.

Wizards' castles—and their country residences—have every
right to be infested with all manner of horrors, but Alyx saw
nothing. The passage wound on, going fairly constantly upward, and as it rose it grew lighter until every now and then she
could see a kind of lighter shape against the blackness and a few
stars. These were windows. There was no sound but her own
breathing and once in a while the complaining rustle of one or
two little creatures she had inadvertently carried with her in a
corner of her cloak. When she stopped she heard nothing. The
fat man was either very quiet or very far away. She hoped it was
quietness. She slung the cloak over her shoulder and began the
climb again.

Then she ran into a wall.

This shocked her, but she gathered herself together and
tried the experiment again. She stepped back, then walked forward and again she ran into a wall, not rock but something
at once elastic and unyielding, and at the very same moment

someone said (as it seemed to her, inside her head) *You cannot get through.*

Alyx swore, religiously. She fell back and nearly lost her balance. She put out one hand and again she touched something impalpable, tingling and elastic; again the voice sounded close behind her ear, with an uncomfortable, frightening intimacy as if she were speaking to herself: *You cannot get through.* "Can't I!" she shouted, quite losing her nerve, and drew her sword; it plunged forward without the slightest resistance, but something again stopped her bare hand and the voice repeated with idiot softness, over and over *You cannot get through. You cannot get through—*

"Who are you!" said she, but there was no answer. She backed down the stairs, sword drawn, and waited. Nothing happened. Round her the stone walls glimmered, barely visible, for the moon was rising outside; patiently she waited, pressing the corner of her cloak with her foot, for as it lay on the floor one of the crabs had chewed his way to freedom and had given her ankle a tremendous nip on the way out. The light increased.

There was nothing there. The crab, who had scuttled busily ahead on the landing of the stair, seemed to come to the place himself and stood here, fiddling. There was absolutely nothing there. Then Alyx, who had been watching the little animal with something close to hopeless calm, gave an exclamation and threw herself flat on the stairs—for the crab had begun to climb upward between floor and ceiling and what it was climbing on was nothing. Tears forced themselves to her eyes. Swimming behind her lids she could see her husband's face, appearing first in one place, then in another, as if frozen on the black box the fat man had showed her the first day they met. She laid herself on the stone and cried. Then she got up, for the face seemed to settle on the other side of the landing and it occurred to her that she must go through. She was still crying. She took off one of her sandals and pushed it through the something-nothing (the crab still climbed in the air with perfect comfort). It went through easily. She grew nauseated at the thought of touching the crab and the thing it climbed on, but she put one hand involuntarily over her face and made a grab with the other (*You cannot* said the voice). When she had got the struggling animal thoroughly in her grasp, she dashed it against the rocky side wall of the tunnel and flung it forward with all her strength. It fell clattering twenty feet further on.

The distinction then, she thought, *is between life and death*, and she sat down hopelessly on the steps to figure this out, for the problem of dying so as to get through and yet getting through without dying, struck her as insoluble. Twenty feet down the tunnel (the spot was in darkness and she could not see what it was) something rustled. It sounded remarkably like a crab that had been stunned and was now recovering, for these animals think of nothing but food and disappointments only seem to give them fresh strength for the search. Alyx gaped into the dark. She felt the hairs rise on the back of her neck. She would have given a great deal to see into that spot, for it seemed to her that she now guessed at the principle of the fat man's demon, which kept out any conscious mind—as it had spoken in hers—but perhaps would let through . . . She pondered. This cynical woman had been a religious enthusiast before circumstances forced her into a drier way of thinking; thus it was that she now slung her cloak ahead of her on the ground to break her fall and leaned deliberately, from head to feet, into the horrid, springy net she could not see. Closing her eyes and pressing the fingers of both hands over an artery in the back of her neck, she began to repeat to herself a formula that she had learned in those prehistoric years, one that has to be altered slightly each time it is repeated—almost as effective a self-hypnotic device as counting backward. And the voice, too, whispering over and over *You cannot get through, you cannot get through—cannot—cannot—*

Something gave her a terrific shock through teeth, bones and flesh, and she woke to find the floor of the landing tilted two inches from her eyes. One knee was twisted under her and the left side of her face ached dizzily, warm and wet under a cushion of numbness. She guessed that her face had been laid open in the fall and her knee sprained, if not broken.

But she was through.

She found the fat man in a room at the very top of the tower, sitting in a pair of shorts in a square of light at the end of a corridor; and, as she made her way limping towards him, he grew (unconscious and busy) to the size of a human being, until at last she stood inside the room, vaguely aware of blood along her arm and a stinging on her face where she had tried to wipe her wound with her cloak. The room was full of machinery. The fat man (he had been jiggling some little arrangement of wires and blocks on his lap) looked up, saw her, registered surprise and then broke into a great grin.

"So it's you," he said.

She said nothing. She put one arm along the wall to steady herself.

"You are amazing," he said, "perfectly amazing. Come here," and he rose and sent his stool spinning away with a touch. He came up to where she stood, wet and shivering, staining the floor and wall, and for a long minute he studied her. Then he said softly:

"Poor animal. Poor little wretch."

Her breathing was ragged. She glanced rapidly about her, taking in the size of the room (it broadened to encompass the whole width of the tower) and the four great windows that opened to the four winds, and the strange things in the shadows: multitudes of little tables, boards hung on the walls, knobs and switches and winking lights innumerable. But she did not move or speak.

"Poor animal," he said again. He walked back and surveyed her contemptuously, both arms akimbo, and then he said, "Do you believe the world was once a lump of rock?"

"Yes," she said.

"Many years ago," he said, "many more years than your mind can comprehend, before there were trees—or cities—or women—I came to this lump of rock. Do you believe that?"

She nodded.

"I came here," said he gently, "in the satisfaction of a certain hobby, and I made all that you see in this room—all the little things you were looking at a moment ago—and I made the tower, too. Sometimes I make it new inside and sometimes I make it look old. Do you understand that, little one?"

She said nothing.

"And when the whim hits me," he said, "I make it new and comfortable and I settle into it, and once I have settled into it

I begin to practice my hobby. Do you know what my hobby is?" He chuckled.

"My hobby, little one," he said, "came from this tower and this machinery, for this machinery can reach all over the world and then things happen exactly as I choose. Now do you know what my hobby is? My hobby is world-making. I make worlds, little one."

She took a quick breath, like a sigh, but she did not speak. He smiled at her.

"Poor beast," he said, "you are dreadfully cut about the face and I believe you have sprained one of your limbs. Hunting animals are always doing that. But it won't last. Look," he said, "look again," and he moved one fat hand in a slow circle around him. "It is I, little one," he said, "who made everything that your eyes have ever rested on. Apes and peacocks, tides and times" (he laughed) "and the fire and the rain. I made you. I made your husband. Come," and he ambled off into the shadows. The circle of light that had rested on him when Alyx first entered the room now followed him, continually keeping him at its center, and although her hair rose to see it, she forced herself to follow, limping in pain past the tables, through stacks of tubing and wire and between square shapes the size of stoves. The light fled always before her. Then he stopped, and as she came up to the light, he said:

"You know, I am not angry at you."

Alyx winced as her foot struck something, and grabbed her knee.

"No, I am not," he said. "It has been delightful—except for tonight, which demonstrates, between ourselves, that the whole thing was something of a mistake and shouldn't be indulged in again—but you must understand that I cannot allow a creation of mine, a paring of my fingernail, if you take my meaning, to rebel in this silly fashion." He grinned. "No, no," he said, "that I cannot do. And so" (here he picked up a glass cube from the table in back of him) "I have decided" (here he joggled the cube a little) "that tonight—why, my dear, what is the matter with you? You are standing there with the veins in your fists knotted as if you would like to strike me, even though your knee is giving you a great deal of trouble just at present and you would be better employed in supporting some of your weight with your hands or I am very much mistaken." And he held out to her—though not far enough for her to reach it—the glass cube, which contained an image of her husband in little, unnaturally sharp, like a picture let into crystal. "See?" he said. "When I turn the lever to the right, the little beasties rioting in his bones grow ever more calm and that does him good. A great deal of good. But when I turn the lever to the left—"

"Devil!" said she.

"Ah, I've gotten something out of you at last!" he said, coming closer. "At last you know! Ah, little one, many and many a time I have seen you wondering whether the world might not be better off if you stabbed me in the back, eh? But you can't, you know. Why don't you try it?" He patted her on the shoulder. "Here I am, you see, quite close enough to you, peering, in fact, into those tragic, blazing eyes—wouldn't it be natural to try and put an end to me? But you can't, you know. You'd be puzzled if you tried. I wear an armor plate, little beast, that any beast might envy, and you could throw me from a ten-thousand-foot mountain, or fry me in a furnace, or do a hundred and one other deadly things to me without the least effect. My armor plate has *in-er-tial dis-crim-in-a-tion*, little savage, which means that it lets nothing too fast and nothing too heavy get through. So you cannot hurt me at all. To murder me, you would have to strike me, but that is too fast and too heavy and so is the ground that hits me when I fall and so is fire. Come here."

She did not move.

"Come here, monkey," he said. "I'm going to kill your man and then I will send you away; though since you operate so well in the dark, I think I'll bless you and make that your permanent condition. What do you think you're doing?" for she had put her fingers to her sleeve; and while he stood, smiling a little with the cube in his hand, she drew her dagger and fell upon him, stabbing him again and again.

"There," he said complacently, "do you see?"

"I see," she said hoarsely, finding her tongue.

"Do you understand?"

"I understand," she said.

"Then move off," he said, "I have got to finish," and he brought the cube up to the level of his eyes. She saw her man, behind the glass as in a refracting prism, break into a multiplicity of images; she saw him reach out grotesquely to the surface; she saw his fingertips strike at the surface as if to erupt into the air; and while the fat man took the lever between thumb and forefinger and—prissily and precisely, his lips pursed into wrinkles, prepared to move it all the way to the left—

She put her fingers in his eyes and then, taking advantage of his pain and blindness, took the cube from him and bent him over the edge of a table in such a way as to break his back. This all took place inside the body. His face worked spasmodically, one eye closed and unclosed in a hideous parody of a wink, his fingers paddled feebly on the tabletop and he fell to the floor.

"My dear!" he gasped.

She looked at him expressionlessly.

"Help me," he whispered, "eh?" His fingers fluttered. "Over there," he said eagerly, "medicines. Make me well, eh? Good and fast. I'll give you half."

"All," she said.

"Yes, yes, all," he said breathlessly, "all—explain all—fascinating hobby—spend most of my time in this room—get the medicine—"

"First show me," she said, "how to turn it off."

"Off?" he said. He watched her, bright-eyed.

"First," she said patiently, "I will turn it all off. And then I will cure you."

"No," he said, "no, no! Never!" She knelt down beside him.

"Come," she said softly, "do you think I want to destroy it? I am as fascinated by it as you are. I only want to make sure you can't do anything to me, that's all. You must explain it all first until I am master of it, too, and then we will turn it on."

"No, no," he repeated suspiciously.

"You must," she said, "or you'll die. What do you think I plan to do? I have to cure you, because otherwise how can I learn to work all this? But I must be safe, too. Show me how to turn it off."

He pointed, doubtfully.

"Is that it?" she said.

"Yes," he said, "but—"

"*Is that it?*"

"Yes, but—no—wait!" for Alyx sprang to her feet and fetched from his stool the pillow on which he had been sitting, the purpose of which he did not at first seem to comprehend, but then his eyes went wide with horror, for she had got the pillow in order to smother him, and that is just what she did.

When she got to her feet, her legs were trembling. Stumbling and pressing both hands together as if in prayer to subdue their shaking, she took the cube that held her husband's picture and carefully—oh, how carefully!—turned the lever to the right. Then she began to sob. It was not the weeping of grief, but a kind of reaction and triumph, all mixed; in the middle of that eerie room she stood, and threw her head back and yelled. The light burned steadily on. In the shadows she found the fat man's master switch, and leaning against the wall, put one finger—only one—on it and caught her breath. Would the world end? She did not know. After a few minutes' search she found a candle and flint hidden away in a cupboard and with this she made herself a light; then, with eyes closed, with a long shudder, she leaned—no, sagged—against the switch, and stood for a long moment, expecting and believing nothing.

But the world did not end. From outside came the wind and the sound of the sea-wash (though louder now, as if some indistinct and not quite audible humming had just ended) and inside fantastic shadows leapt about the candle—the lights had gone out. Alyx began to laugh, catching her breath. She set the candle down and searched until she found a length of metal tubing that stood against the wall, and then she went from machine to machine, smashing, prying, tearing, toppling tables and breaking controls. Then she took the candle in her unsteady hand and stood over the body of the fat man, a phantasmagoric lump on the floor, badly lit at last. Her shadow loomed on the wall. She leaned over him and studied his face, that face that had made out of agony and death the most appalling trivialities. She thought:

Make the world? You hadn't the imagination. You didn't even make these machines; that shiny finish is for customers, not craftsmen, and controls that work by little pictures are for children. You are a child yourself, a child and a horror, and I would ten times rather be subject to your machinery than master of it.

Aloud she said:

"Never confuse the weapon and the arm," and taking the candle, she went away and left him in the dark.

She got home at dawn and, as her man lay asleep in bed, it seemed to her that he was made out of the light of the dawn that streamed through his fingers and his hair, irradiating him with gold. She kissed him and he opened his eyes.

"You've come home," he said.

"So I have," said she.

"I fought all night," she added, "with the Old Man of the Mountain," for you must know that this demon is a legend in Ourdh; he is the god of this world who dwells in a cave containing the whole world in little, and from his cave he rules the fates of men.

"Who won?" said her husband, laughing, for in the sunrise when everything is suffused with light it is difficult to see the seriousness of injuries.

"I did!" said she. "The man is dead." She smiled, splitting open the wound on her cheek, which began to bleed afresh. "He died," she said, "for two reasons only: because he was a fool. And because we are not."

She added, "I'll tell you all about it."

But that's another story.

Picnic on Paradise

SHE WAS a soft-spoken, dark-haired, small-boned woman, not even coming up to their shoulders, like a kind of dwarf or miniature—but that was normal enough for a Mediterranean Greek of nearly four millennia ago, before super-diets and hybridization from seventy colonized planets had turned all humanity (so she had been told) into Scandinavian giants. The young lieutenant, who was two meters and a third tall, or three heads more than herself, very handsome and ebony-skinned, said "I'm sorry, ma'am, but I cannot believe you're the proper Trans-Temporal Agent; I think—" and he finished his thought on the floor, his head under one of his ankles and this slight young woman (or was she young? Trans-Temp did such strange things sometimes!) somehow holding him down in a position he could not get out of without hurting himself to excruciation. She let him go. She sat down on the balloon-inflated thing they provided for sitting on in these strange times, looking curiously at the super-men and super-women, and said, "I am the Agent. My name is Alyx," and smiled. She was in a rather good humor. It still amused her to watch this whole place, the transparent columns the women wore instead of clothing, the parts of the walls that pulsated in and out and changed color, the strange floor that waved like grass, the three-dimensional vortices that kept springing to life on what would have been the ceiling if it had only stayed in one place (but it never did) and the general air of unhappy, dogged, insistent, sad restlessness. "A little bit of home," the lieutenant had called it. He had seemed to find particular cause for nostalgia in a lime-green coil that sprang out of the floor whenever anybody dropped anything, to eat it up, but it was "not in proper order" and sometimes you had to fight it for something you wanted to keep. The people moved her a little closer to laughter. One of them leaned toward her now.

"Pardon me," said this one effusively—it was one of the ladies— "but is that face yours? I've heard Trans-Temp does all sorts of cosmetic work and I thought they might—"

"Why yes," said Alyx, hoping against hope to be impolite. "Are those breasts yours? I can't help noticing—"

"Not at all!" cried the lady happily. "Aren't they wonderful? They're Adrian's. I mean they're by Adrian."

"I think that's enough," said the lieutenant.

"Only we *rather wondered*," said the lady, elevating her indigo brows at what she seemed to have taken as an insult, "why you keep yourself so covered up. Is it a tribal rite? Are you deformed? Why don't you get cosmetic treatment; you could have asked for it, you know, I mean I think you could—" but here everybody went pale and turned aside, just as if she had finally managed to do something offensive and *All I did*, she thought, *was take off my shift*.

One of the nuns fell to praying.

"All right, Agent," said the lieutenant, his voice a bare whisper, "we believe you. Please put on your clothes.

"Please, Agent," he said again, as if his voice were failing him, but she did not move, only sat naked and cross-legged with the old scars on her ribs and belly showing in a perfectly natural and expectable way, sat and looked at them one by one: the two nuns, the lady, the young girl with her mouth hanging open and the iridescent beads wound through three feet of hair, the bald-headed boy with some contraption strapped down over his ears, eyes and nose, the artist and the middle-aged political man, whose right cheek had begun to jump. The artist was leaning forward with his hand cupped under one eye in the old-fashioned and nearly unbelievable pose of someone who has just misplaced a contact lens. He blinked and looked up at her through a flood of mechanical tears.

"The lieutenant," he said, coughing a little, "is thinking of anaesthetics and the lady of surgery—I really think you had better put your clothes back on, by the way—and as to what the others think I'm not so sure. I myself have only had my usual trouble with these damned things and I don't really mind—"

"Please, Agent," said the young officer.

"But I don't think," said the artist, massaging one eye, "that you quite understand the effect you're creating."

"None of *you* has anything on," said Alyx.

"You have on your history," said the artist, "and we're not used to that, believe me. Not to history. Not to old she-wolves with livid marks running up their ribs and arms, and not to the idea of fights in which people are neither painlessly killed nor painlessly fixed up but linger on and die—slowly—or heal —slowly.

"Well!" he added, in a very curious tone of voice, "after all, we may all look like that before this is over."

"Buddha, no!" gasped a nun.

Alyx put her clothes on, tying the black belt around the black dress. "You may not look as bad," she said a bit sourly. "But you will certainly smell worse.

"And I," she added conversationally, "don't like pieces of plastic in people's teeth. I think it disgusting."

"Refined sugar," said the officer, "one of our minor vices," and then, with an amazed expression, he burst into tears.

"Well, well," muttered the young girl, "we'd better get on with it."

"Yes," said the middle-aged man, laughing nervously, "'People for Every Need,' you know," and before he could be thoroughly rebuked for quoting the blazon of the Trans-Temporal Military Authority (Alyx heard the older woman begin lecturing him on the nastiness of calling anyone even by insinuation a thing, an agency, a means or an instrument, *anything* but a People, or as she said "a People People") he began to lead the file toward the door, with the girl coming next, a green tube in the middle of her mouth, the two nuns clinging together in shock, the bald-headed boy swaying a little as he walked, as if to unheard music, the lieutenant and the artist—who lingered.

"Where'd they pick you up?" he said, blinking again and fingering one eye.

"Off Tyre," said Alyx. "Where'd they pick *you* up?"

"We," said the artist, "are rich tourists. Can you believe it? Or refugees, rather. Caught up in a local war. A war on the surface of a planet, mind you; I don't believe I've heard of that in my lifetime."

"I have," said Alyx, "quite a few times," and with the lightest of light pushes she guided him toward the thing that passed for a decent door; the kind of thing she had run through, roaring with laughter, time after time at her first day at Trans-Temp, just for the pleasure of seeing it open up like a giant mouth and then pucker shut in an enormous expression of disgust.

"Babies!" she said.

"By the way," called back the artist, "I'm a flat-color man. What was your profession?"

"Murderer," said Alyx, and she stepped through the door.

"Raydos is the flat-color man," said the lieutenant, his feet up on what looked gratifyingly like a table. "Used to do wrap-arounds and walk-ins—very good walk-ins, too, I have a little education in that line myself—but he's gone wild about something called pigment on flats. Says the other stuff's too easy."

"Flats whats?" said Alyx.

"I don't know, any flat surface, I suppose," said the lieutenant. "And he's got those machines in his eyes which keep coming out, but he won't get retinotherapy. Says he likes having two kinds of vision. Most of us are born myopic nowadays, you know."

"I wasn't," said Alyx.

"Iris," the lieutenant went on, palming something and then holding it to his ear, "is pretty typical, though: young, pretty stable, ditto the older woman—oh yes, her name's Maudey—and Gavrily's a conamon, of course."

"Conamon?" said Alyx, with some difficulty.

"Influence," said the lieutenant, his face darkening a little. "Influence, you know. I don't like the man. That's too personal an evaluation, of course, but damn it, I'm a decent man. If I don't like him, I say I don't like him. He'd honor me for it."

"Wouldn't he kick your teeth in?" said Alyx.

"How much did they teach you at Trans-Temp?" said the lieutenant, after a pause.

"Not much," said Alyx.

"Well, anyway," said the lieutenant, a little desperately, "you've got Gavrily and he's a conamon, then Maudey—the one with the blue eyebrows, you know—"

"Dyed?" asked Alyx politely.

"Of course. Permanently. And the wienie—"

"Well, well!" said Alyx.

"You know," said the lieutenant, with sarcastic restraint, "you can't drink that stuff like wine. It's distilled. Do you know what distilled means?"

"Yes," said Alyx. "I found out the hard way."

"All right," said the lieutenant, jumping to his feet, "all right! A wienie is a wienie. He's the one with the bald head. He calls himself Machine because he's an idiotic adolescent rebel and he wears that—that Trivia on his head to give himself twenty-four hours a day of solid nirvana, station NOTHING, turns off all stimuli when you want it to, operates psionically. We call it a Trivia because that's what it is and because forty years ago it was a Tri-V and I *despise* bald young inexistential rebels who refuse to relate!"

"Well, well," she said again.

"And the nuns," he said, "are nuns, whatever that means to you. It means nothing to me; I am not a religious man. You have got to get them from here to there, 'across the border' as they used to say, because they had money and they came to see Paradise and Paradise turned into—" He stopped and turned to her.

"You know all this," he said accusingly.

She shook her head.

"Trans-Temp—"

"Told me nothing."

"Well," said the lieutenant, "perhaps it's best. Perhaps it's best. What we need is a person who knows nothing. Perhaps that's exactly what we need."

"Shall I go home?" said Alyx.

"Wait," he said harshly, "and don't joke with me. Paradise is the world you're on. It's in the middle of a commercial war. I said commercial war; I'm military and I have nothing to do here except get killed trying to make sure the civilians are out of the way. That's what you're for. You get them" (he pressed something in the wall and it turned into a map; she recognized it instantly, even though there were no sea-monsters and no four winds puffing at the corners, which was rather a loss) "from here to here," he said. "B is a neutral base. They can get you off-planet."

"Is that all?"

"No, that's not all. Listen to me. If you want to exterminate a world, you blanket it with hell-bombs and for the next few weeks you've got a beautiful incandescent disk in the sky, very ornamental and very dead, and that's that. And if you want to strip-mine, you use something a little less deadly and four weeks later you go down in heavy shielding and dig up any damn thing you like, and *that's* that. And if you want to colonize, we have something that kills every form of animal and plant life on the planet and then you go down and cart off the local flora and fauna if they're poisonous or use them as mulch if they're usable. But you can't do any of that on Paradise."

She took another drink. She was not drunk.

"There is," he said, "every reason not to exterminate Paradise. There is every reason to keep her just as she is. The air and the gravity are near perfect, but you can't farm Paradise."

"Why not?" said Alyx.

"Why not?" said he. "Because it's all up and down and nothing, that's why. It's glaciers and mountains and coral reefs; it's rainbows of inedible fish in continental slopes; it's deserts, cacti, waterfalls going nowhere, rivers that end in lakes of mud and skies—and sunsets—and that's all it is. That's *all*." He sat down.

"Paradise," he said, "is impossible to colonize, but it's still too valuable to mess up. It's too beautiful." He took a deep breath. "It happens," he said, "to be a tourist resort."

Alyx began to giggle. She put her hand in front of her mouth but only giggled the more; then she let go and hoorawed, snorting derisively, bellowing, weeping with laughter.

"That," said the lieutenant stiffly, "is pretty ghastly." She said she was sorry.

"I don't know," he said, rising formally, "just what they are going to fight this war with. Sound on the buildings, probably; they're not worth much; and for the people every nasty form of explosive or neuronic hand-weapon that's ever been devised. But no radiation. No viruses. No heat. Nothing to mess up the landscape or the ecological balance. Only they've got a net stretched around the planet that monitors everything up and down the electromagnetic spectrum. Automatically, each millisecond. If you went out in those mountains, young woman, and merely sharpened your knife on a rock, the sparks would bring a radio homer in on you in fifteen seconds. No, less."

"Thank you for telling me," said she, elevating her eyebrows.

"No fires," he said, "no weapons, no transportation, no automatic heating, no food processing, nothing airborne. They'll have some infrared from you but they'll probably think you're local wildlife. But by the way, if you hear anything or see anything overhead, we think the best thing for all of you would be to get down on all fours and pretend to be yaks. I'm not fooling."

"Poseidon!" said she, under her breath.

"Oh, one other thing," he said. "We can't have induction currents, you know. Might happen. You'll have to give up everything metal. The knife, please."

She handed it over, thinking *If I don't get that back—*

"Trans-Temp sent a synthetic substitute, of course," the lieutenant went on briskly. "And crossbows—same stuff—and packs, and we'll give you all the irradiated food we can get you. And insulated suits."

"And ignorance," said she. His eyebrows went up.

"Sheer ignorance," she repeated. "The most valuable commodity of all. Me. No familiarity with mechanical transportation or the whatchamacallits. Stupid. Can't read. Used to walking. Never used a compass in my life. Right?"

"Your skill—" he began.

From each of her low sandals she drew out what had looked like part of the ornamentation and flipped both knives expertly at the map on the wall—both hands, simultaneously—striking precisely at point A and point B.

"You can have those, too," she said.

The lieutenant bowed. He pressed the wall again. The knives hung in a cloudy swirl, then in nothing, clear as air, while outside appeared the frosty blue sky, the snowy foothills drawing up to the long, easy swelling crests of Paradise's oldest mountain chain—old and easy, not like some of the others, and most unluckily, only two thousand meters high.

"By God!" said Alyx, fascinated, "I don't believe I've ever seen snow before."

There was a sound behind her, and she turned. The lieutenant had fainted.

*

They weren't right. She had palmed them a hundred times, flipped them, tested their balance, and they weren't right. Her aim was off. They felt soapy. She complained to the lieutenant, who said you couldn't expect exactly the same densities in synthetics, and sat shivering in her insulated suit in the shed, nodding now and again at the workers assembling their packs, while the lieutenant appeared and disappeared into the walls, a little frantically. "Those are just androids," said Iris good-humoredly. "Don't nod to them. Don't you think it's *fun*?"

"Go cut your hair," said Alyx.

Iris's eyes widened.

"And tell that other woman to do the same," Alyx added.

"Zap!" said Iris cryptically, and ambled off. It was detestably chilly. The crossbows impressed her, but she had had no time to practice with them (*Which will be remedied by every one of you bastards*, she thought) and no time to get used to the cold, which all the rest of them seemed to like. She felt stupid. She began to wonder about something and tried to catch the lieutenant by the arm, cursing herself in her own language, trying to think in her own language and failing, giving up on the knives and finally herding everyone outside into the snow to practice with the crossbows. The wienie was surprisingly good. He stayed at it two hours after the others drifted off, repeating and repeating; Iris came back with her cut hair hanging around her face and confided that she had been named after part of a camera; the lieutenant's hands began to shake a little on each appearance; and Machine became a dead shot. She stared at him. All the time he had kept the thing he wore on his head clamped over ears and eyes and nose. "He can see through it if he wants to," said Iris. Maudey was talking earnestly in a corner with Gavrily, the middle-aged politician, and the whole thing was taking on the air of a picnic. Alyx grew exasperated. She pinched a nerve in the lieutenant's arm the next time he darted across the shed and stopped him, he going "aaah!" and rubbing his arm; he said, "I'm very sorry, but—" She did it again.

"Look here," she said, "I may be stupid, but I'm not that stupid—"

"Sorry," he said, and was gone again, into one of the walls, right into one of the walls.

"He's busy," said Raydos, the flat-color man. "They're sending someone else through and he's trying to talk them out of it."

"Joy," said Alyx.

"Have you noticed," said Raydos, "how your vocabulary keeps expanding? That's the effect of hypnotic language training; they can't give you the whole context consciously, you see, only the sectors where the languages overlap so you keep coming up against these unconscious, 'buried' areas where a sudden context triggers off a whole pre-implanted pattern. It's like packing your frazzle; you always remember where it is when you need it, but of course it's always at the bottom. You'll be feeling rather stupid for a few days, but it'll wear off."

"A frazzle?" said Maudey, drifting over. "Why, I imagine she doesn't even know what a frazzle is."

"I told you to cut your hair," said Alyx.

"A frazzle," said Gavrily, "is the greatest invention of the last two centuries, let me assure you. Only in some cities, of course; they have a decibel limit on most. And of course it's frazzl*es*, one for each ear; they neutralize the sound-waves, you know, absolute silence, although" (he went on and everybody giggled) "I have had them used against *me* at times!"

"I would use one against your campaigns all the time," said Iris, joining them. "See, I cut my hair! Isn't it *fun*?" and with a sudden jerk she swung her head down at Alyx to show her short, silver hair, swinging it back and forth and giggling hysterically while Gavrily laughed and tried to catch at it. They were all between two and two-and-a-half meters tall. It was intolerable. They were grabbing at Iris's hair and explaining to each other about the different frazzles they had used and the sound-baffles of the apartments they had been in, and simulated forests with walls that went *tweet-tweet* and how utterly lag it was to install free-fall in your bathroom (if only you could afford it) and take a bath in a bubble, though you must be careful not to use *too* large a bubble or you might suffocate. She dove between them, unnoticed, into the snow where Machine practiced shooting bolts at a target, his eyes hooded in lenses, his ears muffled, his feet never moving. He was on his way to becoming a master. There was a sudden rise in the excited gabble from inside, and turning, Alyx saw someone come out of the far wall with the lieutenant, the first blond person she had seen so far, for everyone except the lieutenant seemed to be some kind of indeterminate, mixed racial type, except for Maudey and Iris, who had what Alyx would have called a dash of the Asiatic. Everyone was a little darker than herself and a little more pronounced in feature, as if they had crossbred in a hundred ways to even out at last, but here came the lieutenant with what Alyx would have called a freak Northman, another giant (she did not give a damn), and then left him inside and came out and sat down on the outside bench.

"Lieutenant," said Alyx, "why are you sending me on this picnic?"

He made a vague gesture, looking back into the shed, fidgeting like a man who has a hundred things to do and cannot make up his mind where to start.

"An explorer," said the lieutenant, "amateur. Very famous."

"Why don't you send them with him and stop this nonsense, then!" she exploded.

"It's not nonsense," he said. "Oh, no."

"Isn't it? A ten-day walk over those foothills? No large predators? An enemy that doesn't give a damn about us? A path a ten-year-old could follow. An explorer right to hand. *And how much do I cost?*"

"Agent," said the lieutenant, "I know civilians," and he looked back in the shed again, where the newcomer had seized Iris and was kissing her, trying to get his hands inside her suit while Gavrily danced around the couple. Maudey was chatting with Raydos, who made sketches on a pad. "Maybe, Agent," said the lieutenant, very quietly, "I know how much you cost, and maybe it is very important to get these people out of here before one of them is killed, and maybe, Agent, there is more to it than that when you take people away from their—from their electromagnetic spectrum, shall we say. That man" (and he indicated the blond) "has never been away from a doctor and armor and helpers and vehicles and cameras in his life." He looked down into the snow. "I shall have to take their drugs away from them," he said. "They won't like that. They are going to walk on their own feet for two hundred and forty kilometers. That may be ten days to you but you will see how far you get with them. You cost more than you think, Agent, and let me tell you something else" (here he lifted his face intently) "which may help you to understand, and that is, Agent, that this is the first time the Trans-Temporal Authority—which is a military authority, thanks be for that—has ever transported anyone from the past for any purpose whatsoever. And that was accidental—I can't explain that now. All this talk about Agents here and Agents there is purely mythological, fictional, you might say, though why people insist on these silly stories I don't know, for there is only one Agent and that is the first and the last Agent and that, Agent—is you. But don't try to tell them. They won't believe you."

"Is that why you're beginning with a picnic?" said Alyx.

"It will not be a picnic," he said and he looked at the snow again, at Machine's tracks, at Machine, who stood patiently sending bolt after bolt into the paint-sprayed target, his eyes and nose and ears shut to the whole human world.

"What will happen to you?" said Alyx, finally.

"I?" said the young officer. "Oh, I shall die! but that's nothing to you," and he went back into the shed immediately, giving instructions to what Iris had called androids, clapping the giant Northerner on the back, calling Alyx to come in. "This is Gunnar," he said. They shook hands. It seemed an odd custom to Alyx and apparently to everyone else, for they sniggered. He flashed a smile at everyone as the pack was fitted onto his back. "Here," he said, holding out a box, "*Cannabis*," and Iris, making a face, handed over a crumpled bundle of her green cylinders. "I hope I don't have to give these up," said Raydos quietly, stowing his sketchbook into his pack. "They are not power tools, you know," and he watched dispassionately while Maudey argued for a few minutes, looked a bit sulky and finally produced a tiny, ornate orange cylinder. She took a sniff from it and handed it over to the lieutenant. Iris looked malicious. Gavrily confessed he had nothing. The nuns, of course, said everybody, had nothing and would not carry weapons. Everyone had almost forgotten about them. They all straggled out into the snow to where Machine was picking up the last of his bolts. He turned to face them, like a man who would be contaminated by the very air of humankind, nothing showing under the hood of his suit but his mouth and the goggled lenses and snout of another species.

"I must have that, too," said Alyx, planting both feet on the ground.

"Well, after all," said Maudey, "you can't expect—"

"Teach the young fellow a lesson!" said Gavrily.

"Shall I take it off?" remarked the amateur explorer (*And actor*, thought Alyx) striding forward, smile flashing while Machine bent slowly for the last of his bolts, fitting it back into the carrying case, not looking at anyone or hearing anything, for all she knew, off on station N-O-T-H-I-N-G twenty-four hours each Earth day, the boy who called himself Machine because he hated the lot of them.

"If you touch him," said Alyx evenly, "I shall kill you," and as they gasped and giggled (Gunnar gave a rueful smile; he had been outplayed) she walked over to him and held out her hand. The boy took off his Trivia and dropped it into the snow; the showing of any face would have been a shock but his was completely denuded of hair, according (she supposed) to the fashion he followed: eyebrows, eyelashes and scalp, and his eyes were a staring, brilliant, shattering, liquescent blue. "You're a good shot," she said. He was not interested. He looked at them without the slightest emotion. "He hardly *ever* talks," said Maudey. They formed a straggling line, walking off toward the low hills and Alyx, a thought suddenly coming to her, said off-handedly before she knew it, "You're mother and daughter, aren't you?"

The entire line stopped. Maudey had instantly turned away, Iris looked furiously angry, Gunnar extremely surprised and only Raydos patiently waited, as usual, watching them all. Machine remained Machine. The nuns were hiding their mouths, shocked, with both hands.

"I thought—"

"If you must—"

"Don't you ever—!"

The voices came at her from all sides.

"Shut up," she said, "and march. I'll do worse yet." The column began again. "Faster," she said. "You know," she added cruelly, carefully listening for the effect of her words, "one of you may die." Behind her there was a stiffening, a gasp, a terrified murmur at such bad, bad taste. "Yes, yes," she said, hammering it in, "one of us may very well die before this trip is over," and quickened her pace in the powdery snow, the even, crisp, shallow snow, as easy to walk in as if put down expressly for a pleasure jaunt, a lovely picnic under the beautiful blue heaven of this best of all possible tourist resorts. "Any of us," she repeated carefully, "any one of us at all," and all of a sudden she thought *Why, that's true. That's very true.* She sighed. "Come on," she said.

At first she had trouble keeping up with them; then, as they straggled and loitered, she had no trouble at all; and finally they had trouble keeping up with her. The joking and bantering had stopped. She let them halt fairly early (the lieutenant had started them out—wisely, she thought—late in the afternoon) under an overhanging rock. Mountains so old and smooth should not have many caves and outflung walls where a climbing party can rest, but the mountains of Paradise had them. The late, late shadows were violet blue and the sunlight going up the farthest peaks went up like the sunlight in a children's book, with a purity and perfection of color changing into color and the snow melting into cobalt evening which Alyx watched with—

Wonder. Awe. Suspicion. But nobody was about. However, they were making trouble when she got back. They were huddled together, rather irritable, talking insatiably as if they had to make up for their few silent hours in the afternoon's march. It was ten degrees below freezing and would not drop much lower at this time of year, the lieutenant had promised, even though there might be snow, a fact (she thought) for which they might at least look properly thankful.

"Well?" she said, and everyone smiled.

"We've been talking," said Maudey brightly. "About what to do."

"What to do what?" said Alyx.

"What to do next," said Gavrily, surprised. "What else?"

The two nuns smiled.

"We think," said Maudey, "that we ought to go much more slowly and straight across, you know, and Gunnar wants to take photographs—"

"Manual," said the explorer, flashing his teeth.

"And not through the mountains," said Maudey. "It's so up-and-down, you know."

"And *hard*," said Iris.

"And we voted," said Maudey, "and Gunnar won."

"Won what?" said Alyx.

"Well, *won*," said Gavrily, "you know."

"Won what?" repeated Alyx, a little sharply; they all looked embarrassed, not (she thought, surprised) for themselves but for her. Definitely for her.

"They want Gunnar to lead them." No one knew who had spoken. Alyx looked from one to the other but they were as surprised as she; then she whirled around sharply, for it was Machine who had spoken, Machine who had never before said one word. He squatted in the snow, his back against the rock, looking past them. He spoke precisely and without the slightest inflection.

"Thank you," said Alyx. "Is that what you all want?"

"Not I," said Raydos.

"I do," said Maudey.

"And I do," said Iris. "I think—"

"I do," said Gavrily.

"We think—" the nuns began.

She was prepared to blast their ears off, to tell them just what she thought of them. She was shaking all over. She began in her own language, however, and had to switch clumsily into theirs, trying to impress upon them things for which she could not find words, things for which she did not believe the language had words at all: that she was in charge of them, that this was not a pleasure party, that they might die, that it was her job to be responsible for them, and that whoever led them, or how, or why, or in what way, was none of their business. She kept saying it over and over that it was none of their business.

"Oh, everything is everybody's business," said Gavrily cheerfully, as if her feeling that way were quite natural, quite wrong and also completely irrelevant, and they all began to chat again. Gunnar came up to her sympathetically and took hold of her hands. She twisted in his grasp, instinctively beginning a movement that would have ended in the pit of his stomach, but he grasped each of her wrists, saying "No, no, you're not big enough," and holding her indulgently away from him with his big, straight, steady arms. He had begun to laugh, saying "I know this kind of thing too, you see!" when she turned in his grip, taking hold of his wrists in the double hold used by certain circus performers, and bearing down sharply on his arms (he kept them steady for just long enough, thinking he was still holding her off) she lifted herself up as if on a gate, swung under his guard and kicked him right under the arch of the ribs. Luckily the suit cushioned the blow a little. The silence that followed—except for his gasping—was complete. They had never, she supposed, seen Gunnar on the ground that way before. Or anyone else. Then Maudey threw up.

"I am sorry," said Alyx, "but I cannot talk to you. You will do as I say," and she walked away from them and sat down near Machine, whose eyes had never left the snow in front of him, who was making furrows in it with one hand. She sat there, listening to the frightened whispers in back of her, knowing she had behaved badly and wanting to behave even worse all over again, trembling from head to foot with rage, knowing they were only children, cursing herself abominably —and the Trans-Temporal Authority—and her own idiot helplessness and the "commercial war," whatever that might be, and each one of her charges, individually and collectively, until the last of the unfamiliar stars came out and the sky turned black. She fell asleep in her wonderful insulated suit, as did they all, thinking *Oh, God, not even keeping a watch*, and not caring; but she woke from time to time to hear their secure breathing, and then the refrain of a poem came to her in the language of Phoenician Tyre, those great traders who had gone even to the gates of Britain for tin, where the savages painted themselves blue and believed stones to be sacred, not having anything else, the poor bastards. The refrain of the poem was *What will become of me?* which she changed to *What will become of them?* until she realized that nothing at all would become of them, for they did not have to understand her. *But I*, she thought, *will have to understand them.*

And then, sang the merchants of Tyre, that great city, *what, O God, will become of me?*

*

She had no trouble controlling them the next day; they were much too afraid of her. Gunnar, however, plainly admired her and this made her furious. She was getting into her stride now, over the easy snow, getting used to the pack resting on some queer contraption not on her back but on her hips, as they all did, and finding the snow easy to walk over. The sun of Paradise shone in an impossibly blue sky, which she found upsetting. But the air was good; the air was wonderful. She was getting used to walking. She took to outpacing them, long-legged as they were, and sitting in the snow twenty meters away, cross-legged like a monk, until they caught up, then watching them expressionlessly—like a trail-marker—until they passed her, casting back looks that were far from pleasant; and then re-peating the whole thing all over again. After the noon meal she stopped that; it was too cruel. They sat down in the mid-dle of a kind of tilted wasteland—it was the side of a hill but one's up-and-down got easily mixed in the mountains—and ate everything in the plastic bags marked Two-B, none of it dried and all of it magnificent; Alyx had never had such food in her life on a trip before: fruits and spicy little buns, things like sausages, curls of candy that sprung round your finger and smelled of ginger, and for drinking, the bags you filled with snow and hung inside your suit to melt. Chilly, but efficient. She ate half of everything and put the rest back, out of habit. With venomous looks, everybody else ate everything. "She's tinier than we are," Gunnar said, trying to smooth things over, "and I'm sure there's more than enough!" Alyx reached inside her suit and scratched one arm. "There may not be enough," she said, "can't tell," and returned the rest to her pack, won-dering why you couldn't trust adults to eat one meal at a time without marking it with something. She could not actually read the numbers. But perhaps it was a custom or a ritual. *A primitive ritual*, she thought. She was in much better spirits. *A primitive ritual*, she repeated to herself, *practiced through inveterate and age-old superstition*. She dearly longed to play with the curly candy again. She suddenly remembered the ep-igram made one Mediterranean evening by the Prince of Tyre on the palace roof over a game of chess and began sponta-neously to tell it to them, with all that had accompanied it: the sails in the bay hanging disembodied and white like the flowers in the royal garden just before the last light goes, the smell of the bay at low tide, not as bad as inlanders think but oddly stimulating, bringing to one's mind the complex processes of decay and life, the ins and outs of things, the ins and outs of herself who could speak six dialects from the gutter to the palace, and five languages, one of them the old Egyptian; and how she had filched the rather valuable chess set later, for the Tyrians were more than a little ostentatious despite their reputation for tough-mindedness, odd people, the adventurers, the traders, the merchants of the Mediterranean, halfway in their habits between the cumbersome dignities of royal Egypt and the people of Crete, who knew how to live if anyone ever had, decorating their eggshell-thin bowls with sea-creatures made unbelievably graceful or with musicians lying in beds of anemones and singing and playing on the flute. She laughed and quoted the epigram itself, which had been superb, a double pun in two languages, almost a pity to deprive a man like that of a chess set worth—

Nobody was listening. She turned around and stared at them. For a moment she could not think, only smell and stare, and then something shifted abruptly inside her head and she could name them again: Gunnar, Machine, Raydos, Maudey, Iris, Gavrily, the two nuns. She had been talking in her own language. They shambled along, leaning forward against the pull of the hip-packs, ploughing up the snow in their exhaustion, these huge, soft people to whom one could not say anything of any consequence. Their faces were drawn with fatigue. She motioned them to stop and they toppled down into the snow without a word, Iris's cheek right in the cold stuff itself and the two nuns collapsed across each other in a criss-cross. They had worn, she believed, a symbol on a chain around their necks something like the symbol . . . but she did not want to fall back into her own speech again. She felt extremely stupid. "I am sorry that you're tired," she said.

"No, no," muttered Gunnar, his legs straight out in the snow, staring ahead.

"We'll take a break," she said, wondering where the phrase had come from all of a sudden. The sun was hardly halfway down in the sky. She let them rest for an hour or more until

they began to talk; then she forced them to their feet and began it all again, the nightmare of stumbling, slipping, sliding,
the unmistakable agonies of plodding along with cramped legs
and a drained body, the endless pull of the weight at one's
back. . . . She remembered what the lieutenant had said
about people deprived of their electromagnetic spectrum.
Long before nightfall she stopped them and let them revive
while she scouted around for animal tracks—or human tracks
—or anything—but found nothing. Paradise was a winter
sportsman's—well, paradise. She asked about animals, but nobody knew for certain or nobody was telling, although Gunnar volunteered the information that Paradise had not been
extensively mapped. Maudey complained of a headache. They
ate again, this time from a bag marked Two-C, still with nothing dried (*Why carry all that weight in water?* Alyx thought,
remembering how the desert people would ride for weeks on
nothing but ground wheat), stowed empty, deflated Two-C
into their packs and lay down—right in the middle of a vast,
empty snow-field. It gave them all the chills. Alyx lay a little
apart, to let them talk about her as she was sure they would,
and then crept closer. They were talking about her. She made a
face and retreated again. A little later she got them up and into
the hills above until at sunset it looked as if they would have
to sleep in the open. She left them huddled together and went
looking about for a cave, but found nothing, until, coming
around the path at the edge of a rather sharp drop, she met
Machine coming the other way.

"What the devil—!" she exclaimed, planting herself in his
way, arms akimbo, face tilted up to look into his.

"Cave," he said blandly and walked up the side of the hill
with his long legs, around above her, and down on to the path.
He even got back to the others faster than she did, though
sweat was running from under his hood.

"All right," said Alyx as she rejoined them, "it's found a
cave," but she found them all standing up ready to go, most
yawning, all trying not to stagger, and Gunnar beaming heartily in a way that made her wish she had hit him lower down,
much lower down, when she had the chance. *Professional*, she
thought. "He told us," said Maudey with her head in the air,
"before you came," and the troop of them marched—more

or less—after the bald-headed boy, who had found a shallow depression in the rock where they could gather in relative comfort. If there had been a wind, although there was no wind on Paradise, the place would have sheltered them; if it had been snowing, although it was not snowing on Paradise, the place would have protected them; and if anyone had been looking for them, although apparently no one was, the place would have afforded a partial concealment. They all got together; they sat down; some of them threw back their hoods; and then they began to talk. They talked and talked and talked. They discussed whether Maudey had behaved impatiently towards Iris, or whether Iris had tried to attract Gunnar, or whether the nuns were participating enough in the group interaction, with due allowance made for their religious faith, of course, and whether the relationship between Raydos and Gunnar was competitive, and what Gavrily felt about the younger men, and whether he wanted to sleep with Iris, and on and on and on about how they felt about each other and how they ought to feel about each other and how they had felt about each other with an insatiability that stunned Alyx and a wealth of detail that fascinated her, considering that all these interactions had been expressed by people staggering with fatigue, under a load of eleven kilos per person, and exposed to a great deal of unaccustomed exercise. She felt sorry for Machine. She wished she had a Trivia herself. She lay at the mouth of the cave until she could not stand it; then she retreated to the back and lay on her stomach until her elbows galled her; then she took off into the snow in front of the cave where there was a little light and lay on her back, watching the strange stars.

"We do it all the time, I'm afraid," said a man's voice beside her. *Raydos*, she thought instantly. *Machine would have said "they."*

"It doesn't—" he went on, "it doesn't mean—well, it doesn't mean anything, really. It's a kind of habit."

She said nothing.

"I came out," he said, "to apologize for us and to ask you about the watch. I've explained it to the others. I will take the first watch.

"I have read about such things," he added proudly.

Still she said nothing.

"I wish you would repeat to me," he went on slowly, and she realized he was trying to talk simply to her, "what you said this morning in the other language."

"I can't," she said, and then she added, feeling stupid, "the witty saying of . . . of the Prince of Tyre."

"The epigram," he said patiently.

"Epigram," she repeated.

"What did the Prince of Tyre say?"

"He said," she translated, feeling her way desperately, "that in any . . . time . . . any time you . . . have something, whatever tendencies—whatever factors in a situation you have, whatever of these can—can unpredict—"

"Can go wrong," said he.

"Can go wrong," she parroted, caught halfway between two worlds. "Can wrong itself. It—" but here the man beside her burst into such a roar of laughter that she turned to look at him.

"The proverbial Third Law," he said. "Whatever can go wrong, will," and he burst into laughter again. He was big, but they were all big; in the faint glimmer of the snow-field . . .

His hood was back; his hair was pale.

Gunnar.

Alone once more, she lay several meters farther out with her arms wrapped about herself, thinking a bit savagely that the "witty saying" of His Highness had been expressed in two words, not five, both of them punning, both rhymed and each with a triple internal assonance that exactly contrasted with the other.

Damned barbarians! she snapped to herself, and fell asleep.

The next day it began to snow, the soft, even snow of Paradise, hiding their footprints and the little bags of excrement they buried here and there. The insulated suits were ingenious. Her people began to talk to her, just a little, condescendingly but trying to be affable, more and more cheerful as they neared Point B, where they would need her no more, where she could dwindle into a memory, an anecdote, a party conversation: "Did you know, I once met the most *fascinating*—" They really had very little imagination, Alyx thought. In their place she would be asking everything: where she came from, who she

was, how she lived, the desert people who worshiped the wind
god, what the Tyrians ate, their economic system, their families, their beliefs, their feelings, their clothes, the Egyptians, the
Minoans, how the Minoans made those thin, dyed bowls, how
they traded ostrich eggs and perfumes from Egypt, what sort of
ships they sailed, how it felt to rob a house, how it felt to cut a
throat. . . . But all they did was talk about themselves.

"You ought to have cosmetic surgery," said Maudey. "I've
had it on my face and my breasts. It's ingenious. Of course I
had a good doctor. And you have to be careful dyeing eyebrows and eyelashes, although the genetic alterations are usually pretty stable. But they might *spread*, you know. Can you
imagine having a *blue forehead*?"

"I ran away from home," said Iris, "at the age of fifteen and
joined a Youth Core. Almost everyone has Youth Cores, although mine wasn't a delinquent Youth Core and some people
will tell you that doesn't count. But let me tell you, it changed
my life. It's better than hypnotic psychotherapy. They call it a
Core because it forms the core of your adolescent rebellion,
don't you see, and I would have been nobody without it, absolutely nobody, it changed my whole life and all my values. Did
you ever run away from home?"

"Yes," said Alyx. "I starved."

"Nobody starves any more," said Iris. "A Youth Core to fit
each need. I joined a middle-status Youth Core. Once you're
past fourteen you needn't drag—um—your family into everything. We forget about that. It's much better."

"Some people call me a Conamon," said Gavrily, "but where
would we be without them? There are commercial wars and
wars; you know all about that. The point is there are no more
wars. I mean real wars. That would be a terrible thing. And if
you get caught in a commercial war, it's your own fault, you see.
Mixed interests. Mixed economy. I deal in people. Sounds bad,
doesn't it? Some people would say I manage people, but *I* say I
help them. I work *with* them. I form values. Can you imagine
what it would be like without us? No one to bring your group
interests to. No one to mediate between you and the army or
you and business or you and government. Why, there wouldn't
be any local government, really, though of course I'm not Gov;
I'm Con. Mixed interests. It's the only way."

"Wrap-arounds!" said Raydos contemptuously. "Anybody can build a wrap-around. Simplest thing in the world. The problem is to recover the purity of the medium—I hope I'm not boring you—and to recover the purity of the medium you have to withdraw within its boundaries, not stretch them until they crack. I've done environments until I'm sick of them. I want something you can walk around, not something that walks around you. Lights geared to heartbeats, drug combinations, vertigo—I'm through with all that; it's mere vulgarity. Have you ever tried to draw something? Just draw something? Wait a minute; stand still." (And he sketched a few lines on a piece of paper.) "There! *That's* avant-garde for you!"

"The consciousness," said the nuns, speaking softly one after the other, "must be expanded to include the All. That is the only true church. Of course, that is what *we* believe. We do not wish to force our beliefs on others. We are the ancient church of consciousness and Buddha, nearly six hundred years old; I do hope that when we get back you'll attend a service with us. Sex is only part of the ceremony. The drugs are the main part. Of course we're not using them now, but we do carry them. The lieutenant knew we would never touch them. Not while there's the possibility of violence. The essence of violence violates consciousness while the consciousness of expanded consciousness correlates with the essence of the All which is Love, extended Love and the deepening and expanding of experience implied by the consciousness-expanded consciousness."

"You *do* understand," they chorused anxiously, "don't you?"

"Yes," said Alyx, "perfectly."

Gunnar talked passionately about electronics.

"Now there must be some way," he said, "to neutralize this electromagnetic watch-grid they've set up or to polarize it. Do you think polarization would ring the alarm? It might be damn fun! We're only behaving like parts of the landscape now—you *will* stop me if you don't understand, won't you —but there must be regions in the infra-bass where the shock waves—damn! Paradise doesn't have faults and quakes—well, then, the ultra-hard—they must have the cosmic rays down to the twentieth place—somehow— If I had only brought—you know, I think I could rig up some kind of interference—of course they'd spot that—but just think of the equipment—"

Machine said nothing at all. She took to walking with Machine. They walked through the soft, falling snow of Paradise in absolute silence under a sky that dropped feathers like the sky in a fairy tale, like a sky she had never seen before that made endless pillows and hummocks of the rounded stones of Paradise, stones just large enough to sit on, as if someone had been before them all the way providing armchairs and tables. Machine was very restful. On the tenth day she took his arm and leaned against him briefly; on the eleventh day he said:

"Where do you come from?"

"I come," she said softly, "from great cities and palaces and back-alleys and cemeteries and rotten ships.

"And where," she added, "do you come from?"

"Nowhere!" said Machine—and he spat on the snow.

On the sixteenth day of their ten-day journey they found Base B. Everyone had been excited all day—"picnicky" Alyx called it. Maudey had been digging her fingers into her hair and lamenting the absence of something called an electric tease; Gavrily was poking both women, a little short of breath; and Gunnar displayed his smile—that splendid smile—a little too often to be accounted for by the usual circumstances and laughed a good deal to himself.

"Oh golly, oh gosh, oh golly, oh golly, oh gosh!" sang Iris.

"Is that what they taught you at your Core?" said Raydos dryly.

"Yes," said Iris sniffishly. "*Do* you mind?" and she went on singing the words while Raydos made a face. "Didn't you go to a Core?" said Iris and when Raydos informed her that he had gone to a School (whatever that was) instead, Iris sang "Oh golly, oh gosh" so loud that Alyx told her to stop.

"Animals don't sing," said Alyx.

"Well, I hope you're not being moralistic—" Iris began.

"Animals," said Alyx, "don't sing. People sing. People can be caught. People can be killed. Stop singing."

"But we're so near," said Gunnar.

"Come on," said Gavrily. He began to run. Maudey was shepherding the nuns, chattering excitedly; everything was there—the line of boulders, the hill, a little dip in the snow, up another hill (a steep one this time) and there was Base B.

Everybody could go home now. It was all over. They ran up to the top of the hill and nearly tumbled over one another in confusion, Gavrily with his arms spread out against the sky, one of the nuns fallen on one knee and Iris nearly knocking Maudey over.

Base B was gone. In the little dell where there should have been a metal shed with a metal door leading underground, to safety, to home, to the Army, to a room where the ceiling whirled so familiarly ("a little bit of home") and coiled thingamajigs which ate whatever you dropped on the grassy floor, there was no metal shed and no metal door. There was something like a splotch of metal foil smashed flat and a ragged hole in the middle of it, and as they watched, something indeterminate came out of the hole. There was a faint noise in the sky.

"Scatter!" cried Alyx. "Down on your knees!" and as they stood there gaping, she slammed the three nearest across the face and then the others so that when the air vehicle—no one looked up to get a clear view of it—came barreling over the horizon, they were all down on their hands and knees, pretending to be animals. Alyx got down just in time. When the thing had gone, she dared to look into the dell again, where the indeterminate thing had split into four things, which stood at the edges of an exact square while a box the size of a small room floated slowly down between them. The moment it landed they burrowed into it, or were taking it apart; she could not tell. "Lie flat," said Alyx softly. "Don't talk. Gunnar, use your binoculars." *No decent knife*, she thought wryly, *not even a fire, but these marvelous things we do have.*

"I don't see—" began Iris spiritedly.

"Shut up," said Alyx. He was focusing the binoculars. She knew about lenses because she had learned to do it with her own pair. Finally he took them away from his eyes and stared for a few moments into the snow. Then he said, "You can stand up now."

"Is it safe?" cried one of the nuns. "Can we go down now?"

"The snow makes it hard to see," said Gunnar slowly, "but I do not think so. No, I do not think so. Those are commercial usuforms, unpacking a food storage container. They are not Army. Army never uses commercial equipment."

"I think," he said, "that Base B has been taken," and he began quite openly and unashamedly to cry. The snow of Paradise (for it had begun to snow) fell on his cheeks and mingled with his tears, fell as beautifully as feathers from pillows, as if Hera were shaking out the feather quilts of Heaven while the amateur explorer cried and the seven people who had looked to him as their last hope looked first at each other—but there was no help there—and finally—hesitantly—but frightened, oh were they frightened!—at Alyx.

"All right," she said, "it's my show.

"Come on, come on!" she snapped, with all the contempt she could muster, "what's the matter with the lot of you? You're not dead; you're not paralyzed; look alive, will you? I've been in tighter spots than this and I've come out; you there" (she indicated Machine) "pinch them awake, will you! Oh, *will* you snap out of it!" and she shook Gunnar violently, thinking him the most likely to have already recovered. He, at least, had cried. She felt surrounded by enormous puppies.

"Yes—yes—I'm all right," he said at last.

"Listen," she said, "I want to know about those things. When will there be another air vehicle?"

"I don't know," he said.

"How long will it take them to unpack, unload, whatever?"

"About . . . about an hour, I think," he said.

"Then there won't be another box for an hour," she said. "How far can they see?"

"See?" said Gunnar helplessly.

"How far can they perceive, then?" persisted Alyx. "Perceive, you idiot, look, see, hear, touch—what the devil, you know what I mean!"

"They—they perceive," said Gunnar slowly, taking a deep breath, "at about three meters. Four meters. They're meant for close work. They're a low form."

"How do you kill them?"

He indicated the center of his chest.

"Can we do it with a crossbow?" she said.

"Ye-es," he said, "very close range, but—"

"Good. If one of them goes, what happens?"

"I'm not sure," he said, sitting up abruptly. "I think nothing would happen for a few seconds. They've—" (he lifted the binoculars to his eyes again) "they've established some kind of unloading pattern. They seem to be working pretty independently. That model—if it is that model—would let one of them lie maybe fifteen-twenty seconds before radioing down for a removal . . . Perhaps longer. They might simply change the pattern."

"And if all four went dead?"

"Why, nothing would happen," he said, "nothing at all. Not —not for about half an hour. Maybe more. Then they'd begin to wonder downstairs why the stuff wasn't coming in. But we do have half an hour."

"So," said Alyx, "you come with me. And Machine. And—"

"I'll come!" said Iris, clasping her hands nervously. Alyx shook her head. "If you're discriminating against me," said Iris wonderingly, "because I'm a *girl*—"

"No, dear, you're a lousy shot," said Alyx. "Gunnar, you take that one; Machine, that one; I take two. All of you! If they fall and nothing happens, you come down that slope like hell and if something does happen, you go the other way twice as fast! We need food. I want dried stuff, light stuff; you'll recognize it, I won't. Everything you can carry. And keep your voices down. Gunnar, what's—"

"Calories," said Machine.

"Yes, yes, lots of that," said Alyx impatiently, "that—that stuff. Come on," and she started down the slope, waving the other two to circle the little dell. Piles of things—they could not see very well through the falling snow—were growing on each side of the box. The box seemed to be slowly collapsing. The moving things left strange tracks, half-human, half-ploughed; she crossed one of them where a thing had wandered up the side of the hollow for some reason of its own. She hoped they did not do that often. She found her bare hands sweating on the stock of the bow, her gloves hanging from her wrists; *if only they had been men!* she thought, and not things that could call for help in a silent voice called radio, or fall down and not be dead, or you didn't know whether they were dead or not. Machine was in position. Gunnar raised his bow. They began to close in silently and slowly until Gunnar stopped; then she sighted on the first and shot. They were headless, with a square protuberance in the middle of the "chest" and an assemblage of many coiled arms that ended in pincers, blades, hooks, what looked like plates. It went down, silently. She turned for the second, carefully reloading the bow, only to find Machine waving and grinning. He had got two. The fourth was also flat on the ground. They ran towards the big box, Alyx involuntarily closing her eyes as she passed the disabled things; then they leaned against the big box, big as a room. Piles of boxes, piles of plastic bladders, bags, cartons, long tubes, stoppers, things that looked like baby round cheese. She waved an arm in the air violently. The others came running, skidding, stumbling down the slope. They began to pick up things under Gunnar's direction and stuff them into each other's packs, whispering a little, talking endlessly, while Alyx squatted down in the snow and kept her bow trained dead-steady on that hole in the ground. There was probably not much sense in doing so, but she did it anyway. She was convinced it was the proper thing to do. Someone was enthusiastically stuffing something into her pack; "Easy, easy," she said, and sighted on that hole in the ground, keeping her aim decent and listening for any improper sounds from above or below until someone said in her ear, "We're done," and she took off immediately up the slope, not looking back. It took the others several minutes to catch up with her. *Thank God it's snowing!* she thought. She counted them. It was all right.

"Now!" she gasped. "We're going into the mountains. Double quick!" and all the rest of the day she pushed them until they were ready to drop, up into the foothills among the increasingly broken rocks where they had to scramble on hands and knees and several people tore holes in their suits. The cold got worse. There were gusts of wind. She took them the long way round, by pure instinct, into the worst kind of country, the place where no one trying to get anywhere—or trying to escape—would go, in a strange, doubled, senseless series of turns and re-turns, crossing their path once, up over obstacles and then in long, leisurely curves on the flattest part of the hills. She kept carefully picturing their relation to the abandoned Base B, telling herself *They'll know someone was there*; and then repeating obsessively *Part of the landscape, part of the landscape* and driving them all the harder, physically shoving them along, striking them, prodding them, telling them in the ugliest way she could that they would die, that they would be eaten, that their minds would be picked, that they would be crippled, deformed, tortured, that they would die, that they would die, die, die, and finally that she would kill them herself if they stopped, if they stopped for a moment, kill them, scar their faces for life, disembowel them, and finally she had to all but torture them herself, bruise them and pinch them in the nerves she alone knew about until it was less painful to go on than to be goaded constantly, to be terrified, to be slapped and threatened and beaten. At sundown she let them collapse out in the open and slept immediately herself. Two hours later she woke up. She shook Gunnar.

"Gunnar!" she said. He came awake with a kind of convulsive leap, struggling horribly. She put an arm around him, crawling tiredly through the snow and leaned against him to quiet him. She felt herself slipping off again and jerked awake. He had his head in both hands, pressing his temples and swinging his head from side to side.

"Gunnar!" she said, "you are the only one who knows anything about this place. Where do we go?"

"All right, all right," he said. He was swaying a little. She reached under the cuff of his suit and pinched the skin on the inside of his forearm; his eyes opened and he looked at her.

"Where . . . what?" he said.

"Where do we go? Is there any neutral area in this—this place?"

"One moment," he said, and he put his head in his hands again. Then he looked up, awake. "I know," he said, "that there is a control Embassy somewhere here. There is always at least one. It's Military, not Gov; you wouldn't understand that but it doesn't matter. We'd be safe there."

"Where is it?" she said.

"I think," he said, "that I know where it is. It's nearer the Pole, I think. Not too far. A few hours by aircraft, I think. Three hours."

"How long," said she, "on foot?"

"Oh," he said, slipping down into the snow onto one arm, "maybe—maybe twice this. Or a little more. Say five hundred kilometers."

"How long," said she insistently, "is that?"

"Oh not much," he said, yawning and speaking fuzzily. "Not much . . . two hours by aircraft." He smiled. "You might have heard it called," he said, "three hundred *miles*, I think. Or a little less." And he rolled over on his side and went to sleep.

Well, that's not so bad, she thought, half asleep, forgetting them all for the moment and thinking only of herself. *Fourteen, fifteen days, that's all. Not bad*. She looked around. Paradise had begun to blow up a little, covering the farthest of her charges with drifts of snow: eight big, fit people with long, long legs. *Oh God of Hell!* she thought suddenly. *Can I get them to do ten miles a day? Is it three hundred miles? A month? Four hundred? And food*—! so she went and kicked Machine awake, telling him to keep the first watch, then call Iris, and have Iris call her.

"You know," she said, "I owe you something."

He said nothing, as usual.

"When I say 'shoot one,'" said Alyx, "I mean shoot one, not two. Do you understand?"

Machine smiled slightly, a smile she suspected he had spent many years in perfecting: cynical, sullen, I-can-do-it-and-you-can't smile. A thoroughly nasty look. She said:

"You stupid bastard, I might have killed you by accident trying to make that second shot!" and leaning forward, she slapped him backhanded across the face, and then the other way forehand as a kind of afterthought because she was tired. She did it very hard. For a moment his face was only the face of a young man, a soft face, shocked and unprotected. Tears sprang to his eyes. Then he began to weep, turning his face away and putting it down on his knees, sobbing harder and harder, clutching at his knees and pressing his face between them to hide his cries, rocking back and forth, then lying on his face with his hands pressed to his eyes, crying out loud to the stars. He subsided slowly, sobbing, calming down, shaken by less and less frequent spasms of tears, and finally was quiet. His face was wet. He lay back in the snow and stretched out his arms, opening his hands loosely as if he had finally let go of something. He smiled at her, quite genuinely. He looked as if he loved her. "Iris," he said.

"Yes, baby," she said, "Iris," and walked back to her place before anything else could happen. There was a neutral place up there—somewhere—if they could find it—where they would be taken in—if they could make it—and where they would be safe—if they could get to it. If they lived.

And if only they don't drown me between the lot of them, she thought irrationally. And fell asleep.

Paradise was not well mapped, as she found out the next morning with Gunnar's help. He did not know the direction. She asked him about the stars and the sun and the time of year, doing some quick calculating, while everyone else tumbled the contents of their packs into the snow, sorting food and putting it back with low-toned remarks that she did not bother to listen to. The snow had lightened and Paradise had begun to blow up a little with sharp gusts that made their suit jackets flap suddenly now and again.

"Winter has begun," said Alyx. She looked sharply at the explorer. "How cold does it get?"

He said he did not know. They stowed back into their packs the detail maps that ended at Base B (*Very efficient,* she thought) because there was no place to bury them among the rocks. They were entirely useless. The other members of the party were eating breakfast—making faces—and Alyx literally had to stand over them while they ate, shutting each bag or box much against the owner's will, even prying those big hands loose (though they were all afraid of her) and then doling out the food she had saved to all of them. The cold had kept it fairly fresh. She told them they would be traveling for three weeks. She ate a couple of handfuls of some dried stuff herself and decided it was not bad. She was regarded dolefully and sulkily by seven pairs of angry eyes.

"Well?" she said.

"It tastes like—like crams," said Iris.

"It's junk," said Gavrily gravely, "dried breakfast food. Made of grains. And some other things."

"Some of it's hard as rocks," said Maudey.

"That's starch," said Raydos, "dried starch kernels."

"I don't know what dried starch kernels is," said Maudey with energy, "but I know what it tastes like. It tastes like—"

"You will put the dried kernels," said Alyx, "or anything else that is hard-as-rocks in your water bottles, where it will stop being hard as rocks. Double handful, please. That's for dinner."

"What do we eat for lunch?" said Iris.

"More junk," said Raydos. "No?"

"Yes," said Alyx. "More junk."

"Kernels," said Raydos, "by the way," and they all got up from the ground complaining, stiff as boards and aching in the joints. She told them to move about a bit but to be careful how they bent over; then she asked those with the torn suits whether they could mend them. Under the skin of the suits was something like thistledown but very little of it, and under that a layer of something silver. You could really sleep in the damn things. People were applying tape to themselves when there was a noise in the air; all dropped heavily to their hands and knees, some grunting—though not on purpose—and the aircraft passed over in the direction of what Alyx had decided to call the south. The equator, anyway. Far to the south and very fast. *Part of the landscape*, she thought. She got them to their feet again, feeling like a coal-heaver, and praised them, saying they had been very quick. Iris looked pleased. Maudey, who was patching up an arm, did not appear to notice; Gavrily was running a tape-strip down the shoulder of one of the nuns and the other was massaging Raydos's back where he had apparently strained something in getting up or down. He looked uncomfortable and uncaring. Gunnar had the professional smile on his face. *My dog*, she thought. Machine was relieving himself off to one side and kicking snow over the spot. He then came over and lifted one cupped hand to his forehead, as if he were trying to take away a headache, which she did not understand. He looked disappointed.

"That's a salute," said Raydos. He grimaced a little and moved his shoulders.

"A what?" said she.

"Army," said Raydos, moving off and flexing his knees. Machine did it again. He stood there expectantly so she did it, too, bringing up one limp hand to her face and down again. They stood awkwardly, smiling at one another, or not perhaps awkwardly, only waiting, until Raydos stuck his tall head over her shoulder and said, "Army salute. He admires the army. I think he likes you," and Machine turned his back instantly, everything going out of his face.

I cannot, thought Alyx, *tell that bum to shut up merely for clearing up a simple point. On the other hand, I cannot possibly— and if I have to keep restraining myself—I will not let—I cannot, will not, will not let that interfering fool—*

Iris burst into pure song.

"OH, SHUT UP!" shouted Alyx, "FOR GOD'S SAKE!" and marshaled them into some kind of line, abjuring them for Heaven's sake to hurry up and be quiet. She wished she had never gotten into this. She wished three or four of them would die and make it easier for her to keep track of them. She wished several would throw themselves off cliffs. She wished there were cliffs they could throw themselves off of. She was imagining these deaths in detail when one of them loomed beside her and an arm slid into hers. It was Raydos.

"I won't interfere again," he said, "all right?" and then he faded back into the line, silent, uncaring, as if Machine's thoughts had somehow become his own. Perhaps they were swapping minds. It occurred to her that she ought to ask the painter to apologize to the boy, not for interfering, but for talking about him as if he weren't there; then she saw the two of them (she thought it was them) conferring briefly together. Perhaps it had been done. She looked up at the bleary spot in the sky that was the sun and ran down the line, motioning them all to one side, telling them to keep the sun to their left and that Gunnar would show them what constellations to follow that night, if it was clear. Don't wander. Keep your eyes open. Think. Watch it. Machine joined her and walked silently by her side, his eyes on his feet. Paradise, which had sloped gently, began to climb, and they climbed with it, some of them falling down. She went to the head of the line and led them for an hour, then dropped back to allow Gunnar, the amateur mountain-climber, to lead the way. She discussed directions with him. The wind was getting worse. Paradise began to show bare rock. They stopped for a cold and miserable lunch and Alyx saw that everyone's bow was unsprung and packed, except for hers; "Can't have you shooting yourselves in the feet," she said. She told Gunnar it might look less suspicious if. "If," he said. Neither finished the thought. They tramped through the afternoon, colder and colder, with the sun receding early into the mountains, struggled on, climbing slopes that a professional would have laughed at. They found the hoof-prints of something like a goat and Alyx thought *I could live on this country for a year*. She dropped back in the line and joined Machine again, again silent, unspeaking for hours. Then suddenly she said:

"What's a pre-school conditioning director?"

"A teacher," said Machine in a surprisingly serene voice, "of very small children."

"It came into my mind," she said, "all of a sudden, that I was a *pre-school conditioning director*."

"Well, you are," he said gravely, "aren't you?"

He seemed to find this funny and laughed on and off, quietly, for the rest of the afternoon. She did not.

That was the night Maudey insisted on telling the story of her life. She sat in the half-gloom of the cave they had found, clasping her hands in front of her, and went through a feverish and unstoppable list of her marriages: the line marriage, the double marriage, the trial marriage, the period marriage, the group marriage. Alyx did not know what she was talking about. Then Maudey began to lament her troubles with her unstable self-image and at first Alyx thought that she had no soul and therefore no reflection in a mirror, but she knew that was nonsense; so soon she perceived it was one of *their points* (by then she had taken to classifying certain things as *their points*) and tried not to listen, as all gathered around Maudey and analyzed her self-image, using terms Trans-Temp had apparently left out of Alyx's vocabulary, perhaps on purpose. Gunnar was especially active in the discussion. They crowded around her, talking solemnly while Maudey twisted her hands in the middle, but nobody touched her; it occurred to Alyx that although several of them had touched herself, they did not seem to like to get too close to one another. Then it occurred to her that there was something odd in Maudey's posture and something unpleasantly reminiscent in the breathiness of her voice; she decided Maudey had a fever. She wormed her way into the group and seized the woman by the arm, putting her other hand on Maudey's face, which was indeed unnaturally hot.

"She's sick," said Alyx.

"Oh no," said everybody else.

"She's got a fever," said Alyx.

"No, no," said one of the nuns, "it's the drug."

"What—drug?" said Alyx, controlling her temper. How these people could manage to get into such scrapes—

"It's Re-Juv," said Gavrily. "She's been taking Re-Juv and of course the withdrawal symptoms don't come on for a couple of weeks. But she'll be all right."

"It's an unparalleled therapeutic opportunity," said the other nun. Maudey was moaning that nobody cared about her, that nobody had ever paid any attention to her, and whereas other people's dolls were normal when they were little, hers had only had a limited stock of tapes and could only say the same things over and over, just like a person. She said she had always known it wasn't real. No one touched her. They urged her to integrate this perception with her unstable self-image.

"Are you going," said Alyx, "to let her go on like that *all night*?"

"We wouldn't think of stopping her," said Gavrily in a shocked voice and they all went back to talking. "Why wasn't your doll alive?" said one of the nuns in a soft voice. "Think, now; tell us, why do you feel—" Alyx pushed past two of them to try to touch the woman or take her hand, but at this point Maudey got swiftly up and walked out of the cave.

"Eight gods and seven devils!" shouted Alyx in her own language. She realized a nun was clinging to each arm.

"Please don't be distressed," they said, "she'll come back," like twins in unison, only one actually said "She'll return" and the other "She'll come back." Voices pursued her from the cave, everlastingly those damned voices; she wondered if they knew how far an insane woman could wander in a snowstorm. Insane she was, drug or no drug; Alyx had seen too many people behave too oddly under too many different circumstances to draw unnecessary distinctions. She found Maudey some thirty meters along the rock-face, crouching against it.

"Maudey, you must come back," said Alyx.

"Oh, I know *you*," said Maudey, in a superior tone.

"You will get lost in the snow," said Alyx softly, carefully freeing one hand from its glove, "and you won't be comfortable and warm and get a good night's sleep. Now come along."

Maudey smirked and cowered and said nothing.

"Come back and be comfortable and warm," said Alyx. "Come back and go to sleep. Come, dear; come on, dear," and she caught Maudey's arm with her gloved hand and with the other pressed a blood vessel at the base of her neck. The woman passed out immediately and fell down in the snow. Alyx kneeled over her, holding one arm back against the joint, just in case Maudey should decide to get contentious. *And how*, she thought, *do you get her back now when she weighs twice as much as you, clever one?* The wind gave them a nasty shove, then gusted in the other direction. Maudey was beginning to stir. She was saying something louder and louder; finally Alyx heard it.

"I'm a living doll," Maudey was saying, "I'm a living doll, I'm a living doll, I'm a living doll!" interspersed with terrible sobs.

They do tell the truth, thought Alyx, *sometimes*. "You," she said firmly, "are a woman. A woman. A woman."

"I'm a doll!" cried Maudey.

"You," said Alyx, "are a woman. A woman with dyed hair. A silly woman. But a woman. A woman!"

"No I'm not," said Maudey stubbornly, like an older Iris.

"Oh, you're a damned fool!" snapped Alyx, peering nervously about and hoping that their voices would not attract anything. She did not expect people, but she knew that where there are goats or things like goats there are things that eat the things that are like goats.

"Am I damned?" said Maudey. "What's damned?"

"Lost," said Alyx absently, and slipping her gloved hand free, she lifted the crossbow from its loop on her back, loaded it and pointed it away at the ground. Maudey was wiggling her freed arm, with an expression of pain. "You hurt me," she said. Then she saw the bow and sat up in the snow, terrified, shrinking away.

"Will you shoot me, will you shoot me?" she cried.

"Shoot you?" said Alyx.

"You'll shoot me, you hate me!" wailed Maudey, clawing at the rock-face. "You hate me, you hate me, you'll kill me!"

"I think I will," said Alyx simply, "unless you go back to the cave."

"No, no, no," said Maudey.

"If you don't go back to the cave," said Alyx carefully, "I am going to shoot you," and she drove the big woman in front of her, step by step, back along the narrow side of the mountain, back on her own tracks that the snow had already half-obliterated, back through Paradise to the opening of the cave. She trained the crossbow on Maudey until the woman stepped into the group of people inside; then she stood there, blocking the entrance, the bow in her hand.

"One of you," she said, "tie her wrists together."

"You are doing incalculable harm," said one of the nuns.

"Machine," she said, "take rope from your pack. Tie that woman's wrists together and then tie them to Gavrily's feet and the nuns' feet and Iris's. Give them plenty of room but make the knots fast."

"I hear and obey," said Raydos dryly, answering for the boy, who was apparently doing what she had told him to.

"You and Raydos and I and Gunnar will stand watch," she said.

"What's there to watch, for heaven's sake," muttered Iris. Alyx thought she probably did not like being connected to Maudey in any way at all, not even for safety.

"Really," said Gavrily, "she would have come back, you know! I think you might try to understand that!"

"I would have come back," said Maudey in a surprisingly clear and sensible tone, "of course I would have come back, don't be silly," and this statement precipitated such a clamor of discussion, vilification, self-justification and complaints that Alyx stepped outside the cave with her blood pounding in her ears and her hands grasping the stock of the crossbow. She asked the gods to give her strength, although she did not believe in them and never had. Her jaws felt like iron; she was shaking with fury.

Then she saw the bear. It was not twenty meters away.

"Quiet!" she hissed. They went on talking loudly.

"QUIET!" she shouted, and as the talk died down to an injured and peevish mutter, she saw that the bear—if it was a bear—had heard them and was slowly, curiously, calmly, coming over to investigate. It seemed to be grayish-white, like the snow, and longer in the neck than it should be.

"Don't move," she said very softly, "there is an animal out here," and in the silence that followed she saw the creature hesitate, swaying a little or lumbering from side to side. It might very well pass them by. It stopped, sniffed about and stood there for what seemed three or four minutes, then fell clumsily on to all fours and began to move slowly away.

Then Maudey screamed. Undecided no longer, the animal turned and flowed swiftly towards them, unbelievably graceful over the broken ground and the sharply sloping hillside. Alyx stood very still. She said, "Machine, your bow," and heard Gunnar whisper "Kill it, kill it, why don't you kill it!" The beast was almost upon her. At the last moment she knelt and sent a bolt between its eyes; then she dropped down automatically and swiftly, rolling to one side, dropping the bow. She snatched her knives from both her sleeves and threw herself under the swaying animal, driving up between the ribs first with one hand and then the other. The thing fell on her immediately like a dead weight; it was too enormous, too heavy for her to move; she lay there trying to breathe, slowly blacking out and feeling her ribs begin to give way. Then she fainted and came to to find Gunnar and Machine rolling the enormous carcass off her. She lay, a swarm of black sparks in front of her eyes. Machine wiped the beast's blood off her suit—it came off absolutely clean with a handful of snow—and carried her like a doll to a patch of clean snow where she began to breathe. The blood rushed back to her head. She could think again.

"It's dead," said Gunnar unsteadily, "I think it died at once from the bolt."

"Oh you devils!" gasped Alyx.

"*I* came out at once," said Machine, with some relish. "He didn't." He began pressing his hands rhythmically against her sides. She felt better.

"The boy—the boy put a second bolt in it," said Gunnar, after a moment's hesitation. "I was afraid," he added. "I'm sorry."

"Who let that woman scream?" said Alyx.

Gunnar shrugged helplessly.

"Always know anatomy," said Machine, with astonishing cheerfulness. "You see, the human body is a machine. I know some things," and he began to drag the animal away.

"Wait," said Alyx. She found she could walk. She went over and looked at the thing. It was a bear but like none she had ever seen or heard of: a white bear with a long, snaky neck, almost four meters high if it had chosen to stand. The fur was very thick.

"It's a polar bear," said Gunnar.

She wanted to know what that was.

"It's an Old Earth animal," he said, "but it must have been adapted. They usually live in the sea, I think. They have been stocking Paradise with Old Earth animals. I thought you knew."

"*I did not know*," said Alyx.

"I'm—I'm sorry," he said, "but I never—never thought of it. I didn't think it would matter." He looked down at the enormous corpse. "Animals do not attack people," he said. Even in the dim light she could see his expression; he knew that what he had said was idiotic.

"Oh no," she said deliberately, "oh no, of course not," and kneeling beside the corpse she extracted both her knives, cleaned them in the snow and put them back in the sheaths attached to her forearms under the suit. Convenient not to have water rust the blades. She studied the bear's claws for a few minutes, feeling them and trying as well as she could to see them in the dim light. Then she sent Machine into the cave for Raydos's artists' tools, and choosing the small, thin knife that he used to sharpen his pencils (some day, she thought, she would have to ask him what a pencils was) she slashed the animal's belly and neck, imitating the slash of claws and disguising the wounds made by her knives. She had seen bears fight once, in a circus, and had heard tales of what they did to one another. She hoped the stories had been accurate. With Raydos's knife she also ripped open one of the animal's shoulders and attempted to simulate the bite of its teeth, being careful to open a main artery. The damned thing had such a layer of fat that she had trouble getting to it. When cut, the vessel pumped slowly; there was not the pool of blood there should be, but *What the devil*, she thought, *no one may ever find it and if they do, will they be able to tell the difference? Probably not.* They could dig out the bolts tomorrow. She cleaned Raydos's knife, returned it to Machine and went back to the cave.

No one said a word.

"I have," said Alyx, "just killed a bear. It was eleven feet high and could have eaten the lot of you. If anyone talks loud again, any time, for any reason, I shall ram his unspeakable teeth down his unspeakable throat."

Maudey began to mutter, sobbing a little.

"Machine," she said, "make that woman stop," and she watched, dead tired, while Machine took something from his pack, pressed it to Maudey's nose, and laid her gently on the floor. "She'll sleep," he said.

"That was not kindly done," remarked one of the nuns.

Alyx bit her own hand; she bit it hard, leaving marks; she told Machine, Raydos and Gunnar about the watch; she and they brought more snow into the cave to cushion the others, although the wind had half done their job for them. Everyone was quiet. All the same, she put her fingers in her ears but that pushed her hood back and made her head get cold; then she rolled over against the cave wall. Finally she did what she had been doing for the past seventeen nights. She went out into the snow and slept by herself, against the rock wall two meters from the drop, with Machine nearby, dim and comforting in the falling snow. She dreamed of the sun of the Tyrian seas, of clouds and ships and Mediterranean heat—and then of nothing at all.

The next morning when the East—she had decided to call it the East—brightened enough to see by, Alyx ended her watch. It had begun to clear during the night and the sky was showing signs of turning a pale winter blue, very uncomfortable-looking. She woke Gunnar, making the others huddled near him stir and mutter in their sleep, for it had gotten colder, too, during the night, and with Gunnar she sat down in the snow and went over the contents of their two packs, item by item. She figured that what they had in common everyone would have. She made him explain everything: the sun-glasses, the drugs that slowed you down if you were hurt, the bottle Machine had used that was for unconsciousness in cases of pain, the different kinds of dried foods, the binoculars, a bottle of something you put on wounds to make new flesh (it said "nu-flesh" and she tried to memorize the letters on it), the knives, the grooved barrel of the crossbow (but that impressed her greatly), the water containers, the suit-mending tape, fluff you could add to your suit if you lost fluff from it and a coil of extremely thin, extremely strong rope that she measured by solemnly telling it out from her outstretched hand to her nose and so on and so on and so on until she had figured the length. Gunnar seemed to find this very funny. There was also something that she recognized as long underwear (though she did not think she would bring it to anybody's attention just yet) and at the bottom a packet of something she could not make head or tail of; Gunnar said it was to unfold and clean yourself with.

"Everyone's used theirs up," said he, "I'm afraid."

"A ritual, no doubt," said she, "in this cold. I told them they'd stink."

He sat there, wrinkling his brow for a moment, and then he said:

"There are no stimulants and there are no euphorics."

She asked what those were and he explained. "Ah, a Greek root," she said. He started to talk about how worried he was that there were no stimulants and no euphorics; these should have been included; they could hardly expect them to finish a weekend without them, let alone a seven-weeks' trip; in fact, he said, there was something odd about the whole thing. By now Alyx had ambled over to the dead bear and was digging the bolts out of it; she asked him over her shoulder, "Do *they* travel by night or day?"

"They?" he said, puzzled, and then "Oh, them! No, it makes no difference to them."

"Then it will make no difference to us," she said, cleaning the bolts in the snow. "Can they follow our tracks at night?"

"Why not?" said he, and she nodded.

"Do you think," said he, after a moment's silence, "that they are trying something out on us?"

"They?" she said. "Oh, them! Trans-Temp. Possibly. Quite possibly." *But probably not*, she added to herself, *unfortunately.* And she packed the bolts neatly away.

"*I* think," said Gunnar, skirting the bear's carcass where the blood still showed under the trodden snow, "that it is very odd that we have nothing else with us. I'm inclined to—" (*Good*

Lord, he's nervous, she thought) "I'm inclined to believe," he said, settling ponderously in a clean patch of snow and leaning towards her so as to make himself heard, for he was speaking in a low voice, "that this is some kind of experiment. Or carelessness. Criminal carelessness. When we get back—" and he stopped, staring into the snow.

"If we get back," said Alyx cheerfully, getting to her feet, "you can lodge a complaint or declare a tort, or whatever it is you do. Here," and she handed him a wad of fluff she had picked out of her pack.

"What I should have done last night," she said, "half-obliterating our tracks around the carcass so they don't look so damned human. With luck" (she glanced up) "the snow won't stop for an hour yet."

"How can you tell?" said he, his mouth open.

"Because it is still coming down," said Alyx, and she gave him a push in the back. She had to reach up to do it. He bent and the two of them backed away, drawing the wads of fluff across the snow like brooms. It worked, but not well.

"How about those nuns," said Alyx. "Don't they have some damned thing or other with them?"

"Oh, you have to be careful!" he said in a whisper. "You have to be careful about *that!*" and with this he worked his way to the mouth of the cave.

The sleepers were coming out.

Waking up by themselves for the first time, they filed out of the cave and stood in a row in the opening staring down at the corpse of the animal they had not even seen the night before. She suspected the story had gotten around. *Twenty hand-spans*, she thought, *of bear*. The nuns started back, making some kind of complicated sign on their foreheads and breasts. Raydos bowed admiringly, half ironically. The two older people were plainly frightened, even though Maudey had begun to crane forward for a better look; suddenly her whole body jerked and she flung out one arm; she would have overbalanced herself and fallen if Gavrily had not caught her. "After-effects," he said.

"How long do these go on?" said Alyx, a little wearily.

"A couple of days," he said quickly, holding on to the frightened woman, "only a couple of days. They get better."

"Then take care of her until they do," said Alyx, and she was about to add the usual signal for the morning (COME ON!) when a voice somewhere above her head said:

"Agent?"

It was Iris, that great lolloping girl, almost as high as the bear, looking down at her with the unfathomable expression of the very young, twisting and twisting a lock of silver hair that had escaped from her hood. She was really very pretty.

"Agent," blurted Iris, her eyes big, "will you teach me how to shoot?"

"Yes, my dear," said Alyx, "indeed I will."

"Come on!" she bawled then. They came on.

Later in the morning, when she allowed them to stop and eat the soggiest of their protein and dried starch kernels for breakfast, one of the nuns came up to her, squatted gracefully in the snow and made the complicated sign thrice: once on her own forehead, once on her own breast and once in the air between her and the little woman who had shot the bear.

"Violence," said the nun earnestly, "is deplorable. It is always deplorable. It corrupts love, you see, and love is the expansion of consciousness while violence is the restriction of love so that violence, which restricts love and consciousness, is always bad, as consciousness is always good and the consciousness of the All is the best and only good, and to restrict what may lead to the consciousness of the All is unwise and unkind. Therefore to die is only to merge with the All so that actually violence is not justifiable in the postponing of death, as we must all die, and dying is the final good if it is a dying into the All and not a dying away from it, as in violence.

"But," she said, "the recognition of consciousness and the value of expression of consciousness go hand in hand; there is no evil in expressing the impulses of the nature of consciousness, so that there can be no evil in action and action is not violence. Action is actually an expansion of the consciousness, as one becomes more aware of one's particular true nature and thence slowly more aware of one's ultimate all-embracing Nature which unites one with the All. Action is therefore a good. It is not, of course, the same thing as the true religion, but some of us go the slow path and some the quick, and who will attain Enlightenment first? Who knows? What is, is, as the sage said: One way is not another. I hope you will attend our services when we return home."

"Yes," said Alyx. "Indeed I will." The tall lady made the sign again, this time on Alyx's forehead and breast, and went sedately back to her breakfast.

And that, thought Alyx, *is the damndest way of saying Bravo that I have ever heard!*

She decided to teach them all to shoot, including the nuns. It was understood, of course, that the nuns would shoot only bears.

Later in the afternoon, when the snow had stopped and before visibility became bad, she lined all of them up on a relatively level snow-field, assigning the two nuns to Gunnar, Gavrily and Raydos to Machine and herself teaching Iris. Maudey rested, a little dazed from the nervous spasms that had been shaking her all day, though perfectly clear in her mind. Most of them tired of the business after the first hour, except for Raydos, who seemed to enjoy handling the new thing again, and Iris, who kept saying "Just a little more, just a little more; I'm not good enough." When Machine laughed at her, she loftily explained that it was "rather like dancing."

"Which you have never done for pleasure, I am sure," she added.

During the late afternoon they slogged up an ever-narrowing path between cliffs, towards what Gunnar swore was a pass in the mountains. It seemed, however, as if these mountains had no pass but only plateaus; no, not plateaus, only peaks; that even the peaks had no down but only up, and on and on they kept in the red light of the setting winter sun, holding the glare always to the proper side of them, plodding up a steeper and steeper path until the red light turned purple and dim, and died, until each of them saw the other as a dim hulk marching in front of him.

She called a halt. They sat down. For the first time during the whole trip they bunched together, actually touching body to body, with only Maudey a little away from them, for she was still having her trouble. (Alyx had one of the nuns put her to sleep and the spasms stopped instantly.) It was very cold, with the stars splendid, icy points and the whole tumbled waste of jagged rock shining faintly around them. They did not, as they usually did, begin to analyze the events of the day, but only half-sat, half-lay in silence, feeling the still air around them drain away their warmth, which (Iris said) "seemed to flow right up into the sky." They watched the stars. Then out of nowhere, for no reason at all, Gavrily began to sing in a reedy tenor a few lines of what he called a "baby-song" and this nursery tune—for it was not, Alyx was made to understand, real music—put them all into tears. They sobbed companionably for a little while. It got colder and colder. Gunnar suggested that they pack the snow around them to keep in the heat and Alyx, who had noticed that her buttocks seemed to be the warmest place about her, agreed, so they all built a round wall of snow, with Maudey in the middle of it, and then crawled in around her and pulled the whole thing down on top of them, each packing himself in his own little heap. Then it all had to be disrupted and put right again because the first watch had to climb out. This was Iris. She still seemed very excited, whispering to Alyx "Was I good enough? Will you teach me again?" over and over until somebody poked her and she exclaimed "Ow!" There was yawning, sighing, breathing.

"Will you," said Iris, bending over the little heap of persons, "teach me again? Will you tell me all about yourself? Will you tell me everything? Will you? Will you?"

"Oh, be quiet," said Machine crossly, and Iris took her bow and went a little aside, to sit watch.

It was the eighteenth night.

The nineteenth. The twentieth. The twenty-first. They were very quiet. They were idealizing, trusting, companionable, almost happy. It made Alyx nervous, and the more they looked at her, asked her about her and listened to her the more unnerved she became. She did not think they understood what was happening. She told them about her life with one ear on the sounds about them, instantly alert, ready to spring up, with her crossbow always across her knees; so that they asked her what the matter was. She said "Nothing." She told them legends, fairy tales, religious stories, but they didn't want to hear those; they wanted to hear about her; what she ate, what she drank, what she wore, what her house was like, whom she knew, all the particulars of the business, the alleyways, the gutters, the finest houses and the worst houses in Tyre. She felt it was all being dragged out of her against her will. They were among the mountains now and going very slowly, very badly; they went far into the night now whenever it was clear and as soon as they settled down for the night (everyone had got into the long underwear one clear and frosty morning, hopping about from one bare foot to another, and discovering wrapped within it what they declared to be artificial arches) they bunched up together against the cold, interlacing arms and legs and squirming together as close as they could, saying:

"Tell us about—"

She told them.

On the twenty-fourth night, when she woke Machine to take the dawn watch, he said to her "Do you want to climb it?"

"Climb what?" muttered Alyx. She was chilled and uncomfortable, stirring around to get her blood up.

"Do you want to climb it?" said Machine patiently.

"Wait a minute," she said, "let me think." Then she said "You'd better not use slang; I don't think I'm programmed for it."

He translated. He added—off-handedly—"You don't have to worry about pregnancy; Trans-Temp's taken care of it. Or they will, when we get back."

"Well, no," said Alyx. "No, I don't think I do want to— climb it." He looked, as far as she could tell in the dim light, a little surprised; but he did not touch her, he did not ask again or laugh or stir or even move. He sat with his arms around his knees as if considering something and then he said "All right." He repeated it decisively, staring at her with eyes that were just beginning to turn blue with the dawn; then he smiled, pulled back the spring on his crossbow and got to his feet.

"And keep your eyes open," she said, on her way back to the snow-heaped nest of the others.

"Don't I always?" he said, and as she turned away she heard an unmistakable sound. He had laughed.

The next day Raydos started to sketch her at every halt. He took out his materials and worked swiftly but easily, like a man who thinks himself safe. It was intolerable. She told him that if anything happened or anyone came he would either have to drop his sketchbook or put it in his pack; that if he took the time to put it into his pack he might die or betray the lot of them and that if he dropped it, someone might find it.

"They won't know what it is," he said. "It's archaic, you see."

"They'll know it's not an animal," she said. "Put it away."

He went on sketching. She walked over to him, took the book of papers and the length of black thing he was using away from him and stowed them away in her own pack. He smiled and blinked in the sunlight. The thing was not real charcoal or gum or even chalky; she considered asking him about it and then she shuddered. She stood there for a moment, shading her eyes against the sun and being frightened, as if she had to be frightened for the whole crew of them as well as herself, as if she were alone, more alone than by herself, and the more they liked her, the more they obeyed, the more they talked of "when we get back," the more frightened she would have to become.

"All right, come on," she heard herself say.

"All right, come on.

"Come on!"

Time after time after time.

On the twenty-ninth afternoon Maudey died. She died suddenly and by accident. They were into the pass that Gunnar had spoken of, half blinded by the glare of ice on the rock walls to either side, following a path that dropped almost sheer from the left. It was wide enough for two or three and Machine had charge of Maudey that day, for although her nervous fits had grown less frequent, they had never entirely gone away. He walked on the outside, she on the inside. Behind them Iris was humming softly to herself. It was icy in parts and the going was slow. They stopped for a moment and Machine cautiously let go of Maudey's arm; at the same time Iris began to sing softly, the same drab tune over and over again, the way she had said to Alyx they danced at the drug palaces, over and over to put themselves into trances, over and over.

"Stop that filthy song," said Maudey. "I'm tired."

Iris continued insultingly to sing.

"I'm tired!" said Maudey desperately, "I'm tired! I'm tired!" and in turning she slipped and fell on the slippery path to her knees. She was still in balance, however. Iris had arched her eyebrows and was silently mouthing something when Machine, who had been watching Maudey intently, bent down to take hold of her, but at that instant Maudey's whole right arm threw itself out over nothing and she fell over the side of the path. Machine flung himself after her and was only stopped from falling over in his turn by fetching up against someone's foot—it happened to be one of the nuns—and they both went down, teetering for a moment over the side. The nun was sprawled on the path in a patch of gravel and Machine hung shoulders down over the verge. They pulled him back and got the other one to her feet.

"Well, what happened?" said Iris in surprise. Alyx had grabbed Gunnar by the arm. Iris shrugged at them all elaborately and sat down, her chin on her knees, while Alyx got the rope from all the packs as swiftly as possible, knotted it, pushed the nun off the patch of dry gravel and set Machine on it. "Can you hold him?" she said. Machine nodded. She looped the rope about a projecting point in the wall above them and gave it to Machine; the other end she knotted under Gunnar's arms. They sent him down to bring Maudey up, which he did, and they laid her down on the path. She was dead.

"Well, how is she?" said Iris, looking at them all over her shoulder.

"She's dead," said Alyx.

"That," said Iris brightly, "is not the right answer," and she came over to inspect things for herself, coquettishly twisting and untwisting a lock of her straight silver hair. She knelt by the body. Maudey's head lay almost flat against her shoulder for her neck was broken; her eyes were wide open. Alyx closed them, saying again "Little girl, she's dead." Iris looked away, then up at them, then down again. She made a careless face. She said "Mo-Maudey was old, you know; d'you think they can fix her when we get back?"

"She is dead," said Alyx. Iris was drawing lines in the snow. She shrugged and looked covertly at the body, then she turned to it and her face began to change; she moved nearer on her knees. "Mo—Mother," she said, then grabbed at the woman with the funny, twisted neck, screaming the word "Mother" over and over, grabbing at the clothing and the limbs and even the purple hair where the hood had fallen back, screaming without stopping. Machine said quickly, "I can put her out." Alyx shook her head. She put one hand over Iris's mouth to muffle the noise. She sat with the great big girl as Iris threw herself on top of dead Maudey, trying to burrow into her, her screaming turning to sobbing, great gasping sobs that seemed to dislocate her whole body, just as vanity and age had thrown her mother about so terribly between them and had finally thrown her over a cliff. As soon as the girl began to cry, Alyx put both arms about her and rocked with her, back and forth. One of the nuns came up with a thing in her hand, a white pill.

"It would be unkind," said the nun, "it would be most unkind, most unkind—"

"Go to hell," said Alyx in Greek.

"I must insist," said the nun softly, "I must, must insist," in a tangle of hisses like a snake. "I must, must, I must—"

"Get out!" shouted Alyx to the startled woman, who did not even understand the words. With her arms around Iris, big as Iris was, with little Iris in agonies, Alyx talked to her in Greek, soothed her in Greek, talked just to be talking, rocked her back and forth. Finally there came a moment when Iris stopped.

Everyone looked very surprised.

"Your mother," said Alyx, carefully pointing to the body, "is dead." This provoked a fresh outburst. Three more times. Four times. Alyx said it again. For several hours she repeated the whole thing, she did not know how often, holding the girl each time, then holding only her hand, then finally drawing her to her feet and away from the dead woman while the men took the food and equipment out of Maudey's pack to divide it among themselves and threw the body over the path, to hide it. There was a kind of tittering, whispering chatter behind Alyx. She walked all day with the girl, talking to her, arm clumsily about her, making her walk while she shook with fits of weeping, making her walk when she wanted to sit down, making her walk as she talked of her mother, of running away from home—"not like you did" said Iris—of hating her, loving her, hating her, being reasonable, being rational, being grown up, fighting ("but it's natural!"), not being able to stand her, being able to stand her, loving her, always fighting with her (and here a fresh fit of weeping) and then—then—

"I killed her!" cried Iris, stock-still on the path. "Oh my God, I killed her! I! I!"

"Bullshit," said Alyx shortly, her hypnotic vocabulary coming to the rescue at the eleventh instant.

"But I did, I did," said Iris. "Didn't you see? I upset her, I made—"

"Ass!" said Alyx.

"Then why didn't you rope them together," cried Iris, planting herself hysterically in front of Alyx, arms akimbo, "why didn't you? You knew she could fall! You wanted to kill her!"

"If you say that again—" said Alyx, getting ready.

"I see it, I see it," whispered Iris wildly, putting her arms around herself, her eyes narrowing. "Yesss, you wanted her dead—you didn't want the *trouble*—"

Alyx hit her across the face. She threw her down, sat on her and proceeded to pound at her while the others watched, shocked and scandalized. She took good care not to hurt her. When Iris had stopped, she rubbed snow roughly over the girl's face and hauled her to her feet, "and no more trouble out of you!" she said.

"I'm all right," said Iris uncertainly. She took a step. "Yes," she said. Alyx did not hold her any more but walked next to her, giving her a slight touch now and then when she seemed to waver.

"Yes, I am all right," said Iris. Then she added, in her normal voice, "I know Maudey is dead."

"Yes," said Alyx.

"I know," said Iris, her voice wobbling a little, "that you didn't put them together because they both would have gone over."

She added, "I am going to cry."

"Cry away," said Alyx, and the rest of the afternoon Iris marched steadily ahead, weeping silently, trying to mop her face and her nose with the cleaning cloth Alyx had given her, breaking out now and again into suppressed, racking sobs. They camped for the night in a kind of hollow between two rising slopes with Iris jammed securely into the middle of everybody and Alyx next to her. In the dim never-dark of the snow fields, long after everyone else had fallen asleep, someone brushed Alyx across the face, an oddly unctuous sort of touch, at once gentle and unpleasant. She knew at once who it was.

"If you do not," she said, "take that devil's stuff out of here *at once*—!" The hand withdrew.

"I must insist," said the familiar whisper, "I must, must insist. You do not understand—it is not—"

"If you touch her," said Alyx between her teeth, "I will kill you—both of you—and I will take those little pills you are so fond of and defecate upon each and every one of them, upon my soul I swear that I will!"

"But—but—" She could feel the woman trembling with shock.

"If you so much as touch her," said Alyx, "you will have caused me to commit two murders and a sacrilege. Now get out!" and she got up in the dim light, pulled the pack off every grunting, protesting sleeper's back—except the two women who had withdrawn to a little distance together—and piled them like a barricade around Iris, who was sleeping with her face to the stars and her mouth open. *Let them trip over that*, she thought vindictively. *Damn it! Damn them all! Boots without spikes, damn them! What do they expect us to do, swim over the mountains?* She did not sleep for a long time, and when she did it seemed that everyone was climbing over her, stepping on top of her and sliding off just for fun. She dreamed she was what Gunnar had described as a ski-slide. Then she dreamed that the first stepped on to her back and then the second on to his and so on and so on until they formed a human ladder, when the whole snow-field slowly tilted upside down. Everyone fell off. She came to with a start; it was Gavrily, waking her for the dawn watch. She saw him fall asleep in seconds, then trudged a little aside and sat cross-legged, her bow on her knees. The two nuns had moved back to the group, asleep, sprawled out and breathing softly with the others. She watched the sky lighten to the left, become transparent, take on color. Pale blue. Winter blue.

"All right," she said, "everyone up!" and slipped off her pack for the usual handfuls of breakfast food.

The first thing she noticed, with exasperation, was that Raydos had stolen back his art equipment, for it was gone.

The second was that there were only six figures sitting up and munching out of their cupped hands, not seven; she thought *that's right, Maudey's dead*, then ran them over in her head: *Gunnar, Gavrily, Raydos, Machine, the Twins, Iris*—

But Iris was missing.

Her first thought was that the girl had somehow been spirited away, or made to disappear by The Holy Twins, who had stopped eating with their hands halfway to their mouths, like people about to pour a sacrifice of grain on to the ground for Mother Earth. Both of them were watching her. Her second thought was unprintable and almost—but not quite—unspeakable, and so instantaneous that she had leapt into the circle of breakfasters before she half knew where she was, shoving their packs and themselves out of her way. She dislodged one of Raydos's eye lenses; he clapped his hand to his eye and began to grope in the snow. "What the devil—!" said Gunnar.

Iris was lying on her back among the packs, looking up into the sky. She had shut one eye and the other was moving up and down in a regular pattern. Alyx fell over her. When she scrambled to her knees, Iris had not moved and her one open eye still made the regular transit of nothing, up and down, up and down.

"Iris," said Alyx.

"Byootiful," said Iris. Alyx shook her. "Byootiful," crooned the girl, "all byootiful" and very slowly she opened her closed eye, shut the other and began again to scan the something or nothing up in the sky, up and down, up and down. Alyx tried to pull the big girl to her feet, but she was too heavy; then with astonishing lightness Iris herself sat up, put her head to one side and looked at Alyx with absolute calm and complete relaxation. It seemed to Alyx that the touch of one finger would send her down on her back again. "Mother," said Iris clearly, opening both eyes, "mother. Too lovely," and she continued to look at Alyx as she had at the sky. She bent her head down on to one shoulder, as Maudey's head had been bent in death with a broken neck.

"Mother is lovely," said Iris conversationally. "There she is. You are lovely. Here you are. He is lovely. There he is. She is lovely. We are lovely. They are lovely. I am lovely. Love is lovely. Lovely lovely lovely lovely—" she went on talking to herself as

Alyx stood up. One of the nuns came walking across the trampled snow with her hands clasped nervously in front of her; she came up to the little woman and took a breath; then she said:

"You may kill me if you like."

"I love shoes," said Iris, lying down on her back, "I love sky. I love clouds. I love hair. I love zippers. I love food. I love my mother. I love feet. I love bathrooms. I love walking. I love people. I love sleep. I love breathing. I love tape. I love books. I love pictures. I love air. I love rolls. I love hands. I love—"

"Shut up!" shouted Alyx, as the girl continued with her inexhaustible catalogue. "Shut up, for God's sake!" and turned away, only to find herself looking up at the face of the nun, who had quickly moved about to be in front of her and who still repeated, "You may kill us both if you like," with an unbearable mixture of nervousness and superiority. Iris had begun to repeat the word "love" over and over and over again in a soft, unchanging voice.

"Is this not kinder?" said the nun.

"Go away before I kill you!" said Alyx.

"She is happy," said the nun.

"She is an idiot!"

"She will be happy for a day," said the nun, "and then less happy and then even less happy, but she will have her memory of the All and when the sadness comes back—as it will in a day or so, I am sorry to say, but some day we will find out how—"

"Get out!" said Alyx.

"However, it will be an altered sadness," continued the nun rapidly, "an eased sadness with the All in its infinite All—"

"Get out of here before I alter *you* into the All!" Alyx shouted, losing control of herself. The nun hurried away and Alyx, clapping both hands over her ears, walked rapidly away from Iris, who had begun to say "*I've* been to the moon but *you* won't. *I've* been to the sun but *you* won't, *I've* been to—" and over and over and over again with ascending and descending variations.

"Messing up the machinery," said Machine, next to her.

"Leave me alone," said Alyx, her hands still over her ears. The ground had unaccountably jumped up and was swimming in front of her; she knew she was crying.

"I don't approve of messing up the machinery," said Machine

softly. "I have a respect for the machinery; I do not like to see it abused and if they touch the girl again you need not kill them. I will."

"No killing," said Alyx, as levelly as she could.

"Religion?" said Machine sarcastically.

"No," said Alyx, lifting her head abruptly, "but no killing. Not my people." She turned to go, but he caught her gently by the arm, looking into her face with a half-mocking smile, conveying somehow by his touch that her arm was not inside an insulated suit but was bare, and that he was stroking it. The trip had given him back his eyebrows and eyelashes; the hair on his head was a wiry black brush; for Machine did not, apparently, believe in tampering irreversibly with the Machinery. She thought *I won't get involved with any of these people.* She found herself saying idiotically "Your hair's growing in." He smiled and took her other arm, holding her as if he were going to lift her off the ground, she hotter and dizzier every moment, feeling little, feeling light, feeling like a woman who has had no luxury for a long, long time. She said, "Put me down, if you please."

"Tiny," he said, "you *are* down," and putting his hands around her waist, he lifted her easily to the height of his face. "I think you will climb it," he said.

"No," said Alyx. It did not seem to bother him to keep holding her up in the air.

"I think you will," he said, smiling, and still smiling, he kissed her with a sort of dispassionate, calm pleasure, taking his time, holding her closely and carefully, using the thoughtful, practiced, craftsmanly thoroughness that Machine brought to everything that Machine did. Then he put her down and simply walked away.

"Ah, go find someone your own size!" she called after him, but then she remembered that the only girl his size was Iris, and that Iris was lying on her back in the snow in a world where everything was lovely, lovely, lovely due to a little white pill. She swore. She could see Iris in the distance, still talking. She took a knife out of her sleeve and tried the feel of it but the feel was wrong, just as the boots attached to their suits had no spikes, just as their maps stopped at Base B, just as Paradise itself had turned into—but no, that was not so. The place was all right, quite all right. *The place*, she thought, *is all right.* She started back to the group of picnickers who were slipping their packs back on and stamping the snow off their boots; some were dusting off the rear ends of others where they had sat in the snow. She saw one of The Heavenly Twins say something in Iris's ear and Iris get obediently to her feet, still talking; then the other nun said something and Iris's mouth stopped moving.

Bury it deep, thought Alyx, *never let it heal.* She joined them, feeling like a mule-driver.

"D'you know," said Gunnar conversationally, "that we've been out here thirty days? Not bad, eh?"

"I'll say!" said Gavrily.

"And only one death," said Alyx sharply, "not bad, eh?"

"That's not our fault," said Gavrily. They were all staring at her.

"No," she said, "it's not our fault. It's mine."

"Come on," she added.

On the thirty-second day Paradise still offered them the semblance of a path, though Gunnar could not find his mountain pass and grew scared and irritable trying to lead them another way. Paradise tilted and zigzagged around them. At times they had to sit down, or slide down, or even crawl, and he waited for them with deep impatience, telling them haughtily how a professional would be able to handle this sort of thing without getting down on his ——— to go down a slope. Alyx said nothing. Iris spoke to nobody. Only Gavrily talked incessantly about People's Capitalism, as if he had been stung by a bug, explaining at great and unnecessary length how the Government was a check on the Military, the Military was a check on Government, and both were a check on Business which in turn checked the other two. He called it the three-part system of checks and balances. Alyx listened politely. Finally she said:

"What's a—?"

Gavrily explained, disapprovingly.

"Ah," said Alyx, smiling.

Iris still said nothing.

They camped early for the night, sprawled about a narrow sort of table-land, as far away from each other as they could get and complaining loudly. The sun had not been down for fifteen minutes and there was still light in the sky: rose, lavender, yellow, apple-green, violet. It made a beautiful show. It was getting extremely cold. Gunnar insisted that they could go on, in spite of their complaints; he clenched his big hands and ordered them to get up (which they did not do); then he turned to Alyx.

"You too," he said. "You can go on for another hour."

"I'd prefer not to go on in the dark," she said. She was lying down with her hands under her head, watching the colors in the sky.

"There's light enough to last us all night!" he said. "*Will* you come on?"

"No," said Alyx.

"God damn it!" he said, "do you think I don't know what I'm doing? Do you think I don't know where I'm taking you? You lazy sons of bitches, get up!"

"That's enough," said Alyx, half on her feet.

"Oh no it isn't," he said. "Oh no it isn't! You all get up, all of you! You're not going to waste the hour that's left!"

"I prefer," said Alyx quietly, "not to sleep with my head wedged in a chasm, if you don't mind." She rose to her feet.

"Do I have to kick you in the stomach again?" she said calmly.

Gunnar was silent. He stood with his hands balled into fists.

"Do I?" she said. "Do I have to kick you in the groin? Do I have to gouge your eyes out?"

"Do I have to dive between your legs and throw you head foremost on the rocks so you're knocked out?" she said.

"So your nose gets broken?

"So your cheekbones get bloody and your chin bruised?"

She turned to the others.

"I suggest that we keep together," she said, "to take advantage of each other's warmth; otherwise you are bound to stiffen up as you get colder; it is going to be a devil of a night."

She joined the others as they packed snow about themselves —it was more like frozen dust than snow, and there was not much of it; they were too high up—and settled in against Iris, who was unreadable, with the beautiful sky above them dying into deep rose, into dusty rose, into dirty rose. She did not look at Gunnar. She felt sorry for him. He was to take the first watch anyway, *though* (she thought) *what we are watching for I do not know and what we could do if we saw it, God only knows. And then what I am watching for . . . What I would do . . . No food . . . Too high up . . . No good . . .*

She woke under the night sky, which was brilliant with stars: enormous, shining, empty and cold. The stars were unrecognizable, not constellations she knew any more but planes upon planes, shifting trapezoids, tilted pyramids like the mountains themselves, all reaching off into spaces she could not even begin to comprehend: distant suns upon suns. The air was very cold.

Someone was gently shaking her, moving her limbs, trying to untangle her from the mass of human bodies. She said, "Lemme sleep" and tried to turn over. Then she felt a shocking draught at her neck and breast and a hand inside her suit; she said sleepily, "Oh dear, it's too cold."

"You had better get up," whispered Machine reasonably. "I believe I'm standing on somebody.

"I'm trying not to," he added solemnly, "but everyone's so close together that it's rather difficult."

Alyx giggled. The sound startled her. *Well, I'll talk to you,* she said. *No,* she thought, *I didn't say it, did I?* She articulated clearly "I—will—talk—to you," and sat up, leaning her head against his knee to wake up. She pushed his hand away and closed up her suit. "I'm cross," she said, "you hear that?"

"I hear and obey," whispered Machine, grinning, and taking her up in his arms like a baby, he carried her through the mass of sleepers, picking his way carefully, for they were indeed packed very close together. He set her down a little distance away.

"You're supposed to be on watch," she protested. He shook his head. He knelt beside her and pointed to the watch—Gunnar—some fifteen meters away. *A noble figure,* thought Alyx. She began to laugh uncontrollably, muffling her mouth on her knees. Machine's shoulders were shaking gleefully. He scooped her up with one arm and walked her behind a little wall of snow someone had built, a little wall about one meter high and three meters long—"Did you—?" said Alyx.

"I did," said the young man. He reached out with one

forefinger and rapidly slid it down the opening of her suit from her neck to her—

"Eeeey, it's too cold!" cried Alyx, rolling away and pressing the opening shut again.

"Sssh!" he said. "No it's not."

"He'll see us," said Alyx, straightening out distrustfully.

"No he won't."

"Yes he will."

"No he won't."

"Yes he *will*!" and she got up, shook the snow off herself and immediately started away. Machine did not move.

"Well, aren't you—" she said, nettled.

He shook his head. He sat down, crossed his legs in some unaccountable fashion so the feet ended up on top, crossed his arms, and sat immobile as an Oriental statue. She came back and sat next to him, resting her head against him (as much as she could with one of his knees in the way), feeling soulful, trustful, silly. She could feel him chuckling. "How *do* you do that with the feet?" she said. He wriggled his toes inside his boots.

"I dare not do anything else," he said, "because of your deadly abilities with groin-kicking, eye-gouging, head-cracking and the like, Agent."

"Oh, shut up!" said Alyx. She put her arms around him. He uncrossed his own arms, then used them to carefully uncross his legs; then lay down with her in the snow, insulated suit to insulated suit, kissing her time after time. Then he stopped.

"You're scared, aren't you?" he whispered.

She nodded.

"Goddammit, I've had men before!" she whispered. He put his finger over her lips. With the other hand he pressed together the ends of the thongs that could hold a suit loosely together at the collarbone—first his suit, then hers—and then, with the same hand, rapidly opened both suits from the neck in front to the base of the spine in back and ditto with the long underwear: "Ugly but useful," he remarked. Alyx began to giggle again. She tried to press against him, shivering with cold. "Wait!" he said, "and watch, O Agent," and very carefully, biting one lip, he pressed together the righthand edges of both suits and then the left, making for the two of them a personal blanket, a double tent, a spot of warmth under the enormous starry sky.

"And they don't," he said triumphantly, "come apart by pulling. They *only* come apart by prying! And see? You can move your arms and legs in! Isn't it marvelous?" And he gave her a proud kiss—a big, delighted, impersonal smack on the cheek. Alyx began to laugh. She laughed as she pulled her arms and legs in to hug him; she laughed as he talked to her, as he buried his face in her neck, as he began to caress her; she laughed until her laughter turned to sobbing under his expert hands, his too-expert hands, his calm deliberateness; she raked his back with her fingernails; she screamed at him to hurry up and called him a pig and an actor and the son of a whore (for these epithets were of more or less equal value in her own country); and finally, when at his own good time the stars exploded—and she realized that *nova* meant—that *nova* meant (though she had closed her eyes a long time before)—someone had said *nova* the other day—she came to herself as if rocking in the shallows of a prodigious tide, yawning, lazily extending her toes—and with a vague but disquieting sense of having done something or said something she should not have said or done. She knew she hated him there, for a while; she was afraid she might have hurt him or hurt his feelings.

"What language were you speaking?" said Machine with interest.

"Greek!" said Alyx, and she laughed with relief and would have kissed him, only it was really too much effort.

He shook her. "Don't go to sleep," he said.

"Mmmm."

"Don't go to sleep!" and he shook her harder.

"Why not?" she said.

"Because," said Machine, "I am going to begin again."

"All right," said Alyx, complaisantly and raised her knees. He began, as before, to kiss her neck, her shoulders and so on down et cetera et cetera, in short to do everything he had done before on the same schedule until it occurred to her that he was doing everything just as he had done it before and on the same schedule, until she tried to push him away, exclaiming angrily, feeling like a statuette or a picture, frightened and furious. At first he would not stop; finally she bit him.

"What the devil is the matter!" he cried.

"You," she said, "stop it. Let me out." They had been to-gether and now they were sewed up in a sack; it was awful; she started to open the jointure of the suits but he grabbed her hands.

"What is it?" he said, "what is it? Don't you want it? Don't you see that I'm trying?"

"Trying?" said Alyx stupidly.

"Yes, trying!" he said vehemently. "Trying! Do you think that comes by nature?"

"I don't understand," she said. "I'm sorry." They lay silently for a few minutes.

"I was trying," he said in a thick, bitter voice, "to give you a good time. I like you. I did the best I could. Apparently it wasn't good enough."

"But I don't—" said Alyx.

"You don't want it," he said; "all right," and pushing her hands away, he began to open the suits himself. She closed them. He opened them and she closed them several times. Then he began to cry and she put her arms around him.

"I had the best time in my life," she said. He continued to sob, silently, through clenched teeth, turning away his face.

"I had," she repeated, "the best time in my life. I did. I did! But I don't want—"

"All right," he said.

"But I don't," she said. "I don't want—I don't—"

He tried to get away from her and, of course could not; he thrashed about, forgetting that the suits had to be slit and could not be pulled apart; he pushed against the material until he frightened her for she thought she was going to be hurt; finally she cried out:

"Darling, stop it! Please!"

Machine stopped, leaning on his knees and clenched fists, his face stubbornly turned away.

"It's you I want," she said. "D'you see? I don't want a—performance. I want *you*."

"I don't know what you're talking about," he said, more calmly.

"Well, I don't know what *you're* talking about," said Alyx reasonably.

"Look," he said, turning his head back so that they were nose to nose, "when you do something, you do it right, don't you?"

"No," said Alyx promptly.

"Well, what's the good of doing it then!" he shouted.

"Because you want to, idiot!" she snapped, "any five-year-old child—"

"Oh, now I'm a five-year-old child, am I?"

"Just a minute, just a minute, athlete! I never said—"

"Athlete! By God—"

She pinched him.

He pinched her.

She grabbed at what there was of his hair and pulled it; he howled and twisted her hand; then both of them pushed and the result was that he lost his balance and carried her over on to one side with him, the impromptu sleeping-bag obligingly going with them. They both got a faceful of snow. They wrestled silently for a few minutes, each trying to grab some part of the other, Machine muttering, Alyx kicking, Machine pushing her head down into the bag, Alyx trying to bite his finger, Machine yelling, Alyx trying to butt her head into his stomach. There was, however, no room to do anything properly. After a few minutes they stopped.

He sighed. It was rather peaceful, actually.

"Look, dear," he said quietly, "I've done my best. But if you want me, myself, you'll have to do without; I've heard that too often. Do you think they don't want me out there? Sure they do! They want me to open up my" (she could not catch the word) "like a God damned" (or that one) "and show them everything that's inside, all my feelings, or what they call feelings. I don't believe they have feelings. They talk about their complexities and their reactions and their impressions and their interactions and their patterns and their neuroses and their childhoods and their rebellions and their utterly unspeakable insides until I want to vomit. I have no insides. I will not have any. I certainly will not let anyone see any. I do things and I do them well; that's all. If you want that, you can have it. Otherwise, my love, I am simply not at home. Understood?"

"Understood," she said. She took his face in her hands. "You are splendid," she said thickly. "You are splendid and beautiful and superb. I love your performance. Perform me."

And if I let slip any emotion, she thought, *it will—thank God —be in Greek!*

He performed again—rather badly. But it turned out well just the same.

When Machine had gone to take over the watch from Gunnar, Alyx returned to the sleepers. Iris was sitting up. Not only was it possible to identify her face in the starlight reflected from the snow; she had thrown back her hood in the bitter cold and her silver hair glowed uncannily. She waited until Alyx reached her; then she said:

"Talk to me."

"Did you know I was up?" said Alyx. Iris giggled, but an uncertain, odd sort of giggle as if she were fighting for breath; she said in the same queer voice, "Yes, you woke me up. You were both shouting."

Gunnar must know, thought Alyx and dismissed the thought. She wondered if these people were jealous. She turned to go back to her own sleeping place but Iris clutched at her arm, repeating, "Talk to me!"

"What about, love?" said Alyx.

"Tell me—tell me bad things," said Iris, catching her breath and moving her head in the collar of her suit as if it were choking her. "Put your hood on," said Alyx, but the girl shook her head, declaring she wanted it that way. She said, "Tell me —horrors."

"What?" said Alyx in surprise, sitting down.

"I want to hear bad things," said Iris monotonously. "I want to hear awful things. I can't stand it. I keep slipping," and she giggled again, saying "Everybody could hear you all over camp," and then putting one hand to her face, catching her breath, and holding on to Alyx's arm as if she were drowning. "Tell me horrors!" she cried.

"Sssh," said Alyx, "ssssh, I'll tell you anything you like, baby, anything you like."

"My mother's dead," said Iris with sudden emotion. "My mother's dead. I've got to remember that. I've got to!"

"Yes, yes, she's dead," said Alyx.

"Please, please," said Iris, "keep me here. I keep sliding away."

"Horrors," said Alyx. "Good Lord, I don't think I know any tonight."

"It's like feathers," said Iris suddenly, dreamily, looking up in the sky, "it's like pillows, it's like air cushions under those things, you know, it's like—like—"

"All right, all right," said Alyx quickly, "your mother broke her neck. I'll tell you about it again. I might as well; you're all making me soft as wax, the whole lot of you."

"Don't, don't," said Iris, moaning. "Don't say soft. I keep trying, I thought the cold—yes, yes, that's good—" and with sudden decision she began to strip off her suit. Alyx grabbed her and wrestled her to the ground, fastening the suit again and shoving the hood on for good measure. She thought suddenly *She's still fighting the drug*. "You touch that again and I'll smash you," said Alyx steadily. "I'll beat your damned teeth in."

"It's too hot," said Iris feverishly, "too—to—" She relapsed into looking at the stars.

"Look at me," said Alyx, grabbing her head and pulling it down. "Look at me, baby."

"I'm not a baby," said Iris lazily. "I'm not a—a—baby. I'm a woman."

Alyx shook her.

"I am almost grown up," said Iris, not bothered by her head wobbling while she was being shaken. "I am very grown up. I am thirty-three."

Alyx dropped her hands.

"I am thirty-three already," continued Iris, trying to focus her eyes. "I am, I am" (she said this uncomfortably, with great concentration) "and—and Ma—Machine is thirty-six and Gunnar is fifty-eight—yes, that's right—and Maudey was my mother. She was my mother. She was ninety. But she didn't look it. She's dead. She didn't look it, did she? She took that stuff. She didn't look it."

"Baby," said Alyx, finding her voice, "look at me."

"Why?" said Iris in a whisper.

"Because," said Alyx, "I am going to tell you something horrible. Now look at me. You know what I look like. You've seen me in the daylight. I have lines in my face, the first lines, the ones that tell you for the first time that you're going to die. There's gray in my hair, just a little, just enough to see in a strong light, a little around my ears and one streak starting at my forehead. Do you remember it?"

Iris nodded solemnly.

"I am getting old," said Alyx, "and my skin is getting coarse and tough. I tire more easily. I am withering a little. It will go faster and faster from now on and soon I will die.

"Iris," she said with difficulty, "how old am I?"

"Fifty?" said Iris.

Alyx shook her head.

"Sixty?" said Iris hopefully.

Alyx shook her head again.

"Well, how old are you?" said Iris, a little impatiently.

"Twenty-six," said Alyx. Iris put her hands over her eyes.

"Twenty-six," said Alyx steadily. "Think of that, you thirty-three-year-old adolescent! Twenty-six and dead at fifty. Dead! There's a whole world of people who live like that. We don't eat the way you do, we don't have whatever it is the doctors give you, we work like hell, we get sick, we lose arms or legs or eyes and nobody gives us new ones, we die in the plague, one-third of our babies die before they're a year old and one time out of five the mother dies, too, in giving them birth."

"But it's so long ago!" wailed little Iris.

"Oh no it's not," said Alyx. "It's *right now*. It's going on right now. I lived in it and I came here. It's in the next room. I was in that room and now I'm in this one. There are people still in that other room. They are living *now*. They are suffering *now*. And they always live and always suffer because *everything keeps on happening*. You can't say it's all over and done with because it isn't; it keeps going on. It all keeps going on. Shall I tell you about the plague? That's one nice thing. Shall I tell you about the fevers, the boils, the spasms, the fear, the burst blood vessels, the sores? Shall I tell you what's going on right now, right here, right in this place?"

"Y—yes! Yes! Yes!" cried Iris, her hands over her ears. Alyx caught the hands in her own, massaging them (for they were bare), slipping Iris's gloves back on and pressing the little tabs that kept them shut.

"Be quiet," she said, "and listen, for I am going to tell you about the Black Death."

And for the next half hour she did until Iris's eyes came back into focus and Iris began to breathe normally and at last Iris fell asleep.

Don't have nightmares, baby, said Alyx to herself, stroking one lock of silver hair that stuck out from under the girl's hood. *Don't have nightmares, thirty-three-year-old baby*. She did not know exactly what she herself felt. She bedded down in her own place, leaving all that for the next day, thinking first of her own children: the two put out to nurse, the third abandoned in the hills when she had run away from her husband at seventeen and (she thought) not to a Youth Core. She smiled in the dark. She wondered if Gunnar had known who was carrying on so. She wondered if he minded. She thought again of Iris, of Machine, of the comfort it was to hear human breathing around you at night, the real comfort.

I've got two of them, she thought, *and damn Gunnar anyway*. She fell asleep.

The thirty-fifth day was the day they lost Raydos. They did not lose him to the cats, although they found big paw-prints around their camp the next morning and met one of the spotted animals at about noon, circling it carefully at a distance while it stood hissing and spitting on a rocky eminence, obviously unsure whether to come any closer or not. It was less than a meter high and had enormous padded paws: a little animal and a lot of irritation; Alyx dropped to the rear to watch it stalk them for the next three hours, keeping her crossbow ready and making abrupt movements from time to time to make it duck out of sight. Gunnar was up front, leading the way. Its persistence rather amused her at first but she supposed that it could do a lot of damage in spite of its size and was beginning to wonder whether she could risk a loud shout—or a shot into the rocks—to drive it off, when for no reason at all that she could see, the animal's tufted ears perked forward, it crouched down abruptly, gave a kind of hoarse, alarmed growl and bounded awkwardly away. The whole column in front of her had halted. She made her way to the front where Gunnar stood like a huge statue, his big arm pointing up straight into the sky, as visible as the Colossus of Rhodes.

"Look," he said, pleased, "a bird." She yanked at his arm, pulling him to the ground, shouting "Down, everyone!" and all of them fell on to their hands and knees, ducking their heads. The theory was that the white suits and white packs would blend into the snow as long as they kept their faces hidden, or that they would look like animals and that any reading of body heat would be disregarded as such. She wondered if there was any sense to it. She thought that it might be a bird. It occurred to her that distances were hard to judge in a cloudless sky. It also occurred to her that the birds she knew did not come straight down, and certainly not that fast, and that the snow-shoed cat had been running away from something snow-shoed cats did not like. So it might be just as well to occupy their ridiculous position on the ground until whatever it was satisfied its curiosity and went away, even though her knees and elbows hurt and she was getting the cramp, even though things were absolutely silent, even though nothing at all seemed to be happening . . .

"Well?" said Gunnar. There was a stir all along the line.

"Sssh," said Alyx. Nothing happened.

"We've been down on our knees," said Gunnar a bit testily, "for five minutes. I have been looking at my watch."

"All right, I'll take a look up," said Alyx, and leaning on one arm, she used her free hand to pull her hood as far over her face as possible. Slowly she tilted her head and looked.

"Tell us the color of its beak," said Gunnar.

There was a man hanging in the air forty meters above them. Forty meters up in the sky he sat on nothing, totally unsupported, wearing some kind of green suit with a harness around his waist. She could have sworn that he was grinning. He put out one bare hand and punched the air with his finger; then he came down with such speed that it seemed to Alyx as if he must crash; then he stopped just as abruptly, a meter above the snow and two in front of them. He grinned. Now that he was down she could see the faint outline of what he was traveling in: a transparent bubble, just big enough for one, a transparent shelf of a seat, a transparent panel fixed to the wall. The thing made a slight depression in the snow. She supposed that she could see it because it was not entirely clean. The stranger took out of his harness what even she could recognize as a weapon, all too obviously shaped for the human hand to do God knew what to the human body. He pushed at the wall in front of him and stepped out—swaggering.

"Well?" said Gunnar in a strained whisper.

"His beak," said Alyx distinctly, "is green and he's got a gun. Get up," and they all rocketed to their feet, quickly moving back; she could hear them scrambling behind her. The stranger pointed his weapon and favored them with a most unpleasant smile. He lounged against the side of his ship. It occurred to Alyx with a certain relief that she had known him before, that she had known him in two separate millennia and eight languages, and that he had been the same fool each time; she only hoped mightily that no one would get hurt. She hugged herself as if in fear, taking advantage of the position to take off her gloves and loosen the knives in her sleeves while Machine held his crossbow casually and clumsily in one hand. He was gaping at the stranger like an idiot. Gunnar had drawn himself up, half a head above all of them, again the colossus, his face pale and muscles working around his mouth.

"Well, well," said the stranger with heavy sarcasm, "break my ———" (she did not understand this) "I'm just cruising around and what do I find? A bloody circus!"

Someone—probably a nun—was crying quietly in the back.

"And what's *that*?" said the stranger. "A dwarf? The Herculean Infant?" He laughed loudly. "Maybe I'll leave it alone. Maybe if it's female, I'll tuck it under my arm after I've ticked the rest of you and take it away with me for convenience. Some ———!" and again a word Alyx did not understand. Out of the corner of her eye she saw Machine redden. The stranger was idly kicking the snow in front of him; then with his free hand he pointed negligently at Machine's crossbow. "What's that thing?" he said. Machine looked stupid.

"Hey come on, come on, don't waste my time," said the stranger. "What is it? I can tick you first, you know. Start telling."

"It's a d-d-directional f-f-inder," Machine stammered, blushing furiously.

"It's a what?" said the man suspiciously.

"It's t-to tell direction," Machine blurted out. "Only it doesn't work," he added stiffly.

"Give it here," said the stranger. Machine obligingly stepped forward, the crossbow hanging clumsily from his hand.

"*Stay back!*" cried the man, jerking up his gun. "*Don't come near me!*" Machine held out the crossbow, his jaw hanging.

"Stuff it," said the stranger, trying to sound cool, "I'll look at it after you're dead," and added, "Get in line, Civs," as if nothing at all had happened. *Ah yes*, thought Alyx. They moved slowly into line, Alyx throwing her arms around Machine as he stepped back, incidentally affording him the cover to pull back the bow's spring and giving herself the two seconds to say "Belly." She was going to try to get his gun hand. She got her balance as near perfect as she could while the stranger backed away from them to survey the whole line; she planned to throw from her knees and deflect his arm upward while he shot at the place she had been, and to this end she called out "Mister, what are you going to do with us?"

He walked back along the line, looking her up and down —mostly down, for he was as tall as the rest of them; possibly a woman as small as herself was a kind of expensive rarity. He said, "I'm not going to do anything to *you*."

"No," he said, "not to you; I'll leave you here and pick you up later, Infant. We can all use you." She looked innocent.

"After I tick these Ops," he went on, "after we get 'em melted—you're going to see it, Infant—then I'll wrap you up and come back for you later. Or maybe take a little now. We'll see.

"The question," he added, "is which of you I will tick first. The question is which of you feather-loving Ops I will turn to ashes first and I think, after mature judgment and a lot of decisions and maybe just turning it over in my head, I say I think—"

Gunnar threw himself at the man.

He did so just as Alyx flashed to her knees and turned into an instant blur, just as Machine whipped up the crossbow and let go the bolt, just as Gunnar should have stood still and prayed to whatever gods guard amateur explorers—just at this moment he flung himself forward at the stranger's feet. There was a flash of light and a high-pitched, horrible scream. Gunnar lay sprawled in the snow. The stranger, weapon dangling from one hand, bleeding in one small line from the belly where Machine's bolt had hit him, sat in the snow and stared at nothing. Then he bent over and slid onto his side. Alyx ran to the man and snatched the gun from his grasp but he was unmistakably dead; she pulled one of her knives out of his forearm where it had hit him—but high, much too high, damn the balance of the stupid things!—hardly even spoiling his aim—and the other from his neck, grimacing horribly and leaping aside to keep from getting drenched. The corpse fell over on its face. Then she turned to Gunnar.

Gunnar was getting up.

"Well, well," said Machine from between his teeth, "what —do—you—know!"

"How the devil could I tell you were going to do anything!" shouted Gunnar.

"Did you make that noise for effect," said Machine, "or was it merely fright?"

"Shut up, you!" cried Gunnar, his face pale.

"Did you wish to engage our sympathies?" said Machine, "or did you intend to confuse the enemy? Was it electronic noise? Is it designed to foul up radar? Does it contribute to the electromagnetic spectrum? Has it a pattern? Does it scan?"

Gunnar stepped forward, his big hands swinging. Machine raised the bow. Both men bent a little at the knees. Then in between them, pale and calm, stepped one of the nuns, looking first at one and then at the other until Gunnar turned his back and Machine—making a face—broke apart the crossbow and draped both parts over his shoulder.

"Someone is hurt," said the nun.

Gunnar turned back. "That's impossible!" he said. "Anyone in the way of that beam would be dead, not hurt."

"Someone," repeated the nun, "is hurt," and she walked back towards the little knot the others had formed in the snow, clustering about someone on the ground. Gunnar shouted, "It's not possible!"

"It's Raydos," said Machine quietly, somewhere next to Alyx. "It's not Iris. He just got the edge. The bastard had put it on diffuse. He's alive," and taking her by the elbow, he propelled her to the end of the line, where Raydos had been standing almost but not quite in profile, where the stranger had shot when his arm was knocked away and up from his aim on Gunnar, when he had already turned his weapon down on Gunnar because Gunnar was acting like a hero, and not tried to shoot Alyx, who could have dropped beneath the beam, twisted away and killed him before he could shoot again. Strike a man's arm up into the air and it follows a sweeping curve.

Right over Raydos's face.

And Raydos's eyes.

She refused to look at him after the first time. She pushed through the others to take a long look at the unconscious man's face where he lay, his arms thrown out, in the snow: the precise line where his face began, the precise line where it ended, the fine, powdery, black char that had been carefully laid across the rest of it. Stirred by their breath, the black powder rose in fine spirals. Then she saw the fused circles of Raydos's eye lenses: black, shiny black, little puddles resting as if in a valley; they still gave out an intense heat. She heard Gunnar say nervously "Put—put snow on it," and she turned her back remarking, "Snow. And do what you have to do." She walked slowly over to the transparent bubble. In the distance she could see some kind of activity going on over Raydos, things being brought out of his pack, all sorts of conferring going on. She carefully kicked snow over the dead body. She reflected that Paradise must know them all very well, must know them intimately, in fact, to find the levers to open them one by one until none of them were left or only she was left or none of them were left. Maudey. She stood aside carefully as Gunnar and Machine carried up something that was lacking a face—or rather, his face had turned lumpy and white—and put him in the transparent bubble. That is, Gunnar put him in, getting half in with him for the thing would not hold more than the head and arms of another occupant. Gunnar was taping Raydos to the seat and the walls and working on the control board. Then he said, "I'll set the automatic location signal to turn itself off an hour after sundown; he did say he was cruising."

"So you know something," said Machine. Gunnar went on, his voice a little high:

"I can coordinate it for the Pole station."

"So you are worth something," said Machine.

"They won't shoot him down," said Gunnar quickly. "They would but I've set it for a distress call at the coordinate location. They'll try to trap him.

"That's not easy," he added, "but I think it'll work. It's a kind of paradox, but there's an override. I've slowed him down as much as I can without shutting him off altogether, he may last, and I've tried to put in some indication of where we are and where we're headed but it's not equipped for that; I can't send out a Standard call or *they'll* come and pick him up, I mean the others, of course, they must have this section pretty well under control or they wouldn't be sending loners around here. And of course the heat burst registered, but they'll think it's him; he did say—"

"Why don't you write it, you bastard?" said Machine.

"Write?" said Gunnar.

"Write it on a piece of paper," said Machine. "Do you know what paper is? He has it in his pack. That stuff he uses for drawing is paper. Write on it!"

"I don't have anything to write with," said Gunnar.

"You stupid bastard," said Machine slowly, turning Raydos's pack upside down so that everything fell out of it: pens, black stuff, packets of things taped together, food, a kind of hinged manuscript, all the medicine. "You stupid, electronic bastard," he said, ripping a sheet from the manuscript, "this is paper. And this" (holding it out) "is artist's charcoal. Take the charcoal and write on the paper. If you know how to write."

"That's unnecessary," said Gunnar, but he took the writing materials, removed his gloves and wrote laboriously on the paper, his hands shaking a little. He did not seem to be used to writing.

"Now tape it to the wall," said Machine. "No, the inside wall. Thank you. Thank you for everything. Thank you for your heroism. Thank you for your stupidity. Thank you—"

"I'll kill you!" cried Gunnar. Alyx threw up her arm and cracked him under the chin. He gasped and stumbled back. She turned to Machine. "You too," she said, "you too. Now finish it." Gunnar climbed half inside the bubble again and commenced clumsily making some last adjustments on the bank of instruments that hung in the air. The sun was setting: a short day. She watched the snow turn ruddy, ruddy all around, the fingerprints and smears on the bubble gone in a general, faint glow as the light diffused and failed, the sun sank, the man inside—who looked dead—wobbled back and forth as Gunnar's weight changed the balance of the delicate little ship. It looked like an ornament almost, something to set on top of a spire, someone's pearl.

"Is he dead?" said Alyx. Machine shook his head. "Frozen," he said. "We all have it in the packs. Slows you down. He may last."

"His eyes?" said Alyx.

"Why, I didn't think you cared," said Machine, trying to make it light.

"*His eyes!*"

Machine shrugged a little uncomfortably. "Maybe yes, maybe no," he said, "but" (here he laughed) "one would think you were in love with the man."

"I don't know him," said Alyx. "I never knew him."

"Then why all the fuss, Tiny?" he said.

"You don't have a word for it."

"The hell I don't!" said Machine somewhat brutally. "I have words for everything. So the man was what we call an artist. All right. He used color on flat. So what? He can use sound. He can use things you stick your fingers into and they give you a jolt. He can use wires. He can use textures. He can use pulse-beats. He can use things that climb over you while you close your eyes. He can use combinations of drugs. He can use direct brain stimulation. He can use hypnosis. He can use things you walk on barefoot for all I care. It's all respectable; if he gets stuck in a little backwater of his field, that's his business; he can get out of it."

"Put his sketches in with him," said Alyx.

"Why?" said Machine.

"Because you don't have a word for it," she said. He shrugged, a little sadly. He riffled the book that had come from Raydos's pack, tearing out about half of it, and passed the sheets in to Gunnar. They were taped to Raydos's feet.

"Hell, he can still do a lot of things," said Machine, trying to smile.

"Yes," said Alyx, "and you will come out of this paralyzed from the neck down." He stopped smiling.

"But you will do a lot of things," she said. "Yes, you will get out of it. You will lose your body and Gunnar will lose his—his self-respect; he will make one more ghastly mistake and then another and another and in the end he will lose his soul at the very least and perhaps his life."

"You know all this," said Machine.

"Of course," said Alyx, "of course I do. I know it all. I know that Gavrily will do something generous and brave and silly and because he never in his life has learned how to do it, we will lose Gavrily. And then Iris—no, Iris has had it already, I think, and of course the Heavenly Twins will lose nothing because they have nothing to lose. Maybe they will lose their religion or drop their pills down a hole. And I—well, I —my profession, perhaps, or whatever loose junk I have lying around, because this blasted place is too good, you see, too easy; we don't meet animals, we don't meet paid professional murderers, all we meet is our own stupidity. Over and over. It's a picnic. It's a damned picnic. And Iris will come through because she never lives above her means. And a picnic is just her style."

"What will you lose?" said Machine, folding his arms across his chest.

"I will lose you," she said unsteadily, "what do you think of that?" He caught her in his arms, crushing the breath out of her.

"I like it," he whispered sardonically. "I like it, Tiny, because I am jealous. I am much too jealous. If I thought you didn't like me, I'd kill myself and if I thought you liked Iris more than me, I'd kill her. Do you hear me?"

"Don't be an ass," she said. "Let me go."

"I'll never let you go. Never. I'll die. With you."

Gunnar backed ponderously out of the bubble. He closed the door, running his hands carefully over the place where the door joined the rest of the ship until the crack disappeared. He seemed satisfied with it then. He watched it, although nothing seemed to happen for a few minutes; then the bubble rose noiselessly off the snow, went up faster and faster into the evening sky as if sliding along a cable and disappeared into the afterglow. It was going north. Alyx tried to pull away but Machine held on to her, grinning at his rival as the latter turned around, absently dusting his hands together. Then Gunnar groped for his gloves, put them on, absently looking at the two, at the others who had shared the contents of Raydos's pack and were flattening the pack itself into a shape that could be carried in an empty food container. There was the corpse, the man everyone had forgotten. Gunnar looked at it impersonally. He looked at Iris, the nuns, Gavrily, the other two: only seven of them now. His gloved hands dusted themselves together. He looked at nothing.

"Well?" drawled Machine.

"I think we will travel a little now," said Gunnar; "I think we will travel by starlight." He repeated the phrase, as if it pleased him. "By starlight," he said, "yes."

"By snowlight?" said Machine, raising his eyebrows.

"That too," said Gunnar, looking at something in the distance, "yes—that too—"

"Gunnar!" said Alyx sharply. His gaze settled on her.

"I'm all right," he said quietly. "I don't care who you play with," and he plodded over to the others, bent over, very big.

"I shall take you tonight," said Machine between his teeth; "I shall take you right before the eyes of that man!"

She brought the point of her elbow up into his ribs hard enough to double him over; then she ran through the powdery snow to the front of the little line that had already formed. Gunnar was leading them. Her hands were icy. She took his arm—it was unresponsive, nothing but a heavy piece of meat —and said, controlling her breathing, for she did not want him to know that she had been running—"I believe it is getting warmer."

He said nothing.

"I mention this to you," Alyx went on, "because you are the only one of us who knows anything about weather. Or about machinery. We would be in a bad way without you."

He still said nothing.

"I am very grateful," she said, "for what you did with the ship. There is nobody here who knows a damn thing about that ship, you know. No one but you could have—" (she was about to say *saved Raydos's life*) "done anything with the control board. I am grateful. We are all grateful.

"Is it going to snow?" she added desperately, "is it going to snow?"

"Yes," said Gunnar. "I believe it is."

"Can you tell me why?" said she. "I know nothing about it. I would appreciate it very much if you could tell me why."

"Because it is getting warmer."

"*Gunnar!*" she cried. "*Did you hear us?*"

Gunnar stopped walking. He turned to her slowly and slowly looked down at her, blankly, a little puzzled, frowning a little.

"I don't remember hearing anything," he said. Then he added sensibly, "That ship is a very good ship; it's insulated; you don't hear anything inside."

"Tell me about it," said Alyx, her voice almost failing, "and tell me why it's going to snow."

He told her, and she hung on his arm, pretending to listen, for hours.

They walked by starlight until a haze covered the stars; it got warmer, it got slippery. She tried to remember their destination by the stars. They stopped on Paradise's baby mountains, under the vast, ill-defined shadow of something going up, up, a slope going up until it melted into the gray sky, for the cloud cover shone a little, just as the snow shone a little, the light just enough to see by and not enough to see anything at all. When they lay down there was a pervasive feeling of falling to the left. Iris kept trying to clutch at the snow. Alyx told them to put their feet downhill and so they did, lying in a line and trying to hold each other's hands. Gunnar went off a little to one side, to watch—or rather to listen. Everything was indistinct. Five minutes after everyone had settled down—she could still hear their small readjustments, the moving about, the occasional whispering—she discerned someone squatting at her feet, his arms about his knees, balanced just so. She held out one arm and he pulled her to her feet, putting his arms around her: Machine's face, very close in the white darkness. "Over there," he said, jerking his head towards the place where Gunnar was, perhaps sitting, perhaps standing, a kind of blot against the gray sky.

"No," said Alyx.

"Why not?" said Machine in a low, mocking voice. "Do you think he doesn't know?"

She said nothing.

"Do you think there's anyone here who doesn't know?" Machine continued, a trifle brutally. "When you go off, you raise enough hell to wake the dead."

She nudged him lightly in the ribs, in the sore place, just enough to loosen his arms; and then she presented him with the handle of one of her knives, nudging him with that also, making him take step after step backwards, while he whispered angrily:

"What the hell!

"Stop it!

"What are you doing!

"What the devil!"

Then they were on the other side of the line of sleepers, several meters away.

"Here," she whispered, holding out the knife, "take it, take it. Finish him off. Cut off his head."

"I don't know what you're talking about!" snapped Machine.

"But not with me," she said; "oh, no!" and when he threw her down onto the snow and climbed on top of her, shaking her furiously, she only laughed, calling him a baby, teasing him, tickling him through his suit, murmuring mocking love-words, half in Greek, the better to infuriate him. He wound his arms around her and pulled, crushing her ribs, her fingers, smothering her with his weight, the knees of his long legs digging one into her shin and one into her thigh; there would be spectacular bruises tomorrow.

"Kill me," she whispered ecstatically. "Go on, kill me, kill me! Do what you want!" He let her go, lifting himself up on his hands, moving his weight off her. He stared down at her, the mask of a very angry young man. When she had got her breath back a little, she said:

"My God, you're strong!"

"Don't make fun of me," he said.

"But you are strong," she said breathlessly. "You're strong. You're enormous. I adore you."

"Like hell," said Machine shortly and began to get up. She flung both arms around him and held on.

"Do it again," she said, "do it again. Only please, please, more carefully!" He pulled away, making a face, then stayed where he was.

"If you're making fun of me—" he said.

She said nothing, only kissed his chin.

"I hate that man!" he burst out. "I hate his damned 'acceptable' oddities and his—his conventional heroism and his—the bloody amateur!

"He's spent his life being praised for individualism," he went on, "*his* individualism, good God! Big show. Make the Civs feel happy. Never two steps from trans and ports and flyers. Medicine. High-powered this. High-powered that. 'Ooooh, isn't he marvel! Isn't he brave! Let's get a tape and go shooting warts with Gunnar! Let's get a tape and go swimming undersea with Gunnar!' He records his own brain impulses, did you know that?"

"No," said Alyx.

"Yes," said Machine, "he records them and sells them. Gunnar's battle with the monsters. Gunnar's narrow escape. Gunnar's great adventure. All that heroism. That's what they want. That's why he's rich!"

"Well, they certainly wouldn't want the real thing," said Alyx softly, "now would they?"

He stared at her for a moment.

"No," he said more quietly, "I suppose they wouldn't."

"And I doubt," said Alyx, moving closer to him, "that Gunnar is recording anything just now; I think, my dear, that he's very close to the edge now."

"Let him fall in," said Machine.

"Are you rich?" said Alyx. Machine began to weep. He rolled to one side, half laughing, half sobbing.

"I!" he said, "I! Oh, that's a joke!"

"I don't have a damn thing," he said. "I knew there would be a flash here—*they* knew but they thought they could get away—so I came. To get lost. Spent everything. But you can't get lost, you know. You can't get lost anywhere any more, not even in a—a—you would call it a war, Agent."

"Funny war," said Alyx.

"Yes, very funny. A war in a tourist resort. I hope we don't make it. I hope I die here."

She slid her finger down the front of his suit. "I hope not," she said. "No," she said (walking both hands up and down his chest, beneath the long underwear, her little moist palms) "I certainly hope not."

"You're a single-minded woman," said Machine dryly.

She shook her head. She was thoughtfully making the tent of the night before. He helped her.

"Listen, love," she said, "I have no money, either, but I have something else; I am a Project. I think I have cost a lot of money. If we get through this, one of the things this Project will need to keep it happy so it can go on doing whatever it's supposed to do is you. So don't worry about that."

"And you think they'll let you," said Machine. It was a flat, sad statement.

"No," she said, "but nobody ever let me do anything in my life before and I never let that stop me." They were lying on their sides face to face now; she smiled up at him. "I am going to disappear into this damned suit if you don't pull me up," she said. He lifted her up a little under the arms and kissed her. His face looked as if something were hurting him.

"Well?" she said.

"The Machine," he said stiffly, "is—the Machine is fond of the Project."

"The Project loves the Machine," she said, "so—?"

"I can't," he said.

She put her arm around the back of his neck and rubbed her cheek against his. "We'll sleep," she said. They lay together for some time, a little uncomfortable because both were balanced on their sides, until he turned over on his back and she lay half on him and half off, her head butting into his armpit. She began to fall asleep, then accidentally moved so that his arm cut off her breathing, then snorted. She made a little, dissatisfied noise.

"What?" he said.

"Too hot," she said sleepily, "blasted underwear," so with difficulty she took it off—and he took off his—and they wormed it out of the top of the suits where the hoods tied together and chucked it into the snow. She was breathing into his neck. She had half fallen asleep again when all of a sudden she woke to a kind of earthquake: knees in a tangle, jouncing, bruising, some quiet, vehement swearing and a voice telling her for God's sake to wake up. Machine was trying to turn over. Finally he did.

"Aaaaaah—um," said Alyx, now on her back, yawning.

"Wake up!" he insisted, grabbing her by both hips.

"Yes, yes, I am," said Alyx. She opened her eyes. He seemed to be trembling all over and very upset; he was holding her too hard, also.

"What is it?" she whispered.

"This is not going to be a good one," said Machine, "do you know what I mean?"

"No," said Alyx. He swore.

"Listen," he said shakily, "I don't know what's the matter with me; I'm falling apart. I can't explain it, but it's going to be a bad one; you'll just have to wait through it."

"All right, all right," she said, "give me a minute," and she lay quietly, thinking, rubbing his hair—looked Oriental, like a brush now, growing into a peak on his forehead—began kissing various parts of his face, put her arms around his back, felt his hands on her hips (too hard; she thought *I'll be black and blue tomorrow*), concentrated on those hands, and then began to rub herself against him, over and over and over, until she was falling apart herself, dizzy, head swimming, completely out of control.

"God damn it, you're making it worse!" he shouted.

"Can't help it," said Alyx. "Got to—come on."

"It's not fair," he said, "not fair to you. Sorry."

"Forgiven," Alyx managed to say as he plunged in, as she diffused over the landscape—sixty leagues in each direction—and then turned into a drum, a Greek one, hourglass-shaped with the thumped in-and-out of both skins so extreme that they finally met in the middle, so that she then turned inside-out, upside-down and switched right-and-left sides, every cell, both hands, each lobe of her brain, all at once, while someone (anonymous) picked her up by the navel and shook her violently in all directions, remarking "If you don't make them cry, they won't live." She came to herself with the idea that Machine was digging up rocks. He was banging her on the head with his chin. Then after a while he stopped and she could feel him struggle back to self-possession; he took several deep, even breaths; he opened the suit hoods and pushed his face over her shoulder into the snow; then he opened one side of the little tent and let in a blast of cold air.

"Help!" said Alyx. He closed the suits. He leaned on his elbows. He said "I like you. I like you too much. I'm sorry." His face was wet to her touch: snow, tears or sweat. He said "I'm sorry, I'm sorry. We'll do it again."

"Oh no, no, no," she whispered weakly.

"Yes, don't worry," he said. "I'll control myself, it's not fair. No technique."

"If you use any more technique," she managed to get out, "there'll be nothing left of me in the morning but a pair of gloves and a small, damp spot."

"Don't lie," said Machine calmly.

She shook her head. She plucked at his arms, trying to bring his full weight down on her, but he remained propped on his elbows, regarding her face intently. Finally he said:

"Is that pleasure?"

"Is what?" whispered Alyx.

"Is it a pleasure," he said slowly, "or is it merely some detestable intrusion, some unbearable invasion, this being picked up and shaken, this being helpless and—and smashed and shattered into pieces when somebody lights a fuse at the bottom of one's brain!"

"It was pleasure for me," said Alyx softly.

"Was it the same for you?"

She nodded.

"I hate it," he said abruptly. "It was never like this before. Not like this. I hate it and I hate you."

She only nodded again. He watched her somberly.

"I think," he added finally, "that one doesn't like it or dislike it; one loves it. That is, something picked me up by the neck and pushed me into you. Ergo, I love you."

"I know," she said.

"It was not what I wanted."

"I know." She added, "It gets easier." He looked at her again; again she tried to pull him down. Then he remarked "We'll see," and smiled a little; he closed his eyes and smiled.

He let his whole weight down on her carefully, saying, "You'll have to scramble out when I get too heavy, Tiny."

"Will."

"And tomorrow night," he added grimly, "I'll tell you the story of my life."

"Nice," she said, "yes, oh that will be . . . nice . . ." and she sank down deliciously into a sleep of feathers, into the swan's-down and duck's-down and peacock's-down that made up the snow of Paradise, into the sleep and snow of Paradise . . .

The next day Paradise threw hell at them. It was the first real weather. It began with fat, heavy flakes just before dawn so that Gavrily (who had taken the dawn watch) was half buried himself and had to dig out some of the sleepers before he could rouse them; they were so used to the feeling of the stuff against their faces or leaking into their hoods and up their arms that they slept right through it. It turned colder as they ate breakfast, standing around and stamping and brushing themselves; then the snow got smaller and harder and then the first wind blasted around an outcropping of rock. It threw Alyx flat on her back. Gunnar said expressionlessly "You're smaller than we are." The others immediately huddled together. Goggles had not been packed with their equipment. They started out with the wind slamming them from side to side as if they had been toys, changing direction every few seconds and driving into their faces and down their necks stinging grains of rice. Gunnar insisted they were in a pass. They stumbled and fell more often than not, unable to see ten feet on either side, reaching in front of them, holding on to each other and sometimes falling onto hands and knees. Gunnar had faced away from the wind and was holding with both bare hands onto a map he had made from some of Raydos's things. He said "This is the pass." One of the nuns slipped and sprained her back. Gunnar was holding the map close to his eyes, moving it from side to side as if trying to puzzle something out. He said again:

"This is the pass. What are you waiting for?"

"What do you think, you flit!" snapped Iris. She was on one side of the sister and Gavrily on the other, trying to haul the woman to her feet. Gunnar opened his mouth again. Before he could speak, Alyx was at him (clawing at the bottom of his jacket to keep from falling in the wind) and crushing the map into a ball in his hand. "All right, all right!" she shouted through the snow, "it's the pass. Machine, come on," and the three of them plodded ahead, feeling and scrambling over hidden rocks, up a slope they could not see, veiled in snow that whipped about and rammed them, edging on their hands and knees around what seemed like a wall.

Then the wind stopped and Machine disappeared at the same time. She could not see where he had gone for a moment; then the wind returned—at their backs—and blasted the snow clear for a moment, hurrying it off the rock wall in sheets and revealing what looked like a well in the rock and a great, flattened slide of snow near it. It looked as if something had been dragged across it. Then the snow swept back, leaving only a dark hole.

"Chimney!" said Gunnar. Alyx flung herself on the ground and began to inch towards the dark hole in the snow. "I can't see," she said. She went as close as she dared. Gunnar stood back at a little distance, bracing himself against the wall. She risked lifting one hand to wave him closer, but he did not move. "Gunnar!" she shouted. He began to move slowly towards her, hugging the wall; then he stopped where the wall appeared to stop, taking from inside his glove the crumpled map and examining it, bracing himself automatically as the wind rocked him back and forth, and tracing something on the map with one finger as if there were something that puzzled him.

"Gunnar," said Alyx, flattening herself against the ground, "Gunnar, this hole is too broad for me. I can't climb down it."

Gunnar did not move.

"Gunnar," said Alyx desperately, "you're a mountain climber. You're an expert. You can climb down."

He raised his eyes from the map and looked at her without interest.

"You can climb down it," continued Alyx, digging her fingers into the snow. "You can tie a rope to him and then you can climb up and we'll pull him up."

"Well, I don't think so," he said. He came a little closer, apparently not at all bothered by the wind, and peered into the hole; then he repeated in a tone of finality, "No, I don't think so."

"You've got to," said Alyx. He balled up the map again and put it back into his glove. He had turned and was beginning to plod back towards the place where they had left the others, bent halfway into the wind, when she shouted his name and he stopped. He came back and looked into the hole with his hands clasped behind his back; then he said:

"Well, I don't think I'll try that."

"He's dying," said Alyx.

"No, I think that's a little risky," Gunnar added reasonably. He continued to look into the hole. "I'll let you down," he said finally. "Is that all right?"

"Yes, that's all right," said Alyx, shutting her eyes. She considered kicking him or tripping him so that he'd fall in himself but he was keeping a very prudent distance from the edge, and besides, there was no telling where he would fall or how badly Machine was hurt. He might fall on Machine. She said, "That's fine, thanks." She rolled over and half sat up, slipping off her pack; clinging to it, she got out the length of rope they all carried and tied it under her arms. She was very clumsy in the wind; Gunnar watched her without offering to help, and when she was finished he took the free end and held it laxly in one hand. "Your weight won't be too much," he said.

"Gunnar," she said, "hold that thing right." He shook himself a little and took a better hold on the rope. Coming closer, he said "Wait a minute," rummaged in her pack and handed her a kind of bulb which she tucked into her sleeve. It looked like the medicine he had once shown her, the kind they had used on Raydos. He said "Put it in the crook of his arm and press it. A little at a time." She nodded, afraid to speak to him. She crawled toward the edge of the well where the snow had suddenly collapsed under Machine, and throwing her arms over the ground, let herself down into the dark. The rope held and Gunnar did not let go. She imagined that he would wait for her to shout and then throw down his own rope; she wrapped her arms around her head for the hole was too wide for her to brace herself and she spun slowly around —or rather, the walls did, hitting her now and then—until the chimney narrowed. She climbed part of the way down, arms and legs wide as if crucified. She had once seen an acrobat roll on a wheel that way. The darkness seemed to lighten a little and she thought she could see something light at the bottom, so she shouted "Gunnar!" up the shaft. As she had expected, a coil of rope came whispering down, settled about her shoulders, slid off to one side and hung about her like a necklace, the free end dangling down into the half-dark.

But when she pulled at it, she found that the other end was fastened under her own arms.

She did not think. She was careful about that. She descended further, to where Machine lay wedged like a piece of broken goods, his eyes shut, one arm bent at an unnatural angle, his head covered with blood. She could not get at his pack because it was under him. She found a kind of half-shelf next to him that she could stay on by bracing her feet against the opposite wall, and sitting there, she took from her sleeve the bulb Gunnar had given her. She could not get at either of Machine's arms without moving him, for the other one was twisted under him and jammed against the rock, but she knew that a major blood vessel was in the crook of the arm, so she pressed the nose of the bulb against a vessel in his neck and squeezed the bulb twice. Nothing happened. She thought: *Gunnar has gone to get the others.* She squeezed the medicine again and then was afraid, because it might be too much; someone had said "I've given Raydos all he can take"; so she put the thing back in her sleeve. Her legs ached. She could just about reach Machine. She took off a glove and put one hand in front of his mouth to satisfy herself that he was breathing, and then she tried feeling for a pulse in his throat and got something cold, possibly from the medicine bottle. But he had a pulse. His eyes remained closed. In her own pack was a time-telling device called a watch—she supposed vaguely that they called it that from the watches they had to keep at night, or perhaps they called it that for some other reason— but that was up top. She could not get to it. She began to put her weight first on one leg and then on the other, to rest a little, and then she found she could move closer to Machine, who still lay with his face upward, his eyes shut. He had fallen until the narrow part of the chimney stopped him. She was beginning to be able to see better and she touched his face with her bare hand; then she tried to feel about his head, where he was hurt, where the blood that came out increased ever so little, every moment, steadily black and black. The light was very dim. She felt gashes but nothing deep; she thought it must have been a blow or something internal in the body, so she put the medicine bulb to his neck again and squeezed it. Nothing happened. *They'll be back*, she thought. She looked at the bottle but could not see well enough to tell what was written on it so she put it back into her sleeve. It occurred to her then that they had never taught her to read, although they had taught her to speak. Lines came into her mind, *We are done for if we fall asleep*, something she must have heard; for she was growing numb and beginning to fall asleep, or not sleep exactly but some kind of retreat, and the dim, squirming walls around her began to close in and draw back, the way things do when one can barely see. She put both hands on Machine's face where the blood had begun to congeal in the cold, drew them over his face, talked to him steadily to keep herself awake, talked to him to wake him up. She thought *He has concussion*, the word coming from somewhere in that hypnotic hoard they had put into her head. She began to nod and woke with a jerk. She said softly "What's your name?" but Machine did not move. "No, tell me your name," she persisted gently, "tell me your name," drawing her hands over his face, unable to feel from the knees down, trying not to sink into sleep, passing her fingers through his hair while she nodded with sleep, talking to him, whispering against his cheek, feeling again and again for his hurts, trying to move her legs and coming close enough to him to see his face in the dim, dim light; to put her hands against his cheeks and speak to him in her own language, wondering why she should mind so much that he was dying, she who had had three children and other men past counting, wondering how there could be so much to these people and so little, so much and so little, like the coat of snow that made everything seem equal, both the up and the down, like the blowing snow that hid the most abysmal poverty and the precious things down under the earth. She jerked awake. Snow was sifting down on her shoulders and something snaky revolved in the air above her.

But Machine had stopped breathing some time before.

She managed to wind her own rope loosely around her neck and climb the other by bracing herself against the side of the well: not as smoothly as she liked, for the rope wavered a little and tightened unsteadily while Alyx cursed and shouted up to them to mind their bloody business if they didn't want to get it in a few minutes. Gavrily pulled her up over the edge.

"Well?" he said. She was blinking. The four others were all on the rope. She smiled at them briefly, slapping her gloves one against the other. Her hands were rubbed raw. The wind, having done its job, had fallen, and the snow fell straight as silk sheets.

"Well?" said Gavrily again, anxiously, and she shook her head. She could see on the faces of all of them a strange expression, a kind of mixed look as if they did not know what to feel or show. Of course; they had not liked him. She jerked her head towards the pass. Gavrily looked as if he were about to say something, and Iris as if she were about to cry suddenly, but Alyx only shook her head again and started off behind Gunnar. She saw one of the nuns looking back fearfully at the hole. They walked for a while and then Alyx took Gunnar's arm, gently holding on to the unresponsive arm of the big, big man, her lips curling back over her teeth on one side, involuntarily, horribly. She said:

"Gunnar, you did well."

He said nothing.

"You ought to have lived in my country," she said. "Oh yes! you would have been a hero there."

She got in front of him, smiling, clasping her hands together, saying "You think I'm fooling, don't you?" Gunnar stopped.

"It was your job," he said expressionlessly.

"Well, of course," she said sweetly, "of course it was," and crossing her hands wrist to wrist as she had done a thousand times before, she suddenly bent them in and then flipped them wide, each hand holding a knife. She bent her knees slightly; he was two heads taller and twice as heavy, easily. He put one hand stupidly up to his head.

"You can't do this," he said.

"Oh, there's a risk," she said, "there's that, of course," and she began to turn him back towards the others as he automatically stepped away from her, turning him in a complete circle to within sight of the others, while his face grew frightened, more and more awake, until he finally cried out:

"Oh God, Agent, what will you do!"

She shifted a little on her feet.

"I'm not like you!" he said, "I can't help it, what do you expect of me?"

"He came and got us," said Iris, frightened.

"None of us," said Gunnar quickly, "can help the way we are brought up, Agent. You are a creature of your world, believe me, just as I am of mine; I can't help it; I wanted to be like you but I'm not, can I help that? I did what I could! What can a man do? What do you expect me to do? What could I do!"

"Nothing. It's not your job," said Alyx.

"I am ashamed," said Gunnar, stammering, "I am ashamed, Agent, I admit I did the wrong thing. I should have gone down, yes, I should have—put those things away, for God's sake!—forgive me, please, hate me but forgive me; I am what I am, I am only what I am! For Heaven's sake! For God's sake!"

"Defend yourself," said Alyx, and when he did not—for it did not seem to occur to him that this was possible—she slashed the fabric of his suit with her left-hand knife and with the right she drove Trans-Temp's synthetic steel up to the hilt between Gunnar's ribs. It did not kill him; he staggered back a few steps, holding his chest. She tripped him onto his back and then cut his suit open while the madman did not even move, all this in an instant, and when he tried to rise she slashed him through the belly and then—lest the others intrude—pulled back his head by the pale hair and cut his throat from ear to ear. She did not spring back from the blood but stood in it, her face strained in the same involuntary grimace as before, the cords standing out on her neck. Iris grabbed her arm and pulled her away.

"He came and got us," whispered Iris, terrified, "he did, he did, really."

"He took his time," said Gavrily slowly. The five of them stood watching Gunnar, who lay in a red lake. The giant was dead. Alyx watched him until Iris turned her around; she followed obediently for a few steps, then stopped and knelt and wiped her hands in the snow. Then putting on her gloves, she took handfuls of snow and rubbed them over her suit, up and down, up and down. She cleaned herself carefully and automatically, like a cat. Then she put the knives away and silently followed the four others up the pass, floundering and slipping through the still-falling snow, hunched a little, her fists clenched. At dusk they found a shallow cave at the bottom of a long slope, not a rock cave but soft rock and frozen soil. Gavrily said they were over the pass. They sat as far back against the cave wall as they could, watching the snow fall across the opening and glancing now and again at Alyx. She was feeling a kind of pressure at the back of her neck, something insistent like a forgotten thought, but she could not remember what it was; then she took the medicine bulb out of her sleeve and began playing with it, tossing it up and down in her hand. That was what she had been trying to remember. Finally Iris giggled nervously and said:

"What are you doing with that?"

"Put it in your pack," said Alyx, and she held it out to the girl.

"*My* pack?" said Iris, astonished. "Why?"

"We may need it," said Alyx.

"Oh, Lord," said Iris uncomfortably, "we've still got enough to eat, haven't we?"

"Eat?" said Alyx.

"Sure," said Iris, "that's lecithin. From synthetic milk," and then she clapped both hands across her mouth as Alyx leapt to her feet and threw the thing out into the falling snow. It seemed to Alyx that she had suddenly walked into an enormous snake, or a thing like one of the things that cleaned up houses in civilized countries: something long, strong and elastic that winds around you and is everywhere the same, everywhere equally strong so that there is no relief from it, no shifting it or getting away from it. She could not bear it. She did not think of Machine but only walked up and down for a few minutes, trying to change her position so that there would be a few minutes when it would not hurt; then she thought of a funnel and something at the bottom of it; and then finally she saw him. Wedged in like broken goods. She thought *Wedged in like broken goods.* She put her hands over her eyes. The same face.

The same face. Iris had gotten up in alarm and put one hand on Alyx's shoulder; Alyx managed to whisper "Iris!"

"Yes? Yes?" said Iris anxiously.

"Get those damned women," said Alyx hoarsely for now he was all over the cave, pale, eyes shut, on every wall, irretrievably lost, a smashed machine with a broken arm at the bottom of a rock chimney somewhere. It was intolerable. For a moment she thought that she was bleeding, that her arms and legs were cut away. Then that disappeared. She put out her hands to touch his face, to stay awake, to wake him up, again and again and again, and then this would not stop but went on and on in a kind of round dance that she could not control, over and over in complete silence with the cold of the rock-chimney and the dim light and the smell of the place, with Machine still dead, no matter what she did, lying on top of his pack and not speaking, wedged into the rock like a broken toy with one leg dangling. It kept happening. She thought *I never lost anything before.* She cried out in her own language.

When the sister came with the pill-box to comfort her, Alyx wrenched the box out of the woman's hand, swallowed three of the things, shoved the box up her own sleeve—above the knife-harness—and waited for death.

But the only thing that happened was that the nuns got frightened and retreated to the other end of the cave.

And Alyx fell asleep almost instantly.

She woke up all at once, standing, like a board hit with a hoe; Paradise—which had been stable—turned over once and settled itself. This was interesting but not novel. She looked outside the cave, forgot what she had seen, walked over to the nuns and pulled one of them up by the hair, which was very amusing; she did it to the other, too, and then when the noise they made had waked up Iris and Gavrily, she said "Damn it, Gavrily, you better be careful, this place has it in for me."

He only blinked at her. She pulled him outside by one arm and whispered it fiercely into his ear, pulling him down and standing on her toes to do so, but he remained silent. She pushed him away. She looked at his frightened face and said contemptuously "Oh, you! you can't hear," and dropped her pack into the snow; then when somebody put it on her back she dropped it again; only the third time she lost interest. They put it on again and she forgot about it. By then they were all up and facing out onto the plains, a flat land covered with hard snow, a little dirty, like pulverized ice, and a brown haze over the sky so that the sun showed through it in an unpleasant smear: she wanted to look at it and would not go anywhere until someone pushed her. It was not an attractive landscape and it was not an unattractive one; it was fascinating. Behind her Gavrily began to sing:

> When I woke up, my darling dear,
> When I woke up and found you near,
> I thought you were an awful cutie
> And you will always be my sweetie.

She turned around and shouted at him. Someone gave a shocked gasp. They prodded her again. She found Iris at her elbow, quite unexpectedly pushing her along, and began to explain that her feet were doing that part of the work. She was very civil. Then she added:

"You see, I am not like you; I am not doing anything idiotic or lying in the snow making faces. I haven't lost my head and I'm going on in a perfectly rational manner; I can still talk and I can still think and I wish to the devil you would stop working my elbow like a pump; it is very annoying, besides being entirely unnecessary. You are not a nice girl."

"I don't know that language," said Iris helplessly, "what are you saying?"

"Well, you're young," said Alyx serenely, "after all."

At midday they let her look at the sky.

She lay down flat in the snow and watched it as the others ate, through a pair of binoculars she had gotten from someone's pack, concentrating on the detail work and spinning the little wheel in the middle until Iris grabbed her hands and hoisted her to her feet. This made her cross and she bit Iris in the arm, getting a mouthful of insulated suit. She seriously considered that Iris had played a trick on her. She looked for the binoculars but they were not around; she lagged after Iris with her gloves dangling from her wrists and her bare fingers making circles around her eyes; she tried to tell Iris to look at that over there, which is what that which it is, and then a terrible suspicion flashed into her mind in one sentence:

You are going out of your mind.

Immediately she ran to Iris, tugging at Iris's arm, holding her hand, crying out "Iris, Iris, I'm not going out of my mind, am I? Am I going out of my mind? Am I?" and Iris said "No, you're not; come on, *please*," (crying a little) and the voice of one of the Hellish Duo sounded, like an infernal wind instrument creeping along the bottom of the snow, in a mean, meaching, nasty tone, just like the nasty blur in the brown sky, an altogether unpleasant, exceptionable and disgusting tone:

"She's coming out of it."

"How can I come on if I'm coming out?" demanded Alyx, going stiff all over with rage.

"Oh, please!" said Iris.

"How," repeated Alyx in a fury, "can I come on if I'm coming out? How? I'd like you to explain that"—her voice rising shrilly—"that—conundrum, that impossibility, that flat perversion of the laws of nature; it is absolutely and utterly impossible and you are nothing but an excuse, an evasion, a cheap substitute for a human being and a little tin whore!"

Iris turned away.

"But how can I!" exploded Alyx. "How can I be on and out? How can I? It's ridiculous!"

Iris began to cry. Alyx folded her arms around herself and sunk her head on her chest; then she went over to Iris and patted Iris with her mittens; she would have given up even the sky if it made Iris unhappy. She said reassuringly "There, there."

"Just come on, please," said Iris. Subdued, Alyx followed her. A great while after, when she had put down the other foot, Alyx said "You understand, don't you?" She took Iris's arm, companionably.

"It's only the pills," said Iris, "that's all."

"I never take them," said Alyx.

"Of course not," said Iris.

Curiously Alyx said, "Why are you shaking?"

They walked on.

*

Towards evening, long after the immense day had sunk and
even the diffused light died out so that the bottom of the
plain was nothing but a black pit, though even then the snow-
luminescence glowed about them vaguely, not enough to see
by *but enough* (Alyx thought) *to make you take a chance and
break your neck*—she realized that they had been handing her
about from one to the other all day. She supposed it was the
pills. They came and went in waves of unreason, oddly detached from herself; she dozed between them as she walked,
not thinking of suggesting to the others that they stop, and
when they did stop she merely sat down on the snow, put her
arms around her knees and stared off into the darkness. Eventually the light from the snow failed. She felt for the box in her
sleeve and laughed a little; someone near her stirred and whispered "What? What?" and then yawned. The breathing fell
again into its soft, regular rhythm. Alyx laughed again, dreamily, then felt something in back of her, then turned around to
look for it, then found nothing. It was in back of her again.
She yawned. The darkness was becoming uncomfortable. She
fought the desire to sleep. She felt about and nudged the person nearest her, who immediately sat up—to judge from the
sound—and gave out a kind of "Ha!" like a bellows. Alyx
laughed.

"Wha'—huh!" said Gavrily.

"Look," she said sensibly, "about these pills. What do they
do to you?"

"Muh," said Gavrily.

"Well, how many can I take?" said Alyx, amused.

"Take what?"

"Take pills," said Alyx.

"What? Don't take any," he said. He sounded a little more
awake.

"How many," said Alyx patiently, "can I take without hurting myself?"

"None," said Gavrily. "Bad for the liver. Meta—metabol—
give 'em back."

"You won't get them," said Alyx. "Don't try. How many can
I take without making a nuisance of myself?"

"Huh?" said Gavrily.

"How many?" repeated Alyx. "One?"

"No, no," said Gavrily stupidly, "none," and he muttered something else, turned over in the dark and apparently fell asleep. She heard him snore; then it was turned off into a strangled, explosive snort and he breathed like a human being. Alyx sat peering keenly into the dark, feeling them come closer and closer and smiling to herself. When the world was about to touch her—and she would not stand for that—she took out her little box. She broke a pill and swallowed half. She came to the surface nonetheless, as one does when breaking the surface of water, blinded, chilled, shocked by the emptiness of air; the snow solidified under her, her suit began to take shape and grate like iron, the sleepers next to her emerged piecemeal out of the fog, grotesquely in separate limbs, in disconnected sounds, there were flashes of realization, whole moments of absolute reality. It simply would not do. She grinned nervously and hugged her knees. She blinked into the darkness as if her eyes were dazzled; she held on to her knees as a swimmer holds on to the piles of a jetty with his fingertips, she who had never been drunk in her life because it impaired the reason. She stuffed the box back up her sleeve. Eventually something happened—she shook her head as if to get rid of a fly or a nervous tic—the water rose. It closed over her head. She yawned. With her mouth wide open, water inside, water outside, she slid down, and down, and down, singing like a mermaid: *I care for nobody, no, not I.* She slept.

And nobody cares for me.

The false dawn came over the flats, bringing nothing with it.

She sat and considered her sins.

That they were vast was undeniably true, a mental land as flat and bare as a world-sized table, and yet with here and there those disturbing dips and slides: concave surfaces that somehow remained flat, hills that slid the other way, like the squares on a chessboard which bend and produce nausea. Such places exist.

Her sins were terrible. She was staring at a pink marble bathtub, full of water, a bathtub in which she had once bathed in the palace of Knossos on Crete, and which now hung on the ceiling overhead. The water was slipping. She was going to be drowned. The ocean stuck to the sky, heaving. In her youth she had walked town streets and city streets, stolen things, been immensely popular; it had all come to nothing. Nothing had come out of nothing. She did not regret a single life lost. In the snow appeared a chessboard and on the chessboard figures, and these figures one by one slid down into squares in the board and disappeared. The squares puckered and became flat. She put her fingers into them but they would not take her, which was natural enough in a woman who had not even loved her own children. You could not trust anyone in those times. The electromagnetic spectrum was increasing. Slowly the plains filled with air, as a pool with water; an enormous racket went on below the cliff that was the edge of the earth; and finally the sun threw up one hand to grasp the cliff, climbed, clung, rose, mounted and sailed brilliantly white and clear into a brilliant sky.

It said to her, in the voice of Iris: "You are frozen through and through. You are a detestable woman."

She fell back against the snow, dead.

When the dawn came, bringing a false truce, Alyx was sitting up with her arms clasped about her knees and watching the others wake up. She was again, as before, delicately iced over, on the line between reason and unreason. She thought she would keep it that way. She ate with the others, saying nothing, doing nothing, watching the murky haze in the sky and the spreading thumbprint in it that was the sun. The landscape was geometric and very pleasing. In the middle of the morning they passed a boulder someone or something had put out on the waste: to one side of it was a patch of crushed snow and brown moss showing through. Later in the day the world became more natural, though no less pleasant, and they stopped to eat once more, sitting in the middle of the plain that spread out to nowhere in particular. Iris was leaning over and eating out of one hand, utterly beautiful as were all the others, the six or seven or eight of them, all very beautiful and the scenery too, all of which Alyx explained, and that at very great length.

"What do you mean!" cried Iris suddenly. "What do you mean you're going to go along without us, what do you mean by that!"

"Huh?" said Alyx.

"And don't call me names," said Iris, trembling visibly. "I've had enough," and she went off and sat by somebody else. *What have you had enough of?* thought Alyx curiously, but she followed her anyway, to see that she came to no harm. Iris was sitting by one of the nuns. Her face was half turned away and there was a perceptible shadow on it. The nun was saying "Well, I told you." The shadow on Iris's face seemed to grow into a skin disease, something puckered or blistered like the lichens on a rock, a very interesting purple shadow; then it contracted into a small patch on her face and looked as if it were about to go out, but finally it turned into something.

Iris had a black eye.

"Where'd you get that?" said Alyx, with interest.

Iris put her hand over her eye.

"Well, where'd you get it?" said Alyx. "Who gave it to you? Did you fall against a rock?

"I think you're making it up," she added frankly, but the words did not come out quite right. The black eye wavered as if it were going to turn into a skin disease again. "Well?" demanded Alyx. "How'd you get it out here in the middle of the desert? Huh? How did you? Come on!"

"You gave it to me," said Iris.

"Oh, she won't understand anything!" exclaimed one of the nuns contemptuously. Alyx sat down in the snow and tucked her feet under her. She put her arms around herself. Iris was turning away again, nursing the puffy flesh around her blood-shot eye: it was a purple bruise beginning to turn yellow and a remarkable sight, the focus of the entire plain, which had begun to wheel slowly and majestically around it. However, it looked more like a black eye every moment.

"*Me?*" Alyx said finally.

"In your sleep," answered one of the nuns. "You are certainly a practiced woman. I believe you are a bad woman. We have all tried to take the pills away from you and the only issue of it is that Iris has a black eye and Gavrily a sprained wrist. Myself, I wash my hands of it.

"Of course," she added with some satisfaction, "it is too late now. Much too late. You have been eating them all along. You can't stop now; you would die, you know. Metabolic balances."

"What, in one night!" said Alyx.

"No," said the other. "Five."

"I think we are running out of food," said Iris. "We had better go on."

"Come on," she added, getting up.

They went on.

She took command two days later when she had become more habituated to the stuff, and although someone followed them constantly (but out of sight) there were no more hallucinations and her decisions were—on the whole—sensible. She thought the whole thing was a grand joke. When the food disappeared from out of the bottomless bags, she turned them inside out and licked the dust off them, and the others did the same; when she bent down, supporting herself on one arm, and looked over the brown sky for aircraft, the others did the same; and when she held up two fingers against one eye to take the visual diameter of the bleary sun and then moved the two fingers three times to one side—using her other hand as a marker—to find out their way, so did they, though they did not know why. There was no moss, no food, hardly any light, and bad pains in the stomach. Snow held them up for a day when the sun went out altogether. They sat together and did not talk. The next day the sky lifted a little and they went on, still not talking. When the middle of the day came and they had rested a while, they refused to get up; so she had to pummel them and kick them to their feet. She said she saw a thing up ahead that was probably the Pole station; she said they had bad eyes and bad ears and bad minds and could not expect to see it. They went on for the rest of the day and the next morning had to be kicked and cuffed again until they got up, and so they walked slowly on, leaving always the same footprints in the thin snow, a line of footprints behind exactly matching the fresh line in front, added one by one, like a line of stitching. Iris said there was a hobby machine that did that with only a single foot, faster than the eye could follow, over and over again, depositing now a rose, now a face, again a lily, a dragon, a tower, a shield. . . .

*

On the fifty-seventh day they reached the Pole station.

It sprawled over five acres of strangely irregular ground: cut-stone blocks in heaps, stone paths that led nowhere, stone walls that enclosed nothing, a ruined city, entirely roofless. Through their binoculars nothing looked taller than any of them. Nothing was moving. They stood staring at it but could make no sense of it. One of the nuns flopped down in the snow. Gavrily said:

"Someone ought to let them know we're here."

"They know," said Alyx.

"They don't know," he said.

"They know," said Alyx. She was looking through the binoculars. She had her feet planted wide apart in the snow and was fiddling with the focus knob, trying to find something in the ruins. Around her the women lay like big dolls. She knew it was the Pole because of the position of the sun; she knew it was not a city and had never been a city but something the lieutenant had long ago called a giant aerial code and she knew that if someone does not come out to greet you, you do not run to greet him. She said "Stay here," and hung the binoculars around her neck.

"No, Agent," said Gavrily. He was swaying a little on his feet.

"Stay here," she repeated, tucking the binoculars inside her suit, and dropping to her knees, she began to crawl forward. Gavrily, smiling, walked past her towards the giant anagram laid out on the snow; smiling, he turned and waved, saying something she could not catch; and resolutely marching forward—because he could talk to people best, she supposed, although he was stumbling a little and his face was gray—he kept on walking in the direction of the Pole station, over the flat plain, until his head was blown off.

It was done silently and bloodlessly, in a flash of light. Gavrily threw up both arms, stood still, and toppled over. Behind her Alyx heard someone gasp repeatedly, in a fit of hiccoughs. Silence.

"Iris, give me your pack," said Alyx.

"Oh, no, no, no, no, no, no, no, no," said Iris.

"I want to go away," said someone else, tiredly.

Alyx had to kick them to get the packs off them; then she had to push Iris's face into the snow until the girl stopped grabbing at her; she dragged all four packs over the snow like sleds, and stopping a few feet from Gavrily's body, she dumped all four onto the ground and pulled Gavrily back by the feet. *Marker*, she thought. Cursing automatically, she wrenched the packs open and lobbed a few bottles at the town at random. They vanished in a glitter two meters from the ground. She thought for a moment and then rapidly assembled a crossbow; bolts fired from it met the same fate; the crossbow itself, carefully lifted into the air, flared at the tip and the whole thing became so hot that she had to drop it. Her gloves were charred. Wrapping bandages from one of the packs around the bow, she lifted it again, this time ten paces to one side; again the tip vanished; ten paces to the other side and the same thing happened; crawling forward with her sunglasses on, she held it up in front of her and watched the zone of disappearance move slowly down to the grip. She tried it with another, twenty paces to the left. Twenty paces to the right. Her palms were blistered, the gloves burned off. The thing got closer and closer to the ground; there would be no crawling under it. She retreated to Gavrily's body and found Iris behind it, holding on to one of the packs to keep herself steady, whispering "What is it, what is it, what is it?"

"It's a fence," said Alyx, thrusting her stinging hands into the snow, "and whoever's running it doesn't have the sense to turn it off."

"Oh no, it's a machine," whispered Iris, laying her head against the pack, "it's a machine, it's no use, there's nobody there."

"If there were nobody there," said Alyx, "I do not think they would need a fence—Iris!" and she began shaking the girl, who seemed to be falling asleep.

"Doesn't know anything," said Iris, barely audible. "Idiots. Doesn't care."

"Iris!" shouted Alyx, slapping her, "Iris!"

"Only numbers," said Iris, and passed out. Alyx pulled her over by one shoulder and rubbed snow on her face. She fed her snow and put her forefingers under the girl's ears, pressing hard into the glands under them. The pain brought the girl around; "Only numbers," she said again.

"Iris," said Alyx, "give me some numbers."

"I.D.," said Iris, "on my back. Microscopic."

"Iris," said Alyx slowly and distinctly, "I cannot read. You must count something out for me. You must count it out while I show those bastards that there is somebody out here. Otherwise we will never get in. We are not supposed to be recognized and we won't be. We are camouflaged. You must give me some numbers."

"Don't know any," said Iris. Alyx propped her up against what was left of one of the packs. She dozed off. Alyx brought her out of it again and the girl began to cry, tears going effortlessly down her cheeks, busily one after the other. Then she said "In the Youth Core we had a number."

"Yes?" said Alyx.

"It was the number of our Core and it meant the Jolly Pippin," said Iris weakly. "It went like this—" and she recited it.

"I don't know what those words mean," said Alyx; "you must show me," and holding up Iris's hand, she watched while the girl slowly stuck up fingers: five seven seven, five two, seven five five six. Leaving Iris with her head propped against the pack, Alyx wound everything she could around the base of one of the crossbows, and lifting it upwards slowly spelled out five seven seven, five two, seven five five six, until everything was gone, when she wound another pack around another bow, leaving the first in the snow to cool, and again spelled out the number over and over until she could not move either hand, both hurt so abominably, and Iris had passed out for the second time.

Then something glittered in the middle of the Pole station and figures in snowsuits came running through the heaps of stone and the incomplete stone walls. Alyx thought dryly *It's about time.* She turned her head and saw the nuns tottering towards her, she thought suddenly *God, how thin!* and feeling perfectly well, she got up to wave the nuns on, to urge them to greet the real human beings, the actual living people who had finally come out in response to Iris's Jolly Pippin. A phrase she had heard sometime during the trip came to her mind: The Old School Yell. She stepped forward smartly and gestured to one of the men, but as he came closer—two others were picking up Iris, she saw, and still others racing towards the nuns

—she realized that he had no face, or none to speak of, really, a rather amusing travesty or approximation, that he was, in fact, a machine like the workers she had seen in the sheds when they had first set out on their picnic. Someone had told her then "They're androids. Don't nod." She continued to wave. She turned around for a last look at Paradise and there, only a few meters away, as large as life, stood Machine with his arms crossed over his chest. She said to him "What's a machine?" but he did not answer. With an air of finality, with the simplicity and severity of a dying god, he pulled over his blue eyes the goggled lenses and snout of another species, rejecting her, rejecting all of them; and tuned in to station Nothing (twenty-four hours a day every day, someone had said) he turned and began to walk away, fading as he walked, walking as he went away, listening to Trivia between the earth and the air until he walked himself right into a cloud, into nothing, into the blue, blue sky.

Ah, but I feel fine! thought Alyx, and walking forward, smiling as Gavrily had done, she saw under the hood of her android the face of a real man. She collapsed immediately.

Three weeks later Alyx was saying goodbye to Iris on the Moondrom on Old Earth, a vast idiot dome full of mist and show-lights, with people of all sorts rising and falling on streams of smoke. Iris was going the cheap way to the Moon for a conventional weekend with a strange young man. She was fashionably dressed all in silver, for that was the color that month: silver eyes, silvered eyelids, a cut-out glassene dress with a matching cloak, and her silver luggage and coiffure, both vaguely spherical, bobbing half a meter in the air behind their owner. It would have been less unnerving if the hair had been attached to Iris's head; as it was, Alyx could not keep her eyes off it.

Moreover, Iris was having hysterics for the seventh time in the middle of the Moondrom because her old friend who had gone through so much with her, and had taught her to shoot, and had saved her life, would not tell her anything—anything —anything!

"Can I help it if you refuse to believe me?" said Alyx.

"Oh, you think I'll tell *him!*" snapped Iris scornfully, referring to her escort whom neither of them had yet met. She was searching behind her in the air for something that was apparently supposed to come out of her luggage, but didn't. Then they sat down, on nothing.

"Listen, baby," said Alyx, "just listen. For the thirty-third time, Trans-Temp is not the Great Trans-Temporal Cadre of Heroes and Heroines and don't shake your head at me because it *isn't*. It's a study complex for archaeologists, that's all it is, and they fish around blindfold in the past, love, just as you would with a bent pin; though they're very careful where and when they fish because they have an unholy horror of even chipping the bottom off a canoe. They think the world will blow up or something. They stay thirty feet above the top of the sea and twenty feet below it and outside city limits and so on and so on, just about everything you can think of. And they can't even let through anything that's alive. Only one day they were fishing in the Bay of Tyre a good forty feet down and they just happened to receive twenty-odd cubic meters of sea-water complete with a small, rather inept Greek thief who had just pinched an expensive chess set from the Prince of Tyre, who between ourselves is no gentleman. They tell me I was attached to a rope attached to knots attached to a rather large boulder with all of us considerably more dead than alive, just dead enough, in fact, to come through at all, and just alive enough to be salvageable. That is, I was. They also tell me that this is one chance in several billion billion so there is only one of me, my dear, only one, and there never will be any more, prehistoric or heroic or unheroic or otherwise, and if you would only please, please oblige your escort by telling—"

"They'll send you back!" said Iris, clasping her hands with wonderful intensity.

"They can't," said Alyx.

"They'll cut you up and study you!"

"They won't."

"They'll shut you up in a cage and make you teach them things!"

"They tried," said Alyx. "The Army—"

Here Iris jumped up, her mouth open, her face clouded over. She was fingering something behind her ear.

"I have to go," she said absently. She smiled a little sadly. "That's a very good story," she said.

"Iris—" began Alyx, getting up.

"I'll send you something," said Iris hastily. "I'll send you a piece of the Moon; see if I don't."

"The historical sites," said Alyx. She was about to say something more, something light, but at that moment Iris—snatching frantically in the air behind her for whatever it was that had not come out the first time and showed no signs of doing so the second—burst into passionate tears.

"How will you manage?" she cried, "oh, how will you, you're seven years younger than I am, you're just a *baby*!" and weeping in a swirl of silver cloak, and hair, and luggage, in a storm of violently crackling sparks that turned gold and silver and ran off the both of them like water, little Iris swooped down, threw her arms around her littler friend, wept some more, and immediately afterward rose rapidly into the air, waving goodbye like mad. Halfway up to the foggy roof she produced what she had apparently been trying to get from her luggage all along: a small silver flag, a jaunty square with which she blew her nose and then proceeded to wave goodbye again, smiling brilliantly. It was a handkerchief.

Send me a piece of the Moon, said Alyx silently, *send me something I can keep*, and turning away she started out between the walls of the Moondrom, which are walls that one cannot see, through the cave that looks like an enormous sea of fog; and if you forget that it was made for civilized beings, it begins to look, once you have lost your way, like an endless cave, an endless fog, through which you will wander forever.

But of course she found her way out, finally.

At the exit—and it was the right exit, the one with billowing smoke that shone ten thousand colors from the lights in the floor and gave you, as you crossed it, the faint, unpleasant sensation of being turned slowly upside down, there where ladies' cloaks billowed and transparent clothing seemed to dissolve in streams of fire—

Stood Machine. Her heart stopped for a moment, automatically. The fifth or sixth time that day, she estimated.

"God save you, mister," she said.

He did not move.

"They tell me you'll be gone in a few weeks," she said. "I'll be sorry."

He said nothing.

"They also tell me," she went on, "that I am going to teach my special and peculiar skills in a special and peculiar little school, for they seem to think our pilgrimage a success, despite its being full of their own inexcusable blunders, and they also seem to think that my special and peculiar skills are detachable from my special and peculiar attitudes. Like Iris's hair. I think they will find they are wrong."

He began to dissolve.

"Raydos is blind," she said, "stone blind, did you know that? Some kind of immune reaction; when you ask them, they pull a long face and say that medicine can't be expected to do everything. A foolproof world and full of fools. And then they tape wires on my head and ask me how it feels to be away from home; and they shake their heads when I tell them that I am not away from home; and then they laugh a little—just a little —when I tell them that I have never had a home.

"And then," she said, "I tell them that you are dead."

He disappeared.

"We'll give them a run for their money," she said. "Oh yes we will! By God we will! Eh, love?" and she stepped through the smoke, which now contained nothing except the faint, unpleasant sensation of being turned slowly upside down.

Iris may turn out to be surprisingly accurate, she thought, *about the Great Trans-Temporal Cadre of Heroes and Heroines.*

Even if the only thing trans-temporal about them is their attitudes. The attitudes that are not detachable from my special and peculiar skills.

If I have anything to say about it.

But that's another story.

The Second Inquisition

*If a man can resist the influences of his townsfolk, if he can
cut free from the tyranny of neighborhood gossip, the world
has no terrors for him; there is no second inquisition.*

—John Jay Chapman

I OFTEN WATCHED our visitor reading in the living room,
sitting under the floor lamp near the new, standing Philco
radio, with her long, long legs stretched out in front of her
and the pool of light on her book revealing so little of her
face: brownish, coppery features so marked that she seemed
to be a kind of freak and hair that was reddish black but so
rough that it looked like the things my mother used for scour-
ing pots and pans. She read a great deal, that summer. If I
ventured out of the archway, where I was not exactly hiding
but only keeping in the shadow to watch her read, she would
often raise her face and smile silently at me before beginning
to read again, and her skin would take on an abrupt, surprising pallor as it moved into the light. When she got up
and went into the kitchen with the gracefulness of a stork,
for something to eat, she was almost too tall for the door-
ways; she went on legs like a spider's, with long swinging
arms and a little body in the middle, the strange proportions
of the very tall. She looked down at my mother's plates and
dishes from a great, gentle height, remarkably absorbed; and
asking me a few odd questions, she would bend down over
whatever she was going to eat, meditate on it for a few moments like a giraffe, and then straightening up back into the
stratosphere, she would pick up the plate in one thin hand,
curling around it fingers like legs, and go back gracefully into
the living room. She would lower herself into the chair that
was always too small, curl her legs around it, become dissatisfied, settle herself, stretch them out again—I remember so
well those long, hard, unladylike legs—and begin again to
read.

She used to ask, "What is that? What is that? And what is this?" but that was only at first.

My mother, who disliked her, said she was from the circus and we ought to try to understand and be kind. My father made jokes. He did not like big women or short hair—which was still new in places like ours—or women who read, although she was interested in his carpentry and he liked that.

But she was six feet four inches tall; this was in 1925.

My father was an accountant who built furniture as a hobby; we had a gas stove which he actually fixed once when it broke down and some outdoor tables and chairs he had built in the back yard. Before our visitor came on the train for her vacation with us, I used to spend all my time in the back yard, being underfoot, but once we had met her at the station and she shook hands with my father—I think she hurt him when she shook hands—I would watch her read and wish that she might talk to me.

She said: "You are finishing high school?"

I was in the archway, as usual; I answered yes.

She looked up at me again, then down at her book. She said, "This is a very bad book." I said nothing. Without looking up, she tapped one finger on the shabby hassock on which she had put her feet. Then she looked up and smiled at me. I stepped tentatively from the floor to the rug, as reluctantly as if I were crossing the Sahara; she swung her feet away and I sat down. At close view her face looked as if every race in the world had been mixed and only the worst of each kept; an American Indian might look like that, or Ikhnaton from the encyclopedia, or a Swedish African, a Maori princess with the jaw of a Slav. It occurred to me suddenly that she might be a Negro, but no one else had ever seemed to think so, possibly because nobody in our town had ever seen a Negro. We had none. They were "colored people."

She said, "You are not pretty, yes?"

I got up. I said, "My father thinks you're a freak."

"You are sixteen," she said, "sit down," and I sat down. I crossed my arms over my breasts because they were too big, like balloons. Then she said, "I am reading a very stupid book. You will take it away from me, yes?"

"No," I said.

"You must," she said, "or it will poison me, sure as God," and from her lap she plucked up *The Green Hat: A Romance*, gold letters on green binding, last year's bestseller which I had had to swear never to read, and she held it out to me, leaning back in her chair with that long arm doing all the work, the book enclosed in a cage of fingers wrapped completely around it. I think she could have put those fingers around a basketball. I did not take it.

"Go on," she said, "read it, go on, go away," and I found myself at the archway, by the foot of the stairs with *The Green Hat: A Romance* in my hand. I turned it so the title was hidden. She was smiling at me and had her arms folded back under her head. "Don't worry," she said. "Your body will be in fashion by the time of the next war." I met my mother at the top of the stairs and had to hide the book from her; my mother said, "Oh, the poor woman!" She was carrying some sheets. I went to my room and read through almost the whole night, hiding the book in the bedclothes when I was through. When I slept, I dreamt of Hispano-Suizas, of shingled hair and tragic eyes; of women with painted lips who had Affairs, who went night after night with Jews to low dives, who lived as they pleased, who had miscarriages in expensive Swiss clinics; of midnight swims, of desperation, of money, of illicit love, of a beautiful Englishman and getting into a taxi with him while wearing a cloth-of-silver cloak and a silver turban like the ones shown in the society pages of the New York City newspapers.

Unfortunately our guest's face kept recurring in my dream, and because I could not make out whether she was amused or bitter or very much of both, it really spoiled everything.

My mother discovered the book the next morning. I found it next to my plate at breakfast. Neither my mother nor my father made any remark about it; only my mother kept putting out the breakfast things with a kind of tender, reluctant smile. We all sat down, finally, when she had put out everything, and my father helped me to rolls and eggs and ham. Then he took off his glasses and folded them next to his plate. He leaned back in his chair and crossed his legs. Then he looked at the book and said in a tone of mock surprise, "Well! What's this?"

I didn't say anything. I only looked at my plate.

"I believe I've seen this before," he said. "Yes, I believe I have." Then he asked my mother, "Have you seen this before?" My mother made a kind of vague movement with her head. She had begun to butter some toast and was putting it on my plate. I knew she was not supposed to discipline me; only my father was. "Eat your egg," she said. My father, who had continued to look at *The Green Hat: A Romance* with the same expression of unvarying surprise, finally said:

"Well! This isn't a very pleasant thing to find on a Saturday morning, is it?"

I still didn't say anything, only looked at my food. I heard my mother say worriedly, "She's not eating, Ben," and my father put his hand on the back of my chair so I couldn't push it away from the table, as I was trying to do.

"Of course you have an explanation for this," he said. "Don't you?"

I said nothing.

"Of course she does," he said, "doesn't she, Bess? You wouldn't hurt your mother like this. You wouldn't hurt your mother by stealing a book that you knew you weren't supposed to read and for very good reason, too. You know we don't punish you. We talk things over with you. We try to explain. Don't we?"

I nodded.

"Good," he said. "Then where did this book come from?"

I muttered something; I don't know what.

"Is my daughter angry?" said my father. "Is my daughter *being rebellious*?"

"She told you all about it!" I blurted out. My father's face turned red.

"Don't you dare talk about your mother that way!" he shouted, standing up. "Don't you *dare* refer to your mother in that way!"

"Now, Ben—" said my mother.

"Your mother is the soul of unselfishness," said my father, "and don't you forget it, missy; your mother has worried about you since the day you were born and if you don't appreciate that, you can damn well—"

"Ben!" said my mother, shocked.

"I'm sorry," I said, and then I said, "I'm very sorry, Mother." My father sat down. My father had a mustache and his hair was parted in the middle and slicked down; now one lock fell over the part in front and his whole face was gray and quivering. He was staring fixedly at his coffee cup. My mother came over and poured coffee for him; then she took the coffeepot into the kitchen and when she came back she had milk for me. She put the glass of milk on the table near my plate. Then she sat down again. She smiled tremblingly at my father; then she put her hand over mine on the table and said:

"Darling, why did you read that book?"

"Well?" said my father from across the table.

There was a moment's silence. Then:

"Good morning!"

and

"Good morning!"

and

"Good morning!"

said our guest cheerfully, crossing the dining room in two strides, and folding herself carefully down into her breakfast chair, from where her knees stuck out, she reached across the table, picked up *The Green Hat*, propped it up next to her plate and began to read it with great absorption. Then she looked up. "You have a very progressive library," she said. "I took the liberty of recommending this exciting book to your daughter. You told me it was your favorite. You sent all the way to New York City on purpose for it, yes?"

"I don't—I quite—" said my mother, pushing back her chair from the table. My mother was trembling from head to foot and her face was set in an expression of fixed distaste. Our visitor regarded first my mother and then my father, bending over them tenderly and with exquisite interest. She said:

"I hope you do not mind my using your library."

"No no no," muttered my father.

"I eat almost for two," said our visitor modestly, "because of my height. I hope you do not mind that?"

"No, of course not," said my father, regaining control of himself.

"Good. It is all considered in the bill," said the visitor, and looking about at my shrunken parents, each hurried, each spooning in the food and avoiding her gaze, she added deliberately:

"I took also another liberty. I removed from the endpapers certain—ah—drawings that I did not think bore any relation to the text. You do not mind?"

And as my father and mother looked in shocked surprise and utter consternation—at each other—she said to me in a low voice, "Don't eat. You'll make yourself sick," and then smiled warmly at the two of them when my mother went off into the kitchen and my father remembered he was late for work. She waved at them. I jumped up as soon as they were out of the room.

"There was no drawings in that book!" I whispered.

"Then we must make some," said she, and taking a pencil off the whatnot, she drew in the endpapers of the book a series of sketches: the heroine sipping a soda in an ice-cream parlor, showing her legs and very chic; in a sloppy bathing suit and big grin, holding up a large fish; driving her Hispano-Suiza into a tree only to be catapulted straight up into the air; and in the last sketch landing demure and coy in the arms of the hero, who looked violently surprised. Then she drew a white mouse putting on lipstick, getting married to another white mouse in a church, the two entangled in some manner I thought I should not look at, the lady mouse with a big belly and two little mice inside (who were playing chess), then the little mice coming out in separate envelopes and finally the whole family having a picnic, with some things around the picnic basket that I did not recognize and underneath in capital letters "I did not bring up my children to test cigarettes." This left me blank. She laughed and rubbed it out, saying that it was out of date. Then she drew a white mouse with a rolled-up umbrella chasing my mother. I picked that up and looked at it for a while; then I tore it into pieces, and tore the others into pieces as well. I said, "I don't think you have the slightest right to—" and stopped. She was looking at me with—not anger exactly—not warning exactly—I found I had to sit down. I began to cry.

"Ah! The results of practical psychology," she said dryly, gathering up the pieces of her sketches. She took matches off the whatnot and set fire to the pieces in a saucer. She held up the smoking match between her thumb and forefinger, saying,

"You see? The finger is—shall we say, perception?—but the thumb is money. The thumb is hard."

"You oughtn't to treat my parents that way!" I said, crying.

"You ought not to tear up my sketches," she said calmly.

"Why not! Why not!" I shouted.

"Because they are worth money," she said, "in some quarters. I won't draw you any more," and indifferently taking the saucer with the ashes in it in one palm, she went into the kitchen. I heard her voice and then my mother's, and then my mother's again, and then our visitor's in a tone that would've made a rock weep, but I never found out what they said.

I passed our guest's room many times at night that summer, going by in the hall past her rented room where the second-floor windows gave out onto the dark garden. The electric lights were always on brilliantly. My mother had sewn the white curtains because she did everything like that and had bought the furniture at a sale: a marble-topped bureau, the wardrobe, the iron bedstead, an old Victrola against the wall. There was usually an open book on the bed. I would stand in the shadow of the open doorway and look across the bare wood floor, too much of it and all as slippery as the sea, bare wood waxed and shining in the electric light. A black dress hung on the front of the wardrobe and a pair of shoes like my mother's, T-strap shoes with thick heels. I used to wonder if she had silver evening slippers inside the wardrobe. Sometimes the open book on the bed was Wells's *The Time Machine* and then I would talk to the black glass of the window, I would say to the transparent reflections and the black branches of trees that moved beyond it.

"I'm only sixteen."

"You look eighteen," she would say.

"I know," I would say. "I'd like to be eighteen. I'd like to go away to college. To Radcliffe, I think."

She would say nothing, out of surprise.

"Are you reading Wells?" I would say then, leaning against the door jamb. "I think that's funny. Nobody in this town reads anything; they just think about social life. I read a lot, however. I would like to learn a great deal."

She would smile then, across the room.

"I did something funny once," I would go on. "I mean

funny ha-ha, not funny peculiar." It was a real line, very popular. "I read *The Time Machine* and then I went around asking
people were they Eloi or were they Morlocks; everyone liked
it. The point is which you would be if you could, like being
an optimist or a pessimist or do you like bobbed hair." Then I
would add, "Which are you?" and she would only shrug and
smile a little more. She would prop her chin on one long, long
hand and look into my eyes with her black Egyptian eyes and
then she would say in her curious hoarse voice:

"It is you who must say it first."

"I think," I would say, "that you are a Morlock," and sitting
on the bed in my mother's rented room with *The Time Machine* open beside her, she would say:

"You are exactly right. I am a Morlock. I am a Morlock on
vacation. I have come from the last Morlock meeting, which
is held out between the stars in a big goldfish bowl, so all the
Morlocks have to cling to the inside walls like a flock of black
bats, some right side up, some upside down, for there is no
up and down there, clinging like a flock of black crows, like
a chestnut burr turned inside out. There are half a thousand
Morlocks and we rule the worlds. My black uniform is in the
wardrobe."

"I knew I was right," I would say.

"You are always right," she would say, "and you know the
rest of it, too. You know what murderers we are and how terribly we live. We are waiting for the big bang when everything
falls over and even the Morlocks will be destroyed; meanwhile
I stay here waiting for the signal and I leave messages clipped
to the frame of your mother's amateur oil painting of Main
Street because it will be in a museum some day and my friends
can find it; meanwhile I read *The Time Machine*."

Then I would say, "Can I come with you?" leaning against
the door.

"Without you," she would say gravely, "all is lost," and taking
out from the wardrobe a black dress glittering with stars and
a pair of silver sandals with high heels, she would say, "These
are yours. They were my great-grandmother's, who founded
the Order. In the name of Trans-Temporal Military Authority."
And I would put them on.

It was almost a pity she was not really there.

*

Every year in the middle of August the Country Club gave a dance, not just for the rich families who were members but also for the "nice" people who lived in frame houses in town and even for some of the smart, economical young couples who lived in apartments, just as if they had been in the city. There was one new, red-brick apartment building downtown, four stories high, with a courtyard. We were supposed to go, because I was old enough that year, but the day before the dance my father became ill with pains in his left side and my mother had to stay home to take care of him. He was propped up on pillows on the living-room daybed, which we had pulled out into the room so he could watch what my mother was doing with the garden out back and call to her once in a while through the windows. He could also see the walk leading up to the front door. He kept insisting that she was doing things all wrong. I did not even ask if I could go to the dance alone. My father said:

"Why don't you go out and help your mother?"

"She doesn't want me to," I said. "I'm supposed to stay here," and then he shouted angrily, "Bess! Bess!" and began to give her instructions through the window. I saw another pair of hands appear in the window next to my mother's and then our guest—squatting back on her heels and smoking a cigarette—pulling up weeds. She was working quickly and efficiently, the cigarette between her teeth. "No, not that way!" shouted my father, pulling on the blanket that my mother had put over him. "Don't you know what you're doing! Bess, you're ruining everything! Stop it! Do it right!" My mother looked bewildered and upset; she passed out of the window and our visitor took her place; she waved to my father and he subsided, pulling the blanket up around his neck. "I don't like women who smoke," he muttered irritably. I slipped out through the kitchen.

My father's toolshed and working space took up the farther half of the back yard; the garden was spread over the nearer half, part kitchen garden, part flowers, and then extended down either side of the house where we had fifteen feet or so of space before a white slat fence and the next people's side yard. It was an on-and-offish garden, and the house was beginning to need paint. My mother was working in the kitchen garden,

kneeling. Our guest was standing, pruning the lilac trees, still
smoking. I said:

"Mother, can't I go, can't I *go!*" in a low voice.

My mother passed her hand over her forehead and called
"Yes, Ben!" to my father.

"Why *can't* I go!" I whispered. "Ruth's mother and Betty's
mother will be there. Why couldn't you call Ruth's mother and
Betty's mother?"

"*Not that way!*" came a blast from the living-room window.
My mother sighed briefly and then smiled a cheerful smile.
"Yes, Ben!" she called brightly. "I'm listening." My father be-
gan to give some more instructions.

"Mother," I said desperately, "why couldn't you—"

"Your father wouldn't approve," she said, and again she produced a bright smile and called encouragingly to my father. I
wandered over to the lilac trees where our visitor, in her usual
nondescript black dress, was piling the dead wood under the
tree. She took a last puff on her cigarette, holding it between
thumb and forefinger, then ground it out in the grass and
picked up in both arms the entire lot of dead wood. She carried
it over to the fence and dumped it.

"My father says you shouldn't prune trees in August," I
blurted suddenly.

"Oh?" she said.

"It hurts them," I whispered.

"Oh," she said. She had on gardening gloves, though much
too small; she picked up the pruning shears and began snip-
ping again through inch-thick trunks and dead branches that
snapped explosively when they broke and whipped out at your
face. She was efficient and very quick.

I said nothing at all, only watched her face.

She shook her head decisively.

"But Ruth's mother and Betty's mother—" I began, faltering.

"I never go out," she said.

"You needn't stay," I said, placating.

"Never," she said. "Never at all," and snapping free a particularly large, dead, silvery branch from the lilac tree, she put it
in my arms. She stood there looking at me and her look was
suddenly very severe, very unpleasant, something foreign, like
the look of somebody who had seen people go off to battle

to die, the "movies" look but hard, hard as nails. I knew I wouldn't get to go anywhere. I thought she might have seen battles in the Great War, maybe even been in some of it. I said, although I could barely speak:

"Were you in the Great War?"

"Which great war?" said our visitor. Then she said, "No, I never go out," and returned to scissoring the trees.

On the night of the dance my mother told me to get dressed, and I did. There was a mirror on the back of my door, but the window was better; it softened everything; it hung me out in the middle of a black space and made my eyes into mysterious shadows. I was wearing pink organdy and a bunch of daisies from the garden, not the wild kind. I came downstairs and found our visitor waiting for me at the bottom: tall, bare-armed, almost beautiful, for she'd done something to her impossible hair and the rusty reddish black curled slickly like the best photographs. Then she moved and I thought she was altogether beautiful, all black and rippling silver like a Paris dress or better still a New York dress, with a silver band around her forehead like an Indian princess's and silver shoes with the chunky heels and the one strap over the instep.

She said, "Ah! don't you look nice," and then in a whisper, taking my arm and looking down at me with curious gentleness, "I'm going to be a bad chaperone. I'm going to disappear."

"Well!" said I, inwardly shaking, "I hope I can take care of myself, I should think." But I hoped she wouldn't leave me alone and I hoped that no one would laugh at her. She was really incredibly tall.

"Your father's going to sleep at ten," said my mother. "Be back by eleven. Be happy." And she kissed me.

But Ruth's father, who drove Ruth and I and Ruth's mother and our guest to the Country Club, did not laugh. And neither did anyone else. Our visitor seemed to have put on a strange gracefulness with her dress, and a strange sort of kindliness, too, so that Ruth, who had never seen her but had only heard rumors about her, cried out, "Your friend's lovely!" and Ruth's father, who taught mathematics at high school, said (clearing his throat), "It must be lonely staying in," and our visitor said only, "Yes. Oh yes. It is," resting one immensely long, thin, elegant hand on his shoulder like some kind of unwinking spider, while his words and hers went echoing out into the night, back and forth, back and forth, losing themselves in the trees that rushed past the headlights and massed blackly to each side.

"Ruth wants to join a circus!" cried Ruth's mother, laughing.

"I do *not!*" said Ruth.

"You *will* not," said her father.

"I'll do exactly as I please," said Ruth with her nose in the air, and she took a chocolate cream out of her handbag and put it in her mouth.

"You will *not!*" said Ruth's father, scandalized.

"Daddy, you know I will too," said Ruth, serenely though somewhat muffled, and under cover of the dark she wormed over to me in the back seat and passed, from her hot hand to mine, another chocolate cream. I ate it; it was unpleasantly and piercingly sweet.

"Isn't it *glorious?*" said Ruth.

The Country Club was much more bare than I had expected, really only a big frame building with a veranda three-quarters of the way around it and not much lawn, but there was a path down front to two stone pillars that made a kind of gate and somebody had strung the gate and the whole path with colored Chinese lanterns. That part was lovely. Inside the whole first story was one room, with a varnished floor like the high school gym, and a punch table at one end and ribbons and Chinese lanterns hung all over the ceiling. It did not look quite like the movies but everything was beautifully painted. I had noticed that there were wicker armchairs scattered on the veranda. I decided it was "nice." Behind the punch table was a flight of stairs that led to a gallery full of tables where the grown-ups could go and drink (Ruth insisted they would be bringing real liquor for "mixes," although of course the Country Club had to pretend not to know about that) and on both sides of the big room French windows that opened onto the veranda and the Chinese lanterns, swinging a little in the breeze. Ruth was wearing a better dress than mine. We went over to the punch table and drank punch while she asked me about our visitor and I made up a lot of lies. "You don't know anything," said Ruth. She waved across the room to some friends of hers; then I could see her start dancing with

a boy in front of the band, which was at the other end of the
room. Older people were dancing and people's parents, some
older boys and girls. I stayed by the punch table. People who
knew my parents came over and talked to me; they asked me
how I was and I said I was fine; then they asked me how my
father was and I said he was fine. Someone offered to introduce me to someone but I said I knew him. I hoped somebody
would come over. I thought I would skirt around the dance
floor and try to talk to some of the girls I knew, but then
I thought I wouldn't; I imagined myself going up the stairs
with Iris March's lover from *The Green Hat* to sit at a table
and smoke a cigarette or drink something. I stepped behind
the punch table and went out through the French windows.
Our guest was a few chairs away with her feet stretched out,
resting on the lowest rung of the veranda. She was reading a
magazine with the aid of a small flashlight. The flowers planted
around the veranda showed up a little in the light from the
Chinese lanterns: shadowy clumps and masses of petunias, a
few of the white ones springing into life as she turned the page
of her book and the beam of the flashlight moved in her hand.
I decided I would have my cigarette in a long holder. The
moon was coming up over the woods past the Country Club
lawns, but it was a cloudy night and all I could see was a vague
lightening of the sky in that direction. It was rather warm. I
remembered something about *an ivory cigarette holder flaunt-
ing at the moon*. Our visitor turned another page. I thought
that she must have been aware of me. I thought again of Iris
March's lover, coming out to get me on the "terrace" when
somebody tapped me on the shoulder; it was Ruth's father. He
took me by the wrist and led me to our visitor, who looked
up and smiled vaguely, dreamily, in the dark under the colored
lanterns. Then Ruth's father said:

"What do you know? There's a relative of yours inside!" She
continued to smile but her face stopped moving; she smiled
gently and with tenderness at the space next to his head for the
barely perceptible part of a moment. Then she completed the
swing of her head and looked at him, still smiling, but everything had gone out of it.

"How lovely," she said. Then she said, "Who is it?"

"I don't know," said Ruth's father, "but he's tall, looks just like you—beg pardon. He says he's your cousin."

"*Por nada,*" said our guest absently, and getting up, she shook hands with Ruth's father. The three of us went back inside. She left the magazine and flashlight on the chair; they seemed to belong to the Club. Inside, Ruth's father took us up the steps to the gallery and there, at the end of it, sitting at one of the tables, was a man even taller than our visitor, tall even sitting down. He was in evening dress while half the men at the dance were in business suits. He did not really look like her in the face; he was a little darker and a little flatter of feature; but as we approached him, he stood up. He almost reached the ceiling. He was a giant. He and our visitor did not shake hands. The both of them looked at Ruth's father, smiling formally, and Ruth's father left us; then the stranger looked quizzically at me but our guest had already sunk into a nearby seat, all willowiness, all grace. They made a handsome couple. The stranger brought a silver-inlaid flask out of his hip pocket; he took the pitcher of water that stood on the table and poured some into a clean glass. Then he added whisky from the flask, but our visitor did not take it. She only turned it aside, amused, with one finger, and said to me, "Sit down, child," which I did. Then she said:

"Cousin, how did you find me?"

"*Par chance,* cousin," said the stranger. "By luck." He screwed the top back on the flask very deliberately and put the whole thing back in his pocket. He began to stir the drink he had made with a wooden muddler provided by the Country Club.

"I have endured much annoyance," he said, "from that man to whom you spoke. There is not a single specialized here; they are all half-brained: scattered and stupid."

"He is a kind and clever man," said she. "He teaches mathematics."

"The more fool he," said the stranger, "for the mathematics he thinks he teaches!" and he drank his own drink. Then he said, "I think we will go home now."

"Eh! This person?" said my friend, drawing up the ends of her lips half scornfully, half amused. "Not this person!"

"Why not this person, who knows me?" said the strange man.

"Because," said our visitor, and turning deliberately away from me, she put her face next to his and began to whisper mischievously in his ear. She was watching the dancers on the floor below, half the men in business suits, half the couples middle-aged. Ruth and Betty and some of their friends, and some vacationing college boys. The band was playing the fox-trot. The strange man's face altered just a little, it darkened; he finished his drink, put it down, and then swung massively in his seat to face me.

"Does she go out?" he said sharply.

"Well?" said our visitor idly.

"Yes," I said. "Yes, she goes out. Every day."

"By car or on foot?" I looked at her but she was doing nothing. Her thumb and finger formed a circle on the table.

"I don't know," I said.

"Does she go on foot?" he said.

"No," I blurted suddenly, "no, by car. Always by car!" He sat back in his seat.

"You would do anything," he said conversationally. "The lot of you."

"I?" she said. "I'm not dedicated. I can be reasoned with."

After a moment of silence he said, "We'll talk."

She shrugged. "Why not?"

"This girl's home," he said. "I'll leave fifteen minutes after you. Give me your hand."

"Why?" she said. "You know where I live. I am not going to hide in the woods like an animal."

"Give me your hand," he repeated. "For old time's sake." She reached across the table. They clasped hands and she winced momentarily. Then they both rose. She smiled dazzlingly. She took me by the wrist and led me down the stairs while the strange man called after us, as if the phrase pleased him, "For old time's sake!" and then "Good health, cousin! Long life!" while the band struck up a march in ragtime. She stopped to talk to five or six people, including Ruth's father who taught mathematics in the high school, and the band leader, and Betty, who was drinking punch with a boy from our class. Betty said to me under her breath, "Your daisies are coming loose. They're gonna fall off." We walked through the parked cars until we reached one that she seemed to like; they were all open and some owners left the keys in them; she got in behind the wheel and started up.

"But this *isn't your car!*" I said. "You can't just—"

"Get in!" I slid in next to her.

"It's after ten o'clock," I said. "You'll wake up my father. Who—"

"Shut up!"

I did. She drove very fast and very badly. Halfway home she began to slow down. Then suddenly she laughed out loud and said very confidentially, not to me but as if to somebody else:

"I told him I had planted a Neilsen loop around here that would put half of Greene County out of phase. A dead man's control. I had to go out and stop it every week."

"What's a Neilsen loop?" I said.

"Jam yesterday, jam tomorrow, but never jam today," she quoted.

"What," said I emphatically, "is a—"

"I've told you, baby," she said, "and you'll never know more, God willing," and pulling into our driveway with a screech that would have wakened the dead, she vaulted out of the car and through the back door into the kitchen, just as if my mother and father had both been asleep or in a cataleptic trance, like those in the works of E. A. Poe. Then she told me to get the iron poker from the garbage burner in the back yard and find out if the end was still hot; when I brought the thing in, she laid the hot end over one of the flames of the gas stove. Then she rummaged around under the sink and came up with a bottle of my mother's Clear Household Ammonia.

"That stuff's awful," I said. "If you let that get in your eyes—"

"Pour some in the water glass," she said, handing it to me. "Two-thirds full. Cover it with a saucer. Get another glass and another saucer and put all of them on the kitchen table. Fill your mother's water pitcher, cover that, and put that on the table."

"Are you going to *drink* that?" I cried, horrified, halfway to the table with the covered glass. She merely pushed me. I got everything set up, and also pulled three chairs up to the kitchen table; I then went to turn off the gas flame, but she took me by the hand and placed me so that I hid the stove from the window and the door. She said, "Baby, what is the specific heat of iron?"

"What?" I said.

"You know it, baby," she said. "What is it?"

I only stared at her.

"But you know it, baby," she said. "You know it better than I. You know that your mother was burning garbage today and the poker would still be hot. And you know better than to touch the iron pots when they come fresh from the oven, even though the flame is off, because iron takes a long time to heat up and a long time to cool off, isn't that so?"

I nodded.

"And you don't know," she added, "how long it takes for aluminum pots to become cold because nobody uses aluminum for pots yet. And if I told you how scarce the heavy metals are, and what a radionic oven is, and how the heat can go *through* the glass and the plastic and even the ceramic lattice, you wouldn't know what I was talking about, would you?"

"No," I said, suddenly frightened, "no, no, no."

"Then you know more than some," she said. "You know more than me. Remember how I used to burn myself, fiddling with your mother's things?" She looked at her palm and made a face. "He's coming," she said. "Stand in front of the stove. When he asks you to turn off the gas, turn it off. When I say 'Now,' hit him with the poker."

"I can't," I whispered. "He's too big."

"He can't hurt you," she said. "He doesn't dare; that would be an anachronism. Just do as I say."

"What are you going to *do*?" I cried.

"When I say 'Now,'" she repeated serenely, "hit him with the poker," and sitting down by the table, she reached into a jam-jar of odds and ends my mother kept on the windowsill and began to buff her nails with a Lady Marlene emery stick. Two minutes passed by the kitchen clock. Nothing happened. I stood there with my hand on the cold end of the poker, doing nothing until I felt I had to speak, so I said, "Why are you making a face? Does something hurt?"

"The splinter in my palm," she said calmly. "The bastard."

"Why don't you take it out?"

"It will blow up the house."

He stepped in through the open kitchen door.

Without a word she put both arms palm upward on the kitchen table and without a word he took off the black cummerbund of his formal dress and flicked it at her. It settled over both her arms and then began to draw tight, molding itself over her arms and the table like a piece of black adhesive, pulling her almost down onto it and whipping one end around the table edge until the wood almost cracked. It seemed to paralyze her arms. He put his finger to his tongue and then to her palm, where there was a small black spot. The spot disappeared. He laughed and told me to turn off the flame, so I did.

"Take it off," she said then.

He said, "Too bad you are in hiding or you too could carry weapons," and then, as the edge of the table let out a startling sound like a pistol shot, he flicked the black tape off her arms, returning it to himself, where it disappeared into his evening clothes.

"Now that I have used this, everyone knows where we are," he said, and he sat down in a kitchen chair that was much too small for him and lounged back in it, his knees sticking up into the air.

Then she said something I could not understand. She took the saucer off the empty glass and poured water into it; she said something unintelligible again and held it out to him, but he motioned it away. She shrugged and drank the water herself. "Flies," she said, and put the saucer back on. They sat in silence for several minutes. I did not know what to do; I knew I was supposed to wait for the word "Now" and then hit him with the poker, but no one seemed to be saying or doing anything. The kitchen clock, which I had forgotten to wind that morning, was running down at ten minutes to eleven. There was a cricket making a noise close outside the window and I was afraid the ammonia smell would get out somehow; then, just as I was getting a cramp in my legs from standing still, our visitor nodded. She sighed, too, regretfully. The strange man got to his feet, moved his chair carefully out of the way and pronounced:

"Good. I'll call them."

"Now?" said she.

I couldn't do it. I brought the poker in front of me and stood there with it, holding it in both hands. The stranger —who almost had to stoop to avoid our ceiling—wasted only a glance on me, as if I were hardly worth looking at, and then concentrated his attention on her. She had her chin in her hands. Then she closed her eyes.

"Put that down, please," she said tiredly.

I did not know what to do. She opened her eyes and took the saucer off the other glass on the table.

"Put that down right now," she said, and raised the glass of ammonia to her lips.

I swung at him clumsily with the poker. I was not sure what happened next, but I think he laughed and seized the end—the hot end—and then threw me off balance just as he screamed, because the next thing I knew I was down on all fours watching her trip him as he threw himself at her, his eyes screwed horribly shut, choking and coughing and just missing her. The ammonia glass was lying empty and broken on the floor; a brown stain showed where it had rolled off the white table-cloth on the kitchen table. When he fell, she kicked him in the side of the head. Then she stepped carefully away from him and held out her hand to me; I gave her the poker, which she took with the folded edge of the tablecloth, and reversing it so that she held the cold end, she brought it down with immense force—not on his head, as I had expected, but on his windpipe. When he was still, she touched the hot end of the poker to several places on his jacket, passed it across where his belt would be, and to two places on both of his shoes. Then she said to me, "Get out."

I did, but not before I saw her finishing the job on his throat, not with the poker but with the thick heel of her silver shoe.

When I came back in, there was nobody there. There was a clean, rinsed glass on the drainboard next to the sink and the poker was propped up in one corner of the sink with cold water running on it. Our visitor was at the stove, brewing tea in my mother's brown teapot. She was standing under the Dutch cloth calendar my mother, who was very modern, kept hanging on the wall. My mother pinned messages on it; one of them read "Be Careful. Except for the Bathroom, More Accidents Occur in the Kitchen Than in Any Other Part of the House."

"Where—" I said, "where is—is—"

"Sit down," she said. "Sit down here," and she put me into *his* seat at the kitchen table. But there was no *he* anywhere. She said, "Don't think too much." Then she went back to the tea and just as it was ready to pour, my mother came in from the living room, with a blanket around her shoulders, smiling foolishly and saying, "Goodness, I've been asleep, haven't I?"

"Tea?" said our visitor.

"I fell asleep just like that," said my mother, sitting down.

"I forgot," said our visitor. "I borrowed a car. I felt ill. I must call them on the telephone," and she went out into the hall, for we had been among the first to have a telephone. She came back a few minutes later. "Is it all right?" said my mother. We drank our tea in silence.

"Tell me," said our visitor at length. "How is your radio reception?"

"It's perfectly fine," said my mother, a bit offended.

"That's fine," said our visitor, and then, as if she couldn't control herself, "because you live in a dead area, you know, thank God, a dead area!"

My mother said, alarmed, "I beg your par—"

"Excuse me," said our visitor, "I'm ill," and she put her cup into her saucer with a clatter, got up and went out of the kitchen. My mother put one hand caressingly over mine.

"Did anyone . . . insult her at the dance?" said my mother, softly.

"Oh no," I said.

"Are you sure?" my mother insisted. "Are you perfectly sure? Did anyone comment? Did anyone say anything about her appearance? About her height? Anything that was not nice?"

"Ruth did," I said. "Ruth said she looked like a giraffe." My mother's hand slid off mine; gratified, she got up and began to gather up the tea things. She put them into the sink. She clucked her tongue over the poker and put it away in the kitchen closet. Then she began to dry the glass that our visitor had previously rinsed and put on the drainboard, the glass that had held ammonia.

"The poor woman," said my mother, drying it. "Oh, the poor woman."

*

Nothing much happened after that. I began to get my books ready for high school. Blue cornflowers sprang up along the sides of the house and my father, who was better now, cut them down with a scythe. My mother was growing hybrid ones in the back flower garden, twice as tall and twice as big as any of the wild ones; she explained to me about hybrids and why they were bigger, but I forgot it. Our visitor took up with a man, not a nice man, really, because he worked in the town garage and was Polish. She didn't go out but used to see him in the kitchen at night. He was a thickset, stocky man, very blond, with a real Polish name, but everyone called him Bogalusa Joe because he had spent fifteen years in Bogalusa, Louisiana (he called it "Loosiana") and he talked about it all the time. He had a theory, that the colored people were just like us and that in a hundred years everybody would be all mixed up, you couldn't tell them apart. My mother was very advanced in her views but she wouldn't ever let me talk to him. He was very respectful; he called her "Ma'am," and didn't use any bad language, but he never came into the living room. He would always meet our visitor in the kitchen or sometimes on the swing in the back garden. They would drink coffee; they would play cards. Sometimes she would say to him, "Tell me a story, Joe. I love a good story," and he would talk about hiding out in Loosiana; he had had to hide out from somebody or something for three years in the middle of the Negroes and they had let him in and let him work and took care of him. He said, "The coloreds are like anybody." Then he said, "The nigras are smarter. They got to be. They ain't nobody's fool. I had a black girl for two years once was the smartest woman in the world. Beautiful woman. Not beautiful like a white, though, not the same."

"Give us a hundred years," he added, "and it'll all be mixed."

"Two hundred?" said our visitor, pouring coffee. He put a lot of sugar in his; then he remarked that he had learned that in Bogalusa. She sat down. She was leaning her elbows on the table, smiling at him. She was stirring her own coffee with a spoon. He looked at her a moment, and then he said softly:

"A black woman, smartest woman in the world. You're black, woman, ain't you?"

"Part," she said.

"Beautiful woman," he said. "Nobody knows?"

"They know in the circus," she said. "But there they don't care. Shall I tell you what we circus people think of you?"

"Of who?" he said, looking surprised.

"Of all of you," she said. "All who aren't in the circus. All who can't do what we can do, who aren't the biggest or the best, who can't kill a man barehanded or learn a new language in six weeks or slit a man's jugular at fifteen yards with nothing but a pocketknife or climb the Greene County National Bank from the first story to the sixth with no equipment. I can do all that."

"I'll be damned," said Bogalusa Joe softly.

"We despise you," she said. "That's what we do. We think you're slobs. The scum of the earth! The world's fertilizer, Joe, that's what you are."

"Baby, you're blue," he said, "you're blue tonight," and then he took her hand across the table, but not the way they did it in the movies, not the way they did it in the books; there was a look on his face I had never seen on anyone's before, not the high school boys when they put a line over on a girl, not on grown-ups, not even on the brides and grooms because all that was romantic or showing off or "lust" and he only looked infinitely kind, infinitely concerned. She pulled her hand out of his. With the same faint, detached smile she had had all night, she pushed back her chair and stood up. She said flatly:

"All I can do! What good is it?" She shrugged. She added, "I've got to leave tomorrow." He got up and put his arm around her shoulders. I thought that looked bad because he was actually a couple of inches shorter than she was.

He said, "Baby, you don't have to go." She was staring out into the back garden, as if looking miles away, miles out, far away into our vegetable patch or our swing or my mother's hybrids, into something nobody could see. He said urgently, "Honey, look—" and then, when she continued to stare, pulling her face around so she had to look at him, both his broad, mechanic's hands under her chin, "Baby, you can stay with me." He brought his face closer to hers. "Marry me," he said suddenly. She began to laugh. I had never heard her laugh like that before. Then she began to choke. He put his arms around her and she leaned against him, choking, making funny noises like someone with asthma, finally clapping her hands over her face, then biting her palm, heaving up and down as if she were sick. It took me several seconds to realize that she was crying. He looked very troubled. They stood there: she cried, he, distressed—and I hiding, watching all of it. They began to walk slowly toward the kitchen door. When they had gone out and put out the light, I followed them out into the back garden, to the swing my father had rigged up under the one big tree: cushions and springs to the ground like a piece of furniture, big enough to hold four people. Bushes screened it. There was a kerosene lantern my father had mounted on a post, but it was out. I could just about see them. They sat for a few minutes, saying nothing, looking up through the tree into the darkness. The swing creaked a little as our visitor crossed and uncrossed her long legs. She took out a cigarette and lit it, obscuring their faces with even that little glow: an orange spot that wavered up and down as she smoked, making the darkness more black. Then it disappeared. She had ground it out underfoot in the grass. I could see them again. Bogalusa Joe, the garage mechanic, said:

"Tomorrow?"

"Tomorrow," she said. Then they kissed each other. I liked that; it was all right; I had seen it before. She leaned back against the cushions of the swing and seemed to spread her feet in the invisible grass; she let her head and arms fall back onto the cushion. Without saying a word, he lifted her skirt far above her knees and put his hand between her legs. There was a great deal more of the same business and I watched it all, from the first twistings to the stabbings, the noises, the life-and-death battle in the dark. The word *Epilepsy* kept repeating itself in my head. They got dressed and again began to smoke, talking in tones I could not hear. I crouched in the bushes, my heart beating violently.

I was horribly frightened.

She did not leave the next day, or the next or the next; and she even took a dress to my mother and asked if she could have it altered somewhere in town. My school clothes were out, being aired in the back yard to get the mothball smell out of them. I put covers on all my books. I came down one morning to ask my mother whether I couldn't have a jumper taken up at the hem because the magazines said it was all right for young girls. I expected a fight over it. I couldn't find my mother in the hall or the kitchen so I tried the living room, but before I had got halfway through the living-room arch, someone said, "Stop there," and I saw both my parents sitting on two chairs near the front door, both with their hands in their laps, both staring straight ahead, motionless as zombies.

I said, "Oh for heaven's sake, what're you—"

"Stop there," said the same voice. My parents did not move. My mother was smiling her social smile. There was no one else in the room. I waited for a little while, my parents continuing to be dead, and then from some corner on my left, near the new Philco, our visitor came gliding out, wrapped in my mother's spring coat, stepping softly across the rug and looking carefully at all the living-room windows. She grinned when she saw me. She tapped the top of the Philco radio and motioned me in. Then she took off the coat and draped it over the radio.

She was in black from head to foot.

I thought *black*, but black was not the word; the word was *blackness*, dark beyond dark, dark that drained the eyesight, something I could never have imagined even in my dreams, a black in which there was no detail, no sight, no nothing, only an awful, desperate dizziness, for her body—the thing was skintight, like a diver's costume or an acrobat's—had actually disappeared, completely blotted out except for its outline. Her head and bare hands floated in the air. She said, "Pretty, yes?" Then she sat crosslegged on our radio. She said, "Please pull the curtains," and I did, going from one to the other and drawing them shut, circling my frozen parents and then stopping short in the middle of the quaking floor. I said, "I'm going to faint." She was off the radio and into my mother's coat in an instant; holding me by the arm, she got me onto the living-room couch and put her arm around me, massaging my back. She said, "Your parents are asleep." Then she said, "You have known some of this. You are a wonderful little pickup but you get mixed up, yes? All about the Morlocks? The Trans-Temporal Military Authority?"

I began to say "Oh oh oh oh—" and she massaged my back again.

"Nothing will hurt you," she said. "Nothing will hurt your parents. Think how exciting it is! Think! The rebel Morlocks, the revolution in the Trans-Temporal Military Authority."

"But I—I—" I said.

"We are friends," she continued gravely, taking my hands, "we are real friends. You helped me. We will not forget that," and slinging my mother's coat off onto the couch, she went and stood in front of the archway. She put her hands on her hips, then began rubbing the back of her neck nervously and clearing her throat. She turned around to give me one last look.

"Are you calm?" she said. I nodded. She smiled at me. "Be calm," she said softly, "*sois tranquille*. We're friends," and then she put herself to watching the archway. She said once, almost sadly, "Friends," and then stepped back and smiled again at me.

The archway was turning into a mirror. It got misty, then bright, like a cloud of bright dust, then almost like a curtain; and then it was a mirror, although all I could see in it was our visitor and myself, not my parents, not the furniture, not the living room.

Then the first Morlock stepped through.

And the second.

And the third.

And the others.

Oh, the living room was filled with giants! They were like her, like her in the face, like her in the bodies of the very tall, like her in the black uniforms, men and women of all the races of the earth, everything mixed and huge as my mother's hybrid flowers but a foot taller than our visitor, a flock of black ravens, black bats, black wolves, the professionals of the future world, perched on our furniture, on the Philco radio, some on the very walls and drapes of the windows as if they could fly, hovering in the air as if they were out in space where the Morlocks meet, half a thousand in a bubble between the stars.

Who rule the worlds.

Two came through the mirror who crawled on the rug, both in diving suits and goldfish-bowl helmets, a man and a woman, fat and shaped like seals. They lay on the rug breathing water (for I saw the specks flowing in it, in and out of strange frills around their necks, the way dust moves in air) and looking up at the rest with tallowy faces. Their suits bulged. One of the Morlocks said something to one of the seals and one of the seals answered, fingering a thing attached to the barrels on its back, gurgling.

Then they all began to talk.

Even if I'd known what language it was, I think it would have been too fast for me; it was very fast, very hard-sounding, very urgent, like the numbers pilots call in to the ground or something like that, like a code that everybody knows, to get things done as fast as you can. Only the seal-people talked slowly, and they gurgled and stank like a dirty beach. They did not even move their faces except to make little round mouths, like fish. I think I was put to sleep for a while (or maybe I just fell asleep) and then it was something about the seal-people, with the Morlock who was seated on the radio joining in—and then general enough—and then something going round the whole room—and then that fast, hard urgent talk between one of the Morlocks and my friend. It was still business, but they looked at *me*; it was awful to be looked at and yet I felt numb; I wished I were asleep; I wanted to cry because I could not understand a word they were saying. Then my friend suddenly shouted; she stepped back and threw both arms out, hands extended and fingers spread, shaking violently. She was shouting instead of talking, shouting desperately about something, pounding one fist into her palm, her face contorted, just as if it was not business. The other Morlock was breathing quickly and had gone pale with rage. He whispered something, something very venomous. He took from his black uniform, which could have hidden anything, a silver dime, and holding it up between thumb and forefinger, he said in perfectly clear English, while looking at me:

"In the name of the war against the Trans-Tempor—"

She had jumped him in an instant. I scrambled up; I saw her close his fist about the dime with her own; then it was all a blur on the floor until the two of them stood up again, as far as they could get from each other, because it was perfectly clear that they hated each other. She said very distinctly, "*I do insist.*" He shrugged. He said something short and sharp. She took out of her own darkness a knife—only a knife—and looked

slowly about the room at each person in it. Nobody moved.
She raised her eyebrows.

"*Tcha! grozny?*"

The seal-woman hissed on the floor, like steam coming out
of a leaky radiator. She did not get up but lay on her back, eyes
blinking, a woman encased in fat.

"You?" said my friend insultingly. "You will stain the carpet."

The seal-woman hissed again. Slowly my friend walked
toward her, the others watching. She did not bend down, as
I had expected, but dove down abruptly with a kind of sidewise roll, driving herself into the seal-woman's side. She had
planted one heel on the stomach of the woman's diving suit;
she seemed to be trying to tear it. The seal-woman caught my
friend's knife-hand with one glove and was trying to turn it on
my friend while she wrapped the other gloved arm around my
friend's neck. She was trying to strangle her. My friend's free
arm was extended on the rug; it seemed to me that she was
either leaning on the floor or trying to pull herself free. Then
again everything went into a sudden blur. There was a gasp,
a loud, mechanical click; my friend vaulted up and backward,
dropping her knife and clapping one hand to her left eye. The
seal-woman was turning from side to side on the floor, a kind
of shudder running from her feet to her head, an expressionless flexing of her body and face. Bubbles were forming in the
goldfish-bowl helmet. The other seal-person did not move. As
I watched, the water began falling in the seal-woman's helmet
and then it was all air. I supposed she was dead. My friend, our
visitor, was standing in the middle of the room, blood welling
from under her hand; she was bent over with pain and her face
was horribly distorted but not one person in that room moved
to touch her.

"Life—" she gasped, "for life. Yours," and then she crashed
to the rug. The seal-woman had slashed open her eye. Two of
the Morlocks rushed to her then and picked up her and her
knife; they were dragging her toward the mirror in the archway
when she began muttering something.

"Damn your sketches!" shouted the Morlock she had fought
with, completely losing control of himself. "We are at war;
Trans-Temp is at our heels; do you think we have time for dilet-
tantism? You presume on being that woman's granddaughter!
We are fighting for the freedom of fifty billions of people, not

for your scribbles!" and motioning to the others, who immediately dragged the body of the seal-woman through the mirror and began to follow it themselves, he turned to me.

"You!" he snapped. "You will speak to nobody of this. Nobody!"

I put my arms around myself.

"Do not try to impress anyone with stories," he added contemptuously, "you are lucky to live," and without another look he followed the last of the Morlocks through the mirror, which promptly disappeared. There was blood on the rug, a few inches from my feet. I bent down and put my fingertips in it, and then with no clear reason, I put my fingers to my face.

"—come back," said my mother. I turned to face them, the wax manikins who had seen nothing.

"Who the devil drew the curtains!" shouted my father. "I've told you" (to me) "that I don't like tricks, young lady, and if it weren't for your mother's—"

"Oh, Ben, Ben! She's had a nosebleed!" cried my mother.

They told me later that I fainted.

I was in bed a few days, because of the nosebleed, but then they let me up. My parents said I probably had had anemia. They also said they had seen our visitor off at the railroad station that morning, and that she had boarded the train as they watched her; tall, frizzy-haired, freakish, dressed in black down to between the knees and ankles, legged like a stork and carrying all her belongings in a small valise. "Gone to the circus," said my mother. There was nothing in the room that had been hers, nothing in the attic, no reflection in the window at which she had stood, brilliantly lit against the black night, nothing in the kitchen and nothing at the Country Club but tennis courts overgrown with weeds. Joe never came back to our house. The week before school I looked through all my books, starting with *The Time Machine* and ending with *The Green Hat*; then I went downstairs and looked through every book in the house. There was nothing. I was invited to a party; my mother would not let me go. Cornflowers grew around the house. Betty came over once and was bored. One afternoon at the end of summer, with the wind blowing through the empty house from top to bottom and everybody away, nobody next door, my parents in the back yard, the people on the other side of us gone

swimming, everybody silent or sleeping or off somewhere—
except for someone down the block whom I could hear mowing the lawn—I decided to sort and try on all my shoes. I did
this in front of a full-length mirror fastened to the inside of
my closet door. I had been taking off and putting on various
of my winter dresses, too, and I was putting one particular one
away in a box on the floor of the closet when I chanced to look
up at the inside of the closet door.

She was standing in the mirror. It was all black behind her,
like velvet. She was wearing something black and silver, half-
draped, half-nude, and there were lines on her face that made
it look sectioned off, or like a cobweb; she had one eye. The
dead eye radiated spinning white light, like a Catherine wheel.
She said:

"Did you ever think to go back and take care of yourself
when you are little? Give yourself advice?"

I couldn't say anything.

"I am not you," she said, "but I have had the same thought
and now I have come back four hundred and fifty years. Only
there is nothing to say. There is never anything to say. It is a
pity, but natural, no doubt."

"Oh, please!" I whispered. "Stay!" She put one foot up on
the edge of the mirror as if it were the threshold of a door. The
silver sandal she had worn at the Country Club dance almost
came into my bedroom: thick-heeled, squat, flaking, as ugly
as sin; new lines formed on her face and all over her bare skin,
ornamenting her all over. Then she stepped back; she shook
her head, amused; the dead eye waned, filled again, exploded
in sparks and went out, showing the naked socket, ugly, shocking, and horrible.

"Tcha!" she said, "my grandma thought she would bring
something hard to a world that was soft and silly but nice, and
now it's silly and not so nice and the hard has got too hard and
the soft too soft and my great-grandma—it is she who founded
the order—is dead. Not that it matters. Nothing ends, you see.
Just keeps going on and on."

"But you can't *see*!" I managed. She poked herself in the
temple and the eye went on again.

"Bizarre," she said. "Interesting. Attractive. Stone blind is
twice as good. I'll tell you my sketches."

"But you don't—you can't—" I said.

"The first," she said, lines crawling all over her, "is an Eloi having the Go-Jollies, and that is a bald, fat man in a toga, a frilled bib, a sunbonnet and shoes you would not believe, who has a crystal ball in his lap and from it wires plugged into his eyes and his nose and his ears and his tongue and his head, just like your lamps. That is an Eloi having the Go-Jollies."

I began to cry.

"The second," she went on, "is a Morlock working; and that is myself holding a skull, like *Hamlet*, only if you look closely at the skull you will see it is the world, with funny things sticking out of the seas and the polar ice caps, and that it is full of people. Much too full. There are too many of the worlds, too."

"If you'll *stop*—!" I cried.

"They are all pushing each other off," she continued, "and some are falling into the sea, which is a pity, no doubt, but quite natural, and if you will look closely at all these Eloi you will see that each one is holding his crystal ball, or running after an animated machine which runs faster than he, or watching another Eloi on a screen who is cleverer and looks fascinating, and you will see that under the fat the man or woman is screaming, screaming and dying.

"And my third sketch," she said, "which is a very little one, shows a goldfish bowl full of people in black. Behind that is a smaller goldfish bowl full of people in black, which is going after the first goldfish bowl, and behind the second is a third, which is going after the second, and so on, or perhaps they alternate; that would be more economical. Or perhaps I am only bitter because I lost my eye. It's a personal problem."

I got to my feet. I was so close I could have touched her. She crossed her arms across her breast and looked down at me; she then said softly, "My dear, I wished to take you with me, but that's impossible. I'm very sorry," and looking for the first time both serious and tender, she disappeared behind a swarm of sparks.

I was looking at myself. I had recently made, passionately and in secret, the uniform of the Trans-Temporal Military Authority as I thought it ought to look: a black tunic over black sleeves and black tights. The tights were from a high school play I had been in the year before and the rest was cut out of the lining of an old winter coat. That was what I was wearing that afternoon. I had also fastened a silver curling-iron to my waist with a piece of cord. I put one foot up in the air, as if on the threshold of the mirror, and a girl in ragged black stared back at me. She turned and frantically searched the entire room, looking for sketches, for notes, for specks of silver paint, for anything at all. Then she sat down on my bed. She did not cry. She said to me, "You look idiotic." Someone was still mowing the lawn outside, probably my father. My mother would be clipping, patching, rooting up weeds; she never stopped. Someday I would join a circus, travel to the moon, write a book; after all, I had helped kill a man. I had been somebody. It was all nonsense. I took off the curling-iron and laid it on the bed. Then I undressed and got into my middy-blouse and skirt and I put the costume on the bed in a heap. As I walked toward the door of the room, I turned to take one last look at myself in the mirror and at my strange collection of old clothes. For a moment something else moved in the mirror, or I thought it did, something behind me or to one side, something menacing, something half-blind, something heaving slowly like a shadow, leaving perhaps behind it faint silver flakes like the shadow of a shadow or some carelessly dropped coins, something glittering, something somebody had left on the edge of vision, dropped by accident in the dust and cobwebs of an attic. I wished for it violently; I stood and clenched my fists; I almost cried; I wanted something to come out of the mirror and strike me dead. If I could not have a protector, I wanted a monster, a mutation, a horror, a murderous disease, anything! anything at all to accompany me downstairs so that I would not have to go down alone.

Nothing came. Nothing good, nothing bad. I heard the lawnmower going on. I would have to face by myself my father's red face, his heart disease, his temper, his nasty insistencies. I would have to face my mother's sick smile, looking up from the flower-bed she was weeding, always on her knees somehow, saying before she was ever asked, "Oh the poor woman. Oh the poor woman."

And quite alone.

No more stories.

A Game of Vlet

I N OURDH, near the sea, on a summer's night so hot and still that the marble blocks of the Governor's mansion sweated as if the earth itself were respiring through the stone—which is exactly what certain wise men maintain to be the case—the Governor's palace guard caught an assassin trying to enter the Governor's palace through a secret passage too many unfortunates have thought they alone knew. This one, his arm caught and twisted by the Captain, beads of sweat starting out on his pale, black-bearded face, was a thin young man in aristocratic robes, followed by the oddest company one could possibly meet—even in Ourdh—a cook, a servant girl, a couple of waterfront beggars, a battered hulk of a man who looked like a professional bodyguard fallen on evil days, and five peasants. These persons remained timidly silent while the Captain tightened his grip on the young man's arm; the young man made an inarticulate sound between his teeth but did not cry out; the Captain shook him, causing him to fall to his knees; then the Captain said, "Who are you, scum!" and the young man answered, "I am Rav." His followers all nodded in concert, like mechanical mice.

"He is," said one of the guards, "he's a magician. I seen him at the banquet a year ago," and the Captain let go, allowing the young man to get to his feet. Perhaps they were a little afraid of magicians, or perhaps they felt a rudimentary shame at harming someone known to the Governor—though the magician had been out of favor for the last eleven zodiacal signs of the year—but this seems unlikely. Humanity, of course, they did not have. The Captain motioned his men back and stepped back himself, silent in the main hall of the Governor's villa, waiting to hear what the young nobleman had to say. What he said was most surprising. He said (with difficulty):

"I am a champion player of Vlet."

It was then that the Lady appeared. She appeared quite silently, unseen by anybody, between two of the Governor's imported marble pillars, which were tapered toward the base and set in wreaths of carved and tinted anemones and lilies. She

607

stood a little behind one of the nearby torches, which had been
set into a bracket decorated with a group of stylized young
women known to aristrocratic Ourdh as The Female Virtues:
Modesty, Chastity, Fecundity and Tolerance, a common motif
in art, and from this vantage point she watched the scene before her. She heard Rav declare his intention of having come
only to play a game of Vlet with the Governor, which was not
believed, to say the least; she saw the servant girl blurt out a
flurry of deaf-and-dumb signs; she heard the guards laugh until
they cried, hush each other for fear of waking the Governor,
laugh themselves sick again, and finally decide to begin by flay-
ing the peasants to relieve the tedium of the night watch.

It was then that she stepped forward.

"You woke up Sweetie," she said.

That she was not a Lady in truth and in verity might have
been seen from certain small signs in a better light—the heaviness of her sandals, for instance, or the less-than-perfect fit of
her elaborate, jeweled coiffure, or the streaking and blurring of
the gold paint on her face (as if she had applied cosmetics in
haste or desperation)—but she wore the semitransparent, elaborately gold-embroidered black robe Ourdh calls "the gown
of the night" (which is to be sharply distinguished from "the
gown of the evening"), and as she came forward, this fell open,
revealing that she wore nothing at all underneath. Her sandals
were not noticed. She closed the robe again. The Captain, who
had hesitated between anticipations of a bribe and a dressing
down from the Governor, hesitated no longer. He put out his
hand for money. Several guards might have wondered why the
Governor had chosen such an ordinary-looking young woman,
but just at that moment—as she came into the light, which
was (after all) pretty bad—the Lady yawned daintily like a cat,
stretched from top to bottom, smiled a little to herself and
gave each of the five guards in turn a glance of such deep understanding, such utter promise, and such extraordinary good
humor, that one actually blushed. Skill pays for all.

"Poor Sweetie," she said.

"Madam—" began the Captain, a little unnerved.

"I said to Sweetie," went on the Lady, unperturbed, "that
his little villa was just the quietest place in the city and so cutey
darling that I could stay here forever. And then *you* came in."

"Madam—" said the Captain.

"Sweetie doesn't like noise," said the Lady, and she sat down on the Governor's gilded audience bench, crossing her knees so that her robe fell away, leaving one leg bare to the thigh. She began to swing this bare leg in and out of the shadows so confusingly that none could have sworn later whether it were beautiful or merely passable; moreover, something sparkled regularly at her knee with such hypnotic precision that a junior guard's head began to bob a little, like a pendulum, and he had to be elbowed in the ribs by a comrade. She gave the man a sharp, somehow disappointed look. Then she appeared to notice Rav.

"Who's that?" she said carelessly.

"An assassin," said the Captain.

"No, no," said the Lady, drawling impatiently, "the cute one, the one with the little beard. Who's *he*?"

"I said—" began the Captain with asperity.

"Rav, Madam," interrupted the young man, holding his sore arm carefully and wincing a little (for he had bowed to her automatically), "an unhappy wretch formerly patronized by the Governor, his 'magician,' as he was pleased to call me, but no Mage, Madam, no Grandmaster, only a player with trifles, a composer of little tricks; however, I have found out something, if only that, and I came here tonight to offer it to His Excellentness. I am, my Lady, as you may be yourself, an addict of that wonderful game called Vlet, and I came here tonight to offer to the Governor the most extraordinary board and pieces for the game that have ever been made. That is all; but these gentlemen misinterpreted me and declare that I have come to assassinate His Excellentness, the which" (he took a shuddering breath) "is the farthest from my thoughts. I abhor the shedding of blood, as any of my intimates can tell you. I came only to play a game of Vlet."

"Oooooh!" said the Lady. "Vlet! I adore Vlet!"

"I have been away," continued Rav, "for nearly a year, making this most uncommon board and pieces, as I know the Governor's passion for the game. This is no ordinary set, Madam, but a virgin board and virgin pieces which no human hands have ever touched. You may have heard—as all of us have, my Lady—of the virgin speculum or mirror made by certain

powerful Mages, and which can be used once—but only once
—to look anywhere in the world. Such a mirror must be made
of previously unworked ore, fitted in the dark so that no ray
of light ever falls upon it, polished in the dark by blind pol-
ishers so that no human sight ever contaminates it, and under
these conditions, and these conditions only, can the first person
who looks into the mirror look anywhere and see anything he
wishes. A Vlet board and pieces, similarly made from unworked
stone, and without the touch of human hands, is similarly
magical, and the first game played on such a board, with such
pieces, can control anything in the world, just as the user of the
virgin speculum can look anywhere in the world. This gentleman with me" (he indicated the ex-bodyguard) "is a virtuoso
contortionist, taught the art under the urgings of the lash. He
has performed all the carvings of the pieces with his feet so
that we may truly say no human hands have touched them.
That gentleman over there" (he motioned toward the cook)
"lost a hand in an accident in the Governor's kitchens, and
these" (he waved at the peasants) "have had their right hands
removed for evading the taxes. The beggars have been similarly
deformed by their parents for the practice of their abominable
and degrading trade, and the young lady is totally deaf from
repeated boxings on the ears given her by her mistress. It is
she who crushed the ore for us so that no human ears might
hear the sounds of the working. This Vlet board has never been
touched by human hands and neither have the pieces. They are
entirely virgin. You may notice, as I take them from my sleeve,
that they are wrapped in oiled silk, to prevent my touch from
contaminating them. I wished only to present this board and
pieces to the Governor, in the hope that the gift might restore
me to his favor. I have been out of it, as you know. I am an
indifferent player of Vlet but a powerful and sound student,
and I have worked out a classical game in the last year in which
the Governor could—without the least risk to himself—defeat
all his enemies and become emperor of the world. He will play
(as one player must) in his own person; I declare that I am his
enemies *in toto*, and then we play the game, in which, of course,
he defeats me. It is that simple."

"Assassin!" growled the Captain of the Guard. "Liar!" But
the Lady, who had been gliding slowly towards the magician

as he talked, with a perfectly practical and unnoticeable magic of her own, here slipped the board and pieces right out of his hands and said, with a toss of her head:

"You will play against *me*."

The young man turned pale.

"Oh, I know you, I know you," said the Lady, slowly unwrapping the oiled silk from the set of Vlet. "You're the one who kept pestering poor Sweetie about justice and taxes and cutting off people's heads and all sorts of things that were none of your business. Don't interrupt. You're a liar, and you undoubtedly came here to kill Sweetie, but you're terribly inept and very cute, and so" (here she caught her breath and smiled at him) "sit down and play with me." And she touched the first piece.

Now it is often said that in Vlet experienced players lose sight of everything but the game itself, and so passionate is their absorption in this intellectual haze that they forget to eat or drink, and sometimes even to breathe in the intensity of their concentration (this is why Grandmasters are always provided with chamber pots during an especially arduous game), but never before had such a thing actually happened to the Lady. As she touched the first piece—it was a black one—all the sounds in the hall died away, and everyone there, the guards, the pitiful band this misguided magician had brought with him and the great hall itself, the pillars, the fitted blocks of the floor, the frescoes, the torches, everything faded and dissolved into mist. Only she herself existed, she and the board of Vlet, the pieces of Vlet, which stood before her in unnatural distinctness, as if she were looking down from a mountain at the camps of two opposing armies. One army was red and one was black, and on the other side of the great, smoky plain sat the magician, himself the size of a mountain or a god, his lean, pale face working and his black beard standing out like ink. He held in one hand a piece of Red. He looked over the board as if he looked into an abyss, and he smiled pitifully at her, not with fear, but with some intense, fearful hope that was very close to it.

"You are playing for your life," she said, "for I declare myself to be the Government of Ourdh."

"I play," said he, "for the Revolution. As I planned."

And he moved his first piece.

Outside, in the night, five hundred farmers moved against the city gates.

She moved all her Common Persons at once, which was a popular way to open the game. They move one square at a time.

So did he.

In back of her Common Persons she put her Strongbox, which is a very strong offensive piece but weak on the defense; she moved her Archpriest—the sliding piece—in front of her Governor, who is the ultimate object of the game, and brought her Elephant to the side, keeping it in reserve. She went to move a set of Common Persons and discovered with a shock that she seemed to have no Common Persons at all and her opponent nothing else; then she saw that all her black Common Persons had fled to the other side of the board and that they had all turned red. In those days it was possible —depending on the direction from which your piece came —either to take an enemy's piece out of the game—"kill it," they said—or convert it to your own use. One signaled this by standing the piece on its head. The Lady had occasionally lost a game to her own converted Vlet pieces, but never in her life before had she seen ones that literally changed color, or ones that slipped away by themselves when you were not looking, or pieces that made noise, for something across the board was making the oddest noise she had ever heard, a shrill, keening sound, a sort of tinny whistling like insects buzzing or all the little Common Persons singing together. Then the Lady gasped and gripped the edge of the Vlet board until her knuckles turned white, for that was exactly what was happening; across the board her enemy's little red pieces of Vlet, Common Persons all, were moving their miniature knees up and down and singing heartily, and what they were singing was:

The pee-pul!
The pee-pul!

"An ancient verse," said Rav, mountainous across the board. "Make your move," and she saw her own hand, huge as a

giant's, move down into that valley, where transparent buildings and streets seemed to spring up all over the board. She
moved her Strongbox closer to the Governor, playing for time.

*Lights on late in the Councilors' House; much talk; someone
has gone for the Assassins . . .*

He moved another set of Common Persons.

*A baker looked out at his house door in Bread Street. In the
Street of Conspicuous Display torches flicker and are gone around
the buildings. "Is it tonight?" "Tonight!" Someone is scared; someone wants to go home; "Look here, my wife—"*

Her Tax-Collector was caught and

*stabbed in the back in an alley while the rising simmer of the
city, crowds spilling, not quite so aimlessly, into the main boule-
vards*

Rav horrified

"We've got to play a clean game! Out in the open! No—"

While she moved the Archpriest

*Governor's barricades going up around the Treasury, men
called out, they say the priests are behind*

And in horror watched him shake his fist at her and stand
sullenly grimacing in the square where she had put him; then,
before she could stop him, he had hopped two more squares,
knocked flat a couple of commoners whose blood and intestines flowed tinily out on to the board, jeered at her, hopped
two more and killed a third man before she could get her fingers on him.

"He killed a man! With his own hands!"

"Who?"

"The Archpriest!"

"Get him!"

So she picked up the squirming, congested Archpriest,
younger son of a younger son, stupid, spiteful, ambitious (she
knew him personally) and thrust him across the board, deep
into enemy territory.

*Trying to flee the city by water, looks up from under a bale of
hides, miserably stinking—*

Where the Commons could pothook him to their hearts'
content

*Sees those faces, bearded and unwashed, a flash of pride among
the awful fear, cowers—*

"We don't do things that way," said Rav, his voice rolling godlike across the valley, across the towers and terraces, across the parties held on whitewashed roofs where ladies ate cherries and pelted gentlemen with flowers, where aristocratic persons played at darts, embroidered, smoked hemp and behaved as nobles should. One couple was even playing—so tiny as to be almost invisible—a miniature game of Vlet.

"We play a clean game," said Rav.

Which is so difficult (she thought) that only a Grandmaster of Grandmasters attempts it more than once a year. Pieces must be converted but not killed.

The crowd on Market Street is turned back by the troops.

Her Elephant, which she immobilized

Men killed, children crushed, a dreadful silence, in which someone screams, while the troops, not knowing why

and set her Nobles to killing one another, which an inept player can actually do in Vlet

stand immobilized, the Captains gone; some secret fear or failure of will breathes through the city, and again the crowds surge forward, but cannot bring themselves to

She threw away piece after piece

not even to touch, perhaps thinking: these are our natural masters? or: where are we going? What are we doing?

Gave him the opportunity for a Fool's Kill, which he did not take

The Viceroy to the Governor walks untouched through superstitious awe, through the silent crowd; he mounts the steps of the Temple—

Exposed every piece

begins to address the crowd

While Rav smiled pitifully, and far away, out in the city suburbs, in the hovels of peasant freeholds that surrounded the real city, out in the real night she could hear a rumble, a rising voice, thunder; she finds herself surrounding

Arrest that man

the Red Governor, who wasn't a Governor but a Leader, a little piece with Rav's features and with the same pitiful, nervous, gallant smile.

"Check" said the Lady, "and Mate." She did not want to do it. A guard in the room laughed. Out in the city all was

quiet. Then, quite beside herself, the strange Lady in the black
gown of the night, seeing a Red Assassin with her own features
scream furiously from the other side of the board and dart
violently across it, took the board in both hands and threw
the game high into the air. Around her everything whirled:
board, pieces, the magician, who was one moment huge, the
next moment tiny, the onlookers, the guards, the very stone
blocks of the hall seemed to spin. The torches blazed hugely.
The pieces, released from the board, were fighting in midair.
Then the Lady fell to her knees, rearranging the game, surrounding the last remnant of Black, snatching the Red Leader
out of his trap, muttering desperately to herself as Rav cried,
"What are you doing? What are you doing?" and around them
the palace shook, the walls fell, the very earth shuddered on its
foundations.

"Check," said the Lady, "and Mate." A rock came sailing
lazily past them, shattering the glass of the Governor's foreign
window, brought at enormous expense over sea and marsh in a
chest full of sawdust, the only piece of transparent glass in the
city. "Trust a mob to find a window!" said the Lady, laughing.
Outside could be heard a huge tramping of feet, the concerted
breathing of hundreds, thousands, a mob, a storm, a heaving
sea of Common Persons, and all were singing:

"Come on, children of the national unity!
The glorious diurnal period has arrived.
Let us move immediately against tyranny;
The bloody flag is hauled up!"

"My God!" cried Rav, "you don't understand!" as the Lady
—with un-Ladylike precision—whipped off her coiffure and
slammed it across the face of the nearest guard. Her real hair
was a good deal shorter. "Wonderful things—fifteen pounds'
weight—" she shouted, and ripping off the robe of night,
tripped the next guard, grabbed his sword and put herself back
to back with the ex-bodyguard who had another guard's neck
between his hands and was slowly and methodically throttling
the man to death. The servant girl was beating someone's head
against the wall. The Lady wrapped a soldier's cloak around
herself and belted it; then she threw the jeweled wig at one of
the peasants, who caught it, knocked over the two remaining
guards, who were still struggling feebly, not against anyone in

the room but against something in the air, like flies in treacle. None had offered the slightest resistance. She took the magician by the arm, laughing hugely with relief.

"Let me introduce myself," she said. "I—"

"Look out!" said Rav.

"Come on!" she shouted, and as the mob poured through the Governor's famous decorated archway, made entirely—piece by piece—of precious stones collected at exorbitant cost from tax defaulters and convicted blackmailers, she cut off the head of an already dead guard and held it high, shouting, "The Pee-pul! The Pee-pul!" and shoved Rav into position beside her. He looked sick but he smiled. The People roared past them. He had, in his hands, the pieces and board of their game of Vlet, and to judge from his expression, they were causing him considerable discomfort. He winced as tiny lances, knives, pothooks, plough blades and swords bristled through his fingers like porcupine quills. They seemed to be jabbing at each other and getting his palms instead.

"Can't you stop them!" she whispered. The last of the mob was disappearing through the inverted pillars.

"No!" he said. "The game's not over. You cheated—" and with a yell he dropped the whole thing convulsively, board and all. The pieces hit the floor and rolled in all directions, punching, jabbing, chasing each other, screaming in tiny voices, crawling under the board, buzzing and dying like a horde of wasps. The Lady and the magician dropped to their knees—they were alone in the room by now—and tried to sweep the pieces together, but they continued to fight, and some ran under the dead guards or under the curtains.

"We must—we *must* play the game through," said Rav in a hoarse voice. "Otherwise anyone—anyone who gets hold of them can—"

He did not finish the sentence.

"Then we'll play it through, O Rav," she said. "But this time, dammit, you make the moves *I* tell you to make!"

"I told you," he began fiercely, "that I abhor bloodshed. That is true. I will not be a party to it, not even for—"

"Listen," she said, holding up her hand, and there on the floor they crouched while the sounds of riot and looting echoed distantly from all parts of the city. The south windows of the hall began to glow. The poor quarter was on fire. Someone nearby shouted; something struck the ground; and closer and closer came the heavy sound of surf, a hoarse, confused babble.

He began to gather up the pieces.

A little while later the board was only a board, and the pieces had degenerated into the sixty-four pieces of the popular game of Vlet. They were not, she noticed, particularly artistically carved. She walked out with Rav into the Governor's garden, among the roses, and there—with the sound of the horrors in the city growing ever fainter as the dawn increased—they sat down, she with her head on her knees, he leaning his back against a peach tree.

"I'd better go," she said finally.

"Not back to the Governor," said Rav, shuddering. "Not now!" She giggled.

"Hardly," she said, "after tying him and his mistress up with the sheets and stealing her clothes. I fancy he's rather upset. You surprised me at my work, magician."

"One of *us*!" said the magician, amazed. "You're a—"

"One of them," said she, "because I live off them. I'm a parasite. I didn't *quite* end that last game with a win, as I said I did. It didn't seem fair somehow. Your future state would have no place for me, and I do have myself to look after, after all. Besides, none of your damned peasants can play Vlet, and I enjoy the game." She yawned involuntarily.

"I ended that last game," she said, "with a stalemate.

"Ah, don't worry, my dear," she added, patting the stricken man's cheek and turning up to him her soot-stained, blood-stained, paint-stained little face. "You can always make another virgin Vlet board, and I'll play you another game. I'll even trick the Governor if you can find a place for me on the board. Some day. A clean game. Perhaps. Perhaps it's possible, eh?"

But that's another story.

OTHER STORIES

When It Changed

KATY DRIVES like a maniac; we must have been doing over 120 km/hr on those turns. She's good, though, extremely good, and I've seen her take the whole car apart and put it together again in a day. My birthplace on Whileaway was largely given to farm machinery and I refuse to wrestle with a five-gear shift at unholy speeds, not having been brought up to it, but even on those turns in the middle of the night, on a country road as bad as only our district can make them, Katy's driving didn't scare me. The funny thing about my wife, though: she will not handle guns. She has even gone hiking in the forests above the 48th parallel without firearms, for days at a time. And that *does* scare me.

Katy and I have three children between us, one of hers and two of mine. Yuriko, my eldest, was asleep in the back seat, dreaming twelve-year-old dreams of love and war: running away to sea, hunting in the North, dreams of strangely beautiful people in strangely beautiful places, all the wonderful guff you think up when you're turning twelve and the glands start going. Some day soon, like all of them, she will disappear for weeks on end to come back grimy and proud, having knifed her first cougar or shot her first bear, dragging some abominably dangerous dead beastie behind her, which I will never forgive for what it might have done to my daughter. Yuriko says Katy's driving puts her to sleep.

For someone who has fought three duels, I am afraid of far, far too much. I'm getting old. I told this to my wife.

"You're thirty-four," she said. Laconic to the point of silence, that one. She flipped the lights on, on the dash—three km. to go and the road getting worse all the time. Far out in the country. Electric-green trees rushed into our headlights and around the car. I reached down next to me where we bolt the carrier panel to the door and eased my rifle into my lap. Yuriko stirred in the back. My height but Katy's eyes, Katy's face. The car engine is so quiet, Katy says, that you can hear breathing in the back seat. Yuki had been alone in the car when the message came, enthusiastically decoding her dot-dashes (silly to mount a wide-frequency transceiver near an I.C. engine, but most of Whileaway is on steam). She had thrown herself out of the car, my gangly and gaudy offspring, shouting at the top of her lungs, so of course she had had to come along. We've been intellectually prepared for this ever since the Colony was founded, ever since it was abandoned, but this is different. This is awful.

"Men!" Yuki had screamed, leaping over the car door. "They've come back! Real Earth men!"

We met them in the kitchen of the farmhouse near the place where they had landed; the windows were open, the night air very mild. We had passed all sorts of transportation when we parked outside, steam tractors, trucks, an I.C. flatbed, even a bicycle. Lydia, the district biologist, had come out of her Northern taciturnity long enough to take blood and urine samples and was sitting in a corner of the kitchen shaking her head in astonishment over the results; she even forced herself (very big, very fair, very shy, always painfully blushing) to dig up the old language manuals—though I can talk the old tongues in my sleep. And do. Lydia is uneasy with us; we're Southerners and too flamboyant. I counted twenty people in that kitchen, all the brains of North Continent. Phyllis Spet, I think, had come in by glider. Yuki was the only child there.

Then I saw the four of them.

They are bigger than we are. They are bigger and broader. Two were taller than me, and I am extremely tall, 1m, 80 cm in my bare feet. They are obviously of our species but *off*, indescribably off, and as my eyes could not and still cannot quite comprehend the lines of those alien bodies, I could not, then, bring myself to touch them, though the one who spoke Russian—what voices they have!—wanted to "shake hands," a custom from the past, I imagine. I can only say they were apes with human faces. He seemed to mean well, but I found myself shuddering back almost the length of the kitchen—and then I laughed apologetically—and then to set a good example (*interstellar amity*, I thought) did "shake hands" finally. A hard, hard hand. They are heavy as draft horses. Blurred, deep voices. Yuriko had sneaked in between the adults and was gazing at *the men* with her mouth open.

He turned *his* head—those words have not been in our language for six hundred years—and said, in bad Russian:

"Who's that?"

"My daughter," I said, and added (with that irrational attention to good manners we sometimes employ in moments of insanity), "My daughter, Yuriko Janetson. We use the patronymic. You would say matronymic."

He laughed, involuntarily. Yuki exclaimed, "I thought they would be *good-looking!*" greatly disappointed at this reception of herself. Phyllis Helgason Spet, whom someday I shall kill, gave me across the room a cold, level, venomous look, as if to say: *Watch what you say. You know what I can do.* It's true that I have little formal status, but Madam President will get herself in serious trouble with both me and her own staff if she continues to consider industrial espionage good clean fun. Wars and rumors of wars, as it says in one of our ancestors' books. I translated Yuki's words into *the man's* dog-Russian, once our *lingua franca*, and *the man* laughed again.

"Where are all your people?" he said conversationally.

I translated again and watched the faces around the room; Lydia embarrassed (as usual), Spet narrowing her eyes with some damned scheme, Katy very pale.

"This is Whileaway," I said.

He continued to look unenlightened.

"Whileaway," I said. "Do you remember? Do you have records? There was a plague on Whileaway."

He looked moderately interested. Heads turned in the back of the room, and I caught a glimpse of the local professions-parliament delegate; by morning every town meeting, every district caucus, would be in full session.

"Plague?" he said. "That's most unfortunate."

"Yes," I said. "Most unfortunate. We lost half our population in one generation."

He looked properly impressed.

"Whileaway was lucky," I said. "We had a big initial gene pool, we had been chosen for extreme intelligence, we had a high technology and a large remaining population in which every adult was two-or-three experts in one. The soil is good. The climate is blessedly easy. There are thirty millions of us now. Things are beginning to snowball in industry—do you

understand?—give us seventy years and we'll have more than
one real city, more than a few industrial centers, full-time
professions, full-time radio operators, full-time machinists,
give us seventy years and not everyone will have to spend
three quarters of a lifetime on the farm." And I tried to explain how hard it is when artists can practice full-time only in
old age, when there are so few, so very few who can be free,
like Katy and myself. I tried also to outline our government,
the two houses, the one by professions and the geographic
one; I told him the district caucuses handled problems too
big for the individual towns. And that population control
was not a political issue, not yet, though give us time and it
would be. This was a delicate point in our history; give us
time. There was no need to sacrifice the quality of life for an
insane rush into industrialization. Let us go our own pace.
Give us time.

"Where are all the people?" said that monomaniac.

I realized then that he did not mean people, he meant *men*,
and he was giving the word the meaning it had not had on
Whileaway for six centuries.

"They died," I said. "Thirty generations ago."

I thought we had poleaxed him. He caught his breath. He
made as if to get out of the chair he was sitting in; he put his
hand to his chest; he looked around at us with the strangest
blend of awe and sentimental tenderness. Then he said, solemnly and earnestly:

"A great tragedy."

I waited, not quite understanding.

"Yes," he said, catching his breath again with that queer
smile, that adult-to-child smile that tells you something is being hidden and will be presently produced with cries of encour-
agement and joy, "a great tragedy. But it's over." And again he
looked around at all of us with the strangest deference. As if
we were invalids.

"You've adapted amazingly," he said.

"To what?" I said. He looked embarrassed. He looked inane.
Finally he said, "Where I come from, the women don't dress
so plainly."

"Like you?" I said. "Like a bride?" for the men were wearing
silver from head to foot. I had never seen anything so gaudy.

He made as if to answer and then apparently thought better of it; he laughed at me again. With an odd exhilaration—as if we were something childish and something wonderful, as if he were doing us an enormous favor—he took one shaky breath and said, "Well, we're here."

I looked at Spet, Spet looked at Lydia, Lydia looked at Amalia, who is the head of the local town meeting, Amalia looked at I don't know who. My throat was raw. I cannot stand local beer, which the farmers swill as if their stomachs had iridium linings, but I took it anyway, from Amalia (it was her bicycle we had seen outside as we parked), and swallowed it all. This was going to take a long time. I said, "Yes, here you are," and smiled (feeling like a fool), and wondered seriously if male Earth people's minds worked so very differently from female Earth people's minds, but that couldn't be so or the race would have died out long ago. The radio network had got the news around-planet by now and we had another Russian speaker, flown in from Varna; I decided to cut out when *the man* passed around pictures of his wife, who looked like the priestess of some arcane cult. He proposed to question Yuki, so I barreled her into a back room in spite of her furious protests, and went out on the front porch. As I left, Lydia was explaining the difference between parthenogenesis (which is so easy that anyone can practice it) and what we do, which is the merging of ova. That is why Katy's baby looks like me. Lydia went on to the Ansky Process and Katy Ansky, our one full-polymath genius and the great-great-I don't know how many times great-grandmother of my own Katharina.

A dot-dash transmitter in one of the outbuildings chattered faintly to itself: operators flirting and passing jokes down the line.

There was a man on the porch. The other tall man. I watched him for a few minutes—I can move very quietly when I want to—and when I allowed him to see me, he stopped talking into the little machine hung around his neck. Then he said calmly, in excellent Russian, "Did you know that sexual equality has been re-established on Earth?"

"You're the real one," I said, "aren't you? The other one's for show." It was a great relief to get things cleared up. He nodded affably.

"As a people, we are not very bright," he said. "There's been too much genetic damage in the last few centuries. Radiation. Drugs. We can use Whileaway's genes, Janet." Strangers do not call strangers by the first name.

"You can have cells enough to drown in," I said. "Breed your own."

He smiled. "That's not the way we want to do it." Behind him I saw Katy come into the square of light that was the screened-in door. He went on, low and urbane, not mocking me, I think, but with the self-confidence of someone who has always had money and strength to spare, who doesn't know what it is to be second-class or provincial. Which is very odd, because the day before, I would have said that was an exact description of me.

"I'm talking to you, Janet," he said, "because I suspect you have more popular influence than anyone else here. You know as well as I do that parthenogenetic culture has all sorts of inherent defects, and we do not—if we can help it—mean to use you for anything of the sort. Pardon me; I should not have said 'use.' But surely you can see that this kind of society is unnatural."

"Humanity is unnatural," said Katy. She had my rifle under her left arm. The top of that silky head does not quite come up to my collar-bone, but she is as tough as steel; he began to move, again with that queer smiling deference (which his fellow had showed to me but he had not) and the gun slid into Katy's grip as if she had shot with it all her life.

"I agree," said the man. "Humanity is unnatural. I should know. I have metal in my teeth and metal pins here." He touched his shoulder. "Seals are harem animals," he added, "and so are men; apes are promiscuous and so are men; doves are monogamous and so are men; there are even celibate men and homosexual men. There are homosexual cows, I believe. But Whileaway is still missing something." He gave a dry chuckle. I will give him the credit of believing that it had something to do with nerves.

"I miss nothing," said Katy, "except that life isn't endless."

"You are—?" said the man, nodding from me to her.

"Wives," said Katy. "We're married." Again the dry chuckle.

"A good economic arrangement," he said, "for working and taking care of the children. And as good an arrangement as any for randomizing heredity, if your reproduction is made to follow the same pattern. But think, Katharina Michaelason, if there isn't something better that you might secure for your daughters. I believe in instincts, even in Man, and I can't think that the two of you—a machinist, are you? and I gather you are some sort of chief of police—don't feel somehow what even you must miss. You know it intellectually, of course. There is only half a species here. Men must come back to Whileaway."

Katy said nothing.

"I should think, Katharina Michaelason," said the man gently, "that you, of all people, would benefit most from such a change," and he walked past Katy's rifle into the square of light coming from the door. I think it was then that he noticed my scar, which really does not show unless the light is from the side: a fine line that runs from temple to chin. Most people don't even know about it.

"Where did you get that?" he said, and I answered with an involuntary grin, "In my last duel." We stood there bristling at each other for several seconds (this is absurd but true) until he went inside and shut the screen door behind him. Katy said in a brittle voice, "You damned fool, don't you know when we've been insulted?" and swung up the rifle to shoot him through the screen, but I got to her before she could fire and knocked the rifle out of aim; it burned a hole through the porch floor. Katy was shaking. She kept whispering over and over, "That's why I never touched it, because I knew I'd kill someone, I knew I'd kill someone." The first man—the one I'd spoken with first—was still talking inside the house, something about the grand movement to re-colonize and re-discover all that Earth had lost. He stressed the advantages to Whileaway: trade, exchange of ideas, education. He too said that sexual equality had been re-established on Earth.

Katy was right, of course; we should have burned them down where they stood. Men are coming to Whileaway. When one culture has the big guns and the other has none, there is a certain predictability about the outcome. Maybe men would have come eventually in any case. I like to think that a hundred

years from now my great-grandchildren could have stood them
off or fought them to a standstill, but even that's no odds; I will
remember all my life those four people I first met who were
muscled like bulls and who made me—if only for a moment
—feel small. A neurotic reaction, Katy says. I remember everything that happened that night; I remember Yuki's excitement
in the car, I remember Katy's sobbing when we got home as if
her heart would break, I remember her lovemaking, a little pe-
remptory as always, but wonderfully soothing and comforting.
I remember prowling restlessly around the house after Katy fell
asleep with one bare arm flung into a patch of light from the
hall. The muscles of her forearms are like metal bars from all
that driving and testing of her machines. Sometimes I dream
about Katy's arms. I remember wandering into the nursery and
picking up my wife's baby, dozing for a while with the poignant, amazing warmth of an infant in my lap, and finally returning to the kitchen to find Yuriko fixing herself a late snack.
My daughter eats like a Great Dane.

"Yuki," I said, "do you think you could fall in love with a
man?" and she whooped derisively. "With a ten-foot toad!"
said my tactful child.

But men are coming to Whileaway. Lately I sit up nights and
worry about the men who will come to this planet, about my
two daughters and Betta Katharinason, about what will happen
to Katy, to me, to my life. Our ancestors' journals are one long
cry of pain and I suppose I ought to be glad now but one can't
throw away six centuries, or even (as I have lately discovered)
thirty-four years. Sometimes I laugh at the question those four
men hedged about all evening and never quite dared to ask,
looking at the lot of us, hicks in overalls, farmers in canvas pants
and plain shirts: *Which of you plays the role of the man?* As if we
had to produce a carbon copy of their mistakes! I doubt very
much that sexual equality has been re-established on Earth. I
do not like to think of myself mocked, of Katy deferred to as
if she were weak, of Yuki made to feel unimportant or silly, of
my other children cheated of their full humanity or turned into
strangers. And I'm afraid that my own achievements will dwindle from what they were—or what I thought they were—to
the not-very-interesting curiosa of the human race, the oddities you read about in the back of the book, things to laugh at

sometimes because they are so exotic, quaint but not impressive, charming but not useful. I find this more painful than I can say. You will agree that for a woman who has fought three duels, all of them kills, indulging in such fears is ludicrous. But what's around the corner now is a duel so big that I don't think I have the guts for it; in Faust's words: *Verweile doch, du bist so schoen!* Keep it as it is. Don't change.

Sometimes at night I remember the original name of this planet, changed by the first generation of our ancestors, those curious women for whom, I suppose, the real name was too painful a reminder after the men died. I find it amusing, in a grim way, to see it all so completely turned around. This too shall pass. All good things must come to an end.

Take my life but don't take away the meaning of my life.

For-A-While.

Souls

*Deprived of other Banquet
I entertained myself—*

—Emily Dickinson

THIS IS the tale of the Abbess Radegunde and what happened when the Norsemen came. I tell it not as it was told to me but as I saw it, for I was a child then and the Abbess had made a pet and errand boy of me, although the stern old Wardress, Cunigunt, who had outlived the previous Abbess, said I was more in the Abbey than out of it and a scandal. But the Abbess would only say mildly, "Dear Cunigunt, a scandal at the age of seven?" which was turning it off with a joke, for she knew how harsh and disliking my new stepmother was to me and my father did not care and I with no sisters or brothers. You must understand that joking and calling people "dear" and "my dear" was only her manner; she was in every way an unusual woman. The previous Abbess, Herrade, had found that Radegunde, who had been given to her to be fostered, had great gifts and so sent the child south to be taught, and that has never happened here before. The story has it that the Abbess Herrade found Radegunde seeming to read the great illuminated book in the Abbess's study; the child had somehow pulled it off its stand and was sitting on the floor with the volume in her lap, sucking her thumb, and turning the pages with her other hand just as if she were reading.

"Little two-years," said the Abbess Herrade, who was a kind woman, "what are you doing?" She thought it amusing, I suppose, that Radegunde should pretend to read this great book, the largest and finest in the Abbey, which had many, many books more than any other nunnery or monastery I have ever heard of: a full forty then, as I remember. And then little Radegunde was doing the book no harm.

"Reading, Mother," said the little girl.

"Oh, reading?" said the Abbess, smiling. "Then tell me what you are reading," and she pointed to the page.

"This," said Radegunde, "is a great *D* with flowers and other beautiful things about it, which is to show that *Dominus*, our Lord God, is the greatest thing and the most beautiful and makes everything to grow and be beautiful, and then it goes on to say *Domine nobis pacem*, which means *Give peace to us, O Lord*."

Then the Abbess began to be frightened but she said only, "Who showed you this?" thinking that Radegunde had heard someone read and tell the words or had been pestering the nuns on the sly.

"No one," said the child. "Shall I go on?" and she read page after page of the Latin, in each case telling what the words meant.

There is more to the story, but I will say only that after many prayers the Abbess Herrade sent her foster daughter far southwards, even to Poitiers, where Saint Radegunde had ruled an Abbey before, and some say even to Rome, and in these places Radegunde was taught all learning, for all learning there is in the world remains in these places. Radegunde came back a grown woman and nursed the Abbess through her last illness and then became Abbess in her turn. They say that the great folk of the Church down there in the south wanted to keep her because she was such a prodigy of female piety and learning, there where life is safe and comfortable and less rude than it is here, but she said that the gray skies and flooding winters of her birthplace called to her very soul. She often told me the story when I was a child: how headstrong she had been and how defiant, and how she had sickened so desperately for her native land that they had sent her back, deciding that a rude life in the mud of a northern village would be a good cure for such a rebellious soul as hers.

"And so it was," she would say, patting my cheek or tweaking my ear. "See how humble I am now?" for you understand, all this about her rebellious girlhood, twenty years back, was a kind of joke between us. "Don't you do it," she would tell me and we would laugh together, I so heartily at the very idea of my being a pious monk full of learning that I would hold my sides and be unable to speak.

She was kind to everyone. She knew all the languages, not only ours, but the Irish too and the tongues folk speak to the

north and south, and Latin and Greek also, and all the other
languages in the world, both to read and write. She knew
how to cure sickness, both the old women's way with herbs
or leeches and out of books also. And never was there a more
pious woman! Some speak ill of her now she's gone and say she
was too merry to be a good Abbess, but she would say, "Merriment is God's flowers," and when the winter wind blew her
headdress awry and showed the gray hair—which happened
once; I was there and saw the shocked faces of the Sisters with
her—she merely tapped the band back into place, smiling and
saying, "Impudent wind! Thou showest thou hast power which
is more than our silly human power, for it is from God"—and
this quite satisfied the girls with her.

No one ever saw her angry. She was impatient sometimes,
but in a kindly way, as if her mind were elsewhere. It was in
Heaven, I used to think, for I have seen her pray for hours or
sink to her knees—right in the marsh!—to see the wild duck
fly south, her hands clasped and a kind of wild joy on her face,
only to rise a moment later, looking at the mud on her habit
and crying half-ruefully, half in laughter, "Oh, what will Sister
Laundress say to me? I am hopeless! Dear child, tell no one; I
will say I fell," and then she would clap her hand to her mouth,
turning red and laughing even harder, saying, "I *am* hopeless,
telling lies!"

The town thought her a saint, of course. We were all happy
then, or so it seems to me now, and all lucky and well, with this
happiness of having her amongst us burning and blooming in
our midst like a great fire around which we could all warm ourselves, even those who didn't know why life seemed so good.
There was less illness; the food was better; the very weather
stayed mild; and people did not quarrel as they had before
her time and do again now. Nor do I think, considering what
happened at the end, that all this was nothing but the fancy of
a boy who's found his mother, for that's what she was to me; I
brought her all the gossip and ran errands when I could, and
she called me Boy News in Latin; I was happier than I have
ever been.

And then one day those terrible, beaked prows appeared in
our river.

I was with her when the warning came, in the main room

of the Abbey tower just after the first fire of the year had been lit in the great hearth; we thought ourselves safe, for they had never been seen so far south and it was too late in the year for any sensible shipman to be in our waters. The Abbey was host to three Irish priests who turned pale when young Sister Sibihd burst in with the news, crying and wringing her hands; one of the brothers exclaimed a thing in Latin which means "God protect us!" for they had been telling us stories of the terrible sack of the monastery of Saint Columbanus and how everyone had run away with the precious manuscripts or had hidden in the woods, and that was how Father Cairbre and the two others had decided to go "walk the world," for this (the Abbess had been telling it all to me, for I had no Latin) is what the Irish say when they leave their native land to travel elsewhere.

"God protects our souls, not our bodies," said the Abbess Radegunde briskly. She had been talking with the priests in their own language or in the Latin, but this she said in ours so even the women workers from the village would understand. Then she said, "Father Cairbre, take your friends and the younger Sisters to the underground passages; Sister Diemud, open the gates to the villagers; half of them will be trying to get behind the Abbey walls and the others will be fleeing to the marsh. You, Boy News, down to the cellars with the girls." But I did not go and she never saw it; she was up and looking out one of the window slits instantly. So was I. I had always thought the Norsemen's big ships came right up on land—on legs, I supposed—and was disappointed to see that after they came up our river they stayed in the water like other ships and the men were coming ashore in little boats, which they were busy pulling up on shore through the sand and mud. Then the Abbess repeated her order—"Quickly! Quickly!"—and before anyone knew what had happened, she was gone from the room. I watched from the tower window; in the turmoil nobody bothered about me. Below, the Abbey grounds and gardens were packed with folk, all stepping on the herb plots and the Abbess's paestum roses, and great logs were being dragged to bar the door set in the stone walls round the Abbey, not high walls, to tell truth, and Radegunde was going quickly through the crowd, crying: Do this! Do that! Stay, thou! Go, thou! and like things.

Then she reached the door and motioned Sister Oddha, the doorkeeper, aside—the old Sister actually fell to her knees in entreaty—and all this, you must understand, was wonderfully pleasant to me. I had no more idea of danger than a puppy. There was some tumult by the door—I think the men with the logs were trying to get in her way—and Abbess Radegunde took out from the neck of her habit her silver crucifix, brought all the way from Rome, and shook it impatiently at those who would keep her in. So of course they let her through at once.

I settled into my corner of the window, waiting for the Abbess's crucifix to bring down God's lightning on those tall, fair men who defied Our Savior and the law and were supposed to wear animal horns on their heads, though these did not (and I found out later that's just a story; that is not what the Norse do). I did hope that the Abbess, or Our Lord, would wait just a little while before destroying them, for I wanted to get a good look at them before they all died, you understand. I was somewhat disappointed, as they seemed to be wearing breeches with leggings under them and tunics on top, like ordinary folk, and cloaks also, though some did carry swords and axes and there were round shields piled on the beach at one place. But the long hair they had was fine, and the bright colors of their clothes, and the monsters growing out of the heads of the ships were splendid and very frightening, even though one could see that they were only painted, like the pictures in the Abbess's books.

I decided that God had provided me with enough edification and could now strike down the impious strangers.

But He did not.

Instead the Abbess walked alone towards these fierce men, over the stony river bank, as calmly as if she were on a picnic with her girls. She was singing a little song, a pretty tune that I repeated many years later, and a well-traveled man said it was a Norse cradle-song. I didn't know that then, but only that the terrible, fair men, who had looked up in surprise at seeing one lone woman come out of the Abbey (which was barred behind her; I could see that), now began a sort of whispering astonishment among themselves. I saw the Abbess's gaze go quickly from one to the other—we often said that she could tell what was hidden in the soul from one look at the face—and then she picked the skirt of her habit up with one hand and daintily went among the rocks to one of the men, one older than the others, as it proved later, though I could not see so well at the time—and said to him, in his own language:

"Welcome, Thorvald Einarsson, and what do you, good farmer, so far from your own place, with the harvest ripe and the great autumn storms coming on over the sea?" (You may wonder how I knew what she said when I had no Norse; the truth is that Father Cairbre, who had not gone to the cellars after all, was looking out the top of the window while I was barely able to peep out the bottom, and he repeated everything that was said for the folk in the room, who all kept very quiet.)

Now you could see that the pirates were dumfounded to hear her speak their own language and even more so that she called one by his name; some stepped backwards and made strange signs in the air and others unsheathed axes or swords and came running towards the Abbess. But this Thorvald Einarsson put up his hand for them to stop and laughed heartily.

"Think!" he said. "There's no magic here, only cleverness —what pair of ears could miss my name with the lot of you bawling out 'Thorvald Einarsson, help me with this oar;' 'Thorvald Einarsson, my leggings are wet to the knees;' 'Thorvald Einarsson, this stream is as cold as a Fimbul-winter!'"

The Abbess Radegunde nodded and smiled. Then she sat down plump on the river bank. She scratched behind one ear, as I had often seen her do when she was deep in thought. Then she said (and I am sure that this talk was carried on in a loud voice so that we in the Abbey could hear it):

"Good friend Thorvald, you are as clever as the tale I heard of you from your sister's son, Ranulf, from whom I learnt the Norse when I was in Rome, and to show you it was he, he always swore by his gray horse, Lamefoot, and he had a difficulty in his speech; he could not say the sounds as we do and so spoke of you always as 'Torvald.' Is not that so?"

I did not realize it then, being only a child, but the Abbess was—by this speech—claiming hospitality from the man and had also picked by chance or inspiration the cleverest among these thieves, for his next words were:

"I am not the leader. There are no leaders here."

He was warning her that they were not his men to control, you see. So she scratched behind her ear again and got up. Then she began to wander, as if she did not know what to do, from one to the other of these uneasy folk—for some backed off and made signs at her still, and some took out their knives —singing her little tune again and walking slowly, more bent over and older and infirm-looking than we had ever seen her, one helpless little woman in black before all those fierce men. One wild young pirate snatched the headdress from her as she passed, leaving her short gray hair bare to the wind; the others laughed and he that had done it cried out:

"Grandmother, are you not ashamed?"

"Why, good friend, of what?" said she mildly.

"Thou art married to thy Christ," he said, holding the head-covering behind his back, "but this bridegroom of thine cannot even defend thee against the shame of having thy head uncovered! Now if thou wert married to me—"

There was much laughter. The Abbess Radegunde waited until it was over. Then she scratched her bare head and made as if to turn away, but suddenly she turned back upon him with the age and infirmity dropping from her as if they had been a cloak, seeming taller and very grand, as if lit from within by some great fire. She looked directly into his face. This thing she did was something we had all seen, of course, but they had not, nor had they heard that great, grand voice with which she sometimes read the Scriptures to us or talked with us of the wrath of God. I think the young man was frightened, for all his daring. And I know now what I did not then: that the Norse admire courage above all things and that—to be blunt —everyone likes a good story, especially if it happens right in front of your eyes.

"Grandson!"—and her voice tolled like the great bell of God; I think folk must have heard her all the way to the marsh!—"Little grandchild, thinkest thou that the Creator of the World who made the stars and the moon and the sun and our bodies, too and the change of the seasons and the very earth we stand on—yea, even unto the shit in thy belly!— thinkest thou that such a being has a big house in the sky where he keeps his wives and goes in to fuck them as thou wouldst thyself or like the King of Turkey? Do not dishonor the wit of the mother who bore thee! We are the servants of God, not his wives, and if we tell our silly girls they are married to the Christus, it is to make them understand that they must not run off and marry Otto Farmer or Ekkehard Blacksmith, but stick to their work, as they promised. If I told them they were married to an Idea, they would not understand me, and neither dost thou."

(Here Father Cairbre, above me in the window, muttered in a protesting way about something.)

Then the Abbess snatched the silver cross from around her neck and put it into the boy's hand, saying: "Give this to thy mother with my pity. She must pull out her hair over such a child."

But he let it fall to the ground. He was red in the face and breathing hard.

"Take it up," she said more kindly, "take it up, boy; it will not hurt thee and there's no magic in it. It's only pure silver and good workmanship; it will make thee rich." When she saw that he would not—his hand went to his knife—she *tched* to herself in a motherly way (or I believe she did, for she waved one hand back and forth as she always did when she made that sound) and got down on her knees—with more difficulty than was truth, I think—saying loudly, "I will stoop, then; I will stoop," and got up, holding it out to him, saying, "Take. Two sticks tied with a cord would serve me as well."

The boy cried, his voice breaking, "My mother is dead and thou art a witch!" and in an instant he had one arm around the Abbess's neck and with the other his knife at her throat. The man Thorvald Einarsson roared "Thorfinn!" but the Abbess only said clearly, "Let him be. I have shamed this man but did not mean to. He is right to be angry."

The boy released her and turned his back. I remember wondering if these strangers could weep. Later I heard—and I swear that the Abbess must have somehow known this or felt it, for although she was no witch, she could probe a man until she found the sore places in him and that very quickly—that this boy's mother had been known for an adulteress and that no man would own him as a son. It is one thing among those people for a man to have what the Abbess called a concubine and they do not hold the children of such in scorn as we do, but it is a different thing when a married woman has more than one man. Such was Thorfinn's case; I suppose that was what had sent him *viking*. But all this came later; what I saw then —with my nose barely above the window slit—was that the Abbess slipped her crucifix over the hilt of the boy's sword— she really wished him to have it, you see—and then walked to a place near the walls of the Abbey but far from the Norsemen. I think she meant them to come to her. I saw her pick up her skirts like a peasant woman, sit down with legs crossed, and say in a loud voice:

"Come! Who will bargain with me?"

A few strolled over, laughing, and sat down with her.

"All!" she said, gesturing them closer.

"And why should we all come?" said one who was farthest away.

"Because you will miss a bargain," said the Abbess.

"Why should we bargain when we can take?" said another.

"Because you will only get half," said the Abbess. "The rest you will not find."

"We will ransack the Abbey," said a third.

"Half the treasure is not in the Abbey," said she.

"And where is it then?"

She tapped her forehead. They were drifting over by twos and threes. I have heard since that the Norse love riddles and this was a sort of riddle; she was giving them good fun.

"If it is in your head," said the man Thorvald, who was standing behind the others, arms crossed, "we can get it out, can we not?" And he tapped the hilt of his knife.

"If you frighten me, I shall become confused and remember nothing," said the Abbess calmly. "Besides, do you wish to play that old game? You saw how well it worked the last time. I am surprised at you, Ranulf mother's-brother."

"I will bargain then," said the man Thorvald, smiling.

"And the rest of you?" said Radegunde. "It must be all or none; decide for yourselves whether you wish to save yourselves trouble and danger and be rich," and she deliberately turned her back on them. The men moved down to the river's edge and began to talk among themselves, dropping their voices so that we could not hear them any more. Father Cairbre, who was old and short-sighted, cried, "I cannot hear them. What are they doing?" and I cleverly said, "I have good eyes, Father Cairbre," and he held me up to see. So it was just at the time that the Abbess Radegunde was facing the Abbey tower that I appeared in the window. She clapped one hand across her mouth. Then she walked to the gate and called (in a voice I had learned not to disregard; it had often got me a smacked bottom), "Boy News, down! Come down to me here *at once*! And bring Father Cairbre with you."

I was overjoyed. I had no idea that she might want to protect me if anything went wrong. My only thought was that I was going to see it all from wonderfully close by. So I wormed my way, half-suffocated, through the folk in the tower room, stepping on feet and skirts, and having to say every few seconds, "But I *have* to! The Abbess wants me," and meanwhile she was calling outside like an Empress, "Let that boy through! Make a place for that boy! Let the Irish priest through!" until I crept and pushed and complained my way to the very wall itself—no one was going to open the gate for us, of course—and there was a great fuss and finally someone brought a ladder. I was over at once, but the old priest took a longer time, although it was a low wall, as I've said, the builders having been somewhat of two minds about making the Abbey into a true fortress.

Once outside it was lovely, away from all that crowd, and I ran, gloriously pleased, to the Abbess, who said only, "Stay by me, whatever happens," and immediately turned her attention away from me. It had taken so long to get Father Cairbre outside the walls that the tall, foreign men had finished their talking and were coming back—all twenty or thirty of them —towards the Abbey and the Abbess Radegunde, and most especially of all, me. I could see Father Cairbre tremble. They did look grim, close by, with their long, wild hair and the brightness of their strange clothes. I remember that they smelled different from us, but cannot remember how after all these years. Then the Abbess spoke to them in that outlandish language of theirs, so strangely light and lilting to hear from their bearded lips, and then she said something in Latin to Father Cairbre, and he said, with a shake in his voice:

"This is the priest, Father Cairbre, who will say our bargains aloud in our own tongue so that my people may hear. I cannot deal behind their backs. And this is my foster baby, who is very dear to me and who is now having his curiosity rather too much satisfied, I think." (I was trying to stand tall like a man but had one hand secretly holding onto her skirt; so that was what the foreign men had chuckled at!) The talk went on, but I will tell it as if I had understood the Norse, for to repeat everything twice would be tedious.

The Abbess Radegunde said, "Will you bargain?"

There was a general nodding of heads, with a look of: After all, why not?

"And who will speak for you?" said she.

A man stepped forward; I recognized Thorvald Einarsson.

"Ah, yes," said the Abbess dryly. "The company that has no leaders. Is this leaderless company agreed? Will it abide by its word? I want no treachery-planners, no Breakwords here!"

There was a general mutter at this. The Thorvald man (he *was* big, close up!) said mildly, "I sail with none such. Let's begin."

We all sat down.

"Now," said Thorvald Einarsson, raising his eyebrows, "according to my knowledge of this thing, you begin. And according to my knowledge, you will begin by saying that you are very poor."

"But, no," said the Abbess, "we are rich." Father Cairbre groaned. A groan answered him from behind the Abbey walls. Only the Abbess and Thorvald Einarsson seemed unmoved; it was as if these two were joking in some way that no one else understood. The Abbess went on, saying, "We are very rich. Within is much silver, much gold, many pearls, and much embroidered cloth, much fine-woven cloth, much carved and painted wood, and many books with gold upon their pages and jewels set into their covers. All this is yours. But we have more and better: herbs and medicines, ways to keep food from spoiling, the knowledge of how to cure the sick; all this is yours. And we have more and better even than this: we have the knowledge of Christ and the perfect understanding of the soul, which is yours too, any time you wish; you have only to accept it."

Thorvald Einarsson held up his hand. "We will stop with the first," he said, "and perhaps a little of the second. That is more practical."

"And foolish," said the Abbess politely, "in the usual way." And again I had the odd feeling that these two were sharing a joke no one else even saw. She added, "There is one thing you may not have, and that is the most precious of all."

Thorvald Einarsson looked inquiring.

"*My people.* Their safety is dearer to me than myself. They are not to be touched, not a hair on their heads, not for any reason. Think: you can fight your way into the Abbey easily enough, but the folk in there are very frightened of you, and some of the men are armed. Even a good fighter is cumbered in a crowd. You will slip and fall upon each other without meaning to or knowing that you do so. Heed my counsel. Why play butcher when you can have treasure poured into your laps like kings, without work? And after that there will be as much again, when I lead you to the hidden place. An earl's mountain of treasure. Think of it! And to give all this up for slaves, half of whom will get sick and die before you get them home—and will need to be fed if they are to be any good. Shame on you for bad advice-takers! Imagine what you will say to your wives and families: Here are a few miserable bolts of cloth with blood spots that won't come out, here are some pearls and jewels smashed to powder in the fighting, here is a torn piece of embroidery which was whole until someone stepped on it in the battle, and I had slaves but they died of illness and I fucked a pretty young nun and meant to bring her back, but she leapt into the sea. And, oh, yes, there was twice as much again and all of it whole but we decided not to take that. Too much trouble, you see."

This was a lively story and the Norsemen enjoyed it. Radegunde held up her hand.

"People!" she called in German, adding, "Sea-rovers, hear what I say; I will repeat it for you in your tongue." (And so she did.) "*People, if the Norsemen fight us, do not defend yourselves but smash everything! Wives, take your cooking knives and shred the valuable cloth to pieces! Men, with your axes and hammers hew the altars and the carved wood to fragments! All, grind the pearls and smash the jewels against the stone floors! Break the bottles of wine! Pound the gold and silver to shapelessness! Tear to pieces the illuminated books! Tear down the hangings and burn them!*

"But" (she added, her voice suddenly mild) "if these wise men will accept our gifts, let us heap untouched and spotless at their feet all that we have and hold nothing back, so that their kinsfolk will marvel and wonder at the shining and glistering of the wealth they bring back, though it leave us nothing but our bare stone walls."

If anyone had ever doubted that the Abbess Radegunde was inspired by God, their doubts must have vanished away, for who could resist the fiery vigor of her first speech or the beneficent unction of her second? The Norsemen sat there with their mouths open. I saw tears on Father Cairbre's cheeks. Then Thorvald said, "Abbess—"

He stopped. He tried again but again stopped. Then he shook himself, as a man who has been under a spell, and said:

"Abbess, my men have been without women for a long time."

Radegunde looked surprised. She looked as if she could not believe what she had heard. She looked the pirate up and down, as if puzzled, and then walked around him as if taking his measure. She did this several times, looking at every part of his big body as if she were summing him up while he got redder and redder. Then she backed off and surveyed him again, and with her arms akimbo like a peasant, announced very loudly in both Norse and German:

"What! Have they lost the use of their hands?"

It was irresistible, in its way. The Norse laughed. Our people laughed. Even Thorvald laughed. I did too, though I was not sure what everyone was laughing about. The laughter would die down and then begin again behind the Abbey walls, helplessly, and again die down and again begin. The Abbess waited until the Norsemen had stopped laughing and then called for silence in German until there were only a few snickers here and there. She then said:

"These good men—Father Cairbre, tell the people—these good men will forgive my silly joke. I meant no scandal, truly, and no harm, but laughter is good; it settles the body's waters, as the physicians say. And my people know that I am not always as solemn and good as I ought to be. Indeed I am a very great sinner and scandal-maker. Thorvald Einarsson, do we do business?"

The big man—who had not been so pleased as the others, I can tell you!—looked at his men and seemed to see what he needed to know. He said, "I go in with five men to see what you have. Then we let the poor folk on the grounds go, but not those inside the Abbey. Then we search again. The gates will be locked and guarded by the rest of us; if there's any treachery, the bargain's off."

"Then I will go with you," said Radegunde. "That is very just and my presence will calm the people. To see us together will assure them that no harm is meant. You are a good man, Torvald—forgive me; I call you as your nephew did so often. Come, Boy News, hold on to me."

"Open the gates!" she called then. "All is safe!" and with the five men (one of whom was that young Thorfinn who had hated her so) we waited while the great logs were pulled back. There was little space within, but the people shrank back at the sight of those fierce warriors and opened a place for us.

I looked back and the Norsemen had come in and were standing just inside the walls, on either side the gate, with their swords out and their shields up. The crowd parted for us more slowly as we reached the main tower, with the Abbess repeating constantly, "Be calm, people, be calm. All is well," and deftly speaking by name to this one or that. It was much harder when the people gasped upon hearing the big logs pushed shut with a noise like thunder, and it was very close on the stairs; I heard her say something like an apology in the queer foreign tongue. Something that probably meant, "I'm sorry that we must wait." It seemed an age until the stairs were even partly clear and I saw what the Abbess had meant by the cumbering of a crowd; a man might swing a weapon in the press of people, but not very far, and it was more likely he would simply fall over someone and crack his head. We gained the great room with the big crucifix of painted wood and the little one of pearls and gold, and the scarlet hangings worked in gold thread that I had played robbers behind so often before I learned what real robbers were: these tall, frightening men whose eyes glistened with greed at what I had fancied every village had. Most of the Sisters had stayed in the great room, but somehow it was not so crowded, as the folk had huddled back against the walls when the Norsemen came in. The youngest girls were all in a corner, terrified—one could smell it, as one can in people—and when that young Thorfinn went for the little gold-and-pearl cross, Sister Sibihd cried in a high, cracked voice, "It is the body of our Christ!" and leapt up, snatching it from the wall before he could get to it.

"Sibihd!" exclaimed the Abbess, in as sharp a voice as I had ever heard her use. "Put that back or you will feel the weight of my hand, I tell you!"

Now it is odd, is it not, that a young woman desperate enough not to care about death at the hands of a Norse pirate should nonetheless be frightened away at the threat of getting a few slaps from her Abbess? But folk are like that. Sister Sibihd returned the cross to its place (from whence young Thorfinn took it) and fell back among the nuns, sobbing, "He desecrates our Lord God!"

"Foolish girl!" snapped the Abbess. "God only can consecrate or desecrate; man cannot. That is a piece of metal."

Thorvald said something sharp to Thorfinn, who slowly put the cross back on its hook with a sulky look which said, plainer than words: Nobody gives me what I want. Nothing else went wrong in the big room or the Abbess's study or the store-rooms, or out in the kitchens. The Norsemen were silent and kept their hands on their swords, but the Abbess kept talking in a calm way in both tongues; to our folk she said, "See? It is all right but everyone must keep still. God will protect us." Her face was steady and clear, and I believed her a saint, for she had saved Sister Sibihd and the rest of us.

But this peacefulness did not last, of course. Something had to go wrong in all that press of people; to this day I do not know what. We were in a corner of the long refectory, which is the place where the Sisters or Brothers eat in an Abbey, when something pushed me into the wall and I fell, almost suffocated by the Abbess's lying on top of me. My head was ringing and on all sides there was a terrible roaring sound with curses and screams, a dreadful tumult as if the walls had come apart and were falling on everyone. I could hear the Abbess whispering something in Latin over and over in my ear. There were dull, ripe sounds, worse than the rest, which I know now to have been the noise steel makes when it is thrust into bodies. This all seemed to go on forever and then it seemed to me that the floor was wet. Then all became quiet. I felt the Abbess Radegunde get off me. She said:

"So this is how you wash your floors up North." When I lifted my head from the rushes and saw what she meant, I was very sick into the corner. Then she picked me up in her arms and held my face against her bosom so that I would not see, but it was no use; I had already seen: all the people lying sprawled on the floor with their bellies coming out, like heaps of dead fish, old Walafrid with an axe handle standing out of his chest—he was sitting up with his eyes shut in a press of bodies that gave him no room to lie down—and the young beekeeper, Uta, from the village, who had been so merry, lying on her back with her long braids and her gown all dabbled in red dye and a great stain of it on her belly. She was breathing fast and her eyes were wide open. As we passed her, the noise of her breathing ceased.

The Abbess said mildly, "Thy people are thorough house-keepers, Earl Split-gut."

Thorvald Einarsson roared something at us, and the Abbess replied softly, "Forgive me, good friend. You protected me and the boy and I am grateful. But nothing betrays a man's knowledge of the German like a word that bites, is it not so? And I had to be sure."

It came to me then that she had called him "Torvald" and reminded him of his sister's son so that he would feel he must protect us if anything went wrong. But now she would make him angry, I thought, and I shut my eyes tight. Instead he laughed and said in odd, light German, "I did no housekeeping but to stand over you and your pet. Are you not grateful?"

"Oh, very, thank you," said the Abbess with such warmth as she might show to a Sister who had brought her a rose from the garden, or another who copied her work well, or when I told her news, or if Ita the cook made a good soup. But he did not know that the warmth was for everyone and so seemed satisfied. By now we were in the garden and the air was less foul; she put me down, although my limbs were shaking, and I clung to her gown, crumpled, stiff, and blood-reeking though it was. She said, "Oh my God, what a deal of washing hast Thou given us!" She started to walk towards the gate, and Thorvald Einarsson took a step towards her. She said, without turning round: "Do not insist, Thorvald, there is no reason to lock me up. I am forty years old and not likely to be running away into the swamp, what with my rheumatism and the pain in my knees and the folk needing me as they do."

There was a moment's silence. I could see something odd come into the big man's face. He said quietly:

"I did not speak, Abbess."

She turned, surprised. "But you did. I heard you."

He said strangely, "I did not."

Children can guess sometimes what is wrong and what to do about it without knowing how; I remember saying, very quickly, "Oh, she does that sometimes. My stepmother says old age has addled her wits," and then, "Abbess, may I go to my stepmother and my father?"

"Yes, of course," she said, "run along, Boy News—" and then stopped, looking into the air as if seeing in it something we could not. Then she said very gently, "No, my dear, you had better stay here with me," and I knew, as surely as if I had seen it with my own eyes, that I was not to go to my stepmother or my father because both were dead.

She did things like that, too, sometimes.

For a while it seemed that everyone was dead. I did not feel grieved or frightened in the least, but I think I must have been, for I had only one idea in my head: that if I let the Abbess out of my sight, I would die. So I followed her everywhere. She was let to move about and comfort people, especially the mad Sibihd, who would do nothing but rock and wail, but towards nightfall, when the Abbey had been stripped of its treasures, Thorvald Einarsson put her and me in her study, now bare of its grand furniture, on a straw pallet on the floor, and bolted the door on the outside. She said:

"Boy News, would you like to go to Constantinople, where the Turkish Sultan is, and the domes of gold and all the splendid pagans? For that is where this man will take me to sell me."

"Oh, yes!" said I, and then: "But will he take me, too?"

"Of course," said the Abbess, and so it was settled. Then in came Thorvald Einarsson, saying:

"Thorfinn is asking for you." I found out later that they were waiting for him to die; none other of the Norse had been wounded, but a farmer had crushed Thorfinn's chest with an axe, and he was expected to die before morning. The Abbess said:

"Is that a good reason to go?" She added, "I mean that he hates me; will not his anger at my presence make him worse?"

Thorvald said slowly, "The folk here say you can sit by the sick and heal them. Can you do that?"

"To my own knowledge, not at all," said the Abbess Radegunde, "but if they believe so, perhaps that calms them and makes them better. Christians are quite as foolish as other people, you know. I will come if you want," and though I saw that she was pale with tiredness, she got to her feet. I should say that she was in a plain, brown gown taken from one of the peasant women because her own was being washed clean, but to me she had the same majesty as always. And for him too, I think.

Thorvald said, "Will you pray for him or damn him?"

She said, "I do not pray, Thorvald, and I never damn anybody; I merely sit." She added, "Oh, let him; he'll scream your ears off if you don't," and this meant me, for I was ready to yell for my life if they tried to keep me from her.

They had put Thorfinn in the chapel, a little stone room with nothing left in it now but a plain wooden cross, not worth carrying off. He was lying, his eyes closed, on the stone altar with furs under him, and his face was gray. Every time he breathed, there was a bubbling sound, a little, thin, reedy sound; and as I crept closer, I saw why, for in the young man's chest was a great red hole with sharp pink things sticking out of it, all crushed, and in the hole one could see something jump and fall, jump and fall, over and over again. It was his heart beating. Blood kept coming from his lips in a froth. I do not know, of course, what either said, for they spoke in the Norse, but I saw what they did and heard much of it talked of between the Abbess and Thorvald Einarsson later. So I will tell it as if I knew.

The first thing the Abbess did was to stop suddenly on the threshold and raise both hands to her mouth as if in horror. Then she cried furiously to the two guards:

"Do you wish to kill your comrade with the cold and damp? Is this how you treat one another? Get fire in here and some woollen cloth to put over him! No, not more skins, you idiots, *wool* to mold to his body and take up the wet. Run now!"

One said sullenly, "We don't take orders from you, Grandma."

"Oh, no?" said she. "Then I shall strip this wool dress from my old body and put it over that boy and then sit here all night in my flabby, naked skin! What will this child's soul say when it enters the Valhall? That his friends would not give up a little of their booty so that he might fight for life? Is this your fellow-ship? Do it, or I will strip myself and shame you both for the rest of your lives!"

"Well, take it from his share," said the one in a low voice, and the other ran out. Soon there was a fire on the hearth and russet-colored woollen cloth—"From my own share," said one of them loudly, though it was a color the least costly, not like blue or red—and the Abbess laid it loosely over the boy, carefully putting it close to his sides but not moving him. He did not look to be in any pain, but his color got no better. But then he opened his eyes and said in such a little voice as a ghost might have, a whisper as thin and reedy and bubbling as his breath:

"You . . . old witch. But I beat you . . . in the end."

"Did you, my dear?" said the Abbess. "How?"

"Treasure," he said, "for my kinfolk. And I lived as a man at last. Fought . . . and had a woman . . . the one here with the big breasts, Sibihd. . . . Whether she liked it or not. That was good."

"Yes, Sibihd," said the Abbess mildly. "Sibihd has gone mad. She hears no one and speaks to no one. She only sits and rocks and moans and soils herself and will not feed herself, although if one puts food in her mouth with a spoon, she will swallow."

The boy tried to frown. "Stupid," he said at last. "Stupid nuns. The beasts do it."

"Do they?" said the Abbess, as if this were a new idea to her. "Now that is very odd. For never yet heard I of a gander that blacked the goose's eye or hit her over the head with a stone or stuck a knife in her entrails when he was through. When God puts it into their hearts to desire one another, she squats and he comes running. And a bitch in heat will jump through the window if you lock the door. Poor fools! Why didn't you camp three hours' down-river and wait? In a week half the young married women in the village would have been slipping away at night to see what the foreigners were like. Yes, and some unmarried ones, and some of my own girls, too. But you couldn't wait, could you?"

"No," said the boy, with the ghost of a brag. "Better . . . this way."

"*This* way," said she. "Oh, yes, my dear, old Granny knows about *this* way! Pleasure for the count of three or four, and the rest of it as much joy as rolling a stone uphill."

He smiled a ghostly smile. "You're a whore, Grandma."

She began to stroke his forehead. "No, Grandbaby," she said, "but all Latin is not the Church Fathers, you know, great as they are. One can find a great deal in those strange books written by the ones who died centuries before our Lord was born. Listen," and she leaned closer to him and said quietly:

> Syrian dancing girl, how subtly
>   you sway those sensuous limbs,
> Half-drunk in the smoky tavern,
>   lascivious and wanton,
> Your long hair bound back in the
>   Greek way, clashing the castanets
>   in your hands—

The boy was too weak to do anything but look astonished. Then she said this:

"I love you so that anyone permitted to sit near you and talk to you seems to me like a god; when I am near you my spirit is broken, my heart shakes, my voice dies, and I can't even speak. Under my skin I flame up all over and I can't see; there's thunder in my ears and I break out in a sweat, as if from fever; I turn paler than cut grass and feel that I am utterly changed; I feel that Death has come near me."

He said, as if frightened, "Nobody feels like that."

"They do," she said.

He said, in feeble alarm, "You're trying to kill me!"

She said, "No, my dear. I simply don't want you to die a virgin."

It was odd, his saying those things and yet holding on to her hand where he had got at it through the woollen cloth; she stroked his head and he whispered, "Save me, old witch."

"I'll do my best," she said. "You shall do your best by not talking and I by not tormenting you any more, and we'll both try to sleep."

"Pray," said the boy.

"Very well," said she, "but I'll need a chair," and the guards —seeing I suppose, that he was holding her hand—brought in one of the great wooden chairs from the Abbey, which were too plain and heavy to carry off, I think. Then the Abbess Radegunde sat in the chair and closed her eyes. Thorfinn seemed to fall asleep. I crept nearer her on the floor and must have fallen asleep myself almost at once, for the next thing I knew a gray light filled the chapel, the fire had gone out, and someone was shaking Radegunde, who still slept in her chair, her head leaning to one side. It was Thorvald Einarsson and he was shouting with excitement in his strange German, "Woman, how did you do it! How did you do it!"

"Do what?" said the Abbess thickly. "Is he dead?"

"Dead?" exclaimed the Norseman. "He is healed! Healed! The lung is whole and all is closed up about the heart and the shattered pieces of the ribs are grown together! Even the muscles of the chest are beginning to heal!"

"That's good," said the Abbess, still half asleep. "Let me be."

Thorvald shook her again. She said again, "Oh, let me sleep." This time he hauled her to her feet and she shrieked, "My back, my back! Oh, the saints, my rheumatism!" and at the same time a sick voice from under the blue woollens—a sick voice but a man's voice, not a ghost's—said something in Norse.

"Yes, I hear you," said the Abbess. "You must become a follower of the White Christ right away, this very minute. But Dominus noster, please do. You put it into these brawny heads that I must have a tub of hot water with pennyroyal in it? I am too old to sleep all night in a chair, and I am one ache from head to foot."

Thorfinn got louder.

"Tell him," said the Abbess Radegunde to Thorvald in German, "that I will not baptize him and I will not shrive him until he is a different man. All that child wants is someone more powerful than your Odin god or your Thor god to pull him out of the next scrape he gets into. Ask him: Will he adopt Sibihd as his sister? Will he clean her when she soils herself and feed her and sit with his arm about her, talking to her gently and lovingly until she is well again? The Christ does not wipe out our sins only to have us commit them all over again, and that is what he wants and what you all want, a God that gives and gives and gives, but God does not give; He takes and takes and takes. He takes away everything that is not God until there is nothing left but God, and none of you will understand that! There is no remission of sins; there is only change, and Thorfinn must change before God will have him."

"Abbess, you are eloquent," said Thorvald, smiling, "but why do you not tell him all this yourself?"

"Because I ache so!" said Radegunde; "Oh, do get me into some hot water!" and Thorvald half led and half supported her as she hobbled out. That morning, after she had had her soak—when I cried, they let me stay just outside the door—she undertook to cure Sibihd, first by rocking her in her arms and talking to her, telling her she was safe now, and promising that the Northmen would go soon, and then when Sibihd became quieter, leading her out into the woods with Thorvald as a bodyguard to see that we did not run away, and little, dark Sister Hedwic, who had stayed with Sibihd and cared for her. The Abbess would walk for a while in the mild autumn sunshine, and then she would direct Sibihd's face upwards by touching her gently under the chin and say, "See? There is God's sky still," and then, "Look, there are God's trees; they have not changed," and tell her that the world was just the same and God still kindly to folk, only a few more souls had joined the Blessed and were happier waiting for us in Heaven than we could ever be, or even imagine being, on the poor earth. Sister Hedwic kept hold of Sibihd's hand. No one paid more attention to me than if I had been a dog, but every time poor Sister Sibihd saw Thorvald she would shrink away, and you could see that Hedwic could not bear to look at him at all; every time he came in her sight she turned her face aside, shut her eyes hard, and bit her lower lip. It was a quiet, almost warm day, as autumn can be sometimes, and the Abbess found a few little blue late flowers growing in a sheltered place against a log and put them into Sibihd's hand, speaking of how beautifully and cunningly God had made all things. Sister Sibihd had enough wit to hold on to the flowers, but her eyes stared and she would have stumbled and fallen if Hedwic had not led her.

Sister Hedwic said timidly, "Perhaps she suffers because she has been defiled, Abbess," and then looked ashamed. For a moment the Abbess looked shrewdly at young Sister Hedwic and then at the mad Sibihd. Then she said:

"Dear daughter Sibihd and dear daughter Hedwic, I am now going to tell you something about myself that I have never told to a single living soul but my confessor. Do you know that as a young woman I studied at Avignon and from there was sent to Rome, so that I might gather much learning? Well, in Avignon I read mightily our Christian Fathers but also in the pagan poets, for as it has been said by Ermenrich of Ellwangen: As dung spread upon a field enriches it to good harvest, thus one cannot produce divine eloquence without the filthy writings of the pagan poets. This is true but perilous, only I thought not so, for I was very proud and fancied that if the pagan poems of love left me unmoved, that was because I had the gift of chastity right from God Himself, and I scorned sensual pleasures and those tempted by them. I had forgotten, you see, that chastity is not given once and for all like a wedding ring that is put on never to be taken off, but is a garden which each day must be weeded, watered, and trimmed anew, or soon there will be only brambles and wilderness.

"As I have said, the words of the poets did not tempt me, for words are only marks on the page with no life save what we give them. But in Rome there were not only the old books, daughters, but something much worse.

"There were statues. Now you must understand that these are not such as you can imagine from our books, like Saint John or the Virgin; the ancients wrought so cunningly in stone that it is like magic; one stands before the marble holding one's breath, waiting for it to move and speak. They are not statues at all but beautiful, naked men and women. It is a city of sea-gods pouring water, daughter Sibihd and daughter Hedwic, of athletes about to throw the discus, and runners and wrestlers and young emperors, and the favorites of kings; but they do not walk the streets like real men, for they are all of stone.

"There was one Apollo, all naked, which I knew I should not look on but which I always made some excuse to my companions to pass by, and this statue, although three miles distant from my dwelling, drew me as if by magic. Oh, he was fair to look on! Fairer than any youth alive now in Germany, or in the world, I think. And then all the old loves of the pagan poets came back to me: Dido and Aeneas, the taking of Venus and Mars, the love of the moon, Diana, for the shepherd boy—and I thought that if my statue could only come to life, he would utter honeyed love-words from the old poets and would be wise and brave, too, and what woman could resist him?"

Here she stopped and looked at Sister Sibihd but Sibihd only stared on, holding the little blue flowers. It was Sister Hedwic who cried, one hand pressed to her heart:

"Did you pray, Abbess?"

"I did," said Radegunde solemnly, "and yet my prayers kept becoming something else. I would pray to be delivered from the temptation that was in the statue, and then, of course, I would have to think of the statue itself, and then I would tell myself that I must run, like the nymph Daphne, to be armored and sheltered within a laurel tree, but my feet seemed to be already rooted to the ground, and then at the last minute I would flee and be back at my prayers again. But it grew harder each time, and at last the day came when I did not flee."

"Abbess, *you?*" cried Hedwic, with a gasp. Thorvald, keeping his watch a little way from us, looked surprised. I was very pleased—I loved to see the Abbess astonish people; it was one of her gifts—and at seven I had no knowledge of lust except that my little thing felt good sometimes when I handled it to make water, and what had that to do with statues coming to life or women turning into laurel trees? I was more interested in mad Sibihd, the way children are; I did not know what she might do, or if I should be afraid of her, or if I should go mad myself, what it would be like. But the Abbess was laughing gently at Hedwic's amazement.

"Why not me?" said the Abbess. "I was young and healthy and had no special grace from God any more than the hens or the cows do! Indeed, I burned so with desire for that handsome young hero—for so I had made him in my mind, as a woman might do with a man she has seen a few times on the street—that thoughts of him tormented me waking and sleeping. It seemed to me that because of my vows I could not give myself to this Apollo of my own free will. So I would dream that he took me against my will, and, oh, what an exquisite pleasure that was!"

Here Hedwic's blood came all to her face and she covered it with her hands. I could see Thorvald grinning, back where he watched us.

"And then," said the Abbess, as if she had not seen either of them, "a terrible fear came to my heart that God might punish me by sending a ravisher who would use me unlawfully, as I had dreamed my Apollo did, and that I would not even wish to resist him and would feel the pleasures of a base lust and would know myself a whore and a false nun forever after. This fear both tormented and drew me. I began to steal looks at young men in the streets, not letting the other Sisters see me do it, thinking: Will it be he? Or he? Or he?

"And then it happened. I had lingered behind the others at a melon seller's, thinking of no Apollos or handsome heroes but only of the convent's dinner, when I saw my companions disappearing round a corner. I hastened to catch up with them—and made a wrong turning—and was suddenly lost in a narrow street—and at that very moment a young fellow took hold of my habit and threw me to the ground! You may wonder why he should do such a mad thing, but as I found out afterwards, there are prostitutes in Rome who affect our way of dress to please the appetites of certain men who are depraved enough to—well, really, I do not know how to say it! Seeing me alone, he had thought I was one of them and would be glad of a customer and a bit of play. So there was a reason for it.

"Well, there I was on my back with this young fellow, sent as a vengeance by God, as I thought, trying to do exactly what I had dreamed, night after night, that my statue should do. And do you know, it was nothing in the least like my dream! The stones at my back hurt me, for one thing. And instead of melting with delight, I was screaming my head off in terror and kicking at him as he tried to pull up my skirts, and praying to

God that this insane man might not break any of my bones in his rage!

"My screams brought a crowd of people and he went running. So I got off with nothing worse than a bruised back and a sprained knee. But the strangest thing of all was that while I was cured forever of lusting after my Apollo, instead I began to be tormented by a new fear—that I had lusted after *him*, that foolish young man with the foul breath and the one tooth missing!—and I felt strange creepings and crawlings over my body that were half like desire and half like fear and half like disgust and shame with all sorts of other things mixed in—I know that is too many halves but it is how I felt—and nothing at all like the burning desire I had felt for my Apollo. I went to see the statue once more before I left Rome, and it seemed to look at me sadly, as if to say: Don't blame me, poor girl; I'm only a piece of stone. And that was the last time I was so proud as to believe that God had singled me out for a special gift, like chastity—or a special sin, either—or that being thrown down on the ground and hurt had anything to do with any sin of mine, no matter how I mixed the two together in my mind. I dare say you did not find it a great pleasure yesterday, did you?"

Hedwic shook her head. She was crying quietly. She said, "Thank you, Abbess," and the Abbess embraced her. They both seemed happier, but then all of a sudden Sibihd muttered something, so low that one could not hear her.

"The—" she whispered and then she brought it out but still in a whisper: "The blood."

"What, dear, your blood?" said Radegunde.

"No, mother," said Sibihd, beginning to tremble, "The blood. All over us. Walafrid and—and Uta—and Sister Hildegarde—and everyone broken and spilled out like a dish! And none of us had done anything but I could smell it all over me and the children screaming because they were being trampled down, and those demons come up from Hell though we had done nothing and—and—I understand, mother, about the rest, but I will never, ever forget it, oh Christus, it is all around me now, oh, mother, the *blood*!"

Then Sister Sibihd dropped to her knees on the fallen leaves and began to scream, not covering her face as Sister Hedwic had done, but staring ahead with her wide eyes as if she were blind or could see something we could not. The Abbess knelt down and embraced her, rocking her back and forth, saying, "Yes, yes, dear, but we are here; we are here now; that is gone now," but Sibihd continued to scream, covering her ears as if the scream were someone else's and she could hide herself from it.

Thorvald said, looking, I thought, a little uncomfortable, "Cannot your Christ cure this?"

"No," said the Abbess. "Only by undoing the past. And that is the one thing He never does, it seems. She is in Hell now and must go back there many times before she can forget."

"She would make a bad slave," said the Norseman, with a glance at Sister Sibihd, who had fallen silent and was staring ahead of her again. "You need not fear that anyone will want her."

"God," said the Abbess Radegunde calmly, "is merciful."

Thorvald Einarsson said, "Abbess, I am not a bad man."

"For a good man," said the Abbess Radegunde, "you keep surprisingly bad company."

He said angrily, "I did not choose my shipmates. I have had bad luck!"

"Ours has," said the Abbess, "been worse, I think."

"Luck is luck," said Thorvald, clenching his fists. "It comes to some folk and not to others."

"As you came to us," said the Abbess mildly. "Yes, yes, I see, Thorvald Einarsson; one may say that luck is Thor's doing or Odin's doing, but you must know that our bad luck is your own doing and not some god's. You are our bad luck, Thorvald Einarsson. It's true that you're not as wicked as your friends, for they kill for pleasure and you do it without feeling, as a business, the way one hews down grain. Perhaps you have seen today some of the grain you have cut. If you had a man's soul, you would not have gone *viking*, luck or no luck, and if your soul were bigger still, you would have tried to stop your shipmates, just as I talk honestly to you now, despite your anger, and just as Christus himself told the truth and was nailed on the cross. If you were a beast you could not break God's law, and if you were a man you would not, but you are neither, and that makes you a kind of monster that spoils everything it touches and never knows the reason, and that is why I will never forgive you until you become a man, a true man with a true soul. As for your friends—"

Here Thorvald Einarsson struck the Abbess on the face with his open hand and knocked her down. I heard Sister Hedwic gasp in horror and behind us Sister Sibihd began to moan. But the Abbess only sat there, rubbing her jaw and smiling a little. Then she said:

"Oh, dear, have I been at it again? I am ashamed of myself. You are quite right to be angry, Torvald; no one can stand me when I go on in that way, least of all myself; it is such a bore. Still, I cannot seem to stop it; I am too used to being the Abbess Radegunde, that is clear. I promise never to torment you again, but you, Thorvald, must never strike me again, because you will be very sorry if you do."

He took a step forward.

"No, no, my dear man," the Abbess said merrily, "I mean no threat—how could I threaten you?—I mean only that I will never tell you any jokes, my spirits will droop, and I will become as dull as any other woman. Confess it now: I am the most interesting thing that has happened to you in years and I have entertained you better, sharp tongue and all, than all the *skalds* at the Court of Norway. And I know more tales and stories than they do—more than anyone in the whole world—for I make new ones when the old ones wear out.

"Shall I tell you a story now?"

"About your Christ?" said he, the anger still in his face.

"No," said she, "about living men and women. Tell me, Torvald what do you men want from us women?"

"To be talked to death," said he, and I could see there was some anger in him still, but he was turning it to play also.

The Abbess laughed in delight. "Very witty!" she said, springing to her feet and brushing the leaves off her skirt. "You are a very clever man, Torvald. I beg your pardon, Thorvald. I keep forgetting. But as to what men want from women, if you asked the young men, they would only wink and dig one another in the ribs, but that is only how they deceive themselves. That is only body calling to body. They want something quite different and they want it so much that it frightens them. So they pretend it is anything and everything else: pleasure, comfort, a servant in the home. Do you know what it is that they want?"

"What?" said Thorvald.

"The mother," said Radegunde, "as women do, too; we all want the mother. When I walked before you on the riverbank yesterday, I was playing the mother. Now you did nothing, for you are no young fool, but I knew that sooner or later one of you, so tormented by his longing that he would hate me for it, would reveal himself. And so he did: Thorfinn, with his thoughts all mixed up between witches and grannies and what not. I knew I could frighten him, and through him, most of you. That was the beginning of my bargaining. You Norse have too much of the father in your country and not enough mother; that is why you die so well and kill other folk so well —and live so very, very badly."

"You are doing it again," said Thorvald, but I think he wanted to listen all the same.

"Your pardon, friend," said the Abbess. "You are brave men; I don't deny it. But I know your *sagas* and they are all about fighting and dying and afterwards not Heavenly happiness but the end of the world: everything, even the gods, eaten by the Fenris Wolf and the Midgaard snake! What a pity, to die bravely only because life is not worth living! The Irish know better. The pagan Irish were heroes, with their Queens leading them to battle as often as not, and Father Cairbre, God rest his soul, was complaining only two days ago that the common Irish folk were blasphemously making a goddess out of God's mother, for do they build shrines to Christ or Our Lord or pray to them? No! It is Our Lady of the Rocks and Our Lady of the Sea and Our Lady of the Grove and Our Lady of this or that from one end of the land to the other. And even here it is only the Abbey folk who speak of God the Father and of Christ. In the village if one is sick or another in trouble it is: Holy Mother, save me! and: *Miriam Virginem*, intercede for me, and: Blessed Virgin, blind my husband's eyes! and: Our Lady, preserve my crops, and so on, men and women both. We all need the mother."

"You, too?"

"More than most," said the Abbess.

"And I?"

"Oh, no," said the Abbess, stopping suddenly, for we had all been walking back towards the village as she spoke. "No, and that is what drew me to you at once. I saw it in you and knew you were the leader. It is followers who make leaders, you know, and your shipmates have made you leader, whether you know it or not. What you want is—how shall I say it? You are a clever man, Thorvald, perhaps the cleverest man I have ever met, more even than the scholars I knew in my youth. But your cleverness has had no food. It is a cleverness of the world and not of books. You want to travel and know about folk and their customs, and what strange places are like, and what has happened to men and women in the past. If you take me to Constantinople, it will not be to get a price for me but merely to go there; you went seafaring because this longing itched at you until you could bear it not a year more; I know that."

"Then you are a witch," said he, and he was not smiling.

"No, I only saw what was in your face when you spoke of that city," said she. "Also there is gossip that you spent much time in Göteborg as a young man, idling and marveling at the ships and markets when you should have been at your farm."

She said, "Thorvald, I can feed that cleverness. I am the wisest woman in the world. I know everything—everything! I know more than my teachers; I make it up or it comes to me, I don't know how, but it is real—real!—and I know more than anyone. Take me from here, as your slave if you wish but as your friend also, and let us go to Constantinople and see the domes of gold, and the walls all inlaid with gold, and the people so wealthy you cannot imagine it, and the whole city so gilded it seems to be on fire, pictures as high as a wall, set right in the wall and all made of jewels so there is nothing else like them, redder than the reddest rose, greener than the grass, and with a blue that makes the sky pale!"

"You are indeed a witch," said he, "and not the Abbess Radegunde."

She said slowly, "I think I am forgetting how to be the Abbess Radegunde."

"Then you will not care about them any more," said he, and pointed to Sister Hedwic, who was still leading the stumbling Sister Sibihd.

The Abbess's face was still and mild. She said, "I care. Do not strike me, Thorvald, not ever again, and I will be a good friend to you. Try to control the worst of your men and leave as many of my people free as you can—I know them and will tell you which can be taken away with the least hurt to themselves or others—and I will feed that curiosity and cleverness of yours until you will not recognize this old world any more for the sheer wonder and awe of it; I swear this on my life."

"Done," said he, adding, "but with my luck, your life is somewhere else, locked in a box on top of a mountain, like the troll's in the story, or you will die of old age while we are still at sea."

"Nonsense," she said, "I am a healthy, mortal woman with all my teeth, and I mean to gather many wrinkles yet."

He put his hand out and she took it; then he said, shaking his head in wonder, "If I sold you in Constantinople, within a year you would become Queen of the place!"

The Abbess laughed merrily and I cried in fear, "Me, too! Take me too!" and she said "Oh, yes, we must not forget little Boy News," and lifted me into her arms.

The frightening, tall man, with his face close to mine, said in his strange, sing-song German:

"Boy, would you like to see the whales leaping in the open sea and the seals barking on the rocks? And cliffs so high that a giant could stretch his arms up and not reach their tops? And the sun shining at midnight?"

"Yes!" said I.

"But you will be a slave," he said, "and may be ill-treated and will always have to do as you are bid. Would you like that?"

"No!" I cried lustily, from the safety of the Abbess's arms, "I'll fight!"

He laughed a mighty, roaring laugh and tousled my head —rather too hard, I thought—and said, "I will not be a bad master, for I am named for Thor Red-beard and he is strong and quick to fight but good-natured, too, and so am I," and the Abbess put me down, and so we walked back to the village, Thorvald and the Abbess Radegunde talking of the glories of this world and Sister Hedwic saying softly, "She is a saint, our Abbess, a saint, to sacrifice herself for the good of the people," and all the time behind us, like a memory, came the low, witless sobbing of Sister Sibihd, who was in Hell.

When we got back we found that Thorfinn was better and the Norsemen were to leave in the morning. Thorvald had a second pallet brought into the Abbess's study and slept on the floor with us that night. You might think his men would laugh at this, for the Abbess was an old woman, but I think he had been with one of the young ones before he came to us. He had that look about him. There was no bedding for the Abbess but an old brown cloak with holes in it, and she and I were wrapped in it when he came in and threw himself down, whistling, on the other pallet. Then he said:

"Tomorrow, before we sail, you will show me the old Abbess's treasure."

"No," said she. "That agreement was broken."

He had been playing with his knife and now ran his thumb along the edge of it. "I can make you do it."

"No," said she patiently, "and now I am going to sleep."

"So you make light of death?" he said. "Good! That is what a brave woman should do, as the *skalds* sing, and not move, even when the keen sword cuts off her eyelashes. But what if I put this knife here not to your throat but to your little boy's? You would tell me then quick enough!"

The Abbess turned away from him, yawning and saying, "No, Thorvald, because you would not. And if you did, I would despise you for a cowardly oath-breaker and not tell you for that reason. Good night."

He laughed and whistled again for a bit. Then he said:

"Was all that true?"

"All what?" said the Abbess. "Oh, about the statue. Yes, but there was no ravisher. I put him in the tale for poor Sister Hedwic."

Thorvald snorted, as if in disappointment. "Tale? You tell lies, Abbess!"

The Abbess drew the old brown cloak over her head and closed her eyes. "It helped her."

Then there was a silence, but the big Norseman did not seem able to lie still. He shifted his body again as if the straw bothered him, and again turned over. He finally burst out, "But what happened!"

She sat up. Then she shut her eyes. She said, "Maybe it does not come into your man's thoughts that an old woman gets tired and that the work of dealing with folk is hard work, or even that it is work at all. Well!

"Nothing 'happened,' Thorvald. Must something happen only if this one fucks that one or one bangs in another's head? I desired my statue to the point of such foolishness that I determined to find a real, human lover, but when I raised my eyes from my fancies to the real, human men of Rome and unstopped my ears to listen to their talk, I realized that the thing was completely and eternally impossible. Oh, those younger sons with their skulking, jealous hatred of the rich, and the rich ones with their noses in the air because they thought themselves of such great consequence because of their silly money, and the timidity of the priests to their superiors, and their superiors' pride, and the artisans' hatred of the peasants, and the peasants being worked like animals from morning until night, and half the men I saw beating their wives and the other half out to cheat some poor girl of her money or her virginity or both—this was enough to put out any fire! And the women doing less harm only because they had less power to do harm, or so it seemed to me then. So I put all away, as one does with any disappointment. Men are not such bad folk when one stops expecting them to be gods, but they are not for me. If that state is chastity, then a weak stomach is temperance, I think. But whatever it is, I have it, and that's the end of the matter."

"*All* men?" said Thorvald Einarsson with his head to one side, and it came to me that he had been drinking, though he seemed sober.

"Thorvald," said the Abbess, "what you want with this middle-aged wreck of a body I cannot imagine, but if you lust after my wrinkles and flabby breasts and lean, withered flanks, do whatever you want quickly and then, for Heaven's sake, let me sleep. I am tired to death."

He said in a low voice, "I need to have power over you."

She spread her hands in a helpless gesture. "Oh, Thorvald, Thorvald, I am a weak little woman over forty years old! Where is the power? All I can do is talk!"

He said, "That's it. That's how you do it. You talk and talk and talk and everyone does just as you please; I have seen it!"

The Abbess said, looking sharply at him, "Very well. If you must. *But if I were you, Norseman, I would as soon bed my own mother.* Remember that as you pull my skirts up."

That stopped him. He swore under his breath, turning over on his side, away from us. Then he thrust his knife into the edge of his pallet, time after time. Then he put the knife under the rolled-up cloth he was using as a pillow. We had no pillow and so I tried to make mine out of the edge of the cloak and failed. Then I thought that the Norseman was afraid of God working in Radegunde, and then I thought of Sister Hedwic's changing color and wondered why. And then I thought of the leaping whales and the seals, which must be like great dogs because of the barking, and then the seals jumped on land and ran to my pallet and lapped at me with great, icy tongues of water so that I shivered and jumped, and then I woke up.

The Abbess Radegunde had left the pallet—it was her warmth I had missed—and was walking about the room. She would step and pause, her skirts making a small noise as she did so. She was careful not to touch the sleeping Thorvald. There was a dim light in the room from the embers that still glowed under the ashes in the hearth, but no light came from between the shutters of the study window, now shut against the cold. I saw the Abbess kneel under the plain wooden cross which hung on the study wall and heard her say a few words in Latin; I thought she was praying. But then she said in a low voice:

"'Do not call upon Apollo and the Muses, for they are deaf things and vain.' But so are you, Pierced Man, deaf and vain."

Then she got up and began to pace again. Thinking of it now frightens me, for it was the middle of the night and no one to hear her—except me, but she thought I was asleep—and yet she went on and on in that low, even voice as if it were broad day and she were explaining something to someone, as if things that had been in her thoughts for years must finally come out. But I did not find anything alarming in it then, for I thought that perhaps all Abbesses had to do such things, and besides she did not seem angry or hurried or afraid; she sounded as calm as if she were discussing the profits from the Abbey's beekeeping—which I had heard her do—or the

accounts for the wine cellars—which I had also heard—and
there was nothing alarming in that. So I listened as she continued walking about the room in the dark. She said:

"Talk, talk, talk, and always to myself. But one can't abandon the kittens and puppies; that would be cruel. And being
the Abbess Radegunde at least gives one something to do. But
I am so sick of the good Abbess Radegunde; I have put on
Radegunde every morning of my life as easily as I put on my
smock, and then I have had to hear the stupid creature praised
all day!—sainted Radegunde, just Radegunde who is never
angry or greedy or jealous, kindly Radegunde who sacrifices
herself for others, and always the talk, talk, talk, bubbling and
boiling in my head with no one to hear or understand, and no
one to answer. No, not even in the south, only a line here or
a line there, and all written by the dead. Did they feel as I do?
That the world is a giant nursery full of squabbles over toys and
the babes thinking me some kind of goddess because I'm not
greedy for their dolls or bits of straw or their horses made of
tied-together sticks?

"Poor people, if only they knew! It's so easy to be temperate
when one enjoys nothing, so easy to be kind when one loves
nothing, so easy to be fearless when one's life is no better than
one's death. And so easy to scheme when the success doesn't
matter.

"Would they be surprised, I wonder, to find out what my
real thoughts were when Thorfinn's knife was at my throat?
Curiosity! But he would not do it, of course; he does everything for show. And they would think I was twice holy, not to
care about death.

"Then why not kill yourself, impious Sister Radegunde? Is
it your religion which stops you? Oh, you mean the holy wells,
and the holy trees, and the blessed saints with their blessed
relics, and the stupidity that shamed Sister Hedwic, and the
promises of safety that drove poor Sibihd mad when the
blessed body of her Lord did not protect her and the blessed
love of the blessed Mary turned away the sharp point of not
one knife? Trash! Idle leaves and sticks, reeds and rushes, filth
we sweep off our floors when it grows too thick. As if holiness
had anything to do with all of that. As if every place were not
as holy as every other and every thing as holy as every other,

from the shit in Thorfinn's bowels to the rocks on the ground. As if all places and things were not clouds placed in front of our weak eyes, to keep us from being blinded by that glory, that eternal shining, that blazing all about us, the torrent of light that is everything and is in everything! That is what keeps me from the river, but it never speaks to me or tells me what to do, and to it good and evil are the same—no, it is something else than good or evil; it *is*, only—so it is not God. That I know.

"So, people, is your Radegunde a witch or a demon? Is she full of pride or is Radegunde abject? Perhaps she is a witch. Once, long ago, I confessed to old Gerbertus that I could see things that were far away merely by closing my eyes, and I proved it to him, too, and he wept over me and gave me much penance, crying, "If it come of itself it may be a gift of God, daughter, but it is more likely the work of a demon, so do not do it!" And then we prayed and I told him the power had left me, to make the poor old puppy less troubled in its mind, but that was not true, of course. I could still see Turkey as easily as I could see him, and places far beyond: the squat, wild men of the plains on their ponies, and the strange, tall people beyond that with their great cities and odd eyes, as if one pulled one's eyelid up on a slant, and then the seas with the great, wild lands and the cities more full of gold than Constantinople, and water again until one comes back home, for the world's a ball, as the ancients said.

"But I did stop somehow, over the years. Radegunde never had time, I suppose. Besides, when I opened that door it was only pictures, as in a book, and all to no purpose, and after a while I had seen them all and no longer cared for them. It is the other door that draws me, when it opens itself but a crack and strange things peep through, like Ranulf sister's son and the name of his horse. That door is good but very heavy; it always swings back after a little. I shall have to be on my death-bed to open it all the way, I think.

"The fox is asleep. He is the cleverest yet; there is something in him so that at times one can almost talk to him. But still a fox, for the most part. Perhaps in time. . . .

"But let me see; yes, he is asleep. And the Sibihd puppy is asleep, though it will be having a bad dream soon, I think, and the Thorfinn kitten is asleep, as full of fright as when it wakes, with its claws going in and out, in and out, lest something strangle it in its sleep."

Then the Abbess fell silent and moved to the shuttered window as if she were looking out, so I thought that she was indeed looking out—but not with her eyes—at all the sleeping folk, and this was something she had done every night of her life to see if they were safe and sound. But would she not know that *I* was awake? Should I not try very hard to get to sleep before she caught me? Then it seemed to me that she smiled in the dark, although I could not see it. She said in that same low, even voice: "Sleep or wake, Boy News; it is all one to me. Thou hast heard nothing of any importance, only the silly Abbess talking to herself, only Radegunde saying good-bye to Radegunde, only Radegunde going away—don't cry, Boy News; I am still here—but there: Radegunde has gone. This Norseman and I are alike in one way: our minds are like great houses with many of the rooms locked shut. We crowd in a miserable, huddled few, like poor folk, when we might move freely among them all, as gracious as princes. It is fate that locked away so much of the Norseman—see, Boy News, I do not say his name, not even softly, for that wakes folks—but I wonder if the one who bolted me in was not Radegunde herself, she and old Gerbertus—whom I partly believed—they and the years and years of having to be Radegunde and do the things Radegunde did and pretend to have the thoughts Radegunde had and the endless, endless lies Radegunde must tell everyone, and Radegunde's utter and unbearable loneliness."

She fell silent again. I wondered at the Abbess's talk this time: saying she was not there when she was, and about living locked up in small rooms—for surely the Abbey was the most splendid house in all the world, and the biggest—and how could she be lonely when all the folk loved her? But then she said in a voice so low that I could hardly hear it:

"Poor Radegunde! So weary of the lies she tells and the fooling of men and women with the collars round their necks and bribes of food for good behavior and a careful twitch of the leash that they do not even see or feel. And with the Norseman it will be all the same: lies and flattery and all of it work that never ends and no one ever even sees, so that finally Radegunde will lie down like an ape in a cage, weak and sick from hunger, and will never get up.

"Let her die now. There: Radegunde is dead. Radegunde is gone. Perhaps the door was heavy only because she was on the other side of it, pushing against me. Perhaps it will open all the way now. I have looked in all directions: to the east, to the north and south, and to the west, but there is one place I have never looked and now I will: away from the ball, straight out. Let us see—"

She stopped speaking all of a sudden. I had been falling asleep but this silence woke me. Then I heard the Abbess gasp terribly, like one mortally stricken, and then she said in a whisper so keen and thrilling that it made the hair stand up on my head: *Where art thou?* The next moment she had torn the shutters open and was crying out with all her voice: *Help me! Find me! Oh, come, come, come, or I die!*

This waked Thorvald. With some Norse oath he stumbled up and flung on his sword belt and then put his hand to his dagger; I had noticed this thing with the dagger was a thing Norsemen liked to do. The Abbess was silent. He let out his breath in an oof! and went to light the tallow dip at the live embers under the hearth ashes; when the dip had smoked up, he put it on its shelf on the wall.

He said in German, "What the devil, woman! What has happened?"

She turned round. She looked as if she could not see us, as if she had been dazed by a joy too big to hold, like one who has looked into the sun and is still dazzled by it so that everything seems changed, and the world seems all God's and everything in it like Heaven. She said softly, with her arms around herself, hugging herself: "My people. The real people."

"What are you talking of!" said he.

She seemed to see him then, but only as Sibihd had beheld us; I do not mean in horror as Sibihd had, but beholding through something else, like someone who comes from a vision of bliss which still lingers about her. She said in the same soft voice, "They are coming for me, Thorvald. Is it not wonderful? I knew all this year that something would happen, but I did not know it would be the one thing I wanted in all the world."

He grasped his hair. "*Who* is coming?"

"My people," she said, laughing softly. "Do you not feel them? I do. We must wait three days for they come from very far away. But then—oh, you will see!"

He said, "You've been dreaming. We sail tomorrow."

"Oh, no," said the Abbess simply, "you cannot do that for it would not be right. They told me to wait; they said if I went away, they might not find me."

He said slowly, "You've gone mad. Or it's a trick."

"Oh, no, Thorvald," said she. "How could I trick you? I am your friend. And you will wait these three days, will you not, because you are my friend also."

"You're mad," he said, and started for the door of the study, but she stepped in front of him and threw herself on her knees. All her cunning seemed to have deserted her, or perhaps it was Radegunde who had been the cunning one. This one was like a child. She clasped her hands and tears came out of her eyes; she begged him, saying:

"Such a little thing, Thorvald, only three days! And if they do not come, why then we will go anywhere you like, but if they do come you will not regret it, I promise you; they are not like the folk here and that place is like nothing here. It is what the soul craves, Thorvald!"

He said, "Get up, woman for God's sake!"

She said, smiling in a sly, frightened way through her blubbered face, "If you let me stay, I will show you the old Abbess's buried treasure, Thorvald."

He stepped back, the anger clear in him. "So this is the brave old witch who cares nothing for death!" he said. Then he made for the door, but she was up again, as quick as a snake, and had flung herself across it.

She said, still with that strange innocence, "Do not strike me. Do not push me. I am your friend!"

He said, "You mean that you lead me by a string around the neck, like a goose. Well, I am tired of that!"

"But I cannot do that any more," said the Abbess breathlessly, "not since the door opened. I am not able now." He raised his arm to strike her and she cowered, wailing, "Do not strike me! Do not push me! Do not, Thorvald!"

He said, "Out of my way then, old witch!"

She began to cry in sobs and gulps. She said, "One is here but another will come! One is buried but another will rise! She will come, Thorvald!" and then in a low, quick voice, "Do not push open this last door. There is one behind it who is evil and I am afraid—" but one could see that he was angry and disappointed and would not listen. He struck her for the second time and again she fell, but with a desperate cry, covering her face with her hands. He unbolted the door and stepped over her and I heard his footsteps go down the corridor. I could see the Abbess clearly—at that time I did not wonder how this could be, with the shadows from the tallow dip half hiding everything in their drunken dance—but I saw every line in her face as if it had been full day, and in that light I saw Radegunde go away from us at last.

Have you ever been at some great king's court or some earl's and heard the storytellers? There are those so skilled in the art that they not only speak for you what the person in the tale said and did, but they also make an action with their faces and bodies as if they truly were that man or woman, so that it is a great surprise to you when the tale ceases, for you almost believe that you have seen the tale happen in front of your very eyes, and it is as if a real man or woman had suddenly ceased to exist, for you forget that all this was only a teller and a tale.

So it was with the woman who had been Radegunde. She did not change; it was still Radegunde's gray hairs and wrinkled face and old body in the peasant woman's brown dress, and yet at the same time it was a stranger who stepped out of the Abbess Radegunde as out of a gown dropped to the floor. This stranger was without feeling, though Radegunde's tears still stood on her cheeks, and there was no kindness or joy in her. She got up without taking care of her dress where the dirty rushes stuck to it; it was as if the dress were an accident and did not concern her. She said in a voice I had never heard before, one with no feeling in it, as if I did not concern her, or Thorvald Einarsson either, as if neither of us were worth a second glance:

"Thorvald, turn around."

Far up in the hall something stirred.

"Now come back. This way."

There were footsteps, coming closer. Then the big Norseman walked clumsily into the room—jerk! jerk! jerk! at every step as if he were being pulled by a rope. Sweat beaded his face. He said, "You—how?"

"By my nature," she said. "Put up your right arm, fox. Now the left. Now both down. Good."

"You—troll!" he said.

"That is so," she said. "Now listen to me, you. There's a man inside you but he's not worth getting at; I tried moments ago when I was new-hatched and he's buried too deep, but now I have grown beak and claws and care nothing for him. It's almost dawn and your boys are stirring; you will go out and tell them that we must stay here another three days. You are weather-wise; make up some story they will believe. And don't try to tell anyone what happened here tonight; you will find that you cannot."

"Folk—come," said he, trying to turn his head, but the effort only made him sweat.

She raised her eyebrows. "Why should they? No one has heard anything. Nothing has happened. You will go out and be as you always are and I will play Radegunde. For three days only. Then you are free."

He did not move. One could see that to remain still was very hard for him; the sweat poured and he strained until every muscle stood out. She said:

"Fox, don't hurt yourself. And don't push me; I am not fond of you. My hand is light upon you only because you still seem to me a little less unhuman than the rest; do not force me to make it heavier. To be plain: I have just broken Thorfinn's neck, for I find that the change improves him. Do not make me do the same to you."

"No worse—than death," Thorvald brought out.

"Ah, no?" said she, and in a moment he was screaming and clawing at his eyes. She said, "Open them, open them; your sight is back," and then, "I do not wish to bother myself thinking up worse things, like worms in your guts. Or do you wish dead sons and a dead wife? Now go.

"*As you always do,*" she added sharply, and the big man turned and walked out. One could not have told from looking at him that anything was wrong.

I had not been sorry to see such a bad man punished, one whose friends had killed our folk and would have taken for slaves—and yet I was sorry, too, in a way, because of the seals barking and the whales—and he *was* splendid, after a fashion—and yet truly I forgot all about that the moment he was gone, for I was terrified of this strange person or demon or whatever it was, for I knew that whoever was in the room with me was not the Abbess Radegunde. I knew also that it could tell where I was and what I was doing, even if I made no sound, and was in a terrible riddle as to what I ought to do when soft fingers touched my face. It was the demon, reaching swiftly and silently behind her.

And do you know, all of a sudden everything was all right! I don't mean that she was the Abbess again—I still had very serious suspicions about that—but all at once I felt light as air and nothing seemed to matter very much because my stomach was full of bubbles of happiness, just as if I had been drunk, only nicer. If the Abbess Radegunde were really a demon, what a joke that was on her people! And she did not, now that I came to think of it, seem a bad sort of demon, more the frightening kind than the killing kind, except for Thorfinn, of course, but then Thorfinn had been a very wicked man. And did not the angels of the Lord smite down the wicked? So perhaps the Abbess was an angel of the Lord and not a demon, but if she were truly an angel, why had she not smitten the Norsemen down when they first came and so saved all our folk? And then I thought that whether angel or demon, she was no longer the Abbess and would love me no longer, and if I had not been so full of the silly happiness which kept tickling about inside me, this thought would have made me weep.

I said, "Will the bad Thorvald get free, demon?"

"No," she said. "Not even if I sleep."

I thought: *But she does not love me.*

"I love thee," said the strange voice, but it was not the Abbess Radegunde's and so was without meaning, but again those soft fingers touched me and there was some kindness in them, even if it was a stranger's kindness.

Sleep, they said.

So I did.

The next three days I had much secret mirth to see the folk bow down to the demon and kiss its hands and weep over it because it had sold itself to ransom them. That is what Sister

Hedwic told them. Young Thorfinn had gone out in the night
to piss and had fallen over a stone in the dark and broken his
neck, which secretly rejoiced our folk, but his comrades did
not seem to mind much either, save for one young fellow who
had been Thorfinn's friend, I think, and so went about with a
long face. Thorvald locked me up in the Abbess's study with
the demon every night and went out—or so folk said—to one
of the young women, but on those nights the demon was silent, and I lay there with the secret tickle of merriment in my
stomach, caring about nothing.

On the third morning I woke sober. The demon—or the
Abbess—for in the day she was so like the Abbess Radegunde
that I wondered—took my hand and walked us up to Thorvald, who was out picking the people to go aboard the Norsemen's boats at the riverbank to be slaves. Folk were standing
about weeping and wringing their hands; I thought this strange
because of the Abbess's promise to pick those whose going
would hurt least, but I know now that least is not none. The
weather was bad, cold rain out of mist, and some of Thorvald's
companions were speaking sourly to him in the Norse, but he
talked them down—bluff and hearty—as if making light of the
weather. The demon stood by him and said, in German, in a
low voice so that none might hear: "You will say we go to find
the Abbess's treasure and then you will go with us into the
woods."

He spoke to his fellows in Norse and they frowned, but the
end of it was that two must come with us, for the demon said
it was such a treasure as three might carry. The demon had the
voice and manner of the Abbess Radegunde, all smiles, so they
were fooled. Thus we started out into the trees behind the village, with the rain worse and the ground beginning to soften
underfoot. As soon as the village was out of sight, the two
Norsemen fell behind, but Thorvald did not seem to notice
this; I looked back and saw the first man standing in the mud
with one foot up, like a goose, and the second with his head
lifted and his mouth open so that the rain fell in it. We walked
on, the earth sucking at our shoes and all of us getting wet:
Thorvald's hair stuck fast against his face, and the demon's old
brown cloak clinging to its body. Then suddenly the demon
began to breathe harshly and it put its hand to its side with a

cry. Its cloak fell off and it stumbled before us between the wet trees, not weeping but breathing hard. Then I saw, ahead of us through the pelting rain, a kind of shining among the bare tree trunks, and as we came nearer the shining became more clear until it was very plain to see, not a blazing thing like a fire at night but a mild and even brightness as though the sunlight were coming through the clouds pleasantly but without strength, as it often does at the beginning of the year.

And then there were folk inside the brightness, both men and women, all dressed in white, and they held out their arms to us, and the demon ran to them, crying out loudly and weeping but paying no mind to the tree branches which struck it across the face and body. Sometimes it fell but it quickly got up again. When it reached the strange folk they embraced it, and I thought that the filth and mud of its gown would stain their white clothing, but the foulness dropped off and would not cling to those clean garments. None of the strange folk spoke a word, nor did the Abbess—I knew then that she was no demon, whatever she was—but I felt them talk to one another, as if in my mind, although I know not how this could be nor the sense of what they said. An odd thing was that as I came closer I could see they were not standing on the ground, as in the way of nature, but higher up, inside the shining, and that their white robes were nothing at all like ours, for they clung to the body so that one might see the people's legs all the way up to the place where the legs joined, even the women's. And some of the folk were like us, but most had a darker color, and some looked as if they had been smeared with soot —there are such persons in the far parts of the world, you know, as I found out later; it is their own natural color—and there were some with the odd eyes the Abbess had spoken of —but the oddest thing of all I will not tell you now. When the Abbess had embraced and kissed them all and all had wept, she turned and looked down upon us: Thorvald standing there as if held by a rope and I, who had lost my fear and had crept close in pure awe, for there was such a joy about these people, like the light about them, mild as spring light and yet as strong as in a spring where the winter has gone forever.

"Come to me, Thorvald," said the Abbess, and one could not see from her face if she loved or hated him. He moved closer—jerk! jerk!—and she reached down and touched his forehead with her fingertips, at which one side of his lip lifted, as a dog's does when it snarls.

"As thou knowest," said the Abbess quietly, "I hate thee and would be revenged upon thee. Thus I swore to myself three days ago, and such vows are not lightly broken."

I saw him snarl again and he turned his eyes from her.

"I must go soon," said the Abbess, unmoved, "for I could stay here long years only as Radegunde, and Radegunde is no more; none of us can remain here long as our proper selves or even in our true bodies, for if we do we go mad like Sibihd or walk into the river and drown or stop our own hearts, so miserable, wicked, and brutish does your world seem to us. Nor may we come in large companies, for we are few and our strength is not great and we have much to learn and study of thy folk so that we may teach and help without marring all in our ignorance. And ignorant or wise, we can do naught except thy folk aid us.

"Here is my revenge," said the Abbess, and he seemed to writhe under the touch of her fingers, for all they were so light. "Henceforth be not Thorvald Farmer nor yet Thorvald Sea-farer but Thorvald Peacemaker, Thorvald War-hater, put into anguish by bloodshed and agonized at cruelty. I cannot make long thy life—that gift is beyond me—but I give thee this: to the end of thy days, long or short, thou wilt know the Presence about thee always, as I do, and thou wilt know that it is neither good nor evil, as I do, and this knowing will trouble and frighten thee always, as it does me, and so about this one thing, as about many another, Thorvald Peacemaker will never have peace.

"Now, Thorvald, go back to the village and tell thy comrades I was assumed into the company of the saints, straight up to Heaven. Thou mayst believe it, if thou wilt. That is all my revenge."

Then she took away her hand, and he turned and walked from us like a man in a dream, holding out his hands as if to feel the rain and stumbling now and again, as one who wakes from a vision.

Then I began to grieve, for I knew she would be going away with the strange people, and it was to me as if all the love and care and light in the world were leaving me. I crept close to her, meaning to spring secretly onto the shining place and so go away with them, but she spied me and said, "Silly Radulphus, you cannot," and that *you* hurt me more than anything else so that I began to bawl.

"Child," said the Abbess, "come to me," and loudly weeping I leaned against her knees. I felt the shining around me, all bright and good and warm, that wiped away all grief, and then the Abbess's touch on my hair.

She said, "Remember me. And be . . . content."

I nodded, wishing I dared to look up at her face, but when I did, she had already gone with her friends. Not up into the sky, you understand, but as if they moved very swiftly backwards among the trees—although the trees were still behind them somehow—and as they moved, the shining and the people faded away into the rain until there was nothing left.

Then there was no rain. I do not mean that the clouds parted or the sun came out; I mean that one moment it was raining and cold and the next the sky was clear blue from side to side, and it was splendid, sunny, breezy, bright, sailing weather. I had the oddest thought that the strange folk were not agreed about doing such a big miracle—and it was hard for them, too—but they had decided that no one would believe this more than all the other miracles folk speak of, I suppose. And it would surely make Thorvald's lot easier when he came back with wild words about saints and Heaven, as indeed it did, later.

Well, that is the tale, really. She said to me "Be content" and so I am; they call me Radulf the Happy now. I have had my share of trouble and sickness, but always somewhere in me there is a little spot of warmth and joy to make it all easier, like a traveler's fire burning out in the wilderness on a cold night. When I am in real sorrow or distress, I remember her fingers touching my hair and that takes part of the pain away, somehow. So perhaps I got the best gift, after all. And she said also, "Remember me," and thus I have, every little thing, although it all happened when I was the age my own grandson is now, and that is how I can tell you this tale today.

And the rest? Three days after the Norsemen left, Sibihd got back her wits and no one knew how, though I think I do! And as for Thorvald Einarsson, I have heard that after his wife died in Norway he went to England and ended his days there as a monk, but whether this story be true or not I do not know.

I know this: they may call me Happy Radulf all they like, but there is much that troubles me. Was the Abbess Radegunde a demon, as the new priest says? I cannot believe this, although he called half her sayings nonsense and the other half blasphemy when I asked him. Father Cairbre, before the Norse killed him, told us stories about the Sidhe, that is, the Irish fairy people, who leave changelings in human cradles; and for a while it seemed to me that Radegunde must be a woman of the Sidhe when I remembered that she could read Latin at the age of two and was such a marvel of learning when so young, for the changelings the fairies leave are not their own children, you understand, but one of the fairy folk themselves, who are hundreds upon hundreds of years old, and the other fairy folk always come back for their own in the end. And yet this could not have been, for Father Cairbre said also that the Sidhe are wanton and cruel and without souls, and neither the Abbess Radegunde nor the people who came for her were one blessed bit like that, although she did break Thorfinn's neck—but then it may be that Thorfinn broke his own neck by chance, just as we all thought at the time, and she told this to Thorvald afterwards, as if she had done it herself, only to frighten him. She had more of a soul with a soul's griefs and joys than most of us, no matter what the new priest says. He never saw her or felt her sorrow and lonesomeness, or heard her talk of the blazing light all around us—and what can that be but God Himself? Even though she did call the crucifix a deaf thing and vain, she must have meant not Christ, you see, but only the piece of wood itself, for she was always telling the Sisters that Christ was in Heaven and not on the wall. And if she said the light was not good or evil, well, there is a traveling Irish scholar who told me of a holy Christian monk named Augustinus who tells us that all which is, is good, and evil is only a lack of the good, like an empty place not filled up. And if the Abbess truly said there was no God, I say it was the sin of despair, and even saints may sin, if only they repent, which I believe she did at the end.

So I tell myself, and yet I know the Abbess Radegunde was no saint, for are the saints few and weak, as she said? Surely not! And then there is a thing I held back in my telling, a small thing, and it will make you laugh and perhaps means nothing one way or the other, but it is this:

Are the saints bald?

These folk in white had young faces but they were like eggs; there was not a stitch of hair on their domes! Well, God may shave His saints if He pleases, I suppose.

But I know she was no saint. And then I believe that she did kill Thorfinn and the light was not God and she not even a Christian or maybe even human, and I remember how Radegunde was to her only a gown to step out of at will, and how she truly hated and scorned Thorvald until she was happy and safe with her own people. Or perhaps it was like her talk about living in a house with the rooms shut up; when she stopped being Radegunde, first one part of her came back and then the other—the joyful part that could not lie or plan and then the angry part—and then they were all together when she was back among her own folk. And then I give up trying to weigh this matter and go back to warm my soul at the little fire she lit in me, that one warm, bright place in the wide and windy dark.

But something troubles me even there and will not be put to rest by the memory of the Abbess's touch on my hair. As I grow older it troubles me more and more. It was the very last thing she said to me, which I have not told you but will now. When she had given me the gift of contentment, I became so happy that I said, "Abbess, you said you would be revenged on Thorvald, but all you did was change him into a good man. That is no revenge!"

What this saying did to her astonished me, for all the color went out of her face and left it gray. She looked suddenly old, like a death's-head, even standing there among her own true folk with love and joy coming from them so strongly that I myself might feel it. She said, "I did not change him. I lent him my eyes, that is all." Then she looked beyond me, as if at our village, at the Norsemen loading their boats with weeping slaves, at all the villages of Germany and England and France where the poor folk sweat from dawn to dark so that the great lords may do battle with one another, at castles under siege with the starving folk within eating mice and rats and sometimes each other, at the women carried off or raped or beaten, at the mothers wailing for their little ones, and beyond this at the great wide world itself with all its battles which I had used to think so grand, and the misery and greediness and fear and jealousy and hatred of folk one for the other, save—perhaps—for a few small bands of savages, but they were so far from us that one could scarcely see them. She said: *No revenge? Thinkest thou so, boy?* And then she said as one who believes absolutely, as one who has seen all the folk at their living and dying, not for one year but for many, not in one place but in all places, as one who knows it all over the whole wide earth:

Think again. . . .

CHRONOLOGY

NOTE ON THE TEXTS

NOTES

Chronology

1937–41   Born Joanna Ruth Russ on February 22, 1937, in the Bronx, New York, the only child of Evarett Ira Russ, twenty-nine, and Bertha (Zinner) Russ, thirty. Father, the eldest of two children of New York–born parents, teaches high-school industrial arts; mother, the second of three children of Russian-born parents, is an elementary-school teacher who writes fiction. Paternal grandfather ran a candy stand in the lobby of 1 Wall Street; maternal grandfather was a plumber, and grandmother made wigs for a time. Married in 1930, Evarett and Bertha are both active members of the New York City teachers' union. They rent an apartment on Barnes Avenue in the Bronx, in a working-class, Ashkenazi community. Describes childhood as secular, "but with the emphasis on ethics and social action typical of the secular Jews of my parents' generation."

1942–44   Writes her first story, "Bubble Land," at age five. Mother reads poetry to her, and they play a game about guessing poems from their first lines. Father is interested in science and makes his own telescope, through which he and Russ look at the moon, Jupiter, and Saturn. Later, she recalls, "From him I learned how marvelous the universe was."

1945–47   Father teaches her to sew, and she makes several hand-sewn illustrated books. Writes poetry and stories. Father develops angina; he "was scared & could not say & so began to bully my ma, who got more and more passive-aggressive."

1948   Begins to come out to herself as lesbian, only to "go back in" a few years afterward. Later writes, "I tried to find information, I tried to find people who would know about it, and I couldn't. It was totally taboo. I read *The Well of Loneliness* and thought, I'm not masculine, you know. I mean, I'm tall, but I hunch over, and I'm not physically strong, and I'm not athletic, and I don't ride, and I don't fence, and I don't have lots of money, so this isn't for me."

1949–50   Skips three grades in elementary school. Earns a place at the prestigious Bronx High School of Science, but instead starts at William Howard Taft Public High School. "At about 12," she later remembers, "I sprouted hugely, where upon my mother decided she didn't have to take care of me anymore (which had always made her jittery and guilty) but I had to take care of *her*." Begins reading *Love Comics* and science fiction, including Robert Heinlein and her mother's Groff Conklin anthologies. Also reads Mark Twain's story "A Medieval Romance," which, as she later relates to Samuel R. Delany, "became an extremely important part of my fantasy life for decades afterward." Decides to be a writer who will "tell the truth no matter what."

1951–52   Reads S. J. Perelman, horror, and science fiction. Also reads *Mademoiselle de Maupin* by Théophile Gautier; of Gautier and Twain, later writes that "for close to a decade my knowledge of Lesbianism was limited to these two fictions, one of them a parody." Writes the story "Little Tales from Nature" and a story about two lesbians, which ends in suicide; begins a novel that adapts the story into a heterosexual relationship.

1953   As a senior in high school, at age fifteen, is selected as a top-ten finalist in the Westinghouse Science Talent Search for a project titled "Growth of Certain Fungi Under Colored Light and in Darkness"; she is the only female finalist. In the fall, starts at Cornell University in Ithaca, New York, with a partial scholarship; pursues literature over science. Publishes a poem, "Sunset," in the first issue of *The Cornell Writer*, the university's triannual student-run literary magazine, edited by fellow student Ronald Sukenick. Struggles to reconcile her sexual feelings with the world: "It wasn't real. It didn't count, except in my own inner world in which I could not only love women but also fly, ride the lightning, be Alexander the Great, live forever, etc., all of which occurred in my poetry. I regarded this inner life as crucially important and totally trivial, the source of all my vitality and yet something completely sealed off from 'reality.'"

1954   Joins the Cornell Dramatic Club and plays small parts in student productions: the revue *Dark of the Moon*, Archibald MacLeish's verse-play *This Music Crept by Me Upon* the Waters, *The Male Animal* by James Thurber and Eliot Nugent, and Christopher Fry's *Thor, with Angels*. Writes two plays of her own, *Those That I Fight* and *The Time Ran*, and publishes poems in *The Cornell Writer*.

1955   Chosen for the editorial board of *The Cornell Writer*. Writes the play *Henry and the Mimzies* and wins second prize in a university-wide playwriting contest. Joins other students from the English department's creative writing program in a public poetry reading.

1956   Publishes two poems in *Epoch*, a triannual literary magazine published by Cornell's Department of English. Wins the Morrison Poetry Prize for undergraduate verse; becomes prose editor for *The Cornell Writer*. Acts in *All Summer Long* by Robert Anderson, and *Bernadine* by Mary Chase.

1957   In February directs *The Bet*, a one-act play by fellow undergraduate David Seidler. Studies creative writing with Vladimir Nabokov. Writes her last poems. Receives a B.A. with Distinction and High Honors in English from Cornell, a member of Phi Beta Kappa. Wins the Barnes Prize for the best prose essay on the writings of Shakespeare and the Corson Browning Prize for the best essay on Robert Browning. Enrolls at Yale University School of Drama in the fall.

1958–59   Studies drama at Yale and acts in local productions; writes plays, television scripts, and (for the first time) science fiction. Publishes her first commercial story, "Nor Custom Stale," in the September 1959 issue of *The Magazine of Fantasy and Science Fiction*. Writes the play *There and Back Again: A Hobbit's Holiday*; J.R.R. Tolkien doesn't approve the adaptation of his novel *The Hobbit*, and the play is never performed.

1960   "Nor Custom Stale" appears in the French magazine *Fiction* in June, her first work of many to be published in translation. Receives an M.F.A. in Playwriting and Dramatic Literature from Yale University; her master's thesis is a play titled *The Death of Alexander the Great*.

1961   Moves to Brooklyn Heights, New York, where she continues acting in amateur theater: plays the Wicked Stepmother in *Cinderella* at the Heights Players Theatre for Children, and appears in other small roles.

1962   Publishes "My Dear Emily," a nineteenth-century vam-
            pire story with lesbian undertones, in *The Magazine of
            Fantasy and Science Fiction*.

1963   Marries Albert Amateau, a "short, gentle, retiring, pleas-
            ant man" she first met at Cornell; writes later that "I had
            done it partly because I was running out of money and
            couldn't stand working, a motive of which I was bitterly
            ashamed and which I never told anybody." Begins work-
            ing a series of office and secretarial jobs and starts psy-
            choanalysis. In September, publishes "There Is Another
            Shore You Know, upon the Other Side," an English ghost
            story, in *The Magazine of Fantasy and Science Fiction*.

1964–65   Reads Jean Genet and André Gide. Publishes the
            Lovecraft-inspired gothic "I Had Vacantly Crumpled It
            into My Pocket . . ." in the August 1964 issue of *The
            Magazine of Fantasy and Science Fiction*; the following
            year, "Come Closer" appears in the *Magazine of Horror*
            and "Life in a Furniture Store" in *Epoch*.

1966   Publishes "The New Men," a vampire story set in com-
            munist Poland, in *The Magazine of Fantasy and Science
            Fiction* in February and "This Night at My Fire" in *Ep-
            och* in the Winter issue. Separates from Amateau. Begins
            teaching at Queensborough Community College in Bay-
            side, New York. Over the summer, at the invitation of
            Damon Knight, attends her first Milford Writers' Confer-
            ence, in Milford, Pennsylvania; meets Delany and other
            science fiction writers. In December, begins writing re-
            views for *The Magazine of Fantasy and Science Fiction*.
            In 1981, recalls, "I have been a workaholic ever since I
            started teaching (& writing much more), have wanted
            to get involved with people *via* politics, have felt I must
            respond to the demands of everyone. The result of be-
            ing an only child with a rather awful, martyred, clinging
            mother, I suppose."

1967   Adapts *Nightmare Abbey*, the satirical eighteenth-century
            novel by Thomas Love Peacock, for WBAI's 99.5 Radio
            Theatre, where she meets Baird Searles, drama and lit-
            erature director for WBAI-FM; later, Baird serves as the
            model for Jai Vedh, the protagonist of her novel *And
            Chaos Died*. Her "protest play," *Those That I Fight*, is
            staged at the Theater Intime, at Princeton University.
            Sees the Czech film *Late August at the Hotel Ozone*, which

later influences her novel *The Female Man*. Divorces Amateau, quits psychoanalysis, and is hired as an instructor in the creative writing program at Cornell University. Publishes "I Thought She Was Afeard Till She Stroked My Beard" and "Bluestocking" in Damon Knight's anthology *Orbit 2* (where they are retitled "I Gave Her Sack and Sherry" and "The Adventuress"). Serves as dialogue director on WBAI-FM's multipart radio-play version of Christopher Morley's *The Trojan Horse*. Publishes the feminist story "Visiting" in *Manhattan Review*.

1968   Publishes the fantasy story "This Afternoon" in *Cimarron Review*. In June, "The Barbarian" appears in Damon Knight's anthology *Orbit 3*. Her first novella, *Picnic on Paradise*, comes out as an Ace paperback; originally titled "Picnic in Paradise," her editor Terry Carr suggests changing the preposition so that readers will know it is science fiction. *Picnic* is nominated for a Nebula Award for Best Novel. On New Year's Eve, Delany moves to San Francisco, and she begins an extensive correspondence with him that continues through her final years.

1969   Is offered the position of books editor at *The Magazine of Fantasy and Science Fiction*, following Judith Merril's resignation, but declines the job. In January, writes "When It Changed" a few weeks after attending the Cornell Conference on Women, which features Betty Friedan and Kate Millett, among others; later recalls, "It was the first time feminism had hit Ithaca . . . Marriages broke up; people screamed at each other who had been friends for years. It absolutely astonished me. The skies flew open." Six months later, attends a gay-liberation meeting and starts to write *The Female Man*. Her plays *Home Life* and *Rose of My Heart* are performed at Cornell, and *Window Dressing*, *Scenes from Domestic Life*, and *The Inner Circle* at Manhattan's Theatre East. (*Window Dressing* is later anthologized in Honor Moore's 1977 anthology *The New Women's Theatre* and frequently performed; she also adapts it as a short story, with the same title.) Publishes the stories "A Short and Happy Life" in *The Magazine of Fantasy and Science Fiction* and "The Throaways," a satire, in *Consumption*. In December, publishes the essay "Daydream Literature and Science Fiction" in *Extrapolation: A Journal of Science Fiction and Fantasy*.

1970   In a letter to *The Ithaca Journal* in January, urges readers
         to support proposed legislation that would repeal New
         York's criminal abortion laws. Is promoted to assistant
         professor in the creative writing program at Cornell.
         Over the summer, lectures at the Clarion Science Fic-
         tion and Fantasy Writers' Workshop at Clarion State Col-
         lege in Clarion, Pennsylvania. Publishes "The Man Who
         Could Not See Devils" in *Alchemy and Academe*, edited
         by Anne McCaffrey; "Visiting Day" in *South 2*; "The
         View from This Window" in the first issue of *Quark*, an
         anthology of American avant-garde science fiction ed-
         ited by Delany and Marilyn Hacker; and "The Second
         Inquisition"—later a finalist for a Nebula Award—in *Or-
         bit 6*. In the fall, has a three-month stint as prose editor of
         Epoch. Her essay "The Image of Women in Science Fic-
         tion" appears in *Red Clay Reader* in November. Comes
         out "a second time" at age thirty-three.

1971   In January, Ace Books publishes *And Chaos Died*, which
         is nominated for the Nebula Award for Best Novel; her
         story "Poor Man, Beggar Man" is a Nebula nominee for
         Best Novelette. At Cornell, cosponsors the course The
         Representation of Women in Literature, telling the *Cor-
         nell Daily Sun*, "Without a feminist or anti-feminist per-
         spective you don't have anything to talk about." Reads
         from her work during a three-day Women's Festival in
         Ithaca. Publishes "The Zanzibar Cat" in *Quark 3* and
         "Gleepsite" in *Orbit 9*. Over the summer, joins Delany,
         Harlan Ellison, and Ursula K. Le Guin as an instructor
         at the Clarion West speculative fiction workshop in Se-
         attle. Finishes a manuscript of *The Female Man*. Writes
         the essay "The Wearing Out of Genre Materials," pub-
         lished in *College English*. Reads Monique Wittig's *Les
         Guérillères*.

1972   The story "When It Changed" is published in the an-
         thology *Again, Dangerous Visions*, edited by Harlan El-
         lison; it wins the Nebula Award for Best Short Story and
         is nominated for a Hugo Award in 1973. Comes out to
         poet Marilyn Hacker. Through her agent, sends *The Fe-
         male Man* to editor Diane Cleaver at Doubleday. Moves
         to Binghamton, New York, in August, where she begins
         teaching at SUNY Binghamton (now Binghamton Uni-
         versity). Receives fan mail from James Tiptree Jr. (aka Al-
         ice Sheldon); they correspond frequently until Tiptree's

death in 1987 but never meet in person. Discusses "The Image of Women in Science Fiction" on WBAI radio in December.

1973   Publishes the essays "Speculations on the Subjunctivity of Science Fiction" in *Extrapolation: A Journal of Science Fiction and Fantasy* and "Somebody's Trying to Kill Me and I Think It's My Husband: The Modern Gothic" in *The Journal of Popular Culture*. In June, reviews two books on marriage for the *Village Voice*. Again, attends the Clarion West workshop as an instructor.

1974   Wins an inaugural Florence Howe Award for feminist scholarship for her 1972 essay "What Can a Heroine Do?: or, Why Women Can't Write." Receives a National Endowment for the Humanities fellowship, giving her time off from teaching. Publishes "Reasonable People" in *Orbit 14*, "A Game of Vlet" in *The Magazine of Fantasy and Science Fiction*, and the essay "Dear Colleague: I Am Not an Honorary Man" in *Colloquy*. Over the summer, begins the novel *We Who Are About To . . .* In July, joins Le Guin at Oregon State University for a public discussion about the future of nonsexist education. In October, participates in "Women in Science Fiction: A Symposium," or what became known as the *Khatru* symposium, as the edited results of the conversation are published in Jeff Smith's quarterly *Khatru* in November 1975; the symposium, which runs from October 9, 1974, to May 8, 1975, involves the exchange and circulation of letters among a panel of participants: Suzy McKee Charnas, Samuel R. Delany, Virginia Kidd, Ursula K. Le Guin, Vonda McIntyre, Raylyn Moore, Joanna Russ, James Tiptree Jr., Luise White, Kate Wilhelm, and Chelsea Quinn Yarbro. Finishes manuscript of *On Strike Against God*. Writes what Philip K. Dick describes as "the nastiest letter I've ever received" in response to his recently published antiabortion story "The Pre-Persons." Writes to her local paper, the Binghamton *Evening Press*, criticizing the antiabortion efforts of New York senator James L. Buckley.

1975   After numerous rejections by mainstream publishing firms since its completion in 1971, *The Female Man* appears in paperback from Bantam Books in February, having been acquired by its science fiction editor Frederik Pohl "the minute he saw it." At Russ's insistence, the publisher sends copies to the heads of every state chapter of the National Organization for Women, and to feminist bookstores; the novel is subsequently nominated for the Nebula Award, and by 1986 is reported to have sold more than 500,000 copies. In the spring, publishes "Daddy's Little Girl" in *Epoch*. Reviews Ursula Le Guin's novel *The Dispossessed* for *The Magazine of Fantasy and Science Fiction* and, in April, several introductory books on science fiction, including a high-school textbook, *Political Science Fiction*, which she criticizes for its sexist language (the use of "man" and "men" for "humankind"). In July, the essay "Towards an Aesthetic of Science Fiction" appears in the journal *Science Fiction Studies*. Moves to Boulder in the fall and begins teaching at the University of Colorado. Publishes the story "The Autobiography of My Mother" in *Epoch*.

1976   Gregg Press publishes *Alyx*, which contains *Picnic on Paradise* and four of her Alyx stories. Sees Ntozake Shange's *For Colored Girls Who Have Considered Suicide/When the Rainbow Is Enuf* in New York with Marilyn Hacker. Publishes "My Boat" in *The Magazine of Fantasy and Science Fiction*, an "affectionate tribute" to H. P. Lovecraft and an homage to Cicely Tyson's performance in *The Autobiography of Miss Jean Pittman*. ("They're an unlikely couple," she later says of Lovecraft and Tyson, "but when you put unlikely things together you can get some very nice results sometimes.") The novel *We Who Are About To . . .* is serialized in the January and February issues of *Galaxy*. In November, returns to reviewing books for *The Magazine of Fantasy and Science Fiction* after an eighteen-month hiatus. Finishes the manuscript of *The Two of Them* by the end of the year. Reads "When It Changed" and other stories on *Joanna Russ Interpreting Her Stories*, an Alternate World Recordings vinyl LP.

1977   Vicki Wilson at Knopf rejects *The Two of Them*. Wins an O. Henry Prize for her story "The Autobiography of My Mother." In June, thinks about coming out to her parents in anticipation of the publication of *We Who Are About To . . .* and *On Strike Against God*. Works on a middle-grade novel, *Kittatinny: A Tale of Magic*. Is hired as an associate professor of English at the University of Washington; moves to Seattle. In July, father suffers a stroke and is hospitalized. Dell publishes *We Who Are About To . . .* the same month, but *On Strike Against God* is delayed so that its publisher, Out & Out Books—a small lesbian-feminist press in Brooklyn, New York—can raise money for typesetting.

1978   Gives readings at benefit concerts in Olympia, Washington, and in Seattle for the lesbian-feminist publisher Diana Press. In April, becomes bedridden with intense nerve pain from a slipped disc, but continues to write and edit from a rented hospital bed. In May, Berkley/Putnam publishes *The Two of Them*, her last science fiction novel; she is briefly hospitalized later that month and remains mostly bedridden until December. (Writes to Delany, "I feel like a Heinlein character, only I'm *not* being rewarded with immortality, money, love & omnipotence.") Publishes *Kittatinny: A Tale of Magic* with Daughters Publishing Co., with illustrations by Loretta Li, and starts work on *How to Suppress Women's Writing*, a critical account of sexism in publishing. Has exploratory back surgery in November and must write and read standing up and relearn how to write by hand; the pain and difficulty of concentration limit her ability to work. Comments on the recently released blockbuster *Star Wars* in an essay, "SF and Technology as Mystification," in *Science Fiction Studies*: "sold to the public as 'fun'," the movie "is, in fact, racist, grossly sexist, not apolitical in the least but authoritarian and morally imbecile, all of this both denied and enforced by the opportunism of camp (which the youngsters in the audience cannot spot, by the way) and spiced up by technical wonders and marvels, some of which are interesting, many of which are old hat to those used to science fiction." Complains of inability to find a place in Seattle's lesbian community.

1979   Reviews Rosemary Rogers's Avon romance novel *The Insiders* in *The Washington Post*'s "Book World" section in January; it is the first of a half dozen reviews she will write for the *Post* over the next few years. *And Chaos Died* is published in a new edition by Berkley Books in May, which she revises, making its main character, Jai, asexual rather than homosexual. In June, father is hospitalized after a stroke and dies in Miami on June 14; she is unable to travel to see him before he dies because she is ill. In September, "The Extraordinary Voyages of Amélie Bertrand" is published in *The Magazine of Fantasy and Science Fiction* and is nominated for a Nebula Award for Best Short Story.

1980   Out & Out Books publishes *On Strike Against God*. ("It was my coming-out novel," she later says.) Writes last review for *The Magazine of Fantasy and Science Fiction* in February. Spends six weeks in bed in the spring, with back and hip flexor problems. The essay "Amor Vincit Foeminam: The Battle of the Sexes in Science Fiction" appears in *Science Fiction Studies*. Another "coming out piece," "Not for Years but for Decades," is included in *The Coming Out Stories*, edited by Julie Penelope Stanley and Susan J. Wolfe. In August, goes on medical leave for a year. Publishes the essay "On the Fascination of Horror-Stories, Including Lovecraft's" in *Science Fiction Studies* in November.

1981   Publishes the essays "Recent Feminist Utopias" in *Future Females: A Critical Anthology*, edited by Marleen Barr, and "Power and Helplessness in the Women's Movement" in *Sinister Wisdom*. Is hospitalized for two weeks in October to treat foot and back pain. Signs herself into the psychiatric unit of Seattle's Providence Hospital, where she receives shock treatment for depression.

1982   Publishes "Being Against Pornography" in *13th Moon*. The novella "Souls" is published in *The Magazine of Fantasy and Science Fiction*; it wins the Hugo Award for Best Novella and the Locus Award for Best Novella in 1983 and is nominated for a Nebula Award. "The Little Dirty Girl" appears in *Elsewhere* and "The Mystery of the Young Gentleman" in the anthology *Speculations 17*, edited by Isaac Asimov and Alice Laurance; the latter is nominated for the Nebula Award for Best Novelette. Discovers K/S, fan-written erotic and pornographic stories, novels, and poems about the relationship between Kirk and Spock of *Star Trek*. In November, publishes "Elf Hill," her last story for *The Magazine of Fantasy and Science Fiction*. After years of chronic health problems and numerous side effects from medications, she writes to Alice Sheldon, "I have finally mustered up the courage to call myself 'disabled'."

1983   St. Martin's Press acquires *Extra (Ordinary) People* (tentatively titled "The Lesson for Today"). One of the book's stories, "What Did You Do During the Revolution, Grandma?," appears in *The Seattle Review*. Publishes three books: *How to Suppress Women's Writing* (University of Texas Press), which she dedicates to her students; a new edition of *The Adventures of Alyx* (Timespace/Pocket Books); and the story collection *The Zanzibar Cat* (Arkham House). Begins writing her own K/S stories. Publishes the stories "Main Street: 1953" in *Sinister Wisdom* and "Sword Blades and Poppy Seeds" in the anthology *Heroic Visions*. Begins work on the book that will become *What Are We Fighting For: Sex, Race, Class, and the Future of Feminism*; it is tentatively titled "Putting It All Together: Conversations Among Feminists."

1984   Begins to develop arthritis. Publishes "Pornography and the Doubleness of Sex for Women" in *13th Moon*. Presents her theories on K/S in a solo panel at Norwescon 7 and develops these ideas into the essay "Another Addict Raves About K/S," which is published in *Nome* in 1985. Under the pseudonym Janet Alyx, publishes her first K/S stories: "Invasion" in the zine *T'hy'la 4*, and "Domestic Affections" and "Break Thou My Sanctuary" in *Out of Bounds: Gypsies, Tramps and Thieves*. Is promoted to full professor at the University of Washington. Story "The Clichés from Outer Space" appears in *Women's Studies International Forum*. Publishes *Extra (Ordinary) People*, "a set of stories which were written as a series intended to fit together to form a kind of novel." Dedicates book to her mother, "whose love of literature started it all."

1985   Reads from her work at the National Women's Studies Conference in Seattle in June; discusses "Women of Ideas and What Men Have Done to Them" on a panel with Susan Koppelman and Dale Spender. The following month, Crossing Press publishes her new collection *Magic Mommas, Trembling Sisters, Puritans and Perverts: Feminist Essays*. Publishes the K/S story "The Matchmaker" in *T'hy'la 5*. Bantam sells back the rights to *The Female Man*, and she looks for a new publisher.

1986   Jack Zipes includes her 1978 story "Russalka or the Seacoast of Bohemia" in *Don't Bet on the Prince: Contemporary Feminist Fairy Tales in North America and England*. Develops tendonitis from swimming.

1987   In January, St. Martin's Press publishes her story collection *The Hidden Side of the Moon*. Begins to experience the symptoms of Chronic Fatigue Immune Deficiency Syndrome (CFIDS).

1988   Donates to the Freedom Day Committee organizing Seattle's LGBT Pride march. Receives a Pilgrim Award from the Science Fiction Research Association for her critical writing.

1989–92   Symptoms of CFIDS intensify: "I have constantly to ration my sitting and my standing and switch from one pain to another . . . There are sieges of other illnesses, usually the result of medications, and then sometimes I can't write for months. (Two years recently.) So I'm always juggling illnesses, energies and time. Having to live with disabilities is like running a small business." By the end of 1990, she is unable to work, and in 1991, she retires from teaching.

1993   Tells an interviewer: "I'm an outsider in every way but one. I'm a woman, first of all. I'm a lesbian. For the last fifteen years, I'm a disabled lesbian. I'm sort of an outsider in being an Ashkenazi. I am starting to think that is much more important than I did. I was also something of an outsider via class, which I didn't realize until I moved to the West Coast. . . . I am trying to write a book now which relates all of these things to each other." Reads Gloria Anzaldua's *Making Face, Making Soul*. In October, writes a letter of protest to NBC-TV about *The Defense Rests*, their tribute to the recently deceased Raymond Burr, which conceals the actor's homosexuality: "I am disgusted and angry with your lies and I doubt very much that I am alone in reacting like this. Remember how many of us there are in the United States—at least 1 in 10."

1994   Moves to Tucson, Arizona, in January, hoping to find relief for ongoing health problems, including arthritis and seasonal affective disorder. Joins several poets at an August benefit reading in Tucson for Kitchen Table: Women of Color Press.

1995   Publishes *To Write Like a Woman: Essays in Feminism and Science Fiction*, which is nominated for a Hugo Award in 1996.

1996   Last published story, "Invasion," appears in *Isaac Asimov's Science Fiction Magazine*. *The Female Man* and "When It Changed" are awarded retrospective James Tiptree Jr. Memorial Awards.

1997   In March, St. Martin's Press publishes *What Are We Fighting For?: Sex, Race, Class, and the Future of Feminism*, Russ's call for a return to feminist roots. Begins watching *Buffy the Vampire Slayer*, which she later buys on DVD. Participates in TusCon 24, in Tucson.

1998–2010 In continuing ill health, writes little during her sixties and early seventies. Mother dies in 1999, in Florida. Reads and signs books at Reader's Oasis bookstore in Tucson on a couple of occasions, and in 2002 joins in a panel discussion there about women in science fiction. In 2006, attends WisCon30—her last SF convention— via telephone, in a live interview with Delany. In 2007, Liverpool University Press gathers her previously uncollected essays, reviews, and letters in *The Country You Have Never Seen*, for which she contributes new notes and commentary.

2011   Suffers a stroke in February and on April 27 is admitted into hospice care. Dies in Tucson on April 29, at age seventy-four. Her remains are cremated. Two years later, she is posthumously inducted into the Science Fiction and Fantasy Hall of Fame; the following year she receives the Kate Wilhelm Solstice Award for significant impact on speculative fiction.

Note on the Texts

This volume contains Joanna Russ's novels *The Female Man* (1975), *We Who Are About To . . .* (1977), and *On Strike Against God* (1980), followed by the first complete collection of her "Alyx" stories, including her short novel *Picnic on Paradise* (1968). It concludes with two additional stories, "When It Changed" and "Souls." The texts of the novels have been taken from first book printings, and of the Alyx stories, with one exception, from *The Adventures of Alyx* (1983). Texts of the remaining stories have been taken from their original periodical and anthology appearances, as described below.

The Female Man. Russ began writing *The Female Man* in 1969 and finished in 1971, but the novel did not appear in print until 1975. Almost all of her previous works had been published in genre magazines or by presses specializing in speculative fiction. Along with her agent, she hoped to find a mainstream literary publisher for the new novel, but to no avail. Having been "branded" an SF author—as she explained to Larry McCaffery in an interview in 1986—she found it difficult to be "looked at seriously." Other firms declined on the grounds that they had "already published [their] feminist novel this year" and didn't "want another." After many similar rejections, she sent the book to Frederik Pohl, who quickly agreed to publish it in a paperback science fiction series he was then editing for Bantam Books. By the late 1980s it had sold over 500,000 copies.

The novel appeared in at least two additional Bantam printings without alteration after its initial publication in February 1975, and several publishers—Gregg Press in 1977, Beacon Press in 1986 and 2000, and The Women's Press in London in 1985 and 2002 —subsequently reissued it without resetting the type, reproducing that of the Bantam edition in photofacsimile. Russ is not known to have corrected or revised the book when it was published, sometimes with small changes, by others, including W. H. Allen/Star in 1977, The Easton Press in 1994, and Victor Gollancz/Orion in 2010. The text of *The Female Man* in the present volume is that of the 1975 Bantam first printing.

We Who Are About To . . . . Begun during the summer of 1974, *We Who Are About To . . .* was first published in two parts, in the magazine *Galaxy*, in January and February 1976. It first appeared in book form—unchanged, with the exception of some minor differences in paragraphing—as a Dell paperback in July 1977. After a second Dell printing in May 1978, the book was published by several firms, both in the United States and the United Kingdom, including Magnum (1978), Gregg Press (1978), The Women's Press (1987), and Wesleyan University Press (2005). Russ is not known to have sought to revise her novel on any of these occasions. The text of *We Who Are About To . . .* in the present volume is that of the Dell first printing of July 1977.

On Strike Against God. Russ started working on what she later called her "coming-out novel," *On Strike Against God*, as early as 1973, and completed it in 1977, but publication was delayed until 1980; she had promised the novel to a small lesbian-feminist press in Brooklyn, Out & Out Books, and they needed time to raise money to typeset and print it. The novel was published again on two subsequent occasions while Russ was alive, first in 1985 by The Crossing Press in Trumansburg, New York, and then in 1987 by The Women's Press in London, both firms reproducing the Out & Out typesetting in photofacsimile. The addition of the subtitle *A Lesbian Love Story* to the cover (but not the title page or subsequent text) of The Crossing Press printing is not known to have been made at Russ's suggestion; similarly, a posthumous ebook edition published by Open Road Integrated Media in 2021 bears the probably nonauthorial subtitle *A Love Story*. The text of *On Strike Against God* in the present volume is that of the 1980 Out & Out Books printing.

The Complete Alyx Stories. For the first time, this volume gathers all six of Russ's "Alyx" stories, including her short novel *Picnic on Paradise*. Four of these six originally appeared in the *Orbit* anthology series, edited by Damon Knight and published by G. P. Putnam's Sons in New York: "Bluestocking" and "I Thought She Was Afeard Till She Stroked My Beard" in *Orbit 2* in June 1967 (under the variant titles "The Adventuress" and "I Gave Her Sack and Sherry"); "The Barbarian" in *Orbit 3* in June 1968; and "The Second Inquisition" in *Orbit 6* in March 1970. *Picnic on Paradise*, first published as an Ace paperback on July 6, 1968, appeared shortly after "The Barbarian," and "A Game of Vlet" last of all, in the February 1974 issue of *The Magazine of Fantasy and Science Fiction*. Russ collected these stories twice, in both cases without "A Game of Vlet": first in the Gregg Press volume *Alyx*, published in June 1976 and not subsequently reprinted, and then in *The Adventures of Alyx*, published by Timescape/Pocket Books in August 1983. The latter edition was reissued in September 1985 by The Women's Press in London, and by Baen in New York the following year, with no resetting of the type.

The Gregg Press *Alyx* reproduces both the original *Orbit* printings and the Ace *Picnic on Paradise* in photofacsimile, and in chronological order of first publication (but with "I Gave Her Sack and Sherry" and "The Adventuress," from *Orbit 2*, reversed). The text of *The Adventures of Alyx*, newly typeset, differs in a number of ways that suggest Russ's involvement. While the stories are presented in the same chronological order, two are retitled, "The Adventuress" becoming "Bluestocking" and "I Gave Her Sack and Sherry" becoming "I Thought She Was Afeard Till She Stroked My Beard." Manuscript drafts of these stories now among Russ's papers at Bowling Green State University, one undated and the other dated to 1968, bear the same titles as in *The Adventures of Alyx*; it may be that Damon Knight had altered them in *Orbit 2*, and that she was restoring her preferred original titles in the new collection (as had been done, presumably at her request, in her friend Samuel R. Delany's introduction to *Alyx*). Along with about a dozen possibly authorial changes, all told, in punctuation, hyphenation, and capitalization in *The Adventures of Alyx*, two stories also show revisions apparently intended to help unify the collection. In *Orbit 3*, the final sentence of "The Barbarian" reads, "And all the birds in the courtyard broke out shouting at once." In *The Adventures of Alyx*, and on page 473, lines 22–23 of the present volume, this is replaced with: "She added, 'I'll tell you all about it.' / But that's another story." Similarly, *Picnic on Paradise* gains an additional final sentence in *The Adventures of Alyx*, and on page 575, line 30 herein: "*But that's another story.*" With these revisions, the refrain "But that's another story" concludes every Alyx story, including "A Game of Vlet," except for "The Second Inquisition," which ends "No more stories."

Russ later described her Alyx stories as part of a loose "mythos, or whatever you want to call it"; when her editor James Blish noted inconsistencies among them, she is reported to have replied "the hell with it." She may have left "A Game of Vlet" out of *Alyx* and *The Adventures of Alyx* deliberately, but may simply have neglected to add it to the group. Instead, she included it in her second story collection, *The Zanzibar Cat*, published by Arkham House in October 1983 and subsequently by Baen, without revision, in September 1984. The *Zanzibar Cat* text of the story differs from that of the original magazine printing at just under two dozen points, in punctuation, capitalization, and hyphenation, but substantively only once: the sentence "'I play'," said he, 'for the Revolution. As I planned.'"—included in *The Magazine of Fantasy and Science Fiction* and on page 611, line 40, herein—becomes "'I play'," said he, 'for myself and for the Revolution. As I planned.'" In the absence of external evidence, the source of these differences is unknown, but substantive errors elsewhere in *The Zanzibar Cat*—as in the case of "When It Changed," noted below—suggest that an editor or typesetter, rather than Russ herself, may have been responsible for them. The text of "A Game of Vlet" in the present volume has been taken from the February 1974 issue of *The Magazine of Fantasy and Science Fiction*, and of the remaining Alyx stories from the August 1983 first printing of *The Adventures of Alyx*.

Other Stories. This volume concludes with two stories not part of the Alyx universe, "When It Changed" and "Souls." The former, which won a 1973 Nebula Award, first appeared in the Harlan Ellison anthology *Again, Dangerous Visions*, published by Doubleday in New York in March 1972; Russ later included it in her collection *The Zanzibar Cat* (1983), where, along with just under a dozen changes in punctuation, capitalization, and hyphenation suggesting the application of a house style, a typographical error is introduced ("while" for "which," at 621.23 herein), and an apparent miscorrection is made ("matronymic" and "patronymic" are reversed, at 623.6–7). The other story, "Souls"—a winner of the 1983 Hugo and Locus Awards—was first published in *The Magazine of Fantasy and Science Fiction* in January 1982, and subsequently in Russ's collection *Extra (Ordinary) People* (New York: St. Martin's Press, 1984), without change. Both stories were included in numerous anthologies during Russ's lifetime as well, but she is not known to have sought or to have had the opportunity to revise either story. The text of "When It Changed" in the present volume has been taken from the 1972 first printing of *Again, Dangerous Visions*, and the text of "Souls" from *The Magazine of Fantasy and Science Fiction* of January 1982.

This volume presents the texts of the original printings chosen for inclusion here, but it does not attempt to reproduce nontextual features of their typographic design. The texts are presented without change, except for the correction of typographical errors. Spelling, punctuation, and capitalization are often expressive features and are not altered, even when inconsistent or irregular. The following is a list of typographical errors corrected, cited by page and line number: 6.20, bye-street; 8.8, le savate; 10.18, what; 21.18, But; 47.25, IV; 51.2, mapping; 53.14, alas.; 81.25, Whilewayan; 102.17, brother"); 124.24, who everything; 134.27, *and*; 142.16, "An; 170.8, *it*; 190.37, Millet; 232.28, me; 243.28, (I; 297.31, specie; 304.25, Kenny; 304.31, Kenny; 319.11, dowtown; 321.26, Manv; 326.13–14, acquanitances; 326.38, makup; 334.11, kincknack; 342.18, that he we; 349.6, sturmbannsfeuhrer; 350.3, your; 351.10, D,; 353.20, scuplture; 353.30, cannot cannot; 358.7, go the the; 359.17, convinction; 364.38, ecstacies; 377.2, unconsicous; 381.13, they're—"; 381.31, Selby's; 382.16, Selbys; 384.31, hair?); 384.32, said. I; 385.9–10, unsympathetic; 386.35, mother's;

386.38, ideas—"; 387.8, finshed; 390.16 and 18, Ezeckial; 397.17, "'Tis; 408.2, hankerchiefs; 411.9, adsolutely; 433.15, hand?"; 440.6, tree; 496.26, Irish; 528.30, broken?"; 529.13–14, tryin; 541.33, hurts, and; 549.17, in Gunnar!'; 563.19, —"that—; 582.13, in by; 590.40, breath.; 601.6, They they; 610.17, there"; 638.5–6, sword she; 638.30, nothing."; 641.36, *fragkments!*; 644.8, you!; 648.12, out..; 650.36, do You; 661.30, Abbess,; 668.6, simply.; 672.14–15, Norseman's; 672.38, aginast.

Notes

In the notes below, the reference numbers denote page and line of this volume (the line count includes headings but not blank lines). References to Shakespeare are keyed to *The Riverside Shakespeare*, ed. G. Blakemore Evans (Boston: Houghton Mifflin, 1974) and biblical references to the King James Version. For further information about Russ's life and works, and references to other studies, see Jeanne Cortiel, *Demand My Writing: Joanna Russ, Feminism, Science Fiction* (Liverpool: Liverpool University Press, 1999); Gwyneth A. Jones, *Joanna Russ* (Urbana: University of Illinois Press, 2019); Brit Mandelo, *We Wuz Pushed: On Joanna Russ and Radical Truth-Telling* (Seattle: Aqueduct Press, 2012); Farah Mendelsohn, *On Joanna Russ* (Middletown: Wesleyan University Press, 2009).

THE FEMALE MAN

5.9   travois] Sledge consisting of two trailing poles that bear a load over distances, used by Native peoples in the Plains region of North America.

5.28   Stanford-Binet] An intelligence test, originally developed by French psychologists Alfred Binet and Théodore Simon beginning in 1904 and adapted by psychologists at Stanford University in 1916.

6.3   the W.P.A.] The Works Progress Administration, a New Deal public works agency founded in 1935 and closed in 1943.

8.8   la savate] French: literally "the old shoe," but also *la boxe française,* a form of kickboxing.

16.23–24   the Vittore Emmanuele monument] A large neoclassical monument in Rome, constructed beginning in 1885, honoring Victor Emmanuel II (1820–1878), the first modern king of a unified Italy.

22.14   Watteau] Jean-Antoine Watteau (1684–1721), French painter.

27.3   Madam Chiang] Soong Mei-ling (1898–2003), first lady of the Republic of China from 1950 to 1975.

28.8   Chiang Kai-shek] Chiang (1887–1979) led the Republic of China from 1928 until his death, beginning in 1950 from Taiwan.

33.31   *nicht wahr*?] German: is that not so?

46.36   tohu-bohu] Chaos, confusion.

49.31   waldoes] Remotely manipulated mechanical devices (from Robert A. Heinlein's 1940 short story "Waldo").

51.37   ha-has] Sunken fences, used in landscape design.

59.15–16   Janet's ears . . . like Death in the poem] At the end of the *Copa*, a Latin elegy (c. 50 CE?) sometimes translated as "The Female Tavern Keeper" and historically attributed to Virgil, Death plucks a traveler by the ears and whispers, "Live now. I'm on my way."

60.34–35   "The life so short . . . *I mene love.*] See the opening lines of "The Parliament of Fowls" (c. 1381–82) by Geoffrey Chaucer.

61.32–33   *et patati et patata*] French: and so on and so forth; blah, blah, blah.

79.19   a Grange supper] The Grange, founded in 1867, is a national community organization; its local chapters, often in rural areas, host potluck suppers and agricultural fairs.

86.18–19   *The Second Sex*] A pioneering book of feminist philosophy by Simone de Beauvoir (1908–1986), first published as *Le Deuxième Sexe* in 1949 and then in English in 1953.

86.20–23   We all have the impulse . . . know better] Irving Howe (1920–1993), a literary critic, published the biography *Thomas Hardy* (1967) and several occasional pieces about Hardy; Abraham Maslow (1908–1970), a founder of humanistic psychiatry, was the author of *The Psychology of Science: A Reconnaissance* (1966) and other works on scientific accomplishment. Russ paraphrases rather than quotes.

87.19   *Pogo*] A syndicated newspaper comic strip (1948–75) by American newspaper columnist Walt Kelly (1913–1973).

100.32   frowsty] Stuffy, musty.

108.31   I'm Marie of Rumania] See Dorothy Parker's poem "Comment," from her collection *Enough Rope* (1926): "Oh, life is a glorious cycle of song, / A medley of extemporanea; / And love is a thing that can never go wrong; / And I am Marie of Roumania."

110.26   "Charley's Aunt."] A popular three-act comedy by British actor and songwriter Brandon Thomas, first staged in 1892.

119.31   Atropos] In Greek mythology, one of the three Fates or goddesses of destiny, who cuts the threads of human lives.

120.9–10   Uriah Heep] A sycophantic character in Charles Dickens's novel *David Copperfield* (1850).

121.20   "forever feminine," as the man says] Possibly a reference to Robert A. Wilson's *Feminine Forever* (1966), about hormone replacement therapy.

122.6   Grendel's mother] A monster or demon, otherwise unnamed, in the Old English poem *Beowulf* (c. 700–1000 CE).

122.8   Rodan] A dragon-like monster, based on the prehistoric pterosaur genus *Pteranodon*, introduced in the Japanese movie *Rodan* (1956).

122.14–15   as Shaw . . . loves and nestings] See Shaw's *Man and Superman* (1903), act 3.

122.30   Buster Crabbe] Crabbe (1908–1983), who won medals in swimming at the 1928 and 1932 Olympics, starred in *Flash Gordon* (1936), *Flash Gordon's Trip to Mars* (1938), and *Flash Gordon Conquers the Universe* (1940), and subsequently served as aquatics director for a Catskills resort hotel.

124.13   Sir Thomas Nasshe] Probably Thomas Nashe (1567–c. 1601), Elizabethan poet and playwright.

134.26–28   Gunnar Myrdal's . . . *1948*] Myrdal published *An American Dilemma*, subtitled *The Negro Problem and Modern Democracy*, in 1944; the remainder of the title appears to be of Russ's invention.

152.24   Mary Janes] Also known as doll shoes, a shoe style popular among women in the 1920s, and often associated with girlhood.

161.40   Et patati et patata] See note 61.32–33.

162.24   Puli] A Hungarian herding dog breed.

162.34   shoon] An archaic or dialectical plural of *shoe*.

165.5   the Second Brandenberg] One of six concertos by Johann Sebastian Bach (1685–1750), dedicated to the Margrave of Brandenburg-Schwedt in 1721.

165.12   Baba Yaga's hut] In Slavic mythology, the witchlike Baba Yaga often lives in a forest hut that revolves on chicken legs.

169.23   afreets] In Arabic mythology, evil spirits or monstrous demons.

171.15–16   as Blake says . . . Wisdom] See "The Proverbs of Hell" in Blake's *Marriage of Heaven and Hell* (1790–93).

172.11   *geas*] In Irish folklore, a magically imposed obligation or taboo.

174.35–36   Luther . . . NON SUM!] In his *Commentaria de actis et scriptis Martin Lutheri Saxonis* (1549), published after the famous theologian's death in 1546, Johannes Cochlaeus describes a fit Luther is supposed to have had in his twenties, on reading the biblical story, in Mark 9:17, of a child possessed by a devil.

180.25   the mater dolorosa] The sorrowful mother (said especially of the Virgin Mary mourning Jesus).

181.28–29   Victoria de los Angeles] De los Ángeles (1923–2005) was a Spanish lyric soprano.

187.31   Schrafft's] A chain of moderately priced restaurants in Boston, New York, and Philadelphia, particularly popular among women, founded in 1898; its parent company was sold in 1968.

188.18–19   no Four Seasons . . . Chambord] High-end French restaurants, the Four Seasons (1959–2019) and Chambord (1936–1964) in New York, and Maxim's (est. 1893) in Paris.

190.36–37   Friedan . . . Firestone] Feminist writers Betty Friedan (1921–2006), Kate Millett (1934–2017), Germaine Greer (b. 1939), and Shulamith Firestone (1945–2012).

191.13–14   *Spicy Western Stories . . . Son of the Sheik*] *Spicy Western Stories* was a pulp magazine, published from 1936 to 1942; *Elsie Dinsmore* was an 1867 novel, the first of a series by Martha Finley (1828–1909); and *The Son of the Sheik* was a silent movie of 1926, based on the romance novel *The Sons of the Sheik* (1925) by Edith Maud Hull (1880–1947).

WE WHO ARE ABOUT TO . . .

197.8   Hors de combat] French: Out of action due to injury, illness, or damage.

198.7   Graustark] A fictional Eastern European country that provided the setting for a series of novels by George Barr McCutcheon, beginning with *Graustark: The Story of a Love Behind a Throne* (1901), subsequently adapted for film in *Graustark* (1929), directed by Dimitri Buchowetzki.

198.8   shako] A stiff military hat with a high crown and plume.

198.18   Anne Bradstreet] British-born Puritan poet (1612–1672) who was the first writer to be published in the American colonies.

198.24   cache-sexe] A small article of clothing worn to cover the genitalia.

201.23   megatheria] *Megatherium* is a genus of now-extinct giant ground sloths.

204.22   Status asthmaticus] An acute severe form of asthma that does not respond to conventional treatment.

205.27   clairaudience] An ability to perceive sounds unavailable to the ear.

206.3   O pioneers] Title of a 1913 novel by Willa Cather.

211.1   Trembler] A derisive nickname, like "Quaker," given to members of the Religious Society of Friends.

213.29–30   "I'm Nobody . . . too?] "I'm Nobody, who are you?" (260) by Emily Dickinson, lines 1–2.

213.39–40   "the heart . . . know it?"] Jeremiah 17:9.

214.13   George Fox . . . heart.] Fox (1624–1691), an English Dissenter and a founder of the Religious Society of Friends, rebelled against what he saw as the rigid doctrines of the Anglican Church; he believed that the bells calling worshippers to service were akin to those of the marketplace.

219.26   Scarlatti] Italian composer Giuseppe Domenico Scarlatti (1685–1757).

222.22–23   melancholy Dowland . . . *semper dolens.*] English Renaissance composer John Dowland (1563–1626); the consort piece "Semper Dowland, semper Dolens" is part of his instrumental work *Lachrimae, or Seaven Teares*, for viols and lute.

223.39   travois] See note 5.9.

224.19–21   Blue desert . . . Song"?] Possibly "The Desert Song," from the eponymous 1926 operetta, with music by Sigmund Romberg and lyrics by Oscar Hammerstein II, Otto Harbach, and Frank Mandel; the song's chorus includes the line "Blue heaven and you and I."

228.2–4   Gilbert and Sullivan . . . apposite] "If Somebody There Chanced to Be," an aria from the Gilbert and Sullivan opera *Ruddigore; or, The Witch's Curse*, first performed in 1887.

247.2   Megatherium] See note 201.23.

251.2–3   peplum] A draped, body-length garment worn in ancient Greece.

257.33–38   We're off . . . we are!] An English children's ditty, often sung on school outings.

264.5   *When I'm calling yoo-hoo-hoo-hoo-hoo-hoo-hoo*] From the song "By a Waterfall," with music by Sammy Fain and lyrics by Irving Kahal, composed for the Busby Berkeley film *Footlight Parade* (1933).

275.27   G.E.V.] Ground-effect vehicle.

279.4–5   Fra Angelico] Italian painter (1395–1455) best known for a series of frescoes for the convent at San Marco, in Florence.

286.26   Kachina-mask-dancing] Among the tribes of the Pueblo people of the American Southwest, masked dancers are transformed by kachinas, or ancestral spirits, during ceremonial dances.

286.37–38   Old poem . . . bones gone] "And Death Shall Have No Dominion" (1933) by Dylan Thomas: "When their bones are picked clean and the clean bones gone."

298.8   fledermausen?"] German: bats?"

301.39   *Since by Man came death*] See George Frideric Handel's oratorio *Messiah* (1741), part 3.

306.6   *Death, thou shalt die*] John Donne, "Death, be not proud" (1609), line 14.

306.8   *The City of Dreadful Night*] Poem by James Thomson written between 1870 and 1873.

306.8   *Eternity as a bath house full of spiders*] In Dostoyevsky's novel *Crime and Punishment* (1866), Svidrigailov tells Raskolnikov of his vision of eternity as "a bath house in the country, black and grimy and spiders in every corner."

306.9   *The Celestial City*] In John Bunyan's allegory *The Pilgrim's Progress from This World, to That Which Is to Come* (1678), the book's protagonist, Christian, travels from the City of Destruction to the Celestial City, or Heaven, on Mount Zion.

306.10   *Gehenna*] Generally, a place or state of misery; in Jewish and Christian eschatology, it is the locus of the afterlife where the damned reside.

306.11   *History is a nightmare . . . awaken*] In James Joyce's novel *Ulysses* (1922), Stephen Dedalus describes history as "a nightmare from which I am trying to awake."

306.14   *Death is not part . . . lived through*] See Ludwig Wittgenstein's *Tractatus Logico-Philosophicus* (1921).

ON STRIKE AGAINST GOD

313.7   Rilke] Austrian poet Rainer Maria Rilke (1875–1926).

315.2–3   C. P. Snow and the "two cultures"] Snow delivered "Two Cultures and the Scientific Revolution" as the Rede Lecture at the University of Cambridge in 1959; he laments the polarization between literary intellectuals and the scientific community.

319.2   Danny Kaye] American dancer, comedic actor, and singer (1911–1987).

319.18   H. Rider Haggard] Henry Rider Haggard (1856–1925), an English novelist whose adventure romances are frequently set in Africa.

319.27   Phagocytus Giganticus] A phagocyte is a cell that can ingest bacteria, small particles, and other matter, protecting the body from infection and disease.

319.39–40   three interlocking . . . beer ad] Ballantine beer.

322.35–36   King Solomon's Mines] Adventure novel (1885) by H. Rider Haggard in which the big-game hunter Allan Quatermain quests for the eponymous fabled mines.

326.11   mesomorphs] People with husky, muscular builds.

327.23   Finagle's Constant] "Finagle's law" is an invented mathematical constant characterized as changing the universe to fit the equation.

327.27–328.8   Mary Ann Evans' . . . B--l-y] Evans (1819–1880) wrote under the name George Eliot; Emily Brontë (1818–1848), English writer; Charlotte Brontë (1816–1855), English writer; Virginia Woolf (1882–1941), English writer; Murasaki Shikibu (c. 978–c. 1040), Japanese writer; Hrosvitha (c. 935–c. 1000), German poet; Jane Austen (1775–1817), English novelist; Sappho (c. 615–c. 550 BCE), Greek poet; Corinna, ancient Greek poet; Olive Schreiner (1855–1920), South African writer; Kate Chopin (1851–1904), American writer; Mary Shelley (1797–1851), American writer; Charlotte Perkins Gilman (1860–1935), American writer; Phillis Wheatley (1753–1784), American poet; Ann Radcliffe (1764–1823), English writer; Margaret Cavendish (1623–1673), English writer and scientist; Emma Dorothy Eliza Nevitte Southworth, aka E.D.E.N. Southworth (1819–1899), American writer; Sarah Elizabeth Downs, aka Mrs. Georgie Sheldon (1843–1926), American novelist; Georgette Heyer (1902–1974), English writer; Barbara Cartland (1901–2000), English writer; "Unfortunate Miss Bailey," a ballad credited to George Colman the elder (1732–1794) and George Colman the younger (1762–1836).

330.7   Theda Bara] American silent film and stage actress (1885–1955).

330.8   Zorra] Female version of Zorro, a masked vigilante created by pulp writer Johnston McCulley in 1919.

330.10–11   Juana la Loca] Joanna (1479–1555), often referred to as Joanna the Mad, queen of Castile from 1504 to 1555.

330.26–27   Boadicea . . . Sheldon] Boadicea (d. c. 61 CE), queen of the Iceni tribe of Celtic Britons, who led a rebellion against the Roman Empire; Tomyris, queen of the Massagetai whose armies, according to Herodotus, defeated the forces of Cyrus II the Great of Persia in 529 BCE; Cartisman-dua, queen of the Brigantes nation, in northern England between c. 43 and 69; Artemisia, queen of Halicarnassus, a Greco-Carian city, at the time of the Persian Wars (499–449); Corinna, ancient Greek poet; Eva, possibly a reference to Janet Evanson's mother, after whom she is named, in *The Female Man*; Mrs. Georgie Sheldon (1843–1926), American novelist.

330.29   Queen Esther] Jewish wife of the Persian king Ahasuerus (Xerxes I) who convinced her husband to spare the empire's Jewish people from massacre.

333.12   Uriah Heep] A scheming, sycophantic character in Charles Dickens's *David Copperfield* (1850).

337.31   Die Walküre] The second epic drama of Richard Wagner's opera *Der Ring des Nibelungen* (*The Ring of the Nibelung*), first performed separately in 1870.

340.18   Ivy Compton-Burnett] English novelist (1884–1969) whose narra-tives about the upper classes develop through extensive passages of dialogue.

340.20   Atreidae] In Greek mythology, the entrance to the house of Atreus, king of Mycenae, whose sons are Agamemnon and Menelaus.

340.31   Valkyrie] In Norse mythology, a maiden of Odin who guides the spir-its of heroes killed in battle to Valhalla.

343.25   Bergen-Belsen] A Nazi concentration camp in northern Germany.

344.27–28   railroad-engineer's cap . . . French movie] Probably Jeanne Moreau in *Jules and Jim* (1962), directed by François Truffaut.

346.26   Ophelia] See *Hamlet*, IV.5.

347.4   Lucia di Lammermoor] Heroine of Italian composer Gaetano Doni-zetti's 1835 opera.

348.31–32 "All Of Me . . . Thing."] "All of Me," written by Gerald Marks and Seymour Simons in 1931, has been performed by many artists, including Louis Armstrong, Billie Holliday, and Willie Nelson; "Love Is a Many-Splendored Thing," by Sammy Fain and Paul Francis Webster, debuted in a 1955 film of the same title.

352.2–4 that book . . . *better.*] See *Self-Mastery Through Conscious Autosuggestion* (1920) by Emile Coué.

353.29 Bear of Little Brain] See *The House at Pooh Corner* (1928) by A. A. Milne.

353.30–31 the Nut Brown Maid or the Pretty Lady] An English medieval ballad of unknown authorship about a young woman's love and constancy, and a novel (1918) by Arnold Bennett, about an unrepentant French prostitute in London.

358.15 page 1] See page 309 in the present volume.

366.36 Madama Butterfly] Opera (1904) by Giacomo Puccini.

369.6 like Scarlett] Scarlett O'Hara in Margaret Mitchell's novel *Gone with the Wind* (1936).

370.25 *The Green Hat*] A best-selling novel by Michael Arlen published in 1924 about a rich, fashionable set in the interwar years in London.

371.7 *Swan Lake*] Ballet (1875–76) by Russian composer Pyotr Ilyich Tchaikovsky (1840–1893).

374.16 Fred Astaire . . . the Thief"] A 1945 musical comedy directed by Vincente Minnelli and starring Fred Astaire and Lucille Bremer.

377.20 Charles Addams] American cartoonist (1912–1988) whose work is characterized by a mix of humor and the macabre, and who is most often remembered for his creation of the Addams Family.

379.39 Alice Liddell's] As a child, Liddell (1852–1934) was friends with the author Lewis Carroll and helped to inspire his book *Alice's Adventures in Wonderland*.

386.13 T.S. Eliot] Anglo-American modernist poet and winner of the 1948 Nobel Prize in Literature.

386.30 Malcolm no-name] Perhaps a reference to civil rights activist Malcolm X (1925–1965), whose father was killed in a streetcar accident when Malcolm was six.

390.16–21 Ezekiel . . . God] "Ezekiel Saw the Wheel," an African American spiritual arranged by William L. Dawson (1899–1990).

395.28–29 *A Romance . . . Puritan's Daughter*] *A Romance of the Pyrenees* (1803) by English novelist Catherine Cuthbertson; perhaps a conflation of the anonymously written novels *Marianna, or Modern Manners* (1808) and *The Protector's Secret, or, the Puritan's Daughter* (1849).

395.38 Mrs. Defoe's journal] Mary Tuffley, wife of writer Daniel Defoe, gave birth to eight children between around 1689 and 1701.

396.1–2 Mrs. Pepys's dress allowance] The English diarist Samuel Pepys (1633–1703) gave his wife Elisabeth an allowance for clothing and expenses in 1669, after fourteen years of marriage.

396.2–3 "How are we fall'n . . . rules!"] See "The Introduction" (1690s), a poem by Anne Finch, Countess of Winchilsea.

396.3–4 "Women live like . . . Worms."] See Margaret Cavendish, *Orations of divers sorts accommodated to divers places* (1662).

396.4–5 "Anyone may blame . . . likes."] See Charlotte Brontë, *Jane Eyre* (1847).

396.5–6 "How good it must . . . travel."] From a letter of May 27, 1862, written by American author Rebecca Harding Davis to her friend Annie Fields.

396.6–7 "John laughs . . . in marriage."] See Charlotte Perkins Gilman, "The Yellow Wallpaper" (1892).

396.7–8 "It had all been . . . a man. . . ."] See Mary McCarthy, "Ghostly Father, I Confess" (1942).

396.8–9 "I / Revolve . . . impossibles—"] See Sylvia Plath's poem "Purdah" (1962).

397.17–18 "'Tis with . . . her own."] Alexander Pope, *An Essay on Criticism* (1711): "'Tis with our judgments as our watches, none / Go just alike, yet each believes his own."

397.38 Jean Harlow] American actress (1911–1937) known as the original "Blonde Bombshell."

398.38 a book I read by C. S. Lewis] See *That Hideous Strength: A Modern Fairy-Tale for Grown-Ups* (1945).

399.35 the Ice Follies] A touring ice show, featuring elaborate productions, founded in 1937.

400.7–8 Buster Crabbe . . . Christopher Lee] Crabbe (1908–1983), an Olympic swimmer and actor; Bogarde (1921–1999), an English actor and writer; Mason (1909–1984), an English actor; Lee (1922–2015), an English actor.

402.30 the Charleston] A frenetic dance popular in the United States during the Roaring Twenties.

405.29–30 Conan . . . Barbarian] A novel by Richard E. Howard published in 1950, and a story collection by John Jakes published in 1968.

406.10 Fool's Mate] In chess, the quickest sequence to checkmate.

407.21 c.r. group] Consciousness-raising group, women-only meetings in which members discussed personal experiences and women's social roles and behavior.

409.15 Anna Magnani] Italian film and stage actress (1908–1973).

410.30 *Les Miserables*] Novel by Victor Hugo, first published in 1862.

THE COMPLETE ALYX STORIES

503.30 crams,"] Masses of dough or paste used for stuffing fowl.

565.24–26 *I care for nobody . . . for me.*] See "The Miller of Dee" or "The Jolly Miller," an English folk song originally published in the ballad opera *Love in the Village* (1762), with music by Thomas Arne (1710–1778) and lyrics by Isaac Bickerstaffe (1733–1812).

576.2–5 *If a man can resist . . .* Chapman] From "The Unity of Human Nature," an address Chapman (1862–1933) delivered before the graduating class at Hobart College in 1900.

576.7–8 Philco radio] A freestanding mahogany cabinet radio made by the Philco company.

577.28 Ikhnaton] Also spelled Akhenaten, an Egyptian pharaoh who reigned c. 1353–1336 BCE.

578.3 *The Green Hat: A Romance*] See note 370.25.

578.20 Hispano-Suizas] A Spanish automotive company founded in 1904 and perhaps best known for its luxury cars of the 1920s and '30s.

582.26–27 Wells's *The Time Machine*] An 1895 science-fiction novella by H. G. Wells in which a time traveler arrives in the year 802,701.

583.3 Eloi . . . Morlocks] In Wells's novella, humanity has evolved into two species—the Eloi, who descend from the wealthy upper classes and live in a utopian society, and the Morlocks, descendants of the lower classes and who live in darkness underground.

588.11 Iris March] The protagonist of *The Green Hat* (see note 370.25).

591.17 "Jam yesterday . . . jam today,"] From *Through the Looking-Glass; and What Alice Found There* (1871) by Lewis Carroll.

OTHER STORIES

621.1 *When It Changed*] When it was first published—in *Again, Dangerous Visions*, in 1972, Russ included an "Afterword" to this story, as follows:

> I find it hard to say anything about this story. The first few paragraphs were dictated to me in a thoughtful, reasonable, whispering tone I had

never heard before; and once the Daemon had vanished—they always do—I had to finish the thing by myself and in a voice not my own.

The premise of the story needs either a book or silence. I'll try to compromise. It seems to me (in the words of the narrator) that sexual equality has not yet been established on Earth and that (in the words of GBS) the only argument that can be made against it is that it has never been tried. I have read SF stories about manless worlds before; they are either full of busty girls in wisps of chiffon who slink about writing with lust (Keith Laumer wrote a charming, funny one called "The War with the Yukks"), or the women have set up a static, bee-like society in imitation of some presumed primitive matriarchy. These stories are written by men. Why women who have been alone for generations should "instinctively" turn their sexual desires toward persons of whom they have only intellectual knowledge, or why female people are presumed to have an innate preference for Byzantine rigidity I don't know. "Progress" is one of the sacred cows of SF so perhaps the latter just goes to show that although women can run a society by themselves, *it isn't a good one.* This is flattering to men, I suppose. Of SF attempts to depict real matriarchies ("He will be my concubine for tonight," said the Empress of Zar coldly) it is better not to speak. I remember one very good post-bomb story by an English writer (another static society, with the Magna Mater literally and supernaturally in existence) but on the whole we had better just tiptoe past the subject.

In my story I have used assumptions that seem to me obviously true. One of them is the idea that almost all the characterological sex differences we take for granted are in fact learned not innate. I do not see how anyone can walk around with both eyes open and both halves of his/her brain functioning and not realize this. Still, the mythology persists in SF, as elsewhere, that women are naturally gentler than men, that they are naturally less creative than men, or less intelligent, or shrewder, or more cowardly, or more dependent, or more self-centered, or more self-sacrificing, or more materialistic, or shyer, or God knows what, whatever is most convenient at the moment. True, you can make people into anything. There are matrons of fifty so domesticated that any venture away from home is a continual flutter: where's the No Smoking sign, is it on, how do I fasten my seat belt, oh dear can you see the stewardess, she's serving the men first, they always do, isn't it awful. And what's so fascinating about all this was that the strong, competent "male" to whom such a lady in distress turned for help recently was Carol Emshwiller. Wowie, zowie, Mr. Wizard! This flutteriness isn't "femininity" (something men are always so anxious women will lose) but pathology.

It's men who get rapturous and yeasty about the wonderful mystery of Woman, lovely Woman (this is getting difficult to write as I keep imagining my reader to be the George-Georgina of the old circuses: half-bearded, half-permanentwaved). There are few women who go around actually feeling: Oh, what a fascinating feminine mystery I am. This makes it clear enough, I think, which sex (in general) has the higher prestige, the more freedom, the more education, the more money, in Sartre's sense which is subject and which is object. Every role in life has its advantages and disadvantages, of course; a fiery feminist student here at Cornell recently told an audience that a man who acquires a wife acquires a "life-long slave" (fierce look) while the audience justifiably giggled and I wondered how I'd ever been inveigled into speaking on a program with such a lackwit. I also believe, like the villain of my story, that human beings are born with instincts (though fuzzy ones) and that being physically weaker than men and having babies makes a difference. But it makes less of a difference now.

Also, the patriarchal society must have considerable survival value. I suspect that it is actually more stable (and more rigid) than the primeval matriarchal societies hypothesized by some anthropologists. I wish somebody knew. To take only one topic: it seems clear that if there is to be a sexual double standard, it must be the one we know and not the opposite; male potency is too biologically precious to repress. A society that made its well-bred men impotent, as Victorian ladies were made frigid, would rapidly become an unpeopled society. Such things ought to be speculated about.

Meanwhile, my story. I did not come from this lecture, of course, but vice versa. I had read a very fine SF novel, Ursula K. Le Guin's *The Left Hand of Darkness*, in which all the characters are humanoid hermaphrodites, and was wondering at the obduracy of the English language, in which everybody is "he" or "she" and "it" is reserved for typewriters. But how can one call a hermaphrodite "he," as Miss Le Guin does? I tried (in my head) changing all the masculine pronouns to feminine ones, and marveled at the difference. And then I wondered why Miss Le Guin's native "hero" is male in *every* important sexual encounter of his life except that with the human male in the book. Weeks later the Daemon suddenly whispered, "Katy drives like a maniac," and I found myself on Whileaway, on a country road at night. I might add (for the benefit of both the bearded and unbearded sides of the reader's cerebrum) that I never write to shock. I consider that as immoral as writing to please. Katharina and Janet are respectable, decent, even conventional people, and if they shock *you*, just think of what a copy of *Playboy* or *Cosmopolitan* would do to *them*. Resentment of the opposite sex (*Cosmo* is worse) is something they have yet to learn, thank God.

Which is why I visit Whileaway—although I do not live there because there are no men there. And if you wonder about my sincerity in saying *that*, George-Georgina, I must give you up as hopeless.

629.6–7   Faust's words: *Verweile doch, du bist so schoen . . . so shoen!*] German: *Stay, you are so beautiful!* (from Goethe's play *Faust*, 1806–32).

630.2–4   *Deprived of other* . . . Dickinson] "Deprived of other Banquet" (773), by Emily Dickinson.

631.16   Poitiers] A city in western France, home during the twelfth century to Eleanor of Aquitaine, who married the future king Louis VII in the Poitiers Cathedral.

633.36   paestum roses] A variety of roses used for ointments and perfumes.

635.24   Fimbul-winter] In Norse mythology, an unusually harsh winter that heralds the apocalyptic events of Ragnarök.

648.7   the Valhall] The afterlife in Norse mythology for slain warriors, depicted as a palace hall presided over by Odin.

657.23   *skalds*] Scandinavian poets or bards.

658.22   the Fenris Wolf and the Midgaard snake] Both children of Loki and the giantess Angrboða, according to Norse mythology: a fearsome wolf who will descend upon the gods at the time of Ragnarök, killing Odin; and a sea serpent who encircles the realm of Midgaard and will kill and be killed by Thor at Ragnarök.

This book is set in 10 point ITC Galliard, a face designed
for digital composition by Matthew Carter and based
on the sixteenth-century face Granjon. The paper is acid-free
lightweight opaque that will not turn yellow or brittle with age.
The binding is sewn, which allows the book to open easily and lie flat.
The binding board is covered in Brillianta, a woven rayon cloth
made by Van Heek–Scholco Textielfabrieken, Holland.
Composition by Dianna Logan, Clearmont, MO.
Printing by Sheridan Grand Rapids, Grand Rapids, MI.
Binding by Dekker Bookbinding, Wyoming, MI.
Designed by Bruce Campbell.